A CLASH OF KINGS

BY GEORGE R. R. MARTIN

A SONG OF ICE AND FIRE
Book One: *A Game of Thrones*
Book Two: *A Clash of Kings*
Book Three: *A Storm of Swords*
Book Four: *A Feast for Crows*

Dying of the Light
Windhaven (with Lisa Tuttle)
Fevre Dream
The Armageddon Rag
Dead Man's Hand (with John J. Miller)

SHORT STORY COLLECTIONS
Dreamsongs: Volume I
Dreamsongs: Volume II
A Song of Lya and Other Stories
Songs of Stars and Shadows
Sandkings
Songs the Dead Men Sing
Nightflyers
Tuf Voyaging
Portraits of His Children

EDITED BY GEORGE R. R. MARTIN
New Voices in Science Fiction, Volumes 1–4
The Science Fiction Weight-Loss Book
(with Isaac Asimov and Martin Harry Greenberg)
The John W. Campbell Awards, Volume 5
Night Visions 3
Wild Card I–XV

A Clash of Kings

Book Two of
A Song of Ice and Fire

George R. R. Martin

BANTAM BOOKS
NEW YORK

2011 Bantam Books Trade Paperback Edition

Copyright © 1999 by George R. R. Martin
Excerpt from *A Storm of Swords* copyright © 2000 by George R. R. Martin
All rights reserved.

Published in the United States by Bantam Books, an imprint of The Random House Publishing Group, a division of Random House, Inc., New York.

BANTAM BOOKS and the rooster colophon are registered trademarks of Random House, Inc.

Originally published in hardcover in the United States by Bantam Spectra, a division of Random House, Inc., in 1999.

Library of Congress Cataloging-in-Publication Data
Martin, George R. R.
A clash of kings : book two of A song of ice and fire / George R. R. Martin.
    p. cm.—(A song of ice and fire, bk. 2)
ISBN 978-0-553-38169-6
eBook ISBN 978-0-553-89785-2
I. Title. II. Series: Martin, George R. R. Song of ice and fire, bk. 2.
PS3563.A7239C58 1999
813'.54—dc21   98-37954

Maps by James Sinclair
Heraldic crests by Virginia Norey

Printed in the United States of America

www.bantamdell.com

19 18

Design by James Sinclair

to John and Gail
for all the meat and mead we've shared

PROLOGUE

The comet's tail spread across the dawn, a red slash that bled above the crags of Dragonstone like a wound in the pink and purple sky.

The maester stood on the windswept balcony outside his chambers. It was here the ravens came, after long flight. Their droppings speckled the gargoyles that rose twelve feet tall on either side of him, a hellhound and a wyvern, two of the thousand that brooded over the walls of the ancient fortress. When first he came to Dragonstone, the army of stone grotesques had made him uneasy, but as the years passed he had grown used to them. Now he thought of them as old friends. The three of them watched the sky together with foreboding.

The maester did not believe in omens. And yet . . . old as he was, Cressen had never seen a comet half so bright, nor yet that color, that terrible color, the color of blood and flame and sunsets. He wondered if his gargoyles had ever seen its like. They had been here so much longer than he had, and would still be here long after he was gone. If stone tongues could speak . . .

Such folly. He leaned against the battlement, the sea crashing beneath him, the black stone rough beneath his fingers. *Talking gargoyles and prophecies in the sky. I am an old done man, grown giddy as a child again.* Had a lifetime's hard-won wisdom fled him along with his health and strength? He was a maester, trained and chained in the great Citadel of Oldtown. What had he come to, when superstition filled his head as if he were an ignorant fieldhand?

And yet . . . and yet . . . the comet burned even by day now, while pale grey steam rose from the hot vents of Dragonmont behind the castle, and yestermorn a white raven had brought word from the Citadel itself, word long-expected but no less fearful for all that, word of summer's end. Omens, all. Too many to deny. *What does it all mean?* he wanted to cry.

"Maester Cressen, we have visitors." Pylos spoke softly, as if loath to disturb Cressen's solemn meditations. Had he known what drivel filled his head, he would have shouted. "The princess would see the white raven." Ever correct, Pylos called her *princess* now, as her lord father was a king. King of a smoking rock in the great salt sea, yet a king nonetheless. "Her fool is with her."

The old man turned away from the dawn, keeping a hand on his wyvern to steady himself. "Help me to my chair and show them in."

Taking his arm, Pylos led him inside. In his youth, Cressen had walked briskly, but he was not far from his eightieth name day now, and his legs were frail and unsteady. Two years past, he had fallen and shattered a hip, and it had never mended properly. Last year when he took ill, the Citadel had sent Pylos out from Oldtown, mere days before Lord Stannis had closed the isle . . . to help him in his labors, it was said, but Cressen knew the truth. Pylos had come to replace him when he died. He did not mind. Someone must take his place, and sooner than he would like . . .

He let the younger man settle him behind his books and papers. "Go bring her. It is ill to keep a lady waiting." He waved a hand, a feeble gesture of haste from a man no longer capable of hastening. His flesh was wrinkled and spotted, the skin so papery thin that he could see the web of veins and the shape of bones beneath. And how they trembled, these hands of his that had once been so sure and deft . . .

When Pylos returned the girl came with him, shy as ever. Behind her, shuffling and hopping in that queer sideways walk of his, came her fool. On his head was a mock helm fashioned from an old tin bucket, with a rack of deer antlers strapped to the crown and hung with cowbells. With his every lurching step, the bells rang, each with a different voice, *clang-a-dang bong-dong ring-a-ling clong clong clong.*

"Who comes to see us so early, Pylos?" Cressen said.

"It's me and Patches, Maester." Guileless blue eyes blinked at him. Hers was not a pretty face, alas. The child had her lord father's square jut of jaw and her mother's unfortunate ears, along with a disfigurement all her own, the legacy of the bout of greyscale that had almost claimed her in the crib. Across half one cheek and well down her neck, her flesh was stiff and dead, the skin cracked and flaking, mottled black and grey and stony to the touch. "Pylos said we might see the white raven."

"Indeed you may," Cressen answered. As if he would ever deny her. She had been denied too often in her time. Her name was Shireen. She would be ten on her next name day, and she was the saddest child that Maester Cressen had ever known. *Her sadness is my shame,* the old man thought, *another mark of my failure.* "Maester Pylos, do me a kindness and bring the bird down from the rookery for the Lady Shireen."

"It would be my pleasure." Pylos was a polite youth, no more than five-and-twenty, yet solemn as a man of sixty. If only he had more humor, more *life* in him; that was what was needed here. Grim places needed lightening, not solemnity, and Dragonstone was grim beyond a doubt, a lonely citadel in the wet waste surrounded by storm and salt, with the smoking shadow of the mountain at its back. A maester must go where he is sent, so Cressen had come here with his lord some twelve years past, and he had served, and served well. Yet he had never loved Dragonstone, nor ever felt truly at home here. Of late, when he woke from restless dreams in which the red woman figured disturbingly, he often did not know where he was.

The fool turned his patched and piebald head to watch Pylos climb the steep iron steps to the rookery. His bells rang with the motion. "Under the sea, the birds have scales for feathers," he said, *clang-a-langing.* "I know, I know, oh, oh, oh."

Even for a fool, Patchface was a sorry thing. Perhaps once he could evoke gales of laughter with a quip, but the sea had taken that power from him, along with half his wits and all his memory. He was soft and obese, subject to twitches and trembles, incoherent as often as not. The girl was the only one who laughed at him now, the only one who cared if he lived or died.

An ugly little girl and a sad fool, and maester makes three . . . now there is a tale to make men weep. "Sit with me, child." Cressen beckoned her closer. "This is early to come calling, scarce past dawn. You should be snug in your bed."

"I had bad dreams," Shireen told him. "About the dragons. They were coming to eat me."

The child had been plagued by nightmares as far back as Maester Cressen could recall. "We have talked of this before," he said gently. "The dragons cannot come to life. They are carved of stone, child. In olden days, our island was the westernmost outpost of the great Freehold of Valyria. It was the Valyrians who raised this citadel, and they had ways of shaping stone since lost to us. A castle must have towers wherever two walls meet at an angle, for defense. The Valyrians fashioned these towers in the shape of dragons to make their fortress seem more fearsome, just as they crowned their walls with a thousand gargoyles instead of simple crenellations." He took her small pink hand in his own frail spotted one and gave it a gentle squeeze. "So you see, there is nothing to fear."

Shireen was unconvinced. "What about the thing in the sky? Dalla and Matrice were talking by the well, and Dalla said she heard the red woman tell Mother that it was dragonsbreath. If the dragons are breathing, doesn't that mean they are coming to life?"

The red woman, Maester Cressen thought sourly. *Ill enough that she's filled the head of the mother with her madness, must she poison the daughter's dreams as well?* He would have a stern word with Dalla, warn her not to spread such tales. "The thing in the sky is a comet, sweet child. A star with a tail, lost in the heavens. It will be gone soon enough, never to be seen again in our lifetimes. Watch and see."

Shireen gave a brave little nod. "Mother said the white raven means it's not summer anymore."

"That is so, my lady. The white ravens fly only from the Citadel." Cressen's fingers went to the chain about his neck, each link forged from a different metal, each symbolizing his mastery of another branch of learning; the maester's collar, mark of his order. In the pride of his youth, he had worn it easily, but now it seemed heavy to him, the metal cold against his skin. "They are larger than other ravens, and more clever, bred to carry only the most important messages. This one came to tell us that the Conclave has met, considered the reports and measurements made by maesters all over the realm, and declared this great summer done at last. Ten years, two turns, and sixteen days it lasted, the longest summer in living memory."

"Will it get cold now?" Shireen was a summer child, and had never known true cold.

"In time," Cressen replied. "If the gods are good, they will grant us a warm autumn and bountiful harvests, so we might prepare for the winter to come." The smallfolk said that a long summer meant an even longer winter, but the maester saw no reason to frighten the child with such tales.

Patchface rang his bells. "It is *always* summer under the sea," he intoned. "The merwives wear nennymoans in their hair and weave gowns of silver seaweed. I know, I know, oh, oh, oh."

Shireen giggled. "I should like a gown of silver seaweed."

"Under the sea, it snows up," said the fool, "and the rain is dry as bone. I know, I know, oh, oh, oh."

"Will it truly snow?" the child asked.

"It will," Cressen said. *But not for years yet, I pray, and then not for long.* "Ah, here is Pylos with the bird."

Shireen gave a cry of delight. Even Cressen had to admit the bird made an impressive sight, white as snow and larger than any hawk, with the bright black eyes that meant it was no mere albino, but a truebred white raven of the Citadel. "Here," he called. The raven spread its wings, leapt into the air, and flapped noisily across the room to land on the table beside him.

"I'll see to your breakfast now," Pylos announced. Cressen nodded. "This is the Lady Shireen," he told the raven. The bird bobbed its pale head up and down, as if it were bowing. *"Lady,"* it croaked. *"Lady."*

The child's mouth gaped open. "It *talks!*"

"A few words. As I said, they are clever, these birds."

"Clever bird, clever man, clever clever fool," said Patchface, jangling. "Oh, clever clever clever fool." He began to sing. *"The shadows come to dance, my lord, dance my lord, dance my lord,"* he sang, hopping from one foot to the other and back again. *"The shadows come to stay, my lord, stay my lord, stay my lord."* He jerked his head with each word, the bells in his antlers sending up a clangor.

The white raven screamed and went flapping away to perch on the iron railing of the rookery stairs. Shireen seemed to grow smaller. "He sings that all the time. I told him to stop but he won't. It makes me scared. Make him stop."

And how do I do that? the old man wondered. *Once I might have silenced him forever, but now . . .*

Patchface had come to them as a boy. Lord Steffon of cherished memory had found him in Volantis, across the narrow sea. The king—the old king, Aerys II Targaryen, who had not been quite so mad in those days— had sent his lordship to seek a bride for Prince Rhaegar, who had no sisters to wed. "We have found the most splendid fool," he wrote Cressen, a fortnight before he was to return home from his fruitless mission. "Only a boy, yet nimble as a monkey and witty as a dozen courtiers. He juggles and riddles and does magic, and he can sing prettily in four tongues. We have bought his freedom and hope to bring him home with us. Robert will be delighted with him, and perhaps in time he will even teach Stannis how to laugh."

It saddened Cressen to remember that letter. No one had ever taught Stannis how to laugh, least of all the boy Patchface. The storm came up suddenly, howling, and Shipbreaker Bay proved the truth of its name. The lord's two-masted galley *Windproud* broke up within sight of his castle. From its parapets his two eldest sons had watched as their father's ship was smashed against the rocks and swallowed by the waters. A hundred oarsmen and sailors went down with Lord Steffon Baratheon and his lady wife, and for days thereafter every tide left a fresh crop of swollen corpses on the strand below Storm's End.

The boy washed up on the third day. Maester Cressen had come down with the rest, to help put names to the dead. When they found the fool he was naked, his skin white and wrinkled and powdered with wet sand. Cressen had thought him another corpse, but when Jommy grabbed his ankles to drag him off to the burial wagon, the boy coughed water and sat up. To his dying day, Jommy had sworn that Patchface's flesh was clammy cold.

No one ever explained those two days the fool had been lost in the sea. The fisherfolk liked to say a mermaid had taught him to breathe water in return for his seed. Patchface himself had said nothing. The witty, clever lad that Lord Steffon had written of never reached Storm's End; the boy they found was someone else, broken in body and mind, hardly capable of speech, much less of wit. Yet his fool's face left no doubt of who he was. It was the fashion in the Free City of Volantis to tattoo the faces of slaves and servants; from neck to scalp the boy's skin had been patterned in squares of red and green motley.

"The wretch is mad, and in pain, and no use to anyone, least of all himself," declared old Ser Harbert, the castellan of Storm's End in those years. "The kindest thing you could do for that one is fill his cup with the milk of the poppy. A painless sleep, and there's an end to it. He'd bless you if he had the wit for it." But Cressen had refused, and in the end he had won. Whether Patchface had gotten any joy of that victory he could not say, not even today, so many years later.

"The shadows come to dance, my lord, dance my lord, dance my lord," the fool sang on, swinging his head and making his bells clang and clatter. *Bong dong, ring-a-ling, bong dong.*

"Lord," the white raven shrieked. *"Lord, lord, lord."*

"A fool sings what he will," the maester told his anxious princess. "You must not take his words to heart. On the morrow he may remember another song, and this one will never be heard again." *He can sing prettily in four tongues,* Lord Steffon had written . . .

Pylos strode through the door. "Maester, pardons."

"You have forgotten the porridge," Cressen said, amused. That was most unlike Pylos.

"Maester, Ser Davos returned last night. They were talking of it in the kitchen. I thought you would want to know at once."

"Davos . . . last night, you say? Where is he?"

"With the king. They have been together most of the night."

There was a time when Lord Stannis would have woken him, no matter the hour, to have him there to give his counsel. "I should have been told," Cressen complained. "I should have been woken." He disentangled his fingers from Shireen's. "Pardons, my lady, but I must speak with your lord father. Pylos, give me your arm. There are too many steps in this castle, and it seems to me they add a few every night, just to vex me."

Shireen and Patchface followed them out, but the child soon grew restless with the old man's creeping pace and dashed ahead, the fool lurching after her with his cowbells clanging madly.

Castles are not friendly places for the frail, Cressen was reminded as he descended the turnpike stairs of Sea Dragon Tower. Lord Stannis would be found in the Chamber of the Painted Table, atop the Stone Drum, Dragonstone's central keep, so named for the way its ancient walls boomed and rumbled during storms. To reach him they must cross the gallery, pass through the middle and inner walls with their guardian gargoyles and black iron gates, and ascend more steps than Cressen cared to contemplate. Young men climbed steps two at a time; for old men with bad hips, every one was a torment. But Lord Stannis would not think to come to him, so the maester resigned himself to the ordeal. He had Pylos to help him, at the least, and for that he was grateful.

Shuffling along the gallery, they passed before a row of tall arched windows with commanding views of the outer bailey, the curtain wall, and the fishing village beyond. In the yard, archers were firing at practice butts to the call of "Notch, draw, loose." Their arrows made a sound like a flock of birds taking wing. Guardsmen strode the wallwalks, peering between the gargoyles on the host camped without. The morning air was hazy with the smoke of cookfires, as three thousand men sat down to break their fasts beneath the banners of their lords. Past the sprawl of the camp, the anchorage was crowded with ships. No craft that had come within sight of Dragonstone this past half year had been allowed to leave again. Lord Stannis's *Fury*, a triple-decked war galley of three hundred oars, looked almost small beside some of the big-bellied carracks and cogs that surrounded her.

The guardsmen outside the Stone Drum knew the maesters by sight, and passed them through. "Wait here," Cressen told Pylos, within. "It's best I see him alone."

"It is a long climb, Maester."

Cressen smiled. "You think I have forgotten? I have climbed these steps so often I know each one by name."

Halfway up, he regretted his decision. He had stopped to catch his breath and ease the pain in his hip when he heard the scuff of boots on stone, and came face-to-face with Ser Davos Seaworth, descending.

Davos was a slight man, his low birth written plain upon a common face. A well-worn green cloak, stained by salt and spray and faded from the sun, draped his thin shoulders, over brown doublet and breeches that matched brown eyes and hair. About his neck a pouch of worn leather hung from a thong. His small beard was well peppered with grey, and he wore a leather glove on his maimed left hand. When he saw Cressen, he checked his descent.

"Ser Davos," the maester said. "When did you return?"

"In the black of morning. My favorite time." It was said that no one had ever handled a ship by night half so well as Davos Shorthand. Before Lord Stannis had knighted him, he had been the most notorious and elusive smuggler in all the Seven Kingdoms.

"And?"

The man shook his head. "It is as you warned him. They will not rise, Maester. Not for him. They do not love him."

No, Cressen thought. *Nor will they ever. He is strong, able, just . . . aye, just past the point of wisdom . . . yet it is not enough. It has never been enough.* "You spoke to them all?"

"All? No. Only those that would see me. They do not love me either, these highborns. To them I'll always be the Onion Knight." His left hand closed, stubby fingers locking into a fist; Stannis had hacked the ends off at the last joint, all but the thumb. "I broke bread with Gulian Swann and old Penrose, and the Tarths consented to a midnight meeting in a grove. The others—well, Beric Dondarrion is gone missing, some say dead, and Lord Caron is with Renly. Bryce the Orange, of the Rainbow Guard."

"The Rainbow Guard?"

"Renly's made his own Kingsguard," the onetime smuggler explained, "but these seven don't wear white. Each one has his own color. Loras Tyrell's their Lord Commander."

It was just the sort of notion that would appeal to Renly Baratheon; a splendid new order of knighthood, with gorgeous new raiment to proclaim it. Even as a boy, Renly had loved bright colors and rich fabrics, and he had loved his games as well. "Look at me!" he would shout as he ran laughing through the halls of Storm's End. "Look at me, I'm a dragon," or "Look at me, I'm a wizard," or "Look at me, look at me, I'm the rain god."

The bold little boy with wild black hair and laughing eyes was a man grown now, one-and-twenty, and still he played his games. *Look at me, I'm a king,* Cressen thought sadly. *Oh, Renly, Renly, dear sweet child, do you know what you are doing? And would you care if you did? Is there anyone who cares for him but me?* "What reasons did the lords give for their refusals?" he asked Ser Davos.

"Well, as to that, some gave me soft words and some blunt, some made excuses, some promises, some only lied." He shrugged. "In the end words are just wind."

"You could bring him no hope?"

"Only the false sort, and I'd not do that," Davos said. "He had the truth from me."

Maester Cressen remembered the day Davos had been knighted, after the siege of Storm's End. Lord Stannis and a small garrison had held the castle for close to a year, against the great host of the Lords Tyrell and Redwyne. Even the sea was closed against them, watched day and night by Redwyne galleys flying the burgundy banners of the Arbor. Within Storm's End, the horses had long since been eaten, the dogs and cats were gone, and the garrison was down to roots and rats. Then came a night when the moon was new and black clouds hid the stars. Cloaked in that darkness, Davos the smuggler had dared the Redwyne cordon and the rocks of Shipbreaker Bay alike. His little ship had a black hull, black sails, black oars, and a hold crammed with onions and salt fish. Little enough, yet it had kept the garrison alive long enough for Eddard Stark to reach Storm's End and break the siege.

Lord Stannis had rewarded Davos with choice lands on Cape Wrath, a small keep, and a knight's honors . . . but he had also decreed that he lose a joint of each finger on his left hand, to pay for all his years of smuggling. Davos had submitted, on the condition that Stannis wield the knife himself; he would accept no punishment from lesser hands. The lord had used a butcher's cleaver, the better to cut clean and true. Afterward, Davos had chosen the name Seaworth for his new-made house, and he took for his banner a black ship on a pale grey field—with an onion on its sails. The onetime smuggler was fond of saying that Lord Stannis had done him a boon, by giving him four less fingernails to clean and trim.

No, Cressen thought, a man like that would give no false hope, nor soften a hard truth. "Ser Davos, truth can be a bitter draught, even for a man like Lord Stannis. He thinks only of returning to King's Landing in the fullness of his power, to tear down his enemies and claim what is rightfully his. Yet now . . ."

"If he takes this meager host to King's Landing, it will be only to die. He does not have the numbers. I told him as much, but you know his pride." Davos held up his gloved hand. "My fingers will grow back before that man bends to sense."

The old man sighed. "You have done all you could. Now I must add my voice to yours." Wearily, he resumed his climb.

Lord Stannis Baratheon's refuge was a great round room with walls of bare black stone and four tall narrow windows that looked out to the four points of the compass. In the center of the chamber was the great table from which it took its name, a massive slab of carved wood fashioned at the command of Aegon Targaryen in the days before the Conquest. The Painted Table was more than fifty feet long, perhaps half that wide at its widest point, but less than four feet across at its narrowest. Aegon's carpenters had shaped it after the land of Westeros, sawing out each bay and peninsula until the table nowhere ran straight. On its surface, darkened by near three hundred years of varnish, were painted the Seven Kingdoms as they had been in Aegon's day; rivers and mountains, castles and cities, lakes and forests.

There was a single chair in the room, carefully positioned in the precise place that Dragonstone occupied off the coast of Westeros, and raised up to give a good view of the tabletop. Seated in the chair was a man in a tight-laced leather jerkin and breeches of roughspun brown wool. When Maester Cressen entered, he glanced up. "I knew *you* would come, old man, whether I summoned you or no." There was no hint of warmth in his voice; there seldom was.

Stannis Baratheon, Lord of Dragonstone and by the grace of the gods rightful heir to the Iron Throne of the Seven Kingdoms of Westeros, was broad of shoulder and sinewy of limb, with a tightness to his face and flesh that spoke of leather cured in the sun until it was as tough as steel. *Hard* was the word men used when they spoke of Stannis, and hard he was. Though he was not yet five-and-thirty, only a fringe of thin black hair remained on his head, circling behind his ears like the shadow of a crown. His brother, the late King Robert, had grown a beard in his final years. Maester Cressen had never seen it, but they said it was a wild thing, thick and fierce. As if in answer, Stannis kept his own whiskers cropped tight and short. They lay like a blue-black shadow across his square jaw and the bony hollows of his cheeks. His eyes were open wounds beneath his heavy brows, a blue as dark as the sea by night. His mouth would have given despair to even the drollest of fools; it was a mouth made for frowns and scowls and sharply worded commands, all thin pale lips and clenched muscles, a mouth that had forgotten how to smile and had never known how to laugh. Sometimes when the world grew very still and silent of a night, Maester Cressen fancied he could hear Lord Stannis grinding his teeth half a castle away.

"Once you would have woken me," the old man said.

"Once you were young. Now you are old and sick, and need your sleep." Stannis had never learned to soften his speech, to dissemble or flatter; he said what he thought, and those that did not like it could be damned. "I knew you'd learn what Davos had to say soon enough. You always do, don't you?"

"I would be of no help to you if I did not," Cressen said. "I met Davos on the stair."

"And he told all, I suppose? I should have had the man's tongue shortened along with his fingers."

"He would have made you a poor envoy then."

"He made me a poor envoy in any case. The storm lords will not rise for me. It seems they do not like me, and the justice of my cause means nothing to them. The cravenly ones will sit behind their walls waiting to see how the wind rises and who is likely to triumph. The bold ones have already declared for Renly. For *Renly*!" He spat out the name like poison on his tongue.

"Your brother has been the Lord of Storm's End these past thirteen years. These lords are his sworn bannermen—"

"*His*," Stannis broke in, "when by rights they should be mine. I never asked for Dragonstone. I never wanted it. I took it because Robert's enemies were here and he commanded me to root them out. I built his fleet and did his work, dutiful as a younger brother should be to an elder, as Renly should be to me. And what was Robert's thanks? He names me Lord of Dragonstone, and gives Storm's End and its incomes to *Renly*. Storm's End belonged to House Baratheon for three hundred years; by rights it should have passed to me when Robert took the Iron Throne."

It was an old grievance, deeply felt, and never more so than now. Here was the heart of his lord's weakness; for Dragonstone, old and strong though it was, commanded the allegiance of only a handful of lesser lords, whose stony island holdings were too thinly peopled to yield up the men that Stannis needed. Even with the sellswords he had brought across the narrow sea from the Free Cities of Myr and Lys, the host camped outside his walls was far too small to bring down the power of House Lannister.

"Robert did you an injustice," Maester Cressen replied carefully, "yet he had sound reasons. Dragonstone had long been the seat of House Targaryen. He needed a man's strength to rule here, and Renly was but a child."

"He is a child still," Stannis declared, his anger ringing loud in the empty hall, "a thieving child who thinks to snatch the crown off my brow. What has Renly ever done to earn a throne? He sits in council and jests with Littlefinger, and at tourneys he dons his splendid suit of armor and allows himself to be knocked off his horse by a better man. That is the sum of my brother Renly, who thinks he ought to be a king. I ask you, why did the gods inflict me with *brothers*?"

"I cannot answer for the gods."

"You seldom answer at all these days, it seems to me. Who maesters for Renly? Perchance I should send for him, I might like his counsel better. What do you think this maester said when my brother decided to steal my crown? What counsel did your colleague offer to this traitor blood of mine?"

"It would surprise me if Lord Renly sought counsel, Your Grace." The youngest of Lord Steffon's three sons had grown into a man bold but heedless, who acted from impulse rather than calculation. In that, as in so much else, Renly was like his brother Robert, and utterly unlike Stannis.

"*Your Grace*," Stannis repeated bitterly. "You mock me with a king's style, yet what am I king of? Dragonstone and a few rocks in the narrow sea, there is my kingdom." He descended the steps of his chair to stand before the table, his shadow falling across the mouth of the Blackwater Rush and the painted forest where King's Landing now stood. There he stood, brooding over the realm he sought to claim, so near at hand and yet so far away. "Tonight I am to sup with my lords bannermen, such as they are. Celtigar, Velaryon, Bar Emmon, the whole paltry lot of them. A poor crop, if truth be told, but they are what my brothers have left me. That Lysene pirate Salladhor Saan will be there with the latest tally of what I owe him, and Morosh the Myrman will caution me with talk of tides and autumn gales, while Lord Sunglass mutters piously of the will of the Seven. Celtigar will want to know which storm lords are joining us. Velaryon will threaten to take his levies home unless we strike at once. What am I to tell them? What must I do now?"

"Your true enemies are the Lannisters, my lord," Maester Cressen answered. "If you and your brother were to make common cause against them—"

"I will not treat with Renly," Stannis answered in a tone that brooked no argument. "Not while he calls himself a king."

"Not Renly, then," the maester yielded. His lord was stubborn and proud; when he had set his mind, there was no changing it. "Others might serve your needs as well. Eddard Stark's son has been proclaimed King in the North, with all the power of Winterfell and Riverrun behind him."

"A green boy," said Stannis, "and another false king. Am I to accept a broken realm?"

"Surely half a kingdom is better than none," Cressen said, "and if you help the boy avenge his father's murder—"

"Why should I avenge Eddard Stark? The man was nothing to me. Oh, *Robert* loved him, to be sure. Loved him as a brother, how often did I hear that? *I* was his brother, not Ned Stark, but you would never have known it by the way he treated me. I held Storm's End for him, watching good men starve while Mace Tyrell and Paxter Redwyne feasted within sight of my walls. Did Robert thank me? No. He thanked *Stark*, for lifting the siege when we were down to rats and radishes. I built a fleet at Robert's command, took Dragonstone in his name. Did he take my hand and say, *Well done, brother, whatever should I do without you?* No, he blamed me for letting Willem Darry steal away Viserys and the babe, as if I could have stopped it. I sat on his council for fifteen years, helping Jon Arryn rule his realm while Robert drank and whored, but when Jon died, did my brother name me his Hand? No, he went galloping off to his dear friend Ned Stark, and offered him the honor. And small good it did either of them."

"Be that as it may, my lord," Maester Cressen said gently. "Great wrongs have been done you, but the past is dust. The future may yet be won if you join with the Starks. There are others you might sound out as well. What of Lady Arryn? If the queen murdered her husband, surely she will want justice for him. She has a young son, Jon Arryn's heir. If you were to betroth Shireen to him—"

"The boy is weak and sickly," Lord Stannis objected. "Even his father saw how it was, when he asked me to foster him on Dragonstone. Service as a page might have done him good, but that damnable Lannister woman had Lord Arryn poisoned before it could be done, and now Lysa hides him in the Eyrie. She'll never part with the boy, I promise you that."

"Then you must send Shireen to the Eyrie," the maester urged. "Dragonstone is a grim home for a child. Let her fool go with her, so she will have a familiar face about her."

"Familiar and hideous." Stannis furrowed his brow in thought. "Still . . . perhaps it is worth the trying . . ."

"Must the rightful Lord of the Seven Kingdoms beg for help from widow women and usurpers?" a woman's voice asked sharply.

Maester Cressen turned, and bowed his head. "My lady," he said, chagrined that he had not heard her enter.

Lord Stannis scowled. "I do not beg. Of anyone. Mind you remember that, woman."

"I am pleased to hear it, my lord." Lady Selyse was as tall as her husband, thin of body and thin of face, with prominent ears, a sharp nose, and the faintest hint of a mustache on her upper lip. She plucked it daily and cursed it regularly, yet it never failed to return. Her eyes were pale, her mouth stern, her voice a whip. She cracked it now. "Lady Arryn owes you her allegiance, as do the Starks, your brother Renly, and all the rest. You are their one true king. It would not be fitting to plead and bargain with them for what is rightfully yours by the grace of god."

God, she said, not *gods*. The red woman had won her, heart and soul, turning her from the gods of the Seven Kingdoms, both old and new, to worship the one they called the Lord of Light.

"Your god can keep his grace," said Lord Stannis, who did not share his wife's fervent new faith. "It's swords I need, not blessings. Do you have an army hidden somewhere that you've not told me of?" There was no affection in his tone. Stannis had always been uncomfortable around

women, even his own wife. When he had gone to King's Landing to sit on
Robert's council, he had left Selyse on Dragonstone with their daughter.
His letters had been few, his visits fewer; he did his duty in the marriage
bed once or twice a year, but took no joy in it, and the sons he had once
hoped for had never come.

"My brothers and uncles and cousins have armies," she told him.
"House Florent will rally to your banner."

"House Florent can field two thousand swords at best." It was said
that Stannis knew the strength of every house in the Seven Kingdoms.
"And you have a deal more faith in your brothers and uncles than I do,
my lady. The Florent lands lie too close to Highgarden for your lord
uncle to risk Mace Tyrell's wrath."

"There is another way." Lady Selyse moved closer. "Look out your
windows, my lord. There is the sign you have waited for, blazoned on the
sky. Red, it is, the red of flame, red for the fiery heart of the true god. It is
his banner—and yours! See how it unfurls across the heavens like a
dragon's hot breath, and you the Lord of Dragonstone. It means your
time has come, Your Grace. Nothing is more certain. You are meant to
sail from this desolate rock as Aegon the Conqueror once sailed, to
sweep all before you as he did. Only say the word, and embrace the
power of the Lord of Light."

"How many swords will the Lord of Light put into my hand?" Stannis
demanded again.

"All you need," his wife promised. "The swords of Storm's End and
Highgarden for a start, and all their lords bannermen."

"Davos would tell you different," Stannis said. "Those swords are
sworn to Renly. They love my charming young brother, as they once
loved Robert . . . and as they have never loved me."

"Yes," she answered, "but if Renly should die . . ."

Stannis looked at his lady with narrowed eyes, until Cressen could not
hold his tongue. "It is not to be thought. Your Grace, whatever follies
Renly has committed—"

"*Follies?* I call them treasons." Stannis turned back to his wife. "My
brother is young and strong, and he has a vast host around him, and these
rainbow knights of his."

"Melisandre has gazed into the flames, and seen him dead."

Cressen was horrorstruck. "Fratricide . . . my lord, this is *evil*, un-
thinkable . . . please, listen to me."

Lady Selyse gave him a measured look. "And what will you tell him,
Maester? How he might win half a kingdom if he goes to the Starks on
his knees and sells our daughter to Lysa Arryn?"

"I have heard your counsel, Cressen," Lord Stannis said. "Now I will
hear hers. You are dismissed."

Maester Cressen bent a stiff knee. He could feel Lady Selyse's eyes on his back as he shuffled slowly across the room. By the time he reached the bottom of the steps it was all he could do to stand erect. "Help me," he said to Pylos.

When he was safe back in his own rooms, Cressen sent the younger man away and limped to his balcony once more, to stand between his gargoyles and stare out to sea. One of Salladhor Saan's warships was sweeping past the castle, her gaily striped hull slicing through the grey-green waters as her oars rose and fell. He watched until she vanished behind a headland. *Would that my fears could vanish so easily.* Had he lived so long for this?

When a maester donned his collar, he put aside the hope of children, yet Cressen had oft felt a father nonetheless. Robert, Stannis, Renly . . . three sons he had raised after the angry sea claimed Lord Steffon. Had he done so ill that now he must watch one kill the other? He could not allow it, *would* not allow it.

The woman was the heart of it. Not the Lady Selyse, the *other* one. The red woman, the servants had named her, afraid to speak her name. "I will speak her name," Cressen told his stone hellhound. "Melisandre. *Her.*" Melisandre of Asshai, sorceress, shadowbinder, and priestess to R'hllor, the Lord of Light, the Heart of Fire, the God of Flame and Shadow. Melisandre, whose madness must not be allowed to spread beyond Dragonstone.

His chambers seemed dim and gloomy after the brightness of the morning. With fumbling hands, the old man lit a candle and carried it to the workroom beneath the rookery stair, where his ointments, potions, and medicines stood neatly on their shelves. On the bottom shelf behind a row of salves in squat clay jars he found a vial of indigo glass, no larger than his little finger. It rattled when he shook it. Cressen blew away a layer of dust and carried it back to his table. Collapsing into his chair, he pulled the stopper and spilled out the vial's contents. A dozen crystals, no larger than seeds, rattled across the parchment he'd been reading. They shone like jewels in the candlelight, so purple that the maester found himself thinking that he had never truly seen the color before.

The chain around his throat felt very heavy. He touched one of the crystals lightly with the tip of his little finger. *Such a small thing to hold the power of life and death.* It was made from a certain plant that grew only on the islands of the Jade Sea, half a world away. The leaves had to be aged, and soaked in a wash of limes and sugar water and certain rare spices from the Summer Isles. Afterward they could be discarded, but the potion must be thickened with ash and allowed to crystallize. The process was slow and difficult, the necessaries costly and hard to acquire. The alchemists of Lys knew the way of it, though, and the Faceless Men of Braavos . . . and the maesters of his order as well, though it was not something talked about beyond the walls of the Citadel. All the world knew that a maester forged his silver link when he learned the art of healing—but the world preferred to forget that men who knew how to heal also knew how to kill.

Cressen no longer recalled the name the Asshai'i gave the leaf, or the Lysene poisoners the crystal. In the Citadel, it was simply called the strangler. Dissolved in wine, it would make the muscles of a man's throat clench tighter than any fist, shutting off his windpipe. They said a victim's face turned as purple as the little crystal seed from which his death was grown, but so too did a man choking on a morsel of food.

And this very night Lord Stannis would feast his bannermen, his lady wife . . . and the red woman, Melisandre of Asshai.

I must rest, Maester Cressen told himself. *I must have all my strength come dark. My hands must not shake, nor my courage flag. It is a dreadful thing I do, yet it must be done. If there are gods, surely they will forgive me.* He had slept so poorly of late. A nap would refresh him for the ordeal ahead. Wearily, he tottered off to his bed. Yet when he closed his eyes, he could still see the light of the comet, red and fiery and vividly alive amidst the darkness of his dreams. *Perhaps it is my comet,* he thought drowsily at the last, just before sleep took him. *An omen of blood, foretelling murder . . . yes . . .*

When he woke it was full dark, his bedchamber was black, and every joint in his body ached. Cressen pushed himself up, his head throbbing. Clutching for his cane, he rose unsteady to his feet. *So late,* he thought. *They did not summon me.* He was always summoned for feasts, seated near the salt, close to Lord Stannis. His lord's face swam up before him, not the man he was but the boy he had been, standing cold in the shadows while the sun shone on his elder brother. Whatever he did, Robert had done first, and better. Poor boy . . . he must hurry, for *his* sake.

The maester found the crystals where he had left them, and scooped them off the parchment. Cressen owned no hollow rings, such as the poisoners of Lys were said to favor, but a myriad of pockets great and small were sewn inside the loose sleeves of his robe. He secreted the strangler seeds in one of them, threw open his door, and called, "Pylos? Where are you?" When he heard no reply, he called again, louder. "Pylos, I need help." Still there came no answer. That was queer; the young maester had his cell only a half turn down the stair, within easy earshot.

In the end, Cressen had to shout for the servants. "Make haste," he told them. "I have slept too long. They will be feasting by now . . . drinking . . . I should have been woken." What had happened to Maester Pylos? Truly, he did not understand.

Again he had to cross the long gallery. A night wind whispered through the great windows, sharp with the smell of the sea. Torches flickered along the walls of Dragonstone, and in the camp beyond, he could see hundreds of cookfires burning, as if a field of stars had fallen to the earth. Above, the comet blazed red and malevolent. *I am too old and wise to fear such things*, the maester told himself.

The doors to the Great Hall were set in the mouth of a stone dragon. He told the servants to leave him outside. It would be better to enter alone; he must not appear feeble. Leaning heavily on his cane, Cressen climbed the last few steps and hobbled beneath the gateway teeth. A pair of guardsmen opened the heavy red doors before him, unleashing a sudden blast of noise and light. Cressen stepped down into the dragon's maw.

Over the clatter of knife and plate and the low mutter of table talk, he heard Patchface singing, ". . . *dance, my lord, dance my lord*," to the accompaniment of jangling cowbells. The same dreadful song he'd sung this morning. *"The shadows come to stay, my lord, stay my lord, stay my lord."* The lower tables were crowded with knights, archers, and sellsword captains, tearing apart loaves of black bread to soak in their fish stew. Here there was no loud laughter, no raucous shouting such as marred the dignity of other men's feasts; Lord Stannis did not permit such.

Cressen made his way toward the raised platform where the lords sat with the king. He had to step wide around Patchface. Dancing, his bells ringing, the fool neither saw nor heard his approach. As he hopped from one leg to the other, Patchface lurched into Cressen, knocking his cane out from under him. They went crashing down together amidst the rushes in a tangle of arms and legs, while a sudden gale of laughter went up around them. No doubt it was a comical sight.

Patchface sprawled half on top of him, motley fool's face pressed close to his own. He had lost his tin helm with its antlers and bells. "Under the sea, you fall *up*," he declared. "I know, I know, oh, oh, oh." Giggling, the fool rolled off, bounded to his feet, and did a little dance.

Trying to make the best of it, the maester smiled feebly and struggled to rise, but his hip was in such pain that for a moment he was half afraid that he had broken it all over again. He felt strong hands grasp him under the arms and lift him back to his feet. "Thank you, ser," he murmured, turning to see which knight had come to his aid . . .

"Maester," said Lady Melisandre, her deep voice flavored with the music of the Jade Sea. "You ought take more care." As ever, she wore red head to heel, a long loose gown of flowing silk as bright as fire, with dagged sleeves and deep slashes in the bodice that showed glimpses of a darker bloodred fabric beneath. Around her throat was a red gold choker tighter than any maester's chain, ornamented with a single great ruby.

Her hair was not the orange or strawberry color of common red-haired men, but a deep burnished copper that shone in the light of the torches. Even her eyes were red . . . but her skin was smooth and white, unblemished, pale as cream. Slender she was, graceful, taller than most knights, with full breasts and narrow waist and a heart-shaped face. Men's eyes that once found her did not quickly look away, not even a maester's eyes. Many called her beautiful. She was not beautiful. She was red, and terrible, and red.

"I . . . thank you, my lady."

"A man your age must look to where he steps," Melisandre said courteously. "The night is dark and full of terrors."

He knew the phrase, some prayer of her faith. *It makes no matter, I have a faith of my own.* "Only children fear the dark," he told her. Yet even as he said the words, he heard Patchface take up his song again. *"The shadows come to dance, my lord, dance my lord, dance my lord."*

"Now here is a riddle," Melisandre said. "A clever fool and a foolish wise man." Bending, she picked up Patchface's helm from where it had fallen and set it on Cressen's head. The cowbells rang softly as the tin bucket slid down over his ears. "A crown to match your chain, Lord Maester," she announced. All around them, men were laughing.

Cressen pressed his lips together and fought to still his rage. She thought he was feeble and helpless, but she would learn otherwise before the night was done. Old he might be, yet he was still a maester of the Citadel. "I need no crown but truth," he told her, removing the fool's helm from his head.

"There are truths in this world that are not taught at Oldtown." Melisandre turned from him in a swirl of red silk and made her way back to the high table, where King Stannis and his queen were seated. Cressen handed the antlered tin bucket back to Patchface, and made to follow.

Maester Pylos sat in his place.

The old man could only stop and stare. "Maester Pylos," he said at last. "You . . . you did not wake me."

"His Grace commanded me to let you rest." Pylos had at least the grace to blush. "He told me you were not needed here."

Cressen looked over the knights and captains and lords sitting silent. Lord Celtigar, aged and sour, wore a mantle patterned with red crabs picked out in garnets. Handsome Lord Velaryon chose sea-green silk, the white gold seahorse at his throat matching his long fair hair. Lord Bar Emmon, that plump boy of fourteen, was swathed in purple velvet trimmed with white seal, Ser Axell Florent remained homely even in russet and fox fur, pious Lord Sunglass wore moonstones at throat and wrist and finger, and the Lysene captain Salladhor Saan was a sunburst of scarlet satin, gold, and jewels. Only Ser Davos dressed simply, in brown doublet and green wool mantle, and only Ser Davos met his gaze, with pity in his eyes.

"You are too ill and too confused to be of use to me, old man." It sounded so like Lord Stannis's voice, but it could not be, it could not. "Pylos will counsel me henceforth. Already he works with the ravens, since you can no longer climb to the rookery. I will not have you kill yourself in my service."

Maester Cressen blinked. *Stannis, my lord, my sad sullen boy, son I never had, you must not do this, don't you know how I have cared for you, lived for you, loved you despite all? Yes, loved you, better than Robert even, or Renly, for you were the one unloved, the one who needed me most.* Yet all he said was, "As you command, my lord, but . . . but I am hungry. Might not I have a place at your table?" *At your side, I belong at your side . . .*

Ser Davos rose from the bench. "I should be honored if the maester would sit here beside me, Your Grace."

"As you will." Lord Stannis turned away to say something to Melisandre, who had seated herself at his right hand, in the place of high honor. Lady Selyse was on his left, flashing a smile as bright and brittle as her jewels.

Too far, Cressen thought dully, looking at where Ser Davos was seated. Half of the lords bannermen were between the smuggler and the high table. *I must be closer to her if I am to get the strangler into her cup, yet how?*

Patchface was capering about as the maester made his slow way around the table to Davos Seaworth. "Here we eat fish," the fool declared happily, waving a cod about like a scepter. "Under the sea, the fish eat us. I know, I know, oh, oh, oh."

Ser Davos moved aside to make room on the bench. "We all should be in motley tonight," he said gloomily as Cressen seated himself, "for this is fool's business we're about. The red woman has seen victory in her flames, so Stannis means to press his claim, no matter what the numbers. Before she's done we're all like to see what Patchface saw, I fear— the bottom of the sea."

Cressen slid his hands up into his sleeves as if for warmth. His fingers found the hard lumps the crystals made in the wool. "Lord Stannis."

Stannis turned from the red woman, but it was Lady Selyse who replied. "*King* Stannis. You forget yourself, Maester."

"He is old, his mind wanders," the king told her gruffly. "What is it, Cressen? Speak your mind."

"As you intend to sail, it is vital that you make common cause with Lord Stark and Lady Arryn . . ."

"I make common cause with no one," Stannis Baratheon said.

"No more than light makes common cause with darkness." Lady Selyse took his hand.

Stannis nodded. "The Starks seek to steal half my kingdom, even as the Lannisters have stolen my throne and my own sweet brother the swords and service and strongholds that are mine by rights. They are all usurpers, and they are all my enemies."

I have lost him, Cressen thought, despairing. If only he could somehow approach Melisandre unseen . . . he needed but an instant's access to her cup. "You are the rightful heir to your brother Robert, the true Lord of the Seven Kingdoms, and King of the Andals, the Rhoynar, and the First Men," he said desperately, "but even so, you cannot hope to triumph without allies."

"He has an ally," Lady Selyse said. "R'hllor, the Lord of Light, the Heart of Fire, the God of Flame and Shadow."

"Gods make uncertain allies at best," the old man insisted, "and *that* one has no power here."

"You think not?" The ruby at Melisandre's throat caught the light as she turned her head, and for an instant it seemed to glow bright as the comet. "If you will speak such folly, Maester, you ought to wear your crown again."

"Yes," Lady Selyse agreed. "Patches's helm. It suits you well, old man. Put it on again, I command you."

"Under the sea, no one wears hats," Patchface said. "I know, I know, oh, oh, oh."

Lord Stannis's eyes were shadowed beneath his heavy brow, his mouth tight as his jaw worked silently. He always ground his teeth when he was angry. "Fool," he growled at last, "my lady wife commands. Give Cressen your helm."

No, the old maester thought, *this is not you, not your way, you were always just, always hard yet never cruel, never, you did not understand mockery, no more than you understood laughter.*

Patchface danced closer, his cowbells ringing, *clang-a-lang, ding-ding, clink-clank-clink-clank.* The maester sat silent while the fool set the antlered bucket on his brow. Cressen bowed his head beneath the weight. His bells clanged. "Perhaps he ought sing his counsel henceforth," Lady Selyse said.

"You go too far, woman," Lord Stannis said. "He is an old man, and he's served me well."

And I will serve you to the last, my sweet lord, my poor lonely son, Cressen thought, for suddenly he saw the way. Ser Davos's cup was before him, still half-full of sour red. He found a hard flake of crystal in his sleeve, held it tight between thumb and forefinger as he reached for the cup. *Smooth motions, deft, I must not fumble now,* he prayed, and the gods were kind. In the blink of an eye, his fingers were empty. His hands had not been so steady for years, nor half so fluid. Davos saw, but no one else, he was certain. Cup in hand, he rose to his feet. "Mayhaps I have been a fool. Lady Melisandre, will you share a cup of wine with me? A cup in honor of your god, your Lord of Light? A cup to toast his power?"

The red woman studied him. "If you wish."

He could feel them all watching him. Davos clutched at him as he left the bench, catching his sleeve with the fingers that Lord Stannis had shortened. "What are you doing?" he whispered.

"A thing that must be done," Maester Cressen answered, "for the sake of the realm, and the soul of my lord." He shook off Davos's hand, spilling a drop of wine on the rushes.

She met him beneath the high table with every man's eyes upon them. But Cressen saw only her. Red silk, red eyes, the ruby red at her throat, red lips curled in a faint smile as she put her hand atop his own, around the cup. Her skin felt hot, feverish. "It is not too late to spill the wine, Maester."

"No," he whispered hoarsely. "No."

"As you will." Melisandre of Asshai took the cup from his hands and drank long and deep. There was only half a swallow of wine remaining when she offered it back to him. "And now you."

His hands were shaking, but he made himself be strong. A maester of the Citadel must not be afraid. The wine was sour on his tongue. He let the empty cup drop from his fingers to shatter on the floor. "He *does* have power here, my lord," the woman said. "And fire cleanses." At her throat, the ruby shimmered redly.

Cressen tried to reply, but his words caught in his throat. His cough became a terrible thin whistle as he strained to suck in air. Iron fingers tightened round his neck. As he sank to his knees, still he shook his head, denying her, denying her power, denying her magic, denying her god. And the cowbells peeled in his antlers, singing *fool, fool, fool* while the red woman looked down on him in pity, the candle flames dancing in her red red eyes.

ARYA

At Winterfell they had called her "Arya Horseface" and she'd thought nothing could be worse, but that was before the orphan boy Lommy Greenhands had named her "Lumpyhead."

Her head *felt* lumpy when she touched it. When Yoren had dragged her into that alley she'd thought he meant to kill her, but the sour old man had only held her tight, sawing through her mats and tangles with his dagger. She remembered how the breeze sent the fistfuls of dirty brown hair skittering across the paving stones, toward the sept where her father had died. "I'm taking men and boys from the city," Yoren growled as the sharp steel scraped at her head. "Now you hold still, *boy*." By the time he had finished, her scalp was nothing but tufts and stubble.

Afterward he told her that from there to Winterfell she'd be Arry the orphan boy. "Gate shouldn't be hard, but the road's another matter. You got a long way to go in bad company. I got thirty this time, men and boys all bound for the Wall, and don't be thinking they're like that bastard brother o' yours." He shook her. "Lord Eddard gave me pick o' the dungeons, and I didn't find no little lordlings down there. This lot, half o' them would turn you over to the queen quick as spit for a pardon and maybe a few silvers. The other half'd do the same, only they'd rape you first. So you keep to yourself and make your water in the woods, alone. That'll be the hardest part, the pissing, so don't drink no more'n you need."

Leaving King's Landing was easy, just like he'd said. The Lannister guardsmen on the gate were stopping everyone, but Yoren called one by name and their wagons were waved through. No one spared Arya a glance. They were looking for a highborn girl, daughter of the King's Hand, not for a skinny boy with his hair chopped off. Arya never looked back. She wished the Rush would rise and wash the whole city away, Flea Bottom and the Red Keep and the Great Sept and *everything*, and every*one* too, especially Prince Joffrey and his mother. But she knew it wouldn't, and anyhow Sansa was still in the city and would wash away too. When she remembered that, Arya decided to wish for Winterfell instead.

Yoren was wrong about the pissing, though. That wasn't the hardest part at all; Lommy Greenhands and Hot Pie were the hardest part. Orphan boys. Yoren had plucked some from the streets with promises of food for their bellies and shoes for their feet. The rest he'd found in chains. "The Watch needs good men," he told them as they set out, "but you lot will have to do."

Yoren had taken grown men from the dungeons as well, thieves and poachers and rapers and the like. The worst were the three he'd found in the black cells who must have scared even him, because he kept them fettered hand and foot in the back of a wagon, and vowed they'd stay in irons all the way to the Wall. One had no nose, only the hole in his face where it had been cut off, and the gross fat bald one with the pointed teeth and the weeping sores on his cheeks had eyes like nothing human.

They took five wagons out of King's Landing, laden with supplies for the Wall: hides and bolts of cloth, bars of pig iron, a cage of ravens, books and paper and ink, a bale of sourleaf, jars of oil, and chests of medicine and spices. Teams of plow horses pulled the wagons, and Yoren had bought two coursers and a half-dozen donkeys for the boys. Arya would have preferred a real horse, but the donkey was better than riding on a wagon.

The men paid her no mind, but she was not so lucky with the boys. She was two years younger than the youngest orphan, not to mention smaller and skinnier, and Lommy and Hot Pie took her silence to mean she was scared, or stupid, or deaf. "Look at that sword Lumpyhead's got there," Lommy said one morning as they made their plodding way past orchards and wheat fields. He'd been a dyer's apprentice before he was caught stealing, and his arms were mottled green to the elbow. When he laughed he brayed like the donkeys they were riding. "Where's a gutter rat like Lumpyhead get him a sword?"

Arya chewed her lip sullenly. She could see the back of Yoren's faded black cloak up ahead of the wagons, but she was determined not to go crying to him for help.

"Maybe he's a little squire," Hot Pie put in. His mother had been a baker before she died, and he'd pushed her cart through the streets all day, shouting *"Hot pies! Hot pies!"* "Some lordy lord's little squire boy, that's it."

"He ain't no squire, look at him. I bet that's not even a real sword. I bet it's just some play sword made of tin."

Arya hated them making fun of Needle. "It's castle-forged steel, you stupid," she snapped, turning in the saddle to glare at them, "and you better shut your mouth."

The orphan boys hooted. "Where'd you get a blade like that, Lumpyface?" Hot Pie wanted to know.

"Lumpy*head*," corrected Lommy. "He prob'ly stole it."

"I did *not!*" she shouted. Jon Snow had given her Needle. Maybe she had to let them call her Lumpyhead, but she wasn't going to let them call Jon a thief.

"If he stole it, we could take it off him," said Hot Pie. "It's not his anyhow. I could use me a sword like that."

Lommy egged him on. "Go on, take it off him, I dare you."

Hot Pie kicked his donkey, riding closer. "Hey, Lumpyface, you gimme that sword." His hair was the color of straw, his fat face all sunburnt and peeling. "You don't know how to use it."

Yes I do, Arya could have said. *I killed a boy, a fat boy like you, I stabbed him in the belly and he died, and I'll kill you too if you don't let me alone.* Only she did not dare. Yoren didn't know about the stable-boy, but she was afraid of what he might do if he found out. Arya was pretty sure that some of the other men were killers too, the three in the manacles for sure, but the queen wasn't looking for *them*, so it wasn't the same.

"Look at him," brayed Lommy Greenhands. "I bet he's going to cry now. You want to cry, Lumpyhead?"

She had cried in her sleep the night before, dreaming of her father. Come morning, she'd woken red-eyed and dry, and could not have shed another tear if her life had hung on it.

"He's going to wet his pants," Hot Pie suggested.

"Leave him be," said the boy with the shaggy black hair who rode behind them. Lommy had named *him* the Bull, on account of this horned helm he had that he polished all the time but never wore. Lommy didn't dare mock the Bull. He was older, and big for his age, with a broad chest and strong-looking arms.

"You better give Hot Pie the sword, Arry," Lommy said. "Hot Pie wants it bad. He kicked a boy to death. He'll do the same to you, I bet."

"I knocked him down and I kicked him in the balls, and I kept kicking him there until he was dead," Hot Pie boasted. "I kicked him all to pieces. His balls were broke open and bloody and his cock turned black. You better gimme the sword."

Arya slid her practice sword from her belt. "You can have this one," she told Hot Pie, not wanting to fight.

"That's just some stick." He rode nearer and tried to reach over for Needle's hilt.

Arya made the stick whistle as she laid the wood across his donkey's hindquarters. The animal *hawed* and bucked, dumping Hot Pie on the ground. She vaulted off her own donkey and poked him in the gut as he tried to get up and he sat back down with a grunt. Then she whacked him across the face and his nose made a *crack* like a branch breaking. Blood dribbled from his nostrils. When Hot Pie began to wail, Arya whirled toward Lommy Greenhands, who was sitting on his donkey openmouthed. "You want some sword too?" she yelled, but he didn't. He raised dyed green hands in front of his face and squealed at her to get away.

The Bull shouted, "Behind you," and Arya spun. Hot Pie was on his knees, his fist closing around a big jagged rock. She let him throw it, ducking her head as it sailed past. Then she flew at him. He raised a hand and she hit it, and then his cheek, and then his knee. He grabbed for her, and she danced aside and bounced the wood off the back of his head. He fell down and got up and stumbled after her, his red face all smeared with dirt and blood. Arya slid into a water dancer's stance and waited. When he came close enough, she lunged, right between his legs, so hard that if her wooden sword had had a point it would have come out between his butt cheeks.

By the time Yoren pulled her off him, Hot Pie was sprawled out on the ground with his breeches brown and smelly, crying as Arya whapped him over and over and over. *"Enough,"* the black brother roared, prying the stick sword from her fingers, "you want to kill the fool?" When Lommy and some others started to squeal, the old man turned on them too. "Shut your mouths, or I'll be shutting them for you. Any more o' this, I'll tie you lot behind the wagons and *drag* you to the Wall." He spat. "And that goes twice for you, Arry. You come with me, boy. *Now.*"

They were all looking at her, even the three chained and manacled in the back of the wagon. The fat one snapped his pointy teeth together and *hissed*, but Arya ignored him.

The old man dragged her well off the road into a tangle of trees, cursing and muttering all the while. "If I had a thimble o' sense, I would've left you in King's Landing. You hear me, *boy?*" He always snarled that word, putting a bite in it so she would be certain to hear. "Unlace your breeches and pull 'em down. Go on, there's no one here to see. Do it."

Sullenly, Arya did as he said. "Over there, against the oak. Yes, like that." She wrapped her arms around the trunk and pressed her face to the rough wood. "You scream now. You scream loud."

I won't, Arya thought stubbornly, but when Yoren laid the wood against the back of her bare thighs, the shriek burst out of her anyway. "Think that hurt?" he said. "Try this one." The stick came whistling. Arya shrieked again, clutching the tree to keep from falling. "One more." She held on tight, chewing her lip, flinching when she heard it coming. The stroke made her jump and howl. *I won't cry*, she thought, *I won't do that. I'm a Stark of Winterfell, our sigil is the direwolf, direwolves don't cry.* She could feel a thin trickle of blood running down her left leg. Her thighs and cheeks were ablaze with pain. "Might be I got your attention now," Yoren said. "Next time you take that stick to one of your brothers, you'll get twice what you give, you hear me? Now cover yourself."

They're not my brothers, Arya thought as she bent to yank up her breeches, but she knew better than to say so. Her hands fumbled with her belt and laces.

Yoren was looking at her. "You hurt?"

Calm as still water, she told herself, the way Syrio Forel had taught her. "Some."

He spat. "That pie boy's hurting worse. It wasn't him as killed your father, girl, nor that thieving Lommy neither. Hitting them won't bring him back."

"I know," Arya muttered sullenly.

"Here's something you don't know. It wasn't supposed to happen like it did. I was set to leave, wagons bought and loaded, and a man comes with a boy for me, and a purse of coin, and a message, never mind who it's from. Lord Eddard's to take the black, he says to me, wait, he'll be going with you. Why d'you think I was there? Only something went queer."

"Joffrey," Arya breathed. "Someone should kill *him!*"

"Someone will, but it won't be me, nor you neither." Yoren tossed back her stick sword. "Got sourleaf back at the wagons," he said as they made their way back to the road. "You'll chew some, it'll help with the sting."

It did help, some, though the taste of it was foul and it made her spit look like blood. Even so, she walked for the rest of that day, and the day after, and the day after *that*, too raw to sit a donkey. Hot Pie was worse off; Yoren had to shift some barrels around so he could lie in the back of a wagon on some sacks of barley, and he whimpered every time the wheels hit a rock. Lommy Greenhands wasn't even hurt, yet he stayed as far away from Arya as he could get. "Every time you look at him, he twitches," the Bull told her as she walked beside his donkey. She did not answer. It seemed safer not to talk to anyone.

That night she lay upon her thin blanket on the hard ground, staring up at the great red comet. The comet was splendid and scary all at once. "The Red Sword," the Bull named it; he claimed it looked like a sword, the blade still red-hot from the forge. When Arya squinted the right way she could see the sword too, only it wasn't a new sword, it was Ice, her father's greatsword, all ripply Valyrian steel, and the red was Lord Eddard's blood on the blade after Ser Ilyn the King's Justice had cut off his head. Yoren had made her look away when it happened, yet it seemed to her that the comet looked like Ice must have, after.

When at last she slept, she dreamed of home. The kingsroad wound its way past Winterfell on its way to the Wall, and Yoren had promised he'd leave her there with no one any wiser about who she'd been. She yearned to see her mother again, and Robb and Bran and Rickon . . . but it was Jon Snow she thought of most. She wished somehow they could come to the Wall *before* Winterfell, so Jon might muss up her hair and call her "little sister." She'd tell him, "I missed you," and he'd say it too at the very same moment, the way they always used to say things together. She would have liked that. She would have liked that better than anything.

SANSA

T he morning of King Joffrey's name day dawned bright and windy, with the long tail of the great comet visible through the high scuttling clouds. Sansa was watching it from her tower window when Ser Arys Oakheart arrived to escort her down to the tourney grounds. "What do you think it means?" she asked him.

"Glory to your betrothed," Ser Arys answered at once. "See how it flames across the sky today on His Grace's name day, as if the gods themselves had raised a banner in his honor. The smallfolk have named it King Joffrey's Comet."

Doubtless that was what they told Joffrey; Sansa was not so sure. "I've heard servants calling it the Dragon's Tail."

"King Joffrey sits where Aegon the Dragon once sat, in the castle built by his son," Ser Arys said. "He is the dragon's heir—and crimson is the color of House Lannister, another sign. This comet is sent to herald Joffrey's ascent to the throne, I have no doubt. It means that he will triumph over his enemies."

Is it true? she wondered. *Would the gods be so cruel?* Her mother was one of Joffrey's enemies now, her brother Robb another. Her father had died by the king's command. Must Robb and her lady mother die next? The comet *was* red, but Joffrey was Baratheon as much as Lannister, and their sigil was a black stag on a golden field. Shouldn't the gods have sent Joff a golden comet?

Sansa closed the shutters and turned sharply away from the window. "You look very lovely today, my lady," Ser Arys said.

"Thank you, ser." Knowing that Joffrey would require her to attend the tourney in his honor, Sansa had taken special care with her face and clothes. She wore a gown of pale purple silk and a moonstone hair net that had been a gift from Joffrey. The gown had long sleeves to hide the bruises on her arms. Those were Joffrey's gifts as well. When they told him that Robb had been proclaimed King in the North, his rage had been a fearsome thing, and he had sent Ser Boros to beat her.

"Shall we go?" Ser Arys offered his arm and she let him lead her from her chamber. If she must have one of the Kingsguard dogging her steps, Sansa preferred that it be him. Ser Boros was short-tempered, Ser Meryn cold, and Ser Mandon's strange dead eyes made her uneasy, while Ser Preston treated her like a lackwit child. Arys Oakheart was courteous, and would talk to her cordially. Once he even objected when Joffrey commanded him to hit her. He *did* hit her in the end, but not hard as Ser Meryn or Ser Boros might have, and at least he had argued. The others obeyed without question . . . except for the Hound, but Joff never asked the Hound to punish her. He used the other five for that.

Ser Arys had light brown hair and a face that was not unpleasant to look upon. Today he made quite the dashing figure, with his white silk cloak fastened at the shoulder by a golden leaf, and a spreading oak tree worked upon the breast of his tunic in shining gold thread. "Who do you think will win the day's honors?" Sansa asked as they descended the steps arm in arm.

"I will," Ser Arys answered, smiling. "Yet I fear the triumph will have no savor. This will be a small field, and poor. No more than two score will enter the lists, including squires and freeriders. There is small honor in unhorsing green boys."

The last tourney had been different, Sansa reflected. King Robert had staged it in her father's honor. High lords and fabled champions had come from all over the realm to compete, and the whole city had turned out to watch. She remembered the splendor of it: the field of pavilions along the river with a knight's shield hung before each door, the long rows of silken pennants waving in the wind, the gleam of sunlight on bright steel and gilded spurs. The days had rung to the sounds of trumpets and pounding hooves, and the nights had been full of feasts and song. Those had been the most magical days of her life, but they seemed a memory from another age now. Robert Baratheon was dead, and her father as well, beheaded for a traitor on the steps of the Great Sept of Baelor. Now there were three kings in the land, and war raged beyond the Trident while the city filled with desperate men. Small wonder that they had to hold Joff's tournament behind the thick stone walls of the Red Keep.

"Will the queen attend, do you think?" Sansa always felt safer when Cersei was there to restrain her son.

"I fear not, my lady. The council is meeting, some urgent business." Ser Arys dropped his voice. "Lord Tywin has gone to ground at Harrenhal instead of bringing his army to the city as the queen commanded. Her Grace is furious." He fell silent as a column of Lannister guardsmen marched past, in crimson cloaks and lion-crested helms. Ser Arys was fond of gossip, but only when he was certain that no one was listening.

The carpenters had erected a gallery and lists in the outer bailey. It was a poor thing indeed, and the meager throng that had gathered to watch filled but half the seats. Most of the spectators were guardsmen in the gold cloaks of the City Watch or the crimson of House Lannister; of lords and ladies there were but a paltry few, the handful that remained at court. Grey-faced Lord Gyles Rosby was coughing into a square of pink silk. Lady Tanda was bracketed by her daughters, placid dull Lollys and acid-tongued Falyse. Ebon-skinned Jalabhar Xho was an exile who had no other refuge, Lady Ermesande a babe seated on her wet nurse's lap. The talk was she would soon be wed to one of the queen's cousins, so the Lannisters might claim her lands.

The king was shaded beneath a crimson canopy, one leg thrown negligently over the carved wooden arm of his chair. Princess Myrcella and Prince Tommen sat behind him. In the back of the royal box, Sandor Clegane stood at guard, his hands resting on his swordbelt. The white cloak of the Kingsguard was draped over his broad shoulders and fastened with a jeweled brooch, the snowy cloth looking somehow unnatural against his brown roughspun tunic and studded leather jerkin. "Lady Sansa," the Hound announced curtly when he saw her. His voice was as rough as the sound of a saw on wood. The burn scars on his face and throat made one side of his mouth twitch when he spoke.

Princess Myrcella nodded a shy greeting at the sound of Sansa's name, but plump little Prince Tommen jumped up eagerly. "Sansa, did you hear? I'm to ride in the tourney today. Mother said I could." Tommen was all of eight. He reminded her of her own little brother, Bran. They were of an age. Bran was back at Winterfell, a cripple, yet safe.

Sansa would have given anything to be with him. "I fear for the life of your foeman," she told Tommen solemnly.

"His foeman will be stuffed with straw," Joff said as he rose. The king was clad in a gilded breastplate with a roaring lion engraved upon its chest, as if he expected the war to engulf them at any moment. He was thirteen today, and tall for his age, with the green eyes and golden hair of the Lannisters.

"Your Grace," she said, dipping in a curtsy.

Ser Arys bowed. "Pray pardon me, Your Grace. I must equip myself for the lists."

Joffrey waved a curt dismissal while he studied Sansa from head to heels. "I'm pleased you wore my stones."

So the king had decided to play the gallant today. Sansa was relieved. "I thank you for them . . . and for your tender words. I pray you a lucky name day, Your Grace."

"Sit," Joff commanded, gesturing her to the empty seat beside his own. "Have you heard? The Beggar King is dead."

"Who?" For a moment Sansa was afraid he meant Robb.

"Viserys. The last son of Mad King Aerys. He's been going about the Free Cities since before I was born, calling himself a king. Well, Mother says the Dothraki finally crowned him. With molten gold." He laughed. "That's funny, don't you think? The dragon was their sigil. It's almost as good as if some wolf killed your traitor brother. Maybe I'll feed him to wolves after I've caught him. Did I tell you, I intend to challenge him to single combat?"

"I should like to see that, Your Grace." *More than you know.* Sansa kept her tone cool and polite, yet even so Joffrey's eyes narrowed as he tried to decide whether she was mocking him. "Will you enter the lists today?" she asked quickly.

The king frowned. "My lady mother said it was not fitting, since the tourney is in my honor. Otherwise I would have been champion. Isn't that so, dog?"

The Hound's mouth twitched. "Against this lot? Why not?"

He had been the champion in her father's tourney, Sansa remembered. "Will you joust today, my lord?" she asked him.

Clegane's voice was thick with contempt. "Wouldn't be worth the bother of arming myself. This is a tournament of gnats."

The king laughed. "My dog has a fierce bark. Perhaps I should command him to fight the day's champion. To the death." Joffrey was fond of making men fight to the death.

"You'd be one knight the poorer." The Hound had never taken a knight's vows. His brother was a knight, and he hated his brother.

A blare of trumpets sounded. The king settled back in his seat and took Sansa's hand. Once that would have set her heart to pounding, but that was before he had answered her plea for mercy by presenting her with her father's head. His touch filled her with revulsion now, but she knew better than to show it. She made herself sit very still.

"*Ser Meryn Trant of the Kingsguard,*" a herald called.

Ser Meryn entered from the west side of the yard, clad in gleaming white plate chased with gold and mounted on a milk-white charger with a flowing grey mane. His cloak streamed behind him like a field of snow. He carried a twelve-foot lance.

"*Ser Hobber of House Redwyne, of the Arbor,*" the herald sang. Ser Hobber trotted in from the east, riding a black stallion caparisoned in burgundy and blue. His lance was striped in the same colors, and his shield bore the grape cluster sigil of his House. The Redwyne twins were the queen's unwilling guests, even as Sansa was. She wondered whose notion it had been for them to ride in Joffrey's tourney. Not their own, she thought.

At a signal from the master of revels, the combatants couched their lances and put their spurs to their mounts. There were shouts from the watching guardsmen and the lords and ladies in the gallery. The knights came together in the center of the yard with a great shock of wood and steel. The white lance and the striped one exploded in splinters within a second of each other. Hobber Redwyne reeled at the impact, yet somehow managed to keep his seat. Wheeling their horses about at the far end of the lists, the knights tossed down their broken lances and accepted replacements from the squires. Ser Horas Redwyne, Ser Hobber's twin, shouted encouragement to his brother.

But on their second pass Ser Meryn swung the point of his lance to strike Ser Hobber in the chest, driving him from the saddle to crash resoundingly to the earth. Ser Horas cursed and ran out to help his battered brother from the field.

"Poorly ridden," declared King Joffrey.

"*Ser Balon Swann, of Stonehelm in the Red Watch,*" came the herald's cry. Wide white wings ornamented Ser Balon's greathelm, and black and white swans fought on his shield. "*Morros of House Slynt, heir to Lord Janos of Harrenhal.*"

"Look at that upjumped oaf," Joff hooted, loud enough for half the yard to hear. Morros, a mere squire and a new-made squire at that, was having difficulty managing lance and shield. The lance was a knight's weapon, Sansa knew, the Slynts lowborn. Lord Janos had been no more than commander of the City Watch before Joffrey had raised him to Harrenhal and the council.

I hope he falls and shames himself, she thought bitterly. *I hope Ser Balon kills him.* When Joffrey proclaimed her father's death, it had been Janos Slynt who seized Lord Eddard's severed head by the hair and raised it on high for king and crowd to behold, while Sansa wept and screamed.

Morros wore a checkered black-and-gold cloak over black armor inlaid with golden scrollwork. On his shield was the bloody spear his father had chosen as the sigil of their new-made house. But he did not seem to know what to do with the shield as he urged his horse forward, and Ser

Balon's point struck the blazon square. Morros dropped his lance, fought for balance, and lost. One foot caught in a stirrup as he fell, and the runaway charger dragged the youth to the end of the lists, head bouncing against the ground. Joff hooted derision. Sansa was appalled, wondering if the gods had heard her vengeful prayer. But when they disentangled Morros Slynt from his horse, they found him bloodied but alive. "Tommen, we picked the wrong foe for you," the king told his brother. "The straw knight jousts better than that one."

Next came Ser Horas Redwyne's turn. He fared better than his twin, vanquishing an elderly knight whose mount was bedecked with silver griffins against a striped blue-and-white field. Splendid as he looked, the old man made a poor contest of it. Joffrey curled his lip. "This is a feeble show."

"I warned you," said the Hound. "Gnats."

The king was growing bored. It made Sansa anxious. She lowered her eyes and resolved to keep quiet, no matter what. When Joffrey Baratheon's mood darkened, any chance word might set off one of his rages.

"*Lothor Brune, freerider in the service of Lord Baelish,*" cried the herald. "*Ser Dontos the Red, of House Hollard.*"

The freerider, a small man in dented plate without device, duly appeared at the west end of the yard, but of his opponent there was no sign. Finally a chestnut stallion trotted into view in a swirl of crimson and scarlet silks, but Ser Dontos was not on it. The knight appeared a moment later, cursing and staggering, clad in breastplate and plumed helm and nothing else. His legs were pale and skinny, and his manhood flopped about obscenely as he chased after his horse. The watchers roared and shouted insults. Catching his horse by the bridle, Ser Dontos tried to mount, but the animal would not stand still and the knight was so drunk that his bare foot kept missing the stirrup.

By then the crowd was howling with laughter . . . all but the king. Joffrey had a look in his eyes that Sansa remembered well, the same look he'd had at the Great Sept of Baelor the day he pronounced death on Lord Eddard Stark. Finally Ser Dontos the Red gave it up for a bad job, sat down in the dirt, and removed his plumed helm. "I lose," he shouted. "Fetch me some wine."

The king stood. "A cask from the cellars! I'll see him drowned in it."

Sansa heard herself gasp. "*No,* you can't."

Joffrey turned his head. "What did you say?"

Sansa could not believe she had spoken. Was she mad? To tell him *no* in front of half the court? She hadn't meant to say anything, only . . . Ser Dontos was drunk and silly and useless, but he meant no harm.

"Did you say I *can't*? Did you?"

"Please," Sansa said, "I only meant . . . it would be ill luck, Your Grace . . . to, to kill a man on your name day."

"You're lying," Joffrey said. "I ought to drown you with him, if you care for him so much."

"I don't care for him, Your Grace." The words tumbled out desperately. "Drown him or have his head off, only . . . kill him on the morrow, if you like, but please . . . not today, not on your name day. I couldn't bear for you to have ill luck . . . terrible luck, even for kings, the singers all say so . . ."

Joffrey scowled. He knew she was lying, she could see it. He would make her bleed for this.

"The girl speaks truly," the Hound rasped. "What a man sows on his name day, he reaps throughout the year." His voice was flat, as if he did not care a whit whether the king believed him or no. Could it be *true*? Sansa had not known. It was just something she'd said, desperate to avoid punishment.

Unhappy, Joffrey shifted in his seat and flicked his fingers at Ser Dontos. "Take him away. I'll have him killed on the morrow, the fool."

"He is," Sansa said. "A fool. You're so clever, to see it. He's better fitted to be a fool than a knight, isn't he? You ought to dress him in motley and make him clown for you. He doesn't deserve the mercy of a quick death."

The king studied her a moment. "Perhaps you're not so stupid as Mother says." He raised his voice. "Did you hear my lady, Dontos? From this day on, you're my new fool. You can sleep with Moon Boy and dress in motley."

Ser Dontos, sobered by his near brush with death, crawled to his knees. "Thank you, Your Grace. And you, my lady. Thank you."

As a brace of Lannister guardsmen led him off, the master of revels approached the box. "Your Grace," he said, "shall I summon a new challenger for Brune, or proceed with the next tilt?"

"Neither. These are gnats, not knights. I'd have them all put to death, only it's my name day. The tourney is done. Get them all out of my sight."

The master of revels bowed, but Prince Tommen was not so obedient. "I'm supposed to ride against the straw man."

"Not today."

"But I want to ride!"

"I don't care what you want."

"Mother *said* I could ride."

"She said," Princess Myrcella agreed.

"Mother *said*," mocked the king. "Don't be childish."

"We're children," Myrcella declared haughtily. "We're *supposed* to be childish."

The Hound laughed. "She has you there."

Joffrey was beaten. "Very well. Even my brother couldn't tilt any worse than these others. Master, bring out the quintain, Tommen wants to be a gnat."

Tommen gave a shout of joy and ran off to be readied, his chubby little legs pumping hard. "Luck," Sansa called to him.

They set up the quintain at the far end of the lists while the prince's pony was being saddled. Tommen's opponent was a child-sized leather warrior stuffed with straw and mounted on a pivot, with a shield in one hand and a padded mace in the other. Someone had fastened a pair of antlers to the knight's head. Joffrey's father King Robert had worn antlers on his helm, Sansa remembered . . . but so did his uncle Lord Renly, Robert's brother, who had turned traitor and crowned himself king.

A pair of squires buckled the prince into his ornate silver-and-crimson armor. A tall plume of red feathers sprouted from the crest of his helm, and the lion of Lannister and crowned stag of Baratheon frolicked together on his shield. The squires helped him mount, and Ser Aron Santagar, the Red Keep's master-at-arms, stepped forward and handed Tommen a blunted silver longsword with a leaf-shaped blade, crafted to fit an eight-year-old hand.

Tommen raised the blade high. "Casterly Rock!" he shouted in a high boyish voice as he put his heels into his pony and started across the hard-packed dirt at the quintain. Lady Tanda and Lord Gyles started a ragged cheer, and Sansa added her voice to theirs. The king brooded in silence.

Tommen got his pony up to a brisk trot, waved his sword vigorously, and struck the knight's shield a solid blow as he went by. The quintain spun, the padded mace flying around to give the prince a mighty whack in the back of his head. Tommen spilled from the saddle, his new armor rattling like a bag of old pots as he hit the ground. His sword went flying, his pony cantered away across the bailey, and a great gale of derision went up. King Joffrey laughed longest and loudest of all.

"Oh," Princess Myrcella cried. She scrambled out of the box and ran to her little brother.

Sansa found herself possessed of a queer giddy courage. "You should go with her," she told the king. "Your brother might be hurt."

Joffrey shrugged. "What if he is?"

"You should help him up and tell him how well he rode." Sansa could not seem to stop herself.

"He got knocked off his horse and fell in the dirt," the king pointed out. "That's not riding well."

"Look," the Hound interrupted. "The boy has courage. He's going to try again."

They were helping Prince Tommen mount his pony. *If only Tommen were the elder instead of Joffrey,* Sansa thought. *I wouldn't mind marrying Tommen.*

The sounds from the gatehouse took them by surprise. Chains rattled as the portcullis was drawn upward, and the great gates opened to the creak of iron hinges. "Who told them to open the gate?" Joff demanded. With the troubles in the city, the gates of the Red Keep had been closed for days.

A column of riders emerged from beneath the portcullis with a clink of steel and a clatter of hooves. Clegane stepped close to the king, one hand on the hilt of his longsword. The visitors were dinted and haggard and dusty, yet the standard they carried was the lion of Lannister, golden on its crimson field. A few wore the red cloaks and mail of Lannister men-at-arms, but more were freeriders and sellswords, armored in oddments and bristling with sharp steel . . . and there were others, monstrous savages out of one of Old Nan's tales, the scary ones Bran used to love. They were clad in shabby skins and boiled leather, with long hair and fierce beards. Some wore bloodstained bandages over their brows or wrapped around their hands, and others were missing eyes, ears, and fingers.

In their midst, riding on a tall red horse in a strange high saddle that cradled him back and front, was the queen's dwarf brother Tyrion Lannister, the one they called the Imp. He had let his beard grow to cover his pushed-in face, until it was a bristly tangle of yellow and black hair, coarse as wire. Down his back flowed a shadowskin cloak, black fur striped with white. He held the reins in his left hand and carried his right arm in a white silk sling, but otherwise looked as grotesque as Sansa remembered from when he had visited Winterfell. With his bulging brow and mismatched eyes, he was still the ugliest man she had ever chanced to look upon.

Yet Tommen put his spurs into his pony and galloped headlong across the yard, shouting with glee. One of the savages, a huge shambling man so hairy that his face was all but lost beneath his whiskers, scooped the boy out of his saddle, armor and all, and deposited him on the ground beside his uncle. Tommen's breathless laughter echoed off the walls as Tyrion clapped him on the backplate, and Sansa was startled to see that the two were of a height. Myrcella came running after her brother, and the dwarf picked her up by the waist and spun her in a circle, squealing.

When he lowered her back to the ground, the little man kissed her lightly on the brow and came waddling across the yard toward Joffrey.

Two of his men followed close behind him; a black-haired black-eyed sellsword who moved like a stalking cat, and a gaunt youth with an empty socket where one eye should have been. Tommen and Myrcella trailed after them.

The dwarf went to one knee before the king. "Your Grace."

"You," Joffrey said.

"Me," the Imp agreed, "although a more courteous greeting might be in order, for an uncle and an elder."

"They said you were dead," the Hound said.

The little man gave the big one a look. One of his eyes was green, one was black, and both were cool. "I was speaking to the king, not to his cur."

"*I'm* glad you're not dead," said Princess Myrcella.

"We share that view, sweet child." Tyrion turned to Sansa. "My lady, I am sorry for your losses. Truly, the gods are cruel."

Sansa could not think of a word to say to him. How could he be sorry for her losses? Was he mocking her? It wasn't the gods who'd been cruel, it was Joffrey.

"I am sorry for your loss as well, Joffrey," the dwarf said.

"What loss?"

"Your royal father? A large fierce man with a black beard; you'll recall him if you try. He was king before you."

"Oh, *him*. Yes, it was very sad, a boar killed him."

"Is that what 'they' say, Your Grace?"

Joffrey frowned. Sansa felt that she ought to say something. What was it that Septa Mordane used to tell her? *A lady's armor is courtesy*, that was it. She donned her armor and said, "I'm sorry my lady mother took you captive, my lord."

"A great many people are sorry for that," Tyrion replied, "and before I am done, some may be a deal sorrier . . . yet I thank you for the sentiment. Joffrey, where might I find your mother?"

"She's with my council," the king answered. "Your brother Jaime keeps losing battles." He gave Sansa an angry look, as if it were *her* fault. "He's been taken by the Starks and we've lost Riverrun and now her stupid brother is calling himself a king."

The dwarf smiled crookedly. "All sorts of people are calling themselves kings these days."

Joff did not know what to make of that, though he looked suspicious and out of sorts. "Yes. Well. I am pleased you're not dead, Uncle. Did you bring me a gift for my name day?"

"I did. My wits."

"I'd sooner have Robb Stark's head," Joff said with a sly glance at Sansa. "Tommen, Myrcella, come."

Sandor Clegane lingered behind a moment. "I'd guard that tongue of yours, little man," he warned, before he strode off after his liege.

Sansa was left with the dwarf and his monsters. She tried to think of what else she might say. "You hurt your arm," she managed at last.

"One of your northmen hit me with a morningstar during the battle on the Green Fork. I escaped him by falling off my horse." His grin turned into something softer as he studied her face. "Is it grief for your lord father that makes you so sad?"

"My father was a traitor," Sansa said at once. "And my brother and lady mother are traitors as well." That reflex she had learned quickly. "I am loyal to my beloved Joffrey."

"No doubt. As loyal as a deer surrounded by wolves."

"Lions," she whispered, without thinking. She glanced about nervously, but there was no one close enough to hear.

Lannister reached out and took her hand, and gave it a squeeze. "I am only a little lion, child, and I vow, I shall not savage you." Bowing, he said, "But now you must excuse me. I have urgent business with queen and council."

Sansa watched him walk off, his body swaying heavily from side to side with every step, like something from a grotesquerie. *He speaks more gently than Joffrey*, she thought, *but the queen spoke to me gently too. He's still a Lannister, her brother and Joff's uncle, and no friend.* Once she had loved Prince Joffrey with all her heart, and admired and trusted his mother, the queen. They had repaid that love and trust with her father's head. Sansa would never make that mistake again.

TYRION

I n the chilly white raiment of the Kingsguard, Ser Mandon Moore
looked like a corpse in a shroud. "Her Grace left orders, the council
in session is not to be disturbed."

"I would be only a small disturbance, ser." Tyrion slid the parchment
from his sleeve. "I bear a letter from my father, Lord Tywin Lannister,
the Hand of the King. There is his seal."

"Her Grace does not wish to be disturbed," Ser Mandon repeated
slowly, as if Tyrion were a dullard who had not heard him the first time.

Jaime had once told him that Moore was the most dangerous of the
Kingsguard—excepting himself, always—because his face gave no hint as
what he might do next. Tyrion would have welcomed a hint. Bronn and
Timett could likely kill the knight if it came to swords, but it would
scarcely bode well if he began by slaying one of Joffrey's protectors. Yet if
he let the man turn him away, where was his authority? He made himself smile. "Ser Mandon, you have not met my companions. This is
Timett son of Timett, a red hand of the Burned Men. And this is Bronn.
Perchance you recall Ser Vardis Egen, who was captain of Lord Arryn's
household guard?"

"I know the man." Ser Mandon's eyes were pale grey, oddly flat and
lifeless.

"Knew," Bronn corrected with a thin smile.

Ser Mandon did not deign to show that he had heard that.

"Be that as it may," Tyrion said lightly, "I truly must see my sister and present my letter, ser. If you would be so kind as to open the door for us?"

The white knight did not respond. Tyrion was almost at the point of trying to force his way past when Ser Mandon abruptly stood aside. "You may enter. They may not."

A small victory, he thought, *but sweet*. He had passed his first test. Tyrion Lannister shouldered through the door, feeling almost tall. Five members of the king's small council broke off their discussion suddenly. "You," his sister Cersei said in a tone that was equal parts disbelief and distaste.

"I can see where Joffrey learned his courtesies." Tyrion paused to admire the pair of Valyrian sphinxes that guarded the door, affecting an air of casual confidence. Cersei could smell weakness the way a dog smells fear.

"What are you doing here?" His sister's lovely green eyes studied him without the least hint of affection.

"Delivering a letter from our lord father." He sauntered to the table and placed the tightly rolled parchment between them.

The eunuch Varys took the letter and turned it in his delicate powdered hands. "How kind of Lord Tywin. And his sealing wax is such a lovely shade of gold." Varys gave the seal a close inspection. "It gives every appearance of being genuine."

"Of course it's genuine." Cersei snatched it out of his hands. She broke the wax and unrolled the parchment.

Tyrion watched her read. His sister had taken the king's seat for herself—he gathered Joffrey did not often trouble to attend council meetings, no more than Robert had—so Tyrion climbed up into the Hand's chair. It seemed only appropriate.

"This is absurd," the queen said at last. "My lord father has sent my brother to sit in his place in this council. He bids us accept Tyrion as the Hand of the King, until such time as he himself can join us."

Grand Maester Pycelle stroked his flowing white beard and nodded ponderously. "It would seem that a welcome is in order."

"Indeed." Jowly, balding Janos Slynt looked rather like a frog, a smug frog who had gotten rather above himself. "We have sore need of you, my lord. Rebellion everywhere, this grim omen in the sky, rioting in the city streets . . ."

"And whose fault is that, Lord Janos?" Cersei lashed out. "Your gold cloaks are charged with keeping order. As to you, Tyrion, you could better serve us on the field of battle."

He laughed. "No, I'm done with fields of battle, thank you. I sit a chair better than a horse, and I'd sooner hold a wine goblet than a battle-axe. All that about the thunder of the drums, sunlight flashing on armor, magnificent destriers snorting and prancing? Well, the drums gave me headaches, the sunlight flashing on my armor cooked me up like a harvest day goose, and those magnificent destriers shit *everywhere*. Not that I am complaining. Compared to the hospitality I enjoyed in the Vale of Arryn, drums, horseshit, and fly bites are my favorite things."

Littlefinger laughed. "Well said, Lannister. A man after my own heart."

Tyrion smiled at him, remembering a certain dagger with a dragonbone hilt and a Valyrian steel blade. *We must have a talk about that, and soon.* He wondered if Lord Petyr would find that subject amusing as well. "Please," he told them, "do let me be of service, in whatever *small* way I can."

Cersei read the letter again. "How many men have you brought with you?"

"A few hundred. My own men, chiefly. Father was loath to part with any of his. He *is* fighting a war, after all."

"What use will your few hundred men be if Renly marches on the city, or Stannis sails from Dragonstone? I ask for an army and my father sends me a dwarf. The *king* names the Hand, with the consent of council. Joffrey named our lord father."

"And our lord father named me."

"He cannot do that. Not without Joff's consent."

"Lord Tywin is at Harrenhal with his host, if you'd care to take it up with him," Tyrion said politely. "My lords, perchance you would permit me a private word with my sister?"

Varys slithered to his feet, smiling in that unctuous way he had. "How you must have yearned for the sound of your sweet sister's voice. My lords, please, let us give them a few moments together. The woes of our troubled realm shall keep."

Janos Slynt rose hesitantly and Grand Maester Pycelle ponderously, yet they rose. Littlefinger was the last. "Shall I tell the steward to prepare chambers in Maegor's Holdfast?"

"My thanks, Lord Petyr, but I will be taking Lord Stark's former quarters in the Tower of the Hand."

Littlefinger laughed. "You're a braver man than me, Lannister. You *do* know the fate of our last two Hands?"

"Two? If you mean to frighten me, why not say four?"

"Four?" Littlefinger raised an eyebrow. "Did the Hands before Lord Arryn meet some dire end in the Tower? I'm afraid I was too young to pay them much mind."

"Aerys Targaryen's last Hand was killed during the Sack of King's Landing, though I doubt he'd had time to settle into the Tower. He was only Hand for a fortnight. The one before him was burned to death. And

before them came two others who died landless and penniless in exile,
and counted themselves lucky. I believe my lord father was the last
Hand to depart King's Landing with his name, properties, and parts all
intact."

"Fascinating," said Littlefinger. "And all the more reason I'd sooner
bed down in the dungeon."

Perhaps you'll get that wish, Tyrion thought, but he said, "Courage and folly are cousins, or so I've heard. Whatever curse may linger
over the Tower of the Hand, I pray I'm small enough to escape its
notice."

Janos Slynt laughed, Littlefinger smiled, and Grand Maester Pycelle
followed them both out, bowing gravely.

"I hope Father did not send you all this way to plague us with history
lessons," his sister said when they were alone.

"How I have yearned for the sound of your sweet voice," Tyrion
sighed to her.

"How I have yearned to have that eunuch's tongue pulled out with
hot pincers," Cersei replied. "Has father lost his senses? Or did you forge
this letter?" She read it once more, with mounting annoyance. "Why
would he inflict *you* on me? I wanted him to come himself." She crushed
Lord Tywin's letter in her fingers. "I am Joffrey's regent, and I sent him a
royal *command*!"

"And he ignored you," Tyrion pointed out. "He has quite a large army,
he can do that. Nor is he the first. Is he?"

Cersei's mouth tightened. He could see her color rising. "If I name this
letter a forgery and tell them to throw you in a dungeon, no one will
ignore *that,* I promise you."

He was walking on rotten ice now, Tyrion knew. One false step and he
would plunge through. "No one," he agreed amiably, "least of all our
father. The one with the army. But why should you want to throw me
into a dungeon, sweet sister, when I've come all this long way to help
you?"

"I do not require *your* help. It was our father's presence that I commanded."

"Yes," he said quietly, "but it's Jaime you want."

His sister fancied herself subtle, but he had grown up with her. He
could read her face like one of his favorite books, and what he read now
was rage, and fear, and despair. "Jaime—"

"—is my brother no less than yours," Tyrion interrupted. "Give me
your support and I promise you, we will have Jaime freed and returned to
us unharmed."

"How?" Cersei demanded. "The Stark boy and his mother are not like
to forget that we beheaded Lord Eddard."

"True," Tyrion agreed, "yet you still hold his daughters, don't you? I saw the older girl out in the yard with Joffrey."

"Sansa," the queen said. "I've given it out that I have the younger brat as well, but it's a lie. I sent Meryn Trant to take her in hand when Robert died, but her wretched dancing master interfered and the girl fled. No one has seen her since. Likely she's dead. A great many people died that day."

Tyrion had hoped for both Stark girls, but he supposed one would have to do. "Tell me about our friends on the council."

His sister glanced at the door. "What of them?"

"Father seems to have taken a dislike to them. When I left him, he was wondering how their heads might look on the wall beside Lord Stark's." He leaned forward across the table. "Are you certain of their loyalty? Do you trust them?"

"I trust no one," Cersei snapped. "I need them. Does Father believe they are playing us false?"

"Suspects, rather."

"Why? What does he know?"

Tyrion shrugged. "He knows that your son's short reign has been a long parade of follies and disasters. That suggests that someone is giving Joffrey some very bad counsel."

Cersei gave him a searching look. "Joff has had no lack of good counsel. He's always been strong-willed. Now that he's king, he believes he should do as he pleases, not as he's bid."

"Crowns do queer things to the heads beneath them," Tyrion agreed. "This business with Eddard Stark . . . Joffrey's work?"

The queen grimaced. "He was instructed to pardon Stark, to allow him to take the black. The man would have been out of our way forever, and we might have made peace with that son of his, but Joff took it upon himself to give the mob a better show. What was I to do? He called for Lord Eddard's head in front of half the city. And Janos Slynt and Ser Ilyn went ahead blithely and shortened the man without a word from me!" Her hand tightened into a fist. "The High Septon claims we profaned Baelor's Sept with blood, after lying to him about our intent."

"It would seem he has a point," said Tyrion. "So this *Lord* Slynt, he was part of it, was he? Tell me, whose fine notion was it to grant him Harrenhal and name him to the council?"

"Littlefinger made the arrangements. We needed Slynt's gold cloaks. Eddard Stark was plotting with Renly and he'd written to Lord Stannis, offering him the throne. We might have lost all. Even so, it was a close thing. If Sansa hadn't come to me and told me all her father's plans . . ."

Tyrion was surprised. "Truly? His own daughter?" Sansa had always seemed such a sweet child, tender and courteous.

"The girl was wet with love. She would have done *anything* for Joffrey, until he cut off her father's head and called it mercy. That put an end to that."

"His Grace has a unique way of winning the hearts of his subjects," Tyrion said with a crooked smile. "Was it Joffrey's wish to dismiss Ser Barristan Selmy from his Kingsguard too?"

Cersei sighed. "Joff wanted someone to blame for Robert's death. Varys suggested Ser Barristan. Why not? It gave Jaime command of the Kingsguard and a seat on the small council, and allowed Joff to throw a bone to his dog. He is very fond of Sandor Clegane. We were prepared to offer Selmy some land and a towerhouse, more than the useless old fool deserved."

"I hear that useless old fool slew two of Slynt's gold cloaks when they tried to seize him at the Mud Gate."

His sister looked very unhappy. "Janos should have sent more men. He is not as competent as might be wished."

"Ser Barristan was the Lord Commander of Robert Baratheon's Kingsguard," Tyrion reminded her pointedly. "He and Jaime are the only survivors of Aerys Targaryen's seven. The smallfolk talk of him in the same way they talk of Serwyn of the Mirror Shield and Prince Aemon the Dragonknight. What do you imagine they'll think when they see Barristan the Bold riding beside Robb Stark or Stannis Baratheon?"

Cersei glanced away. "I had not considered that."

"Father did," said Tyrion. "*That* is why he sent me. To put an end to these follies and bring your son to heel."

"Joff will be no more tractable for you than for me."

"He might."

"Why should he?"

"He knows *you* would never hurt him."

Cersei's eyes narrowed. "If you believe I'd ever allow you to harm my son, you're sick with fever."

Tyrion sighed. She'd missed the point, as she did so often. "Joffrey is as safe with me as he is with you," he assured her, "but so long as the boy *feels* threatened, he'll be more inclined to listen." He took her hand. "I *am* your brother, you know. You need me, whether you care to admit it or no. Your son needs me, if he's to have a hope of retaining that ugly iron chair."

His sister seemed shocked that he would touch her. "You have always been cunning."

"In my own small way." He grinned.

"It may be worth the trying . . . but make no mistake, Tyrion. If I accept you, you shall be the King's Hand in name, but *my* Hand in truth.

You will share all your plans and intentions with me before you act, and you will do *nothing* without my consent. Do you understand?"

"Oh, yes."

"Do you agree?"

"Certainly," he lied. "I am yours, sister." *For as long as I need to be.* "So, now that we are of one purpose, we ought have no more secrets between us. You say Joffrey had Lord Eddard killed, Varys dismissed Ser Barristan, and Littlefinger gifted us with Lord Slynt. Who murdered Jon Arryn?"

Cersei yanked her hand back. "How should I know?"

"The grieving widow in the Eyrie seems to think it was me. Where did she come by that notion, I wonder?"

"I'm sure I don't know. That fool Eddard Stark accused me of the same thing. He hinted that Lord Arryn suspected or . . . well, believed . . ."

"That you were fucking our sweet Jaime?"

She slapped him.

"Did you think I was as blind as Father?" Tyrion rubbed his cheek. "Who you lie with is no matter to me . . . although it doesn't seem quite just that you should open your legs for one brother and not the other."

She slapped him.

"Be gentle, Cersei, I'm only jesting with you. If truth be told, I'd sooner have a nice whore. I never understood what Jaime saw in you, apart from his own reflection."

She slapped him.

His cheeks were red and burning, yet he smiled. "If you keep doing that, I may get angry."

That stayed her hand. "Why should I care if you do?"

"I have some new friends," Tyrion confessed. "You won't like them at all. How did you kill Robert?"

"He did that himself. All we did was help. When Lancel saw that Robert was going after boar, he gave him strongwine. His favorite sour red, but fortified, three times as potent as he was used to. The great stinking fool loved it. He could have stopped swilling it down anytime he cared to, but no, he drained one skin and told Lancel to fetch another. The boar did the rest. You should have been at the feast, Tyrion. There has never been a boar so delicious. They cooked it with mushrooms and apples, and it tasted like triumph."

"Truly, sister, you were born to be a widow." Tyrion had rather liked Robert Baratheon, great blustering oaf that he was . . . doubtless in part because his sister loathed him so. "Now, if you are done slapping me, I will be off." He twisted his legs around and clambered down awkwardly from the chair.

frowned. "I haven't given you leave to depart. I want to know
␣␣␣␣␣ intend to free Jaime."

␣␣␣␣␣ tell you when I know. Schemes are like fruit, they require a
␣␣␣␣␣ ripening. Right now, I have a mind to ride through the streets
and take the measure of this city." Tyrion rested his hand on the head
of the sphinx beside the door. "One parting request. Kindly make certain no harm comes to Sansa Stark. It would not do to lose *both* the
daughters."

Outside the council chamber, Tyrion nodded to Ser Mandon and made
his way down the long vaulted hall. Bronn fell in beside him. Of Timett
son of Timett there was no sign. "Where's our red hand?" Tyrion asked.

"He felt an urge to explore. His kind was not made for waiting about
in halls."

"I hope he doesn't kill anyone important." The clansmen Tyrion had
brought down from their fastnesses in the Mountains of the Moon were
loyal in their own fierce way, but they were proud and quarrelsome as
well, prone to answer insults real or imagined with steel. "Try to find
him. And while you are at it, see that the rest have been quartered and
fed. I want them in the barracks beneath the Tower of the Hand, but
don't let the steward put the Stone Crows near the Moon Brothers, and
tell him the Burned Men must have a hall all to themselves."

"Where will you be?"

"I'm riding back to the Broken Anvil."

Bronn grinned insolently. "Need an escort? The talk is, the streets are
dangerous."

"I'll call upon the captain of my sister's household guard, and remind
him that I am no less a Lannister than she is. He needs to recall that his
oath is to Casterly Rock, not to Cersei or Joffrey."

An hour later, Tyrion rode from the Red Keep accompanied by a dozen
Lannister guardsmen in crimson cloaks and lion-crested halfhelms. As
they passed beneath the portcullis, he noted the heads mounted atop the
walls. Black with rot and old tar, they had long since become unrecognizable. "Captain Vylarr," he called, "I want those taken down on the morrow. Give them to the silent sisters for cleaning." It would be hell to
match them with the bodies, he supposed, yet it must be done. Even in
the midst of war, certain decencies needed to be observed.

Vylarr grew hesitant. "His Grace has told us he wishes the traitors'
heads to remain on the walls until he fills those last three empty spikes
there on the end."

"Let me hazard a wild stab. One is for Robb Stark, the others for Lords
Stannis and Renly. Would that be right?"

"Yes, my lord."

"My nephew is thirteen years old today, Vylarr. Try and recall that. I'll have the heads down on the morrow, or one of those empty spikes may have a different lodger. Do you take my meaning, Captain?"

"I'll see that they're taken down myself, my lord."

"Good." Tyrion put his heels into his horse and trotted away, leaving the red cloaks to follow as best they could.

He had told Cersei he intended to take the measure of the city. That was not entirely a lie. Tyrion Lannister was not pleased by much of what he saw. The streets of King's Landing had always been teeming and raucous and noisy, but now they reeked of danger in a way that he did not recall from past visits. A naked corpse sprawled in the gutter near the Street of Looms, being torn at by a pack of feral dogs, yet no one seemed to care. Watchmen were much in evidence, moving in pairs through the alleys in their gold cloaks and shirts of black ringmail, iron cudgels never far from their hands. The markets were crowded with ragged men selling their household goods for any price they could get . . . and conspicuously empty of farmers selling food. What little produce he did see was three times as costly as it had been a year ago. One peddler was hawking rats roasted on a skewer. *"Fresh rats,"* he cried loudly, *"fresh rats."* Doubtless fresh rats were to be preferred to old stale rotten rats. The frightening thing was, the rats looked more appetizing than most of what the butchers were selling. On the Street of Flour, Tyrion saw guards at every other shop door. When times grew lean, even bakers found sellswords cheaper than bread, he reflected.

"There is no food coming in, is there?" he said to Vylarr.

"Little enough," the captain admitted. "With the war in the riverlands and Lord Renly raising rebels in Highgarden, the roads are closed to south and west."

"And what has my good sister done about this?"

"She is taking steps to restore the king's peace," Vylarr assured him. "Lord Slynt has tripled the size of the City Watch, and the queen has put a thousand craftsmen to work on our defenses. The stonemasons are strengthening the walls, carpenters are building scorpions and catapults by the hundred, fletchers are making arrows, the smiths are forging blades, and the Alchemists' Guild has pledged ten thousand jars of wildfire."

Tyrion shifted uncomfortably in his saddle. He was pleased that Cersei had not been idle, but wildfire was treacherous stuff, and ten thousand jars were enough to turn all of King's Landing into cinders. "Where has my sister found the coin to pay for all of this?" It was no secret that King Robert had left the crown vastly in debt, and alchemists were seldom mistaken for altruists.

"Lord Littlefinger always finds a way, my lord. He has imposed a tax on those wishing to enter the city."

"Yes, that would work," Tyrion said, thinking, *Clever. Clever and cruel.* Tens of thousands had fled the fighting for the supposed safety of King's Landing. He had seen them on the kingsroad, troupes of mothers and children and anxious fathers who had gazed on his horses and wagons with covetous eyes. Once they reached the city they would doubtless pay over all they had to put those high comforting walls between them and the war . . . though they might think twice if they knew about the wildfire.

The inn beneath the sign of the broken anvil stood within sight of those walls, near the Gate of the Gods where they had entered that morning. As they rode into its courtyard, a boy ran out to help Tyrion down from his horse. "Take your men back to the castle," he told Vylarr. "I'll be spending the night here."

The captain looked dubious. "Will you be safe, my lord?"

"Well, as to that, Captain, when I left the inn this morning it was full of Black Ears. One is never quite safe when Chella daughter of Cheyk is about." Tyrion waddled toward the door, leaving Vylarr to puzzle at his meaning.

A gust of merriment greeted him as he shoved into the inn's common room. He recognized Chella's throaty chuckle and the lighter music of Shae's laughter. The girl was seated by the hearth, sipping wine at a round wooden table with three of the Black Ears he'd left to guard her and a plump man whose back was to him. The innkeeper, he assumed . . . until Shae called Tyrion by name and the intruder rose. "My good lord, I am *so* pleased to see you," he gushed, a soft eunuch's smile on his powdered face.

Tyrion stumbled. "Lord Varys. I had not thought to see you here." *The Others take him, how did he find them so quickly?*

"Forgive me if I intrude," Varys said. "I was taken by a sudden urge to meet your young lady."

"Young lady," Shae repeated, savoring the words. "You're half right, m'lord. I'm young."

Eighteen, Tyrion thought. *Eighteen, and a whore, but quick of wit, nimble as a cat between the sheets, with large dark eyes and fine black hair and a sweet, soft, hungry little mouth . . . and mine! Damn you, eunuch.* "I fear I'm the intruder, Lord Varys," he said with forced courtesy. "When I came in, you were in the midst of some merriment."

"M'lord Varys complimented Chella on her ears and said she must have killed many men to have such a fine necklace," Shae explained. It grated on him to hear her call Varys *m'lord* in that tone; that was what she called him in their pillow play. "And Chella told him only cowards kill the vanquished."

"Braver to leave the man alive, with a chance to cleanse his shame by winning back his ear," explained Chella, a small dark woman whose grisly neckware was hung with no less than forty-six dried, wrinkled ears. Tyrion had counted them once. "Only so can you prove you do not fear your enemies."

Shae hooted. "And then m'lord says if he was a Black Ear he'd never sleep, for dreams of one-eared men."

"A problem I will never need face," Tyrion said. "I'm terrified of my enemies, so I kill them all."

Varys giggled. "Will you take some wine with us, my lord?"

"I'll take some wine." Tyrion seated himself beside Shae. He understood what was happening here, if Chella and the girl did not. Varys was delivering a message. When he said, *I was taken by a sudden urge to meet your young lady,* what he meant was, *You tried to hide her, but I knew where she was, and who she was, and here I am.* He wondered who had betrayed him. The innkeeper, that boy in the stable, a guard on the gate . . . or one of his own?

"I always like to return to the city through the Gate of the Gods," Varys told Shae as he filled the wine cups. "The carvings on the gatehouse are exquisite, they make me weep each time I see them. The eyes . . . so expressive, don't you think? They almost seem to follow you as you ride beneath the portcullis."

"I never noticed, m'lord," Shae replied. "I'll look again on the morrow, if it please you."

Don't bother, sweetling, Tyrion thought, swirling the wine in the cup. *He cares not a whit about carvings. The eyes he boasts of are his own. What he means is that he was watching, that he knew we were here the moment we passed through the gates.*

"Do be careful, child," Varys urged. "King's Landing is not wholly safe these days. I know these streets well, and yet I almost feared to come today, alone and unarmed as I was. Lawless men are everywhere in this dark time, oh, yes. Men with cold steel and colder hearts." *Where I can come alone and unarmed, others can come with swords in their fists,* he was saying.

Shae only laughed. "If they try and bother me, they'll be one ear short when Chella runs them off."

Varys hooted as if that was the funniest thing he had ever heard, but there was no laughter in his eyes when he turned them on Tyrion. "Your young lady has an amiable way to her. I should take very good care of her if I were you."

"I intend to. Any man who tries to harm her—well, I'm too small to be a Black Ear, and I make no claims to courage." *See! I speak the same tongue you do, eunuch. Hurt her, and I'll have your head.*

"I will leave you." Varys rose. "I know how weary you must be. I only wished to welcome you, my lord, and tell you how very pleased I am by your arrival. We have dire need of you on the council. Have you seen the comet?"

"I'm short, not blind," Tyrion said. Out on the kingsroad, it had seemed to cover half the sky, outshining the crescent moon.

"In the streets, they call it the Red Messenger," Varys said. "They say it comes as a herald before a king, to warn of fire and blood to follow." The eunuch rubbed his powdered hands together. "May I leave you with a bit of a riddle, Lord Tyrion?" He did not wait for an answer. "In a room sit three great men, a king, a priest, and a rich man with his gold. Between them stands a sellsword, a little man of common birth and no great mind. Each of the great ones bids him slay the other two. 'Do it,' says the king, 'for I am your lawful ruler.' 'Do it,' says the priest, 'for I command you in the names of the gods.' 'Do it,' says the rich man, 'and all this gold shall be yours.' So tell me—who lives and who dies?" Bowing deeply, the eunuch hurried from the common room on soft slippered feet.

When he was gone, Chella gave a snort and Shae wrinkled up her pretty face. "The rich man lives. Doesn't he?"

Tyrion sipped at his wine, thoughtful. "Perhaps. Or not. That would depend on the sellsword, it seems." He set down his cup. "Come, let's go upstairs."

She had to wait for him at the top of the steps, for her legs were slim and supple while his were short and stunted and full of aches. But she was smiling when she reached her. "Did you miss me?" she teased as she took his hand.

"Desperately," Tyrion admitted. Shae only stood a shade over five feet, yet still he must look up to her . . . but in her case he found he did not mind. She was sweet to look up at.

"You'll miss me all the time in your Red Keep," she said as she led him to her room. "All alone in your cold bed in your Tower of the Hand."

"Too true." Tyrion would gladly have kept her with him, but his lord father had forbidden it. *You will not take the whore to court*, Lord Tywin had commanded. Bringing her to the city was as much defiance as he dared. All his authority derived from his father, the girl had to understand that. "You won't be far," he promised. "You'll have a house, with guards and servants, and I'll visit as often as I'm able."

Shae kicked shut the door. Through the cloudy panes of the narrow window, he could make out the Great Sept of Baelor crowning Visenya's Hill, but Tyrion was distracted by a different sight. Bending, Shae took her gown by the hem, drew it over her head, and tossed it aside. She did not believe in smallclothes. "You'll never be able to rest," she said as she stood before him, pink and nude and lovely, one hand braced on her hip. "You'll think of me every time you go to bed. Then you'll get hard and you'll have no one to help you and you'll never be able to sleep unless you"—she grinned that wicked grin Tyrion liked so well—"is *that* why they call it the Tower of the Hand, m'lord?"

"Be quiet and kiss me," he commanded.

He could taste the wine on her lips, and feel her small firm breasts pressed against him as her fingers moved to the lacings of his breeches. "My lion," she whispered when he broke off the kiss to undress. "My sweet lord, my giant of Lannister." Tyrion pushed her toward the bed. When he entered her, she screamed loud enough to wake Baelor the Blessed in his tomb, and her nails left gouges in his back. He'd never had a pain he liked half so well.

Fool, he thought to himself afterward, as they lay in the center of the sagging mattress amidst the rumpled sheets. *Will you never learn, dwarf? She's a whore, damn you, it's your coin she loves, not your cock. Remember Tysha?* Yet when his fingers trailed lightly over one nipple, it stiffened at the touch, and he could see the mark on her breast where he'd bitten her in his passion.

"So what will you do, m'lord, now that you're the Hand of the King?" Shae asked him as he cupped that warm sweet flesh.

"Something Cersei will never expect," Tyrion murmured softly against her slender neck. "I'll do . . . justice."

BRAN

Bran preferred the hard stone of the window seat to the comforts of his featherbed and blankets. Abed, the walls pressed close and the ceiling hung heavy above him; abed, the room was his cell, and Winterfell his prison. Yet outside his window, the wide world still called.

He could not walk, nor climb nor hunt nor fight with a wooden sword as once he had, but he could still *look.* He liked to watch the windows begin to glow all over Winterfell as candles and hearth fires were lit behind the diamond-shaped panes of tower and hall, and he loved to listen to the direwolves sing to the stars.

Of late, he often dreamed of wolves. *They are talking to me, brother to brother,* he told himself when the direwolves howled. He could almost understand them . . . not quite, not truly, but *almost* . . . as if they were singing in a language he had once known and somehow forgotten. The Walders might be scared of them, but the Starks had wolf blood. Old Nan told him so. "Though it is stronger in some than in others," she warned.

Summer's howls were long and sad, full of grief and longing. Shaggydog's were more savage. Their voices echoed through the yards and halls until the castle rang and it seemed as though some great pack of direwolves haunted Winterfell, instead of only two . . . two where there had once been six. *Do they miss their brothers and sisters too?* Bran wondered. *Are they calling to Grey Wind and Ghost, to Nymeria and Lady's Shade? Do they want them to come home and be a pack together?*

"Who can know the mind of a wolf?" Ser Rodrik Cassel said when Bran asked him why they howled. Bran's lady mother had named him castellan of Winterfell in her absence, and his duties left him little time for idle questions.

"It's freedom they're calling for," declared Farlen, who was kennelmaster and had no more love for the direwolves than his hounds did. "They don't like being walled up, and who's to blame them? Wild things belong in the wild, not in a castle."

"They want to hunt," agreed Gage the cook as he tossed cubes of suet in a great kettle of stew. "A wolf smells better'n any man. Like as not, they've caught the scent o' prey."

Maester Luwin did not think so. "Wolves often howl at the moon. These are howling at the comet. See how bright it is, Bran? Perchance they think it *is* the moon."

When Bran repeated that to Osha, she laughed aloud. "Your wolves have more wit than your maester," the wildling woman said. "They know truths the grey man has forgotten." The way she said it made him shiver, and when he asked what the comet meant, she answered, "Blood and fire, boy, and nothing sweet."

Bran asked Septon Chayle about the comet while they were sorting through some scrolls snatched from the library fire. "It is the sword that slays the season," he replied, and soon after the white raven came from Oldtown bringing word of autumn, so doubtless he was right.

Though Old Nan did not think so, and she'd lived longer than any of them. "Dragons," she said, lifting her head and sniffing. She was near blind and could not see the comet, yet she claimed she could *smell* it. "It be dragons, boy," she insisted. Bran got no *princes* from Nan, no more than he ever had.

Hodor said only, "Hodor." That was all he ever said.

And still the direwolves howled. The guards on the walls muttered curses, hounds in the kennels barked furiously, horses kicked at their stalls, the Walders shivered by their fire, and even Maester Luwin complained of sleepless nights. Only Bran did not mind. Ser Rodrik had confined the wolves to the godswood after Shaggydog bit Little Walder, but the stones of Winterfell played queer tricks with sound, and sometimes it sounded as if they were in the yard right below Bran's window. Other times he would have sworn they were up on the curtain walls, loping round like sentries. He wished that he could see them.

He *could* see the comet hanging above the Guards Hall and the Bell Tower, and farther back the First Keep, squat and round, its gargoyles black shapes against the bruised purple dusk. Once Bran had known every stone of those buildings, inside and out; he had climbed them all, scampering up walls as easily as other boys ran down stairs. Their rooftops had been his secret places, and the crows atop the broken tower his special friends.

And then he had fallen.

Bran did not remember falling, yet they said he had, so he supposed it must be true. He had almost died. When he saw the weatherworn gargoyles atop the First Keep where it had happened, he got a queer tight feeling in his belly. And now he could not climb, nor walk nor run nor swordfight, and the dreams he'd dreamed of knighthood had soured in his head.

Summer had howled the day Bran had fallen, and for long after as he lay broken in his bed; Robb had told him so before he went away to war. Summer had mourned for him, and Shaggydog and Grey Wind had joined in his grief. And the night the bloody raven had brought word of their father's death, the wolves had known that too. Bran had been in the maester's turret with Rickon talking of the children of the forest when Summer and Shaggydog had drowned out Luwin with their howls.

Who are they mourning now? Had some enemy slain the King in the North, who used to be his brother Robb? Had his bastard brother Jon Snow fallen from the Wall? Had his mother died, or one of his sisters? Or was this something else, as maester and septon and Old Nan seemed to think?

If I were truly a direwolf, I would understand the song, he thought wistfully. In his wolf dreams, he could race up the sides of mountains, jagged icy mountains taller than any tower, and stand at the summit beneath the full moon with all the world below him, the way it used to be.

"Oooo," Bran cried tentatively. He cupped his hands around his mouth and lifted his head to the comet. "*Ooooooooooooooooooooo, ahoooooooooooooooo,*" he howled. It sounded stupid, high and hollow and quavering, a little boy's howl, not a wolf's. Yet Summer gave answer, his deep voice drowning out Bran's thin one, and Shaggydog made it a chorus. Bran *haroooed* again. They howled together, last of their pack.

The noise brought a guard to his door, Hayhead with the wen on his nose. He peered in, saw Bran howling out the window, and said, "What's this, my prince?"

It made Bran feel queer when they called him prince, though he *was* Robb's heir, and Robb was King in the North now. He turned his head to howl at the guard. "*Ooooooooo. Oo-oo-ooooooooooooo.*"

Hayhead screwed up his face. "Now you stop that there."

"*Ooo-ooo-oooooo. Ooo-ooo-ooooooooooooooooooo.*"

The guardsman retreated. When he came back, Maester Luwin was with him, all in grey, his chain tight about his neck. "Bran, those beasts make sufficient noise without your help." He crossed the room and put his hand on the boy's brow. "The hour grows late, you ought to be fast asleep."

"I'm talking to the wolves." Bran brushed the hand away.

"Shall I have Hayhead carry you to your bed?"

"I can get to bed myself." Mikken had hammered a row of iron bars into the wall, so Bran could pull himself about the room with his arms. It was slow and hard and it made his shoulders ache, but he hated being carried. "Anyway, I don't have to sleep if I don't want to."

"All men must sleep, Bran. Even princes."

"When I sleep I turn into a wolf." Bran turned his face away and looked back out into the night. "Do wolves dream?"

"All creatures dream, I think, yet not as men do."

"Do dead men dream?" Bran asked, thinking of his father. In the dark crypts below Winterfell, a stonemason was chiseling out his father's likeness in granite.

"Some say yes, some no," the maester answered. "The dead themselves are silent on the matter."

"Do trees dream?"

"Trees? No . . ."

"They do," Bran said with sudden certainty. "They dream tree dreams. I dream of a tree sometimes. A weirwood, like the one in the godswood. It calls to me. The wolf dreams are better. I smell things, and sometimes I can taste the blood."

Maester Luwin tugged at his chain where it chafed his neck. "If you would only spend more time with the other children—"

"I hate the other children," Bran said, meaning the Walders. "I commanded you to send them away."

Luwin grew stern. "The Freys are your lady mother's wards, sent here to be fostered at her express command. It is not for you to expel them, nor is it kind. If we turned them out, where would they go?"

"Home. It's their fault you won't let me have Summer."

"The Frey boy did not ask to be attacked," the maester said, "no more than I did."

"That was Shaggydog." Rickon's big black wolf was so wild he even frightened Bran at times. "Summer never bit anyone."

"Summer ripped out a man's throat in this very chamber, or have you forgotten? The truth is, those sweet pups you and your brothers found in the snow have grown into dangerous beasts. The Frey boys are wise to be wary of them."

"We should put the Walders in the godswood. They could play lord of the crossing all they want, and Summer could sleep with me again. If I'm the prince, why won't you heed me? I wanted to ride Dancer, but Alebelly wouldn't let me past the gate."

"And rightly so. The wolfswood is full of danger; your last ride should have taught you that. Would you want some outlaw to take you captive and sell you to the Lannisters?"

"Summer would save me," Bran insisted stubbornly. "Princes should be allowed to sail the sea and hunt boar in the wolfswood and joust with lances."

"Bran, child, why do you torment yourself so? One day you may do some of these things, but now you are only a boy of eight."

"I'd sooner be a wolf. Then I could live in the wood and sleep when I wanted, and I could find Arya and Sansa. I'd *smell* where they were and go save them, and when Robb went to battle I'd fight beside him like Grey Wind. I'd tear out the Kingslayer's throat with my teeth, *rip*, and then the war would be over and everyone would come back to Winterfell. If I was a wolf . . ." He howled. "*Ooo-ooo-oooooooooooo.*"

Luwin raised his voice. "A true prince would welcome—"

"*AAHOOOOOOO,*" Bran howled, louder. "*OOOO-OOOO-OOOO.*"

The maester surrendered. "As you will, child." With a look that was part grief and part disgust, he left the bedchamber.

Howling lost its savor once Bran was alone. After a time he quieted. *I did welcome them*, he told himself, resentful. *I was the lord in Winterfell, a true lord, he can't say I wasn't.* When the Walders had arrived from the Twins, it had been Rickon who wanted them gone. A baby of four, he had screamed that he wanted Mother and Father and Robb, not these strangers. It had been up to Bran to soothe him and bid the Freys welcome. He had offered them meat and mead and a seat by the fire, and even Maester Luwin had said afterward that he'd done well.

Only that was before the game.

The game was played with a log, a staff, a body of water, and a great deal of shouting. The water was the most important, Walder and Walder assured Bran. You could use a plank or even a series of stones, and a branch could be your staff. You didn't *have* to shout. But without water, there was no game. As Maester Luwin and Ser Rodrik were not about to let the children go wandering off into the wolfswood in search of a stream, they made do with one of the murky pools in the godswood. Walder and Walder had never seen hot water bubbling from the ground before, but they both allowed how it would make the game even better.

Both of them were called Walder Frey. Big Walder said there were bunches of Walders at the Twins, all named after the boys' grandfather, Lord Walder Frey. "We have our *own* names at Winterfell," Rickon told them haughtily when he heard that.

The way their game was played, you laid the log across the water, and one player stood in the middle with the stick. He was the lord of the crossing, and when one of the other players came up, he had to say, "I am the lord of the crossing, who goes there?" And the other player had to make up a speech about who they were and why they should be allowed to cross. The lord could make them swear oaths and answer questions. They didn't have to tell the truth, but the oaths were binding unless they said "Mayhaps," so the trick was to say "Mayhaps" so the lord of the crossing didn't notice. Then you could try and knock the lord into the water and *you* got to be lord of the crossing, but only if you'd said "Mayhaps." Otherwise you were out of the game. The lord got to knock anyone in the water anytime he pleased, and he was the only one who got to use a stick.

In practice, the game seemed to come down to mostly shoving, hitting, and falling into the water, along with a lot of loud arguments about whether or not someone had said "Mayhaps." Little Walder was lord of the crossing more often than not.

He was Little Walder even though he was tall and stout, with a red face and a big round belly. Big Walder was sharp-faced and skinny and half a foot shorter. "He's fifty-two days older than me," Little Walder explained, "so he was bigger at first, but I grew faster."

"We're cousins, not brothers," added Big Walder, the little one. "I'm Walder son of Jammos. My father was Lord Walder's son by his fourth wife. He's Walder son of Merrett. His grandmother was Lord Walder's third wife, the Crakehall. He's ahead of me in the line of succession even though I'm older."

"Only by fifty-two days," Little Walder objected. "And neither of us will ever hold the Twins, stupid."

"I will," Big Walder declared. "We're not the only Walders either. Ser Stevron has a grandson, Black Walder, he's fourth in line of succession, and there's Red Walder, Ser Emmon's son, and Bastard Walder, who isn't in the line at all. He's called Walder Rivers not Walder Frey. Plus there's girls named Walda."

"And Tyr. You always forget Tyr."

"He's Waltyr, not Walder," Big Walder said airily. "And he's after us, so he doesn't matter. Anyhow, I never liked him."

Ser Rodrik decreed that they would share Jon Snow's old bedchamber, since Jon was in the Night's Watch and never coming back. Bran hated that; it made him feel as if the Freys were trying to steal Jon's place.

He had watched wistfully while the Walders contested with Turnip the cook's boy and Joseth's girls Bandy and Shyra. The Walders had decreed that Bran should be the judge and decide whether or not people had said "Mayhaps," but as soon as they started playing they forgot all about him.

The shouts and splashes soon drew others: Palla the kennel girl, Cayn's boy Calon, TomToo whose father Fat Tom had died with Bran's father at King's Landing. Before very long, every one of them was soaked and muddy. Palla was brown from head to heel, with moss in her hair, breathless from laughter. Bran had not heard so much laughing since the night the bloody raven came. *If I had my legs, I'd knock all of them into the water*, he thought bitterly. *No one would ever be lord of the crossing but me.*

Finally Rickon came running into the godswood, Shaggydog at his heels. He watched Turnip and Little Walder struggle for the stick until Turnip lost his footing and went in with a huge splash, arms waving. Rickon yelled, "Me! Me now! I want to play!" Little Walder beckoned him on, and Shaggydog started to follow. "No, Shaggy," his brother commanded. "Wolves can't play. You stay with Bran." And he did . . .

. . . until Little Walder had smacked Rickon with the stick, square across his belly. Before Bran could blink, the black wolf was flying over the plank, there was blood in the water, the Walders were shrieking red murder, Rickon sat in the mud laughing, and Hodor came lumbering in shouting "Hodor! Hodor! Hodor!"

After that, oddly, Rickon decided he *liked* the Walders. They never played lord of the crossing again, but they played other games—monsters and maidens, rats and cats, come-into-my-castle, all sorts of things. With Rickon by their side, the Walders plundered the kitchens for pies and honeycombs, raced round the walls, tossed bones to the pups in the kennels, and trained with wooden swords under Ser Rodrik's sharp eye. Rickon even showed them the deep vaults under the earth where the stonemason was carving father's tomb. "You had no right!" Bran screamed at his brother when he heard. "That was our place, a *Stark* place!" But Rickon never cared.

The door to his bedchamber opened. Maester Luwin was carrying a green jar, and this time Osha and Hayhead came with him. "I've made you a sleeping draught, Bran."

Osha scooped him up in her bony arms. She was very tall for a woman, and wiry strong. She bore him effortlessly to his bed.

"This will give you dreamless sleep," Maester Luwin said as he pulled the stopper from the jar. "Sweet, dreamless sleep."

"It will?" Bran said, wanting to believe.

"Yes. Drink."

Bran drank. The potion was thick and chalky, but there was honey in it, so it went down easy.

"Come the morn, you'll feel better." Luwin gave Bran a smile and a pat as he took his leave.

Osha lingered behind. "Is it the wolf dreams again?"

Bran nodded.

"You should not fight so hard, boy. I see you talking to the heart tree. Might be the gods are trying to talk back."

"The gods?" he murmured, drowsy already. Osha's face grew blurry and grey. *Sweet, dreamless sleep,* Bran thought.

Yet when the darkness closed over him, he found himself in the godswood, moving silently beneath green-grey sentinels and gnarled oaks as old as time. *I am walking,* he thought, exulting. Part of him knew that it was only a dream, but even the dream of walking was better than the truth of his bedchamber, walls and ceiling and door.

It was dark amongst the trees, but the comet lit his way, and his feet were sure. He was moving on four *good* legs, strong and swift, and he could feel the ground underfoot, the soft crackling of fallen leaves, thick roots and hard stones, the deep layers of humus. It was a good feeling.

The smells filled his head, alive and intoxicating; the green muddy stink of the hot pools, the perfume of rich rotting earth beneath his paws, the squirrels in the oaks. The scent of squirrel made him remember the taste of hot blood and the way the bones would crack between his teeth. Slaver filled his mouth. He had eaten no more than half a day past, but there was no joy in dead meat, even deer. He could hear the squirrels chittering and rustling above him, safe among their leaves, but they knew better than to come down to where his brother and he were prowling.

He could smell his brother too, a familiar scent, strong and earthy, his scent as black as his coat. His brother was loping around the walls, full of fury. Round and round he went, night after day after night, tireless, searching . . . for prey, for a way out, for his mother, his littermates, his pack . . . searching, searching, and never finding.

Behind the trees the walls rose, piles of dead man-rock that loomed all about this speck of living wood. Speckled grey they rose, and moss-spotted, yet thick and strong and higher than any wolf could hope to leap. Cold iron and splintery wood closed off the only holes through the piled stones that hemmed them in. His brother would stop at every hole and bare his fangs in rage, but the ways stayed closed.

He had done the same the first night, and learned that it was no good. Snarls would open no paths here. Circling the walls would not push them back. Lifting a leg and marking the trees would keep no men away. The world had tightened around them, but beyond the walled wood still stood the great grey caves of man-rock. *Winterfell*, he remembered, the sound coming to him suddenly. Beyond its sky-tall man-cliffs the true world was calling, and he knew he must answer or die.

ARYA

They traveled dawn to dusk, past woods and orchards and neatly tended fields, through small villages, crowded market towns, and stout holdfasts. Come dark, they would make camp and eat by the light of the Red Sword. The men took turns standing watch. Arya would glimpse firelight flickering through the trees from the camps of other travelers. There seemed to be more camps every night, and more traffic on the kingsroad by day.

Morn, noon, and night they came, old folks and little children, big men and small ones, barefoot girls and women with babes at their breasts. Some drove farm wagons or bumped along in the back of ox carts. More rode: draft horses, ponies, mules, donkeys, anything that would walk or run or roll. One woman led a milk cow with a little girl on its back. Arya saw a smith pushing a wheelbarrow with his tools inside, hammers and tongs and even an anvil, and a little while later a different man with a different wheelbarrow, only inside this one were two babies in a blanket. Most came on foot, with their goods on their shoulders and weary, wary looks upon their faces. They walked south, toward the city, toward King's Landing, and only one in a hundred spared so much as a word for Yoren and his charges, traveling north. She wondered why no one else was going the same way as them.

Many of the travelers were armed; Arya saw daggers and dirks, scythes and axes, and here and there a sword. Some had made clubs from tree limbs, or carved knobby staffs. They fingered their weapons and gave lingering looks at the wagons as they rolled by, yet in the end they let the column pass. Thirty was too many, no matter what they had in those wagons.

Look with your eyes, Syrio had said, *listen with your ears.*

One day a madwoman began to scream at them from the side of the road. "Fools! They'll kill you, fools!" She was scarecrow thin, with hollow eyes and bloody feet.

The next morning, a sleek merchant on a grey mare reined up by Yoren and offered to buy his wagons and everything in them for a quarter of their worth. "It's war, they'll take what they want, you'll do better selling to me, my friend." Yoren turned away with a twist of his crooked shoulders, and spat.

Arya noticed the first grave that same day; a small mound beside the road, dug for a child. A crystal had been set in the soft earth, and Lommy wanted to take it until the Bull told him he'd better leave the dead alone. A few leagues farther on, Praed pointed out more graves, a whole row freshly dug. After that, a day hardly passed without one.

One time Arya woke in the dark, frightened for no reason she could name. Above, the Red Sword shared the sky with half a thousand stars. The night seemed oddly quiet to her, though she could hear Yoren's muttered snores, the crackle of the fire, even the muffled stirrings of the donkeys. Yet somehow it felt as though the world were holding its breath, and the silence made her shiver. She went back to sleep clutching Needle.

Come morning, when Praed did not awaken, Arya realized that it had been his coughing she had missed. They dug a grave of their own then, burying the sellsword where he'd slept. Yoren stripped him of his valuables before they threw the dirt on him. One man claimed his boots, another his dagger. His mail shirt and helm were parceled out. His longsword Yoren handed to the Bull. "Arms like yours, might be you can learn to use this," he told him. A boy called Tarber tossed a handful of acorns on top of Praed's body, so an oak might grow to mark his place.

That evening they stopped in a village at an ivy-covered inn. Yoren counted the coins in his purse and decided they had enough for a hot meal. "We'll sleep outside, same as ever, but they got a bathhouse here, if any of you feels the need o' hot water and a lick o' soap."

Arya did not dare, even though she smelled as bad as Yoren by now, all sour and stinky. Some of the creatures living in her clothes had come all the way from Flea Bottom with her; it didn't seem right to drown them. Tarber and Hot Pie and the Bull joined the line of men headed for the tubs. Others settled down in front of the bathhouse. The rest crowded into the common room. Yoren even sent Lommy out with tankards for the three in fetters, who'd been left chained up in the back of their wagon.

Washed and unwashed alike supped on hot pork pies and baked apples. The innkeeper gave them a round of beer on the house. "I had a brother took the black, years ago. Serving boy, clever, but one day he got seen filching pepper from m'lord's table. He liked the taste of it, is all. Just a pinch o' pepper, but Ser Malcolm was a hard man. You get pepper on the Wall?" When Yoren shook his head, the man sighed. "Shame. Lync loved that pepper."

Arya sipped at her tankard cautiously, between spoonfuls of pie still warm from the oven. Her father sometimes let them have a cup of beer, she remembered. Sansa used to make a face at the taste and say that wine was ever so much finer, but Arya had liked it well enough. It made her sad to think of Sansa and her father.

The inn was full of people moving south, and the common room erupted in scorn when Yoren said they were traveling the other way. "You'll be back soon enough," the innkeeper vowed. "There's no going north. Half the fields are burnt, and what folks are left are walled up inside their holdfasts. One bunch rides off at dawn and another one shows up by dusk."

"That's nothing to us," Yoren insisted stubbornly. "Tully or Lannister, makes no matter. The Watch takes no part."

Lord Tully is my grandfather, Arya thought. It mattered to *her,* but she chewed her lip and kept quiet, listening.

"It's more than Lannister and Tully," the innkeeper said. "There's wild men down from the Mountains of the Moon, try telling *them* you take no part. And the Starks are in it too, the young lord's come down, the dead Hand's son . . ."

Arya sat up straight, straining to hear. Did he mean *Robb?*

"I heard the boy rides to battle on a wolf," said a yellow-haired man with a tankard in his hand.

"Fool's talk." Yoren spat.

"The man I heard it from, he saw it himself. A wolf big as a horse, he swore."

"Swearing don't make it true, Hod," the innkeeper said. "You keep swearing you'll pay what you owe me, and I've yet to see a copper." The common room erupted in laughter, and the man with the yellow hair turned red.

"It's been a bad year for wolves," volunteered a sallow man in a travel-stained green cloak. "Around the Gods Eye, the packs have grown bolder'n anyone can remember. Sheep, cows, dogs, makes no matter, they kill as they like, and they got no fear of men. It's worth your life to go into those woods by night."

"Ah, that's more tales, and no more true than the other."

"I heard the same thing from my cousin, and she's not the sort to lie," an old woman said. "She says there's this great pack, hundreds of them, mankillers. The one that leads them is a she-wolf, a bitch from the seventh hell."

A she-wolf. Arya sloshed her beer, wondering. Was the Gods Eye near the Trident? She wished she had a map. It had been near the Trident that she'd left Nymeria. She hadn't wanted to, but Jory said they had no choice, that if the wolf came back with them she'd be killed for biting Joffrey, even though he'd deserved it. They'd had to shout and scream and throw stones, and it wasn't until a few of Arya's stones struck home that the direwolf had finally stopped following them. *She probably wouldn't even know me now,* Arya thought. *Or if she did, she'd hate me.*

The man in the green cloak said, "I heard how this hellbitch walked into a village one day . . . a market day, people everywhere, and she walks in bold as you please and tears a baby from his mother's arms. When the tale reached Lord Mooton, him and his sons swore they'd put an end to her. They tracked her to her lair with a pack of wolfhounds, and barely escaped with their skins. Not one of those dogs came back, not one."

"That's just a story," Arya blurted out before she could stop herself. "Wolves don't eat babies."

"And what would you know about it, lad?" asked the man in the green cloak.

Before she could think of an answer, Yoren had her by the arm. "The boy's greensick on beer, that's all it is."

"No I'm not. They *don't* eat babies . . ."

"Outside, *boy* . . . and see that you stay there until you learn to shut your mouth when men are talking." He gave her a stiff shove, toward the side door that led back to the stables. "Go on now. See that the stableboy has watered our horses."

Arya went outside, stiff with fury. "They *don't,*" she muttered, kicking at a rock as she stalked off. It went rolling and fetched up under the wagons.

"Boy," a friendly voice called out. "Lovely boy."

One of the men in irons was talking to her. Warily, Arya approached the wagon, one hand on Needle's hilt.

The prisoner lifted an empty tankard, his chains rattling. "A man could use another taste of beer. A man has a thirst, wearing these heavy bracelets." He was the youngest of the three, slender, fine-featured, always smiling. His hair was red on one side and white on the other, all matted and filthy from cage and travel. "A man could use a bath too," he said, when he saw the way Arya was looking at him. "A boy could make a friend."

"I have friends," Arya said.

"None I can see," said the one without a nose. He was squat and thick, with huge hands. Black hair covered his arms and legs and chest, even his back. He reminded Arya of a drawing she had once seen in a book, of an ape from the Summer Isles. The hole in his face made it hard to look at him for long.

The bald one opened his mouth and *hissed* like some immense white lizard. When Arya flinched back, startled, he opened his mouth wide and waggled his tongue at her, only it was more a stump than a tongue. "Stop that," she blurted.

"A man does not choose his companions in the black cells," the handsome one with the red-and-white hair said. Something about the way he talked reminded her of Syrio; it was the same, yet different too. "These two, they have no courtesy. A man must ask forgiveness. You are called Arry, is that not so?"

"Lumpyhead," said the noseless one. "Lumpyhead Lumpyface Stickboy. Have a care, Lorath, he'll hit you with his stick."

"A man must be ashamed of the company he keeps, Arry," the handsome one said. "This man has the honor to be Jaqen H'ghar, once of the Free City of Lorath. Would that he were home. This man's ill-bred companions in captivity are named Rorge"—he waved his tankard at the noseless man—"and Biter." Biter *hissed* at her again, displaying a mouthful of yellowed teeth filed into points. "A man must have some name, is that not so? Biter cannot speak and Biter cannot write, yet his teeth are very sharp, so a man calls him Biter and he smiles. Are you charmed?"

Arya backed away from the wagon. "No." *They can't hurt me*, she told herself, *they're all chained up.*

He turned his tankard upside down. "A man must weep."

Rorge, the noseless one, flung his drinking cup at her with a curse. His manacles made him clumsy, yet even so he would have sent the heavy pewter tankard crashing into her head if Arya hadn't leapt aside. "You get us some beer, pimple. *Now!*"

"You shut your mouth!" Arya tried to think what Syrio would have done. She drew her wooden practice sword.

"Come closer," Rorge said, "and I'll shove that stick up your bunghole and fuck you bloody."

Fear cuts deeper than swords. Arya made herself approach the wagon. Every step was harder than the one before. *Fierce as a wolverine, calm as still water.* The words sang in her head. Syrio would not have been afraid. She was almost close enough to touch the wheel when Biter lurched to his feet and grabbed for her, his irons clanking and rattling. The manacles brought his hands up short, half a foot from her face. He *hissed.*

She hit him. Hard, right between his little eyes.

Screaming, Biter reeled back, and then threw all his weight against his chains. The links slithered and turned and grew taut, and Arya heard the creak of old dry wood as the great iron rings strained against the floorboards of the wagon. Huge pale hands groped for her while veins bulged along Biter's arms, but the bonds held, and finally the man collapsed backward. Blood ran from the weeping sores on his cheeks.

"A boy has more courage than sense," the one who had named himself Jaqen H'ghar observed.

Arya edged backward away from the wagon. When she felt the hand on her shoulder, she whirled, bringing up her stick sword again, but it was only the Bull. "What are you doing?"

He raised his hands defensively. "Yoren said none of us should go near those three."

"They don't scare me," Arya said.

"Then you're stupid. They scare *me.*" The Bull's hand fell to the hilt of his sword, and Rorge began to laugh. "Let's get away from them."

Arya scuffed at the ground with her foot, but she let the Bull lead her around to the front of the inn. Rorge's laughter and Biter's hissing followed them. "Want to fight?" she asked the Bull. She wanted to hit something.

He blinked at her, startled. Strands of thick black hair, still wet from the bathhouse, fell across his deep blue eyes. "I'd hurt you."

"You would not."

"You don't know how strong I am."

"You don't know how quick I am."

"You're asking for it, Arry." He drew Praed's longsword. "This is cheap steel, but it's a real sword."

Arya unsheathed Needle. "This is good steel, so it's realer than yours."

The Bull shook his head. "Promise not to cry if I cut you?"

"I'll promise if you will." She turned sideways, into her water dancer's stance, but the Bull did not move. He was looking at something behind her. "What's wrong?"

"Gold cloaks." His face closed up tight.

It couldn't be, Arya thought, but when she glanced back, they were riding up the kingsroad, six in the black ringmail and golden cloaks of the City Watch. One was an officer; he wore a black enamel breastplate ornamented with four golden disks. They drew up in front of the inn.

Look with your eyes, Syrio's voice seemed to whisper. Her eyes saw white lather under their saddles; the horses had been ridden long and hard. Calm as still water, she took the Bull by the arm and drew him back behind a tall flowering hedge.

"What is it?" he asked. "What are you doing? Let go."

"Quiet as a shadow," she whispered, pulling him down.

Some of Yoren's other charges were sitting in front of the bathhouse, waiting their turn at a tub. "You men," one of the gold cloaks shouted. "You the ones left to take the black?"

"We might be," came the cautious answer.

"We'd rather join you boys," old Reysen said. "We hear it's *cold* on that Wall."

The gold cloak officer dismounted. "I have a warrant for a certain boy—"

Yoren stepped out of the inn, fingering his tangled black beard. "Who is it wants this boy?"

The other gold cloaks were dismounting to stand beside their horses. "Why are we hiding?" the Bull whispered.

"It's me they want," Arya whispered back. His ear smelled of soap. "You be quiet."

"The queen wants him, old man, not that it's your concern," the officer said, drawing a ribbon from his belt. "Here, Her Grace's seal and warrant."

Behind the hedge, the Bull shook his head doubtfully. "Why would the queen want *you*, Arry?"

She punched his shoulder. "Be *quiet*!"

Yoren fingered the warrant ribbon with its blob of golden wax. "Pretty." He spit. "Thing is, the boy's in the Night's Watch now. What he done back in the city don't mean piss-all."

"The queen's not interested in your views, old man, and neither am I," the officer said. "I'll have the boy."

Arya thought about running, but she knew she wouldn't get far on her donkey when the gold cloaks had horses. And she was so tired of running. She'd run when Ser Meryn came for her, and again when they killed her father. If she was a real water dancer, she would go out there with Needle and kill all of them, and never run from anyone ever again.

"You'll have no one," Yoren said stubbornly. "There's laws on such things."

The gold cloak drew a shortsword. "Here's your law."

Yoren looked at the blade. "That's no law, just a sword. Happens I got one too."

The officer smiled. "Old fool. I have five men with me."

Yoren spat. "Happens I got thirty."

The gold cloak laughed. "This lot?" said a big lout with a broken nose. "Who's first?" he shouted, showing his steel.

Tarber plucked a pitchfork out of a bale of hay. "I am."

"No, I am," called Cutjack, the plump stonemason, pulling his hammer off the leather apron he always wore.

"Me." Kurz came up off the ground with his skinning knife in hand.

"Me and him." Koss strung his longbow.

"All of us," said Reysen, snatching up the tall hardwood walking staff he carried.

Dobber stepped naked out of the bathhouse with his clothes in a bundle, saw what was happening, and dropped everything but his dagger. "Is it a fight?" he asked.

"I guess," said Hot Pie, scrambling on all fours for a big rock to throw. Arya could not believe what she was seeing. She *hated* Hot Pie! Why would he risk himself for her?

The one with the broken nose still thought it was funny. "You girls put away them rocks and sticks before you get spanked. None of you knows what end of a sword to hold."

"*I do!*" Arya wouldn't let them die for her like Syrio. She wouldn't! Shoving through the hedge with Needle in hand, she slid into a water dancer's stance.

Broken Nose guffawed. The officer looked her up and down. "Put the blade away, little girl, no one wants to hurt you."

"I'm *not* a girl!" she yelled, furious. What was wrong with them? They rode all this way for her and here she was and they were just smiling at her. "I'm the one you want."

"*He's* the one we want." The officer jabbed his shortsword toward the Bull, who'd come forward to stand beside her, Praed's cheap steel in his hand.

But it was a mistake to take his eyes off Yoren, even for an instant. Quick as that, the black brother's sword was pressed to the apple of the officer's throat. "Neither's the one you get, less you want me to see if your apple's ripe yet. I got me ten, fifteen more brothers in that inn, if you still need convincing. I was you, I'd let loose of that gutcutter, spread my cheeks over that fat little horse, and gallop on back to the city." He spat, and poked harder with the point of his sword. "Now."

The officer's fingers uncurled. His sword fell in the dust.

"We'll just keep that," Yoren said. "Good steel's always needed on the Wall."

"As you say. For now. Men." The gold cloaks sheathed and mounted up. "You'd best scamper up to that Wall of yours in a hurry, old man.

The next time I catch you, I believe I'll have your head to go with the bastard boy's."

"Better men than you have tried." Yoren slapped the rump of the officer's horse with the flat of his sword and sent him reeling off down the kingsroad. His men followed.

When they were out of sight, Hot Pie began to whoop, but Yoren looked angrier than ever. "Fool! You think he's done with us? Next time he won't prance up and hand me no damn ribbon. Get the rest out o' them baths, we need to be moving. Ride all night, maybe we can stay ahead o' them for a bit." He scooped up the shortsword the officer had dropped. "Who wants this?"

"Me!" Hot Pie yelled.

"Don't be using it on Arry." He handed the boy the sword, hilt first, and walked over to Arya, but it was the Bull he spoke to. "Queen wants you bad, boy."

Arya was lost. "Why should she want *him*?"

The Bull scowled at her. "Why should she want *you*? You're nothing but a little gutter rat!"

"Well, you're nothing but a bastard boy!" Or maybe he was only *pretending* to be a bastard boy. "What's your true name?"

"Gendry," he said, like he wasn't quite sure.

"Don't see why no one wants neither o' you," Yoren said, "but they can't have you regardless. You ride them two coursers. First sight of a gold cloak, make for the Wall like a dragon's on your tail. The rest o' us don't mean spit to them."

"Except for you," Arya pointed out. "That man said he'd take your head too."

"Well, as to that," Yoren said, "if he can get it off my shoulders, he's welcome to it."

JON

"S am?" Jon called softly.

The air smelled of paper and dust and years. Before him, tall wooden shelves rose up into dimness, crammed with leather-bound books and bins of ancient scrolls. A faint yellow glow filtered through the stacks from some hidden lamp. Jon blew out the taper he carried, preferring not to risk an open flame amidst so much old dry paper. Instead he followed the light, wending his way down the narrow aisles beneath barrel-vaulted ceilings. All in black, he was a shadow among shadows, dark of hair, long of face, grey of eye. Black moleskin gloves covered his hands; the right because it was burned, the left because a man felt half a fool wearing only one glove.

Samwell Tarly sat hunched over a table in a niche carved into the stone of the wall. The glow came from the lamp hung over his head. He looked up at the sound of Jon's steps.

"Have you been here all night?"

"Have I?" Sam looked startled.

"You didn't break your fast with us, and your bed hadn't been slept in." Rast suggested that maybe Sam had deserted, but Jon never believed it. Desertion required its own sort of courage, and Sam had little enough of that.

"Is it morning? Down here there's no way to know."

"Sam, you're a sweet fool," Jon said. "You'll miss that bed when we're sleeping on the cold hard ground, I promise you."

Sam yawned. "Maester Aemon sent me to find maps for the Lord Commander. I never thought . . . Jon, the *books*, have you ever seen their like? There are *thousands*!"

He gazed about him. "The library at Winterfell has more than a hundred. Did you find the maps?"

"Oh, yes." Sam's hand swept over the table, fingers plump as sausages indicating the clutter of books and scrolls before him. "A dozen, at the least." He unfolded a square of parchment. "The paint has faded, but you can see where the mapmaker marked the sites of wildling villages, and there's another book . . . where is it now? I was reading it a moment ago." He shoved some scrolls aside to reveal a dusty volume bound in rotted leather. "*This*," he said reverently, "is the account of a journey from the Shadow Tower all the way to Lorn Point on the Frozen Shore, written by a ranger named Redwyn. It's not dated, but he mentions a Dorren Stark as King in the North, so it must be from before the Conquest. Jon, they fought *giants*! Redwyn even traded with the children of the forest, it's all here." Ever so delicately, he turned pages with a finger. "He drew maps as well, see . . ."

"Maybe you could write an account of our ranging, Sam."

He'd meant to sound encouraging, but it was the wrong thing to say. The last thing Sam needed was to be reminded of what faced them on the morrow. He shuffled the scrolls about aimlessly. "There's more maps. If I had time to search . . . everything's a jumble. *I* could set it all to order, though; I know I could, but it would take time . . . well, *years*, in truth."

"Mormont wanted those maps a little sooner than that." Jon plucked a scroll from a bin, blew off the worst of the dust. A corner flaked off between his fingers as he unrolled it. "Look, this one is crumbling," he said, frowning over the faded script.

"Be gentle." Sam came around the table and took the scroll from his hand, holding it as if it were a wounded animal. "The important books used to be copied over when they needed them. Some of the oldest have been copied half a hundred times, probably."

"Well, don't bother copying that one. Twenty-three barrels of pickled cod, eighteen jars of fish oil, a cask of salt . . ."

"An inventory," Sam said, "or perhaps a bill of sale."

"Who cares how much pickled cod they ate six hundred years ago?" Jon wondered.

"I would." Sam carefully replaced the scroll in the bin from which Jon had plucked it. "You can learn so much from ledgers like that, truly you can. It can tell you how many men were in the Night's Watch then, how they lived, what they ate . . ."

"They ate food," said Jon, "and they lived as we live."

"You'd be surprised. This vault is a treasure, Jon."

"If you say so." Jon was doubtful. Treasure meant gold, silver, and jewels, not dust, spiders, and rotting leather.

"I do," the fat boy blurted. He was older than Jon, a man grown by law, but it was hard to think of him as anything but a boy. "I found drawings of the faces in the trees, and a book about the tongue of the children of the forest . . . works that even the Citadel doesn't have, scrolls from old Valyria, counts of the seasons written by maesters dead a thousand years . . ."

"The books will still be here when we return."

"*If* we return . . ."

"The Old Bear is taking two hundred seasoned men, three-quarters of them rangers. Qhorin Halfhand will be bringing another hundred brothers from the Shadow Tower. You'll be as safe as if you were back in your lord father's castle at Horn Hill."

Samwell Tarly managed a sad little smile. "I was never very safe in my father's castle either."

The gods play cruel jests, Jon thought. Pyp and Toad, all a lather to be a part of the great ranging, were to remain at Castle Black. It was Samwell Tarly, the self-proclaimed coward, grossly fat, timid, and near as bad a rider as he was with a sword, who must face the haunted forest. The Old Bear was taking two cages of ravens, so they might send back word as they went. Maester Aemon was blind and far too frail to ride with them, so his steward must go in his place. "We need you for the ravens, Sam. And someone has to help me keep Grenn humble."

Sam's chins quivered. "You could care for the ravens, or Grenn could, or *anyone*," he said with a thin edge of desperation in his voice. "I could show you how. You know your letters too, you could write down Lord Mormont's messages as well as I."

"I'm the Old Bear's steward. I'll need to squire for him, tend his horse, set up his tent; I won't have time to watch over birds as well. Sam, you said the words. You're a brother of the Night's Watch now."

"A brother of the Night's Watch shouldn't be so scared."

"We're all scared. We'd be fools if we weren't." Too many rangers had been lost the past two years, even Benjen Stark, Jon's uncle. They had found two of his uncle's men in the wood, slain, but the corpses had risen in the chill of night. Jon's burnt fingers twitched as he remembered. He still saw the wight in his dreams, dead Othor with the burning blue eyes and the cold black hands, but that was the last thing Sam needed to be reminded of. "There's no shame in fear, my father told me, what matters is how we face it. Come, I'll help you gather up the maps."

Sam nodded unhappily. The shelves were so closely spaced that they had to walk single file as they left. The vault opened onto one of the tunnels the brothers called the wormwalks, winding subterranean passages that linked the keeps and towers of Castle Black under the earth. In summer the wormwalks were seldom used, save by rats and other vermin, but winter was a different matter. When the snows drifted forty and fifty feet high and the ice winds came howling out of the north, the tunnels were all that held Castle Black together.

Soon, Jon thought as they climbed. He'd seen the harbinger that had come to Maester Aemon with word of summer's end, the great raven of the Citadel, white and silent as Ghost. He had seen a winter once, when he was very young, but everyone agreed that it had been a short one, and mild. This one would be different. He could feel it in his bones.

The steep stone steps had Sam puffing like a blacksmith's bellows by the time they reached the surface. They emerged into a brisk wind that made Jon's cloak swirl and snap. Ghost was stretched out asleep beneath the wattle-and-daub wall of the granary, but he woke when Jon appeared, bushy white tail held stiffly upright as he trotted to them.

Sam squinted up at the Wall. It loomed above them, an icy cliff seven hundred feet high. Sometimes it seemed to Jon almost a living thing, with moods of its own. The color of the ice was wont to change with every shift of the light. Now it was the deep blue of frozen rivers, now the dirty white of old snow, and when a cloud passed before the sun it darkened to the pale grey of pitted stone. The Wall stretched east and west as far as the eye could see, so huge that it shrunk the timbered keeps and stone towers of the castle to insignificance. It was the end of the world.

And we are going beyond it.

The morning sky was streaked by thin grey clouds, but the pale red line was there behind them. The black brothers had dubbed the wanderer Mormont's Torch, saying (only half in jest) that the gods must have sent it to light the old man's way through the haunted forest.

"The comet's so bright you can see it by day now," Sam said, shading his eyes with a fistful of books.

"Never mind about comets, it's maps the Old Bear wants."

Ghost loped ahead of them. The grounds seemed deserted this morning, with so many rangers off at the brothel in Mole's Town, digging for buried treasure and drinking themselves blind. Grenn had gone with them. Pyp and Halder and Toad had offered to buy him his first woman to celebrate his first ranging. They'd wanted Jon and Sam to come as well, but Sam was almost as frightened of whores as he was of the haunted forest, and Jon had wanted no part of it. "Do what you want," he told Toad, "I took a vow."

As they passed the sept, he heard voices raised in song. *Some men want whores on the eve of battle, and some want gods.* Jon wondered who felt better afterward. The sept tempted him no more than the brothel; his own gods kept their temples in the wild places, where the weirwoods spread their bone-white branches. *The Seven have no power beyond the Wall*, he thought, *but my gods will be waiting.*

Outside the armory, Ser Endrew Tarth was working with some raw recruits. They'd come in last night with Conwy, one of the wandering crows who roamed the Seven Kingdoms collecting men for the Wall. This new crop consisted of a greybeard leaning on a staff, two blond boys with the look of brothers, a foppish youth in soiled satin, a raggy man with a clubfoot, and some grinning loon who must have fancied himself a warrior. Ser Endrew was showing him the error of that presumption. He was a gentler master-at-arms than Ser Alliser Thorne had been, but his lessons would still raise bruises. Sam winced at every blow, but Jon Snow watched the swordplay closely.

"What do you make of them, Snow?" Donal Noye stood in the door of his armory, bare-chested under a leather apron, the stump of his left arm uncovered for once. With his big gut and barrel chest, his flat nose and bristly black jaw, Noye did not make a pretty sight, but he was a welcome one nonetheless. The armorer had proved himself a good friend.

"They smell of summer," Jon said as Ser Endrew bullrushed his foe and knocked him sprawling. "Where did Conwy find them?"

"A lord's dungeon near Gulltown," the smith replied. "A brigand, a barber, a beggar, two orphans, and a boy whore. With such do we defend the realms of men."

"They'll do." Jon gave Sam a private smile. "We did."

Noye drew him closer. "You've heard these tidings of your brother?"

"Last night." Conwy and his charges had brought the news north with them, and the talk in the common room had been of little else. Jon was still not certain how he felt about it. Robb a king? The brother he'd played with, fought with, shared his first cup of wine with? *But not mother's milk, no. So now Robb will sip summerwine from jeweled goblets, while I'm kneeling beside some stream sucking snowmelt from cupped hands.* "Robb will make a good king," he said loyally.

"Will he now?" The smith eyed him frankly. "I hope that's so, boy, but once I might have said the same of Robert."

"They say you forged his warhammer," Jon remembered.

"Aye. I was his man, a Baratheon man, smith and armorer at Storm's End until I lost the arm. I'm old enough to remember Lord Steffon before the sea took him, and I knew those three sons of his since they got their names. I tell you this—Robert was never the same after he put on that crown. Some men are like swords, made for fighting. Hang them up and they go to rust."

"And his brothers?" Jon asked.

The armorer considered that a moment. "Robert was the true steel. Stannis is pure iron, black and hard and strong, yes, but brittle, the way iron gets. He'll break before he bends. And Renly, that one, he's copper, bright and shiny, pretty to look at but not worth all that much at the end of the day."

And what metal is Robb? Jon did not ask. Noye was a Baratheon man; likely he thought Joffrey the lawful king and Robb a traitor. Among the brotherhood of the Night's Watch, there was an unspoken pact never to probe too deeply into such matters. Men came to the Wall from all of the Seven Kingdoms, and old loves and loyalties were not easily forgotten, no matter how many oaths a man swore . . . as Jon himself had good reason to know. Even Sam—his father's House was sworn to Highgarden, whose Lord Tyrell supported King Renly. Best not to talk of such things. The Night's Watch took no sides. "Lord Mormont awaits us," Jon said.

"I won't keep you from the Old Bear." Noye clapped him on the shoulder and smiled. "May the gods go with you on the morrow, Snow. You bring back that uncle of yours, you hear?"

"We will," Jon promised him.

Lord Commander Mormont had taken up residence in the King's Tower after the fire had gutted his own. Jon left Ghost with the guards outside the door. "More stairs," said Sam miserably as they started up. "I hate stairs."

"Well, that's one thing we won't face in the wood."

When they entered the solar, the raven spied them at once. *"Snow!"* the bird shrieked. Mormont broke off his conversation. "Took you long enough with those maps." He pushed the remains of breakfast out of the way to make room on the table. "Put them here. I'll have a look at them later."

Thoren Smallwood, a sinewy ranger with a weak chin and a weaker mouth hidden under a thin scraggle of beard, gave Jon and Sam a cool look. He had been one of Alliser Thorne's henchmen, and had no love for either of them. "The Lord Commander's place is at Castle Black, lording and commanding," he told Mormont, ignoring the newcomers, "it seems to me."

The raven flapped big black wings. *"Me, me, me."*

"If you are ever Lord Commander, you may do as you please," Mormont told the ranger, "but it seems to *me* that I have not died yet, nor have the brothers put you in my place."

"I'm First Ranger now, with Ben Stark lost and Ser Jaremy killed," Smallwood said stubbornly. "The command should be mine."

Mormont would have none of it. "I sent out Ben Stark, and Ser Waymar before him. I do not mean to send you after them and sit wondering how long I must wait before I give you up for lost as well." He pointed. "And Stark remains First Ranger until we know for a certainty that he is dead. Should that day come, it will be me who names his successor, not you. Now stop wasting my time. We ride at first light, or have you forgotten?"

Smallwood pushed to his feet. "As my lord commands." On the way out, he frowned at Jon, as if it were somehow his fault.

"First Ranger!" The Old Bear's eyes lighted on Sam. "I'd sooner name *you* First Ranger. He has the effrontery to tell me to my face that I'm too old to ride with him. Do I look old to you, boy?" The hair that had retreated from Mormont's spotted scalp had regrouped beneath his chin in a shaggy grey beard that covered much of his chest. He thumped it hard. "Do I look *frail?*"

Sam opened his mouth, gave a little squeak. The Old Bear terrified him. "No, my lord," Jon offered quickly. "You look strong as a . . . a . . ."

"Don't cozen me, Snow, you know I won't have it. Let me have a look at these maps." Mormont pawed through them brusquely, giving each no more than a glance and a grunt. "Was this all you could find?"

"I . . . m-m-my lord," Sam stammered, "there . . . there were more, b-b-but . . . the dis-disorder . . ."

"These are old," Mormont complained, and his raven echoed him with a sharp cry of *"Old, old."*

"The villages may come and go, but the hills and rivers will be in the same places," Jon pointed out.

"True enough. Have you chosen your ravens yet, Tarly?"

"M-m-maester Aemon m-means to p-pick them come evenfall, after the f-f-feeding."

"I'll have his best. Smart birds, and strong."

"Strong," his own bird said, preening. *"Strong, strong."*

"If it happens that we're all butchered out there, I mean for my successor to know where and how we died."

Talk of butchery reduced Samwell Tarly to speechlessness. Mormont leaned forward. "Tarly, when I was a lad half your age, my lady mother told me that if I stood about with my mouth open, a weasel was like to mistake it for his lair and run down my throat. If you have something to say, say it. Otherwise, beware of weasels." He waved a brusque dismissal. "Off with you, I'm too busy for folly. No doubt the maester has some work you can do."

Sam swallowed, stepped back, and scurried out so quickly he almost tripped over the rushes.

"Is that boy as big a fool as he seems?" the Lord Commander asked when he'd gone. *"Fool,"* the raven complained. Mormont did not wait for Jon to answer. "His lord father stands high in King Renly's councils, and I had half a notion to dispatch him . . . no, best not. Renly is not like to heed a quaking fat boy. I'll send Ser Arnell. He's a deal steadier, and his mother was one of the green-apple Fossoways."

"If it please my lord, what would you have of King Renly?"

"The same things I'd have of all of them, lad. Men, horses, swords, armor, grain, cheese, wine, wool, nails . . . the Night's Watch is not proud, we take what is offered." His fingers drummed against the rough-hewn planks of the table. "If the winds have been kind, Ser Alliser should reach King's Landing by the turn of the moon, but whether this boy Joffrey will pay him any heed, I do not know. House Lannister has never been a friend to the Watch."

"Thorne has the wight's hand to show them." A grisly pale thing with black fingers, it was, that twitched and stirred in its jar as if it were still alive.

"Would that we had another hand to send to Renly."

"Dywen says you can find anything beyond the Wall."

"Aye, Dywen says. And the last time he went ranging, he says he saw a bear fifteen feet tall." Mormont snorted. "My sister is said to have taken a bear for her lover. I'd believe *that* before I'd believe one fifteen feet tall. Though in a world where dead come walking . . . . ah, even so, a man must believe his eyes. I have seen the dead walk. I've not seen any giant bears." He gave Jon a long, searching look. "But we were speaking of hands. How is yours?"

"Better." Jon peeled off his moleskin glove and showed him. Scars covered his arm halfway to the elbow, and the mottled pink flesh still felt tight and tender, but it was healing. "It itches, though. Maester Aemon says that's good. He gave me a salve to take with me when we ride."

"You can wield Longclaw despite the pain?"

"Well enough." Jon flexed his fingers, opening and closing his fist the way the maester had shown him. "I'm to work the fingers every day to keep them nimble, as Maester Aemon said."

"Blind he may be, but Aemon knows what he's about. I pray the gods let us keep him another twenty years. Do you know that he might have been king?"

Jon was taken by surprise. "He told me his father was king, but not . . . I thought him perhaps a younger son."

"So he was. His father's father was Daeron Targaryen, the Second of His Name, who brought Dorne into the realm. Part of the pact was that he wed a Dornish princess. She gave him four sons. Aemon's father Maekar was the youngest of those, and Aemon was *his* third son. Mind you, all this happened long before I was born, ancient as Smallwood would make me."

"Maester Aemon was named for the Dragonknight."

"So he was. Some say Prince Aemon was King Daeron's true father, not Aegon the Unworthy. Be that as it may, our Aemon lacked the Dragonknight's martial nature. He likes to say he had a slow sword but quick wits. Small wonder his grandfather packed him off to the Citadel. He was nine or ten, I believe . . . and ninth or tenth in the line of succession as well."

Maester Aemon had counted more than a hundred name days, Jon knew. Frail, shrunken, wizened, and blind, it was hard to imagine him as a little boy no older than Arya.

Mormont continued. "Aemon was at his books when the eldest of his uncles, the heir apparent, was slain in a tourney mishap. He left two sons, but they followed him to the grave not long after, during the Great Spring Sickness. King Daeron was also taken, so the crown passed to Daeron's second son, Aerys."

"The Mad King?" Jon was confused. Aerys had been king before Robert, that wasn't so long ago.

"No, this was Aerys the First. The one Robert deposed was the second of that name."

"How long ago was this?"

"Eighty years or close enough," the Old Bear said, "and no, I *still* hadn't been born, though Aemon had forged half a dozen links of his maester's chain by then. Aerys wed his own sister, as the Targaryens were wont to do, and reigned for ten or twelve years. Aemon took his vows and left the Citadel to serve at some lordling's court . . . until his royal uncle died without issue. The Iron Throne passed to the last of King Daeron's four sons. That was Maekar, Aemon's father. The new king summoned all his sons to court and would have made Aemon part of his councils, but he refused, saying that would usurp the place rightly belonging to the Grand Maester. Instead he served at the keep of his eldest brother, another Daeron. Well, that one died too, leaving only a feeble-witted daughter as heir. Some pox he caught from a whore, I believe. The next brother was Aerion."

"Aerion the Monstrous?" Jon knew that name. "The Prince Who Thought He Was a Dragon" was one of Old Nan's more gruesome tales. His little brother Bran had loved it.

"The very one, though he named himself Aerion Brightflame. One night, in his cups, he drank a jar of wildfire, after telling his friends it would transform him into a dragon, but the gods were kind and it transformed him into a corpse. Not quite a year after, King Maekar died in battle against an outlaw lord."

Jon was not entirely innocent of the history of the realm; his own maester had seen to that. "That was the year of the Great Council," he said. "The lords passed over Prince Aerion's infant son and Prince Daeron's daughter and gave the crown to Aegon."

"Yes and no. First they offered it, quietly, to Aemon. And quietly he refused. The gods meant for him to serve, not to rule, he told them. He had sworn a vow and would not break it, though the High Septon himself offered to absolve him. Well, no sane man wanted any blood of Aerion's on the throne, and Daeron's girl was a lackwit besides being female, so they had no choice but to turn to Aemon's younger brother—Aegon, the Fifth of His Name. Aegon the Unlikely, they called him, born the fourth son of a fourth son. Aemon knew, and rightly, that if he remained at court those who disliked his brother's rule would seek to use him, so he came to the Wall. And here he has remained, while his brother and his brother's son and *his* son each reigned and died in turn, until Jaime Lannister put an end to the line of the Dragonkings."

"*King*," croaked the raven. The bird flapped across the solar to land on Mormont's shoulder. "*King*," it said again, strutting back and forth.

"He likes that word," Jon said, smiling.

"An easy word to say. An easy word to like."

"*King*," the bird said again.

"I think he means for you to have a crown, my lord."

"The realm has three kings already, and that's two too many for my liking." Mormont stroked the raven under the beak with a finger, but all the while his eyes never left Jon Snow.

It made him feel odd. "My lord, why have you told me this, about Maester Aemon?"

"Must I have a reason?" Mormont shifted in his seat, frowning. "Your brother Robb has been crowned King in the North. You and Aemon have that in common. A king for a brother."

"And this too," said Jon. "A vow."

The Old Bear gave a loud snort, and the raven took flight, flapping in a circle about the room. "Give me a man for every vow I've seen broken and the Wall will never lack for defenders."

"I've always known that Robb would be Lord of Winterfell."

Mormont gave a whistle, and the bird flew to him again and settled on his arm. "A lord's one thing, a king's another." He offered the raven a handful of corn from his pocket. "They will garb your brother Robb in silks, satins, and velvets of a hundred different colors, while you live and die in black ringmail. He will wed some beautiful princess and father sons on her. You'll have no wife, nor will you ever hold a child of your own blood in your arms. Robb will rule, you will serve. Men will call you a crow. Him they'll call *Your Grace*. Singers will praise every little thing he does, while your greatest deeds all go unsung. Tell me that none of this troubles you, Jon . . . and I'll name you a liar, and know I have the truth of it."

Jon drew himself up, taut as a bowstring. "And if it *did* trouble me, what might I do, bastard as I am?"

"What *will* you do?" Mormont asked. "Bastard as you are?"

"Be troubled," said Jon, "and keep my vows."

CATELYN

Her son's crown was fresh from the forge, and it seemed to Catelyn Stark that the weight of it pressed heavy on Robb's head. The ancient crown of the Kings of Winter had been lost three centuries ago, yielded up to Aegon the Conqueror when Torrhen Stark knelt in submission. What Aegon had done with it no man could say. Lord Hoster's smith had done his work well, and Robb's crown looked much as the other was said to have looked in the tales told of the Stark kings of old; an open circlet of hammered bronze incised with the runes of the First Men, surmounted by nine black iron spikes wrought in the shape of longswords. Of gold and silver and gemstones, it had none; bronze and iron were the metals of winter, dark and strong to fight against the cold.

As they waited in Riverrun's Great Hall for the prisoner to be brought before them, she saw Robb push back the crown so it rested upon the thick auburn mop of his hair; moments later, he moved it forward again; later he gave it a quarter turn, as if that might make it sit more easily on his brow. *It is no easy thing to wear a crown*, Catelyn thought, watching, *especially for a boy of fifteen years.*

When the guards brought in the captive, Robb called for his sword. Olyvar Frey offered it up hilt first, and her son drew the blade and laid it bare across his knees, a threat plain for all to see. "Your Grace, here is the man you asked for," announced Ser Robin Ryger, captain of the Tully household guard.

"Kneel before the king, Lannister!" Theon Greyjoy shouted. Ser Robin forced the prisoner to his knees.

He did not look a lion, Catelyn reflected. This Ser Cleos Frey was a son of the Lady Genna who was sister to Lord Tywin Lannister, but he had none of the fabled Lannister beauty, the fair hair and green eyes. Instead he had inherited the stringy brown locks, weak chin, and thin face of his sire, Ser Emmon Frey, old Lord Walder's second son. His eyes were pale and watery and he could not seem to stop blinking, but perhaps that was only the light. The cells below Riverrun were dark and damp . . . and these days crowded as well.

"Rise, Ser Cleos." Her son's voice was not as icy as his father's would have been, but he did not sound a boy of fifteen either. War had made a man of him before his time. Morning light glimmered faintly against the edge of the steel across his knees.

Yet it was not the sword that made Ser Cleos Frey anxious; it was the beast. Grey Wind, her son had named him. A direwolf large as any elkhound, lean and smoke-dark, with eyes like molten gold. When the beast padded forward and sniffed at the captive knight, every man in that hall could smell the scent of fear. Ser Cleos had been taken during the battle in the Whispering Wood, where Grey Wind had ripped out the throats of half a dozen men.

The knight scrambled up, edging away with such alacrity that some of the watchers laughed aloud. "Thank you, my lord."

"Your Grace," barked Lord Umber, the Greatjon, ever the loudest of Robb's northern bannermen . . . and the truest and fiercest as well, or so he insisted. He had been the first to proclaim her son King in the North, and he would brook no slight to the honor of his new-made sovereign.

"Your Grace," Ser Cleos corrected hastily. "Pardons."

He is not a bold man, this one, Catelyn thought. More of a Frey than a Lannister, in truth. His cousin the Kingslayer would have been a much different matter. They would never have gotten that honorific through Ser Jaime Lannister's perfect teeth.

"I brought you from your cell to carry my message to your cousin Cersei Lannister in King's Landing. You'll travel under a peace banner, with thirty of my best men to escort you."

Ser Cleos was visibly relieved. "Then I should be most glad to bring His Grace's message to the queen."

"Understand," Robb said, "I am not giving you your freedom. Your grandfather Lord Walder pledged me his support and that of House Frey. Many of your cousins and uncles rode with us in the Whispering Wood, but *you* chose to fight beneath the lion banner. That makes you a Lannister, not a Frey. I want your pledge, on your honor as a knight, that after you deliver my message you'll return with the queen's reply, and resume your captivity."

Ser Cleos answered at once. "I do so vow."

"Every man in this hall has heard you," warned Catelyn's brother Ser Edmure Tully, who spoke for Riverrun and the lords of the Trident in the place of their dying father. "If you do not return, the whole realm will know you forsworn."

"I will do as I pledged," Ser Cleos replied stiffly. "What is this message?"

"An offer of peace." Robb stood, longsword in hand. Grey Wind moved to his side. The hall grew hushed. "Tell the Queen Regent that if she meets my terms, I will sheath this sword, and make an end to the war between us."

In the back of the hall, Catelyn glimpsed the tall, gaunt figure of Lord Rickard Karstark shove through a rank of guards and out the door. No one else moved. Robb paid the disruption no mind. "Olyvar, the paper," he commanded. The squire took his longsword and handed up a rolled parchment.

Robb unrolled it. "First, the queen must release my sisters and provide them with transport by sea from King's Landing to White Harbor. It is to be understood that Sansa's betrothal to Joffrey Baratheon is at an end. When I receive word from my castellan that my sisters have returned unharmed to Winterfell, I will release the queen's cousins, the squire Willem Lannister and your brother Tion Frey, and give them safe escort to Casterly Rock or wheresoever she desires them delivered."

Catelyn Stark wished she could read the thoughts that hid behind each face, each furrowed brow and pair of tightened lips.

"Secondly, my lord father's bones will be returned to us, so he may rest beside his brother and sister in the crypts beneath Winterfell, as he would have wished. The remains of the men of his household guard who died in his service at King's Landing must also be returned."

Living men had gone south, and cold bones would return. *Ned had the truth of it*, she thought. *His place was at Winterfell, he said as much, but would I hear him? No. Go, I told him, you must be Robert's Hand, for the good of our House, for the sake of our children . . . my doing, mine, no other . . .*

"Third, my father's greatsword Ice will be delivered to my hand, here at Riverrun."

She watched her brother Ser Edmure Tully as he stood with his thumbs hooked over his swordbelt, his face as still as stone.

"Fourth, the queen will command her father Lord Tywin to release those knights and lords bannermen of mine that he took captive in the battle on the Green Fork of the Trident. Once he does so, I shall release my own captives taken in the Whispering Wood and the Battle of the Camps, save Jaime Lannister alone, who will remain my hostage for his father's good behavior."

She studied Theon Greyjoy's sly smile, wondering what it meant. That young man had a way of looking as though he knew some secret jest that only he was privy to; Catelyn had never liked it.

"Lastly, King Joffrey and the Queen Regent must renounce all claims to dominion over the north. Henceforth we are no part of their realm, but a free and independent kingdom, as of old. Our domain shall include all the Stark lands north of the Neck, and in addition the lands watered by the River Trident and its vassal streams, bounded by the Golden Tooth to the west and the Mountains of the Moon in the east."

"THE KING IN THE NORTH!" boomed Greatjon Umber, a ham-sized fist hammering at the air as he shouted. *"Stark! Stark! The King in the North!"*

Robb rolled up the parchment again. "Maester Vyman has drawn a map, showing the borders we claim. You shall have a copy for the queen. Lord Tywin must withdraw beyond these borders, and cease his raiding, burning, and pillage. The Queen Regent and her son shall make no claims to taxes, incomes, nor service from my people, and shall free my lords and knights from all oaths of fealty, vows, pledges, debts, and obligations owed to the Iron Throne and the Houses Baratheon and Lannister. Additionally, the Lannisters shall deliver ten highborn hostages, to be mutually agreed upon, as a pledge of peace. These I will treat as honored guests, according to their station. So long as the terms of this pact are abided with faithfully, I shall release two hostages every year, and return them safely to their families." Robb tossed the rolled parchment at the knight's feet. "There are the terms. If she meets them, I'll give her peace. If not"—he whistled, and Grey Wind moved forward snarling—"I'll give her another Whispering Wood."

"Stark!" the Greatjon roared again, and now other voices took up the cry. *"Stark, Stark, King in the North!"* The direwolf threw back his head and howled.

Ser Cleos had gone the color of curdled milk. "The queen shall hear your message, my—Your Grace."

"Good," Robb said. "Ser Robin, see that he has a good meal and clean clothing. He's to ride at first light."

"As you command, Your Grace," Ser Robin Ryger replied.

"Then we are done." The assembled knights and lords bannermen bent their knees as Robb turned to leave, Grey Wind at his heels. Olyvar

Frey scrambled ahead to open the door. Catelyn followed them out, her
brother at her side.

"You did well," she told her son in the gallery that led from the rear of
the hall, "though that business with the wolf was japery more befitting a
boy than a king."

Robb scratched Grey Wind behind the ear. "Did you see the look on
his face, Mother?" he asked, smiling.

"What I saw was Lord Karstark, walking out."

"As did I." Robb lifted off his crown with both hands and gave it to
Olyvar. "Take this thing back to my bedchamber."

"At once, Your Grace." The squire hurried off.

"I'll wager there were others who felt the same as Lord Karstark," her
brother Edmure declared. "How can we talk of peace while the Lannisters spread like a pestilence over my father's domains, stealing his crops
and slaughtering his people? I say again, we ought to be marching on
Harrenhal."

"We lack the strength," Robb said, though unhappily.

Edmure persisted. "Do we grow stronger sitting here? Our host dwin-
dles every day."

"And whose doing is that?" Catelyn snapped at her brother. It had
been at Edmure's insistence that Robb had given the river lords leave to
depart after his crowning, each to defend his own lands. Ser Marq Piper
and Lord Karyl Vance had been the first to go. Lord Jonos Bracken had
followed, vowing to reclaim the burnt shell of his castle and bury his
dead, and now Lord Jason Mallister had announced his intent to return to
his seat at Seagard, still mercifully untouched by the fighting.

"You cannot ask my river lords to remain idle while their fields are
being pillaged and their people put to the sword," Ser Edmure said, "but
Lord Karstark is a northman. It would be an ill thing if he were to leave
us."

"I'll speak with him," said Robb. "He lost two sons in the Whispering
Wood. Who can blame him if he does not want to make peace with their
killers . . . with my father's killers . . ."

"More bloodshed will not bring your father back to us, or Lord Rickard's sons," Catelyn said. "An offer had to be made—though a wiser man
might have offered sweeter terms."

"Any sweeter and I would have gagged." Her son's beard had grown in
redder than his auburn hair. Robb seemed to think it made him look
fierce, royal . . . older. But bearded or no, he was still a youth of fifteen,
and wanted vengeance no less than Rickard Karstark. It had been no easy
thing to convince him to make even this offer, poor as it was.

"Cersei Lannister will *never* consent to trade your sisters for a pair of cousins. It's her brother she'll want, as you know full well." She had told him as much before, but Catelyn was finding that kings do not listen half so attentively as sons.

"I can't release the Kingslayer, not even if I wanted to. My lords would never abide it."

"Your lords made you their king."

"And can *unmake* me just as easy."

"If your crown is the price we must pay to have Arya and Sansa returned safe, we should pay it willingly. Half your lords would like to murder Lannister in his cell. If he should die while he's your prisoner, men will say—"

"—that he well deserved it," Robb finished.

"And your sisters?" Catelyn asked sharply. "Will they deserve their deaths as well? I promise you, if any harm comes to her brother, Cersei will pay us back blood for blood—"

"Lannister won't die," Robb said. "No one so much as speaks to him without my warrant. He has food, water, clean straw, more comfort than he has any right to. But I won't free him, not even for Arya and Sansa."

Her son was looking *down* at her, Catelyn realized. *Was it war that made him grow so fast,* she wondered, *or the crown they had put on his head?* "Are you afraid to have Jaime Lannister in the field again, is that the truth of it?"

Grey Wind growled, as if he sensed Robb's anger, and Edmure Tully put a brotherly hand on Catelyn's shoulder. "Cat, don't. The boy has the right of this."

"Don't call me *the boy*," Robb said, rounding on his uncle, his anger spilling out all at once on poor Edmure, who had only meant to support him. "I'm almost a man grown, and a king—*your* king, ser. And I don't fear Jaime Lannister. I defeated him once, I'll defeat him again if I must, only . . ." He pushed a fall of hair out of his eyes and gave a shake of the head. "I might have been able to trade the Kingslayer for Father, but . . ."

". . . but not for the girls?" Her voice was icy quiet. "Girls are not important enough, are they?"

Robb made no answer, but there was hurt in his eyes. Blue eyes, Tully eyes, eyes she had given him. She had wounded him, but he was too much his father's son to admit it.

That was unworthy of me, she told herself. *Gods be good, what is to become of me? He is doing his best, trying so hard, I know it, I see it, and yet . . . I have lost my Ned, the rock my life was built on, I could not bear to lose the girls as well . . .*

"I'll do all I can for my sisters," Robb said. "If the queen has any sense, she'll accept my terms. If not, I'll make her rue the day she refused me."

Plainly, he'd had enough of the subject. "Mother, are you certain you will not consent to go to the Twins? You would be farther from the fighting, and you could acquaint yourself with Lord Frey's daughters to help me choose my bride when the war is done."

He wants me gone, Catelyn thought wearily. *Kings are not supposed to have mothers, it would seem, and I tell him things he does not want to hear.* "You're old enough to decide which of Lord Walder's girls you prefer without your mother's help, Robb."

"Then go with Theon. He leaves on the morrow. He'll help the Mallisters escort that lot of captives to Seagard and then take ship for the Iron Islands. You could find a ship as well, and be back at Winterfell with a moon's turn, if the winds are kind. Bran and Rickon need you."

And you do not, is that what you mean to say? "My lord father has little enough time remaining him. So long as your grandfather lives, my place is at Riverrun with him."

"I could command you to go. As king. I could."

Catelyn ignored that. "I'll say again, I would sooner you sent someone else to Pyke, and kept Theon close to you."

"Who better to treat with Balon Greyjoy than his son?"

"Jason Mallister," offered Catelyn. "Tytos Blackwood. Stevron Frey. Anyone . . . but not Theon."

Her son squatted beside Grey Wind, ruffling the wolf's fur and incidentally avoiding her eyes. "Theon's fought bravely for us. I told you how he saved Bran from those wildlings in the wolfswood. If the Lannisters won't make peace, I'll have need of Lord Greyjoy's longships."

"You'll have them sooner if you keep his son as hostage."

"He's been a hostage half his life."

"For good reason," Catelyn said. "Balon Greyjoy is not a man to be trusted. He wore a crown himself, remember, if only for a season. He may aspire to wear one again."

Robb stood. "I will not grudge him that. If I'm King in the North, let him be King of the Iron Islands, if that's his desire. I'll give him a crown gladly, so long as he helps us bring down the Lannisters."

"Robb—"

"I'm sending Theon. Good day, Mother. Grey Wind, come." Robb walked off briskly, the direwolf padding beside him.

Catelyn could only watch him go. Her son and now her king. How queer that felt. *Command,* she had told him back in Moat Cailin. And so he did. "I am going to visit Father," she announced abruptly. "Come with me, Edmure."

"I need to have a word with those new bowmen Ser Desmond is training. I'll visit him later."

If he still lives, Catelyn thought, but she said nothing. Her brother would sooner face battle than that sickroom.

The shortest way to the central keep where her father lay dying was through the godswood, with its grass and wildflowers and thick stands of elm and redwood. A wealth of rustling leaves still clung to the branches of the trees, all ignorant of the word the white raven had brought to Riverrun a fortnight past. Autumn had come, the Conclave had declared, but the gods had not seen fit to tell the winds and woods as yet. For that Catelyn was duly grateful. Autumn was always a fearful time, with the specter of winter looming ahead. Even the wisest man never knew whether his next harvest would be the last.

Hoster Tully, Lord of Riverrun, lay abed in his solar, with its commanding view to the east where the rivers Tumblestone and Red Fork met beyond the walls of his castle. He was sleeping when Catelyn entered, his hair and beard as white as his featherbed, his once portly frame turned small and frail by the death that grew within him.

Beside the bed, still dressed in mail hauberk and travel-stained cloak, sat her father's brother, the Blackfish. His boots were dusty and spattered with dried mud. "Does Robb know you are returned, Uncle?" Ser Brynden Tully was Robb's eyes and ears, the commander of his scouts and outriders.

"No. I came here straight from the stables, when they told me the king was holding court. His Grace will want to hear my tidings in private first, I'd think." The Blackfish was a tall, lean man, grey of hair and precise in his movements, his clean-shaven face lined and windburnt. "How is he?" he asked, and she knew he did not mean Robb.

"Much the same. The maester gives him dreamwine and milk of the poppy for his pain, so he sleeps most of the time, and eats too little. He seems weaker with each day that passes."

"Does he speak?"

"Yes . . . but there is less and less sense to the things he says. He talks of his regrets, of unfinished tasks, of people long dead and times long past. Sometimes he does not know what season it is, or who I am. Once he called me by Mother's name."

"He misses her still," Ser Brynden answered. "You have her face. I can see it in your cheekbones, and your jaw . . ."

"You remember more of her than I do. It has been a long time." She seated herself on the bed and brushed away a strand of fine white hair that had fallen across her father's face.

"Each time I ride out, I wonder if I shall find him alive or dead on my return." Despite their quarrels, there was a deep bond between her father and the brother he had once disowned.

"At least you made your peace with him."

They sat for a time in silence, until Catelyn raised her head. "You spoke of tidings that Robb needed to hear?" Lord Hoster moaned and rolled onto his side, almost as if he had heard.

Brynden stood. "Come outside. Best if we do not wake him."

She followed him out onto the stone balcony that jutted three-sided from the solar like the prow of a ship. Her uncle glanced up, frowning. "You can see it by day now. My men call it the Red Messenger . . . but what is the message?"

Catelyn raised her eyes, to where the faint red line of the comet traced a path across the deep blue sky like a long scratch across the face of god. "The Greatjon told Robb that the old gods have unfurled a red flag of vengeance for Ned. Edmure thinks it's an omen of victory for Riverrun— he sees a fish with a long tail, in the Tully colors, red against blue." She sighed. "I wish I had their faith. Crimson is a Lannister color."

"That thing's not crimson," Ser Brynden said. "Nor Tully red, the mud red of the river. That's blood up there, child, smeared across the sky."

"Our blood or theirs?"

"Was there ever a war where only one side bled?" Her uncle gave a shake of the head. "The riverlands are awash in blood and flame all around the Gods Eye. The fighting has spread south to the Blackwater and north across the Trident, almost to the Twins. Marq Piper and Karyl Vance have won some small victories, and this southron lordling Beric Dondarrion has been raiding the raiders, falling upon Lord Tywin's foraging parties and vanishing back into the woods. It's said that Ser Burton Crakehall was boasting that he'd slain Dondarrion, until he led his column into one of Lord Beric's traps and got every man of them killed."

"Some of Ned's guard from King's Landing are with this Lord Beric," Catelyn recalled. "May the gods preserve them."

"Dondarrion and this red priest who rides with him are clever enough to preserve themselves, if the tales be true," her uncle said, "but your father's bannermen make a sadder tale. Robb should never have let them go. They've scattered like quail, each man trying to protect his own, and it's folly, Cat, folly. Jonos Bracken was wounded in the fighting amidst the ruins of his castle, and his nephew Hendry slain. Tytos Blackwood's swept the Lannisters off his lands, but they took every cow and pig and speck of grain and left him nothing to defend but Raventree Hall and a scorched desert. Darry men recaptured their lord's keep but held it less than a fortnight before Gregor Clegane descended on them and put the whole garrison to the sword, even their lord."

Catelyn was horrorstruck. "Darry was only a child."

"Aye, and the last of his line as well. The boy would have brought a fine ransom, but what does gold mean to a frothing dog like Gregor Clegane? That beast's head would make a noble gift for all the people of the realm, I vow."

Catelyn knew Ser Gregor's evil reputation, yet still . . . "Don't speak to me of heads, Uncle. Cersei has mounted Ned's on a spike above the walls of the Red Keep, and left it for the crows and flies." Even now, it was hard for her to believe that he was truly gone. Some nights she would wake in darkness, half-asleep, and for an instant expect to find him there beside her. "Clegane is no more than Lord Tywin's catspaw." For Tywin Lannister—Lord of Casterly Rock, Warden of the West, father to Queen Cersei, Ser Jaime the Kingslayer, and Tyrion the Imp, and grandfather to Joffrey Baratheon, the new-crowned boy king—was the true danger, Catelyn believed.

"True enough," Ser Brynden admitted. "And Tywin Lannister is no man's fool. He sits safe behind the walls of Harrenhal, feeding his host on our harvest and burning what he does not take. Gregor is not the only dog he's loosed. Ser Amory Lorch is in the field as well, and some sellsword out of Qohor who'd sooner maim a man than kill him. I've seen what they leave behind them. Whole villages put to the torch, women raped and mutilated, butchered children left unburied to draw wolves and wild dogs . . . it would sicken even the dead."

"When Edmure hears this, he will rage."

"And that will be just as Lord Tywin desires. Even terror has its purpose, Cat. Lannister wants to provoke us to battle."

"Robb is like to give him that wish," Catelyn said, fretful. "He is restless as a cat sitting here, and Edmure and the Greatjon and the others will urge him on." Her son had won two great victories, smashing Jaime Lannister in the Whispering Wood and routing his leaderless host outside the walls of Riverrun in the Battle of the Camps, but from the way some of his bannermen spoke of him, he might have been Aegon the Conqueror reborn.

Brynden Blackfish arched a bushy grey eyebrow. "More fool they. My first rule of war, Cat—*never* give the enemy his wish. Lord Tywin would like to fight on a field of his own choosing. He wants us to march on Harrenhal."

"Harrenhal." Every child of the Trident knew the tales told of Harrenhal, the vast fortress that King Harren the Black had raised beside the waters of Gods Eye three hundred years past, when the Seven Kingdoms had *been* seven kingdoms, and the riverlands were ruled by the ironmen from the islands. In his pride, Harren had desired the highest hall and tallest towers in all Westeros. Forty years it had taken, rising like a great shadow on the shore of the lake while Harren's armies plundered his neighbors for stone, lumber, gold, and workers. Thousands of captives died in his quarries, chained to his sledges, or laboring on his five colossal towers. Men froze by winter and sweltered in summer. Weirwoods that had stood three thousand years were cut down for beams and rafters. Harren had beggared the riverlands and the Iron Islands alike to ornament his dream. And when at last Harrenhal stood complete, on the very day King Harren took up residence, Aegon the Conqueror had come ashore at King's Landing.

Catelyn could remember hearing Old Nan tell the story to her own children, back at Winterfell. "And King Harren learned that thick walls and high towers are small use against dragons," the tale always ended. "For dragons *fly*." Harren and all his line had perished in the fires that engulfed his monstrous fortress, and every house that held Harrenhal since had come to misfortune. Strong it might be, but it was a dark place, and cursed.

"I would not have Robb fight a battle in the shadow of that keep," Catelyn admitted. "Yet we must do *something*, Uncle."

"And soon," her uncle agreed. "I have not told you the worst of it, child. The men I sent west have brought back word that a new host is gathering at Casterly Rock."

Another Lannister army. The thought made her ill. "Robb must be told at once. Who will command?"

"Ser Stafford Lannister, it's said." He turned to gaze out over the rivers, his red-and-blue cloak stirring in the breeze.

"Another nephew?" The Lannisters of Casterly Rock were a damnably large and fertile house.

"Cousin," Ser Brynden corrected. "Brother to Lord Tywin's late wife, so twice related. An old man and a bit of a dullard, but he has a son, Ser Daven, who is more formidable."

"Then let us hope it is the father and not the son who takes this army into the field."

"We have some time yet before we must face them. This lot will be sellswords, freeriders, and green boys from the stews of Lannisport. Ser Stafford must see that they are armed and drilled before he dare risk battle . . . and make no mistake, Lord Tywin is not the Kingslayer. He will not rush in heedless. He will wait patiently for Ser Stafford to march before he stirs from behind the walls of Harrenhal."

"Unless . . ." said Catelyn.

"Yes?" Ser Brynden prompted.

"Unless he *must* leave Harrenhal," she said, "to face some other threat."

Her uncle looked at her thoughtfully. "Lord Renly."

"*King* Renly." If she would ask help from the man, she would need to grant him the style he had claimed for himself.

"Perhaps." The Blackfish smiled a dangerous smile. "He'll want something, though."

"He'll want what kings always want," she said. "Homage."

TYRION

Janos Slynt was a butcher's son, and he laughed like a man chopping meat. "More wine?" Tyrion asked him.

"I should not object," Lord Janos said, holding out his cup. He was built like a keg, and had a similar capacity. "I should not object at all. That's a fine red. From the Arbor?"

"Dornish." Tyrion gestured, and his serving man poured. But for the servants, he and Lord Janos were alone in the Small Hall, at a small candlelit table surrounded by darkness. "Quite the find. Dornish wines are not often so rich."

"Rich," said the big frog-faced man, taking a healthy gulp. He was not a man for sipping, Janos Slynt. Tyrion had made note of that at once. "Yes, rich, that's the very word I was searching for, the *very* word. You have a gift for words, Lord Tyrion, if I might say so. And you tell a droll tale. Droll, yes."

"I'm pleased you think so . . . but I'm not a lord, as you are. A simple *Tyrion* will suffice for me, Lord Janos."

"As you wish." He took another swallow, dribbling wine on the front of his black satin doublet. He was wearing a cloth-of-gold half cape fastened with a miniature spear, its point enameled in dark red. And he was well and truly drunk.

Tyrion covered his mouth and belched politely. Unlike Lord Janos he had gone easy on the wine, but he was very full. The first thing he had done after taking up residence in the Tower of the Hand was inquire after the finest cook in the city and take her into his service. This evening they had supped on oxtail soup, summer greens tossed with pecans, grapes, red fennel, and crumbled cheese, hot crab pie, spiced squash, and quails drowned in butter. Each dish had come with its own wine. Lord Janos allowed that he had never eaten half so well. "No doubt that will change when you take your seat in Harrenhal," Tyrion said.

"For a certainty. Perhaps I should ask this cook of yours to enter my service, what do you say?"

"Wars have been fought over less," he said, and they both had a good long laugh. "You're a bold man to take Harrenhal for your seat. Such a grim place, and huge . . . costly to maintain. And some say cursed as well."

"Should I fear a pile of stone?" He hooted at the notion. "A bold man, you said. You must be bold, to rise. As I have. To Harrenhal, yes! And why not? You know. You are a bold man too, I sense. Small, mayhap, but bold."

"You are too kind. More wine?"

"No. No, truly, I . . . oh, gods be damned, yes. Why not? A bold man drinks his fill!"

"Truly." Tyrion filled Lord Slynt's cup to the brim. "I have been glancing over the names you put forward to take your place as Commander of the City Watch."

"Good men. Fine men. Any of the six will do, but I'd choose Allar Deem. My right arm. Good good man. Loyal. Pick him and you won't be sorry. If he pleases the king."

"To be sure." Tyrion took a small sip of his own wine. "I had been considering Ser Jacelyn Bywater. He's been captain on the Mud Gate for three years, and he served with valor during Balon Greyjoy's Rebellion. King Robert knighted him at Pyke. And yet his name does not appear on your list."

Lord Janos Slynt took a gulp of wine and sloshed it around in his mouth for a moment before swallowing. "Bywater. Well. Brave man, to be sure, yet . . . he's rigid, that one. A queer dog. The men don't like him. A cripple too, lost his hand at Pyke, that's what got him knighted. A poor trade, if you ask me, a hand for a ser." He laughed. "Ser Jacelyn thinks overmuch of himself and his honor, as I see it. You'll do better leaving that one where he is, my lor—Tyrion. Allar Deem's the man for you."

"Deem is little loved in the streets, I am told."

"He's feared. That's better."

"What was it I heard of him? Some trouble in a brothel?"

"That. Not his fault, my lo—Tyrion. No. He never meant to kill the woman, that was her own doing. He warned her to stand aside and let him do his duty."

"Still . . . mothers and children, he might have expected she'd try to save the babe." Tyrion smiled. "Have some of this cheese, it goes splendidly with the wine. Tell me, why did you choose Deem for that unhappy task?"

"A good commander knows his men, Tyrion. Some are good for one job, some for another. Doing for a babe, and her still on the tit, that takes a certain sort. Not every man'd do it. Even if it was only some whore and her whelp."

"I suppose that's so," said Tyrion, hearing *only some whore* and thinking of Shae, and Tysha long ago, and all the other women who had taken his coin and his seed over the years.

Slynt went on, oblivious. "A hard man for a hard job, is Deem. Does as he's told, and never a word afterward." He cut a slice off the cheese. "This *is* fine. Sharp. Give me a good sharp knife and a good sharp cheese and I'm a happy man."

Tyrion shrugged. "Enjoy it while you can. With the riverlands in flame and Renly king in Highgarden, good cheese will soon be hard to come by. So who sent you after the whore's bastard?"

Lord Janos gave Tyrion a wary look, then laughed and wagged a wedge of cheese at him. "You're a sly one, Tyrion. Thought you could trick me, did you? It takes more than wine and cheese to make Janos Slynt tell more than he should. I pride myself. Never a question, and never a word afterward, not with me."

"As with Deem."

"Just the same. You make him your Commander when I'm off to Harrenhal, and you won't regret it."

Tyrion broke off a nibble of the cheese. It was sharp indeed, and veined with wine, very choice. "Whoever the king names will not have an easy time stepping into *your* armor, I can tell. Lord Mormont faces the same problem."

Lord Janos looked puzzled. "I thought she was a lady. Mormont. Beds down with bears, that's the one?"

"It was her brother I was speaking of. Jeor Mormont, the Lord Commander of the Night's Watch. When I was visiting with him on the Wall, he mentioned how concerned he was about finding a good man to take his place. The Watch gets so few good men these days." Tyrion grinned. "He'd sleep easier if he had a man like you, I imagine. Or the valiant Allar Deem."

Lord Janos roared. "Small chance of that!"

"One would think," Tyrion said, "but life does take queer turns. Consider Eddard Stark, my lord. I don't suppose he ever imagined his life would end on the steps of Baelor's Sept."

"There were damn few as did," Lord Janos allowed, chuckling.

Tyrion chuckled too. "A pity I wasn't here to see it. They say even Varys was surprised."

Lord Janos laughed so hard his gut shook. "The Spider," he said. "Knows everything, they say. Well, he didn't know *that*."

"How could he?" Tyrion put the first hint of a chill in his tone. "He had helped persuade my sister that Stark should be pardoned, on the condition that he take the black."

"Eh?" Janos Slynt blinked vaguely at Tyrion.

"My sister Cersei," Tyrion repeated, a shade more strongly, in case the fool had some doubt who he meant. "The Queen Regent."

"Yes." Slynt took a swallow. "As to that, well . . . the king commanded it, m'lord. The king himself."

"The king is thirteen," Tyrion reminded him.

"Still. He *is* the king." Slynt's jowls quivered when he frowned. "The Lord of the Seven Kingdoms."

"Well, one or two of them, at least," Tyrion said with a sour smile. "Might I have a look at your spear?"

"My spear?" Lord Janos blinked in confusion.

Tyrion pointed. "The clasp that fastens your cape."

Hesitantly, Lord Janos drew out the ornament and handed it to Tyrion.

"We have goldsmiths in Lannisport who do better work," he opined. "The red enamel blood is a shade much, if you don't mind my saying. Tell me, my lord, did you drive the spear into the man's back yourself, or did you only give the command?"

"I gave the command, and I'd give it again. Lord Stark was a traitor." The bald spot in the middle of Slynt's head was beet-red, and his cloth-of-gold cape had slithered off his shoulders onto the floor. "The man tried to buy me."

"Little dreaming that you had already been sold."

Slynt slammed down his wine cup. "Are you drunk? If you think I will sit here and have my honor questioned . . ."

"What honor is that? I do admit, you made a better bargain than Ser Jacelyn. A lordship and a castle for a spear thrust in the back, and you didn't even need to thrust the spear." He tossed the golden ornament back to Janos Slynt. It bounced off his chest and clattered to the floor as the man rose.

"I mislike the tone of your voice, my lo—*Imp*. I am the Lord of Harrenhal and a member of the king's council, who are you to chastise me like this?"

Tyrion cocked his head sideways. "I think you know quite well who I am. How many sons do you have?"

"What are my sons to you, dwarf?"

"*Dwarf?*" His anger flashed. "You should have stopped at Imp. I am Tyrion of House Lannister, and someday, if you have the sense the gods gave a sea slug, you will drop to your knees in thanks that it was me you had to deal with, and not my lord father. Now, *how many sons do you have?*"

Tyrion could see the sudden fear in Janos Slynt's eyes. "Th-three, m'lord. And a daughter. Please, m'lord—"

"You need not beg." He slid off his chair. "You have my word, no harm will come to them. The younger boys will be fostered out as squires. If they serve well and loyally, they may be knights in time. Let it never be said that House Lannister does not reward those who serve it. Your eldest son will inherit the title Lord Slynt, and this appalling sigil of yours." He kicked at the little golden spear and sent it skittering across the floor. "Lands will be found for him, and he can build a seat for himself. It will not be Harrenhal, but it will be sufficient. It will be up to him to make a marriage for the girl."

Janos Slynt's face had gone from red to white. "Wh-what . . . what do you . . . ?" His jowls were quivering like mounds of suet.

"What do I mean to do with *you?*" Tyrion let the oaf tremble for a moment before he answered. "The carrack *Summer's Dream* sails on the morning tide. Her master tells me she will call at Gulltown, the Three Sisters, the isle of Skagos, and Eastwatch-by-the-Sea. When you see Lord Commander Mormont, give him my fond regards, and tell him that I have not forgotten the needs of the Night's Watch. I wish you long life and good service, my lord."

Once Janos Slynt realized he was not to be summarily executed, color returned to his face. He thrust his jaw out. "We will see about this, Imp. *Dwarf.* Perhaps it will be you on that ship, what do you think of that? Perhaps it will be you on the Wall." He gave a bark of anxious laughter. "You and your threats, well, we will see. I am the king's friend, you know. We shall hear what Joffrey has to say about this. And Littlefinger and the queen, oh, yes. Janos Slynt has a good many friends. We will see who goes sailing, I promise you. Indeed we will."

Slynt spun on his heel like the watchman he'd once been, and strode the length of the Small Hall, boots ringing on the stone. He clattered up the steps, threw open the door . . . and came face-to-face with a tall, lantern-jawed man in black breastplate and gold cloak. Strapped to the stump of his right wrist was an iron hand. "Janos," he said, deep-set eyes glinting under a prominent brow ridge and a shock of salt-and-pepper hair. Six gold cloaks moved quietly into the Small Hall behind him as Janos Slynt backed away.

"Lord Slynt," Tyrion called out, "I believe you know Ser Jacelyn Bywater, our new Commander of the City Watch."

"We have a litter waiting for you, my lord," Ser Jacelyn told Slynt. "The docks are dark and distant, and the streets are not safe by night. Men."

As the gold cloaks ushered out their onetime commander, Tyrion called Ser Jacelyn to his side and handed him a roll of parchment. "It's a long voyage, and Lord Slynt will want for company. See that these six join him on the *Summer's Dream.*"

Bywater glanced over the names and smiled. "As you will."

"There's one," Tyrion said quietly. "Deem. Tell the captain it would not be taken amiss if that one should happen to be swept overboard before they reach Eastwatch."

"I'm told those northern waters are very stormy, my lord." Ser Jacelyn bowed and took his leave, his cloak rippling behind him. He trod on Slynt's cloth-of-gold cape on his way.

Tyrion sat alone, sipping at what remained of the fine sweet Dornish wine. Servants came and went, clearing the dishes from the table. He told them to leave the wine. When they were done, Varys came gliding into the hall, wearing flowing lavender robes that matched his smell. "Oh, sweetly done, my good lord."

"Then why do I have this bitter taste in my mouth?" He pressed his fingers into his temples. "I told them to throw Allar Deem into the sea. I am sorely tempted to do the same with you."

"You might be disappointed by the result," Varys replied. "The storms come and go, the waves crash overhead, the big fish eat the little fish, and I keep on paddling. Might I trouble you for a taste of the wine that Lord Slynt enjoyed so much?"

Tyrion waved at the flagon, frowning.

Varys filled a cup. "Ah. Sweet as summer." He took another sip. "I hear the grapes singing on my tongue."

"I wondered what that noise was. Tell the grapes to keep still, my head is about to split. It was my sister. That was what the oh-so-loyal Lord Janos refused to say. *Cersei* sent the gold cloaks to that brothel."

Varys tittered nervously. So he had known all along.

"You left that part out," Tyrion said accusingly.

"Your own sweet sister," Varys said, so grief-stricken he looked close to tears. "It is a hard thing to tell a man, my lord. I was fearful how you might take it. Can you forgive me?"

"No," Tyrion snapped. "Damn you. Damn *her*." He could not touch Cersei, he knew. Not yet, not even if he'd wanted to, and he was far from certain that he did. Yet it rankled, to sit here and make a mummer's show of justice by punishing the sorry likes of Janos Slynt and Allar Deem, while his sister continued on her savage course. "In future, you will tell me what you know, Lord Varys. *All* of what you know."

The eunuch's smile was sly. "That might take rather a long time, my good lord. I know quite a lot."

"Not enough to save this child, it would seem."

"Alas, no. There was another bastard, a boy, older. I took steps to see him removed from harm's way . . . but I confess, I never dreamed the babe would be at risk. A baseborn girl, less than a year old, with a whore for a mother. What threat could she pose?"

"She was Robert's," Tyrion said bitterly. "That was enough for Cersei, it would seem."

"Yes. It is grievous sad. I must blame myself for the poor sweet babe and her mother, who was so young and loved the king."

"Did she?" Tyrion had never seen the dead girl's face, but in his mind she was Shae and Tysha both. "Can a whore truly love anyone, I wonder? No, don't answer. Some things I would rather not know." He had settled Shae in a sprawling stone-and-timber manse, with its own well and stable and garden; he had given her servants to see to her wants, a white bird from the Summer Isles to keep her company, silks and silver and gemstones to adorn her, guards to protect her. And yet she seemed restive. She wanted to be with him more, she told him; she wanted to serve him and help him. "You help me most here, between the sheets," he told her one night after their loving as he lay beside her, his head pillowed against her breast, his groin aching with a sweet soreness. She made no reply, save with her eyes. He could see there that it was not what she'd wanted to hear.

Sighing, Tyrion started to reach for the wine again, then remembered Lord Janos and pushed the flagon away. "It does seem my sister was telling the truth about Stark's death. We have my nephew to thank for that madness."

"King Joffrey gave the command. Janos Slynt and Ser Ilyn Payne carried it out, swiftly, without hesitation . . ."

". . . almost as if they had expected it. Yes, we have been over this ground before, without profit. A folly."

"With the City Watch in hand, my lord, you are well placed to see to it that His Grace commits no further . . . follies? To be sure, there is still the queen's household guard to consider . . ."

"The red cloaks?" Tyrion shrugged. "Vylarr's loyalty is to Casterly Rock. He knows I am here with my father's authority. Cersei would find

it hard to use his men against me . . . besides, they are only a hundred. I
have half again as many men of my own. *And* six thousand gold cloaks,
if Bywater is the man you claim."

"You will find Ser Jacelyn to be courageous, honorable, obedient . . .
and most grateful."

"To whom, I wonder?" Tyrion did not trust Varys, though there was
no denying his value. He knew things, beyond a doubt. "Why *are* you so
helpful, my lord Varys?" he asked, studying the man's soft hands, the
bald powdered face, the slimy little smile.

"You are the Hand. I serve the realm, the king, and you."

"As you served Jon Arryn and Eddard Stark?"

"I served Lord Arryn and Lord Stark as best I could. I was saddened
and horrified by their most untimely deaths."

"Think how *I* feel. I'm like to be next."

"Oh, I think not," Varys said, swirling the wine in his cup. "Power is a
curious thing, my lord. Perchance you have considered the riddle I posed
you that day in the inn?"

"It has crossed my mind a time or two," Tyrion admitted. "The king,
the priest, the rich man—who lives and who dies? Who will the swordsman obey? It's a riddle without an answer, or rather, too many answers.
All depends on the man with the sword."

"And yet he is no one," Varys said. "He has neither crown nor gold nor
favor of the gods, only a piece of pointed steel."

"That piece of steel is the power of life and death."

"Just so . . . yet if it is the swordsmen who rule us in truth, why do
we pretend our kings hold the power? Why should a strong man with a
sword *ever* obey a child king like Joffrey, or a wine-sodden oaf like his
father?"

"Because these child kings and drunken oafs can call other strong
men, with other swords."

"Then these other swordsmen have the true power. Or do they?
Whence came their swords? Why do *they* obey?" Varys smiled. "Some
say knowledge is power. Some tell us that all power comes from the
gods. Others say it derives from law. Yet that day on the steps of Baelor's
Sept, our godly High Septon and the lawful Queen Regent and your ever-
so-knowledgeable servant were as powerless as any cobbler or cooper in
the crowd. Who truly killed Eddard Stark, do you think? Joffrey, who
gave the command? Ser Ilyn Payne, who swung the sword? Or . . . another?"

Tyrion cocked his head sideways. "Did you mean to answer your
damned riddle, or only to make my head ache worse?"

Varys smiled. "Here, then. Power resides where men *believe* it resides.
No more and no less."

"So power is a mummer's trick?"

"A shadow on the wall," Varys murmured, "yet shadows can kill. And ofttimes a very small man can cast a very large shadow."

Tyrion smiled. "Lord Varys, I am growing strangely fond of you. I may kill you yet, but I think I'd feel sad about it."

"I will take that as high praise."

"What are you, Varys?" Tyrion found he truly wanted to know. "A spider, they say."

"Spies and informers are seldom loved, my lord. I am but a loyal servant of the realm."

"And a eunuch. Let us not forget that."

"I seldom do."

"People have called me a halfman too, yet I think the gods have been kinder to me. I am small, my legs are twisted, and women do not look upon me with any great yearning . . . yet I'm still a man. Shae is not the first to grace my bed, and one day I may take a wife and sire a son. If the gods are good, he'll look like his uncle and think like his father. You have no such hope to sustain you. Dwarfs are a jape of the gods . . . but men make eunuchs. Who cut you, Varys? When and why? Who *are* you, truly?"

The eunuch's smile never flickered, but his eyes glittered with something that was not laughter. "You are kind to ask, my lord, but my tale is long and sad, and we have treasons to discuss." He drew a parchment from the sleeve of his robe. "The master of the King's Galley *White Hart* plots to slip anchor three days hence to offer his sword and ship to Lord Stannis."

Tyrion sighed. "I suppose we must make some sort of bloody lesson out of the man?"

"Ser Jacelyn could arrange for him to vanish, but a trial before the king would help assure the continued loyalty of the other captains."

And keep my royal nephew occupied as well. "As you say. Put him down for a dose of Joffrey's justice."

Varys made a mark on the parchment. "Ser Horas and Ser Hobber Redwyne have bribed a guard to let them out a postern gate, the night after next. Arrangements have been made for them to sail on the Pentoshi galley *Moonrunner*, disguised as oarsmen."

"Can we *keep* them on those oars for a few years, see how they fancy it?" He smiled. "No, my sister would be distraught to lose such treasured guests. Inform Ser Jacelyn. Seize the man they bribed and explain what an honor it is to serve as a brother of the Night's Watch. And have men posted around the *Moonrunner*, in case the Redwynes find a second guard short of coin."

"As you will." Another mark on the parchment. "Your man Timett

slew a wineseller's son this evening, at a gambling den on the Street of
Silver. He accused him of cheating at tiles."

"Was it true?"

"Oh, beyond a doubt."

"Then the honest men of the city owe Timett a debt of gratitude. I
shall see that he has the king's thanks."

The eunuch gave a nervous giggle and made another mark. "We also
have a sudden plague of holy men. The comet has brought forth all manner of queer priests, preachers, and prophets, it would seem. They beg in
the winesinks and pot-shops and foretell doom and destruction to anyone who stops to listen."

Tyrion shrugged. "We are close on the three hundredth year since
Aegon's Landing, I suppose it is only to be expected. Let them rant."

"They are spreading fear, my lord."

"I thought that was your job."

Varys covered his mouth with his hand. "You are very cruel to say so.
One last matter. Lady Tanda gave a small supper last night. I have the
menu and the guest list for your inspection. When the wine was poured,
Lord Gyles rose to lift a cup to the king, and Ser Balon Swann was heard
to remark, *'We'll need three cups for that.'* Many laughed . . ."

Tyrion raised a hand. "Enough. Ser Balon made a jest. I am not interested in treasonous table talk, Lord Varys."

"You are as wise as you are gentle, my lord." The parchment vanished
up the eunuch's sleeve. "We both have much to do. I shall leave you."

When the eunuch had departed, Tyrion sat for a long time watching
the candle and wondering how his sister would take the news of Janos
Slynt's dismissal. Not happily, if he was any judge, but beyond sending
an angry protest to Lord Tywin in Harrenhal, he did not see what Cersei
could hope to do about it. Tyrion had the City Watch now, plus a hun-
dred-and-a-half fierce clansmen and a growing force of sellswords recruited by Bronn. He would seem well protected.

Doubtless Eddard Stark thought the same.

The Red Keep was dark and still when Tyrion left the Small Hall.
Bronn was waiting in his solar. "Slynt?" he asked.

"Lord Janos will be sailing for the Wall on the morning tide. Varys
would have me believe that I have replaced one of Joffrey's men with one
of my own. More likely, I have replaced Littlefinger's man with one
belonging to Varys, but so be it."

"You'd best know, Timett killed a man—"

"Varys told me."

The sellsword seemed unsurprised. "The fool figured a one-eyed man
would be easier to cheat. Timett pinned his wrist to the table with a

dagger and ripped out his throat barehanded. He has this trick where he stiffens his fingers—"

"Spare me the grisly details, my supper is sitting badly in my belly," Tyrion said. "How goes your recruiting?"

"Well enough. Three new men tonight."

"How do you know which ones to hire?"

"I look them over. I question them, to learn where they've fought and how well they lie." Bronn smiled. "And then I give them a chance to kill me, while I do the same for them."

"Have you killed any?"

"No one we could have used."

"And if one of them kills you?"

"He'll be one you'll want to hire."

Tyrion was a little drunk, and very tired. "Tell me, Bronn. If I told you to kill a babe . . . an infant girl, say, still at her mother's breast . . . would you do it? Without question?"

"Without question? No." The sellsword rubbed thumb and forefinger together. "I'd ask how much."

And why would I ever need your Allar Deem, Lord Slynt? Tyrion thought. *I have a hundred of my own.* He wanted to laugh; he wanted to weep; most of all, he wanted Shae.

ARYA

The road was little more than two ruts through the weeds.

The good part was, with so little traffic there'd be no one to point the finger and say which way they'd gone. The human flood that had flowed down the kingsroad was only a trickle here.

The bad part was, the road wound back and forth like a snake, tangling with even smaller trails and sometimes seeming to vanish entirely only to reappear half a league farther on when they had all but given up hope. Arya hated it. The land was gentle enough, rolling hills and terraced fields interspersed with meadows and woodlands and little valleys where willows crowded close to slow shallow streams. Even so, the path was so narrow and crooked that their pace had dropped to a crawl.

It was the wagons that slowed them, lumbering along, axles creaking under the weight of their heavy loads. A dozen times a day they had to stop to free a wheel that had stuck in a rut, or double up the teams to climb a muddy slope. Once, in the middle of a dense stand of oak, they came face-to-face with three men pulling a load of firewood in an ox cart, with no way for either to get around. There had been nothing for it but to wait while the foresters unhitched their ox, led him through the trees, spun the cart, hitched the ox up again, and started back the way they'd come. The ox was even *slower* than the wagons, so that day they hardly got anywhere at all.

Arya could not help looking over her shoulder, wondering when the gold cloaks would catch them. At night, she woke at every noise to grab for Needle's hilt. They never made camp without putting out sentries now, but Arya did not trust them, especially the orphan boys. They might have done well enough in the alleys of King's Landing, but out here they were lost. When she was being quiet as a shadow, she could sneak past all of them, flitting out by starlight to make her water in the woods where no one would see. Once, when Lommy Greenhands had the watch, she shimmied up an oak and moved from tree to tree until she was right above his head, and he never saw a thing. She would have jumped down on top of him, but she knew his scream would wake the whole camp, and Yoren might take a stick to her again.

Lommy and the other orphans all treated the Bull like someone special now because the queen wanted his head, though he would have none of it. "I never did nothing to no queen," he said angrily. "I did my work, is all. Bellows and tongs and fetch and carry. I was s'posed to be an armorer, and one day Master Mott says I got to join the Night's Watch, that's all I know." Then he'd go off to polish his helm. It was a beautiful helm, rounded and curved, with a slit visor and two great metal bull's horns. Arya would watch him polish the metal with an oilcloth, shining it so bright you could see the flames of the cookfire reflected in the steel. Yet he never actually put it on his head.

"I bet he's that traitor's bastard," Lommy said one night, in a hushed voice so Gendry would not hear. "The wolf lord, the one they nicked on Baelor's steps."

"He is not," Arya declared. *My father only had one bastard, and that's Jon.* She stalked off into the trees, wishing she could just saddle her horse and ride home. She was a good horse, a chestnut mare with a white blaze on her forehead. And Arya had always been a good rider. She could gallop off and never see any of them, unless she wanted to. Only then she'd have no one to scout ahead of her, or watch behind, or stand guard while she napped, and when the gold cloaks caught her, she'd be all alone. It was safer to stay with Yoren and the others.

"We're not far from Gods Eye," the black brother said one morning. "The kingsroad won't be safe till we're across the Trident. So we'll come up around the lake along the western shore, they're not like to look for us there." At the next spot where two ruts cut cross each other, he turned the wagons west.

Here farmland gave way to forest, the villages and holdfasts were smaller and farther apart, the hills higher and the valleys deeper. Food grew harder to come by. In the city, Yoren had loaded up the wagons with salt fish, hard bread, lard, turnips, sacks of beans and barley, and wheels of yellow cheese, but every bite of it had been eaten. Forced to live off the land, Yoren turned to Koss and Kurz, who'd been taken as poachers. He would send them ahead of the column, into the woods, and

come dusk they would be back with a deer slung between them on a pole
or a brace of quail swinging from their belts. The younger boys would be
set to picking blackberries along the road, or climbing fences to fill a
sack with apples if they happened upon an orchard.

Arya was a skilled climber and a fast picker, and she liked to go off by
herself. One day she came across a rabbit, purely by happenstance. It was
brown and fat, with long ears and a twitchy nose. Rabbits ran faster than
cats, but they couldn't climb trees half so well. She whacked it with her
stick and grabbed it by its ears, and Yoren stewed it with some mushrooms and wild onions. Arya was given a whole leg, since it was her
rabbit. She shared it with Gendry. The rest of them each got a spoonful,
even the three in manacles. Jaqen H'ghar thanked her politely for the
treat, and Biter licked the grease off his dirty fingers with a blissful look,
but Rorge, the noseless one, only laughed and said, "There's a hunter
now. Lumpyface Lumpyhead Rabbitkiller."

Outside a holdfast called Briarwhite, some fieldhands surrounded
them in a cornfield, demanding coin for the ears they'd taken. Yoren
eyed their scythes and tossed them a few coppers. "Time was, a man in
black was feasted from Dorne to Winterfell, and even high lords called it
an honor to shelter him under their roofs," he said bitterly. "Now
cravens like you want hard coin for a bite of wormy apple." He spat.

"It's sweetcorn, better'n a stinking old black bird like you deserves,"
one of them answered roughly. "You get out of our field now, and take
these sneaks and stabbers with you, or we'll stake you up in the corn to
scare the other crows away."

They roasted the sweetcorn in the husk that night, turning the ears
with long forked sticks, and ate it hot right off the cob. Arya thought it
tasted wonderful, but Yoren was too angry to eat. A cloud seemed to
hang over him, ragged and black as his cloak. He paced about the camp
restlessly, muttering to himself.

The next day Koss came racing back to warn Yoren of a camp ahead.
"Twenty or thirty men, in mail and halfhelms," he said. "Some of them
are cut up bad, and one's dying, from the sound of him. With all the noise
he was making, I got right up close. They got spears and shields, but only
one horse, and that's lame. I think they been there awhile, from the stink
of the place."

"See a banner?"

"Spotted treecat, yellow and black, on a mud-brown field."

Yoren folded a sourleaf into his mouth and chewed. "Can't say," he
admitted. "Might be one side, might be t'other. If they're hurt that bad,
likely they'd take our mounts no matter who they are. Might be they'd
take more than that. I believe we'll go wide around them." It took them
miles out of their way, and cost them two days at the least, but the old

man said it was cheap at the price. "You'll have time enough on the Wall. The rest o' your lives, most like. Seems to me there's no rush to get there."

Arya saw men guarding the fields more and more when they turned north again. Often they stood silently beside the road, giving a cold eye to anyone who passed. Elsewhere they patrolled on horses, riding their fence lines with axes strapped to their saddles. At one place, she spotted a man perched up in a dead tree, with a bow in his hand and a quiver hanging from the branch beside him. The moment he spied them, he notched an arrow to his bowstring, and never looked away until the last wagon was out of sight. All the while, Yoren cursed. "Him in his tree, let's see how well he likes it up there when the Others come to take him. He'll scream for the Watch then, that he will."

A day later Dobber spied a red glow against the evening sky. "Either this road went and turned again, or that sun's setting in the north."

Yoren climbed a rise to get a better look. "Fire," he announced. He licked a thumb and held it up. "Wind should blow it away from us. Still bears watching."

And watch it they did. As the world darkened, the fire seemed to grow brighter and brighter, until it looked as though the whole north was ablaze. From time to time, they could even smell the smoke, though the wind held steady and the flames never got any closer. By dawn the fire had burned itself out, but none of them slept very well that night.

It was midday when they arrived at the place where the village had been. The fields were a charred desolation for miles around, the houses blackened shells. The carcasses of burnt and butchered animals dotted the ground, under living blankets of carrion crows that rose, cawing furiously, when disturbed. Smoke still drifted from inside the holdfast. Its timber palisade looked strong from afar, but had not proved strong enough.

Riding out in front of the wagons on her horse, Arya saw burnt bodies impaled on sharpened stakes atop the walls, their hands drawn up tight in front of their faces as if to fight off the flames that had consumed them. Yoren called a halt when they were still some distance off, and told Arya and the other boys to guard the wagons while he and Murch and Cutjack went in on foot. A flock of ravens rose from inside the walls when they climbed through the broken gate, and the caged ravens in their wagons called out to them with *quorks* and raucous shrieks.

"Should we go in after them?" Arya asked Gendry after Yoren and the others had been gone a long time.

"Yoren said wait." Gendry's voice sounded hollow. When Arya turned to look, she saw that he was wearing his helm, all shiny steel and great curving horns.

When they finally returned, Yoren had a little girl in his arms, and Murch and Cutjack were carrying a woman in a sling made of an old torn quilt. The girl was no older than two and she cried all the time, a whimpery sound, like something was caught in her throat. Either she couldn't talk yet or she had forgotten how. The woman's right arm ended in a bloody stump at her elbow, and her eyes didn't seem to see anything, even when she was looking right at it. She talked, but she only said one thing. "Please," she cried, over and over. "Please. Please." Rorge thought that was funny. He laughed through the hole in his face where his nose had been, and Biter started laughing too, until Murch cursed them and told them to shut up.

Yoren had them fix the woman a place in the back of a wagon. "And be quick about it," he said. "Come dark, there'll be wolves here, and worse."

"I'm scared," Hot Pie murmured when he saw the one-armed woman thrashing in the wagon.

"Me too," Arya confessed.

He squeezed her shoulder. "I never truly kicked no boy to death, Arry. I just sold my mommy's pies, is all."

Arya rode as far ahead of the wagons as she dared, so she wouldn't have to hear the little girl crying or listen to the woman whisper, "Please." She remembered a story Old Nan had told once, about a man imprisoned in a dark castle by evil giants. He was very brave and smart and he tricked the giants and escaped . . . but no sooner was he outside the castle than the Others took him, and drank his hot red blood. Now she knew how he must have felt.

The one-armed woman died at evenfall. Gendry and Cutjack dug her grave on a hillside beneath a weeping willow. When the wind blew, Arya thought she could hear the long trailing branches whispering, "Please. Please. Please." The little hairs on the back of her neck rose, and she almost ran from the graveside.

"No fire tonight," Yoren told them. Supper was a handful of wild radishes Koss found, a cup of dry beans, water from a nearby brook. The water had a funny taste to it, and Lommy told them it was the taste of bodies, rotting someplace upstream. Hot Pie would have hit him if old Reysen hadn't pulled them apart.

Arya drank too much water, just to fill her belly with something. She never thought she'd be able to sleep, yet somehow she did. When she woke, it was pitch-black and her bladder was full to bursting. Sleepers huddled all around her, wrapped in blankets and cloaks. Arya found Needle, stood, listened. She heard the soft footfalls of a sentry, men turning in restless sleep, Rorge's rattling snores, and the queer hissing sound that

Biter made when he slept. From a different wagon came the steady rhythmic scrape of steel on stone as Yoren sat, chewing sourleaf and sharpening the edge of his dirk.

Hot Pie was one of the boys on watch. "Where you going?" he asked when he saw Arya heading for the trees.

Arya waved vaguely at the woods.

"No you're not," Hot Pie said. He had gotten bolder again now that he had a sword on his belt, even though it was just a shortsword and he handled it like a cleaver. "The old man said for everyone to stay close tonight."

"I need to make water," Arya explained.

"Well, use that tree right there." He pointed. "You don't know what's out there, Arry. I heard wolves before."

Yoren wouldn't like it if she fought with him. She tried to look afraid. "Wolves? For true?"

"I heard," he assured her.

"I don't think I need to go after all." She went back to her blanket and pretended to sleep until she heard Hot Pie's footsteps going away. Then she rolled over and slipped off into the woods on the other side of the camp, quiet as a shadow. There were sentries out this way too, but Arya had no trouble avoiding them. Just to make sure, she went out twice as far as usual. When she was sure there was no one near, she skinned down her breeches and squatted to do her business.

She was making water, her clothing tangled about her ankles, when she heard rustling from under the trees. *Hot Pie,* she thought in panic, *he followed me.* Then she saw the eyes shining out from the wood, bright with reflected moonlight. Her belly clenched tight as she grabbed for Needle, not caring if she pissed herself, counting eyes, two four eight twelve, a whole pack . . .

One of them came padding out from under the trees. He stared at her, and bared his teeth, and all she could think was how stupid she'd been and how Hot Pie would gloat when they found her half-eaten body the next morning. But the wolf turned and raced back into the darkness, and quick as that the eyes were gone. Trembling, she cleaned herself and laced up and followed a distant scraping sound back to camp, and to Yoren. Arya climbed up into the wagon beside him, shaken. "Wolves," she whispered hoarsely. "In the woods."

"Aye. They would be." He never looked at her.

"They scared me."

"Did they?" He spat. "Seems to me your kind was fond o' wolves."

"Nymeria was a direwolf." Arya hugged herself. "That's different. Anyhow, she's gone. Jory and I threw rocks at her until she ran off, or else the queen would have killed her." It made her sad to talk about it. "I bet if she'd been in the city, she wouldn't have let them cut off Father's head."

"Orphan boys got no fathers," Yoren said, "or did you forget that?" The sourleaf had turned his spit red, so it looked like his mouth was bleeding. "The only wolves we got to fear are the ones wear manskin, like those who done for that village."

"I wish I was home," she said miserably. She tried so hard to be brave, to be fierce as a wolverine and all, but sometimes she felt like she was just a little girl after all.

The black brother peeled a fresh sourleaf from the bale in the wagon and stuffed it into his mouth. "Might be I should of left you where I found you, boy. All of you. Safer in the city, seems to me."

"I don't care. I want to go home."

"Been bringing men to the Wall for close on thirty years." Froth shone on Yoren's lips, like bubbles of blood. "All that time, I only lost three. Old man died of a fever, city boy got snakebit taking a shit, and one fool tried to kill me in my sleep and got a red smile for his trouble." He drew the dirk across his throat, to show her. "Three in thirty years." He spat out the old sourleaf. "A ship now, might have been wiser. No chance o' finding more men on the way, but still . . . clever man, he'd go by ship, but me . . . thirty years I been taking this kingsroad." He sheathed his dirk. "Go to sleep, boy. Hear me?"

She did try. Yet as she lay under her thin blanket, she could hear the wolves howling . . . and another sound, fainter, no more than a whisper on the wind, that might have been screams.

DAVOS

The morning air was dark with the smoke of burning gods.

They were all afire now, Maid and Mother, Warrior and Smith, the Crone with her pearl eyes and the Father with his gilded beard; even the Stranger, carved to look more animal than human. The old dry wood and countless layers of paint and varnish blazed with a fierce hungry light. Heat rose shimmering through the chill air; behind, the gargoyles and stone dragons on the castle walls seemed blurred, as if Davos were seeing them through a veil of tears. *Or as if the beasts were trembling, stirring . . .*

"An ill thing," Allard declared, though at least he had the sense to keep his voice low. Dale muttered agreement.

"Silence," said Davos. "Remember where you are." His sons were good men, but young, and Allard especially was rash. *Had I stayed a smuggler, Allard would have ended on the Wall. Stannis spared him from that end, something else I owe him . . .*

Hundreds had come to the castle gates to bear witness to the burning of the Seven. The smell in the air was ugly. Even for soldiers, it was hard not to feel uneasy at such an affront to the gods most had worshiped all their lives.

The red woman walked round the fire three times, praying once in the speech of Asshai, once in High Valyrian, and once in the Common Tongue. Davos understood only the last. "R'hllor, come to us in our darkness," she called. "Lord of Light, we offer you these false gods, these seven who are one, and him the enemy. Take them and cast your light upon us, for the night is dark and full of terrors." Queen Selyse echoed the words. Beside her, Stannis watched impassively, his jaw hard as stone under the blue-black shadow of his tight-cropped beard. He had dressed more richly than was his wont, as if for the sept.

Dragonstone's sept had been where Aegon the Conqueror knelt to pray the night before he sailed. That had not saved it from the queen's men. They had overturned the altars, pulled down the statues, and smashed the stained glass with warhammers. Septon Barre could only curse them, but Ser Hubard Rambton led his three sons to the sept to defend their gods. The Rambtons had slain four of the queen's men before the others overwhelmed them. Afterward Guncer Sunglass, mildest and most pious of lords, told Stannis he could no longer support his claim. Now he shared a sweltering cell with the septon and Ser Hubard's two surviving sons. The other lords had not been slow to take the lesson.

The gods had never meant much to Davos the smuggler, though like most men he had been known to make offerings to the Warrior before battle, to the Smith when he launched a ship, and to the Mother whenever his wife grew great with child. He felt ill as he watched them burn, and not only from the smoke.

Maester Cressen would have stopped this. The old man had challenged the Lord of Light and been struck down for his impiety, or so the gossips told each other. Davos knew the truth. He had seen the maester slip something into the wine cup. *Poison. What else could it be? He drank a cup of death to free Stannis from Melisandre, but somehow her god shielded her.* He would gladly have killed the red woman for that, yet what chance would he have where a maester of the Citadel had failed? He was only a smuggler raised high, Davos of Flea Bottom, the Onion Knight.

The burning gods cast a pretty light, wreathed in their robes of shifting flame, red and orange and yellow. Septon Barre had once told Davos how they'd been carved from the masts of the ships that had carried the first Targaryens from Valyria. Over the centuries, they had been painted and repainted, gilded, silvered, jeweled. "Their beauty will make them more pleasing to R'hllor," Melisandre said when she told Stannis to pull them down and drag them out the castle gates.

The Maiden lay athwart the Warrior, her arms widespread as if to embrace him. The Mother seemed almost to shudder as the flames came licking up her face. A longsword had been thrust through her heart, and its leather grip was alive with flame. The Father was on the bottom, the first to fall. Davos watched the hand of the Stranger writhe and curl as the fingers blackened and fell away one by one, reduced to so much glowing charcoal. Nearby, Lord Celtigar coughed fitfully and covered his wrinkled face with a square of linen embroidered in red crabs. The Myrmen swapped jokes as they enjoyed the warmth of the fire, but young Lord Bar Emmon had turned a splotchy grey, and Lord Velaryon was watching the king rather than the conflagration.

Davos would have given much to know what he was thinking, but one such as Velaryon would never confide in him. The Lord of the Tides was of the blood of ancient Valyria, and his House had thrice provided brides for Targaryen princes; Davos Seaworth stank of fish and onions. It was the same with the other lordlings. He could trust none of them, nor would they ever include him in their private councils. They scorned his sons as well. *My grandsons will joust with theirs, though, and one day their blood may wed with mine. In time my little black ship will fly as high as Velaryon's seahorse or Celtigar's red crabs.*

That is, if Stannis won his throne. If he lost . . .

Everything I am, I owe to him. Stannis had raised him to knighthood. He had given him a place of honor at his table, a war galley to sail in place of a smuggler's skiff. Dale and Allard captained galleys as well, Maric was oarmaster on the *Fury*, Matthos served his father on *Black Betha*, and the king had taken Devan as a royal squire. One day he would be knighted, and the two little lads as well. Marya was mistress of a small keep on Cape Wrath, with servants who called her m'lady, and Davos could hunt red deer in his own woods. All this he had of Stannis Baratheon, for the price of a few finger joints. *It was just, what he did to me. I had flouted the king's laws all my life. He has earned my loyalty.* Davos touched the little pouch that hung from the leather thong about his neck. His fingers were his luck, and he needed luck now. *As do we all. Lord Stannis most of all.*

Pale flames licked at the grey sky. Dark smoke rose, twisting and curling. When the wind pushed it toward them, men blinked and wept and rubbed their eyes. Allard turned his head away, coughing and cursing. *A taste of things to come*, thought Davos. Many and more would burn before this war was done.

Melisandre was robed all in scarlet satin and blood velvet, her eyes as red as the great ruby that glistened at her throat as if it too were afire. "In ancient books of Asshai it is written that there will come a day after a long summer when the stars bleed and the cold breath of darkness falls heavy on the world. In this dread hour a warrior shall draw from the fire a burning sword. And that sword shall be Lightbringer, the Red Sword of Heroes, and he who clasps it shall be Azor Ahai come again, and the darkness shall flee before him." She lifted her voice, so it carried out over the gathered host. "*Azor Ahai, beloved of R'hllor! The Warrior of Light, the Son of Fire! Come forth, your sword awaits you! Come forth and take it into your hand!*"

Stannis Baratheon strode forward like a soldier marching into battle. His squires stepped up to attend him. Davos watched as his son Devan pulled a long padded glove over the king's right hand. The boy wore a cream-colored doublet with a fiery heart sewn on the breast. Bryen Farring was similarly garbed as he tied a stiff leather cape around His Grace's neck. Behind, Davos heard a faint clank and clatter of bells. "Under the sea, smoke rises in bubbles, and flames burn green and blue and black," Patchface sang somewhere. "I know, I know, oh, oh, oh."

The king plunged into the fire with his teeth clenched, holding the leather cloak before him to keep off the flames. He went straight to the Mother, grasped the sword with his gloved hand, and wrenched it free of the burning wood with a single hard jerk. Then he was retreating, the sword held high, jade-green flames swirling around cherry-red steel. Guards rushed to beat out the cinders that clung to the king's clothing.

"*A sword of fire!*" shouted Queen Selyse. Ser Axell Florent and the other queen's men took up the cry. "*A sword of fire! It burns! It burns! A sword of fire!*"

Melisandre lifted her hands above her head. "*Behold! A sign was promised, and now a sign is seen! Behold Lightbringer! Azor Ahai has come again! All hail the Warrior of Light! All hail the Son of Fire!*"

A ragged wave of shouts gave answer, just as Stannis's glove began to smolder. Cursing, the king thrust the point of the sword into the damp earth and beat out the flames against his leg.

"Lord, cast your light upon us!" Melisandre called out.

"For the night is dark and full of terrors," Selyse and her queen's men replied. *Should I speak the words as well? Davos wondered. Do I owe Stannis that much? Is this fiery god truly his own?* His shortened fingers twitched.

Stannis peeled off the glove and let it fall to the ground. The gods in the pyre were scarcely recognizable anymore. The head fell off the Smith with a puff of ash and embers. Melisandre sang in the tongue of Asshai, her voice rising and falling like the tides of the sea. Stannis untied his singed leather cape and listened in silence. Thrust in the ground, Lightbringer still glowed ruddy hot, but the flames that clung to the sword were dwindling and dying.

By the time the song was done, only charwood remained of the gods, and the king's patience had run its course. He took the queen by the elbow and escorted her back into Dragonstone, leaving Lightbringer where it stood. The red woman remained a moment to watch as Devan knelt with Byren Farring and rolled up the burnt and blackened sword in the king's leather cloak. *The Red Sword of Heroes looks a proper mess,* thought Davos.

A few of the lords lingered to speak in quiet voices upwind of the fire. They fell silent when they saw Davos looking at them. *Should Stannis fall, they will pull me down in an instant.* Neither was he counted one of the queen's men, that group of ambitious knights and minor lordlings who had given themselves to this Lord of Light and so won the favor and patronage of Lady—*no, Queen, remember?*—Selyse.

The fire had started to dwindle by the time Melisandre and the squires departed with the precious sword. Davos and his sons joined the crowd making its way down to the shore and the waiting ships. "Devan acquitted himself well," he said as they went.

"He fetched the glove without dropping it, yes," said Dale.

Allard nodded. "That badge on Devan's doublet, the fiery heart, what was that? The Baratheon sigil is a crowned stag."

"A lord can choose more than one badge," Davos said.

Dale smiled. "A black ship *and* an onion, Father?"

Allard kicked at a stone. "The Others take our onion . . . *and* that flaming heart. It was an ill thing to burn the Seven."

"When did you grow so devout?" Davos said. "What does a smuggler's son know of the doings of gods?"

"I'm a knight's son, Father. If you won't remember, why should they?"

"A knight's son, but not a knight," said Davos. "Nor will you ever be, if you meddle in affairs that do not concern you. Stannis is our rightful king, it is not for us to question him. We sail his ships and do his bidding. That is all."

"As to that, Father," Dale said, "I mislike these water casks they've given me for *Wraith*. Green pine. The water will spoil on a voyage of any length."

"I got the same for *Lady Marya*," said Allard. "The queen's men have laid claim to all the seasoned wood."

"I will speak to the king about it," Davos promised. Better it come from him than from Allard. His sons were good fighters and better sailors, but they did not know how to talk to lords. *They were lowborn, even as I was, but they do not like to recall that. When they look at our banner, all they see is a tall black ship flying on the wind. They close their eyes to the onion.*

The port was as crowded as Davos had ever known it. Every dock teemed with sailors loading provisions, and every inn was packed with soldiers dicing or drinking or looking for a whore . . . a vain search, since Stannis permitted none on his island. Ships lined the strand; war galleys and fishing vessels, stout carracks and fat-bottomed cogs. The best berths had been taken by the largest vessels: Stannis's flagship *Fury* rocking between *Lord Steffon* and *Stag of the Sea*, Lord Velaryon's silver-hulled *Pride of Driftmark* and her three sisters, Lord Celtigar's ornate *Red Claw*, the ponderous *Swordfish* with her long iron prow. Out to sea at anchor rode Salladhor Saan's great *Valyrian* amongst the striped hulls of two dozen smaller Lysene galleys.

A weathered little inn sat on the end of the stone pier where *Black Betha*, *Wraith*, and *Lady Marya* shared mooring space with a half-dozen other galleys of one hundred oars or less. Davos had a thirst. He took his leave of his sons and turned his steps toward the inn. Out front squatted a waist-high gargoyle, so eroded by rain and salt that his features were all but obliterated. He and Davos were old friends, though. He gave a pat to the stone head as he went in. "Luck," he murmured.

Across the noisy common room, Salladhor Saan sat eating grapes from a wooden bowl. When he spied Davos, he beckoned him closer. "Ser knight, come sit with me. Eat a grape. Eat two. They are marvelously sweet." The Lyseni was a sleek, smiling man whose flamboyance was a byword on both sides of the narrow sea. Today he wore flashing cloth-of-silver, with dagged sleeves so long the ends of them pooled on the floor. His buttons were carved jade monkeys, and atop his wispy white curls perched a jaunty green cap decorated with a fan of peacock feathers.

Davos threaded his way through the tables to a chair. In the days before his knighthood, he had often bought cargoes from Salladhor Saan. The Lyseni was a smuggler himself, as well as a trader, a banker, a notorious pirate, and the self-styled Prince of the Narrow Sea. *When a pirate grows rich enough, they make him a prince.* It had been Davos who had made the journey to Lys to recruit the old rogue to Lord Stannis's cause.

"You did not see the gods burn, my lord?" he asked.

"The red priests have a great temple on Lys. Always they are burning this and burning that, crying out to their R'hllor. They bore me with their fires. Soon they will bore King Stannis too, it is to be hoped." He seemed utterly unconcerned that someone might overhear him, eating his grapes and dribbling the seeds out onto his lip, flicking them off with a finger. "My *Bird of Thousand Colors* came in yesterday, good ser. She is not a warship, no, but a trader, and she paid a call on King's Landing. Are you sure you will not have a grape? Children go hungry in the city, it is said." He dangled the grapes before Davos and smiled.

"It's ale I need, and news."

"The men of Westeros are ever rushing," complained Salladhor Saan. "What good is this, I ask you? He who hurries through life hurries to his grave." He belched. "The Lord of Casterly Rock has sent his dwarf to see to King's Landing. Perhaps he hopes that his ugly face will frighten off attackers, eh? Or that we will laugh ourselves dead when the Imp capers on the battlements, who can say? The dwarf has chased off the lout who ruled the gold cloaks and put in his place a knight with an iron hand." He plucked a grape, and squeezed it between thumb and forefinger until the skin burst. Juice ran down between his fingers.

A serving girl pushed her way through, swatting at the hands that groped her as she passed. Davos ordered a tankard of ale, turned back to Saan, and said, "How well is the city defended?"

The other shrugged. "The walls are high and strong, but who will man them? They are building scorpions and spitfires, oh, yes, but the men in the golden cloaks are too few and too green, and there are no others. A swift strike, like a hawk plummeting at a hare, and the great city will be ours. Grant us wind to fill our sails, and your king could sit upon his Iron Throne by evenfall on the morrow. We could dress the dwarf in motley and prick his little cheeks with the points of our spears to make him dance for us, and mayhaps your goodly king would make me a gift of the beautiful Queen Cersei to warm my bed for a night. I have been too long away from my wives, and all in his service."

"Pirate," said Davos. "You have no wives, only concubines, and you have been well paid for every day and every ship."

"Only in promises," said Salladhor Saan mournfully. "Good ser, it is gold I crave, not words on papers." He popped a grape into his mouth.

"You'll have your gold when we take the treasury in King's Landing. No man in the Seven Kingdoms is more honorable than Stannis Baratheon. He will keep his word." Even as Davos spoke, he thought, *This world is twisted beyond hope, when lowborn smugglers must vouch for the honor of kings.*

"So he has said and said. And so I say, let us do this thing. Even these grapes could be no more ripe than that city, my old friend."

The serving girl returned with his ale. Davos gave her a copper. "Might be we could take King's Landing, as you say," he said as he lifted the tankard, "but how long would we hold it? Tywin Lannister is known to be at Harrenhal with a great host, and Lord Renly . . ."

"Ah, yes, the young brother," said Salladhor Saan. "That part is not so good, my friend. King Renly bestirs himself. No, here he is *Lord* Renly, my pardons. So many kings, my tongue grows weary of the word. The brother Renly has left Highgarden with his fair young queen, his flowered lords and shining knights, and a mighty host of foot. He marches up your road of roses toward the very same great city we were speaking of."

"He takes his *bride?*"

The other shrugged. "He did not tell me why. Perhaps he is loath to part with the warm burrow between her thighs, even for a night. Or perhaps he is that certain of his victory."

"The king must be told."

"I have attended to it, good ser. Though His Grace frowns so whenever he does see me that I tremble to come before him. Do you think he would like me better if I wore a hair shirt and never smiled? Well, I will not do it. I am an honest man, he must suffer me in silk and samite. Or else I shall take my ships where I am better loved. That sword was not Lightbringer, my friend."

The sudden shift in subject left Davos uneasy. "Sword?"

"A sword plucked from fire, yes. Men tell me things, it is my pleasant smile. How shall a burnt sword serve Stannis?"

"A *burning* sword," corrected Davos.

"Burnt," said Salladhor Saan, "and be glad of that, my friend. Do you know the tale of the forging of Lightbringer? I shall tell it to you. It was a time when darkness lay heavy on the world. To oppose it, the hero must have a hero's blade, oh, like none that had ever been. And so for thirty days and thirty nights Azor Ahai labored sleepless in the temple, forging a blade in the sacred fires. Heat and hammer and fold, heat and hammer and fold, oh, yes, until the sword was done. Yet when he plunged it into water to temper the steel it burst asunder.

"Being a hero, it was not for him to shrug and go in search of excellent grapes such as these, so again he began. The second time it took him fifty days and fifty nights, and this sword seemed even finer than the first. Azor Ahai captured a lion, to temper the blade by plunging it through the beast's red heart, but once more the steel shattered and split. Great was his woe and great was his sorrow then, for he knew what he must do.

"A hundred days and a hundred nights he labored on the third blade, and as it glowed white-hot in the sacred fires, he summoned his wife. 'Nissa Nissa,' he said to her, for that was her name, 'bare your breast, and know that I love you best of all that is in this world.' She did this thing, why I cannot say, and Azor Ahai thrust the smoking sword through her living heart. It is said that her cry of anguish and ecstasy left a crack across the face of the moon, but her blood and her soul and her strength and her courage all went into the steel. Such is the tale of the forging of Lightbringer, the Red Sword of Heroes.

"Now do you see my meaning? Be glad that it is just a burnt sword that His Grace pulled from that fire. Too much light can hurt the eyes, my friend, and fire *burns*." Salladhor Saan finished the last grape and smacked his lips. "When do you think the king will bid us sail, good ser?"

"Soon, I think," said Davos, "if his god wills it."

"*His* god, ser friend? Not yours? Where is the god of Ser Davos Seaworth, knight of the onion ship?"

Davos sipped his ale to give himself a moment. *The inn is crowded, and you are not Salladhor Saan,* he reminded himself. *Be careful how you answer.* "King Stannis is my god. He made me and blessed me with his trust."

"I will remember." Salladhor Saan got to his feet. "My pardons. These grapes have given me a hunger, and dinner awaits on my *Valyrian*. Minced lamb with pepper and roasted gull stuffed with mushrooms and fennel and onion. Soon we shall eat together in King's Landing, yes? In the Red Keep we shall feast, while the dwarf sings us a jolly tune. When you speak to King Stannis, mention if you would that he will owe me another thirty thousand dragons come the black of the moon. He ought to have given those gods to me. They were too beautiful to burn, and might have brought a noble price in Pentos or Myr. Well, if he grants me Queen Cersei for a night I shall forgive him." The Lyseni clapped Davos on the back, and swaggered from the inn as if he owned it.

Ser Davos Seaworth lingered over his tankard for a good while, thinking. A year ago, he had been with Stannis in King's Landing when King Robert staged a tourney for Prince Joffrey's name day. He remembered the red priest Thoros of Myr, and the flaming sword he had wielded in the melee. The man had made for a colorful spectacle, his red robes flapping while his blade writhed with pale green flames, but everyone knew there was no true magic to it, and in the end his fire had guttered out and Bronze Yohn Royce had brained him with a common mace.

A true sword of fire, now, that would be a wonder to behold. Yet at such a cost . . . When he thought of Nissa Nissa, it was his own Marya he pictured, a good-natured plump woman with sagging breasts and a kindly smile, the best woman in the world. He tried to picture himself driving a sword through her, and shuddered. *I am not made of the stuff of heroes,* he decided. If that was the price of a magic sword, it was more than he cared to pay.

Davos finished his ale, pushed away the tankard, and left the inn. On the way out he patted the gargoyle on the head and muttered, "Luck." They would all need it.

It was well after dark when Devan came down to *Black Betha*, leading a snow-white palfrey. "My lord father," he announced, "His Grace commands you to attend him in the Chamber of the Painted Table. You are to ride the horse and come at once."

It was good to see Devan looking so splendid in his squire's raiment, but the summons made Davos uneasy. *Will he bid us sail?* he wondered. Salladhor Saan was not the only captain who felt that King's Landing was ripe for an attack, but a smuggler must learn patience. *We have no hope of victory. I said as much to Maester Cressen, the day I returned to*

Dragonstone, and nothing has changed. We are too few, the foes too many. If we dip our oars, we die. Nonetheless, he climbed onto the horse.

When Davos arrived at the Stone Drum, a dozen highborn knights and great bannermen were just leaving. Lords Celtigar and Velaryon each gave him a curt nod and walked on while the others ignored him utterly, but Ser Axell Florent stopped for a word.

Queen Selyse's uncle was a keg of a man with thick arms and bandy legs. He had the prominent ears of a Florent, even larger than his niece's. The coarse hair that sprouted from his did not stop him hearing most of what went on in the castle. For ten years Ser Axell had served as castellan of Dragonstone while Stannis sat on Robert's council in King's Landing, but of late he had emerged as the foremost of the queen's men. "Ser Davos, it is good to see you, as ever," he said.

"And you, my lord."

"I made note of you this morning as well. The false gods burned with a merry light, did they not?"

"They burned brightly." Davos did not trust this man, for all his courtesy. House Florent had declared for Renly.

"The Lady Melisandre tells us that sometimes R'hllor permits his faithful servants to glimpse the future in flames. It seemed to me as I watched the fire this morning that I was looking at a dozen beautiful dancers, maidens garbed in yellow silk spinning and swirling before a great king. I think it was a true vision, ser. A glimpse of the glory that awaits His Grace after we take King's Landing and the throne that is his by rights."

Stannis has no taste for such dancing, Davos thought, but he dared not offend the queen's uncle. "I saw only fire," he said, "but the smoke was making my eyes water. You must pardon me, ser, the king awaits." He pushed past, wondering why Ser Axell had troubled himself. *He is a queen's man and I am the king's.*

Stannis sat at his Painted Table with Maester Pylos at his shoulder, an untidy pile of papers before them. "Ser," the king said when Davos entered, "come have a look at this letter."

Obediently, he selected a paper at random. "It looks handsome enough, Your Grace, but I fear I cannot read the words." Davos could decipher maps and charts as well as any, but letters and other writings were beyond his powers. *But my Devan has learned his letters, and young Steffon and Stannis as well.*

"I'd forgotten." A furrow of irritation showed between the king's brows. "Pylos, read it to him."

"Your Grace." The maester took up one of the parchments and cleared his throat. *"All men know me for the trueborn son of Steffon Baratheon,*

Lord of Storm's End, by his lady wife Cassana of House Estermont. I declare upon the honor of my House that my beloved brother Robert, our late king, left no trueborn issue of his body, the boy Joffrey, the boy Tommen, and the girl Myrcella being abominations born of incest between Cersei Lannister and her brother Jaime the Kingslayer. By right of birth and blood, I do this day lay claim to the Iron Throne of the Seven Kingdoms of Westeros. Let all true men declare their loyalty. Done in the Light of the Lord, under the sign and seal of Stannis of House Baratheon, the First of His Name, King of the Andals, the Rhoynar, and the First Men, and Lord of the Seven Kingdoms." The parchment rustled softly as Pylos laid it down.

"Make it *Ser* Jaime the Kingslayer henceforth," Stannis said, frowning. "Whatever else the man may be, he remains a knight. I don't know that we ought to call Robert my *beloved* brother either. He loved me no more than he had to, nor I him."

"A harmless courtesy, Your Grace," Pylos saïd.

"A lie. Take it out." Stannis turned to Davos. "The maester tells me that we have one hundred seventeen ravens on hand. I mean to use them all. One hundred seventeen ravens will carry one hundred seventeen copies of my letter to every corner of the realm, from the Arbor to the Wall. Perhaps a hundred will win through against storm and hawk and arrow. If so, a hundred maesters will read my words to as many lords in as many solars and bedchambers . . . and then the letters will like as not be consigned to the fire, and lips pledged to silence. These great lords love Joffrey, or Renly, or Robb Stark. I am their rightful king, but they will deny me if they can. So I have need of you."

"I am yours to command, my king. As ever."

Stannis nodded. "I mean for you to sail *Black Betha* north, to Gulltown, the Fingers, the Three Sisters, even White Harbor. Your son Dale will go south in *Wraith*, past Cape Wrath and the Broken Arm, all along the coast of Dorne as far as the Arbor. Each of you will carry a chest of letters, and you will deliver one to every port and holdfast and fishing village. Nail them to the doors of septs and inns for every man to read who can."

Davos said, "That will be few enough."

"Ser Davos speaks truly, Your Grace," said Maester Pylos. "It would be better to have the letters read aloud."

"Better, but more dangerous," said Stannis. "These words will not be kindly received."

"Give me knights to do the reading," Davos said. "That will carry more weight than anything I might say."

Stannis seemed well satisfied with that. "I can give you such men, yes. I have a hundred knights who would sooner read than fight. Be open where you can and stealthy where you must. Use every smuggler's trick you know, the black sails, the hidden coves, whatever it requires. If you run short of letters, capture a few septons and set them to copying out more. I mean to use your second son as well. He will take *Lady Marya* across the narrow sea, to Braavos and the other Free Cities, to deliver other letters to the men who rule there. The world will know of my claim, and of Cersei's infamy."

You can tell them, Davos thought, *but will they believe?* He glanced thoughtfully at Maester Pylos. The king caught the look. "Maester, perhaps you ought get to your writing. We will need a great many letters, and soon."

"As you will." Pylos bowed, and took his leave.

The king waited until he was gone before he said, "What is it you would not say in the presence of my maester, Davos?"

"My liege, Pylos is pleasant enough, but I cannot see the chain about his neck without mourning for Maester Cressen."

"Is it his fault the old man died?" Stannis glanced into the fire. "I never wanted Cressen at that feast. He'd angered me, yes, he'd given me bad counsel, but I did not want him dead. I'd hoped he might be granted a few years of ease and comfort. He had earned that much, at least, but"— he ground his teeth together—"but he died. And Pylos serves me ably."

"Pylos is the least of it. The letter . . . What did your lords make of it, I wonder?"

Stannis snorted. "Celtigar pronounced it admirable. If I showed him the contents of my privy, he would declare that admirable as well. The others bobbed their heads up and down like a flock of geese, all but Velaryon, who said that steel would decide the matter, not words on parchment. As if I had never suspected. The Others take my lords, I'll hear your views."

"Your words were blunt and strong."

"And true."

"And true. Yet you have no proof. Of this incest. No more than you did a year ago."

"There's proof of a sort at Storm's End. Robert's bastard. The one he fathered on my wedding night, in the very bed they'd made up for me and my bride. Delena was a Florent, and a maiden when he took her, so Robert acknowledged the babe. Edric Storm, they call him. He is said to be the very image of my brother. If men were to see him, and then look again at Joffrey and Tommen, they could not help but wonder, I would think."

"Yet how are men to see him, if he is at Storm's End?"

Stannis drummed his fingers on the Painted Table. "It is a difficulty. One of many." He raised his eyes. "You have more to say about the letter. Well, get on with it. I did not make you a knight so you could learn to mouth empty courtesies. I have my lords for that. Say what you would say, Davos."

Davos bowed his head. "There was a phrase at the end. How did it go? *Done in the Light of the Lord . . .*"

"Yes." The king's jaw was clenched.

"Your people will mislike those words."

"As you did?" said Stannis sharply.

"If you were to say instead, *Done in the sight of gods and men,* or *By the grace of the gods old and new . . .*"

"Have you gone devout on me, smuggler?"

"That was to be my question for you, my liege."

"Was it now? It sounds as though you love my new god no more than you love my new maester."

"I do not know this Lord of Light," Davos admitted, "but I knew the gods we burned this morning. The Smith has kept my ships safe, while the Mother has given me seven strong sons."

"Your wife has given you seven strong sons. Do you pray to her? It was wood we burned this morning."

"That may be so," Davos said, "but when I was a boy in Flea Bottom begging for a copper, sometimes the septons would feed me."

"*I* feed you now."

"You have given me an honored place at your table. And in return I give you truth. Your people will not love you if you take from them the gods they have always worshiped, and give them one whose very name sounds queer on their tongues."

Stannis stood abruptly. "*R'hllor.* Why is that so hard? They will not love me, you say? When have they ever loved me? How can I lose something I have never owned?" He moved to the south window to gaze out at the moonlit sea. "I stopped believing in gods the day I saw the *Windproud* break up across the bay. Any gods so monstrous as to drown my mother and father would never have *my* worship, I vowed. In King's Landing, the High Septon would prattle at me of how all justice and goodness flowed from the Seven, but all I ever saw of either was made by men."

"If you do not believe in gods—"

"—why trouble with this new one?" Stannis broke in. "I have asked myself as well. I know little and care less of gods, but the red priestess has power."

Yes, but what sort of power? "Cressen had wisdom."

"I trusted in his wisdom and your wiles, and what did they avail me, smuggler? The storm lords sent you packing. I went to them a beggar and they laughed at me. Well, there will be no more begging, and no more laughing either. The Iron Throne is mine by rights, but how am I to take it? There are four kings in the realm, and three of them have more men and more gold than I do. I have ships . . . and I have *her*. The red woman. Half my knights are afraid even to say her name, did you know? If she can do nothing else, a sorceress who can inspire such dread in grown men is not to be despised. A frightened man is a beaten man. And perhaps she *can* do more. I mean to find out.

"When I was a lad I found an injured goshawk and nursed her back to health. *Proudwing*, I named her. She would perch on my shoulder and flutter from room to room after me and take food from my hand, but she would not soar. Time and again I would take her hawking, but she never flew higher than the treetops. Robert called her *Weakwing*. He owned a gyrfalcon named Thunderclap who never missed her strike. One day our great-uncle Ser Harbert told me to try a different bird. I was making a fool of myself with Proudwing, he said, and he was right." Stannis Baratheon turned away from the window, and the ghosts who moved upon the southern sea. "The Seven have never brought me so much as a sparrow. It is time I tried another hawk, Davos. A red hawk."

THEON

There was no safe anchorage at Pyke, but Theon Greyjoy wished to look on his father's castle from the sea, to see it as he had seen it last, ten years before, when Robert Baratheon's war galley had borne him away to be a ward of Eddard Stark. On that day he had stood beside the rail, listening to the stroke of the oars and the pounding of the master's drum while he watched Pyke dwindle in the distance. Now he wanted to see it grow larger, to rise from the sea before him.

Obedient to his wishes, the *Myraham* beat her way past the point with her sails snapping and her captain cursing the wind and his crew and the follies of highborn lordlings. Theon drew the hood of his cloak up against the spray, and looked for home.

The shore was all sharp rocks and glowering cliffs, and the castle seemed one with the rest, its towers and walls and bridges quarried from the same grey-black stone, wet by the same salt waves, festooned with the same spreading patches of dark green lichen, speckled by the droppings of the same seabirds. The point of land on which the Greyjoys had raised their fortress had once thrust like a sword into the bowels of the ocean, but the waves had hammered at it day and night until the land broke and shattered, thousands of years past. All that remained were three bare and barren islands and a dozen towering stacks of rock that rose from the water like the pillars of some sea god's temple, while the angry waves foamed and crashed among them.

Drear, dark, forbidding, Pyke stood atop those islands and pillars, almost a part of them, its curtain wall closing off the headland around the foot of the great stone bridge that leapt from the clifftop to the largest islet, dominated by the massive bulk of the Great Keep. Farther out were the Kitchen Keep and the Bloody Keep, each on its own island. Towers and outbuildings clung to the stacks beyond, linked to each other by covered archways when the pillars stood close, by long swaying walks of wood and rope when they did not.

The Sea Tower rose from the outmost island at the point of the broken sword, the oldest part of the castle, round and tall, the sheer-sided pillar on which it stood half-eaten through by the endless battering of the waves. The base of the tower was white from centuries of salt spray, the upper stories green from the lichen that crawled over it like a thick blanket, the jagged crown black with soot from its nightly watchfire.

Above the Sea Tower snapped his father's banner. The *Myraham* was too far off for Theon to see more than the cloth itself, but he knew the device it bore: the golden kraken of House Greyjoy, arms writhing and reaching against a black field. The banner streamed from an iron mast, shivering and twisting as the wind gusted, like a bird struggling to take flight. And here at least the direwolf of Stark did not fly above, casting its shadow down upon the Greyjoy kraken.

Theon had never seen a more stirring sight. In the sky behind the castle, the fine red tail of the comet was visible through thin, scuttling clouds. All the way from Riverrun to Seagard, the Mallisters had argued about its meaning. *It is my comet*, Theon told himself, sliding a hand into his fur-lined cloak to touch the oilskin pouch snug in its pocket. Inside was the letter Robb Stark had given him, paper as good as a crown.

"Does the castle look as you remember it, milord?" the captain's daughter asked as she pressed herself against his arm.

"It looks smaller," Theon confessed, "though perhaps that is only the distance." The *Myraham* was a fat-bellied southron merchanter up from Oldtown, carrying wine and cloth and seed to trade for iron ore. Her captain was a fat-bellied southron merchanter as well, and the stony sea that foamed at the feet of the castle made his plump lips quiver, so he stayed well out, farther than Theon would have liked. An ironborn captain in a longship would have taken them along the cliffs and under the high bridge that spanned the gap between the gatehouse and the Great Keep, but this plump Oldtowner had neither the craft, the crew, nor the courage to attempt such a thing. So they sailed past at a safe distance, and Theon must content himself with seeing Pyke from afar. Even so, the *Myraham* had to struggle mightily to keep itself off those rocks.

"It must be windy there," the captain's daughter observed.

He laughed. "Windy and cold and damp. A miserable hard place, in truth . . . but my lord father once told me that hard places breed hard men, and hard men rule the world."

The captain's face was as green as the sea when he came bowing up to Theon and asked, "May we make for port now, milord?"

"You may," Theon said, a faint smile playing about his lips. The promise of gold had turned the Oldtowner into a shameless lickspittle. It would have been a much different voyage if a longship from the islands had been waiting at Seagard as he'd hoped. Ironborn captains were proud and willful, and did not go in awe of a man's blood. The islands were too small for awe, and a longship smaller still. If every captain was a king aboard his own ship, as was often said, it was small wonder they named the islands the land of ten thousand kings. And when you have seen your kings shit over the rail and turn green in a storm, it was hard to bend the knee and pretend they were gods. "The Drowned God makes men," old King Urron Redhand had once said, thousands of years ago, "but it's men who make crowns."

A longship would have made the crossing in half the time as well. The *Myraham* was a wallowing tub, if truth be told, and he would not care to be aboard her in a storm. Still, Theon could not be too unhappy. He was here, undrowned, and the voyage had offered certain other amusements. He put an arm around the captain's daughter. "Summon me when we make Lordsport," he told her father. "We'll be below, in my cabin." He led the girl away aft, while her father watched them go in sullen silence.

The cabin was the captain's, in truth, but it had been turned over to Theon's use when they sailed from Seagard. The captain's daughter had not been turned over to his use, but she had come to his bed willingly enough all the same. A cup of wine, a few whispers, and there she was. The girl was a shade plump for his taste, with skin as splotchy as oatmeal, but her breasts filled his hands nicely and she had been a maiden the first time he took her. That was surprising at her age, but Theon found it diverting. He did not think the captain approved, and that was amusing as well, watching the man struggle to swallow his outrage while performing his courtesies to the high lord, the rich purse of gold he'd been promised never far from his thoughts.

As Theon shrugged out of his wet cloak, the girl said, "You must be so happy to see your home again, milord. How many years have you been away?"

"Ten, or close as makes no matter," he told her. "I was a boy of ten when I was taken to Winterfell as a ward of Eddard Stark." A ward in name, a hostage in truth. Half his days a hostage . . . but no longer. His life was his own again, and nowhere a Stark to be seen. He drew the captain's daughter close and kissed her on her ear. "Take off your cloak."

She dropped her eyes, suddenly shy, but did as he bid her. When the heavy garment, sodden with spray, fell from her shoulders to the deck, she gave him a little bow and smiled anxiously. She looked rather stupid when she smiled, but he had never required a woman to be clever. "Come here," he told her.

She did. "I have never seen the Iron Islands."

"Count yourself fortunate." Theon stroked her hair. It was fine and dark, though the wind had made a tangle of it. "The islands are stern and stony places, scant of comfort and bleak of prospect. Death is never far here, and life is mean and meager. Men spend their nights drinking ale and arguing over whose lot is worse, the fisherfolk who fight the sea or the farmers who try and scratch a crop from the poor thin soil. If truth be told, the miners have it worse than either, breaking their backs down in the dark, and for what? Iron, lead, tin, those are our treasures. Small wonder the ironmen of old turned to raiding."

The stupid girl did not seem to be listening. "I could go ashore with you," she said. "I would, if it please you . . ."

"You could go ashore," Theon agreed, squeezing her breast, "but not with me, I fear."

"I'd work in your castle, milord. I can clean fish and bake bread and churn butter. Father says my peppercrab stew is the best he's ever tasted. You could find me a place in your kitchens and I could make you pepper-crab stew."

"And warm my bed by night?" He reached for the laces of her bodice and began to undo them, his fingers deft and practiced. "Once I might have carried you home as a prize, and kept you to wife whether you willed it or no. The ironmen of old did such things. A man had his rock wife, his true bride, ironborn like himself, but he had his salt wives too, women captured on raids."

The girl's eyes grew wide, and not because he had bared her breasts. "I would be your salt wife, milord."

"I fear those days are gone." Theon's finger circled one heavy teat, spiraling in toward the fat brown nipple. "No longer may we ride the wind with fire and sword, taking what we want. Now we scratch in the ground and toss lines in the sea like other men, and count ourselves lucky if we have salt cod and porridge enough to get us through a winter." He took her nipple in his mouth, and bit it until she gasped.

"You can put it in me again, if it please you," she whispered in his ear as he sucked.

When he raised his head from her breast, the skin was dark red where his mouth had marked her. "It would please me to teach you something new. Unlace me and pleasure me with your mouth."

"With my mouth?"

His thumb brushed lightly over her full lips. "It's what those lips were made for, sweetling. If you were my salt wife, you'd do as I command."

She was timid at first, but learned quickly for such a stupid girl, which pleased him. Her mouth was as wet and sweet as her cunt, and this way he did not have to listen to her mindless prattle. *Once I would have kept her as a salt wife in truth*, he thought to himself as he slid his fingers through her tangled hair. *Once. When we still kept the Old Way, lived by the axe instead of the pick, taking what we would, be it wealth, women, or glory.* In those days, the ironborn did not work mines; that was labor for the captives brought back from the hostings, and so too the sorry business of farming and tending goats and sheep. War was an ironman's proper trade. The Drowned God had made them to reave and rape, to carve out kingdoms and write their names in fire and blood and song.

Aegon the Dragon had destroyed the Old Way when he burned Black Harren, gave Harren's kingdom back to the weakling rivermen, and reduced the Iron Islands to an insignificant backwater of a much greater realm. Yet the old red tales were still told around driftwood fires and smoky hearths all across the islands, even behind the high stone halls of Pyke. Theon's father numbered among his titles the style of Lord Reaper, and the Greyjoy words boasted that *We Do Not Sow.*

It had been to bring back the Old Way more than for the empty vanity of a crown that Lord Balon had staged his great rebellion. Robert Baratheon had written a bloody end to that hope, with the help of his friend Eddard Stark, but both men were dead now. Mere boys ruled in their stead, and the realm that Aegon the Conqueror had forged was smashed and sundered. *This is the season*, Theon thought as the captain's daughter slid her lips up and down the length of him, *the season, the year, the day, and I am the man.* He smiled crookedly, wondering what his father would say when Theon told him that he, the last-born, babe and hostage, *he* had succeeded where Lord Balon himself had failed.

His climax came on him sudden as a storm, and he filled the girl's mouth with his seed. Startled, she tried to pull away, but Theon held her tight by the hair. Afterward, she crawled up beside him. "Did I please milord?"

"Well enough," he told her.

"It tasted salty," she murmured.

"Like the sea?"

She nodded. "I have always loved the sea, milord."

"As I have," he said, rolling her nipple idly between his fingers. It was true. The sea meant freedom to the men of the Iron Islands. He had forgotten that until the *Myraham* had raised sail at Seagard. The sounds brought old feelings back; the creak of wood and rope, the captain's shouted commands, the snap of the sails as the wind filled them, each as familiar as the beating of his own heart, and as comforting. *I must remember this,* Theon vowed to himself. *I must never go far from the sea again.*

"Take me with you, milord," the captain's daughter begged. "I don't need to go to your castle. I can stay in some town, and be your salt wife." She reached out to stroke his cheek.

Theon Greyjoy pushed her hand aside and climbed off the bunk. "My place is Pyke, and yours is on this ship."

"I can't stay here now."

He laced up his breeches. "Why not?"

"My father," she told him. "Once you're gone, he'll punish me, milord. He'll call me names and hit me."

Theon swept his cloak off its peg and over his shoulders. "Fathers are like that," he admitted as he pinned the folds with a silver clasp. "Tell him he should be pleased. As many times as I've fucked you, you're likely with child. It's not every man who has the honor of raising a king's bastard." She looked at him stupidly, so he left her there.

The *Myraham* was rounding a wooded point. Below the pine-clad bluffs, a dozen fishing boats were pulling in their nets. The big cog stayed well out from them, tacking. Theon moved to the bow for a better view. He saw the castle first, the stronghold of the Botleys. When he was a boy it had been timber and wattle, but Robert Baratheon had razed that structure to the ground. Lord Sawane had rebuilt in stone, for now a small square keep crowned the hill. Pale green flags drooped from the squat corner towers, each emblazoned with a shoal of silvery fish.

Beneath the dubious protection of the fish-ridden little castle lay the village of Lordsport, its harbor aswarm with ships. When last he'd seen Lordsport, it had been a smoking wasteland, the skeletons of burnt longships and smashed galleys littering the stony shore like the bones of dead leviathans, the houses no more than broken walls and cold ashes. After ten years, few traces of the war remained. The smallfolk had built new hovels with the stones of the old, and cut fresh sod for their roofs. A new inn had risen beside the landing, twice the size of the old one, with a lower story of cut stone and two upper stories of timber. The sept beyond had never been rebuilt, though; only a seven-sided foundation remained where it had stood. Robert Baratheon's fury had soured the ironmen's taste for the new gods, it would seem.

Theon was more interested in ships than gods. Among the masts of countless fishing boats, he spied a Tyroshi trading galley off-loading beside a lumbering Ibbenese cog with her black-tarred hull. A great number of longships, fifty or sixty at the least, stood out to sea or lay beached on the pebbled shore to the north. Some of the sails bore devices from the other islands; the blood moon of Wynch, Lord Goodbrother's banded black warhorn, Harlaw's silver scythe. Theon searched for his uncle Euron's *Silence*. Of that lean and terrible red ship he saw no sign, but his father's *Great Kraken* was there, her bow ornamented with a grey iron ram in the shape of its namesake.

Had Lord Balon anticipated him and called the Greyjoy banners? His hand went inside his cloak again, to the oilskin pouch. No one knew of his letter but Robb Stark; they were no fools, to entrust their secrets to a bird. Still, Lord Balon was no fool either. He might well have guessed why his son was coming home at long last, and acted accordingly.

The thought did not please him. His father's war was long done, and lost. This was Theon's hour—his plan, his glory, and in time his crown. *Yet if the longships are hosting . . .*

It might be only a caution, now that he thought on it. A defensive move, lest the war spill out across the sea. Old men were cautious by nature. His father was old now, and so too his uncle Victarion, who commanded the Iron Fleet. His uncle Euron was a different song, to be sure, but the *Silence* did not seem to be in port. *It's all for the good,* Theon told himself. *This way, I shall be able to strike all the more quickly.*

As the *Myraham* made her way landward, Theon paced the deck restlessly, scanning the shore. He had not thought to find Lord Balon himself at quayside, but surely his father would have sent someone to meet him. Sylas Sourmouth the steward, Lord Botley, perhaps even Dagmer Cleftjaw. It would be good to look on Dagmer's hideous old face again. It was not as though they had no word of his arrival. Robb had sent ravens from Riverrun, and when they'd found no longship at Seagard, Jason Mallister had sent his own birds to Pyke, supposing that Robb's were lost.

Yet he saw no familiar faces, no honor guard waiting to escort him from Lordsport to Pyke, only smallfolk going about their small business. Shorehands rolled casks of wine off the Tyroshi trader, fisherfolk cried the day's catch, children ran and played. A priest in the seawater robes of the Drowned God was leading a pair of horses along the pebbled shore, while above him a slattern leaned out a window in the inn, calling out to some passing Ibbenese sailors.

A handful of Lordsport merchants had gathered to meet the ship. They shouted questions as the *Myraham* was tying up. "We're out of Oldtown," the captain called down, "bearing apples and oranges, wines from the Arbor, feathers from the Summer Isles. I have pepper, woven leathers, a bolt of Myrish lace, mirrors for milady, a pair of Oldtown woodharps sweet as any you ever heard." The gangplank descended with a creak and a thud. "And I've brought your heir back to you."

The Lordsport men gazed on Theon with blank, bovine eyes, and he realized that they did not know who he was. It made him angry. He pressed a golden dragon into the captain's palm. "Have your men bring my things." Without waiting for a reply, he strode down the gangplank. "Innkeeper," he barked, "I require a horse."

"As you say, m'lord," the man responded, without so much as a bow. He had forgotten how bold the ironborn could be. "Happens as I have one might do. Where would you be riding, m'lord?"

"Pyke." The fool *still* did not know him. He should have worn his good doublet, with the kraken embroidered on the breast.

"You'll want to be off soon, to reach Pyke afore dark," the innkeeper said. "My boy will go with you and show you the way."

"Your boy will not be needed," a deep voice called, "nor your horse. I shall see my nephew back to his father's house."

The speaker was the priest he had seen leading the horses along the shoreline. As the man approached, the smallfolk bent the knee, and Theon heard the innkeeper murmur, "Damphair."

Tall and thin, with fierce black eyes and a beak of a nose, the priest was garbed in mottled robes of green and grey and blue, the swirling colors of the Drowned God. A waterskin hung under his arm on a leather strap, and ropes of dried seaweed were braided through his waist-long black hair and untrimmed beard.

A memory prodded at Theon. In one of his rare curt letters, Lord Balon had written of his youngest brother going down in a storm, and turning holy when he washed up safe on shore. "Uncle Aeron?" he said doubtfully.

"Nephew Theon," the priest replied. "Your lord father bid me fetch you. Come."

"In a moment, Uncle." He turned back to the *Myraham*. "My things," he commanded the captain.

A sailor fetched him down his tall yew bow and quiver of arrows, but it was the captain's daughter who brought the pack with his good clothing. "Milord." Her eyes were red. When he took the pack, she made as if to embrace him, there in front of her own father and his priestly uncle and half the island.

Theon turned deftly aside. "You have my thanks."

"Please," she said, "I do love you well, milord."

"I must go." He hurried after his uncle, who was already well down the pier. Theon caught him with a dozen long strides. "I had not looked for you, Uncle. After ten years, I thought perhaps my lord father and lady mother might come themselves, or send Dagmer with an honor guard."

"It is not for you to question the commands of the Lord Reaper of Pyke." The priest's manner was chilly, most unlike the man Theon remembered. Aeron Greyjoy had been the most amiable of his uncles, feckless and quick to laugh, fond of songs, ale, and women. "As to Dagmer, the Cleftjaw is gone to Old Wyk at your father's behest, to roust the Stonehouses and the Drumms."

"To what purpose? Why are the longships hosting?"

"Why have longships ever hosted?" His uncle had left the horses tied up in front of the waterside inn. When they reached them, he turned to Theon. "Tell me true, nephew. Do you pray to the wolf gods now?"

Theon seldom prayed at all, but that was not something you confessed to a priest, even your father's own brother. "Ned Stark prayed to a tree. No, I care nothing for Stark's gods."

"Good. Kneel."

The ground was all stones and mud. "Uncle, I—"

"*Kneel*. Or are you too proud now, a lordling of the green lands come among us?"

Theon knelt. He had a purpose here, and might need Aeron's help to achieve it. A crown was worth a little mud and horseshit on his breeches, he supposed.

"Bow your head." Lifting the skin, his uncle pulled the cork and directed a thin stream of seawater down upon Theon's head. It drenched his hair and ran over his forehead into his eyes. Sheets washed down his cheeks, and a finger crept under his cloak and doublet and down his back, a cold rivulet along his spine. The salt made his eyes burn, until it was all he could do not to cry out. He could taste the ocean on his lips. "Let Theon your servant be born again from the sea, as you were," Aeron Greyjoy intoned. "Bless him with salt, bless him with stone, bless him with steel. Nephew, do you still know the words?"

"What is dead may never die," Theon said, remembering.

"What is dead may never die," his uncle echoed, "but rises again, harder and stronger. Stand."

Theon stood, blinking back tears from the salt in his eyes. Wordless, his uncle corked the waterskin, untied his horse, and mounted. Theon did the same. They set off together, leaving the inn and the harbor behind them, up past the castle of Lord Botley into the stony hills. The priest ventured no further word.

"I have been half my life away from home," Theon ventured at last. "Will I find the islands changed?"

"Men fish the sea, dig in the earth, and die. Women birth children in blood and pain, and die. Night follows day. The winds and tides remain. The islands are as our god made them."

Gods, he has grown grim, Theon thought. "Will I find my sister and my lady mother at Pyke?"

"You will not. Your mother dwells on Harlaw, with her own sister. It is less raw there, and her cough troubles her. Your sister has taken *Black Wind* to Great Wyk, with messages from your lord father. She will return e'er long, you may be sure."

Theon did not need to be told that *Black Wind* was Asha's longship. He had not seen his sister in ten years, but that much he knew of her. Odd that she would call it that, when Robb Stark had a wolf named Grey Wind. "Stark is grey and Greyjoy's black," he murmured, smiling, "but it seems we're both windy."

The priest had nothing to say to that.

"And what of you, Uncle?" Theon asked. "You were no priest when I was taken from Pyke. I remember how you would sing the old reaving songs standing on the table with a horn of ale in hand."

"Young I was, and vain," Aeron Greyjoy said, "but the sea washed my follies and my vanities away. That man drowned, nephew. His lungs filled with seawater, and the fish ate the scales off his eyes. When I rose again, I saw clearly."

He is as mad as he is sour. Theon had liked what he remembered of the old Aeron Greyjoy. "Uncle, why has my father called his swords and sails?"

"Doubtless he will tell you at Pyke."

"I would know his plans now."

"From me, you shall not. We are commanded not to speak of this to any man."

"Even to *me?*" Theon's anger flared. He'd led men in war, hunted with a king, won honor in tourney melees, ridden with Brynden Blackfish and Greatjon Umber, fought in the Whispering Wood, bedded more girls than he could name, and yet this uncle was treating him as though he were still a child of ten. "If my father makes plans for war, I must know of them. I am not *'any man,'* I am heir to Pyke and the Iron Islands."

"As to that," his uncle said, "we shall see."

The words were a slap in the face. *"We shall see?* My brothers are both dead. I am my lord father's only living son."

"Your sister lives."

Asha, he thought, confounded. She was three years older than Theon, yet still . . . "A woman may inherit only if there is no male heir in the direct line," he insisted loudly. "I will not be cheated of my rights, I warn you."

His uncle grunted. "You *warn* a servant of the Drowned God, boy? You have forgotten more than you know. And you are a great fool if you believe your lord father will ever hand these holy islands over to a Stark. Now be silent. The ride is long enough without your magpie chatterings."

Theon held his tongue, though not without struggle. *So that is the way of it*, he thought. As if ten years in Winterfell could make a Stark. Lord Eddard had raised him among his own children, but Theon had never been one of them. The whole castle, from Lady Stark to the lowliest kitchen scullion, knew he was hostage to his father's good behavior, and treated him accordingly. Even the bastard Jon Snow had been accorded more honor than he had.

Lord Eddard had tried to play the father from time to time, but to Theon he had always remained the man who'd brought blood and fire to Pyke and taken him from his home. As a boy, he had lived in fear of Stark's stern face and great dark sword. His wife was, if anything, even more distant and suspicious.

As for their children, the younger ones had been mewling babes for most of his years at Winterfell. Only Robb and his baseborn half brother Jon Snow had been old enough to be worth his notice. The bastard was a sullen boy, quick to sense a slight, jealous of Theon's high birth and Robb's regard for him. For Robb himself, Theon did have a certain affection, as for a younger brother . . . but it would be best not to mention that. In Pyke, it would seem, the old wars were still being fought. That ought not surprise him. The Iron Islands lived in the past; the present was too hard and bitter to be borne. Besides, his father and uncles were old, and the old lords were like that; they took their dusty feuds to the grave, forgetting nothing and forgiving less.

It had been the same with the Mallisters, his companions on the ride from Riverrun to Seagard. Patrek Mallister was not too ill a fellow; they shared a taste for wenches, wine, and hawking. But when old Lord Jason saw his heir growing overly fond of Theon's company, he had taken Patrek aside to remind him that Seagard had been built to defend the coast against reavers from the Iron Islands, the Greyjoys of Pyke chief among them. Their Booming Tower was named for its immense bronze bell, rung of old to call the townsfolk and farmhands into the castle when longships were sighted on the western horizon.

"Never mind that the bell has been rung just once in three hundred years," Patrek had told Theon the day after, as he shared his father's cautions and a jug of green-apple wine.

"When my brother stormed Seagard," Theon said. Lord Jason had slain Rodrik Greyjoy under the walls of the castle, and thrown the ironmen back into the bay. "If your father supposes I bear him some enmity for that, it's only because he never knew Rodrik."

They had a laugh over that as they raced ahead to an amorous young miller's wife that Patrek knew. *Would that Patrek were with me now.* Mallister or no, he was a more amiable riding companion than this sour old priest that his uncle Aeron had turned into.

The path they rode wound up and up, into bare and stony hills. Soon they were out of sight of the sea, though the smell of salt still hung sharp in the damp air. They kept a steady plodding pace, past a shepherd's croft and the abandoned workings of a mine. This new, holy Aeron Greyjoy was not much for talk. They rode in a gloom of silence. Finally Theon could suffer it no longer. "Robb Stark is Lord of Winterfell now," he said.

Aeron rode on. "One wolf is much like the other."

"Robb has broken fealty with the Iron Throne and crowned himself King in the North. There's war."

"The maester's ravens fly over salt as soon as rock. This news is old and cold."

"It means a new day, Uncle."

"Every morning brings a new day, much like the old."

"In Riverrun, they would tell you different. They say the red comet is a herald of a new age. A messenger from the gods."

"A sign it is," the priest agreed, "but from our god, not theirs. A burning brand it is, such as our people carried of old. It is the flame the Drowned God brought from the sea, and it proclaims a rising tide. It is time to hoist our sails and go forth into the world with fire and sword, as he did."

Theon smiled. "I could not agree more."

"A man agrees with god as a raindrop with the storm."

This raindrop will one day be a king, old man. Theon had suffered quite enough of his uncle's gloom. He put his spurs into his horse and trotted on ahead, smiling.

It was nigh on sunset when they reached the walls of Pyke, a crescent of dark stone that ran from cliff to cliff, with the gatehouse in the center and three square towers to either side. Theon could still make out the scars left by the stones of Robert Baratheon's catapults. A new south tower had risen from the ruins of the old, its stone a paler shade of grey, and as yet unmarred by patches of lichen. That was where Robert had made his breach, swarming in over the rubble and corpses with his warhammer in hand and Ned Stark at his side. Theon had watched from the safety of the Sea Tower, and sometimes he still saw the torches in his dreams, and heard the dull thunder of the collapse.

The gates stood open to him, the rusted iron portcullis drawn up. The guards atop the battlements watched with strangers' eyes as Theon Greyjoy came home at last.

Beyond the curtain wall were half a hundred acres of headland hard against the sky and the sea. The stables were here, and the kennels, and a scatter of other outbuildings. Sheep and swine huddled in their pens while the castle dogs ran free. To the south were the cliffs, and the wide stone bridge to the Great Keep. Theon could hear the crashing of waves as he swung down from his saddle. A stableman came to take his horse.

A pair of gaunt children and some thralls stared at him with dull eyes, but there was no sign of his lord father, nor anyone else he recalled from boyhood. *A bleak and bitter homecoming*, he thought.

The priest had not dismounted. "Will you not stay the night and share our meat and mead, Uncle?"

"Bring you, I was told. You are brought. Now I return to our god's business." Aeron Greyjoy turned his horse and rode slowly out beneath the muddy spikes of the portcullis.

A bentback old crone in a shapeless grey dress approached him warily. "M'lord, I am sent to show you to chambers."

"By whose bidding?"

"Your lord father, m'lord."

Theon pulled off his gloves. "So you *do* know who I am. Why is my father not here to greet me?"

"He awaits you in the Sea Tower, m'lord. When you are rested from your trip."

And I thought Ned Stark cold. "And who are you?"

"Helya, who keeps this castle for your lord father."

"Sylas was steward here. They called him Sourmouth." Even now, Theon could recall the winey stench of the old man's breath.

"Dead these five years, m'lord."

"And what of Maester Qalen, where is he?"

"He sleeps in the sea. Wendamyr keeps the ravens now."

It is as if I were a stranger here, Theon thought. *Nothing has changed, and yet everything has changed.* "Show me to my chambers, woman," he commanded. Bowing stiffly, she led him across the headland to the bridge. That at least was as he remembered; the ancient stones slick with spray and spotted by lichen, the sea foaming under their feet like some great wild beast, the salt wind clutching at their clothes.

Whenever he'd imagined his homecoming, he had always pictured himself returning to the snug bedchamber in the Sea Tower, where he'd slept as a child. Instead the old woman led him to the Bloody Keep. The halls here were larger and better furnished, if no less cold nor damp. Theon was given a suite of chilly rooms with ceilings so high that they were lost in gloom. He might have been more impressed if he had not known that these were the very chambers that had given the Bloody Keep its name. A thousand years before, the sons of the River King had been slaughtered here, hacked to bits in their beds so that pieces of their bodies might be sent back to their father on the mainland.

But Greyjoys were not murdered in Pyke except once in a great while by their brothers, and his brothers were both dead. It was not fear of ghosts that made him glance about with distaste. The wall hangings were green with mildew, the mattress musty-smelling and sagging, the rushes old and brittle. Years had come and gone since these chambers had last been opened. The damp went bone deep. "I'll have a basin of hot water and a fire in this hearth," he told the crone. "See that they light braziers in the other rooms to drive out some of the chill. And gods be good, get someone in here at once to change these rushes."

"Yes, m'lord. As you command." She fled.

After some time, they brought the hot water he had asked for. It was only tepid, and soon cold, and seawater in the bargain, but it served to wash the dust of the long ride from his face and hair and hands. While two thralls lit his braziers, Theon stripped off his travel-stained clothing and dressed to meet his father. He chose boots of supple black leather, soft lambswool breeches of silvery-grey, a black velvet doublet with the golden kraken of the Greyjoys embroidered on the breast. Around his throat he fastened a slender gold chain, around his waist a belt of bleached white leather. He hung a dirk at one hip and a longsword at the other, in scabbards striped black-and-gold. Drawing the dirk, he tested its edge with his thumb, pulled a whetstone from his belt pouch, and gave it a few licks. He prided himself on keeping his weapons sharp. "When I return, I shall expect a warm room and clean rushes," he warned the thralls as he drew on a pair of black gloves, the silk decorated with a delicate scrollwork tracery in golden thread.

Theon returned to the Great Keep through a covered stone walkway, the echoes of his footsteps mingling with the ceaseless rumble of the sea below. To get to the Sea Tower on its crooked pillar, he had to cross three further bridges, each narrower than the one before. The last was made of rope and wood, and the wet salt wind made it sway underfoot like a living thing. Theon's heart was in his mouth by the time he was halfway across. A long way below, the waves threw up tall plumes of spray as they crashed against the rock. As a boy, he used to *run* across this bridge, even in the black of night. *Boys believe nothing can hurt them*, his doubt whispered. *Grown men know better.*

The door was grey wood studded with iron, and Theon found it barred from the inside. He hammered on it with a fist, and cursed when a splinter snagged the fabric of his glove. The wood was damp and moldy, the iron studs rusted.

After a moment the door was opened from within by a guard in a black iron breastplate and pothelm. "You are the son?"

"Out of my way, or you'll learn who I am." The man stood aside. Theon climbed the twisting steps to the solar. He found his father seated beside a brazier, beneath a robe of musty sealskins that covered him foot to chin. At the sound of boots on stone, the Lord of the Iron Islands lifted his eyes to behold his last living son. He was smaller than Theon remembered him. And so gaunt. Balon Greyjoy had always been thin, but now he looked as though the gods had put him in a cauldron and boiled every spare ounce of flesh from his bones, until nothing remained but hair and skin. Bone thin and bone hard he was, with a face that might have been chipped from flint. His eyes were flinty too, black and sharp, but the years and the salt winds had turned his hair the grey of a winter sea, flecked with whitecaps. Unbound, it hung past the small of the back.

"Nine years, is it?" Lord Balon said at last.

"Ten," Theon answered, pulling off his torn gloves.

"A boy they took," his father said. "What are you now?"

"A man," Theon answered. "Your blood and your heir."

Lord Balon grunted. "We shall see."

"You shall," Theon promised.

"Ten years, you say. Stark had you as long as I. And now you come as his envoy."

"Not his," Theon said. "Lord Eddard is dead, beheaded by the Lannister queen."

"They are both dead, Stark and that Robert who broke my walls with his stones. I vowed I'd live to see them both in their graves, and I have." He grimaced. "Yet the cold and the damp still make my joints ache, as when they were alive. So what does it serve?"

"It serves." Theon moved closer. "I bring a letter—"

"Did Ned Stark dress you like that?" his father interrupted, squinting up from beneath his robe. "Was it his pleasure to garb you in velvets and silks and make you his own sweet daughter?"

Theon felt the blood rising to his face. "I am no man's daughter. If you mislike my garb, I will change it."

"You will." Throwing off the furs, Lord Balon pushed himself to his feet. He was not so tall as Theon remembered. "That bauble around your neck—was it bought with gold or iron?"

Theon touched the gold chain. He had forgotten. *It has been so long . . .* In the Old Way, women might decorate themselves with ornaments bought with coin, but a warrior wore only the jewelry he took off the corpses of enemies slain by his own hand. *Paying the iron price,* it was called.

"You blush red as a maid, Theon. A question was asked. Is it the gold price you paid, or the iron?"

"The gold," Theon admitted.

His father slid his fingers under the necklace and gave it a yank so hard it was like to take Theon's head off, had the chain not snapped first. "My daughter has taken an axe for a lover," Lord Balon said. "I will not have my son bedeck himself like a whore." He dropped the broken chain onto the brazier, where it slid down among the coals. "It is as I feared. The green lands have made you soft, and the Starks have made you theirs."

"You're wrong. Ned Stark was my gaoler, but my blood is still salt and iron."

Lord Balon turned away to warm his bony hands over the brazier. "Yet the Stark pup sends you to me like a well-trained raven, clutching his little message."

"There is nothing small about the letter I bear," Theon said, "and the offer he makes is one I suggested to him."

"This wolf king heeds your counsel, does he?" The notion seemed to amuse Lord Balon.

"He heeds me, yes. I've hunted with him, trained with him, shared meat and mead with him, warred at his side. I have earned his trust. He looks on me as an older brother, he—"

"No." His father jabbed a finger at his face. "Not here, not in Pyke, not in my hearing, you will not name him brother, this son of the man who put your true brothers to the sword. Or have you forgotten Rodrik and Maron, who were your own blood?"

"I forget nothing." Ned Stark had killed neither of his brothers, in truth. Rodrik had been slain by Lord Jason Mallister at Seagard, Maron crushed in the collapse of the old south tower . . . but Stark would have done for them just as quick had the tide of battle chanced to sweep them together. "I remember my brothers very well," Theon insisted. Chiefly he remembered Rodrik's drunken cuffs and Maron's cruel japes and endless lies. "I remember when my father was a king too." He took out Robb's letter and thrust it forward. "Here. Read it . . . Your Grace."

Lord Balon broke the seal and unfolded the parchment. His black eyes flicked back and forth. "So the boy would give me a crown again," he said, "and all I need do is destroy his enemies." His thin lips twisted in a smile.

"By now Robb is at the Golden Tooth," Theon said. "Once it falls, he'll be through the hills in a day. Lord Tywin's host is at Harrenhal, cut off from the west. The Kingslayer is a captive at Riverrun. Only Ser Stafford Lannister and the raw green levies he's been gathering remain to oppose Robb in the west. Ser Stafford will put himself between Robb's army and Lannisport, which means the city will be undefended when we descend on it by sea. If the gods are with us, even Casterly Rock itself may fall before the Lannisters so much as realize that we are upon them."

Lord Balon grunted. "Casterly Rock has never fallen."

"Until now." Theon smiled. And how sweet that will be.

His father did not return the smile. "So this is why Robb Stark sends you back to me, after so long? So you might win my consent to this plan of his?"

"It is my plan, not Robb's," Theon said proudly. *Mine, as the victory will be mine, and in time the crown.* "I will lead the attack myself, if it please you. As my reward I would ask that you grant me Casterly Rock for my own seat, once we have taken it from the Lannisters." With the Rock, he could hold Lannisport and the golden lands of the west. It would mean wealth and power such as House Greyjoy had never known.

"You reward yourself handsomely for a notion and a few lines of scribbling." His father read the letter again. "The pup says nothing about a reward. Only that you speak for him, and I am to listen, and give him my sails and swords, and in return he will give me a crown." His flinty eyes lifted to meet his son's. "He will *give* me a crown," he repeated, his voice growing sharp.

"A poor choice of words, what is meant is—"

"What is meant is what is said. The boy will *give* me a crown. And what is given can be taken away." Lord Balon tossed the letter onto the brazier, atop the necklace. The parchment curled, blackened, and took flame.

Theon was aghast. "Have you gone mad?"

His father laid a stinging backhand across his cheek. "Mind your tongue. You are not in Winterfell now, and I am not Robb the Boy, that you should speak to me so. I am the Greyjoy, Lord Reaper of Pyke, King of Salt and Rock, Son of the Sea Wind, and no man gives me a crown. I pay the iron price. I will *take* my crown, as Urron Redhand did five thousand years ago."

Theon edged backward, away from the sudden fury in his father's tone. "Take it, then," he spat, his cheek still tingling. "Call yourself King of the Iron Islands, no one will care . . . until the wars are over, and the victor looks about and spies the old fool perched off his shore with an iron crown on his head."

Lord Balon laughed. "Well, at the least you are no craven. No more than I'm a fool. Do you think I gather my ships to watch them rock at anchor? I mean to carve out a kingdom with fire and sword . . . but not from the west, and not at the bidding of King Robb the Boy. Casterly Rock is too strong, and Lord Tywin too cunning by half. Aye, we might take Lannisport, but we should never keep it. No. I hunger for a different plum . . . not so juicy sweet, to be sure, yet it hangs there ripe and undefended."

Where? Theon might have asked, but by then he knew.

DAENERYS

The Dothraki named the comet *shierak qiya*, the Bleeding Star. The old men muttered that it omened ill, but Daenerys Targaryen had seen it first on the night she had burned Khal Drogo, the night her dragons had awakened. *It is the herald of my coming*, she told herself as she gazed up into the night sky with wonder in her heart. *The gods have sent it to show me the way.*

Yet when she put the thought into words, her handmaid Doreah quailed. "That way lies the red lands, *Khaleesi*. A grim place and terrible, the riders say."

"The way the comet points is the way we must go," Dany insisted . . . though in truth, it was the only way open to her.

She dare not turn north onto the vast ocean of grass they called the Dothraki sea. The first *khalasar* they met would swallow up her ragged band, slaying the warriors and slaving the rest. The lands of the Lamb Men south of the river were likewise closed to them. They were too few to defend themselves even against that unwarlike folk, and the Lhazareen had small reason to love them. She might have struck downriver for the ports at Meereen and Yunkai and Astapor, but Rakharo warned her that Pono's *khalasar* had ridden that way, driving thousands of captives before them to sell in the flesh marts that festered like open sores on the shores of Slaver's Bay. "Why should I fear Pono?" Dany objected. "He was Drogo's *ko*, and always spoke me gently."

"Ko Pono spoke you gently," Ser Jorah Mormont said. "Khal Pono will kill you. He was the first to abandon Drogo. Ten thousand warriors went with him. You have a hundred."

No, Dany thought. *I have four. The rest are women, old sick men, and boys whose hair has never been braided.* "I have the dragons," she pointed out.

"Hatchlings," Ser Jorah said. "One swipe from an *arakh* would put an end to them, though Pono is more like to seize them for himself. Your dragon eggs were more precious than rubies. A living dragon is beyond price. In all the world, there are only three. Every man who sees them will want them, my queen."

"They are *mine,*" she said fiercely. They had been born from her faith and her need, given life by the deaths of her husband and unborn son and the *maegi* Mirri Maz Duur. Dany had walked into the flames as they came forth, and they had drunk milk from her swollen breasts. "No man will take them from me while I live."

"You will not live long should you meet Khal Pono. Nor Khal Jhaqo, nor any of the others. You must go where they do not."

Dany had named him the first of her Queensguard . . . and when Mormont's gruff counsel and the omens agreed, her course was clear. She called her people together and mounted her silver mare. Her hair had burned away in Drogo's pyre, so her handmaids garbed her in the skin of the *hrakkar* Drogo had slain, the white lion of the Dothraki sea. Its fearsome head made a hood to cover her naked scalp, its pelt a cloak that flowed across her shoulders and down her back. The cream-colored dragon sunk sharp black claws into the lion's mane and coiled its tail around her arm, while Ser Jorah took his accustomed place by her side.

"We follow the comet," Dany told her *khalasar*. Once it was said, no word was raised against it. They had been Drogo's people, but they were hers now. *The Unburnt,* they called her, and *Mother of Dragons.* Her word was their law.

They rode by night, and by day took refuge from the sun beneath their tents. Soon enough Dany learned the truth of Doreah's words. This was no kindly country. They left a trail of dead and dying horses behind them as they went, for Pono, Jhaqo, and the others had seized the best of Drogo's herds, leaving to Dany the old and the scrawny, the sickly and the lame, the broken animals and the ill-tempered. It was the same with the people. *They are not strong,* she told herself, *so I must be their strength. I must show no fear, no weakness, no doubt. However frightened my heart, when they look upon my face they must see only Drogo's queen.* She felt older than her fourteen years. If ever she had truly been a girl, that time was done.

Three days into the march, the first man died. A toothless oldster with cloudy blue eyes, he fell exhausted from his saddle and could not rise again. An hour later he was done. Blood flies swarmed about his corpse and carried his ill luck to the living. "His time was past," her handmaid Irri declared. "No man should live longer than his teeth." The others agreed. Dany bid them kill the weakest of their dying horses, so the dead man might go mounted into the night lands.

Two nights later, it was an infant girl who perished. Her mother's anguished wailing lasted all day, but there was nothing to be done. The child had been too young to ride, poor thing. Not for her the endless black grasses of the night lands; she must be born again.

There was little forage in the red waste, and less water. It was a sere and desolate land of low hills and barren windswept plains. The rivers they crossed were dry as dead men's bones. Their mounts subsisted on the tough brown devilgrass that grew in clumps at the base of rocks and dead trees. Dany sent outriders ranging ahead of the column, but they found neither wells nor springs, only bitter pools, shallow and stagnant, shrinking in the hot sun. The deeper they rode into the waste, the smaller the pools became, while the distance between them grew. If there were gods in this trackless wilderness of stone and sand and red clay, they were hard dry gods, deaf to prayers for rain.

Wine gave out first, and soon thereafter the clotted mare's milk the horselords loved better than mead. Then their stores of flatbread and dried meat were exhausted as well. Their hunters found no game, and only the flesh of their dead horses filled their bellies. Death followed death. Weak children, wrinkled old women, the sick and the stupid and the heedless, the cruel land claimed them all. Doreah grew gaunt and hollow-eyed, and her soft golden hair turned brittle as straw.

Dany hungered and thirsted with the rest of them. The milk in her breasts dried up, her nipples cracked and bled, and the flesh fell away from her day by day until she was lean and hard as a stick, yet it was her dragons she feared for. Her father had been slain before she was born, and her splendid brother Rhaegar as well. Her mother had died bringing her into the world while the storm screamed outside. Gentle Ser Willem Darry, who must have loved her after a fashion, had been taken by a wasting sickness when she was very young. Her brother Viserys, Khal Drogo who was her sun-and-stars, even her unborn son, the gods had claimed them all. *They will not have my dragons*, Dany vowed. *They will not.*

The dragons were no larger than the scrawny cats she had once seen skulking along the walls of Magister Illyrio's estate in Pentos . . . until they unfolded their wings. Their span was three times their length, each wing a delicate fan of translucent skin, gorgeously colored, stretched taut between long thin bones. When you looked hard, you could see that most of their body was neck, tail, and wing. *Such little things*, she thought as she fed them by hand. Or rather, tried to feed them, for the dragons would not eat. They would hiss and spit at each bloody morsel of horsemeat, steam rising from their nostrils, yet they would not take the food . . . until Dany recalled something Viserys had told her when they were children.

Only dragons and men eat cooked meat, he had said.

When she had her handmaids char the horsemeat black, the dragons ripped at it eagerly, their heads striking like snakes. So long as the meat was seared, they gulped down several times their own weight every day, and at last began to grow larger and stronger. Dany marveled at the smoothness of their scales, and the *heat* that poured off them, so palpable that on cold nights their whole bodies seemed to steam.

Each evenfall as the *khalasar* set out, she would choose a dragon to ride upon her shoulder. Irri and Jhiqui carried the others in a cage of woven wood slung between their mounts, and rode close behind her, so Dany was never out of their sight. It was the only way to keep them quiescent.

"Aegon's dragons were named for the gods of Old Valyria," she told her bloodriders one morning after a long night's journey. "Visenya's dragon was Vhagar, Rhaenys had Meraxes, and Aegon rode Balerion, the Black Dread. It was said that Vhagar's breath was so hot that it could melt a knight's armor and cook the man inside, that Meraxes swallowed horses whole, and Balerion . . . his fire was as black as his scales, his wings so vast that whole towns were swallowed up in their shadow when he passed overhead."

The Dothraki looked at her hatchlings uneasily. The largest of her three was shiny black, his scales slashed with streaks of vivid scarlet to match his wings and horns. "*Khaleesi*," Aggo murmured, "there sits Balerion, come again."

"It may be as you say, blood of my blood," Dany replied gravely, "but he shall have a new name for this new life. I would name them all for those the gods have taken. The green one shall be Rhaegal, for my valiant brother who died on the green banks of the Trident. The cream-and-gold I call Viserion. Viserys was cruel and weak and frightened, yet he was my brother still. His dragon will do what he could not."

"And the black beast?" asked Ser Jorah Mormont.

"The black," she said, "is Drogon."

Yet even as her dragons prospered, her *khalasar* withered and died. Around them the land turned ever more desolate. Even devilgrass grew scant; horses dropped in their tracks, leaving so few that some of her people must trudge along on foot. Doreah took a fever and grew worse with every league they crossed. Her lips and hands broke with blood blisters, her hair came out in clumps, and one evenfall she lacked the strength to mount her horse. Jhogo said they must leave her or bind her to her saddle, but Dany remembered a night on the Dothraki sea, when the Lysene girl had taught her secrets so that Drogo might love her more. She gave Doreah water from her own skin, cooled her brow with a damp cloth, and held her hand until she died, shivering. Only then would she permit the *khalasar* to press on.

They saw no sign of other travelers. The Dothraki began to mutter fearfully that the comet had led them to some hell. Dany went to Ser Jorah one morning as they made camp amidst a jumble of black wind-scoured stones. "Are we lost?" she asked him. "Does this waste have no end to it?"

"It has an end," he answered wearily. "I have seen the maps the traders draw, my queen. Few caravans come this way, that is so, yet there are great kingdoms to the east, and cities full of wonders. Yi Ti, Qarth, Asshai by the Shadow . . ."

"Will we live to see them?"

"I will not lie to you. The way is harder than I dared think." The knight's face was grey and exhausted. The wound he had taken to his hip the night he fought Khal Drogo's bloodriders had never fully healed; she could see how he grimaced when he mounted his horse, and he seemed to slump in his saddle as they rode. "Perhaps we are doomed if we press on . . . but I know for a certainty that we are doomed if we turn back."

Dany kissed him lightly on the cheek. It heartened her to see him smile. *I must be strong for him as well*, she thought grimly. *A knight he may be, but I am the blood of the dragon.*

The next pool they found was scalding hot and stinking of brimstone, but their skins were almost empty. The Dothraki cooled the water in jars and pots and drank it tepid. The taste was no less foul, but water was water, and all of them thirsted. Dany looked at the horizon with despair. They had lost a third of their number, and still the waste stretched before them, bleak and red and endless. *The comet mocks my hopes*, she thought, lifting her eyes to where it scored the sky. *Have I crossed half the world and seen the birth of dragons only to die with them in this hard hot desert?* She would not believe it.

The next day, dawn broke as they were crossing a cracked and fissured plain of hard red earth. Dany was about to command them to make camp when her outriders came racing back at a gallop. "A city, *Khaleesi*," they cried. "A city pale as the moon and lovely as a maid. An hour's ride, no more."

"Show me," she said.

When the city appeared before her, its walls and towers shimmering white behind a veil of heat, it looked so beautiful that Dany was certain it must be a mirage. "Do you know what place this might be?" she asked Ser Jorah.

The exile knight gave a weary shake of the head. "No, my queen. I have never traveled this far east."

The distant white walls promised rest and safety, a chance to heal and grow strong, and Dany wanted nothing so much as to rush toward them. Instead she turned to her bloodriders. "Blood of my blood, go ahead of us and learn the name of this city, and what manner of welcome we should expect."

"*Ai, Khaleesi,*" said Aggo.

Her riders were not long in returning. Rakharo swung down from his saddle. From his medallion belt hung the great curving *arakh* that Dany had bestowed on him when she named him bloodrider. "This city is dead, *Khaleesi*. Nameless and godless we found it, the gates broken, only wind and flies moving through the streets."

Jhiqui shuddered. "When the gods are gone, the evil ghosts feast by night. Such places are best shunned. It is known."

"It is known," Irri agreed.

"Not to me." Dany put her heels into her horse and showed them the way, trotting beneath the shattered arch of an ancient gate and down a silent street. Ser Jorah and her bloodriders followed, and then, more slowly, the rest of the Dothraki.

How long the city had been deserted she could not know, but the white walls, so beautiful from afar, were cracked and crumbling when seen up close. Inside was a maze of narrow crooked alleys. The buildings pressed close, their facades blank, chalky, windowless. Everything was white, as if the people who lived here had known nothing of color. They rode past heaps of sun-washed rubble where houses had fallen in, and elsewhere saw the faded scars of fire. At a place where six alleys came together, Dany passed an empty marble plinth. Dothraki had visited this place before, it would seem. Perhaps even now the missing statue stood among the other stolen gods in Vaes Dothrak. She might have ridden past it a hundred times, never knowing. On her shoulder, Viserion *hissed.*

They made camp before the remnants of a gutted palace, on a wind-swept plaza where devilgrass grew between the paving stones. Dany sent out men to search the ruins. Some went reluctantly, yet they went . . . and one scarred old man returned a brief time later, hopping and grinning, his hands overflowing with figs. They were small, withered things, yet her people grabbed for them greedily, jostling and pushing at each other, stuffing the fruit into their cheeks and chewing blissfully.

Other searchers returned with tales of other fruit trees, hidden behind closed doors in secret gardens. Aggo showed her a courtyard overgrown with twisting vines and tiny green grapes, and Jhogo discovered a well where the water was pure and cold. Yet they found bones too, the skulls of the unburied dead, bleached and broken. "Ghosts," Irri muttered. "Terrible ghosts. We must not stay here, *Khaleesi*, this is their place."

"I fear no ghosts. Dragons are more powerful than ghosts." *And figs are more important.* "Go with Jhiqui and find me some clean sand for a bath, and trouble me no more with silly talk."

In the coolness of her tent, Dany blackened horsemeat over a brazier and reflected on her choices. There was food and water here to sustain them, and enough grass for the horses to regain their strength. How pleasant it would be to wake every day in the same place, to linger among shady gardens, eat figs, and drink cool water, as much as she might desire.

When Irri and Jhiqui returned with pots of white sand, Dany stripped and let them scrub her clean. "Your hair is coming back, *Khaleesi*," Jhiqui said as she scraped sand off her back. Dany ran a hand over the top of her head, feeling the new growth. Dothraki men wore their hair in long oiled braids, and cut them only when defeated. *Perhaps I should do the same,* she thought, *to remind them that Drogo's strength lives within me now.* Khal Drogo had died with his hair uncut, a boast few men could make.

Across the tent, Rhaegal unfolded green wings to flap and flutter a half foot before thumping to the carpet. When he landed, his tail lashed back and forth in fury, and he raised his head and screamed. *If I had wings, I would want to fly too,* Dany thought. The Targaryens of old had ridden upon dragonback when they went to war. She tried to imagine what it would feel like, to straddle a dragon's neck and soar high into the air. *It would be like standing on a mountaintop, only better. The whole world would be spread out below. If I flew high enough, I could even see the Seven Kingdoms, and reach up and touch the comet.*

Irri broke her reverie to tell her that Ser Jorah Mormont was outside, awaiting her pleasure. "Send him in," Dany commanded, sand-scrubbed skin tingling. She wrapped herself in the lionskin. The *hrakkar* had been much bigger than Dany, so the pelt covered everything that wanted covering.

"I've brought you a peach," Ser Jorah said, kneeling. It was so small she could almost hide it in her palm, and overripe too, but when she took the first bite, the flesh was so sweet she almost cried. She ate it slowly, savoring every mouthful, while Ser Jorah told her of the tree it had been plucked from, in a garden near the western wall.

"Fruit and water and shade," Dany said, her cheeks sticky with peach juice. "The gods were good to bring us to this place."

"We should rest here until we are stronger," the knight urged. "The red lands are not kind to the weak."

"My handmaids say there are ghosts here."

"There are ghosts everywhere," Ser Jorah said softly. "We carry them with us wherever we go."

Yes, she thought. *Viserys, Khal Drogo, my son Rhaego, they are with me always.* "Tell me the name of your ghost, Jorah. You know all of mine."

His face grew very still. "Her name was Lynesse."

"Your wife?"

"My second wife."

It pains him to speak of her, Dany saw, but she wanted to know the truth. "Is that all you would say of her?" The lion pelt slid off one shoulder and she tugged it back into place. "Was she beautiful?"

"Very beautiful." Ser Jorah lifted his eyes from her shoulder to her face. "The first time I beheld her, I thought she was a goddess come to earth, the Maid herself made flesh. Her birth was far above my own. She was the youngest daughter of Lord Leyton Hightower of Oldtown. The White Bull who commanded your father's Kingsguard was her great-uncle. The Hightowers are an ancient family, very rich and very proud."

"And loyal," Dany said. "I remember, Viserys said the Hightowers were among those who stayed true to my father."

"That's so," he admitted.

"Did your fathers make the match?"

"No," he said. "Our marriage . . . that makes a long tale and a dull one, Your Grace. I would not trouble you with it."

"I have nowhere to go," she said. "Please."

"As my queen commands." Ser Jorah frowned. "My home . . . you must understand that to understand the rest. Bear Island is beautiful, but remote. Imagine old gnarled oaks and tall pines, flowering thornbushes, grey stones bearded with moss, little creeks running icy down steep hillsides. The hall of the Mormonts is built of huge logs and surrounded by an earthen palisade. Aside from a few crofters, my people live along the coasts and fish the seas. The island lies far to the north, and our winters are more terrible than you can imagine, *Khaleesi.*

"Still, the island suited me well enough, and I never lacked for women. I had my share of fishwives and crofter's daughters, before and after I was wed. I married young, to a bride of my father's choosing, a Glover of Deepwood Motte. Ten years we were wed, or near enough as makes no matter. She was a plain-faced woman, but not unkind. I suppose I came to love her after a fashion, though our relations were dutiful rather than passionate. Three times she miscarried while trying to give me an heir. The last time she never recovered. She died not long after."

Dany put her hand on his and gave his fingers a squeeze. "I am sorry for you, truly."

Ser Jorah nodded. "By then my father had taken the black, so I was Lord of Bear Island in my own right. I had no lack of marriage offers, but before I could reach a decision Lord Balon Greyjoy rose in rebellion against the Usurper, and Ned Stark called his banners to help his friend Robert. The final battle was on Pyke. When Robert's stonethrowers opened a breach in King Balon's wall, a priest from Myr was the first man through, but I was not far behind. For that I won my knighthood.

"To celebrate his victory, Robert ordained that a tourney should be held outside Lannisport. It was there I saw Lynesse, a maid half my age. She had come up from Oldtown with her father to see her brothers joust. I could not take my eyes off her. In a fit of madness, I begged her favor to wear in the tourney, never dreaming she would grant my request, yet she did.

"I fight as well as any man, *Khaleesi*, but I have never been a tourney knight. Yet with Lynesse's favor knotted round my arm, I was a different man. I won joust after joust. Lord Jason Mallister fell before me, and Bronze Yohn Royce. Ser Ryman Frey, his brother Ser Hosteen, Lord Whent, Strongboar, even Ser Boros Blount of the Kingsguard, I unhorsed them all. In the last match, I broke nine lances against Jaime Lannister to no result, and King Robert gave me the champion's laurel. I crowned Lynesse queen of love and beauty, and that very night went to her father and asked for her hand. I was drunk, as much on glory as on wine. By rights I should have gotten a contemptuous refusal, but Lord Leyton accepted my offer. We were married there in Lannisport, and for a fortnight I was the happiest man in the wide world."

"Only a fortnight?" asked Dany. *Even I was given more happiness than that, with Drogo who was my sun-and-stars.*

"A fortnight was how long it took us to sail from Lannisport back to Bear Island. My home was a great disappointment to Lynesse. It was too cold, too damp, too far away, my castle no more than a wooden longhall. We had no masques, no mummer shows, no balls or fairs. Seasons might pass without a singer ever coming to play for us, and there's not a goldsmith on the island. Even meals became a trial. My cook knew little beyond his roasts and stews, and Lynesse soon lost her taste for fish and venison.

"I lived for her smiles, so I sent all the way to Oldtown for a new cook, and brought a harper from Lannisport. Goldsmiths, jewelers, dressmakers, whatever she wanted I found for her, but it was never enough. Bear Island is rich in bears and trees, and poor in aught else. I built a fine ship for her and we sailed to Lannisport and Oldtown for festivals and fairs, and once even to Braavos, where I borrowed heavily from the money-lenders. It was as a tourney champion that I had won her hand and heart, so I entered other tourneys for her sake, but the magic was gone. I never distinguished myself again, and each defeat meant the loss of another charger and another suit of jousting armor, which must needs be ransomed or replaced. The cost could not be borne. Finally I insisted we return home, but there matters soon grew even worse than before. I could no longer pay the cook and the harper, and Lynesse grew wild when I spoke of pawning her jewels.

"The rest . . . I did things it shames me to speak of. For gold. So Lynesse might keep her jewels, her harper, and her cook. In the end it cost me all. When I heard that Eddard Stark was coming to Bear Island, I was so lost to honor that rather than stay and face his judgment, I took her with me into exile. Nothing mattered but our love, I told myself. We fled to Lys, where I sold my ship for gold to keep us."

His voice was thick with grief, and Dany was reluctant to press him any further, yet she had to know how it ended. "Did she die there?" she asked him gently.

"Only to me," he said. "In half a year my gold was gone, and I was obliged to take service as a sellsword. While I was fighting Braavosi on the Rhoyne, Lynesse moved into the manse of a merchant prince named Tregar Ormollen. They say she is his chief concubine now, and even his wife goes in fear of her."

Dany was horrified. "Do you hate her?"

"Almost as much as I love her," Ser Jorah answered. "Pray excuse me, my queen. I find I am very tired."

She gave him leave to go, but as he was lifting the flap of her tent, she could not stop herself calling after him with one last question. "What did she look like, your Lady Lynesse?"

Ser Jorah smiled sadly. "Why, she looked a bit like you, Daenerys." He bowed low. "Sleep well, my queen."

Dany shivered, and pulled the lionskin tight about her. *She looked like me.* It explained much that she had not truly understood. *He wants me*, she realized. *He loves me as he loved her, not as a knight loves his queen but as a man loves a woman.* She tried to imagine herself in Ser Jorah's arms, kissing him, pleasuring him, letting him enter her. It was no good. When she closed her eyes, his face kept changing into Drogo's.

Khal Drogo had been her sun-and-stars, her first, and perhaps he must be her last. The *maegi* Mirri Maz Duur had sworn she should never bear a living child, and what man would want a barren wife? And what man could hope to rival Drogo, who had died with his hair uncut and rode now through the night lands, the stars his *khalasar*?

She had heard the longing in Ser Jorah's voice when he spoke of his Bear Island. *He can never have me, but one day I can give him back his home and honor. That much I can do for him.*

No ghosts troubled her sleep that night. She dreamed of Drogo and the first ride they had taken together on the night they were wed. In the dream it was not horses they rode, but dragons.

The next morn, she summoned her bloodriders. "Blood of my blood," she told the three of them, "I have need of you. Each of you is to choose three horses, the hardiest and healthiest that remain to us. Load as much water and food as your mounts can bear, and ride forth for me. Aggo shall strike southwest, Rakharo due south. Jhogo, you are to follow *shierak qiya* on southeast."

"What shall we seek, *Khaleesi*?" asked Jhogo.

"Whatever there is," Dany answered. "Seek for other cities, living and dead. Seek for caravans and people. Seek for rivers and lakes and the great salt sea. Find how far this waste extends before us, and what lies on the other side. When I leave this place, I do not mean to strike out blind again. I will know where I am bound, and how best to get there."

And so they went, the bells in their hair ringing softly, while Dany settled down with her small band of survivors in the place they named *Vaes Tolorro*, the city of bones. Day followed night followed day. Women harvested fruit from the gardens of the dead. Men groomed their mounts and mended saddles, stirrups, and shoes. Children wandered the twisty alleys and found old bronze coins and bits of purple glass and stone flagons with handles carved like snakes. One woman was stung by a red scorpion, but hers was the only death. The horses began to put on some flesh. Dany tended Ser Jorah's wound herself, and it began to heal.

Rakharo was the first to return. Due south the red waste stretched on and on, he reported, until it ended on a bleak shore beside the poison water. Between here and there lay only swirling sand, wind-scoured rocks, and plants bristly with sharp thorns. He had passed the bones of a dragon, he swore, so immense that he had ridden his horse through its great black jaws. Other than that, he had seen nothing.

Dany gave him charge of a dozen of her strongest men, and set them to pulling up the plaza to get to the earth beneath. If devilgrass could grow between the paving stones, other grasses would grow when the stones were gone. They had wells enough, no lack of water. Given seed, they could make the plaza bloom.

Aggo was back next. The southwest was barren and burnt, he swore. He had found the ruins of two more cities, smaller than Vaes Tolorro but otherwise the same. One was warded by a ring of skulls mounted on rusted iron spears, so he dared not enter, but he had explored the second for as long as he could. He showed Dany an iron bracelet he had found, set with a uncut fire opal the size of her thumb. There were scrolls as well, but they were dry and crumbling and Aggo had left them where they lay.

Dany thanked him and told him to see to the repair of the gates. If enemies had crossed the waste to destroy these cities in ancient days, they might well come again. "If so, we must be ready," she declared.

Jhogo was gone so long that Dany feared him lost, but finally when they had all but ceased to look for him, he came riding up from the southeast. One of the guards that Aggo had posted saw him first and gave a shout, and Dany rushed to the walls to see for herself. It was true. Jhogo came, yet not alone. Behind him rode three queerly garbed strangers atop ugly humped creatures that dwarfed any horse.

They drew rein before the city gates, and looked up to see Dany on the wall above them. "Blood of my blood," Jhogo called, "I have been to the great city Qarth, and returned with three who would look on you with their own eyes."

Dany stared down at the strangers. "Here I stand. Look, if that is your pleasure . . . but first tell me your names."

The pale man with the blue lips replied in guttural Dothraki, "I am Pyat Pree, the great warlock."

The bald man with the jewels in his nose answered in the Valyrian of the Free Cities, "I am Xaro Xhoan Daxos of the Thirteen, a merchant prince of Qarth."

The woman in the lacquered wooden mask said in the Common Tongue of the Seven Kingdoms, "I am Quaithe of the Shadow. We come seeking dragons."

"Seek no more," Daenerys Targaryen told them. "You have found them."

JON

Whitetree, the village was named on Sam's old maps. Jon did not think it much of a village. Four tumbledown one-room houses of unmortared stone surrounded an empty sheepfold and a well. The houses were roofed with sod, the windows shuttered with ragged pieces of hide. And above them loomed the pale limbs and dark red leaves of a monstrous great weirwood.

It was the biggest tree Jon Snow had ever seen, the trunk near eight feet wide, the branches spreading so far that the entire village was shaded beneath their canopy. The size did not disturb him so much as the face . . . the mouth especially, no simple carved slash, but a jagged hollow large enough to swallow a sheep.

Those are not sheep bones, though. Nor is that a sheep's skull in the ashes.

"An old tree." Mormont sat his horse, frowning. *"Old,"* his raven agreed from his shoulder. *"Old, old, old."*

"And powerful." Jon could feel the power.

Thoren Smallwood dismounted beside the trunk, dark in his plate and mail. "Look at that face. Small wonder men feared them, when they first came to Westeros. I'd like to take an axe to the bloody thing myself."

Jon said, "My lord father believed no man could tell a lie in front of a heart tree. The old gods know when men are lying."

"My father believed the same," said the Old Bear. "Let me have a look at that skull."

Jon dismounted. Slung across his back in a black leather shoulder sheath was Longclaw, the hand-and-a-half bastard blade the Old Bear had given him for saving his life. *A bastard sword for a bastard*, the men joked. The hilt had been fashioned new for him, adorned with a wolf's-head pommel in pale stone, but the blade itself was Valyrian steel, old and light and deadly sharp.

He knelt and reached a gloved hand down into the maw. The inside of the hollow was red with dried sap and blackened by fire. Beneath the skull he saw another, smaller, the jaw broken off. It was half-buried in ash and bits of bone.

When he brought the skull to Mormont, the Old Bear lifted it in both hands and stared into the empty sockets. "The wildlings burn their dead. We've always known that. Now I wished I'd asked them why, when there were still a few around to ask."

Jon Snow remembered the wight rising, its eyes shining blue in the pale dead face. He knew why, he was certain.

"Would that bones could talk," the Old Bear grumbled. "This fellow could tell us much. How he died. Who burned him, and why. Where the wildlings have gone." He sighed. "The children of the forest could speak to the dead, it's said. But I can't." He tossed the skull back into the mouth of the tree, where it landed with a puff of fine ash. "Go through all these houses. Giant, get to the top of this tree, have a look. I'll have the hounds brought up too. Perchance this time the trail will be fresher." His tone did not suggest that he held out much hope of the last.

Two men went through each house, to make certain nothing was missed. Jon was paired with dour Eddison Tollett, a squire grey of hair and thin as a pike, whom the other brothers called Dolorous Edd. "Bad enough when the dead come walking," he said to Jon as they crossed the village, "now the Old Bear wants them talking as well? No good will come of *that*, I'll warrant. And who's to say the bones wouldn't lie? Why should death make a man truthful, or even clever? The dead are likely dull fellows, full of tedious complaints—the ground's too cold, my gravestone should be larger, why does *he* get more worms than I do . . ."

Jon had to stoop to pass through the low door. Within he found a packed dirt floor. There were no furnishings, no sign that people had lived here but for some ashes beneath the smoke hole in the roof. "What a dismal place to live," he said.

"I was born in a house much like this," declared Dolorous Edd. "Those were my enchanted years. Later I fell on hard times." A nest of dry straw bedding filled one corner of the room. Edd looked at it with longing. "I'd give all the gold in Casterly Rock to sleep in a bed again."

"You call that a bed?"

"If it's softer than the ground and has a roof over it, I call it a bed."
Dolorous Edd sniffed the air. "I smell dung."

The smell was very faint. "Old dung," said Jon. The house felt as
though it had been empty for some time. Kneeling, he searched through
the straw with his hands to see if anything had been concealed beneath,
then made a round of the walls. It did not take very long. "There's nothing here."

Nothing was what he had expected; Whitetree was the fourth village
they had passed, and it had been the same in all of them. The people
were gone, vanished with their scant possessions and whatever animals
they may have had. None of the villages showed any signs of having been
attacked. They were simply . . . empty. "What do you think happened
to them all?" Jon asked.

"Something worse than we can imagine," suggested Dolorous Edd.
"Well, *I* might be able to imagine it, but I'd sooner not. Bad enough to
know you're going to come to some awful end without thinking about it
aforetime."

Two of the hounds were sniffing around the door as they reemerged.
Other dogs ranged through the village. Chett was cursing them loudly,
his voice thick with the anger he never seemed to put aside. The light
filtering through the red leaves of the weirwood made the boils on his
face look even more inflamed than usual. When he saw Jon his eyes
narrowed; there was no love lost between them.

The other houses had yielded no wisdom. *"Gone,"* cried Mormont's
raven, flapping up into the weirwood to perch above them. *"Gone, gone,
gone."*

"There were wildlings at Whitetree only a year ago." Thoren
Smallwood looked more a lord than Mormont did, clad in Ser Jaremy
Rykker's gleaming black mail and embossed breastplate. His heavy cloak
was richly trimmed with sable, and clasped with the crossed hammers of
the Rykkers, wrought in silver. Ser Jaremy's cloak, once . . . but the
wight had claimed Ser Jaremy, and the Night's Watch wasted nothing.

"A year ago Robert was king, and the realm was at peace," declared
Jarman Buckwell, the square stolid man who commanded the scouts.
"Much can change in a year's time."

"One thing hasn't changed," Ser Mallador Locke insisted. "Fewer
wildlings means fewer worries. I won't mourn, whatever's become of
them. Raiders and murderers, the lot of them."

Jon heard a rustling from the red leaves above. Two branches parted,
and he glimpsed a little man moving from limb to limb as easily as a
squirrel. Bedwyck stood no more than five feet tall, but the grey streaks
in his hair showed his age. The other rangers called him Giant. He sat in
a fork of the tree over their heads and said, "There's water to the north. A

lake, might be. A few flint hills rising to the west, not very high. Nothing else to see, my lords."

"We might camp here tonight," Smallwood suggested.

The Old Bear glanced up, searching for a glimpse of sky through the pale limbs and red leaves of the weirwood. "No," he declared. "Giant, how much daylight remains to us?"

"Three hours, my lord."

"We'll press on north," Mormont decided. "If we reach this lake, we can make camp by the shore, perchance catch a few fish. Jon, fetch me paper, it's past time I wrote Maester Aemon."

Jon found parchment, quill, and ink in his saddlebag and brought them to the Lord Commander. *At Whitetree*, Mormont scrawled. *The fourth village. All empty. The wildlings are gone.* "Find Tarly and see that he gets this on its way," he said as he handed Jon the message. When he whistled, his raven came flapping down to land on his horse's head. *"Corn,"* the raven suggested, bobbing. The horse whickered.

Jon mounted his garron, wheeled him about, and trotted off. Beyond the shade of the great weirwood the men of the Night's Watch stood beneath lesser trees, tending their horses, chewing strips of salt beef, pissing, scratching, and talking. When the command was given to move out again, the talk died, and they climbed back into their saddles. Jarman Buckwell's scouts rode out first, with the vanguard under Thoren Smallwood heading the column proper. Then came the Old Bear with the main force, Ser Mallador Locke with the baggage train and packhorses, and finally Ser Ottyn Wythers and the rear guard. Two hundred men all told, with half again as many mounts.

By day they followed game trails and streambeds, the "ranger's roads" that led them ever deeper into the wilderness of leaf and root. At night they camped beneath a starry sky and gazed up at the comet. The black brothers had left Castle Black in good spirits, joking and trading tales, but of late the brooding silence of the wood seemed to have sombered them all. Jests had grown fewer and tempers shorter. No one would admit to being afraid—they were men of the Night's Watch, after all—but Jon could feel the unease. Four empty villages, no wildlings anywhere, even the game seemingly fled. The haunted forest had never seemed more haunted, even veteran rangers agreed.

As he rode, Jon peeled off his glove to air his burned fingers. *Ugly things.* He remembered suddenly how he used to muss Arya's hair. His little stick of a sister. He wondered how she was faring. It made him a little sad to think that he might never muss her hair again. He began to flex his hand, opening and closing the fingers. If he let his sword hand stiffen and grow clumsy, it well might be the end of him, he knew. A man needed his sword beyond the Wall.

Jon found Samwell Tarly with the other stewards, watering his horses. He had three to tend: his own mount, and two packhorses, each bearing a large wire-and-wicker cage full of ravens. The birds flapped their wings at Jon's approach and screamed at him through the bars. A few shrieks sounded suspiciously like words. "Have you been teaching them to talk?" he asked Sam.

"A few words. Three of them can say *snow*."

"One bird croaking my name was bad enough," said Jon, "and snow's nothing a black brother wants to hear about." Snow often meant death in the north.

"Was there anything in Whitetree?"

"Bones, ashes, and empty houses." Jon handed Sam the roll of parchment. "The Old Bear wants word sent back to Aemon."

Sam took a bird from one of the cages, stroked its feathers, attached the message, and said, "Fly home now, brave one. Home." The raven *quorked* something unintelligible back at him, and Sam tossed it into the air. Flapping, it beat its way skyward through the trees. "I wish he could carry me with him."

"Still?"

"Well," said Sam, "yes, but . . . I'm not as frightened as I was, truly. The first night, every time I heard someone getting up to make water, I thought it was wildlings creeping in to slit my throat. I was afraid that if I closed my eyes, I might never open them again, only . . . well . . . dawn came after all." He managed a wan smile. "I may be craven, but I'm not *stupid*. I'm sore and my back aches from riding and from sleeping on the ground, but I'm hardly scared at all. Look." He held out a hand for Jon to see how steady it was. "I've been working on my maps."

The world is strange, Jon thought. Two hundred brave men had left the Wall, and the only one who was not growing more fearful was Sam, the self-confessed coward. "We'll make a ranger of you yet," he joked. "Next thing, you'll want to be an outrider like Grenn. Shall I speak to the Old Bear?"

"Don't you dare!" Sam pulled up the hood of his enormous black cloak and clambered awkwardly back onto his horse. It was a plow horse, big and slow and clumsy, but better able to bear his weight than the little garrons the rangers rode. "I had hoped we might stay the night in the village," he said wistfully. "It would be nice to sleep under a roof again."

"Too few roofs for all of us." Jon mounted again, gave Sam a parting smile, and rode off. The column was well under way, so he swung wide around the village to avoid the worst of the congestion. He had seen enough of Whitetree.

Ghost emerged from the undergrowth so suddenly that the garron shied and reared. The white wolf hunted well away from the line of march, but he was not having much better fortune than the foragers Smallwood sent out after game. The woods were as empty as the villages, Dywen had told him one night around the fire. "We're a large party," Jon had said. "The game's probably been frightened away by all the noise we make on the march."

"Frightened away by *something*, no doubt," Dywen said.

Once the horse had settled, Ghost loped along easily beside him. Jon caught up to Mormont as he was wending his way around a hawthorn thicket. "Is the bird away?" the Old Bear asked.

"Yes, my lord. Sam is teaching them to talk."

The Old Bear snorted. "He'll regret that. Damned things make a lot of noise, but they never say a thing worth hearing."

They rode in silence, until Jon said, "If my uncle found all these villages empty as well—"

"—he would have made it his purpose to learn why," Lord Mormont finished for him, "and it may well be someone or something did not want that known. Well, we'll be three hundred when Qhorin joins us. Whatever enemy waits out here will not find us so easy to deal with. We will find them, Jon, I promise you."

Or they will find us, thought Jon.

ARYA

The river was a blue-green ribbon shining in the morning sun. Reeds grew thick in the shallows along the banks, and Arya saw a water snake skimming across the surface, ripples spreading out behind it as it went. Overhead a hawk flew in lazy circles.

It seemed a peaceful place . . . until Koss spotted the dead man. "There, in the reeds." He pointed, and Arya saw it. The body of a soldier, shapeless and swollen. His sodden green cloak had hung up on a rotted log, and a school of tiny silver fishes were nibbling at his face. "I told you there was bodies," Lommy announced. "I could taste them in that water."

When Yoren saw the corpse, he spat. "Dobber, see if he's got anything worth the taking. Mail, knife, a bit o' coin, what have you." He spurred his gelding and rode out into the river, but the horse struggled in the soft mud and beyond the reeds the water deepened. Yoren rode back angry, his horse covered in brown slime up to the knees. "We won't be crossing here. Koss, you'll come with me upriver, look for a ford. Woth, Gerren, you go downstream. The rest o' you wait here. Put a guard out."

Dobber found a leather purse in the dead man's belt. Inside were four coppers and a little hank of blond hair tied up with a red ribbon. Lommy and Tarber stripped naked and went wading, and Lommy scooped up handfuls of slimy mud and threw them at Hot Pie, shouting, "Mud Pie! Mud Pie!" In the back of their wagon, Rorge cursed and threatened and told them to unchain him while Yoren was gone, but no one paid him any mind. Kurz caught a fish with his bare hands. Arya saw how he did it, standing over a shallow pool, calm as still water, his hand darting out quick as a snake when the fish swam near. It didn't look as hard as catching cats. Fish didn't have claws.

It was midday when the others returned. Woth reported a wooden bridge half a mile downstream, but someone had burned it up. Yoren peeled a sourleaf off the bale. "Might be we could swim the horses over, maybe the donkeys, but there's no way we'll get those wagons across. And there's smoke to the north and west, more fires, could be this side o' the river's the place we want to be." He picked up a long stick and drew a circle in the mud, a line trailing down from it. "That's Gods Eye, with the river flowing south. We're here." He poked a hole beside the line of the river, under the circle. "We can't go round west of the lake, like I thought. East takes us back to the kingsroad." He moved the stick up to where the line and circle met. "Near as I recall, there's a town here. The holdfast's stone, and there's a lordling got his seat there too, just a towerhouse, but he'll have a guard, might be a knight or two. We follow the river north, should be there before dark. They'll have boats, so I mean to sell all we got and hire us one." He drew the stick up through the circle of the lake, from bottom to top. "Gods be good, we'll find a wind and sail across the Gods Eye to Harrentown." He thrust the point down at the top of the circle. "We can buy new mounts there, or else take shelter at Harrenhal. That's Lady Whent's seat, and she's always been a friend o' the Watch."

Hot Pie's eyes got wide. "There's ghosts in Harrenhal . . ."

Yoren spat. "There's for your ghosts." He tossed the stick down in the mud. "Mount up."

Arya was remembering the stories Old Nan used to tell of Harrenhal. Evil King Harren had walled himself up inside, so Aegon unleashed his dragons and turned the castle into a pyre. Nan said that fiery spirits still haunted the blackened towers. Sometimes men went to sleep safe in their beds and were found dead in the morning, all burnt up. Arya didn't really believe that, and anyhow it had all happened a long time ago. Hot Pie was being silly; it wouldn't be ghosts at Harrenhal, it would be *knights*. Arya could reveal herself to Lady Whent, and the knights would escort her home and keep her safe. That was what knights did; they kept you safe, especially women. Maybe Lady Whent would even help the crying girl.

The river track was no kingsroad, yet it was not half bad for what it was, and for once the wagons rolled along smartly. They saw the first house an hour shy of evenfall, a snug little thatch-roofed cottage surrounded by fields of wheat. Yoren rode out ahead, hallooing, but got no answer. "Dead, might be. Or hiding. Dobber, Rey, with me." The three men went into the cottage. "Pots is gone, no sign o' any coin laid by," Yoren muttered when they returned. "No animals. Run, most like. Might be we met 'em on the kingsroad." At least the house and field had not been burned, and there were no corpses about. Tarber found a garden out back, and they pulled some onions and radishes and filled a sack with cabbages before they went on their way.

A little farther up the road, they glimpsed a forester's cabin surrounded by old trees and neatly stacked logs ready for the splitting, and later a ramshackle stilt-house leaning over the river on poles ten feet tall, both deserted. They passed more fields, wheat and corn and barley ripening in the sun, but here there were no men sitting in trees, nor walking the rows with scythes. Finally the town came into view; a cluster of white houses spread out around the walls of the holdfast, a big sept with a shingled wooden roof, the lord's towerhouse sitting on a small rise to the west . . . and no sign of any people, anywhere.

Yoren sat on his horse, frowning through his tangle of beard. "Don't like it," he said, "but there it is. We'll go have us a look. A *careful* look. See maybe there's some folk hiding. Might be they left a boat behind, or some weapons we can use."

The black brother left ten to guard the wagons and the whimpery little girl, and split the rest of them into four groups of five to search the town. "Keep your eyes and ears open," he warned them, before he rode off to the towerhouse to see if there was any sign of the lordling or his guards.

Arya found herself with Gendry, Hot Pie, and Lommy. Squat, kettle-bellied Woth had pulled an oar on a galley once, which made him the next best thing they had to a sailor, so Yoren told him to take them down to the lakefront and see if they could find a boat. As they rode between the silent white houses, gooseprickles crawled up Arya's arms. This empty town frightened her almost as much as the burnt holdfast where they'd found the crying girl and the one-armed woman. Why would people run off and leave their homes and everything? What could scare them so much?

The sun was low to the west, and the houses cast long dark shadows. A sudden clap of sound made Arya reach for Needle, but it was only a shutter banging in the wind. After the open river shore, the closeness of the town unnerved her.

When she glimpsed the lake ahead between houses and trees, Arya put her knees into her horse, galloping past Woth and Gendry. She burst out onto the grassy sward beside the pebbled shore. The setting sun made the tranquil surface of the water shimmer like a sheet of beaten copper. It was the biggest lake she had ever seen, with no hint of a far shore. She saw a rambling inn to her left, built out over the water on heavy wooden pilings. To her right, a long pier jutted into the lake, and there were other docks farther east, wooden fingers reaching out from the town. But the only boat in view was an upside-down rowboat abandoned on the rocks beneath the inn, its bottom thoroughly rotted out. "They're gone," Arya said, dejected. What would they do now?

"There's an inn," Lommy said, when the others rode up. "Do you think they left any food? Or ale?"

"Let's go see," Hot Pie suggested.

"Never you mind about no inn," snapped Woth. "Yoren said we're to find a boat."

"They took the boats." Somehow Arya knew it was true; they could search the whole town, and they'd find no more than the upside-down rowboat. Despondent, she climbed off her horse and knelt by the lake. The water lapped softly around her legs. A few lantern bugs were coming out, their little lights blinking on and off. The green water was warm as tears, but there was no salt in it. It tasted of summer and mud and growing things. Arya plunged her face down into it to wash off the dust and dirt and sweat of the day. When she leaned back the trickles ran down the back of her neck and under her collar. They felt good. She wished she could take off her clothes and swim, gliding through the warm water like an skinny pink otter. Maybe she could swim all the way to Winterfell.

Woth was shouting at her to help search, so she did, peering into boathouses and sheds while her horse grazed along the shore. They found some sails, some nails, buckets of tar gone hard, and a mother cat with a litter of new-born kittens. But no boats.

The town was as dark as any forest when Yoren and the others reappeared. "Tower's empty," he said. "Lord's gone off to fight maybe, or to get his smallfolk to safety, no telling. Not a horse or pig left in town, but we'll eat. Saw a goose running loose, and some chickens, and there's good fish in the Gods Eye."

"The boats are gone," Arya reported.

"We could patch the bottom of that rowboat," said Koss.

"Might do for four o' us," Yoren said.

"There's nails," Lommy pointed out. "And there's trees all around. We could build us all boats."

Yoren spat. "You know anything 'bout boat-building, dyer's boy?" Lommy looked blank.

"A raft," suggested Gendry. "Anyone can build a raft, and long poles for pushing."

Yoren looked thoughtful. "Lake's too deep to pole across, but if we stayed to the shallows near shore . . . it'd mean leaving the wagons. Might be that's best. I'll sleep on it."

"Can we stay at the inn?" Lommy asked.

"We'll stay in the holdfast, with the gates barred," the old man said. "I like the feel o' stone walls about me when I sleep."

Arya could not keep quiet. "We shouldn't stay here," she blurted. "The people didn't. They all ran off, even their lord."

"Arry's scared," Lommy announced, braying laughter.

"I'm *not*," she snapped back, "but *they* were."

"Smart boy," said Yoren. "Thing is, the folks who lived here were at war, like it or no. We're not. Night's Watch takes no part, so no man's our enemy."

And no man's our friend, she thought, but this time she held her tongue. Lommy and the rest were looking at her, and she did not want to seem craven in front of them.

The holdfast gates were studded with iron nails. Within, they found a pair of iron bars the size of saplings, with post holes in the ground and metal brackets on the gate. When they slotted the bars through the brackets, they made a huge X brace. It was no Red Keep, Yoren announced when they'd explored the holdfast top to bottom, but it was better than most, and should do for a night well enough. The walls were rough unmortared stone ten feet high, with a wooden catwalk inside the battlements. There was a postern gate to the north, and Gerren discovered a trap under the straw in the old wooden barn, leading to a narrow, winding tunnel. He followed it a long way under the earth and came out by the lake. Yoren had them roll a wagon on top of the trap, to make certain no one came in that way. He divided them into three watches, and sent Tarber, Kurz, and Cutjack off to the abandoned towerhouse to keep an eye out from on high. Kurz had a hunting horn to sound if danger threatened.

They drove their wagons and animals inside and barred the gates behind them. The barn was a ramshackle thing, large enough to hold half the animals in the town. The haven, where the townfolk would shelter in times of trouble, was even larger, low and long and built of stone, with a thatched roof. Koss went out the postern gate and brought the goose back, and two chickens as well, and Yoren allowed a cookfire. There was a big kitchen inside the holdfast, though all the pots and kettles had been taken. Gendry, Dobber, and Arya drew cook duty. Dobber told Arya to pluck the fowl while Gendry split wood. "Why can't I split the wood?" she asked, but no one listened. Sullenly, she set to plucking a chicken while Yoren sat on the end of the bench sharpening the edge of his dirk with a whetstone.

When the food was ready, Arya ate a chicken leg and a bit of onion. No one talked much, not even Lommy. Gendry went off by himself afterward, polishing his helm with a look on his face like he wasn't even there. The crying girl whimpered and wept, but when Hot Pie offered her a bit of goose she gobbled it down and looked for more.

Arya drew second watch, so she found a straw pallet in the haven. Sleep did not come easy, so she borrowed Yoren's stone and set to honing Needle. Syrio Forel had said that a dull blade was like a lame horse. Hot Pie squatted on the pallet beside her, watching her work. "Where'd you get a good sword like that?" he asked. When he saw the look she gave him, he raised his hands defensively. "I never said you stole it, I just wanted to know where you got it, is all."

"My brother gave it to me," she muttered.

"I never knew you had no brother."

Arya paused to scratch under her shirt. There were fleas in the straw, though she couldn't see why a few more would bother her. "I have lots of brothers."

"You do? Are they bigger than you, or littler?"

I shouldn't be talking like this. Yoren said I should keep my mouth shut. "Bigger," she lied. "They have swords too, big longswords, and they showed me how to kill people who bother me."

"I was talking, not bothering." Hot Pie went off and let her alone and Arya curled up on her pallet. She could hear the crying girl from the far side of the haven. *I wish she'd just be quiet. Why does she have to cry all the time?*

She must have slept, though she never remembered closing her eyes. She dreamed a wolf was howling, and the sound was so terrible that it woke her at once. Arya sat up on her pallet with her heart thumping. "Hot Pie, wake up." She scrambled to her feet. "Woth, Gendry, didn't you hear?" She pulled on a boot.

All around her, men and boys stirred and crawled from their pallets. "What's wrong?" Hot Pie asked. "Hear what?" Gendry wanted to know. "Arry had a bad dream," someone else said.

"No, I heard it," she insisted. "A wolf."

"Arry has wolves in his head," sneered Lommy. "Let them howl," Gerren said, "they're out there, we're in here." Woth agreed. "Never saw no wolf could storm a holdfast." Hot Pie was saying, "I never heard nothing."

"It was a *wolf*," she shouted at them as she yanked on her second boot. "Something's wrong, someone's coming, get *up!*"

Before they could hoot her down again, the sound came shuddering through the night—only it was no wolf this time, it was Kurz blowing his hunting horn, sounding danger. In a heartbeat, all of them were pulling on clothes and snatching for whatever weapons they owned. Arya ran for the gate as the horn sounded again. As she dashed past the barn, Biter threw himself furiously against his chains, and Jaqen H'ghar called out from the back of their wagon. "Boy! Sweet boy! Is it war, red war? Boy, free us. A man can fight. *Boy!*" She ignored him and plunged on. By then she could hear horses and shouts beyond the wall.

She scrambled up onto the catwalk. The parapets were a bit too high and Arya a bit too short; she had to wedge her toes into the holes between the stones to see over. For a moment she thought the town was full of lantern bugs. Then she realized they were men with torches, galloping between the houses. She saw a roof go up, flames licking at the belly of the night with hot orange tongues as the thatch caught. Another followed, and then another, and soon there were fires blazing everywhere.

Gendry climbed up beside her, wearing his helm. "How many?"

Arya tried to count, but they were riding too fast, torches spinning through the air as they flung them. "A hundred," she said. "Two hundred, I don't know." Over the roar of the flames, she could hear shouts. "They'll come for us soon."

"There," Gendry said, pointing.

A column of riders moved between the burning buildings toward the holdfast. Firelight glittered off metal helms and spattered their mail and plate with orange and yellow highlights. One carried a banner on a tall lance. She thought it was red, but it was hard to tell in the night, with the fires roaring all around. Everything seemed red or black or orange.

The fire leapt from one house to another. Arya saw a tree consumed, the flames creeping across its branches until it stood against the night in robes of living orange. Everyone was awake now, manning the catwalks or struggling with the frightened animals below. She could hear Yoren shouting commands. Something bumped against her leg, and she glanced down to discover the crying girl clutching her. "Get away!" She wrenched her leg free. "What are you doing up here? Run and hide someplace, you stupid." She shoved the girl away.

The riders reined up before the gates. *"You in the holdfast!"* shouted a knight in a tall helm with a spiked crest. *"Open, in the name of the king!"*

"Aye, and which king is that?" old Reysen yelled back down, before Woth cuffed him into silence.

Yoren climbed the battlement beside the gate, his faded black cloak tied to a wooden staff. *"You men hold down here!"* he shouted. *"The townfolk's gone."*

"And who are you, old man? One of Lord Beric's cravens?" called the knight in the spiked helm. "If that fat fool Thoros is in there, ask him how he likes *these* fires."

"Got no such man here," Yoren shouted back. "Only some lads for the

Watch. Got no part o' your war." He hoisted up the staff, so they could all see the color of his cloak. "Have a look. That's black, for the Night's Watch."

"Or black for House Dondarrion," called the man who bore the enemy banner. Arya could see its colors more clearly now in the light of the burning town: a golden lion on red. "Lord Beric's sigil is a purple lightning bolt on a black field."

Suddenly Arya remembered the morning she had thrown the orange in Sansa's face and gotten juice all over her stupid ivory silk gown. There had been some southron lordling at the tourney, her sister's stupid friend Jeyne was in love with him. He had a lightning bolt on his shield and her father had sent him out to behead the Hound's brother. It seemed a thousand years ago now, something that had happened to a different person in a different life . . . to Arya Stark the Hand's daughter, not Arry the orphan boy. How would Arry know lords and such?

"Are you blind, man?" Yoren waved his staff back and forth, making the cloak ripple. "You see a bloody lightning bolt?"

"By night all banners look black," the knight in the spiked helm observed. "Open, or we'll know you for outlaws in league with the king's enemies."

Yoren spat. "Who's got your command?"

"I do." The reflections of burning houses glimmered dully on the armor of his warhorse as the others parted to let him pass. He was a stout man with a manticore on his shield, and ornate scrollwork crawling across his steel breastplate. Through the open visor of his helm, a face pale and piggy peered up. "Ser Amory Lorch, bannerman to Lord Tywin Lannister of Casterly Rock, the Hand of the King. The *true* king, Joffrey." He had a high, thin voice. "In his name, I command you to open these gates."

All around them, the town burned. The night air was full of smoke, and the drifting red embers outnumbered the stars. Yoren scowled. "Don't see the need. Do what you want to the town, it's naught to me, but leave us be. We're no foes to you."

Look with your eyes, Arya wanted to shout at the men below. "Can't they *see* we're no lords or knights?" she whispered.

"I don't think they care, Arry," Gendry whispered back.

And she looked at Ser Amory's face, the way Syrio had taught her to look, and she saw that he was right.

"If you are no traitors, open your gates," Ser Amory called. "We'll make certain you're telling it true and be on our way."

Yoren was chewing sourleaf. "Told you, no one here but us. You got my word on that."

The knight in the spiked helm laughed. "The crow gives us his *word*."

"You lost, old man?" mocked one of the spearmen. "The Wall's a long way north o' here."

"I command you once more, in King Joffrey's name, to prove the loyalty you profess and open these gates," said Ser Amory.

For a long moment Yoren considered, chewing. Then he spat. "Don't think I will."

"So be it. You defy the king's command, and so proclaim yourselves rebels, black cloaks or no."

"Got me young boys in here," Yoren shouted down.

"Young boys and old men die the same." Ser Amory raised a lanquid fist, and a spear came hurtling from the fire-bright shadows behind. Yoren must have been the target, but it was Woth beside him who was hit. The spearhead went in his throat and exploded out the back of his neck, dark and wet. Woth grabbed at the shaft, and fell boneless from the walk.

"Storm the walls and kill them all," Ser Amory said in a bored voice. More spears flew. Arya yanked down Hot Pie by the back of his tunic. From outside came the rattle of armor, the scrape of swords on scabbards, the banging of spears on shields, mingled with curses and the hoofbeats of racing horses. A torch sailed spinning above their heads, trailing fingers of fire as it thumped down in the dirt of the yard.

"*Blades!*" Yoren shouted. "Spread apart, defend the wall wherever they hit. Koss, Urreg, hold the postern. Lommy, pull that spear out of Woth and get up where he was."

Hot Pie dropped his shortsword when he tried to unsheath it. Arya shoved the blade back into his hand. "I don't know how to swordfight," he said, white-eyed.

"It's easy," Arya said, but the lie died in her throat as a *hand* grasped the top of the parapet. She saw it by the light of the burning town, so clear that it was as if time had stopped. The fingers were blunt, callused, wiry black hairs grew between the knuckles, there was dirt under the nail of the thumb. *Fear cuts deeper than swords,* she remembered as the top of a pothelm loomed up behind the hand.

She slashed down hard, and Needle's castle-forged steel bit into the grasping fingers between the knuckles. "*Winterfell!*" she screamed. Blood spurted, fingers flew, and the helmed face vanished as suddenly as it had appeared. "Behind!" Hot Pie yelled. Arya whirled. The second man was bearded and helmetless, his dirk between his teeth to leave both hands free for climbing. As he swung his leg over the parapet, she drove her point at his eyes. Needle never touched him; he reeled backward and fell. *I hope he falls on his face and cuts off his tongue.* "Watch *them*, not me!" she screamed at Hot Pie. The next time someone tried to climb their part of the wall, the boy hacked at his hands with his swordshort until the man dropped away.

Ser Amory had no ladders, but the holdfast walls were rough-cut and unmortared, easy to climb, and there seemed to be no end to the foes. For each one Arya cut or stabbed or shoved back, another was coming over the wall. The knight in the spiked helm reached the rampart, but Yoren tangled his black banner around his spike, and forced the point of his dirk through his armor while the man was fighting the cloth. Every time Arya looked up, more torches were flying, trailing long tongues of flame that lingered behind her eyes. She saw a gold lion on a red banner and thought of Joffrey, wishing he was here so she could drive Needle through his sneery face. When four men assaulted the gate with axes, Koss shot them down with arrows, one by one. Dobber wrestled a man off the walk, and Lommy smashed his head with a rock before he could rise, and hooted until he saw the knife in Dobber's belly and realized he wouldn't be getting up either. Arya jumped over a dead boy no older than Jon, lying with his arm cut off. She didn't think she'd done it, but she wasn't sure. She heard Qyle beg for mercy before a knight with a wasp on his shield smashed his face in with a spiked mace. Everything smelled of blood and smoke and iron and piss, but after a time it seemed like that was only one smell. She never saw how the skinny man got over the wall, but when he did she fell on him with Gendry and Hot Pie. Gendry's sword shattered on the man's helm, tearing it off his head. Underneath he was bald and scared-looking, with missing teeth and a speckly grey beard, but even as she was feeling sorry for him she was killing him, shouting, *"Winterfell! Winterfell!"* while Hot Pie screamed *"Hot Pie!"* beside her as he hacked at the man's scrawny neck.

When the skinny man was dead, Gendry stole his sword and leapt down into the yard to fight some more. Arya looked past him, and saw steel shadows running through the holdfast, firelight shining off mail and blades, and she knew that they'd gotten over the wall somewhere, or broken through at the postern. She jumped down beside Gendry, landing the way Syrio had taught her. The night rang to the clash of steel and the cries of the wounded and dying. For a moment Arya stood uncertain, not knowing which way to go. Death was all around her.

And then Yoren was there, shaking her, screaming in her face. *"Boy!"* he yelled, the way he always yelled it. "Get *out*, it's done, we've lost. Herd up all you can, you and him and the others, the boys, you get them out. *Now!*"

"How?" Arya said.

"That trap," he screamed. "Under the barn."

Quick as that he was gone, off to fight, sword in hand. Arya grabbed

Gendry by the arm. "He said *go*," she shouted, "the barn, the way out." Through the slits of his helm, the Bull's eyes shone with reflected fire. He nodded. They called Hot Pie down from the wall and found Lommy Greenhands where he lay bleeding from a spear thrust through his calf. They found Gerren too, but he was hurt too bad to move. As they were running toward the barn, Arya spied the crying girl sitting in the middle of the chaos, surrounded by smoke and slaughter. She grabbed her by the hand and pulled her to her feet as the others raced ahead. The girl wouldn't walk, even when slapped. Arya dragged her with her right hand while she held Needle in the left. Ahead, the night was a sullen red. *The barn's on fire,* she thought. Flames were licking up its sides from where a torch had fallen on straw, and she could hear the screaming of the animals trapped within. Hot Pie stepped out of the barn. "Arry, *come on!* Lommy's *gone,* leave her if she won't come!"

Stubbornly, Arya dragged all the harder, pulling the crying girl along. Hot Pie scuttled back inside, abandoning them . . . but Gendry came back, the fire shining so bright on his polished helm that the horns seemed to glow orange. He ran to them, and hoisted the crying girl up over his shoulder. *"Run!"*

Rushing through the barn doors was like running into a furnace. The air was swirling with smoke, the back wall a sheet of fire ground to roof. Their horses and donkeys were kicking and rearing and screaming. *The poor animals,* Arya thought. Then she saw the wagon, and the three men manacled to its bed. Biter was flinging himself against the chains, blood running down his arms from where the irons clasped his wrists. Rorge screamed curses, kicking at the wood. "Boy!" called Jaqen H'ghar. "Sweet boy!"

The open trap was only a few feet ahead, but the fire was spreading fast, consuming the old wood and dry straw faster than she would have believed. Arya remembered the Hound's horrible burned face. "Tunnel's narrow," Gendry shouted. "How do we get her through?"

"Pull her," Arya said. "Push her."

"Good boys, kind boys," called Jaqen H'ghar, coughing.

"Get these fucking chains off!" Rorge screamed.

Gendry ignored them. "You go first, then her, then me. Hurry, it's a long way."

"When you split the firewood," Arya remembered, "where did you leave the axe?"

"Out by the haven." He spared a glance for the chained men. "I'd save the donkeys first. There's no time."

"You take her!" she yelled. "You get her out! You do it!" The fire beat at her back with hot red wings as she fled the burning barn. It felt blessedly cool outside, but men were dying all around her. She saw Koss throw down his blade to yield, and she saw them kill him where he stood. Smoke was everywhere. There was no sign of Yoren, but the axe was where Gendry had left it, by the woodpile outside the haven. As she wrenched it free, a mailed hand grabbed her arm. Spinning, Arya drove the head of the axe hard between his legs. She never saw his face, only the dark blood seeping between the links of his hauberk. Going back into that barn was the hardest thing she ever did. Smoke was pouring out the open door like a writhing black snake, and she could hear the screams of the poor animals inside, donkeys and horses and men. She chewed her lip, and darted through the doors, crouched low where the smoke wasn't quite so thick.

A donkey was caught in a ring of fire, shrieking in terror and pain. She could smell the stench of burning hair. The roof was gone up too, and things were falling down, pieces of flaming wood and bits of straw and hay. Arya put a hand over her mouth and nose. She couldn't see the wagon for the smoke, but she could still hear Biter screaming. She crawled toward the sound.

And then a wheel was looming over her. The wagon *jumped* and moved a half foot when Biter threw himself against his chains again. Jaqen saw her, but it was too hard to breathe, let alone talk. She threw the axe into the wagon. Rorge caught it and lifted it over his head, rivers of sooty sweat pouring down his noseless face. Arya was running, coughing. She heard the steel crash through the old wood, and again, again. An instant later came a *crack* as loud as thunder, and the bottom of the wagon came ripping loose in an explosion of splinters.

Arya rolled headfirst into the tunnel and dropped five feet. She got dirt in her mouth but she didn't care, the taste was fine, the taste was mud and water and worms and life. Under the earth the air was cool and dark. Above was nothing but blood and roaring red and choking smoke and the screams of dying horses. She moved her belt around so Needle would not be in her way, and began to crawl. A dozen feet down the tunnel she heard the sound, like the roar of some monstrous beast, and a cloud of hot smoke and black dust came billowing up behind her, smelling of hell. Arya held her breath and kissed the mud on the floor of the tunnel and cried. For whom, she could not say.

TYRION

The queen was not disposed to wait on Varys. "Treason is vile enough," she declared furiously, "but this is barefaced naked villainy, and I do not need that mincing eunuch to tell me what must be done with villains."

Tyrion took the letters from his sister's hand and compared them side by side. There were two copies, the words exactly alike, though they had been written by different hands.

"Maester Frenken received the first missive at Castle Stokeworth," Grand Maester Pycelle explained. "The second copy came through Lord Gyles."

Littlefinger fingered his beard. "If Stannis bothered with *them*, it's past certain every other lord in the Seven Kingdoms saw a copy as well."

"I want these letters burned, every one," Cersei declared. "No hint of this must reach my son's ears, or my father's."

"I imagine Father's heard rather more than a hint by now," Tyrion said dryly. "Doubtless Stannis sent a bird to Casterly Rock, and another to Harrenhal. As for burning the letters, to what point? The song is sung, the wine is spilled, the wench is pregnant. And this is not as dire as it seems, in truth."

Cersei turned on him in green-eyed fury. "Are you utterly witless? Did you read what he says? *The boy Joffrey*, he calls him. And he dares to accuse *me* of incest, adultery, and treason!"

Only because you're guilty. It was astonishing to see how angry Cersei could wax over accusations she knew perfectly well to be true. *If we lose the war, she ought to take up mummery, she has a gift for it.* Tyrion waited until she was done and said, "Stannis must have some pretext to justify his rebellion. What did you expect him to write? 'Joffrey is my brother's trueborn son and heir, but I mean to take his throne for all that'?"

"I will not suffer to be called a whore!"

Why, sister, he never claims Jaime paid you. Tyrion made a show of glancing over the writing again. There had been some niggling phrase . . . "Done in the Light of the Lord," he read. "A queer choice of words, that."

Pycelle cleared his throat. "These words often appear in letters and documents from the Free Cities. They mean no more than, let us say, *written in the sight of god.* The god of the red priests. It is their usage, I do believe."

"Varys told us some years past that Lady Selyse had taken up with a red priest," Littlefinger reminded them.

Tyrion tapped the paper. "And now it would seem her lord husband has done the same. We can use that against him. Urge the High Septon to reveal how Stannis has turned against the gods as well as his rightful king . . ."

"Yes, yes," the queen said impatiently, "but first we must stop this filth from spreading further. The council must issue an edict. Any man heard speaking of incest or calling Joff a bastard should lose his tongue for it."

"A prudent measure," said Grand Maester Pycelle, his chain of office clinking as he nodded.

"A folly," sighed Tyrion. "When you tear out a man's tongue, you are not proving him a liar, you're only telling the world that you fear what he might say."

"So what would *you* have us do?" his sister demanded.

"Very little. Let them whisper, they'll grow bored with the tale soon enough. Any man with a thimble of sense will see it for a clumsy attempt to justify usurping the crown. Does Stannis offer proof? How could he, when it never happened?" Tyrion gave his sister his sweetest smile.

"That's so," she had to say. "Still . . ."

"Your Grace, your brother has the right of this." Petyr Baelish steepled his fingers. "If we attempt to silence this talk, we only lend it credence. Better to treat it with contempt, like the pathetic lie it is. And meantime, fight fire with fire."

Cersei gave him a measuring look. "What sort of fire?"

"A tale of somewhat the same nature, perhaps. But more easily believed. Lord Stannis has spent most of his marriage apart from his wife. Not that I fault him, I'd do the same were I married to Lady Selyse. Nonetheless, if we put it about that her daughter is baseborn and Stannis a cuckold, well . . . the smallfolk are always eager to believe the worst of their lords, particularly those as stern, sour, and prickly proud as Stannis Baratheon."

"He has never been much loved, that's true." Cersei considered a moment. "So we pay him back in his own coin. Yes, I like this. Who can we name as Lady Selyse's lover? She has two brothers, I believe. And one of her uncles has been with her on Dragonstone all this time . . ."

"Ser Axell Florent is her castellan." Loath as Tyrion was to admit it, Littlefinger's scheme had promise. Stannis had never been enamored of his wife, but he was bristly as a hedgehog where his honor was concerned and mistrustful by nature. If they could sow discord between him and his followers, it could only help their cause. "The child has the Florent ears, I'm told."

Littlefinger gestured languidly. "A trade envoy from Lys once observed to me that Lord Stannis must love his daughter very well, since he'd erected hundreds of statues of her all along the walls of Dragonstone. 'My lord,' I had to tell him, 'those are gargoyles.' " He chuckled. "Ser Axell might serve for Shireen's father, but in my experience, the more bizarre and shocking a tale the more apt it is to be repeated. Stannis keeps an especially grotesque fool, a lackwit with a tattooed face."

Grand Maester Pycelle gaped at him, aghast. "Surely you do not mean to suggest that Lady Selyse would bring a *fool* into her bed?"

"You'd have to be a fool to want to bed Selyse Florent," said Littlefinger. "Doubtless Patchface reminded her of Stannis. And the best lies contain within them nuggets of truth, enough to give a listener pause. As it happens, this fool is utterly devoted to the girl and follows her everywhere. They even look somewhat alike. Shireen has a mottled, half-frozen face as well."

Pycelle was lost. "But that is from the greyscale that near killed her as a babe, poor thing."

"I like my tale better," said Littlefinger, "and so will the smallfolk. Most of them believe that if a woman eats rabbit while pregnant, her child will be born with long floppy ears."

Cersei smiled the sort of smile she customarily reserved for Jaime. "Lord Petyr, you are a wicked creature."

"Thank you, Your Grace."

"And a most accomplished liar," Tyrion added, less warmly. *This one is more dangerous than I knew,* he reflected.

Littlefinger's grey-green eyes met the dwarf's mismatched stare with no hint of unease. "We all have our gifts, my lord."

The queen was too caught up in her revenge to take note of the exchange. "Cuckolded by a halfwit fool! Stannis will be laughed at in every winesink this side of the narrow sea."

"The story should not come from us," Tyrion said, "or it will be seen for a self-serving lie." *Which it is, to be sure.*

Once more Littlefinger supplied the answer. "Whores love to gossip, and as it happens I own a brothel or three. And no doubt Varys can plant seeds in the alehouses and pot-shops."

"Varys," Cersei said, frowning. "Where *is* Varys?"

"I have been wondering about that myself, Your Grace."

"The Spider spins his secret webs day and night," Grand Maester Pycelle said ominously. "I mistrust that one, my lords."

"And he speaks so kindly of you." Tyrion pushed himself off his chair. As it happened, he knew what the eunuch was about, but it was nothing the other councillors needed to hear. "Pray excuse me, my lords. Other business calls."

Cersei was instantly suspicious. "King's business?"

"Nothing you need trouble yourself about."

"I'll be the judge of that."

"Would you spoil my surprise?" Tyrion said. "I'm having a gift made for Joffrey. A little chain."

"What does he need with another chain? He has gold chains and silver, more than he can wear. If you think for a moment you can buy Joff's love with gifts—"

"Why, surely I *have* the king's love, as he has mine. And *this* chain I believe he may one day treasure above all others." The little man bowed and waddled to the door.

Bronn was waiting outside the council chambers to escort him back to the Tower of the Hand. "The smiths are in your audience chamber, waiting your pleasure," he said as they crossed the ward.

"Waiting my pleasure. I like the ring of that, Bronn. You almost sound a proper courtier. Next you'll be kneeling."

"Fuck you, dwarf."

"That's Shae's task." Tyrion heard Lady Tanda calling to him merrily from the top of the serpentine steps. Pretending not to notice her, he waddled a bit faster. "See that my litter is readied, I'll be leaving the castle as soon as I'm done here." Two of the Moon Brothers had the door guard. Tyrion greeted them pleasantly, and grimaced before starting up the stairs. The climb to his bedchamber made his legs ache.

Within he found a boy of twelve laying out clothing on the bed; his squire, such that he was. Podrick Payne was so shy he was furtive.

Tyrion had never quite gotten over the suspicion that his father had inflicted the boy on him as a joke.

"Your garb, my lord," the boy mumbled when Tyrion entered, staring down at his boots. Even when he worked up the courage to speak, Pod could never quite manage to look at you. "For the audience. And your chain. The Hand's chain."

"Very good. Help me dress." The doublet was black velvet covered with golden studs in the shape of lions' heads, the chain a loop of solid gold hands, the fingers of each clasping the wrist of the next. Pod brought him a cloak of crimson silk fringed in gold, cut to his height. On a normal man, it would be no more than a half cape.

The Hand's private audience chamber was not so large as the king's, nor a patch on the vastness of the throne room, but Tyrion liked its Myrish rugs, wall hangings, and sense of intimacy. As he entered, his steward cried out, "Tyrion Lannister, Hand of the King." He liked that too. The gaggle of smiths, armorers, and ironmongers that Bronn had collected fell to their knees.

He hoisted himself up into the high seat under the round golden window and bid them rise. "Goodmen, I know you are all busy, so I will be succinct. Pod, if you please." The boy handed him a canvas sack. Tyrion yanked the drawstring and upended the bag. Its contents spilled onto the rug with a muffled *thunk* of metal on wool. "I had these made at the castle forge. I want a thousand more just like them."

One of the smiths knelt to inspect the object: three immense steel links, twisted together. "A mighty chain."

"Mighty, but short," the dwarf replied. "Somewhat like me. I fancy one a good deal longer. Do you have a name?"

"They call me Ironbelly, m'lord." The smith was squat and broad, plainly dressed in wool and leather, but his arms were as thick as a bull's neck.

"I want every forge in King's Landing turned to making these links and joining them. All other work is to be put aside. I want every man who knows the art of working metal set to this task, be he master, journeyman, or apprentice. When I ride up the Street of Steel, I want to hear hammers ringing, night or day. And I want a man, a strong man, to see that all this is done. Are you that man, Goodman Ironbelly?"

"Might be I am, m'lord. But what of the mail and swords the queen was wanting?"

Another smith spoke up. "Her Grace commanded us to make chainmail and armor, swords and daggers and axes, all in great numbers. For arming her new gold cloaks, m'lord."

"That work can wait," Tyrion said. "The chain first."

"M'lord, begging your pardon, Her Grace said those as didn't meet their numbers would have their hands crushed," the anxious smith persisted. "Smashed on their own anvils, she said."

Sweet Cersei, always striving to make the smallfolk love us. "No one will have their hands smashed. You have my word on it."

"Iron is grown dear," Ironbelly declared, "and this chain will be needing much of it, and coke beside, for the fires."

"Lord Baelish will see that you have coin as you need it," Tyrion promised. He could count on Littlefinger for that much, he hoped. "I will command the City Watch to help you find iron. Melt down every horseshoe in this city if you must."

An older man moved forward, richly dressed in a damask tunic with silver fastenings and a cloak lined with foxfur. He knelt to examine the great steel links Tyrion had dumped on the floor. "My lord," he announced gravely, "this is crude work at best. There is no art to it. Suitable labor for common smiths, no doubt, for men who bend horseshoes and hammer out kettles, but I am a master armorer, as it please my lord. This is no work for me, nor my fellow masters. We make swords as sharp as song, armor such as a god might wear. Not *this*."

Tyrion tilted his head to the side and gave the man a dose of his mismatched eyes. "What is your name, master armorer?"

"Salloreon, as it please my lord. If the King's Hand will permit, I should be *most* honored to forge him a suit of armor suitable to his House and high office." Two of the others sniggered, but Salloreon plunged ahead, heedless. "Plate and scale, I think. The scales gilded bright as the sun, the plate enameled a deep Lannister crimson. I would suggest a demon's head for a helm, crowned with tall golden horns. When you ride into battle, men will shrink away in fear."

A demon's head, Tyrion thought ruefully, *now what does that say of me?* "Master Salloreon, I plan to fight the rest of my battles from this chair. It's links I need, not demon horns. So let me put it to you this way. You will make chains, or you will wear them. The choice is yours." He rose, and took his leave with nary a backward glance.

Bronn was waiting by the gate with his litter and an escort of mounted Black Ears. "You know where we're bound," Tyrion told him. He accepted a hand up into the litter. He had done all he could to feed the hungry city—he'd set several hundred carpenters to building fishing boats in place of catapults, opened the kingswood to any hunter who dared to cross the river, even sent gold cloaks foraging to the west and south—yet he still saw accusing eyes everywhere he rode. The litter's curtains shielded him from that, and besides gave him leisure to think.

As they wound their slow way down twisty Shadowblack Lane to the foot of Aegon's High Hill, Tyrion reflected on the events of the morning. His sister's ire had led her to overlook the true significance of Stannis

Baratheon's letter. Without proof, his accusations were nothing; what mattered was that he had named himself a king. *And what will Renly make of that?* They could not *both* sit the Iron Throne.

Idly, he pushed the curtain back a few inches to peer out at the streets. Black Ears rode on both sides of him, their grisly necklaces looped about their throats, while Bronn went in front to clear the way. He watched the passersby watching him, and played a little game with himself, trying to sort the informers from the rest. *The ones who look the most suspicious are likely innocent,* he decided. *It's the ones who look innocent I need to beware.*

His destination was behind the hill of Rhaenys, and the streets were crowded. Almost an hour had passed before the litter swayed to a stop. Tyrion was dozing, but he woke abruptly when the motion ceased, rubbed the sand from his eyes, and accepted Bronn's hand to climb down.

The house was two stories tall, stone below and timber above. A round turret rose from one corner of the structure. Many of the windows were leaded. Over the door swung an ornate lamp, a globe of gilded metal and scarlet glass.

"A brothel," Bronn said. "What do you mean to do here?"

"What does one usually do in a brothel?"

The sellsword laughed. "Shae's not enough?"

"She was pretty enough for a camp follower, but I'm no longer in camp. Little men have big appetites, and I'm told the girls here are fit for a king."

"Is the boy old enough?"

"Not Joffrey. Robert. This house was a great favorite of his." *Although Joffrey may indeed be old enough. An interesting notion, that.* "If you and the Black Ears care to amuse yourselves, feel free, but Chataya's girls are costly. You'll find cheaper houses all along the street. Leave one man here who'll know where to find the others when I wish to return."

Bronn nodded. "As you say." The Black Ears were all grins.

Inside the door, a tall woman in flowing silks was waiting for him. She had ebon skin and sandalwood eyes. "I am Chataya," she announced, bowing deeply. "And you are—"

"Let us not get into the habit of names. Names are dangerous." The air smelled of some exotic spice, and the floor beneath his feet displayed a mosaic of two women entwined in love. "You have a pleasant establishment."

"I have labored long to make it so. I am glad the Hand is pleased." Her voice was flowing amber, liquid with the accents of the distant Summer Isles.

"Titles can be as dangerous as names," Tyrion warned. "Show me a few of your girls."

"It will be my great delight. You will find that they are all as sweet as they are beautiful, and skilled in every art of love." She swept off gracefully, leaving Tyrion to waddle after as best he could on legs half the length of hers.

From behind an ornate Myrish screen carved with flowers and fancies and dreaming maidens, they peered unseen into a common room where an old man was playing a cheerful air on the pipes. In a cushioned alcove, a drunken Tyroshi with a purple beard dandled a buxom young wench on his knee. He'd unlaced her bodice and was tilting his cup to pour a thin trickle of wine over her breasts so he might lap it off. Two other girls sat playing at tiles before a leaded glass window. The freckled one wore a chain of blue flowers in her honeyed hair. The other had skin as smooth and black as polished jet, wide dark eyes, small pointed breasts. They dressed in flowing silks cinched at the waist with beaded belts. The sunlight pouring through the colored glass outlined their sweet young bodies through the thin cloth, and Tyrion felt a stirring in his groin. "I would respectfully suggest the dark-skinned girl," said Chataya.

"She's young."

"She has sixteen years, my lord."

A good age for Joffrey, he thought, remembering what Bronn had said. His first had been even younger. Tyrion remembered how shy she'd seemed as he drew her dress up over her head the first time. Long dark hair and blue eyes you could drown in, and he had. So long ago . . . *What a wretched fool you are, dwarf.* "Does she come from your home lands, this girl?"

"Her blood is the blood of summer, my lord, but my daughter was born here in King's Landing." His surprise must have shown on his face, for Chataya continued, "My people hold that there is no shame to be found in the pillow house. In the Summer Isles, those who are skilled at giving pleasure are greatly esteemed. Many highborn youths and maidens serve for a few years after their flowerings, to honor the gods."

"What do the gods have to do with it?"

"The gods made our bodies as well as our souls, is it not so? They give us voices, so we might worship them with song. They give us hands, so we might build them temples. And they give us desire, so we might mate and worship them in that way."

"Remind me to tell the High Septon," said Tyrion. "If I could pray with my cock, I'd be much more religious." He waved a hand. "I will gladly accept your suggestion."

"I shall summon my daughter. Come."

The girl met him at the foot of the stairs. Taller than Shae, though not so tall as her mother, she had to kneel before Tyrion could kiss her. "My name is Alayaya," she said, with only the slightest hint of her mother's

accent. "Come, my lord." She took him by the hand and drew him up
two flights of stairs, then down a long hall. Gasps and shrieks of pleasure
were coming from behind one of the closed doors, giggles and whispers
from another. Tyrion's cock pressed against the lacings of his breeches.
This could be humiliating, he thought as he followed Alayaya up another stair to the turret room. There was only one door. She led him
through and closed it. Within the room was a great canopied bed, a tall
wardrobe decorated with erotic carvings, and a narrow window of leaded
glass in a pattern of red and yellow diamonds.

"You are very beautiful, Alayaya," Tyrion told her when they were
alone. "From head to heels, every part of you is lovely. Yet just now the
part that interests me most is your tongue."

"My lord will find my tongue well schooled. When I was a girl I
learned when to use it, and when not."

"That pleases me." Tyrion smiled. "So what shall we do now?
Perchance you have some suggestion?"

"Yes," she said. "If my lord will open the wardrobe, he will find what
he seeks."

Tyrion kissed her hand, and climbed inside the empty wardrobe.
Alayaya closed it after him. He groped for the back panel, felt it slide
under his fingers, and pushed it all the way aside. The hollow space
behind the walls was pitch-black, but he fumbled until he felt metal. His
hand closed around the rung of a ladder. He found a lower rung with his
foot, and started down. Well below street level, the shaft opened onto a
slanting earthen tunnel, where he found Varys waiting with candle in
hand.

Varys did not look at all like himself. A scarred face and a stubble of
dark beard showed under his spiked steel cap, and he wore mail over
boiled leather, dirk and shortsword at his belt. "Was Chataya's to your
satisfaction, my lord?"

"Almost too much so," admitted Tyrion. "You're certain this woman
can be relied on?"

"I am certain of nothing in this fickle and treacherous world, my lord.
Chataya has no cause to love the queen, though, and she knows that she
has you to thank for ridding her of Allar Deem. Shall we go?" He started
down the tunnel.

Even his walk is different, Tyrion observed. The scent of sour wine
and garlic clung to Varys instead of lavender. "I like this new garb of
yours," he offered as they went.

"The work I do does not permit me to travel the streets amid a column of knights. So when I leave the castle, I adopt more suitable guises,
and thus live to serve you longer."

"Leather becomes you. You ought to come like this to our next council session."

"Your sister would not approve, my lord."

"My sister would soil her smallclothes." He smiled in the dark. "I saw no signs of any of her spies skulking after me."

"I am pleased to hear it, my lord. Some of your sister's hirelings are mine as well, unbeknownst to her. I should hate to think they had grown so sloppy as to be seen."

"Well, *I'd* hate to think I was climbing through wardrobes and suffering the pangs of frustrated lust all for naught."

"Scarcely for naught," Varys assured him. "They know you are here. Whether any will be bold enough to enter Chataya's in the guise of patrons I cannot say, but I find it best to err on the side of caution."

"How is it a brothel happens to have a secret entrance?"

"The tunnel was dug for another King's Hand, whose honor would not allow him to enter such a house openly. Chataya has closely guarded the knowledge of its existence."

"And yet *you* knew of it."

"Little birds fly through many a dark tunnel. Careful, the steps are steep."

They emerged through a trap at the back of a stable, having come perhaps a distance of three blocks under Rhaenys's Hill. A horse whickered in his stall when Tyrion let the door slam shut. Varys blew out the candle and set it on a beam and Tyrion gazed about. A mule and three horses occupied the stalls. He waddled over to the piebald gelding and took a look at his teeth. "Old," he said, "and I have my doubts about his wind."

"He is not a mount to carry you into battle, true," Varys replied, "but he will serve, and attract no notice. As will the others. And the stableboys see and hear only the animals." The eunuch took a cloak from a peg. It was roughspun, sun-faded, and threadbare, but very ample in its cut. "If you will permit me." When he swept it over Tyrion's shoulders it enveloped him head to heel, with a cowl that could be pulled forward to drown his face in shadows. "Men see what they expect to see," Varys said as he fussed and pulled. "Dwarfs are not so common a sight as children, so a child is what they will see. A boy in an old cloak on his father's horse, going about his father's business. Though it would be best if you came most often by night."

"I plan to . . . after today. At the moment, though, Shae awaits me." He had put her up in a walled manse at the far northeast corner of King's Landing, not far from the sea, but he had not dared visit her there for fear of being followed.

"Which horse will you have?"

Tyrion shrugged. "This one will do well enough."

"I shall saddle him for you." Varys took tack and saddle down from a peg.

Tyrion adjusted the heavy cloak and paced restlessly. "You missed a lively council. Stannis has crowned himself, it seems."

"I know."

"He accuses my brother and sister of incest. I wonder how he came by that suspicion."

"Perhaps he read a book and looked at the color of a bastard's hair, as Ned Stark did, and Jon Arryn before him. Or perhaps someone whispered it in his ear." The eunuch's laugh was not his usual giggle, but deeper and more throaty.

"Someone like you, perchance?"

"Am I suspected? It was not me."

"If it had been, would you admit it?"

"No. But why should I betray a secret I have kept so long? It is one thing to deceive a king, and quite another to hide from the cricket in the rushes and the little bird in the chimney. Besides, the bastards were there for all to see."

"Robert's bastards? What of them?"

"He fathered eight, to the best of my knowing," Varys said as he wrestled with the saddle. "Their mothers were copper and honey, chestnut and butter, yet the babes were all black as ravens . . . and as ill-omened, it would seem. So when Joffrey, Myrcella, and Tommen slid out between your sister's thighs, each as golden as the sun, the truth was not hard to glimpse."

Tyrion shook his head. *If she had borne only one child for her husband, it would have been enough to disarm suspicion . . . but then she would not have been Cersei.* "If you were not this whisperer, who was?"

"Some traitor, doubtless." Varys tightened the cinch.

"Littlefinger?"

"I named no name."

Tyrion let the eunuch help him mount. "Lord Varys," he said from the saddle, "sometimes I feel as though you are the best friend I have in King's Landing, and sometimes I feel you are my worst enemy."

"How odd. I think quite the same of you."

BRAN

Long before the first pale fingers of light pried apart Bran's shutters, his eyes were open.

There were guests in Winterfell, visitors come for the harvest feast. This morning they would be tilting at quintains in the yard. Once that prospect would have filled him with excitement, but that was *before*.

Not now. The Walders would break lances with the squires of Lord Manderly's escort, but Bran would have no part of it. He must play the prince in his father's solar. "Listen, and it may be that you will learn something of what lordship is all about," Maester Luwin had said.

Bran had never asked to be a prince. It was knighthood he had always dreamed of; bright armor and streaming banners, lance and sword, a warhorse between his legs. Why must he waste his days listening to old men speak of things he only half understood? *Because you're broken*, a voice inside reminded him. A lord on his cushioned chair might be crippled—the Walders said their grandfather was so feeble he had to be carried everywhere in a litter—but not a knight on his destrier. Besides, it was his duty. "You are your brother's heir and the Stark in Winterfell," Ser Rodrik said, reminding him of how Robb used to sit with their lord father when his bannermen came to see him.

Lord Wyman Manderly had arrived from White Harbor two days past, traveling by barge and litter, as he was too fat to sit a horse. With him had come a long tail of retainers: knights, squires, lesser lords and ladies, heralds, musicians, even a juggler, all aglitter with banners and surcoats in what seemed half a hundred colors. Bran had welcomed them to Winterfell from his father's high stone seat with the direwolves carved into the arms, and afterward Ser Rodrik had said he'd done well. If that had been the end of it, he would not have minded. But it was only the beginning.

"The feast makes a pleasant pretext," Ser Rodrik explained, "but a man does not cross a hundred leagues for a sliver of duck and a sip of wine. Only those who have matters of import to set before us are like to make the journey."

Bran gazed up at the rough stone ceiling above his head. Robb would tell him not to play the boy, he knew. He could almost hear him, and their lord father as well. *Winter is coming, and you are almost a man grown, Bran. You have a duty.*

When Hodor came bustling in, smiling and humming tunelessly, he found the boy resigned to his fate. Together they got him washed and brushed. "The white wool doublet today," Bran commanded. "And the silver brooch. Ser Rodrik will want me to look lordly." As much as he could, Bran preferred to dress himself, but there were some tasks—pulling on breeches, lacing his boots—that vexed him. They went quicker with Hodor's help. Once he had been taught to do something, he did it deftly. His hands were always gentle, though his strength was astonishing. "You could have been a knight too, I bet," Bran told him. "If the gods hadn't taken your wits, you would have been a great knight."

"Hodor?" Hodor blinked at him with guileless brown eyes, eyes innocent of understanding.

"Yes," said Bran. "Hodor." He pointed.

On the wall beside the door hung a basket, stoutly made of wicker and leather, with holes cut for Bran's legs. Hodor slid his arms through the straps and cinched the wide belt tight around his chest, then knelt beside the bed. Bran used the bars sunk into the wall to support himself as he swung the dead weight of his legs into the basket and through the holes.

"Hodor," Hodor said again, rising. The stableboy stood near seven feet tall all by himself; on his back Bran's head almost brushed the ceiling. He ducked low as they passed through the door. One time Hodor smelled bread baking and *ran* to the kitchens, and Bran got such a crack that Maester Luwin had to sew up his scalp. Mikken had given him a rusty old visorless helm from the armory, but Bran seldom troubled to wear it. The Walders laughed whenever they saw it on his head.

He rested his hands on Hodor's shoulders as they descended the winding stair. Outside, the sounds of sword and shield and horse already rang through the yard. It made a sweet music. *I'll just have a look*, Bran thought, *a quick look, that's all.*

The White Harbor lordlings would emerge later in the morning, with their knights and men-at-arms. Until then, the yard belonged to their squires, who ranged in age from ten to forty. Bran wished he were one of them so badly that his stomach hurt with the wanting.

Two quintains had been erected in the courtyard, each a stout post supporting a spinning crossbeam with a shield at one end and a padded butt at the other. The shields had been painted red-and-gold, though the Lannister lions were lumpy and misshapen, and already well scarred by the first boys to take a tilt at them.

The sight of Bran in his basket drew stares from those who had not seen it before, but he had learned to ignore stares. At least he had a good view; on Hodor's back, he towered over everyone. The Walders were mounting up, he saw. They'd brought fine armor up from the Twins, shining silver plate with enameled blue chasings. Big Walder's crest was shaped like a castle, while Little Walder favored streamers of blue and grey silk. Their shields and surcoats also set them apart from each other. Little Walder quartered the twin towers of Frey with the brindled boar of his grandmother's House and the plowman of his mother's: Crakehall and Darry, respectively. Big Walder's quarterings were the tree-and-ravens of House Blackwood and the twining snakes of the Paeges. *They must be hungry for honor,* Bran thought as he watched them take up their lances. *A Stark needs only the direwolf.*

Their dappled grey coursers were swift, strong, and beautifully trained. Side by side they charged the quintains. Both hit the shields cleanly and were well past before the padded butts came spinning around. Little Walder struck the harder blow, but Bran thought Big Walder sat his horse better. He would have given both his useless legs for the chance to ride against either.

Little Walder cast his splintered lance aside, spied Bran, and reined up. "Now there's an ugly horse," he said of Hodor.

"Hodor's no horse," Bran said.

"Hodor," said Hodor.

Big Walder trotted up to join his cousin. "Well, he's not as *smart* as a horse, that's for certain." A few of the White Harbor lads poked each other and laughed.

"Hodor." Beaming genially, Hodor looked from one Frey to the other, oblivious to their taunting. "Hodor hodor?"

Little Walder's mount whickered. "See, they're talking to each other. Maybe *hodor* means 'I love you' in horse."

"You shut up, Frey." Bran could feel his color rising.

Little Walder spurred his horse closer, giving Hodor a bump that pushed him backward. "What will you do if I don't?"

"He'll set his wolf on you, cousin," warned Big Walder.

"Let him. I always wanted a wolfskin cloak."

"Summer would tear your fat head off," Bran said.

Little Walder banged a mailed fist against his breastplate. "Does your wolf have steel teeth, to bite through plate and mail?"

"*Enough!*" Maester Luwin's voice cracked through the clangor of the yard as loud as a thunderclap. How much he had overheard, Bran could not say . . . but it was enough to anger him, clearly. "These threats are unseemly, and I'll hear no more of them. Is this how you behave at the Twins, Walder Frey?"

"If I want to." Atop his courser, Little Walder gave Luwin a sullen glare, as if to say, *You are only a maester, who are you to reproach a Frey of the Crossing?*

"Well, it is not how Lady Stark's wards ought behave at Winterfell. What's at the root of this?" The maester looked at each boy in turn. "One of you will tell me, I swear, or—"

"We were having a jape with Hodor," confessed Big Walder. "I am sorry if we offended Prince Bran. We only meant to be amusing." He at least had the grace to look abashed.

Little Walder only looked peevish. "And me," he said. "I was only being amusing too."

The bald spot atop the maester's head had turned red, Bran could see; if anything, Luwin was more angry than before. "A good lord comforts and protects the weak and helpless," he told the Freys. "I will not have you making Hodor the butt of cruel jests, do you hear me? He's a good-hearted lad, dutiful and obedient, which is more than I can say for either of you." The maester wagged a finger at Little Walder. "And you will stay *out* of the godswood and away from those wolves, or answer for it." Sleeves flapping, he turned on his heels, stalked off a few paces, and glanced back. "Bran. Come. Lord Wyman awaits."

"Hodor, go with the maester," Bran commanded.

"Hodor," said Hodor. His long strides caught up with the maester's furiously pumping legs on the steps of the Great Keep. Maester Luwin held the door open, and Bran hugged Hodor's neck and ducked as they went through.

"The Walders—" he began.

"I'll hear no more of that, it's done." Maester Luwin looked worn-out and frayed. "You were right to defend Hodor, but you should never have been there. Ser Rodrik and Lord Wyman have broken their fast already while they waited for you. Must I come myself to fetch you, as if you were a little child?"

"No," Bran said, ashamed. "I'm sorry. I only wanted . . ."

"I know what you wanted," Maester Luwin said, more gently. "Would that it could be, Bran. Do you have any questions before we begin this audience?"

"Will we talk of the war?"

"*You* will talk of naught." The sharpness was back in Luwin's voice. "You are still a child of eight . . ."

"Almost nine!"

"Eight," the maester repeated firmly. "Speak nothing but courtesies unless Ser Rodrik or Lord Wyman puts you a question."

Bran nodded. "I'll remember."

"I will say nothing to Ser Rodrik of what passed between you and the Frey boys."

"Thank you."

They put Bran in his father's oak chair with the grey velvet cushions, behind a long plank-and-trestle table. Ser Rodrik sat on his right hand and Maester Luwin to his left, armed with quills and inkpots and a sheaf of blank parchment to write down all that transpired. Bran ran a hand across the rough wood of the table and begged Lord Wyman's pardons for being late.

"Why, no prince is ever late," the Lord of White Harbor responded amiably. "Those who arrive before him have come early, that's all." Wyman Manderly had a great booming laugh. It was small wonder he could not sit a saddle; he looked as if he outweighed most horses. As windy as he was vast, he began by asking Winterfell to confirm the new customs officers he had appointed for White Harbor. The old ones had been holding back silver for King's Landing rather than paying it over to the new King in the North. "King Robb needs his own coinage as well," he declared, "and White Harbor is the very place to mint it." He offered to take charge of the matter, as it please the king, and went from that to speak of how he had strengthened the port's defenses, detailing the cost of every improvement.

In addition to a mint, Lord Manderly also proposed to build Robb a warfleet. "We have had no strength at sea for hundreds of years, since Brandon the Burner put the torch to his father's ships. Grant me the gold and within the year I will float you sufficient galleys to take Dragonstone and King's Landing both."

Bran's interest pricked up at talk of warships. No one asked him, but he thought Lord Wyman's notion a splendid one. In his mind's eye he could see them already. He wondered if a cripple had ever commanded a warship. But Ser Rodrik promised only to send the proposal on to Robb for his consideration, while Maester Luwin scratched at the parchment.

Midday came and went. Maester Luwin sent Poxy Tym down to the kitchens, and they dined in the solar on cheese, capons, and brown oat-bread. While tearing apart a bird with fat fingers, Lord Wyman made polite inquiry after Lady Hornwood, who was a cousin of his. "She was born a Manderly, you know. Perhaps, when her grief has run its course, she would like to be a Manderly again, eh?" He took a bite from a wing, and smiled broadly. "As it happens, I am a widower these past eight years. Past time I took another wife, don't you agree, my lords? A man does get lonely." Tossing the bones aside, he reached for a leg. "Or if the lady fancies a younger lad, well, my son Wendel is unwed as well. He is off south guarding Lady Catelyn, but no doubt he will wish to take a bride on his return. A valiant boy, and jolly. Just the man to teach her to laugh again, eh?" He wiped a bit of grease off his chin with the sleeve of his tunic.

Bran could hear the distant clash of arms through the windows. He cared nothing about marriages. *I wish I was down in the yard.*

His lordship waited until the table had been cleared before he raised the matter of a letter he had received from Lord Tywin Lannister, who held his elder son, Ser Wylis, taken captive on the Green Fork. "He offers him back to me without ransom, provided I withdraw my levies from His Grace and vow to fight no more."

"You will refuse him, of course," said Ser Rodrik.

"Have no fear on that count," the lord assured them. "King Robb has no more loyal servant than Wyman Manderly. I would be loath to see my son languish at Harrenhal any longer than he must, however. That is an ill place. Cursed, they say. Not that I am the sort to swallow such tales, but still, there it is. Look at what's befallen this Janos Slynt. Raised up to Lord of Harrenhal by the queen, and cast down by her brother. Shipped off to the Wall, they say. I pray some equitable exchange of captives can be arranged before too very long. I know Wylis would not want to sit out the rest of the war. Gallant, that son of mine, and fierce as a mastiff."

Bran's shoulders were stiff from sitting in the same chair by the time the audience drew to a close. And that night, as he sat to supper, a horn sounded to herald the arrival of another guest. Lady Donella Hornwood brought no tail of knights and retainers; only herself, and six tired men-at-arms with a moosehead badge on their dusty orange livery. "We are very sorry for all you have suffered, my lady," Bran said when she came before him to speak her words of greetings. Lord Hornwood had been killed in the battle on the Green Fork, their only son cut down in the Whispering Wood. "Winterfell will remember."

"That is good to know." She was a pale husk of a woman, every line of her face etched with grief. "I am very weary, my lord. If I might have leave to rest, I should be thankful."

"To be sure," Ser Rodrik said. "There is time enough for talk on the morrow."

When the morrow came, most of the morning was given over to talk of grains and greens and salting meat. Once the maesters in their Citadel had proclaimed the first of autumn, wise men put away a portion of each harvest . . . though how large a portion was a matter that seemed to require much talk. Lady Hornwood was storing a fifth of her harvest. At Maester Luwin's suggestion, she vowed to increase that to a quarter.

"Bolton's bastard is massing men at the Dreadfort," she warned them. "I hope he means to take them south to join his father at the Twins, but when I sent to ask his intent, he told me that no Bolton would be questioned by a woman. As if he were trueborn and had a right to that name."

"Lord Bolton has never acknowledged the boy, so far as I know," Ser Rodrik said. "I confess, I do not know him."

"Few do," she replied. "He lived with his mother until two years past, when young Domeric died and left Bolton without an heir. That was when he brought his bastard to the Dreadfort. The boy is a sly creature by all accounts, and he has a servant who is almost as cruel as he is. Reek, they call the man. It's said he never bathes. They hunt together, the Bastard and this Reek, and not for deer. I've heard tales, things I can scarce believe, even of a Bolton. And now that my lord husband and my sweet son have gone to the gods, the Bastard looks at my lands hungrily."

Bran wanted to give the lady a hundred men to defend her rights, but Ser Rodrik only said, "He may look, but should he do more I promise you there will be dire retribution. You will be safe enough, my lady . . . though perhaps in time, when your grief is passed, you may find it prudent to wed again."

"I am past my childbearing years, what beauty I had long fled," she replied with a tired half smile, "yet men come sniffing after me as they never did when I was a maid."

"You do not look favorably on these suitors?" asked Luwin.

"I shall wed again if His Grace commands it," Lady Hornwood replied, "but Mors Crowfood is a drunken brute, and older than my father. As for my noble cousin of Manderly, my lord's bed is not large enough to hold one of his majesty, and I am surely too small and frail to lie beneath him."

Bran knew that men slept on top of women when they shared a bed. Sleeping under Lord Manderly would be like sleeping under a fallen horse, he imagined. Ser Rodrik gave the widow a sympathetic nod. "You will have other suitors, my lady. We shall try and find you a prospect more to your taste."

"Perhaps you need not look very far, ser."

After she had taken her leave, Maester Luwin smiled. "Ser Rodrik, I do believe my lady fancies you."

Ser Rodrik cleared his throat and looked uncomfortable.

"She was very sad," said Bran.

Ser Rodrik nodded. "Sad and gentle, and not at all uncomely for a woman of her years, for all her modesty. Yet a danger to the peace of your brother's realm nonetheless."

"Her?" Bran said, astonished.

Maester Luwin answered. "With no direct heir, there are sure to be many claimants contending for the Hornwood lands. The Tallharts, Flints, and Karstarks all have ties to House Hornwood through the female line, and the Glovers are fostering Lord Harys's bastard at Deepwood Motte. The Dreadfort has no claim that I know, but the lands adjoin, and Roose Bolton is not one to overlook such a chance."

Ser Rodrik tugged at his whiskers. "In such cases, her liege lord must find her a suitable match."

"Why *can't* you marry her?" Bran asked. "You said she was comely, and Beth would have a mother."

The old knight put a hand on Bran's arm. "A kindly thought, my prince, but I am only a knight, and besides too old. I might hold her lands for a few years, but as soon as I died Lady Hornwood would find herself back in the same mire, and Beth's prospects might be perilous as well."

"Then let Lord Hornwood's bastard be the heir," Bran said, thinking of his half brother Jon.

Ser Rodrik said, "That would please the Glovers, and perhaps Lord Hornwood's shade as well, but I do not think Lady Hornwood would love us. The boy is not of her blood."

"Still," said Maester Luwin, "it must be considered. Lady Donella is past her fertile years, as she said herself. If not the bastard, who?"

"May I be excused?" Bran could hear the squires at their swordplay in the yard below, the ring of steel on steel.

"As you will, my prince," said Ser Rodrik. "You did well." Bran flushed with pleasure. Being a lord was not so tedious as he had feared, and since Lady Hornwood had been so much briefer than Lord Manderly, he even had a few hours of daylight left to visit with Summer. He liked to spend time with his wolf every day, when Ser Rodrik and the maester allowed it.

No sooner had Hodor entered the godswood than Summer emerged from under an oak, almost as if he had known they were coming. Bran glimpsed a lean black shape watching from the undergrowth as well. "Shaggy," he called. "Here, Shaggydog. To me." But Rickon's wolf vanished as swiftly as he'd appeared.

Hodor knew Bran's favorite place, so he took him to the edge of the pool beneath the great spread of the heart tree, where Lord Eddard used to kneel to pray. Ripples were running across the surface of the water when they arrived, making the reflection of the weirwood shimmer and dance. There was no wind, though. For an instant Bran was baffled.

And then Osha exploded up out of the pool with a great splash, so sudden that even Summer leapt back, snarling. Hodor jumped away, wailing "Hodor, *Hodor*" in dismay until Bran patted his shoulder to soothe his fears. "How can you swim in there?" he asked Osha. "Isn't it cold?"

"As a babe I suckled on icicles, boy. I like the cold." Osha swam to the rocks and rose dripping. She was naked, her skin bumpy with gooseprickles. Summer crept close and sniffed at her. "I wanted to touch the bottom."

"I never knew there was a bottom."

"Might be there isn't." She grinned. "What are you staring at, boy? Never seen a woman before?"

"I have so." Bran had bathed with his sisters hundreds of times and he'd seen serving women in the hot pools too. Osha looked different, though, hard and sharp instead of soft and curvy. Her legs were all sinew, her breasts flat as two empty purses. "You've got a lot of scars."

"Every one hard earned." She picked up her brown shift, shook some leaves off of it, and pulled it down over her head.

"Fighting giants?" Osha claimed there were still giants beyond the Wall. *One day maybe I'll even see one . . .*

"Fighting men." She belted herself with a length of rope. "Black crows, oft as not. Killed me one too," she said, shaking out her hair. It had grown since she'd come to Winterfell, well down past her ears. She looked softer than the woman who had once tried to rob and kill him in the wolfswood. "Heard some yattering in the kitchen today about you and them Freys."

"Who? What did they say?"

She gave him a sour grin. "That it's a fool boy who mocks a giant, and a mad world when a cripple has to defend him."

"Hodor never knew they were mocking him," Bran said. "Anyhow he never fights." He remembered once when he was little, going to the market square with his mother and Septa Mordane. They brought Hodor to carry for them, but he had wandered away, and when they found him some boys had him backed into an alley, poking him with sticks. *"Hodor!"* he kept shouting, cringing and covering himself, but he had never raised a hand against his tormentors. "Septon Chayle says he has a gentle spirit."

"Aye," she said, "and hands strong enough to twist a man's head off his shoulders, if he takes a mind to. All the same, he better watch his back around that Walder. Him and you both. The big one they call little, it comes to me he's well named. Big outside, little inside, and mean down to the bones."

"He'd never dare hurt me. He's scared of Summer, no matter what he says."

"Then might be he's not so stupid as he seems." Osha was always wary around the direwolves. The day she was taken, Summer and Grey Wind between them had torn three wildlings to bloody pieces. "Or might be he is. And that tastes of trouble too." She tied up her hair. "You have more of them wolf dreams?"

"No." He did not like to talk about the dreams.

"A prince should lie better than that." Osha laughed. "Well, your dreams are your business. Mine's in the kitchens, and I'd best be getting back before Gage starts to shouting and waving that big wooden spoon of his. By your leave, my prince."

She should never have talked about the wolf dreams, Bran thought as Hodor carried him up the steps to his bedchamber. He fought against sleep as long as he could, but in the end it took him as it always did. On this night he dreamed of the weirwood. It was looking at him with its deep red eyes, calling to him with its twisted wooden mouth, and from its pale branches the three-eyed crow came flapping, pecking at his face and crying his name in a voice as sharp as swords.

The blast of horns woke him. Bran pushed himself onto his side, grateful for the reprieve. He heard horses and boisterous shouting. *More guests have come, and half-drunk by the noise of them.* Grasping his bars he pulled himself from the bed and over to the window seat. On their banner was a giant in shattered chains that told him that these were Umber men, down from the northlands beyond the Last River.

The next day two of them came together to audience; the Greatjon's uncles, blustery men in the winter of their days with beards as white as the bearskin cloaks they wore. A crow had once taken Mors for dead and pecked out his eye, so he wore a chunk of dragonglass in its stead. As Old Nan told the tale, he'd grabbed the crow in his fist and bitten its head off, so they named him Crowfood. She would never tell Bran why his gaunt brother Hother was called Whoresbane.

No sooner had they been seated than Mors asked for leave to wed Lady Hornwood. "The Greatjon's the Young Wolf's strong right hand, all know that to be true. Who better to protect the widow's lands than an Umber, and what Umber better than me?"

"Lady Donella is still grieving," Maester Luwin said.

"I have a cure for grief under my furs." Mors laughed. Ser Rodrik thanked him courteously and promised to bring the matter before the lady and the king.

Hother wanted ships. "There's wildlings stealing down from the north, more than I've ever seen before. They cross the Bay of Seals in little boats and wash up on our shores. The crows in Eastwatch are too few to stop them, and they go to ground quick as weasels. It's longships we need, aye, and strong men to sail them. The Greatjon took too many. Half our harvest is gone to seed for want of arms to swing the scythes."

Ser Rodrik pulled at his whiskers. "You have forests of tall pine and old oak. Lord Manderly has shipwrights and sailors in plenty. Together you ought to be able to float enough longships to guard both your coasts."

"Manderly?" Mors Umber snorted. "That great waddling sack of suet? His own people mock him as Lord Lamprey, I've heard. The man can scarce walk. If you stuck a sword in his belly, ten thousand eels would wriggle out."

"He is fat," Ser Rodrik admitted, "but he is not stupid. You will work with him, or the king will know the reason why." And to Bran's astonishment, the truculent Umbers agreed to do as he commanded, though not without grumbling.

While they were sitting at audience, the Glover men arrived from Deepwood Motte, and a large party of Tallharts from Torrhen's Square. Galbart and Robett Glover had left Deepwood in the hands of Robett's wife, but it was their steward who came to Winterfell. "My lady begs that you excuse her absence. Her babes are still too young for such a journey, and she was loath to leave them." Bran soon realized that it was the steward, not Lady Glover, who truly ruled at Deepwood Motte. The man allowed that he was at present setting aside only a tenth of his harvest. A hedge wizard had told him there would be a bountiful spirit summer before the cold set in, he claimed. Maester Luwin had a number of choice things to say about hedge wizards. Ser Rodrik commanded the man to set aside a fifth, and questioned the steward closely about Lord Hornwood's bastard, the boy Larence Snow. In the north, all highborn bastards took the surname *Snow*. This lad was near twelve, and the steward praised his wits and courage.

"Your notion about the bastard may have merit, Bran," Maester Luwin said after. "One day you will be a good lord for Winterfell, I think."

"No I won't." Bran knew he would never be a lord, no more than he could be a knight. "Robb's to marry some Frey girl, you told me so yourself, and the Walders say the same. He'll have sons, and they'll be the lords of Winterfell after him, not me."

"It may be so, Bran," Ser Rodrik said, "but I was wed three times and my wives gave me daughters. Now only Beth remains to me. My brother Martyn fathered four strong sons, yet only Jory lived to be a man. When he was slain, Martyn's line died with him. When we speak of the morrow nothing is ever certain."

Leobald Tallhart had his turn the following day. He spoke of weather portents and the slack wits of smallfolk, and told how his nephew itched for battle. "Benfred has raised his own company of lances. Boys, none older than nineteen years, but every one thinks he's another young wolf. When I told them they were only young rabbits, they laughed at me. Now they call themselves the Wild Hares and gallop about the country with rabbitskins tied to the ends of their lances, singing songs of chivalry."

Bran thought that sounded grand. He remembered Benfred Tallhart, a big bluff loud boy who had often visited Winterfell with his father, Ser Helman, and had been friendly with Robb and with Theon Greyjoy. But Ser Rodrik was clearly displeased by what he heard. "If the king were in need of more men, he would send for them," he said. "Instruct your nephew that he is to remain at Torrhen's Square, as his lord father commanded."

"I will, ser," said Leobald, and only then raised the matter of Lady Hornwood. Poor thing, with no husband to defend her lands nor son to inherit. His own lady wife was a Hornwood, sister to the late Lord Halys, doubtless they recalled. "An empty hall is a sad one. I had a thought to send my younger son to Lady Donella to foster as her own. Beren is near ten, a likely lad, and her own nephew. He would cheer her, I am certain, and perhaps he would even take the name Hornwood . . ."

"If he were named heir?" suggested Maester Luwin.

". . . so the House might continue," finished Leobald.

Bran knew what to say. "Thank you for the notion, my lord," he blurted out before Ser Rodrik could speak. "We will bring the matter to my brother Robb. Oh, and Lady Hornwood."

Leobald seemed surprised that he had spoken. "I'm grateful, my prince," he said, but Bran saw pity in his pale blue eyes, mingled perhaps with a little gladness that the cripple was, after all, not *his* son. For a moment he hated the man.

Maester Luwin liked him better, though. "Beren Tallhart may well be our best answer," he told them when Leobald had gone. "By blood he is half Hornwood. If he takes his uncle's name . . ."

". . . he will still be a boy," said Ser Rodrik, "and hard-pressed to hold his lands against the likes of Mors Umber or this bastard of Roose Bolton's. We must think on this carefully. Robb should have our best counsel before he makes his decision."

"It may come down to practicalities," said Maester Luwin. "Which lord he most needs to court. The riverlands are part of his realm, he may wish to cement the alliance by wedding Lady Hornwood to one of the lords of the Trident. A Blackwood, perhaps, or a Frey—"

"Lady Hornwood can have one of our Freys," said Bran. "She can have both of them if she likes."

"You are not kind, my prince," Ser Rodrik chided gently.

Neither are the Walders. Scowling, Bran stared down at the table and said nothing.

In the days that followed, ravens arrived from other lordly houses, bearing regrets. The bastard of the Dreadfort would not be joining them, the Mormonts and Karstarks had all gone south with Robb, Lord Locke was too old to dare the journey, Lady Flint was heavy with child, there was sickness at Widow's Watch. Finally all of the principal vassals of House Stark had been heard from save for Howland Reed the crannogman, who had not set foot outside his swamps for many a year, and the Cerwyns whose castle lay a half day's ride from Winterfell. Lord Cerwyn was a captive of the Lannisters, but his son, a lad of fourteen, arrived one bright, blustery morning at the head of two dozen lances. Bran was riding Dancer around the yard when they came through the gate. He trotted over to greet them. Cley Cerwyn had always been a friend to Bran and his brothers.

"Good morrow, Bran," Cley called out cheerfully. "Or must I call you Prince Bran now?"

"Only if you want."

Cley laughed. "Why not? Everyone else is a king or prince these days. Did Stannis write Winterfell as well?"

"Stannis? I don't know."

"He's a king now too," Cley confided. "He says Queen Cersei bedded her brother, so Joffrey is a bastard."

"Joffrey the Illborn," one of the Cerwyn knights growled. "Small wonder he's faithless, with the Kingslayer for a father."

"Aye," said another, "the gods hate incest. Look how they brought down the Targaryens."

For a moment Bran felt as though he could not breathe. A giant hand was crushing his chest. He felt as though he was falling, and clutched desperately at Dancer's reins.

His terror must have shown on his face. "Bran?" Cley Cerwyn said. "Are you unwell? It's only another king."

"Robb will beat him too." He turned Dancer's head toward the stables, oblivious to the puzzled stares the Cerwyns gave him. His blood was roaring in his ears, and had he not been strapped onto his saddle he might well have fallen.

That night Bran prayed to his father's gods for dreamless sleep. If the gods heard, they mocked his hopes, for the nightmare they sent was worse than any wolf dream.

"Fly or die!" cried the three-eyed crow as it pecked at him. He wept and pleaded but the crow had no pity. It put out his left eye and then his right, and when he was blind in the dark it pecked at his brow, driving its terrible sharp beak deep into his skull. He screamed until he was certain his lungs must burst. The pain was an axe splitting his head apart, but when the crow wrenched out its beak all slimy with bits of bone and brain, Bran could see again. What he saw made him gasp in fear. He was clinging to a tower miles high, and his fingers were slipping, nails scrabbling at the stone, his legs dragging him down, stupid useless dead legs. *"Help me!"* he cried. A golden man appeared in the sky above him and pulled him up. "The things I do for love," he murmured softly as he tossed him out kicking into empty air.

TYRION

I do not sleep as I did when I was younger," Grand Maester Pycelle told him, by way of apology for the dawn meeting. "I would sooner be up, though the world be dark, than lie restless abed, fretting on tasks undone," he said—though his heavy-lidded eyes made him look half-asleep as he said it.

In the airy chambers beneath the rookery, his girl served them boiled eggs, stewed plums, and porridge, while Pycelle served the pontifications. "In these sad times, when so many hunger, I think it only fitting to keep my table spare."

"Commendable," Tyrion admitted, breaking a large brown egg that reminded him unduly of the Grand Maester's bald spotted head. "I take a different view. If there is food I eat it, in case there is none on the morrow." He smiled. "Tell me, are your ravens early risers as well?"

Pycelle stroked the snowy beard that flowed down his chest. "To be sure. Shall I send for quill and ink after we have eaten?"

"No need." Tyrion laid the letters on the table beside his porridge, twin parchments tightly rolled and sealed with wax at both ends. "Send your girl away, so we can talk."

"Leave us, child," Pycelle commanded. The serving girl hurried from the room. "These letters, now . . ."

"For the eyes of Doran Martell, Prince of Dorne." Tyrion peeled the cracked shell away from his egg and took a bite. It wanted salt. "One letter, in two copies. Send your swiftest birds. The matter is of great import."

"I shall dispatch them as soon as we have broken our fast."

"Dispatch them now. Stewed plums will keep. The realm may not. Lord Renly is leading his host up the roseroad, and no one can say when Lord Stannis will sail from Dragonstone."

Pycelle blinked. "If my lord prefers—"

"He does."

"I am here to serve." The maester pushed himself ponderously to his feet, his chain of office clinking softly. It was a heavy thing, a dozen maester's collars threaded around and through each other and ornamented with gemstones. And it seemed to Tyrion that the gold and silver and platinum links far outnumbered those of baser metals.

Pycelle moved so slowly that Tyrion had time to finish his egg and taste the plums—overcooked and watery, to his taste—before the sound of wings prompted him to rise. He spied the raven, dark in the dawn sky, and turned briskly toward the maze of shelves at the far end of the room.

The maester's medicines made an impressive display; dozens of pots sealed with wax, hundreds of stoppered vials, as many milkglass bottles, countless jars of dried herbs, each container neatly labeled in Pycelle's precise hand. *An orderly mind*, Tyrion reflected, and indeed, once you puzzled out the arrangement, it was easy to see that every potion had its place. *And such interesting things.* He noted sweetsleep and nightshade, milk of the poppy, the tears of Lys, powdered greycap, wolfsbane and demon's dance, basilisk venom, blindeye, widow's blood . . .

Standing on his toes and straining upward, he managed to pull a small dusty bottle off the high shelf. When he read the label, he smiled and slipped it up his sleeve.

He was back at the table peeling another egg when Grand Maester Pycelle came creeping down the stairs. "It is done, my lord." The old man seated himself. "A matter like this . . . best done promptly, indeed, indeed . . . of great import, you say?"

"Oh, yes." The porridge was too thick, Tyrion felt, and wanted butter and honey. To be sure, butter and honey were seldom seen in King's Landing of late, though Lord Gyles kept them well supplied in the castle. Half of the food they ate these days came from his lands or Lady Tanda's. Rosby and Stokeworth lay near the city to the north, and were yet untouched by war.

"The Prince of Dorne, himself. Might I ask . . ."

"Best not."

"As you say." Pycelle's curiosity was so ripe that Tyrion could almost taste it. "Mayhaps . . . the king's council . . ."

Tyrion tapped his wooden spoon against the edge of the bowl. "The council exists to *advise* the king, Maester."

"Just so," said Pycelle, "and the king—"

"—is a boy of thirteen. I speak with his voice."

"So you do. Indeed. The King's Own Hand. Yet . . . your most gracious sister, our Queen Regent, she . . ."

". . . bears a great weight upon those lovely white shoulders of hers. I have no wish to add to her burdens. Do you?" Tyrion cocked his head and gave the Grand Maester an inquiring stare.

Pycelle dropped his gaze back to his food. Something about Tyrion's mismatched green-and-black eyes made men squirm; knowing that, he made good use of them. "Ah," the old man muttered into his plums. "Doubtless you have the right of it, my lord. It is most considerate of you to . . . spare her this . . . burden."

"That's just the sort of fellow I am." Tyrion returned to the unsatisfactory porridge. "Considerate. Cersei is my own sweet sister, after all."

"And a woman, to be sure," Grand Maester Pycelle said. "A most uncommon woman, and yet . . . it is no small thing, to tend to all the cares of the realm, despite the frailty of her sex . . ."

Oh, yes, she's a frail dove, just ask Eddard Stark. "I'm pleased you share my concern. And I thank you for the hospitality of your table. But a long day awaits." He swung his legs out and clambered down from his chair. "Be so good as to inform me at once should we receive a reply from Dorne?"

"As you say, my lord."

"And *only* me?"

"Ah . . . to be sure." Pycelle's spotted hand was clutching at his beard the way a drowning man clutches for a rope. It made Tyrion's heart glad. *One,* he thought.

He waddled out into the lower bailey; his stunted legs complained of the steps. The sun was well up now, and the castle was stirring. Guardsmen walked the walls, and knights and men-at-arms were training with blunted weapons. Nearby, Bronn sat on the lip of a well. A pair of comely serving girls sauntered past carrying a wicker basket of rushes between them, but the sellsword never looked. "Bronn, I despair of you." Tyrion gestured at the wenches. "With sweet sights like that before you, all you see is a gaggle of louts raising a clangor."

"There are a hundred whorehouses in this city where a clipped copper will buy me all the cunt I want," Bronn answered, "but one day my life may hang on how close I've watched your louts." He stood. "Who's the boy in the checkered blue surcoat with the three eyes on his shield?"

"Some hedge knight. Tallad, he names himself. Why?"

Bronn pushed a fall of hair from his eyes. "He's the best of them. But watch him, he falls into a rhythm, delivering the same strokes in the same order each time he attacks." He grinned. "That will be the death of him, the day he faces me."

"He's pledged to Joffrey; he's not like to face you." They set off across the bailey, Bronn matching his long stride to Tyrion's short one. These days the sellsword was looking almost respectable. His dark hair was washed and brushed, he was freshly shaved, and he wore the black breastplate of an officer of the City Watch. From his shoulders trailed a cloak of Lannister crimson patterned with golden hands. Tyrion had made him a gift of it when he named him captain of his personal guard. "How many supplicants do we have today?" he inquired.

"Thirty odd," answered Bronn. "Most with complaints, or wanting something, as ever. Your pet was back."

He groaned. "Lady Tanda?"

"Her page. She invites you to sup with her again. There's to be a haunch of venison, she says, a brace of stuffed geese sauced with mulberries, and—"

"—her daughter," Tyrion finished sourly. Since the hour he had arrived in the Red Keep, Lady Tanda had been stalking him, armed with a never-ending arsenal of lamprey pies, wild boars, and savory cream stews. Somehow she had gotten the notion that a dwarf lordling would be the perfect consort for her daughter Lollys, a large, soft, dim-witted girl who rumor said was still a maid at thirty-and-three. "Send her my regrets."

"No taste for stuffed goose?" Bronn grinned evilly.

"Perhaps you should eat the goose and marry the maid. Or better still, send Shagga."

"Shagga's more like to eat the maid and marry the goose," observed Bronn. "Anyway, Lollys outweighs him."

"There is that," Tyrion admitted as they passed under the shadow of a covered walkway between two towers. "Who else wants me?"

The sellsword grew more serious. "There's a moneylender from Braavos, holding fancy papers and the like, requests to see the king about payment on some loan."

"As if Joff could count past twenty. Send the man to Littlefinger, he'll find a way to put him off. Next?"

"A lordling down from the Trident, says your father's men burned his keep, raped his wife, and killed all his peasants."

"I believe they call that *war.*" Tyrion smelled Gregor Clegane's work, or that of Ser Amory Lorch or his father's other pet hellhound, the Qohorik. "What does he want of Joffrey?"

"New peasants," Bronn said. "He walked all this way to sing how loyal he is and beg for recompense."

"I'll make time for him on the morrow." Whether truly loyal or merely desperate, a compliant river lord might have his uses. "See that he's given a comfortable chamber and a hot meal. Send him a new pair of boots as well, good ones, courtesy of King Joffrey." A show of generosity never hurt.

Bronn gave a curt nod. "There's also a great gaggle of bakers, butchers, and greengrocers clamoring to be heard."

"I told them last time, I have nothing to give them." Only a thin trickle of food was coming into King's Landing, most of it earmarked for castle and garrison. Prices had risen sickeningly high on greens, roots, flour, and fruit, and Tyrion did not want to think about what sorts of flesh might be going into the kettles of the pot-shops down in Flea Bottom. Fish, he hoped. They still had the river and the sea . . . at least until Lord Stannis sailed.

"They want protection. Last night a baker was roasted in his own oven. The mob claimed he charged too much for bread."

"Did he?"

"He's not apt to deny it."

"They didn't eat him, did they?"

"Not that I've heard."

"Next time they will," Tyrion said grimly. "I give them what protection I can. The gold cloaks—"

"They claim there were gold cloaks in the mob," Bronn said. "They're demanding to speak to the king himself."

"Fools." Tyrion had sent them off with regrets; his nephew would send them off with whips and spears. He was half-tempted to allow it . . . but no, he dare not. Soon or late, some enemy would march on King's Landing, and the last thing he wanted was willing traitors within the city walls. "Tell them King Joffrey shares their fears and will do all he can for them."

"They want bread, not promises."

"If I give them bread today, on the morrow I'll have twice as many at the gates. Who else?"

"A black brother down from the Wall. The steward says he brought some rotted hand in a jar."

Tyrion smiled wanly. "I'm surprised no one ate it. I suppose I ought to see him. It's not Yoren, perchance?"

"No. Some knight. Thorne."

"Ser *Alliser* Thorne?" Of all the black brothers he'd met on the Wall, Tyrion Lannister had liked Ser Alliser Thorne the least. A bitter, mean-spirited man with too great a sense of his own worth. "Come to think on it, I don't believe I care to see Ser Alliser just now. Find him a snug cell where no one has changed the rushes in a year, and let his hand rot a little more."

Bronn snorted laughter and went his way, while Tyrion struggled up the serpentine steps. As he limped across the outer yard, he heard the portcullis rattling up. His sister and a large party were waiting by the main gate.

Mounted on her white palfrey, Cersei towered high above him, a goddess in green. "Brother," she called out, not warmly. The queen had not been pleased by the way he'd dealt with Janos Slynt.

"Your Grace." Tyrion bowed politely. "You look lovely this morning." Her crown was gold, her cloak ermine. Her retinue sat their mounts behind her: Ser Boros Blount of the Kingsguard, wearing white scale and his favorite scowl; Ser Balon Swann, bow slung from his silver-inlay saddle; Lord Gyles Rosby, his wheezing cough worse than ever; Hallyne the Pyromancer of the Alchemists' Guild; and the queen's newest favorite, their cousin Ser Lancel Lannister, her late husband's squire upjumped to knight at his widow's insistence. Vylarr and twenty guardsmen rode escort. "Where are you bound this day, sister?" Tyrion asked.

"I'm making a round of the gates to inspect the new scorpions and spitfires. I would not have it thought that all of us are as indifferent to the city's defense as you seem to be." Cersei fixed him with those clear green eyes of hers, beautiful even in their contempt. "I am informed that Renly Baratheon has marched from Highgarden. He is making his way up the roseroad, with all his strength behind him."

"Varys gave me the same report."

"He could be here by the full moon."

"Not at his present leisurely pace," Tyrion assured her. "He feasts every night in a different castle, and holds court at every crossroads he passes."

"And every day, more men rally to his banners. His host is now said to be a hundred thousand strong."

"That seems rather high."

"He has the power of Storm's End and Highgarden behind him, you little fool," Cersei snapped down at him. "All the Tyrell bannermen but for the Redwynes, and you have me to thank for that. So long as I hold those poxy twins of his, Lord Paxter will squat on the Arbor and count himself fortunate to be out of it."

"A pity you let the Knight of Flowers slip through your pretty fingers. Still, Renly has other concerns besides us. Our father at Harrenhal, Robb Stark at Riverrun . . . were I he, I would do much as he is doing. Make my progress, flaunt my power for the realm to see, watch, wait. Let my rivals contend while I bide my own sweet time. If Stark defeats us, the south will fall into Renly's hands like a windfall from the gods, and he'll not have lost a man. And if it goes the other way, he can descend on us while we are weakened."

Cersei was not appeased. "I want you to make Father bring his army to King's Landing."

Where it will serve no purpose but to make you feel safe. "When have I ever been able to *make* Father do anything?"

She ignored the question. "And when do you plan to free Jaime? He's worth a hundred of you."

Tyrion grinned crookedly. "Don't tell Lady Stark, I beg you. We don't have a hundred of me to trade."

"Father must have been mad to send you. You're worse than useless." The queen jerked on her reins and wheeled her palfrey around. She rode out the gate at a brisk trot, ermine cloak streaming behind her. Her retinue hastened after.

In truth, Renly Baratheon did not frighten Tyrion half so much as his brother Stannis did. Renly was beloved of the commons, but he had never before led men in war. Stannis was otherwise: hard, cold, inexorable. If only they had some way of knowing what was happening on Dragonstone . . . but not one of the fisherfolk he had paid to spy out the island had ever returned, and even the informers the eunuch claimed to have placed in Stannis's household had been ominously silent. The striped hulls of Lysene war galleys had been seen offshore, though, and Varys had reports from Myr of sellsail captains taking service with Dragonstone. *If Stannis attacks by sea while his brother Renly storms the gates, they'll soon be mounting Joffrey's head on a spike. Worse, mine will be beside him.* A depressing thought. He ought to make plans to get Shae safely out of the city, should the worst seem likely.

Podrick Payne stood at the door of his solar, studying the floor. "He's inside," he announced to Tyrion's belt buckle. "Your solar. My lord. Sorry."

Tyrion sighed. "*Look* at me, Pod. It unnerves me when you talk to my codpiece, especially when I'm not wearing one. Who is inside my solar?"

"Lord Littlefinger." Podrick managed a quick look at his face, then hastily dropped his eyes. "I meant, Lord Petyr. Lord Baelish. The master of coin."

"You make him sound a crowd." The boy hunched down as if struck, making Tyrion feel absurdly guilty.

Lord Petyr was seated on his window seat, languid and elegant in a plush plum-colored doublet and a yellow satin cape, one gloved hand resting on his knee. "The king is fighting hares with a crossbow," he said. "The hares are winning. Come see."

Tyrion had to stand on his toes to get a look. A dead hare lay on the ground below, another, long ears twitching, was about to expire from the bolt in his side. Spent quarrels lay strewn across the hard-packed earth like straws scattered by a storm. "Now!" Joff shouted. The gamesman released the hare he was holding, and he went bounding off. Joffrey jerked the trigger on the crossbow. The bolt missed by two feet. The hare stood on his hind legs and twitched his nose at the king. Cursing, Joff spun the wheel to winch back his string, but the animal was gone before he was loaded. "Another!" The gamesman reached into the hutch. This one made a brown streak against the stones, while Joffrey's hurried shot almost took Ser Preston in the groin.

Littlefinger turned away. "Boy, are you fond of potted hare?" he asked Podrick Payne.

Pod stared at the visitor's boots, lovely things of red-dyed leather ornamented with black scrollwork. "To eat, my lord?"

"Invest in pots," Littlefinger advised. "Hares will soon overrun the castle. We'll be eating hare thrice a day."

"Better than rats on a skewer," said Tyrion. "Pod, leave us. Unless Lord Petyr would care for some refreshment?"

"Thank you, but no." Littlefinger flashed his mocking smile. "Drink with the dwarf, it's said, and you wake up walking the Wall. Black brings out my unhealthy pallor."

Have no fear, my lord, Tyrion thought, *it's not the Wall I have in mind for you.* He seated himself in a high chair piled with cushions and said, "You look very elegant today, my lord."

"I'm wounded. I strive to look elegant *every* day."

"Is the doublet new?"

"It is. You're most observant."

"Plum and yellow. Are those the colors of your House?"

"No. But a man gets bored wearing the same colors day in and day out, or so I've found."

"That's a handsome knife as well."

"Is it?" There was mischief in Littlefinger's eyes. He drew the knife and glanced at it casually, as if he had never seen it before. "Valyrian steel, and a dragonbone hilt. A trifle plain, though. It's yours, if you would like it."

"Mine?" Tyrion gave him a long look. "No. I think not. Never mine." *He knows, the insolent wretch. He knows and he knows that I know, and he thinks that I cannot touch him.*

If ever truly a man had armored himself in gold, it was Petyr Baelish, not Jaime Lannister. Jaime's famous armor was but gilded steel, but

Littlefinger, ah . . . Tyrion had learned a few things about sweet Petyr, to his growing disquiet.

Ten years ago, Jon Arryn had given him a minor sinecure in customs, where Lord Petyr had soon distinguished himself by bringing in three times as much as any of the king's other collectors. King Robert had been a prodigious spender. A man like Petyr Baelish, who had a gift for rubbing two golden dragons together to breed a third, was invaluable to his Hand. Littlefinger's rise had been arrow-swift. Within three years of his coming to court, he was master of coin and a member of the small council, and today the crown's revenues were ten times what they had been under his beleaguered predecessor . . . though the crown's debts had grown vast as well. A master juggler was Petyr Baelish.

Oh, he was clever. He did not simply collect the gold and lock it in a treasure vault, no. He paid the king's debts in promises, and put the king's gold to work. He bought wagons, shops, ships, houses. He bought grain when it was plentiful and sold bread when it was scarce. He bought wool from the north and linen from the south and lace from Lys, stored it, moved it, dyed it, sold it. The golden dragons bred and multiplied, and Littlefinger lent them out and brought them home with hatchlings.

And in the process, he moved his own men into place. The Keepers of the Keys were his, all four. The King's Counter and the King's Scales were men he'd named. The officers in charge of all three mints. Harbormasters, tax farmers, customs sergeants, wool factors, toll collectors, pursers, wine factors; nine of every ten belonged to Littlefinger. They were men of middling birth, by and large; merchants' sons, lesser lordlings, sometimes even foreigners, but judging from their results, far more able than their highborn predecessors.

No one had ever thought to question the appointments, and why should they? Littlefinger was no threat to anyone. A clever, smiling, genial man, everyone's friend, always able to find whatever gold the king or his Hand required, and yet of such undistinguished birth, one step up from a hedge knight, he was not a man to fear. He had no banners to call, no army of retainers, no great stronghold, no holdings to speak of, no prospects of a great marriage.

But do I dare touch him? Tyrion wondered. *Even if he is a traitor?* He was not at all certain he could, least of all now, while the war raged. Given time, he could replace Littlefinger's men with his own in key positions, but . . .

A shout rang up from the yard. "Ah, His Grace has killed a hare," Lord Baelish observed.

"No doubt a slow one," Tyrion said. "My lord, you were fostered at Riverrun. I've heard it said that you grew close to the Tullys."

"You might say so. The girls especially."

"How close?"

"I had their maidenhoods. Is that close enough?"

The lie—Tyrion was fairly certain it was a lie—was delivered with such an air of nonchalance that one could almost believe it. Could it have been Catelyn Stark who lied? About her defloration, and the dagger as well? The longer he lived, the more Tyrion realized that nothing was simple and little was true. "Lord Hoster's daughters do not love me," he confessed. "I doubt they would listen to any proposal I might make. Yet coming from you, the same words might fall more sweetly on their ears."

"That would depend on the words. If you mean to offer Sansa in return for your brother, waste someone else's time. Joffrey will never surrender his plaything, and Lady Catelyn is not so great a fool as to barter the Kingslayer for a slip of a girl."

"I mean to have Arya as well. I have men searching."

"Searching is not finding."

"I'll keep that in mind, my lord. In any case, it was Lady Lysa I hoped you might sway. For her, I have a sweeter offer."

"Lysa is more tractable than Catelyn, true . . . but also more fearful, and I understand she hates you."

"She believes she has good reason. When I was her guest in the Eyrie, she insisted that I'd murdered her husband, and was not inclined to listen to denials." He leaned forward. "If I gave her Jon Arryn's true killer, she might think more kindly of me."

That made Littlefinger sit up. "True killer? I confess, you make me curious. Who do you propose?"

It was Tyrion's turn to smile. "Gifts I give my friends, freely. Lysa Arryn would need to understand that."

"Is it her friendship you require, or her swords?"

"Both."

Littlefinger stroked the neat spike of his beard. "Lysa has woes of her own. Clansmen raiding out of the Mountains of the Moon, in greater numbers than ever before . . . and better armed."

"Distressing," said Tyrion Lannister, who had armed them. "I could help her with that. A word from me . . ."

"And what would this word cost her?"

"I want Lady Lysa and her son to acclaim Joffrey as king, to swear fealty, and to—"

"—make war on the Starks and Tullys?" Littlefinger shook his head. "There's the roach in your pudding, Lannister. Lysa will never send her knights against Riverrun."

"Nor would I ask it. We have no lack of enemies. I'll use her power to oppose Lord Renly, or Lord Stannis, should he stir from Dragonstone. In return, I will give her justice for Jon Arryn and peace in the Vale. I will even name that appalling child of hers Warden of the East, as his father was before him." *I want to see him fly*, a boy's voice whispered faintly in memory. "And to seal the bargain, I will give her my niece."

He had the pleasure of seeing a look of genuine surprise in Petyr Baelish's grey-green eyes. "Myrcella?"

"When she comes of age, she can wed little Lord Robert. Until such time, she'll be Lady Lysa's ward at the Eyrie."

"And what does Her Grace the queen think of this ploy?" When Tyrion shrugged, Littlefinger burst into laughter. "I thought not. You're a dangerous little man, Lannister. Yes, I could sing this song to Lysa." Again the sly smile, the mischief in his glance. "If I cared to."

Tyrion nodded, waiting, knowing Littlefinger could never abide a long silence.

"So," Lord Petyr continued after a pause, utterly unabashed, "what's in your pot for me?"

"Harrenhal."

It was interesting to watch his face. Lord Petyr's father had been the smallest of small lords, his grandfather a landless hedge knight; by birth, he held no more than a few stony acres on the windswept shore of the Fingers. Harrenhal was one of the richest plums in the Seven Kingdoms, its lands broad and rich and fertile, its great castle as formidable as any in the realm . . . and so large as to dwarf Riverrun, where Petyr Baelish had been fostered by House Tully, only to be brusquely expelled when he dared raise his sights to Lord Hoster's daughter.

Littlefinger took a moment to adjust the drape of his cape, but Tyrion had seen the flash of hunger in those sly cat's eyes. *I have him*, he knew. "Harrenhal is cursed," Lord Petyr said after a moment, trying to sound bored.

"Then raze it to the ground and build anew to suit yourself. You'll have no lack of coin. I mean to make you liege lord of the Trident. These river lords have proven they cannot be trusted. Let them do you fealty for their lands."

"Even the Tullys?"

"If there are any Tullys left when we are done."

Littlefinger looked like a boy who had just taken a furtive bite from a honeycomb. He was *trying* to watch for bees, but the honey was so sweet. "Harrenhal and all its lands and incomes," he mused. "With a stroke, you'd make me one of the greatest lords in the realm. Not that I'm ungrateful, my lord, but—why?"

"You served my sister well in the matter of the succession."

"As did Janos Slynt. On whom this same castle of Harrenhal was quite recently bestowed—only to be snatched away when he was no longer of use."

Tyrion laughed. "You have me, my lord. What can I say? I need you to deliver the Lady Lysa. I did not need Janos Slynt." He gave a crooked shrug. "I'd sooner have you seated in Harrenhal than Renly seated on the Iron Throne. What could be plainer?"

"What indeed. You realize that I may need to bed Lysa Arryn again to get her consent to this marriage?"

"I have little doubt you'll be equal to the task."

"I once told Ned Stark that when you find yourself naked with an ugly woman, the only thing to do is close your eyes and get on with it." Littlefinger steepled his fingers and gazed into Tyrion's mismatched eyes. "Give me a fortnight to conclude my affairs and arrange for a ship to carry me to Gulltown."

"That will do nicely."

His guest rose. "This has been quite the pleasant morning, Lannister. And profitable . . . for both of us, I trust." He bowed, his cape a swirl of yellow as he strode out the door.

Two, thought Tyrion.

He went up to his bedchamber to await Varys, who would soon be making an appearance. Evenfall, he guessed. Perhaps as late as moonrise, though he hoped not. He hoped to visit Shae tonight. He was pleasantly surprised when Galt of the Stone Crows informed him not an hour later that the powdered man was at his door. "You are a cruel man, to make the Grand Maester squirm so," the eunuch scolded. "The man cannot abide a secret."

"Is that a crow I hear, calling the raven black? Or would you sooner not hear what I've proposed to Doran Martell?"

Varys giggled. "Perhaps my little birds have told me."

"Have they, indeed?" He wanted to hear this. "Go on."

"The Dornishmen thus far have held aloof from these wars. Doran Martell has called his banners, but no more. His hatred for House Lannister is well known, and it is commonly thought he will join Lord Renly. You wish to dissuade him."

"All this is obvious," said Tyrion.

"The only puzzle is what you might have offered for his allegiance. The prince is a sentimental man, and he still mourns his sister Elia and her sweet babe."

"My father once told me that a lord never lets sentiment get in the way of ambition . . . and it happens we have an empty seat on the small council, now that Lord Janos has taken the black."

"A council seat is not to be despised," Varys admitted, "yet will it be enough to make a proud man forget his sister's murder?"

"Why forget?" Tyrion smiled. "I've promised to deliver his sister's killers, alive or dead, as he prefers. *After* the war is done, to be sure."

Varys gave him a shrewd look. "My little birds tell me that Princess Elia cried a . . . certain name . . . when they came for her."

"Is a secret still a secret if everyone knows it?" In Casterly Rock, it was common knowledge that Gregor Clegane had killed Elia and her babe. They said he had raped the princess with her son's blood and brains still on his hands.

"*This* secret is your lord father's sworn man."

"My father would be the first to tell you that fifty thousand Dornishmen are worth one rabid dog."

Varys stroked a powdered cheek. "And if Prince Doran demands the blood of the lord who gave the command as well as the knight who did the deed . . ."

"Robert Baratheon led the rebellion. All commands came from him, in the end."

"Robert was not at King's Landing."

"Neither was Doran Martell."

"So. Blood for his pride, a chair for his ambition. Gold and land, that goes without saying. A sweet offer . . . yet sweets can be poisoned. If I were the prince, something more would I require before I should reach for this honeycomb. Some token of good faith, some sure safeguard against betrayal." Varys smiled his slimiest smile. "Which one will you give him, I wonder?"

Tyrion sighed. "You know, don't you?"

"Since you put it that way—yes. Tommen. You could scarcely offer Myrcella to Doran Martell and Lysa Arryn both."

"Remind me never to play these guessing games with you again. You cheat."

"Prince Tommen is a good boy."

"If I pry him away from Cersei and Joffrey while he's still young, he may even grow to be a good man."

"And a good king?"

"Joffrey is king."

"And Tommen is heir, should anything ill befall His Grace. Tommen, whose nature is so sweet, and notably . . . tractable."

"You have a suspicious mind, Varys."

"I shall take that as a tribute, my lord. In any case, Prince Doran will hardly be insensible of the great honor you do him. Very deftly done, I would say . . . but for one small flaw."

The dwarf laughed. "Named Cersei?"

"What avails statecraft against the love of a mother for the sweet fruit of her womb? Perhaps, for the glory of her House and the safety of the realm, the queen might be persuaded to send away Tommen or Myrcella. But both of them? Surely not."

"What Cersei does not know will never hurt me."

"And if Her Grace were to discover your intentions before your plans are ripe?"

"Why," he said, "then I would know the man who told her to be my certain enemy." And when Varys giggled, he thought, *Three.*

SANSA

ome to the godswood tonight, if you want to go home.
The words were the same on the hundredth reading as they'd
been on the first, when Sansa had discovered the folded sheet of
parchment beneath her pillow. She did not know how it had gotten there
or who had sent it. The note was unsigned, unsealed, and the hand unfa-
miliar. She crushed the parchment to her chest and whispered the words
to herself. "Come to the godswood tonight, if you want to go home," she
breathed, ever so faintly.

What could it mean? Should she take it to the queen to prove that she
was being good? Nervously, she rubbed her stomach. The angry purple
bruise Ser Meryn had given her had faded to an ugly yellow, but still
hurt. His fist had been mailed when he hit her. It was her own fault. She
must learn to hide her feelings better, so as not to anger Joffrey. When
she heard that the Imp had sent Lord Slynt to the Wall, she had forgotten
herself and said, "I hope the Others get him." The king had not been
pleased.

Come to the godswood tonight, if you want to go home.

Sansa had prayed so hard. Could this be her answer at last, a true
knight sent to save her? Perhaps it was one of the Redwyne twins, or
bold Ser Balon Swann . . . or even Beric Dondarrion, the young lord her
friend Jeyne Poole had loved, with his red-gold hair and the spray of stars
on his black cloak.

Come to the godswood tonight, if you want to go home.

What if it was some cruel jape of Joffrey's, like the day he had taken her up to the battlements to show her Father's head? Or perhaps it was some subtle snare to prove she was not loyal. If she went to the godswood, would she find Ser Ilyn Payne waiting for her, sitting silent under the heart tree with Ice in his hand, his pale eyes watching to see if she'd come?

Come to the godswood tonight, if you want to go home.

When the door opened, she hurriedly stuffed the note under her sheet and sat on it. It was her bedmaid, the mousy one with the limp brown hair. "What do you want?" Sansa demanded.

"Will milady be wanting a bath tonight?"

"A fire, I think . . . I feel a chill." She *was* shivering, though the day had been hot.

"As you wish."

Sansa watched the girl suspiciously. Had she seen the note? Had she put it under the pillow? It did not seem likely; she seemed a stupid girl, not one you'd want delivering secret notes, but Sansa did not know her. The queen had her servants changed every fortnight, to make certain none of them befriended her.

When a fire was blazing in the hearth, Sansa thanked the maid curtly and ordered her out. The girl was quick to obey, as ever, but Sansa decided there was something sly about her eyes. Doubtless, she was scurrying off to report to the queen, or maybe Varys. All her maids spied on her, she was certain.

Once alone, she thrust the note in the flames, watching the parchment curl and blacken. *Come to the godswood tonight, if you want to go home.* She drifted to her window. Below, she could see a short knight in moon-pale armor and a heavy white cloak pacing the drawbridge. From his height, it could only be Ser Preston Greenfield. The queen had given her freedom of the castle, but even so, he would want to know where she was going if she tried to leave Maegor's Holdfast at this time of night. What was she to tell him? Suddenly she was glad she had burned the note.

She unlaced her gown and crawled into her bed, but she did not sleep. *Was he still there?* she wondered. *How long will he wait?* It was so cruel, to send her a note and tell her nothing. The thoughts went round and round in her head.

If only she had someone to tell her what to do. She missed Septa Mordane, and even more Jeyne Poole, her truest friend. The septa had lost her head with the rest, for the crime of serving House Stark. Sansa did not know what had happened to Jeyne, who had disappeared from her rooms afterward, never to be mentioned again. She tried not to think of them too often, yet sometimes the memories came unbidden, and then it was hard to hold back the tears. Once in a while, Sansa even missed her sister. By now Arya was safe back in Winterfell, dancing and sewing, playing with Bran and baby Rickon, even riding through the winter town if she liked. Sansa was allowed to go riding too, but only in the bailey, and it got boring going round in a circle all day.

She was wide awake when she heard the shouting. Distant at first, then growing louder. Many voices yelling together. She could not make out the words. And there were horses as well, and pounding feet, shouts of command. She crept to her window and saw men running on the walls, carrying spears and torches. *Go back to your bed*, Sansa told herself, *this is nothing that concerns you, just some new trouble out in the city.* The talk at the wells had all been of troubles in the city of late. People were crowding in, running from the war, and many had no way to live save by robbing and killing each other. *Go to bed.*

But when she looked, the white knight was gone, the bridge across the dry moat down but undefended.

Sansa turned away without thinking and ran to her wardrobe. *Oh, what am I doing?* she asked herself as she dressed. *This is madness.* She could see the lights of many torches on the curtain walls. Had Stannis and Renly come at last to kill Joffrey and claim their brother's throne? If so, the guards would raise the drawbridge, cutting off Maegor's Holdfast from the outer castle. Sansa threw a plain grey cloak over her shoulders and picked up the knife she used to cut her meat. *If it is some trap, better that I die than let them hurt me more*, she told herself. She hid the blade under her cloak.

A column of red-cloaked swordsmen ran past as she slipped out into the night. She waited until they were well past before she darted across the undefended drawbridge. In the yard, men were buckling on swordbelts and cinching the saddles of their horses. She glimpsed Ser Preston near the stables with three others of the Kingsguard, white cloaks bright as the moon as they helped Joffrey into his armor. Her breath caught in her throat when she saw the king. Thankfully, he did not see her. He was shouting for his sword and crossbow.

The noise receded as she moved deeper into the castle, never daring to look back for fear that Joffrey might be watching . . . or worse, following. The serpentine steps twisted ahead, striped by bars of flickering light from the narrow windows above. Sansa was panting by the time she reached the top. She ran down a shadowy colonnade and pressed herself against a wall to catch her breath. When something brushed against her leg, she almost jumped out of her skin, but it was only a cat, a ragged black tom with a chewed-off ear. The creature spit at her and leapt away.

By the time she reached the godswood, the noises had faded to a faint rattle of steel and a distant shouting. Sansa pulled her cloak tighter. The air was rich with the smells of earth and leaf. *Lady would have liked this place*, she thought. There was something wild about a godswood; even here, in the heart of the castle at the heart of the city, you could feel the old gods watching with a thousand unseen eyes.

Sansa had favored her mother's gods over her father's. She loved the statues, the pictures in leaded glass, the fragrance of burning incense, the septons with their robes and crystals, the magical play of the rainbows over altars inlaid with mother-of-pearl and onyx and lapis lazuli. Yet she could not deny that the godswood had a certain power too. Especially by night. *Help me*, she prayed, *send me a friend, a true knight to champion me . . .*

She moved from tree to tree, feeling the roughness of the bark beneath her fingers. Leaves brushed at her cheeks. Had she come too late? He would not have left so soon, would he? Or had he even been here? Dare she risk calling out? It seemed so hushed and still here . . .

"I feared you would not come, child."

Sansa whirled. A man stepped out of the shadows, heavyset, thick of neck, shambling. He wore a dark grey robe with the cowl pulled forward, but when a thin sliver of moonlight touched his cheek, she knew him at once by the blotchy skin and web of broken veins beneath. "Ser Dontos," she breathed, heartbroken. "Was it you?"

"Yes, my lady." When he moved closer, she could smell the sour stench of wine on his breath. "Me." He reached out a hand.

Sansa shrank back. *"Don't!"* She slid her hand under her cloak, to her hidden knife. "What . . . what do you want with me?"

"Only to help you," Dontos said, "as you helped me."

"You're drunk, aren't you?"

"Only one cup of wine, to help my courage. If they catch me now, they'll strip the skin off my back."

And what will they do to me? Sansa found herself thinking of Lady again. She could smell out falsehood, she *could*, but she was dead, Father had killed her, on account of Arya. She drew the knife and held it before her with both hands.

"Are you going to stab me?" Dontos asked.

"I will," she said. "Tell me who sent you."

"No one, sweet lady. I swear it on my honor as a knight."

"A knight?" Joffrey had decreed that he was to be a knight no longer, only a fool, lower even than Moon Boy. "I prayed to the gods for a knight to come save me," she said. "I prayed and prayed. Why would they send me a drunken old fool?"

"I deserve that, though . . . I know it's queer, but . . . all those years I was a knight, I was truly a fool, and now that I am a fool I think . . . I think I may find it in me to be a knight again, sweet lady.

And all because of you . . . your grace, your courage. You saved me, not only from Joffrey, but from myself." His voice dropped. "The singers say there was another fool once who was the greatest knight of all . . ."

"*Florian*," Sansa whispered. A shiver went through her.

"Sweet lady, I would be your Florian," Dontos said humbly, falling to his knees before her.

Slowly, Sansa lowered the knife. Her head seemed terribly light, as if she were floating. *This is madness, to trust myself to this drunkard, but if I turn away will the chance ever come again?* "How . . . how would you do it? Get me away?"

Ser Dontos raised his face to her. "Taking you from the castle, that will be the hardest. Once you're out, there are ships that would take you home. I'd need to find the coin and make the arrangements, that's all."

"Could we go now?" she asked, hardly daring to hope.

"This very night? No, my lady, I fear not. First I must find a sure way to get you from the castle when the hour is ripe. It will not be easy, nor quick. They watch me as well." He licked his lips nervously. "Will you put away your blade?"

Sansa slipped the knife beneath her cloak. "Rise, ser."

"Thank you, sweet lady." Ser Dontos lurched clumsily to his feet, and brushed earth and leaves from his knees. "Your lord father was as true a man as the realm has ever known, but I stood by and let them slay him. I said nothing, did nothing . . . and yet, when Joffrey would have slain me, you spoke up. Lady, I have never been a hero, no Ryam Redwyne or Barristan the Bold. I've won no tourneys, no renown in war . . . but I *was* a knight once, and you have helped me remember what that meant. My life is a poor thing, but it is yours." Ser Dontos placed a hand on the gnarled bole of the heart tree. He was shaking, she saw. "I vow, with your father's gods as witness, that I shall send you home."

He swore. A solemn oath, before the gods. "Then . . . I will put myself in your hands, ser. But how will I know, when it is time to go? Will you send me another note?"

Ser Dontos glanced about anxiously. "The risk is too great. You must come here, to the godswood. As often as you can. This is the safest place. The *only* safe place. Nowhere else. Not in your chambers nor mine nor on the steps nor in the yard, even if it seems we are alone. The stones have ears in the Red Keep, and only here may we talk freely."

"Only here," Sansa said. "I'll remember."

"And if I should seem cruel or mocking or indifferent when men are watching, forgive me, child. I have a role to play, and you must do the same. One misstep and our heads will adorn the walls as did your father's."

She nodded. "I understand."

"You will need to be brave and strong . . . and patient, patient above all."

"I will be," she promised, "but . . . please . . . make it as soon as you can. I'm afraid . . ."

"So am I," Ser Dontos said, smiling wanly. "And now you must go, before you are missed."

"You will not come with me?"

"Better if we are never seen together."

Nodding, Sansa took a step . . . then spun back, nervous, and softly laid a kiss on his cheek, her eyes closed. "My Florian," she whispered. "The gods heard my prayer."

She flew along the river walk, past the small kitchen, and through the pig yard, her hurried footsteps lost beneath the squealing of the hogs in their pens. *Home,* she thought, *home, he is going to take me home, he'll keep me safe, my Florian.* The songs about Florian and Jonquil were her very favorites. *Florian was homely too, though not so old.*

She was racing headlong down the serpentine steps when a man lurched out of a hidden doorway. Sansa caromed into him and lost her balance. Iron fingers caught her by the wrist before she could fall, and a deep voice rasped at her. "It's a long roll down the serpentine, little bird. Want to kill us both?" His laughter was rough as a saw on stone. "Maybe you do."

The Hound. "No, my lord, pardons, I'd never." Sansa averted her eyes but it was too late, he'd seen her face. "Please, you're hurting me." She tried to wriggle free.

"And what's Joff's little bird doing flying down the serpentine in the black of night?" When she did not answer, he shook her. *"Where were you?"*

"The g-g-godswood, my lord," she said, not daring to lie. "Praying . . . praying for my father, and . . . for the king, praying that he'd not be hurt."

"Think I'm so drunk that I'd believe *that*?" He let go his grip on her arm, swaying slightly as he stood, stripes of light and darkness falling across his terrible burnt face. "You look almost a woman . . . face, teats, and you're taller too, almost . . . ah, you're still a stupid little bird, aren't you? Singing all the songs they taught you . . . sing me a song, why don't you? Go on. Sing to me. Some song about knights and fair maids. You like knights, don't you?"

He was scaring her. "T-true knights, my lord."

"*True* knights," he mocked. "And I'm no lord, no more than I'm a knight. Do I need to beat that into you?" Clegane reeled and almost fell. *"Gods,"* he swore, "too much wine. Do you like wine, little bird? *True* wine? A flagon of sour red, dark as blood, all a man needs. Or a woman."

He laughed, shook his head. "Drunk as a dog, damn me. You come now. Back to your cage, little bird. I'll take you there. Keep you safe for the king." The Hound gave her a push, oddly gentle, and followed her down the steps. By the time they reached the bottom, he had lapsed back into a brooding silence, as if he had forgotten she was there.

When they reached Maegor's Holdfast, she was alarmed to see that it was Ser Boros Blount who now held the bridge. His high white helm turned stiffly at the sound of their footsteps. Sansa flinched away from his gaze. Ser Boros was the worst of the Kingsguard, an ugly man with a foul temper, all scowls and jowls.

"That one is nothing to fear, girl." The Hound laid a heavy hand on her shoulder. "Paint stripes on a toad, he does not become a tiger."

Ser Boros lifted his visor. "Ser, where—"

"Fuck your *ser*, Boros. You're the knight, not me. I'm the king's dog, remember?"

"The king was looking for his dog earlier."

"The dog was drinking. It was your night to shield him, *ser*. You and my other *brothers*."

Ser Boros turned to Sansa. "How is it you are not in your chambers at this hour, lady?"

"I went to the godswood to pray for the safety of the king." The lie sounded better this time, almost true.

"You expect her to sleep with all the noise?" Clegane said. "What was the trouble?"

"Fools at the gate," Ser Boros admitted. "Some loose tongues spread tales of the preparations for Tyrek's wedding feast, and these wretches got it in their heads they should be feasted too. His Grace led a sortie and sent them scurrying."

"A brave boy," Clegane said, mouth twitching.

Let us see how brave he is when he faces my brother, Sansa thought. The Hound escorted her across the drawbridge. As they were winding their way up the steps, she said, "Why do you let people call you a dog? You won't let *anyone* call you a knight."

"I like dogs better than knights. My father's father was kennelmaster at the Rock. One autumn year, Lord Tytos came between a lioness and her prey. The lioness didn't give a shit that she was Lannister's own sigil. Bitch tore into my lord's horse and would have done for my lord too, but my grandfather came up with the hounds. Three of his dogs died running her off. My grandfather lost a leg, so Lannister paid him for it with lands and a towerhouse, and took his son to squire. The three dogs on our banner are the three that died, in the yellow of autumn grass. A hound will die for you, but never lie to you. And he'll look you straight in the face." He cupped her under the jaw, raising her chin, his fingers pinching her painfully. "And that's more than little birds can do, isn't it? I never got my song."

"I . . . I know a song about Florian and Jonquil."

"Florian and Jonquil? A fool and his cunt. Spare me. But one day I'll have a song from you, whether you will it or no."

"I will sing it for you gladly."

Sandor Clegane snorted. "Pretty thing, and such a bad liar. A dog can smell a lie, you know. Look around you, and take a good whiff. They're all liars here . . . and every one better than you."

ARYA

When she climbed all the way up to the highest branch, Arya could see chimneys poking through the trees. Thatched roofs clustered along the shore of the lake and the small stream that emptied into it, and a wooden pier jutted out into the water beside a low long building with a slate roof.

She skinnied farther out, until the branch began to sag under her weight. No boats were tied to the pier, but she could see thin tendrils of smoke rising from some of the chimneys, and part of a wagon jutting out behind a stable.

Someone's there. Arya chewed her lip. All the other places they'd come upon had been empty and desolate. Farms, villages, castles, septs, barns, it made no matter. If it could burn, the Lannisters had burned it; if it could die, they'd killed it. They had even set the woods ablaze where they could, though the leaves were still green and wet from recent rains, and the fires had not spread. "They would have burned the lake if they could have," Gendry had said, and Arya knew he was right. On the night of their escape, the flames of the burning town had shimmered so brightly on the water that it had seemed that the lake *was* afire.

When they finally summoned the nerve to steal back into the ruins the next night, nothing remained but blackened stones, the hollow shells of houses, and corpses. In some places wisps of pale smoke still rose from the ashes. Hot Pie had pleaded with them not to go back, and Lommy called them fools and swore that Ser Amory would catch them and kill

them too, but Lorch and his men had long gone by the time they reached
the holdfast. They found the gates broken down, the walls partly demol-
ished, and the inside strewn with the unburied dead. One look was
enough for Gendry. "They're killed, every one," he said. "And dogs have
been at them too, look."

"Or wolves."

"Dogs, wolves, it makes no matter. It's done here."

But Arya would not leave until they found Yoren. They couldn't have
killed *him*, she told herself, he was too hard and tough, and a brother of
the Night's Watch besides. She said as much to Gendry as they searched
among the corpses.

The axe blow that had killed him had split his skull apart, but the
great tangled beard could be no one else's, or the garb, patched and unwashed and so faded it was more grey than black. Ser Amory Lorch had
given no more thought to burying his own dead than to those he had
murdered, and the corpses of four Lannister men-at-arms were heaped
near Yoren's. Arya wondered how many it had taken to bring him down.

He was going to take me home, she thought as they dug the old man's
hole. There were too many dead to bury them all, but Yoren at least
must have a grave, Arya had insisted. *He was going to bring me safe to
Winterfell, he promised.* Part of her wanted to cry. The other part wanted
to kick him.

It was Gendry who thought of the lord's towerhouse and the three that
Yoren had sent to hold it. They had come under attack as well, but the
round tower had only one entry, a second-story door reached by a ladder.
Once that had been pulled inside, Ser Amory's men could not get at
them. The Lannisters had piled brush around the tower's base and set it
afire, but the stone would not burn, and Lorch did not have the patience
to starve them out. Cutjack opened the door at Gendry's shout, and
when Kurz said they'd be better pressing on north than going back, Arya
had clung to the hope that she still might reach Winterfell.

Well, this village was no Winterfell, but those thatched roofs promised
warmth and shelter and maybe even food, if they were bold enough to
risk them. *Unless it's Lorch there. He had horses; he would have traveled faster than us.*

She watched from the tree for a long time, hoping she might see something; a man, a horse, a banner, anything that would help her know. A
few times she glimpsed motion, but the buildings were so far off it was
hard to be certain. Once, very clearly, she heard the whinny of a horse.

The air was full of birds, crows mostly. From afar, they were no larger
than flies as they wheeled and flapped above the thatched roofs. To the
east, Gods Eye was a sheet of sun-hammered blue that filled half the

world. Some days, as they made their slow way up the muddy shore (Gendry wanted no part of any roads, and even Hot Pie and Lommy saw the sense in that), Arya felt as though the lake were calling her. She wanted to leap into those placid blue waters, to feel clean again, to swim and splash and bask in the sun. But she dare not take off her clothes where the others could see, not even to wash them. At the end of the day she would often sit on a rock and dangle her feet in the cool water. She had finally thrown away her cracked and rotted shoes. Walking barefoot was hard at first, but the blisters had finally broken, the cuts had healed, and her soles had turned to leather. The mud was nice between her toes, and she liked to feel the earth underfoot when she walked.

From up here, she could see a small wooded island off to the northeast. Thirty yards from shore, three black swans were gliding over the water, so serene . . . no one had told them that war had come, and they cared nothing for burning towns and butchered men. She stared at them with yearning. Part of her wanted to be a swan. The other part wanted to eat one. She had broken her fast on some acorn paste and a handful of bugs. Bugs weren't so bad when you got used to them. Worms were worse, but still not as bad as the pain in your belly after days without food. Finding bugs was easy, all you had to do was kick over a rock. Arya had eaten a bug once when she was little, just to make Sansa screech, so she hadn't been afraid to eat another. Weasel wasn't either, but Hot Pie retched up the beetle he tried to swallow, and Lommy and Gendry wouldn't even try. Yesterday Gendry had caught a frog and shared it with Lommy, and, a few days before, Hot Pie had found blackberries and stripped the bush bare, but mostly they had been living on water and acorns. Kurz had told them how to use rocks and make a kind of acorn paste. It tasted awful.

She wished the poacher hadn't died. He'd known more about the woods than all the rest of them together, but he'd taken an arrow through the shoulder pulling in the ladder at the towerhouse. Tarber had packed it with mud and moss from the lake, and for a day or two Kurz swore the wound was nothing, even though the flesh of his throat was turning dark while angry red welts crept up his jaw and down his chest. Then one morning he couldn't find the strength to get up, and by the next he was dead.

They buried him under a mound of stones, and Cutjack had claimed his sword and hunting horn, while Tarber helped himself to bow and boots and knife. They'd taken it all when they left. At first they thought the two had just gone hunting, that they'd soon return with game and feed them all. But they waited and waited, until finally Gendry made them move on. Maybe Tarber and Cutjack figured they would stand a

better chance without a gaggle of orphan boys to herd along. They probably would too, but that didn't stop her hating them for leaving.

Beneath her tree, Hot Pie barked like a dog. Kurz had told them to use
animal sounds to signal to each other. An old poacher's trick, he'd said,
but he'd died before he could teach them how to make the sounds right.
Hot Pie's bird calls were awful. His dog was better, but not much.

Arya hopped from the high branch to one beneath it, her hands out for
balance. *A water dancer never falls.* Lightfoot, her toes curled tight
around the branch, she walked a few feet, hopped down to a larger limb,
then swung hand over hand through the tangle of leaves until she
reached the trunk. The bark was rough beneath her fingers, against her
toes. She descended quickly, jumping down the final six feet, rolling
when she landed.

Gendry gave her a hand to pull her up. "You were up there a long time.
What could you see?"

"A fishing village, just a little place, north along the shore. Twenty-six
thatch roofs and one slate, I counted. I saw part of a wagon. Someone's
there."

At the sound of her voice, Weasel came creeping out from the bushes.
Lommy had named her that. He said she looked like a weasel, which
wasn't true, but they couldn't keep on calling her the crying girl after she
finally stopped crying. Her mouth was filthy. Arya hoped she hadn't
been eating mud again.

"Did you see people?" asked Gendry.

"Mostly just roofs," Arya admitted, "but some chimneys were smoking, and I heard a horse." The Weasel put her arms around her leg,
clutching tight. Sometimes she did that now.

"If there's people, there's food," Hot Pie said, too loudly. Gendry was
always telling him to be more quiet, but it never did any good. "Might be
they'd give us some."

"Might be they'd kill us too," Gendry said.

"Not if we yielded," Hot Pie said hopefully.

"Now you sound like Lommy."

Lommy Greenhands sat propped up between two thick roots at the
foot of an oak. A spear had taken him through his left calf during the
fight at the holdfast. By the end of the next day, he had to limp along
one-legged with an arm around Gendry, and now he couldn't even do
that. They'd hacked branches off trees to make a litter for him, but it
was slow, hard work carrying him along, and he whimpered every time
they jounced him.

"We have to yield," he said. "That's what Yoren should have done. He
should have opened the gates like they said."

Arya was sick of Lommy going on about how Yoren should have yielded. It was all he talked about when they carried him, that and his leg and his empty belly.

Hot Pie agreed. "They *told* Yoren to open the gates, they told him in the king's name. You have to do what they tell you in the king's name. It was that stinky old man's fault. If he'd of yielded, they would have left us be."

Gendry frowned. "Knights and lordlings, they take each other captive and pay ransoms, but they don't care if the likes of you yield or not." He turned to Arya. "What else did you see?"

"If it's a fishing village, they'd sell us fish, I bet," said Hot Pie. The lake teemed with fresh fish, but they had nothing to catch them with. Arya had tried to use her hands, the way she'd seen Koss do, but fish were quicker than pigeons and the water played tricks on her eyes.

"I don't know about fish." Arya tugged at the Weasel's matted hair, thinking it might be best to hack it off. "There's crows down by the water. Something's dead there."

"Fish, washed up on shore," Hot Pie said. "If the crows eat it, I bet we could."

"We should catch some crows, we could eat *them*," said Lommy. "We could make a fire and roast them like chickens."

Gendry looked fierce when he scowled. His beard had grown in thick and black as briar. "I said, no fires."

"Lommy's *hungry*," Hot Pie whined, "and I am too."

"We're all hungry," said Arya.

"*You're* not," Lommy spat from the ground. "Worm breath."

Arya could have kicked him in his wound. "I *said* I'd dig worms for you too, if you wanted."

Lommy made a disgusted face. "If it wasn't for my leg, I'd hunt us some boars."

"Some boars," she mocked. "You need a boarspear to hunt boars, and horses and dogs, and men to flush the boar from its lair." Her father had hunted boar in the wolfswood with Robb and Jon. Once he even took Bran, but never Arya, even though she was older. Septa Mordane said boar hunting was not for ladies, and Mother only promised that when she was older she might have her own hawk. She was older now, but if she had a hawk she'd *eat* it.

"What do *you* know about hunting boars?" said Hot Pie.

"More than you."

Gendry was in no mood to hear it. "Quiet, both of you, I need to think what to do." He always looked pained when he tried to think, like it hurt him something fierce.

"Yield," Lommy said.

"I told you to shut up about the yielding. We don't even know who's in there. Maybe we can steal some food."

"Lommy could steal, if it wasn't for his leg," said Hot Pie. "He was a thief in the city."

"A bad thief," Arya said, "or he wouldn't have got caught."

Gendry squinted up at the sun. "Evenfall will be the best time to sneak in. I'll go scout come dark."

"No, I'll go," Arya said. "You're too noisy."

Gendry got that look on his face. "We'll both go."

"Arry should go," said Lommy. "He's sneakier than you are."

"We'll *both* go, I said."

"But what if you don't come back? Hot Pie can't carry me by himself, you know he can't . . ."

"And there's wolves," Hot Pie said. "I heard them last night, when I had the watch. They sounded close."

Arya had heard them too. She'd been asleep in the branches of an elm, but the howling had woken her. She'd sat awake for a good hour, listening to them, prickles creeping up her spine.

"And you won't even let us have a fire to keep them off," Hot Pie said. "It's not right, leaving us for the wolves."

"No one is leaving you," Gendry said in disgust. "Lommy has his spear if the wolves come, and you'll be with him. We're just going to go see, that's all; we're coming back."

"Whoever it is, you should yield to them," Lommy whined. "I need some potion for my leg, it hurts bad."

"If we see any leg potion, we'll bring it," Gendry said. "Arry, let's go, I want to get near before the sun is down. Hot Pie, you keep Weasel here, I don't want her following."

"Last time she kicked me."

"*I'll* kick you if you don't keep her here." Without waiting for an answer, Gendry donned his steel helm and walked off.

Arya had to scamper to keep up. Gendry was five years older and a foot taller than she was, and long of leg as well. For a while he said nothing, just plowed on through the trees with an angry look on his face, making too much noise. But finally he stopped and said, "I think Lommy's going to die."

She was not surprised. Kurz had died of his wound, and he'd been a lot stronger than Lommy. Whenever it was Arya's turn to help carry him, she could feel how warm his skin was, and smell the stink off his leg. "Maybe we could find a maester . . ."

"You only find maesters in castles, and even if we found one, he wouldn't dirty his hands on the likes of Lommy." Gendry ducked under a low-hanging limb.

"That's not true." Maester Luwin would have helped anyone who came to him, she was certain.

"He's going to die, and the sooner he does it, the better for the rest of us. We should just leave him, like he says. If it was you or me hurt, you know he'd leave us." They scrambled down a steep cut and up the other side, using roots for handholds. "I'm sick of carrying him, and I'm sick of all his talk about yielding too. If he could stand up, I'd knock his teeth in. Lommy's no use to anyone. That crying girl's no use either."

"You leave Weasel alone, she's just scared and hungry is all." Arya glanced back, but the girl was not following for once. Hot Pie must have grabbed her, like Gendry had told him.

"She's no use," Gendry repeated stubbornly. "Her and Hot Pie and Lommy, they're slowing us down, and they're going to get us killed. You're the only one of the bunch who's good for anything. Even if you are a girl."

Arya froze in her steps. *"I'm not a girl!"*

"Yes you are. Do you think I'm as stupid as they are?"

"No, you're stupider. The Night's Watch doesn't take girls, everyone knows that."

"That's true. I don't know why Yoren brought you, but he must have had some reason. You're still a girl."

"I am not!"

"Then pull out your cock and take a piss. Go on."

"I don't need to take a piss. If I wanted to I could."

"Liar. You can't take out your cock because you don't have one. I never noticed before when there were thirty of us, but you always go off in the woods to make your water. You don't see Hot Pie doing that, nor me neither. If you're not a girl, you must be some eunuch."

"You're the eunuch."

"You know I'm not." Gendry smiled. "You want me to take out my cock and prove it? I don't have anything to hide."

"Yes you do," Arya blurted, desperate to escape the subject of the cock she didn't have. "Those gold cloaks were after you at the inn, and you won't tell us why."

"I wish I knew. I think Yoren knew, but he never told me. Why did you think they were after you, though?"

Arya bit her lip. She remembered what Yoren had said, the day he had hacked off her hair. *This lot, half o' them would turn you over to the queen quick as spit for a pardon and maybe a few silvers. The other half'd do the same, only they'd rape you first.* Only Gendry was different, the queen wanted him too. "I'll tell you if you'll tell me," she said warily.

"I would if I knew, Arry . . . is that really what you're called, or do you have some girl's name?"

Arya glared at the gnarled root by her feet. She realized that the pretense was done. Gendry knew, and she had nothing in her pants to convince him otherwise. She could draw Needle and kill him where he stood, or else trust him. She wasn't certain she'd be able to kill him, even if she tried; he had his own sword, and he was a *lot* stronger. All that was left was the truth. "Lommy and Hot Pie can't know," she said.

"They won't," he swore. "Not from me."

"Arya." She raised her eyes to his. "My name is Arya. Of House Stark."

"Of House . . ." It took him a moment before he said, "The King's Hand was named Stark. The one they killed for a traitor."

"He was never a traitor. He was my father."

Gendry's eyes widened. "So *that*'s why you thought . . ."

She nodded. "Yoren was taking me home to Winterfell."

"I . . . you're highborn then, a . . . you'll be a lady . . ."

Arya looked down at her ragged clothes and bare feet, all cracked and callused. She saw the dirt under her nails, the scabs on her elbows, the scratches on her hands. *Septa Mordane wouldn't even know me, I bet. Sansa might, but she'd pretend not to.* "My mother's a lady, and my sister, but I never was."

"Yes you were. You were a lord's daughter and you lived in a castle, didn't you? And you . . . gods be good, I never . . ." All of a sudden Gendry seemed uncertain, almost afraid. "All that about cocks, I never should have said that. And I been pissing in front of you and everything, I . . . I beg your pardon, m'lady."

"Stop that!" Arya hissed. Was he mocking her?

"I know my courtesies, m'lady," Gendry said, stubborn as ever. "Whenever highborn girls came into the shop with their fathers, my master told me I was to bend the knee, and speak only when they spoke to me, and call them *m'lady.*"

"If you start calling me m'lady, even *Hot Pie* is going to notice. And you better keep on pissing the same way too."

"As m'lady commands."

Arya slammed his chest with both hands. He tripped over a stone and sat down with a thump. "What kind of lord's daughter are you?" he said, laughing.

"*This* kind." She kicked him in the side, but it only made him laugh harder. "You laugh all you like. *I'm* going to see who's in the village." The sun had already fallen below the trees; dusk would be on them in no time at all. For once it was Gendry who had to hurry after. "You smell that?" she asked.

He sniffed the air. "Rotten fish?"

"You know it's not."

"We better be careful. I'll go around west, see if there's some road. There must be if you saw a wagon. You take the shore. If you need help, bark like a dog."

"That's stupid. If I need help, I'll shout *help*." She darted away, bare feet silent in the grass. When she glanced back over her shoulder, he was watching her with that pained look on his face that meant he was thinking. *He's probably thinking that he shouldn't be letting m'lady go stealing food.* Arya just knew he was going to be stupid now.

The smell grew stronger as she got closer to the village. It did not smell like rotten fish to her. This stench was ranker, fouler. She wrinkled her nose.

Where the trees began to thin, she used the undergrowth, slipping from bush to bush quiet as a shadow. Every few yards she stopped to listen. The third time, she heard horses, and a man's voice as well. And the smell got worse. *Dead man's stink, that's what it is.* She had smelled it before, with Yoren and the others.

A dense thicket of brambles grew south of the village. By the time she reached it, the long shadows of sunset had begun to fade, and the lantern bugs were coming out. She could see thatched roofs just beyond the hedge. She crept along until she found a gap and squirmed through on her belly, keeping well hidden until she saw what made the smell.

Beside the gently lapping waters of Gods Eye, a long gibbet of raw green wood had been thrown up, and things that had once been men dangled there, their feet in chains, while crows pecked at their flesh and flapped from corpse to corpse. For every crow there were a hundred flies. When the wind blew off the lake, the nearest corpse twisted on its chain, ever so slightly. The crows had eaten most of its face, and something else had been at it as well, something much larger. Throat and chest had been torn apart, and glistening green entrails and ribbons of ragged flesh dangled from where the belly had been opened. One arm had been ripped right off the shoulder; Arya saw the bones a few feet away, gnawed and cracked, picked clean of meat.

She made herself look at the next man and the one beyond him and the one beyond *him*, telling herself she was hard as a stone. Corpses all, so savaged and decayed that it took her a moment to realize they had been stripped before they were hanged. They did not look like naked people; they hardly looked like people at all. The crows had eaten their eyes, and sometimes their faces. Of the sixth in the long row, nothing remained but a single leg, still tangled in its chains, swaying with each breeze..

Fear cuts deeper than swords. Dead men could not hurt her, but whoever had killed them could. Well beyond the gibbet, two men in mail hauberks stood leaning on their spears in front of the long low building by the water, the one with the slate roof. A pair of tall poles had been driven into the muddy ground in front of it, banners drooping from each staff. One looked red and one paler, white or yellow maybe, but both were limp and with the dusk settling, she could not even be certain that red one was Lannister crimson. *I don't need to see the lion, I can see all the dead people, who else would it be but Lannisters!*

Then there was a shout.

The two spearmen turned at the cry, and a third man came into view, shoving a captive before him. It was growing too dark to make out faces, but the prisoner was wearing a shiny steel helm, and when Arya saw the horns she knew it was Gendry. *You stupid stupid stupid STUPID!* she thought. If he'd been here she would have kicked him again.

The guards were talking loudly, but she was too far away to make out the words, especially with the crows gabbling and flapping closer to hand. One of the spearmen snatched the helm off Gendry's head and asked him a question, but he must not have liked the answer, because he smashed him across the face with the butt of his spear and knocked him down. The one who'd captured him gave him a kick, while the second spearman was trying on the bull's-head helm. Finally they pulled him to his feet and marched him off toward the storehouse. When they opened the heavy wooden doors, a small boy darted out, but one of the guards grabbed his arm and flung him back inside. Arya heard sobbing from inside the building, and then a shriek so loud and full of pain that it made her bite her lip.

The guards shoved Gendry inside with the boy and barred the doors behind them. Just then, a breath of wind came sighing off the lake, and the banners stirred and lifted. The one on the tall staff bore the golden lion, as she'd feared. On the other, three sleek black shapes ran across a field as yellow as butter. Dogs, she thought. Arya had seen those dogs before, but where?

It didn't matter. The only thing that mattered was that they had Gendry. Even if he *was* stubborn and stupid, she had to get him out. She wondered if they knew that the queen wanted him.

One of the guards took off his helm and donned Gendry's instead. It made her angry to see him wearing it, but she knew there was nothing she could do to stop him. She thought she heard more screams from inside the windowless storehouse, muffled by the masonry, but it was hard to be certain.

She stayed long enough to see the guard changed, and much more besides. Men came and went. They led their horses down to the stream to drink. A hunting party returned from the wood, carrying a deer's carcass slung from a pole. She watched them clean and gut it and build a cookfire on the far side of the stream, and the smell of cooking meat mingled queerly with the stench of corruption. Her empty belly roiled and she thought she might retch. The prospect of food brought other men out of the houses, near all of them wearing bits of mail or boiled leather. When the deer was cooked, the choicest portions were carried to one of the houses.

She thought that the dark might let her crawl close and free Gendry, but the guards kindled torches off the cookfire. A squire brought meat and bread to the two guarding the storehouse, and later two more men joined them and they all passed a skin of wine from hand to hand. When it was empty the others left, but the two guards remained, leaning on their spears.

Arya's arms and legs were stiff when she finally wriggled out from under the briar into the dark of the wood. It was a black night, with a thin sliver of moon appearing and disappearing as the clouds blew past. *Silent as a shadow,* she told herself as she moved through the trees. In this darkness she dared not run, for fear of tripping on some unseen root or losing her way. On her left Gods Eye lapped calmly against its shores. On her right a wind sighed through the branches, and leaves rustled and stirred. Far off, she heard the howling of wolves.

Lommy and Hot Pie almost shit themselves when she stepped out of the trees behind them. "Quiet," she told them, putting an arm around Weasel when the little girl came running up.

Hot Pie stared at her with big eyes. "We thought you left us." He had his shortsword in hand, the one Yoren had taken off the gold cloak. "I was scared you was a wolf."

"Where's the Bull?" asked Lommy.

"They caught him," Arya whispered. "We have to get him out. Hot Pie, you got to help. We'll sneak up and kill the guards, and then I'll open the door."

Hot Pie and Lommy exchanged a look. "How many?"

"I couldn't count," Arya admitted. "Twenty at least, but only two on the door."

Hot Pie looked as if he were going to cry. "We can't fight *twenty.*"

"You only need to fight *one.* I'll do the other and we'll get Gendry out and run."

"We should yield," Lommy said. "Just go in and yield."

Arya shook her head stubbornly.

"Then just leave him, Arry," Lommy pleaded. "They don't know about the rest of us. If we hide, they'll go away, you know they will. It's not our fault Gendry's captured."

"You're stupid, Lommy," Arya said angrily. "You'll *die* if we don't get Gendry out. Who's going to carry you?"

"You and Hot Pie."

"All the time, with no one else to help? We'll never do it. Gendry was the strong one. Anyhow, I don't care what you say, I'm going back for him." She looked at Hot Pie. "Are you coming?"

Hot Pie glanced at Lommy, at Arya, at Lommy again. "I'll come," he said reluctantly.

"Lommy, you keep Weasel here."

He grabbed the little girl by the hand and pulled her close. "What if the wolves come?"

"Yield," Arya suggested.

Finding their way back to the village seemed to take hours. Hot Pie kept stumbling in the dark and losing his way, and Arya had to wait for him and double back. Finally she took him by the hand and led him along through the trees. "Just be quiet and follow." When they could make out the first faint glow of the village fires against the sky, she said, "There's dead men hanging on the other side of the hedge, but they're nothing to be scared of, just remember fear cuts deeper than swords. We have to go real quiet and slow." Hot Pie nodded.

She wriggled under the briar first and waited for him on the far side, crouched low. Hot Pie emerged pale and panting, face and arms bloody with long scratches. He started to say something, but Arya put a finger to his lips. On hands and knees, they crawled along the gibbet, beneath the swaying dead. Hot Pie never once looked up, nor made a sound.

Until the crow landed on his back, and he gave a muffled gasp. *"Who's there?"* a voice boomed suddenly from the dark.

Hot Pie leapt to his feet. *"I yield!"* He threw away his sword as dozens of crows rose shrieking and complaining to flap about the corpses. Arya grabbed his leg and tried to drag him back down, but he wrenched loose and ran forward, waving his arms. "I yield, I yield."

She bounced up and drew Needle, but by then men were all around her. Arya slashed at the nearest, but he blocked her with a steel-clad arm, and someone else slammed into her and dragged her to the ground, and a third man wrenched the sword from her grasp. When she tried to bite, her teeth snapped shut on cold dirty chainmail. "Oho, a fierce one," the man said, laughing. The blow from his iron-clad fist near knocked her head off.

They talked over her as she lay hurting, but Arya could not seem to understand the words. Her ears rang. When she tried to crawl off, the earth moved beneath her. *They took Needle.* The shame of that hurt worse than the pain, and the pain hurt a lot. Jon had given her that sword. Syrio had taught her to use it.

Finally someone grabbed the front of her jerkin, yanked her to her knees. Hot Pie was kneeling too, before the tallest man Arya had ever seen, a monster from one of Old Nan's stories. She never saw where the giant had come from. Three black dogs raced across his faded yellow surcoat, and his face looked as hard as if it had been cut from stone. Suddenly Arya knew where she had seen those dogs before. The night of the tourney at King's Landing, all the knights had hung their shields outside their pavilions. "That one belongs to the Hound's brother," Sansa had confided when they passed the black dogs on the yellow field. "He's even bigger than Hodor, you'll see. They call him *the Mountain That Rides.*"

Arya let her head droop, only half aware of what was going on around her. Hot Pie was yielding some more. The Mountain said, "You'll lead us to these others," and walked off. Next she was stumbling past the dead men on their gibbet, while Hot Pie told their captors he'd bake them pies and tarts if they didn't hurt him. Four men went with them. One carried a torch, one a longsword; two had spears.

They found Lommy where they'd left him, under the oak. "I yield," he called out at once when he saw them. He'd flung away his own spear and raised his hands, splotchy green with old dye. "I yield. Please."

The man with the torch searched around under the trees. "Are you the last? Baker boy said there was a girl."

"She ran off when she heard you coming," Lommy said. "You made a lot of noise." And Arya thought, *Run, Weasel, run as far as you can, run and hide and never come back.*

"Tell us where we can find that whoreson Dondarrion, and there'll be a hot meal in it for you."

"Who?" said Lommy blankly.

"I told you, this lot don't know no more than those cunts in the village. Waste o' bloody time."

One of the spearmen drifted over to Lommy. "Something wrong with your leg, boy?"

"It got hurt."

"Can you walk?" He sounded concerned.

"No," said Lommy. "You got to carry me."

"Think so?" The man lifted his spear casually and drove the point through the boy's soft throat. Lommy never even had time to yield again. He jerked once, and that was all. When the man pulled his spear loose, blood sprayed out in a dark fountain. "Carry him, he says," he muttered, chuckling.

TYRION

They had warned him to dress warmly. Tyrion Lannister took them at their word. He was garbed in heavy quilted breeches and a woolen doublet, and over it all he had thrown the shadowskin cloak he had acquired in the Mountains of the Moon. The cloak was absurdly long, made for a man twice his height. When he was not ahorse, the only way to wear the thing was to wrap it around him several times, which made him look like a ball of striped fur.

Even so, he was glad he had listened. The chill in the long dank vault went bone deep. Timett had chosen to retreat back up to the cellar after a brief taste of the cold below. They were somewhere under the hill of Rhaenys, behind the Guildhall of the Alchemists. The damp stone walls were splotchy with nitre, and the only light came from the sealed iron-and-glass oil lamp that Hallyne the Pyromancer carried so gingerly.

Gingerly indeed . . . and these would be the ginger jars. Tyrion lifted one for inspection. It was round and ruddy, a fat clay grapefruit. A little big for his hand, but it would fit comfortably in the grip of a normal man, he knew. The pottery was thin, so fragile that even he had been warned not to squeeze too tightly, lest he crush it in his fist. The clay felt roughened, pebbled. Hallyne told him that was intentional. "A smooth pot is more apt to slip from a man's grasp."

The wildfire oozed slowly toward the lip of the jar when Tyrion tilted it to peer inside. The color would be a murky green, he knew, but the poor light made that impossible to confirm. "Thick," he observed.

"That is from the cold, my lord," said Hallyne, a pallid man with soft damp hands and an obsequious manner. He was dressed in striped black-and-scarlet robes trimmed with sable, but the fur looked more than a little patchy and moth-eaten. "As it warms, the substance will flow more easily, like lamp oil."

The substance was the pyromancers' own term for wildfire. They called each other *wisdom* as well, which Tyrion found almost as annoying as their custom of hinting at the vast secret stores of knowledge that they wanted him to think they possessed. Once theirs had been a powerful guild, but in recent centuries the maesters of the Citadel had supplanted the alchemists almost everywhere. Now only a few of the older order remained, and they no longer even pretended to transmute metals . . .

. . . but they *could* make wildfire. "Water will not quench it, I am told."

"That is so. Once it takes fire, the substance will burn fiercely until it is no more. More, it will seep into cloth, wood, leather, even steel, so they take fire as well."

Tyrion remembered the red priest Thoros of Myr and his flaming sword. Even a thin coating of wildfire could burn for an hour. Thoros always needed a new sword after a melee, but Robert had been fond of the man and ever glad to provide one. "Why doesn't it seep into the clay as well?"

"Oh, but it does," said Hallyne. "There is a vault below this one where we store the older pots. Those from King Aerys's day. It was his fancy to have the jars made in the shapes of fruits. Very perilous fruits indeed, my lord Hand, and, hmmm, *riper* now than ever, if you take my meaning. We have sealed them with wax and pumped the lower vault full of water, but even so . . . by rights they ought to have been destroyed, but so many of our masters were murdered during the Sack of King's Landing, the few acolytes who remained were unequal to the task. And much of the stock we made for Aerys was lost. Only last year, two hundred jars were discovered in a storeroom beneath the Great Sept of Baelor. No one could recall how they came there, but I'm sure I do not need to tell you that the High Septon was beside himself with terror. I myself saw that they were safely moved. I had a cart filled with sand, and sent our most able acolytes. We worked only by night, we—"

"—did a splendid job, I have no doubt." Tyrion placed the jar he'd been holding back among its fellows. They covered the table, standing in orderly rows of four and marching away into the subterranean dimness. And there were other tables beyond, many other tables. "These, ah, *fruits* of the late King Aerys, can they still be used?"

"Oh, yes, most certainly . . . but *carefully*, my lord, ever so carefully. As it ages, the substance grows ever more, hmmmm, *fickle*, let us say. Any flame will set it afire. Any spark. Too much heat and jars will blaze up of their own accord. It is not wise to let them sit in sunlight, even for a short time. Once the fire begins within, the heat causes the substance to expand violently, and the jars shortly fly to pieces. If other jars should happen to be stored in the same vicinity, those go up as well, and so—"

"How many jars do you have at present?"

"This morning the Wisdom Munciter told me that we had seven thousand eight hundred and forty. That count includes four thousand jars from King Aerys's day, to be sure."

"Our overripe fruits?"

Hallyne bobbed his head. "Wisdom Malliard believes we shall be able to provide a full ten thousand jars, as was promised the queen. I concur." The pyromancer looked indecently pleased with that prospect.

Assuming our enemies give you the time. The pyromancers kept their recipe for wildfire a closely guarded secret, but Tyrion knew that it was a lengthy, dangerous, and time-consuming process. He had assumed the promise of ten thousand jars was a wild boast, like that of the bannerman who vows to marshal ten thousand swords for his lord and shows up on the day of battle with a hundred and two. *If they can truly give us ten thousand . . .*

He did not know whether he ought to be delighted or terrified. *Perhaps a smidge of both.* "I trust that your guild brothers are not engaging in any unseemly haste, Wisdom. We do not want ten thousand jars of defective wildfire, nor even one . . . and we most certainly do not want any mishaps."

"There will be no mishaps, my lord Hand. The substance is prepared by trained acolytes in a series of bare stone cells, and each jar is removed by an apprentice and carried down here the instant it is ready. Above each work cell is a room filled entirely with sand. A protective spell has been laid on the floors, hmmm, most powerful. Any fire in the cell below causes the floors to fall away, and the sand smothers the blaze at once."

"Not to mention the careless acolyte." By *spell* Tyrion imagined Hallyne meant *clever trick.* He thought he would like to inspect one of these false-ceilinged cells to see how it worked, but this was not the time. Perhaps when the war was won.

"My brethren are never careless," Hallyne insisted. "If I may be, hmmmm, *frank . . .*"

"Oh, do."

"The substance flows through my veins, and lives in the heart of every pyromancer. We respect its power. But the common soldier, hmmmm, the crew of one of the queen's spitfires, say, in the unthinking frenzy of battle . . . any little mistake can bring catastrophe. That cannot be said too often. My father often told King Aerys as much, as *his* father told old King Jaehaerys."

"They must have listened," Tyrion said. "If they had burned the city down, someone would have told me. So your counsel is that we had best be careful?"

"Be *very* careful," said Hallyne. "Be *very very* careful."

"These clay jars . . . do you have an ample supply?"

"We do, my lord, and thank you for asking."

"You won't mind if I take some, then. A few thousand."

"A few *thousand*?"

"Or however many your guild can spare, without interfering with production. It's *empty* pots I'm asking for, understand. Have them sent round to the captains on each of the city gates."

"I will, my lord, but why . . . ?"

Tyrion smiled up at him. "When you tell me to dress warmly, I dress warmly. When you tell me to be careful, well . . ." He gave a shrug. "I've seen enough. Perhaps you would be so good as to escort me back up to my litter?"

"It would be my great, hmmm, pleasure, my lord." Hallyne lifted the lamp and led the way back to the stairs. "It was good of you to visit us. A great honor, hmmm. It has been too long since the King's Hand graced us with his presence. Not since Lord Rossart, and he was of our order. That was back in King Aerys's day. King Aerys took a great interest in our work."

King Aerys used you to roast the flesh off his enemies. His brother Jaime had told him a few stories of the Mad King and his pet pyromancers. "Joffrey will be interested as well, I have no doubt." *Which is why I'd best keep him well away from you.*

"It is our great hope to have the king visit our Guildhall in his own royal person. I have spoken of it to your royal sister. A great feast . . ."

It was growing warmer as they climbed. "His Grace has prohibited all feasting until such time as the war is won." *At my insistence.* "The king does not think it fitting to banquet on choice food while his people go without bread."

"A most, hmmm, *loving* gesture, my lord. Perhaps instead some few of us might call upon the king at the Red Keep. A small demonstration of our powers, as it were, to distract His Grace from his many cares for an evening. Wildfire is but one of the dread secrets of our ancient order. Many and wondrous are the things we might show you."

"I will take it up with my sister." Tyrion had no objection to a few

magic tricks, but Joff's fondness for making men fight to the death was
trial enough; he had no intention of allowing the boy to taste the possibilities of burning them alive.

When at last they reached the top of the steps, Tyrion shrugged out of
his shadowskin fur and folded it over his arm. The Guildhall of the
Alchemists was an imposing warren of black stone, but Hallyne led him
through the twists and turns until they reached the Gallery of the Iron
Torches, a long echoing chamber where columns of green fire danced
around black metal columns twenty feet tall. Ghostly flames shimmered
off the polished black marble of the walls and floor and bathed the hall in
an emerald radiance. Tyrion would have been more impressed if he
hadn't known that the great iron torches had only been lit this morning
in honor of his visit, and would be extinguished the instant the doors
closed behind him. Wildfire was too costly to squander.

They emerged atop the broad curving steps that fronted on the Street
of the Sisters, near the foot of Visenya's Hill. He bid Hallyne farewell and
waddled down to where Timett son of Timett waited with an escort of
Burned Men. Given his purpose today, it had seemed a singularly appropriate choice for his guard. Besides, their scars struck terror in the hearts
of the city rabble. That was all to the good these days. Only three nights
past, another mob had gathered at the gates of the Red Keep, chanting for
food. Joff had unleashed a storm of arrows against them, slaying four, and
then shouted down that they had his leave to eat their dead. *Winning us
still more friends.*

Tyrion was surprised to see Bronn standing beside the litter as well.
"What are you doing here?"

"Delivering your messages," Bronn said. "Ironhand wants you urgently at the Gate of the Gods. He won't say why. And you've been
summoned to Maegor's too."

"*Summoned?*" Tyrion knew of only one person who would presume
to use that word. "And what does Cersei want of me?"

Bronn shrugged. "The queen commands you to return to the castle at
once and attend her in her chambers. That stripling cousin of yours delivered the message. Four hairs on his lip and he thinks he's a man."

"Four hairs and a knighthood. He's *Ser* Lancel now, never forget."
Tyrion knew that Ser Jacelyn would not send for him unless the matter
was of import. "I'd best see what Bywater wants. Inform my sister that I
will attend her on my return."

"She won't like that," Bronn warned.

"Good. The longer Cersei waits, the angrier she'll become, and anger
makes her stupid. I much prefer angry and stupid to composed and cunning." Tyrion tossed his folded cloak into his litter, and Timett helped
him up after it.

The market square inside the Gate of the Gods, which in normal times would have been thronged with farmers selling vegetables, was near deserted when Tyrion crossed it. Ser Jacelyn met him at the gate, and raised his iron hand in brusque salute. "My lord. Your cousin Cleos Frey is here, come from Riverrun under a peace banner with a letter from Robb Stark."

"Peace terms?"

"So he says."

"Sweet cousin. Show me to him."

The gold cloaks had confined Ser Cleos to a windowless guardroom in the gatehouse. He rose when they entered. "Tyrion, you are a most welcome sight."

"That's not something I hear often, cousin."

"Has Cersei come with you?"

"My sister is otherwise occupied. Is this Stark's letter?" He plucked it off the table. "Ser Jacelyn, you may leave us."

Bywater bowed and departed. "I was asked to bring the offer to the Queen Regent," Ser Cleos said as the door shut.

"I shall." Tyrion glanced over the map that Robb Stark had sent with his letter. "All in good time, cousin. Sit. Rest. You look gaunt and haggard." He looked worse than that, in truth.

"Yes." Ser Cleos lowered himself onto a bench. "It is bad in the riverlands, Tyrion. Around the Gods Eye and along the kingsroad especially. The river lords are burning their own crops to try and starve us, and your father's foragers are torching every village they take and putting the smallfolk to the sword."

That was the way of war. The smallfolk were slaughtered, while the highborn were held for ransom. *Remind me to thank the gods that I was born a Lannister.*

Ser Cleos ran a hand through his thin brown hair. "Even with a peace banner, we were attacked twice. Wolves in mail, hungry to savage anyone weaker than themselves. The gods alone know what side they started on, but they're on their own side now. Lost three men, and twice as many wounded."

"What news of our foe?" Tyrion turned his attention back to Stark's terms. *The boy does not want too much. Only half the realm, the release of our captives, hostages, his father's sword . . . oh, yes, and his sisters.*

"The boy sits idle at Riverrun," Ser Cleos said. "I think he fears to face your father in the field. His strength grows less each day. The river lords have departed, each to defend his own lands."

Is this what Father intended? Tyrion rolled up Stark's map. "These terms will never do."

"Will you at least consent to trade the Stark girls for Tion and Willem?" Ser Cleos asked plaintively.

Tion Frey was his younger brother, Tyrion recalled. "No," he said gently, "but we'll propose our own exchange of captives. Let me consult with Cersei and the council. We shall send you back to Riverrun with *our* terms."

Clearly, the prospect did not cheer him. "My lord, I do not believe Robb Stark will yield easily. It is Lady Catelyn who wants this peace, not the boy."

"Lady Catelyn wants her daughters." Tyrion pushed himself down from the bench, letter and map in hand. "Ser Jacelyn will see that you have food and fire. You look in dire need of sleep, cousin. I will send for you when we know more."

He found Ser Jacelyn on the ramparts, watching several hundred new recruits drilling in the field below. With so many seeking refuge in King's Landing, there was no lack of men willing to join the City Watch for a full belly and a bed of straw in the barracks, but Tyrion had no illusions about how well these ragged defenders of theirs would fight if it came to battle.

"You did well to send for me," Tyrion said. "I shall leave Ser Cleos in your hands. He is to have every hospitality."

"And his escort?" the commander wanted to know.

"Give them food and clean garb, and find a maester to see to their hurts. They are not to set foot inside the city, is that understood?" It would never do to have the truth of conditions in King's Landing reach Robb Stark in Riverrun.

"Well understood, my lord."

"Oh, and one more thing. The alchemists will be sending a large supply of clay pots to each of the city gates. You're to use them to train the men who will work your spitfires. Fill the pots with green paint and have them drill at loading and firing. Any man who spatters should be replaced. When they have mastered the paint pots, substitute lamp oil and have them work at lighting the jars and firing them while aflame. Once they learn to do that without burning themselves, they may be ready for wildfire."

Ser Jacelyn scratched at his cheek with his iron hand. "Wise measures. Though I have no love for that alchemist's piss."

"Nor I, but I use what I'm given."

Once back inside his litter, Tyrion Lannister drew the curtains and plumped a cushion under his elbow. Cersei would be displeased to learn that he had intercepted Stark's letter, but his father had sent him here to rule, not to please Cersei.

It seemed to him that Robb Stark had given them a golden chance. Let the boy wait at Riverrun dreaming of an easy peace. Tyrion would reply with terms of his own, giving the King in the North just enough of what he wanted to keep him hopeful. Let Ser Cleos wear out his bony Frey rump riding to and fro with offers and counters. All the while, their cousin Ser Stafford would be training and arming the new host he'd raised at Casterly Rock. Once he was ready, he and Lord Tywin could smash the Tullys and Starks between them.

Now if only Robert's brothers would be so accommodating. Glacial as his progress was, still Renly Baratheon crept north and east with his huge southron host, and scarcely a night passed that Tyrion did not dread being awakened with the news that Lord Stannis was sailing his fleet up the Blackwater Rush. *Well, it would seem I have a goodly stock of wildfire, but still . . .*

The sound of some hubbub in the street intruded on his worries. Tyrion peered out cautiously between the curtains. They were passing through Cobbler's Square, where a sizable crowd had gathered beneath the leather awnings to listen to the rantings of a prophet. A robe of undyed wool belted with a hempen rope marked him for one of the begging brothers.

"Corruption!" the man cried shrilly. "There is the warning! Behold the Father's scourge!" He pointed at the fuzzy red wound in the sky. From this vantage, the distant castle on Aegon's High Hill was directly behind him, with the comet hanging forebodingly over its towers. *A clever choice of stage,* Tyrion reflected. "We have become swollen, bloated, foul. Brother couples with sister in the bed of kings, and the fruit of their incest capers in his palace to the piping of a twisted little monkey demon. Highborn ladies fornicate with fools and give birth to monsters! Even the High Septon has forgotten the gods! He bathes in scented waters and grows fat on lark and lamprey while his people starve! Pride comes before prayer, maggots rule our castles, and gold is all . . . but *no more!* The Rotten Summer is at an end, and the Whoremonger King is brought low! When the boar did open him, a great stench rose to heaven and a thousand snakes slid forth from his belly, hissing and biting!" He jabbed his bony finger back at comet and castle. "There comes the Harbinger! Cleanse yourselves, the gods cry out, lest ye be cleansed! Bathe in the wine of righteousness, or you shall be bathed in fire! *Fire!"*

"Fire!" other voices echoed, but the hoots of derision almost drowned them out. Tyrion took solace from that. He gave the command to continue, and the litter rocked like a ship on a rough sea as the Burned Men cleared a path. *Twisted little monkey demon indeed.* The wretch did have a point about the High Septon, to be sure. What was it that Moon

Boy had said of him the other day? *A pious man who worships the Seven so fervently that he eats a meal for each of them whenever he sits to table.* The memory of the fool's jape made Tyrion smile.

He was pleased to reach the Red Keep without further incident. As he climbed the steps to his chambers, Tyrion felt a deal more hopeful than he had at dawn. *Time, that's all I truly need, time to piece it all together. Once the chain is done . . .* He opened the door to his solar.

Cersei turned away from the window, her skirts swirling around her slender hips. "How *dare* you ignore my summons!"

"Who admitted you to my tower?"

"*Your* tower? This is my son's royal castle."

"So they tell me." Tyrion was not amused. Crawn would be even less so; his Moon Brothers had the guard today. "I was about to come to you, as it happens."

"Were you?"

He swung the door shut behind him. "You doubt me?"

"Always, and with good reason."

"I'm hurt." Tyrion waddled to the sideboard for a cup of wine. He knew no surer way to work up a thirst than talking with Cersei. "If I've given you offense, I would know how."

"What a disgusting little worm you are. Myrcella is my only daughter. Did you truly imagine that I would allow you to sell her like a bag of oats?"

Myrcella, he thought. *Well, that egg has hatched. Let's see what color the chick is.* "Hardly a bag of oats. Myrcella is a princess. Some would say this is what she was born for. Or did you plan to marry her to Tommen?"

Her hand lashed out, knocking the wine cup from his hand to spill on the floor. "Brother or no, I should have your tongue out for that. *I* am Joffrey's regent, not you, and I say that Myrcella will not be shipped off to this Dornishman the way I was shipped to Robert Baratheon."

Tyrion shook wine off his fingers and sighed. "Why not? She'd be a deal safer in Dorne than she is here."

"Are you utterly ignorant or simply perverse? You know as well as I that the Martells have no cause to love us."

"The Martells have every cause to hate us. Nonetheless, I expect them to agree. Prince Doran's grievance against House Lannister goes back only a generation, but the Dornishmen have warred against Storm's End and Highgarden for a thousand years, and Renly has taken Dorne's allegiance for granted. Myrcella is nine, Trystane Martell eleven. I have proposed they wed when she reaches her fourteenth year. Until such time, she would be an honored guest at Sunspear, under Prince Doran's protection."

"A hostage," Cersei said, mouth tightening.

"An honored guest," Tyrion insisted, "and I suspect Martell will treat Myrcella more kindly than Joffrey has treated Sansa Stark. I had in mind to send Ser Arys Oakheart with her. With a knight of the Kingsguard as her sworn shield, no one is like to forget who or what she is."

"Small good Ser Arys will do her if Doran Martell decides that my daughter's death would wash out his sister's."

"Martell is too honorable to murder a nine-year-old girl, particularly one as sweet and innocent as Myrcella. So long as he holds her he can be reasonably certain that we'll keep faith on our side, and the terms are too rich to refuse. Myrcella is the least part of it. I've also offered him his sister's killer, a council seat, some castles on the Marches . . ."

"Too much." Cersei paced away from him, restless as a lioness, skirts swirling. "You've offered too much, and without my authority or consent."

"This is the Prince of Dorne we are speaking of. If I'd offered less, he'd likely spit in my face."

"Too much!" Cersei insisted, whirling back.

"What would *you* have offered him, that hole between your legs?" Tyrion said, his own anger flaring.

This time he saw the slap coming. His head snapped around with a *crack.* "Sweet sweet sister," he said, "I promise you, that was the last time you will ever strike me."

His sister laughed. "Don't threaten me, little man. Do you think Father's letter keeps you safe? A piece of paper. Eddard Stark had a piece of paper too, for all the good it did him."

Eddard Stark did not have the City Watch, Tyrion thought, *nor my clansmen, nor the sellswords that Bronn has hired. I do.* Or so he hoped. Trusting in Varys, in Ser Jacelyn Bywater, in Bronn. Lord Stark had probably had his delusions as well.

Yet he said nothing. A wise man did not pour wildfire on a brazier. Instead he poured a fresh cup of wine. "How safe do you think Myrcella will be if King's Landing falls? Renly and Stannis will mount her head beside yours."

And Cersei began to cry.

Tyrion Lannister could not have been more astonished if Aegon the Conqueror himself had burst into the room, riding on a dragon and juggling lemon pies. He had not seen his sister weep since they were children together at Casterly Rock. Awkwardly, he took a step toward her. When your sister cries, you were supposed to comfort her . . . but this was *Cersei!* He reached a tentative hand for her shoulder.

"Don't *touch* me," she said, wrenching away. It should not have hurt, yet it did, more than any slap. Red-faced, as angry as she was grief-stricken, Cersei struggled for breath. "Don't look at me, not . . . not like this . . . not *you.*"

Politely, Tyrion turned his back. "I did not mean to frighten you. I promise you, nothing will happen to Myrcella."

"Liar," she said behind him. "I'm not a child, to be soothed with empty promises. You told me you would free Jaime too. Well, where is he?"

"In Riverrun, I should imagine. Safe and under guard, until I find a way to free him."

Cersei sniffed. "I should have been born a man. I would have no need of any of you then. None of this would have been allowed to happen. How could Jaime let himself be captured by that *boy*? And Father, I trusted in him, fool that I am, but where is he now that he's wanted? What is he *doing*?"

"Making war."

"From behind the walls of Harrenhal?" she said scornfully. "A curious way of fighting. It looks suspiciously like hiding."

"Look again."

"What else would you call it? Father sits in one castle, and Robb Stark sits in another, and no one *does* anything."

"There is sitting and there is sitting," Tyrion suggested. "Each one waits for the other to move, but the lion is still, poised, his tail twitching, while the fawn is frozen by fear, bowels turned to jelly. No matter which way he bounds, the lion will have him, and he knows it."

"And you're *quite* certain that Father is the lion?"

Tyrion grinned. "It's on all our banners."

She ignored the jest. "If it was Father who'd been taken captive, Jaime would not be sitting by idly, I promise you."

Jaime would be battering his host to bloody bits against the walls of Riverrun, and the Others take their chances. He never did have any patience, no more than you, sweet sister. "Not all of us can be as bold as Jaime, but there are other ways to win wars. Harrenhal is strong and well situated."

"And King's Landing is *not*, as we both know perfectly well. While Father plays lion and fawn with the Stark boy, Renly marches up the roseroad. He could be at our gates any day now!"

"The city will not fall in a day. From Harrenhal it is a straight, swift march down the kingsroad. Renly will scarce have unlimbered his siege engines before Father takes him in the rear. His host will be the hammer, the city walls the anvil. It makes a lovely picture."

Cersei's green eyes bored into him, wary, yet hungry for the reassurance he was feeding her. "And if Robb Stark marches?"

"Harrenhal is close enough to the fords of the Trident so that Roose

Bolton cannot bring the northern foot across to join with the Young
Wolf's horse. Stark cannot march on King's Landing without taking Har-
renhal first, and even with Bolton he is not strong enough to do that."
Tyrion tried his most winning smile. "Meanwhile Father lives off the fat
of the riverlands, while our uncle Stafford gathers fresh levies at the
Rock."

Cersei regarded him suspiciously. "How could you know all this? Did
Father tell you his intentions when he sent you here?"

"No. I glanced at a map."

Her look turned to disdain. "You've conjured up every word of this in
that grotesque head of yours, haven't you, Imp?"

Tyrion tsked. "Sweet sister, I ask you, if we weren't winning, would
the Starks have sued for peace?" He drew out the letter that Ser Cleos
Frey had brought. "The Young Wolf has sent us terms, you see. Unac-
ceptable terms, to be sure, but still, a beginning. Would you care to see
them?"

"Yes." That fast, she was all queen again. "How do you come to have
them? They should have come to me."

"What else is a Hand for, if not to hand you things?" Tyrion handed
her the letter. His cheek still throbbed where Cersei's hand had left its
mark. *Let her flay half my face, it will be a small price to pay for her
consent to the Dornish marriage.* He would have that now, he could
sense it.

And certain knowledge of an informer too . . . well, that was the
plum in his pudding.

BRAN

ancer was draped in bardings of snowy white wool emblazoned with the grey direwolf of House Stark, while Bran wore grey breeches and white doublet, his sleeves and collar trimmed with vair. Over his heart was his wolf's-head brooch of silver and polished jet. He would sooner have had Summer than a silver wolf on his breast, but Ser Rodrik had been unyielding.

The low stone steps balked Dancer only for a moment. When Bran urged her on, she took them easily. Beyond the wide oak-and-iron doors, eight long rows of trestle tables filled Winterfell's Great Hall, four on each side of the center aisle. Men crowded shoulder to shoulder on the benches. "Stark!" they called as Bran trotted past, rising to their feet. "Winterfell! *Winterfell!*"

He was old enough to know that it was not truly *him* they shouted for—it was the harvest they cheered, it was Robb and his victories, it was his lord father and his grandfather and all the Starks going back eight thousand years. Still, it made him swell with pride. For so long as it took him to ride the length of that hall he forgot that he was broken. Yet when he reached the dais, with every eye upon him, Osha and Hodor undid his straps and buckles, lifted him off Dancer's back, and carried him to the high seat of his fathers.

Ser Rodrik was seated to Bran's left, his daughter Beth beside him. Rickon was to his right, his mop of shaggy auburn hair grown so long that it brushed his ermine mantle. He had refused to let anyone cut it since their mother had gone. The last girl to try had been bitten for her efforts. "I wanted to ride too," he said as Hodor led Dancer away. "I ride better than you."

"You don't, so hush up," he told his brother. Ser Rodrik bellowed for quiet. Bran raised his voice. He bid them welcome in the name of his brother, the King in the North, and asked them to thank the gods old and new for Robb's victories and the bounty of the harvest. "May there be a hundred more," he finished, raising his father's silver goblet.

"*A hundred more!*" Pewter tankards, clay cups, and iron-banded drinking horns clashed together. Bran's wine was sweetened with honey and fragrant with cinnamon and cloves, but stronger than he was used to. He could feel its hot snaky fingers wriggling through his chest as he swallowed. By the time he set down the goblet, his head was swimming.

"You did well, Bran," Ser Rodrik told him. "Lord Eddard would have been most proud." Down the table, Maester Luwin nodded his agreement as the servers began to carry in the food.

Such food Bran had never seen; course after course after course, so much that he could not manage more than a bite or two of each dish. There were great joints of aurochs roasted with leeks, venison pies chunky with carrots, bacon, and mushrooms, mutton chops sauced in honey and cloves, savory duck, peppered boar, goose, skewers of pigeon and capon, beef-and-barley stew, cold fruit soup. Lord Wyman had brought twenty casks of fish from White Harbor packed in salt and seaweed; whitefish and winkles, crabs and mussels, clams, herring, cod, salmon, lobster and lampreys. There was black bread and honeycakes and oaten biscuits; there were turnips and pease and beets, beans and squash and huge red onions; there were baked apples and berry tarts and pears poached in strongwine. Wheels of white cheese were set at every table, above and below the salt, and flagons of hot spice wine and chilled autumn ale were passed up and down the tables.

Lord Wyman's musicians played bravely and well, but harp and fiddle and horn were soon drowned beneath a tide of talk and laughter, the clash of cup and plate, and the snarling of hounds fighting for table scraps. The singer sang good songs, "Iron Lances" and "The Burning of the Ships" and "The Bear and the Maiden Fair," but only Hodor seemed to be listening. He stood beside the piper, hopping from one foot to the other.

The noise swelled to a steady rumbling roar, a great heady stew of sound. Ser Rodrik talked with Maester Luwin above Beth's curly head, while Rickon screamed happily at the Walders. Bran had not wanted the Freys at the high table, but the maester reminded him that they would soon be kin. Robb was to marry one of their aunts, and Arya one of their uncles. "She never will," Bran said, "not Arya," but Maester Luwin was unyielding, so there they were beside Rickon.

The serving men brought every dish to Bran first, that he might take the lord's portion if he chose. By the time they reached the ducks, he could eat no more. After that he nodded approval at each course in turn, and waved it away. If the dish smelled especially choice, he would send it to one of the lords on the dais, a gesture of friendship and favor that Maester Luwin told him he must make. He sent some salmon down to poor sad Lady Hornwood, the boar to the boisterous Umbers, a dish of goose-in-berries to Cley Cerwyn, and a huge lobster to Joseth the master of horse, who was neither lord nor guest, but had seen to Dancer's training and made it possible for Bran to ride. He sent sweets to Hodor and Old Nan as well, for no reason but he loved them. Ser Rodrik reminded him to send something to his foster brothers, so he sent Little Walder some boiled beets and Big Walder the buttered turnips.

On the benches below, Winterfell men mixed with smallfolk from the winter town, friends from the nearer holdfasts, and the escorts of their lordly guests. Some faces Bran had never seen before, others he knew as well as his own, yet they all seemed equally foreign to him. He watched them as from a distance, as if he still sat in the window of his bedchamber, looking down on the yard below, seeing everything yet a part of nothing.

Osha moved among the tables, pouring ale. One of Leobald Tallhart's men slid a hand up under her skirts and she broke the flagon over his head, to roars of laughter. Yet Mikken had his hand down some woman's bodice, and she seemed not to mind. Bran watched Farlen make his red bitch beg for bones and smiled at Old Nan plucking at the crust of a hot pie with wrinkled fingers. On the dais, Lord Wyman attacked a steaming plate of lampreys as if they were an enemy host. He was so fat that Ser Rodrik had commanded that a special wide chair be built for him to sit in, but he laughed loud and often, and Bran thought he liked him. Poor wan Lady Hornwood sat beside him, her face a stony mask as she picked listlessly at her food. At the opposite end of the high table, Hothen and Mors were playing a drinking game, slamming their horns together as hard as knights meeting in joust.

It is too hot here, and too noisy, and they are all getting drunk. Bran itched under his grey and white woolens, and suddenly he wished he were anywhere but here. *It is cool in the godswood now. Steam is rising off the hot pools, and the red leaves of the weirwood are rustling. The smells are richer than here, and before long the moon will rise and my brother will sing to it.*

"Bran?" Ser Rodrik said. "You do not eat."

The waking dream had been so vivid, for a moment Bran had not known where he was. "I'll have more later," he said. "My belly's full to bursting."

The old knight's white mustache was pink with wine. "You have done well, Bran. Here, and at the audiences. You will be an especial fine lord one day, I think."

I want to be a knight. Bran took another sip of the spiced honey wine from his father's goblet, grateful for something to clutch. The lifelike head of a snarling direwolf was raised on the side of the cup. He felt the silver muzzle pressing against his palm, and remembered the last time he had seen his lord father drink from this goblet.

It had been the night of the welcoming feast, when King Robert had brought his court to Winterfell. Summer still reigned then. His parents had shared the dais with Robert and his queen, with her brothers beside her. Uncle Benjen had been there too, all in black. Bran and his brothers and sisters sat with the king's children, Joffrey and Tommen and Princess Myrcella, who'd spent the whole meal gazing at Robb with adoring eyes. Arya made faces across the table when no one was looking; Sansa listened raptly while the king's high harper sang songs of chivalry, and Rickon kept asking why Jon wasn't with them. "Because he's a bastard," Bran finally had to whisper to him.

And now they are all gone. It was as if some cruel god had reached down with a great hand and swept them all away, the girls to captivity, Jon to the Wall, Robb and Mother to war, King Robert and Father to their graves, and perhaps Uncle Benjen as well . . .

Even down on the benches, there were new men at the tables. Jory was dead, and Fat Tom, and Porther, Alyn, Desmond, Hullen who had been master of horse, Harwin his son . . . all those who had gone south with his father, even Septa Mordane and Vayon Poole. The rest had ridden to war with Robb, and might soon be dead as well for all Bran knew. He liked Hayhead and Poxy Tym and Skittrick and the other new men well enough, but he missed his old friends.

He looked up and down the benches at all the faces happy and sad, and wondered who would be missing next year and the year after. He might have cried then, but he couldn't. He was the Stark in Winterfell, his father's son and his brother's heir, and almost a man grown.

At the foot of the hall, the doors opened and a gust of cold air made the torches flame brighter for an instant. Alebelly led two new guests into the feast. "The Lady Meera of House Reed," the rotund guardsman bellowed over the clamor. "With her brother, Jojen, of Greywater Watch."

Men looked up from their cups and trenchers to eye the newcomers. Bran heard Little Walder mutter, "Frogeaters," to Big Walder beside him. Ser Rodrik climbed to his feet. "Be welcome, friends, and share this harvest with us." Serving men hurried to lengthen the table on the dais, fetching trestles and chairs.

"Who are *they*?" Rickon asked.

"Mudmen," answered Little Walder disdainfully. "They're thieves and cravens, and they have green teeth from eating frogs."

Maester Luwin crouched beside Bran's seat to whisper counsel in his ear. "You must greet these ones warmly. I had not thought to see them here, but . . . you know who they are?"

Bran nodded. "Crannogmen. From the Neck."

"Howland Reed was a great friend to your father," Ser Rodrik told him. "These two are his, it would seem."

As the newcomers walked the length of the hall, Bran saw that one was indeed a girl, though he would never have known it by her dress. She wore lambskin breeches soft with long use, and a sleeveless jerkin armored in bronze scales. Though near Robb's age, she was slim as a boy, with long brown hair knotted behind her head and only the barest suggestion of breasts. A woven net hung from one slim hip, a long bronze knife from the other; under her arm she carried an old iron greathelm spotted with rust; a frog spear and round leathern shield were strapped to her back.

Her brother was several years younger and bore no weapons. All his garb was green, even to the leather of his boots, and when he came closer Bran saw that his eyes were the color of moss, though his teeth looked as white as anyone else's. Both Reeds were slight of build, slender as swords and scarcely taller than Bran himself. They went to one knee before the dais.

"My lords of Stark," the girl said. "The years have passed in their hundreds and their thousands since my folk first swore their fealty to the King in the North. My lord father has sent us here to say the words again, for all our people."

She is looking at me, Bran realized. He had to make some answer. "My brother Robb is fighting in the south," he said, "but you can say your words to me, if you like."

"To Winterfell we pledge the faith of Greywater," they said together. "Hearth and heart and harvest we yield up to you, my lord. Our swords and spears and arrows are yours to command. Grant mercy to our weak, help to our helpless, and justice to all, and we shall never fail you."

"I swear it by earth and water," said the boy in green.

"I swear it by bronze and iron," his sister said.

"We swear it by ice and fire," they finished together.

Bran groped for words. Was he supposed to swear something back to them? Their oath was not one he had been taught. "May your winters be short and your summers bountiful," he said. That was usually a good thing to say. "Rise. I'm Brandon Stark."

The girl, Meera, got to her feet and helped her brother up. The boy stared at Bran all the while. "We bring you gifts of fish and frog and fowl," he said.

"I thank you." Bran wondered if he would have to eat a frog to be polite. "I offer you the meat and mead of Winterfell." He tried to recall all he had been taught of the crannogmen, who dwelt amongst the bogs of the Neck and seldom left their wetlands. They were a poor folk, fishers and frog-hunters who lived in houses of thatch and woven reeds on floating islands hidden in the deeps of the swamp. It was said that they were a cowardly people who fought with poisoned weapons and preferred to hide from foes rather than face them in open battle. And yet Howland Reed had been one of Father's staunchest companions during the war for King Robert's crown, before Bran was born.

The boy, Jojen, looked about the hall curiously as he took his seat. "Where are the direwolves?"

"In the godswood," Rickon answered. "Shaggy was bad."

"My brother would like to see them," the girl said.

Little Walder spoke up loudly. "He'd best watch they don't see him, or they'll take a bite out of him."

"They won't bite if I'm there." Bran was pleased that they wanted to see the wolves. "Summer won't anyway, and he'll keep Shaggydog away." He was curious about these mudmen. He could not recall ever seeing one before. His father had sent letters to the Lord of Greywater over the years, but none of the crannogmen had ever called at Winterfell. He would have liked to talk to them more, but the Great Hall was so noisy that it was hard to hear anyone who wasn't right beside you.

Ser Rodrik was right beside Bran. "Do they truly eat frogs?" he asked the old knight.

"Aye," Ser Rodrik said. "Frogs and fish and lizard-lions, and all manner of birds."

Maybe they don't have sheep and cattle, Bran thought. He commanded the serving men to bring them mutton chops and a slice off the aurochs and fill their trenchers with beef-and-barley stew. They seemed to like that well enough. The girl caught him staring at her and smiled. Bran blushed and looked away.

Much later, after all the sweets had been served and washed down with gallons of summerwine, the food was cleared and the tables shoved back against the walls to make room for the dancing. The music grew wilder, the drummers joined in, and Hother Umber brought forth a huge curved warhorn banded in silver. When the singer reached the part in

"The Night That Ended" where the Night's Watch rode forth to meet the Others in the Battle for the Dawn, he blew a blast that set all the dogs to barking.

Two Glover men began a spinning skirl on bladder and woodharp. Mors Umber was the first on his feet. He seized a passing serving girl by the arm, knocking the flagon of wine out of her hands to shatter on the floor. Amidst the rushes and bones and bits of bread that littered the stone, he whirled her and spun her and tossed her in the air. The girl squealed with laughter and turned red as her skirts swirled and lifted.

Others soon joined in. Hodor began to dance all by himself, while Lord Wyman asked little Beth Cassel to partner him. For all his size, he moved gracefully. When he tired, Cley Cerwyn danced with the child in his stead. Ser Rodrik approached Lady Hornwood, but she made her excuses and took her leave. Bran watched long enough to be polite, and then had Hodor summoned. He was hot and tired, flushed from the wine, and the dancing made him sad. It was something else he could never do. "I want to go."

"Hodor," Hodor shouted back, kneeling. Maester Luwin and Hayhead lifted him into his basket. The folk of Winterfell had seen this sight half a hundred times, but doubtless it looked queer to the guests, some of whom were more curious than polite. Bran felt the stares.

They went out the rear rather than walk the length of the hall, Bran ducking his head as they passed through the lord's door. In the dim-lit gallery outside the Great Hall, they came upon Joseth the master of horse engaged in a different sort of riding. He had some woman Bran did not know shoved up against the wall, her skirts around her waist. She was giggling until Hodor stopped to watch. Then she screamed. "Leave them be, Hodor," Bran had to tell him. "Take me to my bedchamber."

Hodor carried him up the winding steps to his tower and knelt beside one of the iron bars that Mikken had driven into the wall. Bran used the bars to move himself to the bed, and Hodor pulled off his boots and breeches. "You can go back to the feast now, but don't go bothering Joseth and that woman," Bran said.

"Hodor," Hodor replied, bobbing his head.

When he blew out his bedside candle, darkness covered him like a soft, familiar blanket. The faint sound of music drifted through his shuttered window.

Something his father had told him once when he was little came back to him suddenly. He had asked Lord Eddard if the Kingsguard were truly the finest knights in the Seven Kingdoms. "No longer," he answered, "but once they were a marvel, a shining lesson to the world."

"Was there one who was best of all?"

"The finest knight I ever saw was Ser Arthur Dayne, who fought with a blade called Dawn, forged from the heart of a fallen star. They called him the Sword of the Morning, and he would have killed me but for Howland Reed." Father had gotten sad then, and he would say no more. Bran wished he had asked him what he meant.

He went to sleep with his head full of knights in gleaming armor, fighting with swords that shone like starfire, but when the dream came he was in the godswood again. The smells from the kitchen and the Great Hall were so strong that it was almost as if he had never left the feast. He prowled beneath the trees, his brother close behind him. This night was wildly alive, full of the howling of the man-pack at their play. The sounds made him restless. He wanted to run, to hunt, he wanted to—

The rattle of iron made his ears prick up. His brother heard it too. They raced through the undergrowth toward the sound. Bounding across the still water at the foot of the old white one, he caught the scent of a stranger, the man-smell well mixed with leather and earth and iron.

The intruders had pushed a few yards into the wood when he came upon them, a female and a young male, with no taint of fear to them, even when he showed them the white of his teeth. His brother growled low in his throat, yet still they did not run.

"Here they come," the female said. *Meera,* some part of him whispered, some wisp of the sleeping boy lost in the wolf dream. "Did you know they would be so big?"

"They will be bigger still before they are grown," the young male said, watching them with eyes large, green, and unafraid. "The black one is full of fear and rage, but the grey is strong . . . stronger than he knows . . . can you feel him, sister?"

"No," she said, moving a hand to the hilt of the long brown knife she wore. "Go careful, Jojen."

"He won't hurt me. This is not the day I die." The male walked toward them, unafraid, and reached out for his muzzle, a touch as light as a summer breeze. Yet at the brush of those fingers the wood dissolved and the very ground turned to smoke beneath his feet and swirled away laughing, and then he was spinning and falling, falling, *falling* . . .

CATELYN

As she slept amidst the rolling grasslands, Catelyn dreamt that Bran was whole again, that Arya and Sansa held hands, that Rickon was still a babe at her breast. Robb, crownless, played with a wooden sword, and when all were safe asleep, she found Ned in her bed, smiling.

Sweet it was, sweet and gone too soon. Dawn came cruel, a dagger of light. She woke aching and alone and weary; weary of riding, weary of hurting, weary of duty. *I want to weep*, she thought. *I want to be comforted. I'm so tired of being strong. I want to be foolish and frightened for once. Just for a small while, that's all . . . a day . . . an hour . . .*

Outside her tent, men were stirring. She heard the whicker of horses, Shadd complaining of stiffness in his back, Ser Wendel calling for his bow. Catelyn wished they would all go away. They were good men, loyal, yet she was tired of them all. It was her children she yearned after. One day, she promised herself as she lay abed, one day she would allow herself to be less than strong.

But not today. It could not be today.

Her fingers seemed more clumsy than usual as she fumbled on her clothes. She supposed she ought to be grateful that she had any use of her hands at all. The dagger had been Valyrian steel, and Valyrian steel bites deep and sharp. She had only to look at the scars to remember.

Outside, Shadd was stirring oats into a kettle, while Ser Wendel

Manderly sat stringing his bow. "My lady," he said when Catelyn emerged. "There are birds in this grass. Would you fancy a roast quail to break your fast this morning?"

"Oats and bread are sufficient . . . for all of us, I think. We have many leagues yet to ride, Ser Wendel."

"As you will, my lady." The knight's moon face looked crestfallen, the tips of his great walrus mustache twitching with disappointment. "Oats and bread, and what could be better?" He was one of the fattest men Catelyn had ever known, but howevermuch he loved his food, he loved his honor more.

"Found some nettles and brewed a tea," Shadd announced. "Will m'lady take a cup?"

"Yes, with thanks."

She cradled the tea in her scarred hands and blew on it to cool it. Shadd was one of the Winterfell men. Robb had sent twenty of his best to see her safely to Renly. He had sent five lordlings as well, whose names and high birth would add weight and honor to her mission. As they made their way south, staying well clear of towns and holdfasts, they had seen bands of mailed men more than once, and glimpsed smoke on the eastern horizon, but none had dared molest them. They were too weak to be a threat, too many to be easy prey. Once across the Blackwater, the worst was behind. For the past four days, they had seen no signs of war.

Catelyn had never wanted this. She had told Robb as much, back in Riverrun. "When last I saw Renly, he was a boy no older than Bran. I do not know him. Send someone else. My place is here with my father, for whatever time he has left."

Her son had looked at her unhappily. "There is no one else. I cannot go myself. Your father's too ill. The Blackfish is my eyes and ears, I dare not lose him. Your brother I need to hold Riverrun when we march—"

"March?" No one had said a word to her of marching.

"I cannot sit at Riverrun waiting for peace. It makes me look as if I were afraid to take the field again. When there are no battles to fight, men start to think of hearth and harvest, Father told me that. Even my northmen grow restless."

My northmen, she thought. *He is even starting to talk like a king.* "No one has ever died of restlessness, but rashness is another matter. We've planted seeds, let them grow."

Robb shook his head stubbornly. "We've tossed some seeds in the wind, that's all. If your sister Lysa was coming to aid us, we would have heard by now. How many birds have we sent to the Eyrie, four? I want peace too, but why should the Lannisters give me *anything* if all I do is sit here while my army melts away around me swift as summer snow?"

"So rather than look craven, you will dance to Lord Tywin's pipes?" she threw back. "He *wants* you to march on Harrenhal, ask your uncle Brynden if—"

"I said nothing of Harrenhal," Robb said. "Now, will you go to Renly for me, or must I send the Greatjon?"

The memory brought a wan smile to her face. Such an obvious ploy, that, yet deft for a boy of fifteen. Robb knew how ill-suited a man like Greatjon Umber would be to treat with a man like Renly Baratheon, and he knew that she knew it as well. What could she do but accede, praying that her father would live until her return? Had Lord Hoster been well, he would have gone himself, she knew. Still, that leavetaking was hard, hard. He did not even know her when she came to say farewell. "Minisa," he called her, "where are the children? My little Cat, my sweet Lysa . . ." Catelyn had kissed him on the brow and told him his babes were well. "Wait for me, my lord," she said as his eyes closed. "I waited for you, oh, so many times. Now you must wait for me."

Fate drives me south and south again, Catelyn thought as she sipped the astringent tea, *when it is north I should be going, north to home.* She had written to Bran and Rickon, that last night at Riverrun. *I do not forget you, my sweet ones, you must believe that. It is only that your brother needs me more.*

"We ought to reach the upper Mander today, my lady," Ser Wendel announced while Shadd spooned out the porridge. "Lord Renly will not be far, if the talk be true."

And what do I tell him when I find him? That my son holds him no true king? She did not relish this meeting. They needed friends, not more enemies, yet Robb would never bend the knee in homage to a man he felt had no claim to the throne.

Her bowl was empty, though she could scarce remember tasting the porridge. She laid it aside. "It is time we were away." The sooner she spoke to Renly, the sooner she could turn for home. She was the first one mounted, and she set the pace for the column. Hal Mollen rode beside her, bearing the banner of House Stark, the grey direwolf on an ice-white field.

They were still a half day's ride from Renly's camp when they were taken. Robin Flint had ranged ahead to scout, and he came galloping back with word of a far-eyes watching from the roof of a distant windmill. By the time Catelyn's party reached the mill, the man was long gone. They pressed on, covering not quite a mile before Renly's outriders came swooping down on them, twenty men mailed and mounted, led by a grizzled greybeard of a knight with bluejays on his surcoat.

When he saw her banners, he trotted up to her alone. "My lady," he

called, "I am Ser Colen of Greenpools, as it please you. These are dangerous lands you cross."

"Our business is urgent," she answered him. "I come as envoy from
my son, Robb Stark, the King in the North, to treat with Renly
Baratheon, the King in the South."

"King Renly is the crowned and anointed lord of *all* the Seven Kingdoms, my lady," Ser Colen answered, though courteously enough. "His
Grace is encamped with his host near Bitterbridge, where the roseroad
crosses the Mander. It shall be my great honor to escort you to him." The
knight raised a mailed hand, and his men formed a double column flank-
ing Catelyn and her guard. *Escort or captor?* she wondered. There was
nothing to be done but trust in Ser Colen's honor, and Lord Renly's.

They saw the smoke of the camp's fires when they were still an hour
from the river. Then the sound came drifting across farm and field and
rolling plain, indistinct as the murmur of some distant sea, but swelling
as they rode closer. By the time they caught sight of the Mander's muddy
waters glinting in the sun, they could make out the voices of men, the
clatter of steel, the whinny of horses. Yet neither sound nor smoke prepared them for the host itself.

Thousands of cookfires filled the air with a pale smoky haze. The
horse lines alone stretched out over leagues. A forest had surely been
felled to make the tall staffs that held the banners. Great siege engines
lined the grassy verge of the roseroad, mangonels and trebuchets and
rolling rams mounted on wheels taller than a man on horseback. The
steel points of pikes flamed red with sunlight, as if already blooded,
while the pavilions of the knights and high lords sprouted from the grass
like silken mushrooms. She saw men with spears and men with swords,
men in steel caps and mail shirts, camp followers strutting their charms,
archers fletching arrows, teamsters driving wagons, swineherds driving
pigs, pages running messages, squires honing swords, knights riding pal-
freys, grooms leading ill-tempered destriers. "This is a fearsome lot of
men," Ser Wendel Manderly observed as they crossed the ancient stone
span from which Bitterbridge took its name.

"That it is," Catelyn agreed.

Near all the chivalry of the south had come to Renly's call, it seemed.
The golden rose of Highgarden was seen everywhere: sewn on the right
breast of armsmen and servants, flapping and fluttering from the green
silk banners that adorned lance and pike, painted upon the shields hung
outside the pavilions of the sons and brothers and cousins and uncles of
House Tyrell. As well Catelyn spied the fox-and-flowers of House
Florent, Fossoway apples red and green, Lord Tarly's striding huntsman,
oak leaves for Oakheart, cranes for Crane, a cloud of black-and-orange
butterflies for the Mullendores.

Across the Mander, the storm lords had raised their standards—Renly's own bannermen, sworn to House Baratheon and Storm's End. Catelyn recognized Bryce Caron's nightingales, the Penrose quills, and Lord Estermont's sea turtle, green on green. Yet for every shield she knew, there were a dozen strange to her, borne by the small lords sworn to the bannermen, and by hedge knights and freeriders who had come swarming to make Renly Baratheon a king in fact as well as name.

Renly's own standard flew high over all. From the top of his tallest siege tower, a wheeled oaken immensity covered with rawhides, streamed the largest war banner that Catelyn had ever seen—a cloth big enough to carpet many a hall, shimmering gold, with the crowned stag of Baratheon black upon it, prancing proud and tall.

"My lady, do you hear that noise?" asked Hallis Mollen, trotting close. "What is that?"

She listened. Shouts, and horses screaming, and the clash of steel, and . . . "Cheering," she said. They had been riding up a gentle slope toward a line of brightly colored pavilions on the height. As they passed between them, the press of men grew thicker, the sounds louder. And then she saw.

Below, beneath the stone-and-timber battlements of a small castle, a melee was in progress.

A field had been cleared off, fences and galleries and tilting barriers thrown up. Hundreds were gathered to watch, perhaps thousands. From the looks of the grounds, torn and muddy and littered with bits of dinted armor and broken lances, they had been at it for a day or more, but now the end was near. Fewer than a score of knights remained ahorse, charging and slashing at each other as watchers and fallen combatants cheered them on. She saw two destriers collide in full armor, going down in a tangle of steel and horseflesh. "A tourney," Hal Mollen declared. He had a penchant for loudly announcing the obvious.

"Oh, splendid," Ser Wendel Manderly said as a knight in a rainbow-striped cloak wheeled to deliver a backhand blow with a long-handled axe that shattered the shield of the man pursuing him and sent him reeling in his stirrups.

The press in front of them made further progress difficult. "Lady Stark," Ser Colen said, "if your men would be so good as to wait here, I'll present you to the king."

"As you say." She gave the command, though she had to raise her voice to be heard above the tourney din. Ser Colen walked his horse slowly through the throngs, with Catelyn riding in his wake. A roar went up from the crowd as a helmetless red-bearded man with a griffin on his shield went down before a big knight in blue armor. His steel was a deep cobalt, even the blunt morningstar he wielded with such deadly effect, his mount barded in the quartered sun-and-moon heraldry of House Tarth.

"Red Ronnet's down, gods be damned," a man cursed.

"Loras'll do for that blue—" a companion answered before a roar drowned out the rest of his words.

Another man was fallen, trapped beneath his injured horse, both of them screaming in pain. Squires rushed out to aid them.

This is madness, Catelyn thought. *Real enemies on every side and half the realm in flames, and Renly sits here playing at war like a boy with his first wooden sword.*

The lords and ladies in the gallery were as engrossed in the melee as the men on the ground. Catelyn marked them well. Her father had oft treated with the southron lords, and not a few had been guests at Riverrun. She recognized Lord Mathis Rowan, stouter and more florid than ever, the golden tree of his House spread across his white doublet. Below him sat Lady Oakheart, tiny and delicate, and to her left Lord Randyll Tarly of Horn Hill, his greatsword Heartsbane propped up against the back of his seat. Others she knew only by their sigils, and some not at all.

In their midst, watching and laughing with his young queen by his side, sat a ghost in a golden crown.

Small wonder the lords gather around him with such fervor, she thought, *he is Robert come again.* Renly was handsome as Robert had been handsome; long of limb and broad of shoulder, with the same coal-black hair, fine and straight, the same deep blue eyes, the same easy smile. The slender circlet around his brows seemed to suit him well. It was soft gold, a ring of roses exquisitely wrought; at the front lifted a stag's head of dark green jade, adorned with golden eyes and golden antlers.

The crowned stag decorated the king's green velvet tunic as well, worked in gold thread upon his chest; the Baratheon sigil in the colors of Highgarden. The girl who shared the high seat with him was also of Highgarden: his young queen, Margaery, daughter to Lord Mace Tyrell. Their marriage was the mortar that held the great southron alliance together, Catelyn knew. Renly was one-and-twenty, the girl no older than Robb, very pretty, with a doe's soft eyes and a mane of curling brown hair that fell about her shoulders in lazy ringlets. Her smile was shy and sweet.

Out in the field, another man lost his seat to the knight in the rainbow-striped cloak, and the king shouted approval with the rest. *"Loras!"* she heard him call. *"Loras! Highgarden!"* The queen clapped her hands together in excitement.

Catelyn turned to see the end of it. Only four men were left in the fight now, and there was small doubt whom king and commons favored. She had never met Ser Loras Tyrell, but even in the distant north one heard tales of the prowess of the young Knight of Flowers. Ser Loras rode a tall white stallion in silver mail, and fought with a long-handled axe. A crest of golden roses ran down the center of his helm.

Two of the other survivors had made common cause. They spurred their mounts toward the knight in the cobalt armor. As they closed to either side, the blue knight reined hard, smashing one man full in the face with his splintered shield while his black destrier lashed out with a steel-shod hoof at the other. In a blink, one combatant was unhorsed, the other reeling. The blue knight let his broken shield drop to the ground to free his left arm, and then the Knight of Flowers was on him. The weight of his steel seemed to hardly diminish the grace and quickness with which Ser Loras moved, his rainbow cloak swirling about him.

The white horse and the black one wheeled like lovers at a harvest dance, the riders throwing steel in place of kisses. Longaxe flashed and morningstar whirled. Both weapons were blunted, yet still they raised an awful clangor. Shieldless, the blue knight was getting much the worse of it. Ser Loras rained down blows on his head and shoulders, to shouts of *"Highgarden!"* from the throng. The other gave answer with his morningstar, but whenever the ball came crashing in, Ser Loras interposed his battered green shield, emblazoned with three golden roses. When the longaxe caught the blue knight's hand on the backswing and sent the morningstar flying from his grasp, the crowd screamed like a rutting beast. The Knight of Flowers raised his axe for the final blow.

The blue knight charged into it. The stallions slammed together, the blunted axehead smashed against the scarred blue breastplate . . . but somehow the blue knight had the haft locked between steel-gauntleted fingers. He wrenched it from Ser Loras's hand, and suddenly the two were grappling mount-to-mount, and an instant later they were falling. As their horses pulled apart, they crashed to the ground with bone-jarring force. Loras Tyrell, on the bottom, took the brunt of the impact. The blue knight pulled a long dirk free and flicked open Tyrell's visor. The roar of the crowd was too loud for Catelyn to hear what Ser Loras said, but she saw the word form on his split, bloody lips. *Yield.*

The blue knight climbed unsteady to his feet, and raised his dirk in the direction of Renly Baratheon, the salute of a champion to his king. Squires dashed onto the field to help the vanquished knight to his feet. When they got his helm off, Catelyn was startled to see how young he was. He could not have had more than two years on Robb. The boy might have been as comely as his sister, but the broken lip, unfocused eyes, and blood trickling through his matted hair made it hard to be certain.

"Approach," King Renly called to the champion.

He limped toward the gallery. At close hand, the brilliant blue armor looked rather less splendid; everywhere it showed scars, the dents of mace and warhammer, the long gouges left by swords, chips in the enameled breastplate and helm. His cloak hung in rags. From the way he moved, the man within was no less battered. A few voices hailed him with cries of *"Tarth!"* and, oddly, *"A Beauty! A Beauty!"* but most were silent. The blue knight knelt before the king. "Grace," he said, his voice muffled by his dented greathelm.

"You are all your lord father claimed you were." Renly's voice carried over the field. "I've seen Ser Loras unhorsed once or twice . . . but never quite in *that* fashion."

"That were no proper unhorsing," complained a drunken archer nearby, a Tyrell rose sewn on his jerkin. "A vile trick, pulling the lad down."

The press had begun to open up. "Ser Colen," Catelyn said to her escort, "who is this man, and why do they mislike him so?"

Ser Colen frowned. "Because he is no man, my lady. That's Brienne of Tarth, daughter to Lord Selwyn the Evenstar."

"Daughter?" Catelyn was horrified.

"Brienne the Beauty, they name her . . . though not to her face, lest they be called upon to defend those words with their bodies."

She heard King Renly declare the Lady Brienne of Tarth the victor of the great melee at Bitterbridge, last mounted of one hundred sixteen knights. "As champion, you may ask of me any boon that you desire. If it lies in my power, it is yours."

"Your Grace," Brienne answered, "I ask the honor of a place among your Rainbow Guard. I would be one of your seven, and pledge my life to yours, to go where you go, ride at your side, and keep you safe from all hurt and harm."

"Done," he said. "Rise, and remove your helm."

She did as he bid her. And when the greathelm was lifted, Catelyn understood Ser Colen's words.

Beauty, they called her . . . mocking. The hair beneath the visor was a squirrel's nest of dirty straw, and her face . . . Brienne's eyes were large and very blue, a young girl's eyes, trusting and guileless, but the rest . . . her features were broad and coarse, her teeth prominent and crooked, her mouth too wide, her lips so plump they seemed swollen. A thousand freckles speckled her cheeks and brow, and her nose had been broken more than once. Pity filled Catelyn's heart. *Is there any creature on earth as unfortunate as an ugly woman?*

And yet, when Renly cut away her torn cloak and fastened a rainbow in its place, Brienne of Tarth did not look unfortunate. Her smile lit up her face, and her voice was strong and proud as she said, "My life for yours, Your Grace. From this day on, I am your shield, I swear it by the old gods and the new." The way she looked at the king—looked *down* at him, she was a good hand higher, though Renly was near as tall as his brother had been—was painful to see.

"Your Grace!" Ser Colen of Greenpools swung down off his horse to approach the gallery. "I beg your leave." He went to one knee. "I have the honor to bring you the Lady Catelyn Stark, sent as envoy by her son Robb, Lord of Winterfell."

"Lord of Winterfell and King in the North, ser," Catelyn corrected him. She dismounted and moved to Ser Colen's side.

King Renly looked surprised. "Lady Catelyn? We are most pleased." He turned to his young queen. "Margaery my sweet, this is the Lady Catelyn Stark of Winterfell."

"You are most welcome here, Lady Stark," the girl said, all soft courtesy. "I am sorry for your loss."

"You are kind," said Catelyn.

"My lady, I swear to you, I will see that the Lannisters answer for your husband's murder," the king declared. "When I take King's Landing, I'll send you Cersei's head."

And will that bring my Ned back to me? she thought. "It will be enough to know that justice has been done, my lord."

"*Your Grace,*" Brienne the Blue corrected sharply. "And you should kneel when you approach the king."

"The distance between a *lord* and a *grace* is a small one, my lady," Catelyn said. "Lord Renly wears a crown, as does my son. If you wish, we may stand here in the mud and debate what honors and titles are rightly due to each, but it strikes me that we have more pressing matters to consider."

Some of Renly's lords bristled at that, but the king only laughed. "Well said, my lady. There will be time enough for *grace*s when these wars are done. Tell me, when does your son mean to march against Harrenhal?"

Until she knew whether this king was friend or foe, Catelyn was not about to reveal the least part of Robb's dispositions. "I do not sit on my son's war councils, my lord."

"So long as he leaves a few Lannisters for me, I'll not complain. What has he done with the Kingslayer?"

"Jaime Lannister is held prisoner at Riverrun."

"Still alive?" Lord Mathis Rowan seemed dismayed.

Bemused, Renly said, "It would seem the direwolf is gentler than the lion."

"Gentler than the Lannisters," murmured Lady Oakheart with a bitter smile, "is drier than the sea."

"I call it weak." Lord Randyll Tarly had a short, bristly grey beard and a reputation for blunt speech. "No disrespect to you, Lady Stark, but it would have been more seemly had Lord Robb come to pay homage to the king himself, rather than hiding behind his mother's skirts."

"*King* Robb is warring, my lord," Catelyn replied with icy courtesy, "not playing at tourney."

Renly grinned. "Go softly, Lord Randyll, I fear you're overmatched." He summoned a steward in the livery of Storm's End. "Find a place for the lady's companions, and see that they have every comfort. Lady Catelyn shall have my own pavilion. Since Lord Caswell has been so kind as to give me use of his castle, I have no need of it. My lady, when you are rested, I would be honored if you would share our meat and mead at the feast Lord Caswell is giving us tonight. A farewell feast. I fear his lordship is eager to see the heels of my hungry horde."

"Not true, Your Grace," protested a wispy young man who must have been Caswell. "What is mine is yours."

"Whenever someone said that to my brother Robert, he took them at their word," Renly said. "Do you have daughters?"

"Yes, Your Grace. Two."

"Then thank the gods that I am not Robert. My sweet queen is all the woman I desire." Renly held out his hand to help Margaery to her feet. "We'll talk again when you've had a chance to refresh yourself, Lady Catelyn."

Renly led his bride back toward the castle while his steward conducted Catelyn to the king's green silk pavilion. "If you have need of anything, you have only to ask, my lady."

Catelyn could scarcely imagine what she might need that had not already been provided. The pavilion was larger than the common rooms of many an inn and furnished with every comfort: feather mattress and sleeping furs, a wood-and-copper tub large enough for two, braziers to keep off the night's chill, slung leather camp chairs, a writing table with quills and inkpot, bowls of peaches, plums, and pears, a flagon of wine with a set of matched silver cups, cedar chests packed full of Renly's clothing, books, maps, game boards, a high harp, a tall bow and a quiver of arrows, a pair of red-tailed hunting hawks, a vertible armory of fine weapons. *He does not stint himself, this Renly*, she thought as she looked about. *Small wonder this host moves so slowly.*

Beside the entrance, the king's armor stood sentry; a suit of forest-green plate, its fittings chased with gold, the helm crowned by a great rack of golden antlers. The steel was polished to such a high sheen that she could see her reflection in the breastplate, gazing back at her as if from the bottom of a deep green pond. *The face of a drowned woman,* Catelyn thought. *Can you drown in grief?* She turned away sharply, angry with her own frailty. She had no time for the luxury of self-pity. She must wash the dust from her hair and change into a gown more fitting for a king's feast.

Ser Wendel Manderly, Lucas Blackwood, Ser Perwyn Frey, and the rest of her highborn companions accompanied her to the castle. The great hall of Lord Caswell's keep was great only by courtesy, yet room was found on the crowded benches for Catelyn's men, amidst Renly's own knights. Catelyn was assigned a place on the dais between red-faced Lord Mathis Rowan and genial Ser Jon Fossoway of the green-apple Fossoways. Ser Jon made jests, while Lord Mathis inquired politely after the health of her father, brother, and children.

Brienne of Tarth had been seated at the far end of the high table. She did not gown herself as a lady, but chose a knight's finery instead, a velvet doublet quartered rose-and-azure, breeches and boots and a fine-tooled swordbelt, her new rainbow cloak flowing down her back. No garb could disguise her plainness, though; the huge freckled hands, the wide flat face, the thrust of her teeth. Out of armor, her body seemed ungainly, broad of hip and thick of limb, with hunched muscular shoulders but no bosom to speak of. And it was clear from her every action that Brienne knew it, and suffered for it. She spoke only in answer, and seldom lifted her gaze from her food.

Of food there was plenty. The war had not touched the fabled bounty of Highgarden. While singers sang and tumblers tumbled, they began with pears poached in wine, and went on to tiny savory fish rolled in salt and cooked crisp, and capons stuffed with onions and mushrooms. There were great loaves of brown bread, mounds of turnips and sweetcorn and pease, immense hams and roast geese and trenchers dripping full of venison stewed with beer and barley. For the sweet, Lord Caswell's servants brought down trays of pastries from his castle kitchens, cream swans and spun-sugar unicorns, lemon cakes in the shape of roses, spiced honey biscuits and blackberry tarts, apple crisps and wheels of buttery cheese.

The rich foods made Catelyn queasy, but it would never do to show frailty when so much depended on her strength. She ate sparingly, while she watched this man who would be king. Renly sat with his young bride on his left hand and her brother on the right. Apart from the white linen bandage around his brow, Ser Loras seemed none the worse for the day's misadventures. He was indeed as comely as Catelyn had suspected he might be. When not glazed, his eyes were lively and intelligent, his hair an artless tumble of brown locks that many a maid might have envied. He had replaced his tattered tourney cloak with a new one; the same brilliantly striped silk of Renly's Rainbow Guard, clasped with the golden rose of Highgarden.

From time to time, King Renly would feed Margaery some choice morsel off the point of his dagger, or lean over to plant the lightest of kisses on her cheek, but it was Ser Loras who shared most of his jests and confidences. The king enjoyed his food and drink, that was plain to see, yet he seemed neither glutton nor drunkard. He laughed often, and well, and spoke amiably to highborn lords and lowly serving wenches alike.

Some of his guests were less moderate. They drank too much and boasted too loudly, to her mind. Lord Willum's sons Josua and Elyas disputed heatedly about who would be first over the walls of King's Landing. Lord Varner dandled a serving girl on his lap, nuzzling at her neck while one hand went exploring down her bodice. Guyard the Green, who fancied himself a singer, diddled a harp and gave them a verse about tying lions' tails in knots, parts of which rhymed. Ser Mark Mullendore brought a black-and-white monkey and fed him morsels from his own plate, while Ser Tanton of the red-apple Fossoways climbed on the table and swore to slay Sandor Clegane in single combat. The vow might have been taken more solemnly if Ser Tanton had not had one foot in a gravy boat when he made it.

The height of folly was reached when a plump fool came capering out in gold-painted tin with a cloth lion's head, and chased a dwarf around the tables, whacking him over the head with a bladder. Finally King Renly demanded to know why he was beating his brother. "Why, Your Grace, I'm the Kinslayer," the fool said.

"It's *King*slayer, fool of a fool," Renly said, and the hall rang with laughter.

Lord Rowan beside her did not join the merriment. "They are all so young," he said.

It was true. The Knight of Flowers could not have reached his second name day when Robert slew Prince Rhaegar on the Trident. Few of the others were very much older. They had been babes during the Sack of King's Landing, and no more than boys when Balon Greyjoy raised the Iron Islands in rebellion. *They are still unblooded,* Catelyn thought as she watched Lord Bryce goad Ser Robar into juggling a brace of daggers. *It is all a game to them still, a tourney writ large, and all they see is the chance for glory and honor and spoils. They are boys drunk on song and story, and like all boys, they think themselves immortal.*

"War will make them old," Catelyn said, "as it did us." She had been a girl when Robert and Ned and Jon Arryn raised their banners against Aerys Targaryen, a woman by the time the fighting was done. "I pity them."

"Why?" Lord Rowan asked her. "Look at them. They're young and strong, full of life and laughter. And lust, aye, more lust than they know what to do with. There will be many a bastard bred this night, I promise you. Why pity?"

"Because it will not last," Catelyn answered, sadly. "Because they are the knights of summer, and winter is coming."

"Lady Catelyn, you are wrong." Brienne regarded her with eyes as blue as her armor. "Winter will never come for the likes of us. Should we die in battle, they will surely sing of us, and it's always summer in the songs. In the songs all knights are gallant, all maids are beautiful, and the sun is always shining."

Winter comes for all of us, Catelyn thought. *For me, it came when Ned died. It will come for you too, child, and sooner than you like.* She did not have the heart to say it.

The king saved her. "Lady Catelyn," Renly called down. "I feel the need of some air. Will you walk with me?"

Catelyn stood at once. "I should be honored."

Brienne was on her feet as well. "Your Grace, give me but a moment to don my mail. You should not be without protection."

King Renly smiled. "If I am not safe in the heart of Lord Caswell's castle, with my own host around me, one sword will make no matter . . . not even *your* sword, Brienne. Sit and eat. If I have need of you, I'll send for you."

His words seemed to strike the girl harder than any blow she had taken that afternoon. "As you will, Your Grace." Brienne sat, eyes downcast. Renly took Catelyn's arm and led her from the hall, past a slouching guardsman who straightened so hurriedly that he near dropped his spear. Renly clapped the man on the shoulder and made a jest of it.

"This way, my lady." The king took her through a low door into a stair tower. As they started up, he said, "Perchance, is Ser Barristan Selmy with your son at Riverrun?"

"No," she answered, puzzled. "Is he no longer with Joffrey? He was the Lord Commander of the Kingsguard."

Renly shook his head. "The Lannisters told him he was too old and gave his cloak to the Hound. I'm told he left King's Landing vowing to take up service with the true king. That cloak Brienne claimed today was the one I was keeping for Selmy, in hopes that he might offer me his sword. When he did not turn up at Highgarden, I thought perhaps he had gone to Riverrun instead."

"We have not seen him."

"He was old, yes, but a good man still. I hope he has not come to harm. The Lannisters are great fools." They climbed a few more steps. "On the night of Robert's death, I offered your husband a hundred swords and urged him to take Joffrey into his power. Had he listened, he would be regent today, and there would have been no need for me to claim the throne."

"Ned refused you." She did not have to be told.

"He had sworn to protect Robert's children," Renly said. "I lacked the strength to act alone, so when Lord Eddard turned me away, I had no choice but to flee. Had I stayed, I knew the queen would see to it that I did not long outlive my brother."

Had you stayed, and lent your support to Ned, he might still be alive, Catelyn thought bitterly.

"I liked your husband well enough, my lady. He was a loyal friend to Robert, I know . . . but he would not listen and he would not bend. Here, I wish to show you something." They had reached the top of the stairwell. Renly pushed open a wooden door, and they stepped out onto the roof.

Lord Caswell's keep was scarcely tall enough to call a tower, but the country was low and flat and Catelyn could see for leagues in all directions. Wherever she looked, she saw fires. They covered the earth like fallen stars, and like the stars there was no end to them. "Count them if you like, my lady," Renly said quietly. "You will still be counting when dawn breaks in the east. How many fires burn around Riverrun tonight, I wonder?"

Catelyn could hear faint music drifting from the Great Hall, seeping out into the night. She dare not count the stars.

"I'm told your son crossed the Neck with twenty thousand swords at his back," Renly went on. "Now that the lords of the Trident are with him, perhaps he commands forty thousand."

No, she thought, *not near so many, we have lost men in battle, and others to the harvest.*

"I have twice that number here," Renly said, "and this is only part of my strength. Mace Tyrell remains at Highgarden with another ten thousand, I have a strong garrison holding Storm's End, and soon enough the Dornishmen will join me with all their power. And never forget my brother Stannis, who holds Dragonstone and commands the lords of the narrow sea."

"It would seem that you are the one who has forgotten Stannis," Catelyn said, more sharply than she'd intended.

"His claim, you mean?" Renly laughed. "Let us be blunt, my lady. Stannis would make an appalling king. Nor is he like to become one. Men respect Stannis, even fear him, but precious few have ever loved him."

"He is still your elder brother. If either of you can be said to have a right to the Iron Throne, it must be Lord Stannis."

Renly shrugged. "Tell me, what right did my brother Robert ever have to the Iron Throne?" He did not wait for an answer. "Oh, there was talk of the blood ties between Baratheon and Targaryen, of weddings a hundred years past, of second sons and elder daughters. No one but the maesters care about any of it. Robert won the throne with his warhammer." He swept a hand across the campfires that burned from horizon to horizon. "Well, there is my claim, as good as Robert's ever was. If your son supports me as his father supported Robert, he'll not find me ungenerous. I will gladly confirm him in all his lands, titles, and honors. He can rule in Winterfell as he pleases. He can even go on calling himself King in the North if he likes, so long as he bends the knee and does me homage as his overlord. *King* is only a word, but fealty, loyalty, service . . . those I must have."

"And if he will not give them to you, my lord?"

"I mean to be king, my lady, and not of a broken kingdom. I cannot say it plainer than that. Three hundred years ago, a Stark king knelt to Aegon the Dragon, when he saw he could not hope to prevail. That was wisdom. Your son must be wise as well. Once he joins me, this war is good as done. We—" Renly broke off suddenly, distracted. "What's this now?"

The rattle of chains heralded the raising of the portcullis. Down in the yard below, a rider in a winged helm urged his well-lathered horse under the spikes. "Summon the king!" he called.

Renly vaulted up into a crenel. "I'm here, ser."

"Your Grace." The rider spurred his mount closer. "I came swift as I could. From Storm's End. We are besieged, Your Grace, Ser Cortnay defies them, but . . ."

"But . . . that's not possible. I would have been told if Lord Tywin left Harrenhal."

"These are no Lannisters, my liege. It's Lord Stannis at your gates. *King* Stannis, he calls himself now."

JON

A blowing rain lashed at Jon's face as he spurred his horse across the swollen stream. Beside him, Lord Commander Mormont gave the hood of his cloak a tug, muttering curses on the weather. His raven sat on his shoulder, feathers ruffled, as soaked and grumpy as the Old Bear himself. A gust of wind sent wet leaves flapping round them like a flock of dead birds. *The haunted forest*, Jon thought ruefully. *The drowned forest, more like it.*

He hoped Sam was holding up, back down the column. He was not a good rider even in fair weather, and six days of rain had made the ground treacherous, all soft mud and hidden rocks. When the wind blew, it drove the water right into their eyes. The Wall would be flowing off to the south, the melting ice mingling with warm rain to wash down in sheets and rivers. Pyp and Toad would be sitting near the fire in the common room, drinking cups of mulled wine before their supper. Jon envied them. His wet wool clung to him sodden and itching, his neck and shoulders ached fiercely from the weight of mail and sword, and he was sick of salt cod, salt beef, and hard cheese.

Up ahead a hunting horn sounded a quavering note, half drowned beneath the constant patter of the rain. "Buckwell's horn," the Old Bear announced. "The gods are good; Craster's still there." His raven gave a single flap of his big wings, croaked *"Corn,"* and ruffled his feathers up again.

Jon had often heard the black brothers tell tales of Craster and his keep. Now he would see it with his own eyes. After seven empty villages, they had all come to dread finding Craster's as dead and desolate as the rest, but it seemed they would be spared that. *Perhaps the Old Bear will finally get some answers*, he thought. *Anyway, we'll be out of the rain.*

Thoren Smallwood swore that Craster was a friend to the Watch, despite his unsavory reputation. "The man's half-mad, I won't deny it," he'd told the Old Bear, "but you'd be the same if you'd spent your life in this cursed wood. Even so, he's never turned a ranger away from his fire, nor does he love Mance Rayder. He'll give us good counsel."

So long as he gives us a hot meal and a chance to dry our clothes, I'll be happy. Dywen said Craster was a kinslayer, liar, raper, and craven, and hinted that he trafficked with slavers and demons. "And worse," the old forester would add, clacking his wooden teeth. "There's a *cold* smell to that one, there is."

"Jon," Lord Mormont commanded, "ride back along the column and spread the word. And remind the officers that I want no trouble about Craster's wives. The men are to mind their hands and speak to these women as little as need be."

"Aye, my lord." Jon turned his horse back the way they'd come. It was pleasant to have the rain out of his face, if only for a little while. Everyone he passed seemed to be weeping. The march was strung out through half a mile of woods.

In the midst of the baggage train, Jon passed Samwell Tarly, slumped in his saddle under a wide floppy hat. He was riding one dray horse and leading the others. The drumming of the rain against the hoods of their cages had the ravens squawking and fluttering. "You put a fox in with them?" Jon called out.

Water ran off the brim of Sam's hat as he lifted his head. "Oh, hullo, Jon. No, they just hate the rain, the same as us."

"How are you faring, Sam?"

"Wetly." The fat boy managed a smile. "Nothing has killed me yet, though."

"Good. Craster's Keep is just ahead. If the gods are good, he'll let us sleep by his fire."

Sam looked dubious. "Dolorous Edd says Craster's a terrible savage. He marries his daughters and obeys no laws but those he makes himself. And Dywen told Grenn he's got black blood in his veins. His mother was a wildling woman who lay with a ranger, so he's a bas . . ." Suddenly he realized what he was about to say.

"A bastard," Jon said with a laugh. "You can say it, Sam. I've heard the word before." He put the spurs to his surefooted little garron. "I need to hunt down Ser Ottyn. Be careful around Craster's women." As if

Samwell Tarly needed warning on that score. "We'll talk later, after we've made camp."

Jon carried the word back to Ser Ottyn Wythers, plodding along with the rear guard. A small prune-faced man of an age with Mormont, Ser Ottyn always looked tired, even at Castle Black, and the rain had beaten him down unmercifully. "Welcome tidings," he said. "This wet has soaked my bones, and even my saddle sores complain of saddle sores."

On his way back, Jon swung wide of the column's line of march and took a shorter path through the thick of the wood. The sounds of man and horse diminished, swallowed up by the wet green wild, and soon enough he could hear only the steady wash of rain against leaf and tree and rock. It was midafternoon, yet the forest seemed as dark as dusk. Jon wove a path between rocks and puddles, past great oaks, grey-green sentinels, and black-barked ironwoods. In places the branches wove a canopy overhead and he was given a moment's respite from the drumming of the rain against his head. As he rode past a lightning-blasted chestnut tree overgrown with wild white roses, he heard something rustling in the underbrush. *"Ghost,"* he called out. "Ghost, to me."

But it was Dywen who emerged from the greenery, forking a shaggy grey garron with Grenn ahorse beside him. The Old Bear had deployed outriders to either side of the main column, to screen their march and warn of the approach of any enemies, and even there he took no chances, sending the men out in pairs.

"Ah, it's you, Lord Snow." Dywen smiled an oaken smile; his teeth were carved of wood, and fit badly. "Thought me and the boy had us one o' them Others to deal with. Lose your wolf?"

"He's off hunting." Ghost did not like to travel with the column, but he would not be far. When they made camp for the night, he'd find his way to Jon at the Lord Commander's tent.

"Fishing, I'd call it, in this wet," Dywen said.

"My mother always said rain was good for growing crops," Grenn put in hopefully.

"Aye, a good crop of mildew," Dywen said. "The best thing about a rain like this, it saves a man from taking baths." He made a clacking sound on his wooden teeth.

"Buckwell's found Craster," Jon told them.

"Had he lost him?" Dywen chuckled. "See that you young bucks don't go nosing about Craster's wives, you hear?"

Jon smiled. "Want them all for yourself, Dywen?"

Dywen clacked his teeth some more. "Might be I do. Craster's got ten fingers and one cock, so he don't count but to eleven. He'd never miss a couple."

"How many wives does he have, truly?" Grenn asked.

"More'n you ever will, brother. Well, it's not so hard when you breed your own. There's your beast, Snow."

Ghost was trotting along beside Jon's horse with tail held high, his white fur ruffed up thick against the rain. He moved so silently Jon could not have said just when he appeared. Grenn's mount shied at the scent of him; even now, after more than a year, the horses were uneasy in the presence of the direwolf. "With me, Ghost." Jon spurred off to Craster's Keep.

He had never thought to find a stone castle on the far side of the Wall, but he *had* pictured some sort of motte-and-bailey with a wooden palisade and a timber tower keep. What they found instead was a midden heap, a pigsty, an empty sheepfold, and a windowless daub-and-wattle hall scarce worthy of the name. It was long and low, chinked together from logs and roofed with sod. The compound stood atop a rise too modest to name a hill, surrounded by an earthen dike. Brown rivulets flowed down the slope where the rain had eaten gaping holes in the defenses, to join a rushing brook that curved around to the north, its thick waters turned into a murky torrent by the rains.

On the southwest, he found an open gate flanked by a pair of animal skulls on high poles: a bear to one side, a ram to the other. Bits of flesh still clung to the bear skull, Jon noted as he joined the line riding past. Within, Jarmen Buckwell's scouts and men from Thoren Smallwood's van were setting up horse lines and struggling to raise tents. A host of piglets rooted about three huge sows in the sty. Nearby, a small girl pulled carrots from a garden, naked in the rain, while two women tied a pig for slaughter. The animal's squeals were high and horrible, almost human in their distress. Chett's hounds barked wildly in answer, snarling and snapping despite his curses, with a pair of Craster's dogs barking back. When they saw Ghost, some of the dogs broke off and ran, while others began to bay and growl. The direwolf ignored them, as did Jon.

Well, thirty of us will be warm and dry, Jon thought once he'd gotten a good look at the hall. *Perhaps as many as fifty.* The place was much too small to sleep two hundred men, so most would need to remain outside. And where to put them? The rain had turned half the compound yard to ankle-deep puddles and the rest to sucking mud. Another dismal night was in prospect.

The Lord Commander had entrusted his mount to Dolorous Edd. He was cleaning mud out of the horse's hooves as Jon dismounted. "Lord Mormont's in the hall," he announced. "He said for you to join him. Best leave the wolf outside, he looks hungry enough to eat one of Craster's children. Well, truth be told, *I'm* hungry enough to eat one of Craster's children, so long as he was served hot. Go on, I'll see to your horse. If it's warm and dry inside, don't tell me, I wasn't asked in." He flicked a glob of wet mud out from under a horseshoe. "Does this mud look like shit to you? Could it be that this whole hill is made of Craster's shit?"

Jon smiled. "Well, I hear he's been here a long time."

"You cheer me not. Go see the Old Bear."

"Ghost, stay," he commanded. The door to Craster's Keep was made of two flaps of deerhide. Jon shoved between them, stooping to pass under the low lintel. Two dozen of the chief rangers had preceded him, and were standing around the firepit in the center of the dirt floor while puddles collected about their boots. The hall stank of soot, dung, and wet dog. The air was heavy with smoke, yet somehow still damp. Rain leaked through the smoke hole in the roof. It was all a single room, with a sleeping loft above reached by a pair of splintery ladders.

Jon remembered how he'd felt the day they had left the Wall: nervous as a maiden, but eager to glimpse the mysteries and wonders beyond each new horizon. *Well, here's one of the wonders,* he told himself, gazing about the squalid, foul-smelling hall. The acrid smoke was making his eyes water. *A pity that Pyp and Toad can't see all they're missing.*

Craster sat above the fire, the only man to enjoy his own chair. Even Lord Commander Mormont must seat himself on the common bench, with his raven muttering on his shoulder. Jarman Buckwell stood behind, dripping from patched mail and shiny wet leather, beside Thoren Smallwood in the late Ser Jaremy's heavy breastplate and sable-trimmed cloak.

Craster's sheepskin jerkin and cloak of sewn skins made a shabby contrast, but around one thick wrist was a heavy ring that had the glint of gold. He looked to be a powerful man, though well into the winter of his days now, his mane of hair grey going to white. A flat nose and a drooping mouth gave him a cruel look, and one of his ears was missing. *So this is a wildling.* Jon remembered Old Nan's tales of the savage folk who drank blood from human skulls. Craster seemed to be drinking a thin yellow beer from a chipped stone cup. Perhaps he had not heard the stories.

"I've not seen Benjen Stark for three years," he was telling Mormont. "And if truth be told, I never once missed him." A half-dozen black puppies and the odd pig or two skulked among the benches, while women in ragged deerskins passed horns of beer, stirred the fire, and chopped carrots and onions into a kettle.

"He ought to have passed here last year," said Thoren Smallwood. A dog came sniffing round his leg. He kicked it and sent it off yipping.

Lord Mormont said, "Ben was searching for Ser Waymar Royce, who'd vanished with Gared and young Will."

"Aye, those three I recall. The lordling no older than one of these pups. Too proud to sleep under my roof, him in his sable cloak and black steel. My wives give him big cow eyes all the same." He turned his squint on the nearest of the women. "Gared says they were chasing raiders. I told him, with a commander that green, best not catch 'em. Gared wasn't half-bad, for a crow. Had less ears than me, that one. The 'bite took 'em, same as mine." Craster laughed. "Now I hear he got no head neither. The 'bite do that too?"

Jon remembered a spray of red blood on white snow, and the way Theon Greyjoy had kicked the dead man's head. *The man was a deserter.* On the way back to Winterfell, Jon and Robb had raced, and found six direwolf pups in the snow. A thousand years ago.

"When Ser Waymar left you, where was he bound?"

Craster gave a shrug. "Happens I have better things to do than tend to the comings and goings of crows." He drank a pull of beer and set the cup aside. "Had no good southron wine up here for a bear's night. I could use me some wine, and a new axe. Mine's lost its bite, can't have that, I got me women to protect." He gazed around at his scurrying wives.

"You are few here, and isolated," Mormont said. "If you like, I'll detail some men to escort you south to the Wall."

The raven seemed to like the notion. *"Wall,"* it screamed, spreading black wings like a high collar behind Mormont's head.

Their host gave a nasty smile, showing a mouthful of broken brown teeth. "And what would we do there, serve you at supper? We're free folk here. Craster serves no man."

"These are bad times to dwell alone in the wild. The cold winds are rising."

"Let them rise. My roots are sunk deep." Craster grabbed a passing woman by the wrist. "Tell him, wife. Tell the Lord Crow how well content we are."

The woman licked at thin lips. "This is our place. Craster keeps us safe. Better to die free than live a slave."

"Slave," muttered the raven.

Mormont leaned forward. "Every village we have passed has been abandoned. Yours are the first living faces we've seen since we left the Wall. The people are gone . . . whether dead, fled, or taken, I could not say. The animals as well. Nothing is left. And earlier, we found the bodies of two of Ben Stark's rangers only a few leagues from the Wall. They were pale and cold, with black hands and black feet and wounds that did not bleed. Yet when we took them back to Castle Black they rose in the night and killed. One slew Ser Jaremy Rykker and the other came for me, which tells me that they remember some of what they knew when they lived, but there was no human mercy left in them."

The woman's mouth hung open, a wet pink cave, but Craster only gave a snort. "We've had no such troubles here . . . and I'll thank you not to tell such evil tales under my roof. I'm a godly man, and the gods keep me safe. If wights come walking, I'll know how to send them back to their graves. Though I could use me a sharp new axe." He sent his wife scurrying with a slap on her leg and a shout of "More beer, and be quick about it."

"No trouble from the dead," Jarmen Buckwell said, "but what of the living, my lord? What of your king?"

"*King!*" cried Mormont's raven. "*King, king, king.*"

"That Mance Rayder?" Craster spit into the fire. "King-beyond-the-Wall. What do free folk want with kings?" He turned his squint on Mormont. "There's much I could tell you o' Rayder and his doings, if I had a mind. This o' the empty villages, that's his work. You would have found this hall abandoned as well, if I were a man to scrape to such. He sends a rider, tells me I must leave my own keep to come grovel at his feet. I sent the man back, but kept his tongue. It's nailed to that wall there." He pointed. "Might be that I could tell you where to seek Mance Rayder. If I had a mind." The brown smile again. "But we'll have time enough for that. You'll be wanting to sleep beneath my roof, belike, and eat me out of pigs."

"A roof would be most welcome, my lord," Mormont said. "We've had hard riding, and too much wet."

"Then you'll guest here for a night. No longer, I'm not that fond o' crows. The loft's for me and mine, but you'll have all the floor you like. I've meat and beer for twenty, no more. The rest o' your black crows can peck after their own corn."

"We've packed in our own supplies, my lord," said the Old Bear. "We should be pleased to share our food and wine."

Craster wiped his drooping mouth with the back of a hairy hand. "I'll taste your wine, Lord Crow, that I will. One more thing. Any man lays a hand on my wives, he loses the hand."

"Your roof, your rule," said Thoren Smallwood, and Lord Mormont nodded stiffly, though he looked none too pleased.

"That's settled, then." Craster grudged them a grunt. "D'ya have a man can draw a map?"

"Sam Tarly can." Jon pushed forward. "Sam loves maps."

Mormont beckoned him closer. "Send him here after he's eaten. Have him bring quill and parchment. And find Tollett as well. Tell him to bring my axe. A guest gift for our host."

"Who's this one now?" Craster said before Jon could go. "He has the look of a Stark."

"My steward and squire, Jon Snow."

"A bastard, is it?" Craster looked Jon up and down. "Man wants to bed a woman, seems like he ought to take her to wife. That's what I do." He shooed Jon off with a wave. "Well, run and do your service, bastard, and see that axe is good and sharp now, I've no use for dull steel."

Jon Snow bowed stiffly and took his leave. Ser Ottyn Wythers was coming in as he was leaving, and they almost collided at the deerhide door. Outside, the rain seemed to have slackened. Tents had gone up all over the compound. Jon could see the tops of others under the trees.

Dolorous Edd was feeding the horses. "Give the wildling an axe, why not?" He pointed out Mormont's weapon, a short-hafted battle-axe with gold scrollwork inlaid on the black steel blade. "He'll give it back, I vow. Buried in the Old Bear's skull, like as not. Why not give him *all* our axes, and our swords as well? I mislike the way they clank and rattle as we ride. We'd travel faster without them, straight to hell's door. Does it rain in hell, I wonder? Perhaps Craster would like a nice hat instead."

Jon smiled. "He wants an axe. And wine as well."

"See, the Old Bear's clever. If we get the wildling well and truly drunk, perhaps he'll only cut off an ear when he tries to slay us with that axe. I have two ears but only one head."

"Smallwood says Craster is a friend to the Watch."

"Do you know the difference between a wildling who's a friend to the Watch and one who's not?" asked the dour squire. "Our enemies leave our bodies for the crows and the wolves. Our friends bury us in secret graves. I wonder how long that bear's been nailed up on that gate, and what Craster had there before we came hallooing?" Edd looked at the axe doubtfully, the rain running down his long face. "Is it dry in there?"

"Drier than out here."

"If I lurk about after, not too close to the fire, belike they'll take no note of me till morn. The ones under his roof will be the first he murders, but at least we'll die dry."

Jon had to laugh. "Craster's one man. We're two hundred. I doubt he'll murder anyone."

"You cheer me," said Edd, sounding utterly morose. "And besides, there's much to be said for a good sharp axe. I'd hate to be murdered with a maul. I saw a man hit in the brow with a maul once. Scarce split the skin at all, but his head turned mushy and swelled up big as a gourd, only purply-red. A comely man, but he died ugly. It's good that we're not giving them mauls." Edd walked away shaking his head, his sodden black cloak shedding rain behind him.

Jon got the horses fed before he stopped to think of his own supper. He was wondering where to find Sam when he heard a shout of fear. *"Wolf!"* He sprinted around the hall toward the cry, the earth sucking at his boots. One of Craster's women was backed up against the mud-spattered wall of the keep. "Keep away," she was shouting at Ghost. "You keep away!" The direwolf had a rabbit in his mouth and another dead and bloody on the ground before him. "Get it away, m'lord," she pleaded when she saw him.

"He won't hurt you." He knew at once what had happened; a wooden hutch, its slats shattered, lay on its side in the wet grass. "He must have been hungry. We haven't seen much game." Jon whistled. The direwolf bolted down the rabbit, crunching the small bones between his teeth, and padded over to him.

The woman regarded them with nervous eyes. She was younger than he'd thought at first. A girl of fifteen or sixteen years, he judged, dark hair plastered across a gaunt face by the falling rain, her bare feet muddy to the ankles. The body under the sewn skins was showing in the early turns of pregnancy. "Are you one of Craster's daughters?" he asked.

She put a hand over her belly. "Wife now." Edging away from the wolf, she knelt mournfully beside the broken hutch. "I was going to breed them rabbits. There's no sheep left."

"The Watch will make good for them." Jon had no coin of his own, or he would have offered it to her . . . though he was not sure what good a few coppers or even a silver piece would do her beyond the Wall. "I'll speak to Lord Mormont on the morrow."

She wiped her hands on her skirt. "M'lord—"

"I'm no lord."

But others had come crowding round, drawn by the woman's scream and the crash of the rabbit hutch. "Don't you believe him, girl," called out Lark the Sisterman, a ranger mean as a cur. "That's Lord Snow himself."

"Bastard of Winterfell and brother to kings," mocked Chett, who'd left his hounds to see what the commotion was about.

"That wolf's looking at you hungry, girl," Lark said. "Might be it fancies that tender bit in your belly."

Jon was not amused. "You're scaring her."

"Warning her, more like." Chett's grin was as ugly as the boils that covered most of his face.

"We're not to talk to you," the girl remembered suddenly.

"Wait," Jon said, too late. She bolted, ran.

Lark made a grab for the second rabbit, but Ghost was quicker. When he bared his teeth, the Sisterman slipped in the mud and went down on his bony butt. The others laughed. The direwolf took the rabbit in his mouth and brought it to Jon.

"There was no call to scare the girl," he told them.

"We'll hear no scolds from you, bastard." Chett blamed Jon for the loss of his comfortable position with Maester Aemon, and not without justice. If he had not gone to Aemon about Sam Tarly, Chett would still be tending an old blind man instead of a pack of ill-tempered hunting hounds. "You may be the Lord Commander's pet, but you're not the Lord Commander . . . and you wouldn't talk so bloody bold without that monster of yours always about."

"I'll not fight a brother while we're beyond the Wall," Jon answered, his voice cooler than he felt.

Lark got to one knee. "He's afraid of you, Chett. On the Sisters, we have a name for them like him."

"I know all the names. Save your breath." He walked away, Ghost at his side. The rain had dwindled to a thin drizzle by the time he reached the gate. Dusk would be on them soon, followed by another wet dark dismal night. The clouds would hide moon and stars and Mormont's Torch, turning the woods black as pitch. Every piss would be an adventure, if not quite of the sort Jon Snow had once envisioned.

Out under the trees, some rangers had found enough duff and dry wood to start a fire beneath a slanting ridge of slate. Others had raised tents or made rude shelters by stretching their cloaks over low branches. Giant had crammed himself inside the hollow of a dead oak. "How d'ye like my castle, Lord Snow?"

"It looks snug. You know where Sam is?"

"Keep on the way you were. If you come on Ser Ottyn's pavilion, you've gone too far." Giant smiled. "Unless Sam's found him a tree too. What a tree *that* would be."

It was Ghost who found Sam in the end. The direwolf shot ahead like a quarrel from a crossbow. Under an outcrop of rock that gave some small degree of shelter from the rain, Sam was feeding the ravens. His boots squished when he moved. "My feet are soaked through," he admitted miserably. "When I climbed off my horse, I stepped in a hole and went in up to my knees."

"Take off your boots and dry your stockings. I'll find some dry wood. If the ground's not wet under the rock, we might be able to get a fire burning." Jon showed Sam the rabbit. "And we'll feast."

"Won't you be attending Lord Mormont in the hall?"

"No, but you will. The Old Bear wants you to map for him. Craster says he'll find Mance Rayder for us."

"Oh." Sam did not look anxious to meet Craster, even if it meant a warm fire.

"He said eat first, though. Dry your feet." Jon went to gather fuel, digging down under deadfalls for the drier wood beneath and peeling back layers of sodden pine needles until he found likely kindling. Even then, it seemed to take forever for a spark to catch. He hung his cloak from the rock to keep the rain off his smoky little fire, making them a small snug alcove.

As he knelt to skin the rabbit, Sam pulled off his boots. "I think there's moss growing between my toes," he declared mournfully, wriggling the toes in question. "The rabbit will taste good. I don't even mind about the blood and all." He looked away. "Well, only a little . . ."

Jon spitted the carcass, banked the fire with a pair of rocks, and balanced their meal atop them. The rabbit had been a scrawny thing, but as it cooked it smelled like a king's feast. Other rangers gave them envious looks. Even Ghost looked up hungrily, flames shining in his red eyes as he sniffed. "You had yours before," Jon reminded him.

"Is Craster as savage as the rangers say?" Sam asked. The rabbit was a shade underdone, but tasted wonderful. "What's his castle like?"

"A midden heap with a roof and a firepit." Jon told Sam what he had seen and heard in Craster's Keep.

By the time the telling was done, it was dark outside and Sam was licking his fingers. "That was good, but now I'd like a leg of lamb. A whole leg, just for me, sauced with mint and honey and cloves. Did you see any lambs?"

"There was a sheepfold, but no sheep."

"How does he feed all his men?"

"I didn't see any men. Just Craster and his women and a few small girls. I wonder he's able to hold the place. His defenses were nothing to speak of, only a muddy dike. You had better go up to the hall and draw that map. Can you find the way?"

"If I don't fall in the mud." Sam struggled back into his boots, collected quill and parchment, and shouldered out into the night, the rain pattering down on his cloak and floppy hat.

Ghost laid his head on his paws and went to sleep by the fire. Jon stretched out beside him, grateful for the warmth. He was cold and wet, but not so cold and wet as he'd been a short time before. *Perhaps tonight the Old Bear will learn something that will lead us to Uncle Benjen.*

He woke to the sight of his own breath misting in the cold morning air. When he moved, his bones ached. Ghost was gone, the fire burnt out. Jon reached to pull aside the cloak he'd hung over the rock, and found it stiff and frozen. He crept beneath it and stood up in a forest turned to crystal.

The pale pink light of dawn sparkled on branch and leaf and stone. Every blade of grass was carved from emerald, every drip of water turned to diamond. Flowers and mushrooms alike wore coats of glass. Even the mud puddles had a bright brown sheen. Through the shimmering greenery, the black tents of his brothers were encased in a fine glaze of ice.

So there is magic beyond the Wall after all. He found himself thinking of his sisters, perhaps because he'd dreamed of them last night. Sansa would call this an enchantment, and tears would fill her eyes at the wonder of it, but Arya would run out laughing and shouting, wanting to touch it all.

"Lord Snow?" he heard. Soft and meek. He turned.

Crouched atop the rock that had sheltered him during the night was the rabbit keeper, wrapped in a black cloak so large it drowned her. *Sam's cloak,* Jon realized at once. *Why is she wearing Sam's cloak?* "The fat one told me I'd find you here, m'lord," she said.

"We ate the rabbit, if that's what you came for." The admission made him feel absurdly guilty.

"Old Lord Crow, him with the talking bird, he gave Craster a crossbow worth a hundred rabbits." Her arms closed over the swell of her belly. "Is it true, m'lord? Are you brother to a king?"

"A half brother," he admitted. "I'm Ned Stark's bastard. My brother Robb is the King in the North. Why are you here?"

"The fat one, that Sam, he said to see you. He give me his cloak, so no one would say I didn't belong."

"Won't Craster be angry with you?"

"My father drank overmuch of the Lord Crow's wine last night. He'll sleep most of the day." Her breath frosted the air in small nervous puffs. "They say the king gives justice and protects the weak." She started to climb off the rock, awkwardly, but the ice had made it slippery and her foot went out from under her. Jon caught her before she could fall, and helped her safely down. The woman knelt on the icy ground. "M'lord, I beg you—"

"Don't beg me anything. Go back to your hall, you shouldn't be here. We were commanded not to speak to Craster's women."

"You don't have to speak with me, m'lord. Just take me with you, when you go, that's all I ask."

All she asks, he thought. *As if that were nothing.*

"I'll . . . I'll be your wife, if you like. My father, he's got nineteen now, one less won't hurt him none."

"Black brothers are sworn never to take wives, don't you know that? And we're guests in your father's hall besides."

"Not *you,*" she said. "I watched. You never ate at his board, nor slept by his fire. He never gave you guest-right, so you're not bound to him. It's for the baby I have to go."

"I don't even know your name."

"Gilly, he called me. For the gillyflower."

"That's pretty." He remembered Sansa telling him once that he should say that whenever a lady told him her name. He could not help the girl, but perhaps the courtesy would please her. "Is it Craster who frightens you, Gilly?"

"For the baby, not for me. If it's a girl, that's not so bad, she'll grow a few years and he'll marry her. But Nella says it's to be a boy, and she's had six and knows these things. He gives the boys to the gods. Come the white cold, he does, and of late it comes more often. That's why he started giving them sheep, even though he has a taste for mutton. Only now the sheep's gone too. Next it will be dogs, till . . ." She lowered her eyes and stroked her belly.

"What gods?" Jon was remembering that they'd seen no boys in Craster's Keep, nor men either, save Craster himself.

"The cold gods," she said. "The ones in the night. The white shadows."

And suddenly Jon was back in the Lord Commander's Tower again. A severed hand was climbing his calf and when he pried it off with the point of his longsword, it lay writhing, fingers opening and closing. The dead man rose to his feet, blue eyes shining in that gashed and swollen face. Ropes of torn flesh hung from the great wound in his belly, yet there was no blood.

"What color are their eyes?" he asked her.

"Blue. As bright as blue stars, and as cold."

She has seen them, he thought. *Craster lied.*

"Will you take me? Just so far as the Wall—"

"We do not ride for the Wall. We ride north, after Mance Rayder and these Others, these white shadows and their wights. We *seek* them, Gilly. Your babe would not be safe with us."

Her fear was plain on her face. "You will come back, though. When your warring's done, you'll pass this way again."

"We may." *If any of us still live.* "That's for the Old Bear to say, the one you call the Lord Crow. I'm only his squire. I do not choose the road I ride."

"No." He could hear the defeat in her voice. "Sorry to be of trouble, m'lord. I only . . . they said the king keeps people safe, and I thought . . ." Despairing, she ran, Sam's cloak flapping behind her like great black wings.

Jon watched her go, his joy in the morning's brittle beauty gone. *Damn her*, he thought resentfully, *and damn Sam twice for sending her to me. What did he think I could do for her? We're here to fight wildlings, not save them.*

Other men were crawling from their shelters, yawning and stretching. The magic was already faded, icy brightness turning back to common dew in the light of the rising sun. Someone had gotten a fire started; he could smell woodsmoke drifting through the trees, and the smoky scent of bacon. Jon took down his cloak and snapped it against the rock, shattering the thin crust of ice that had formed in the night, then gathered up Longclaw and shrugged an arm through a shoulder strap. A few yards away he made water into a frozen bush, his piss steaming in the cold air and melting the ice wherever it fell. Afterward he laced up his black wool breeches and followed the smells.

Grenn and Dywen were among the brothers who had gathered round the fire. Hake handed Jon a hollow heel of bread filled with burnt bacon and chunks of salt fish warmed in bacon grease. He wolfed it down while listening to Dywen boast of having three of Craster's women during the night.

"You did not," Grenn said, scowling. "I would have seen."

Dywen whapped him up alongside his ear with the back of his hand. "You? Seen? You're blind as Maester Aemon. You never even saw that bear."

"What bear? Was there a bear?"

"There's always a bear," declared Dolorous Edd in his usual tone of gloomy resignation. "One killed my brother when I was young. Afterward it wore his teeth around its neck on a leather thong. And they were good teeth too, better than mine. I've had nothing but trouble with my teeth."

"Did Sam sleep in the hall last night?" Jon asked him.

"I'd not call it sleeping. The ground was hard, the rushes ill-smelling, and my brothers snore frightfully. Speak of bears if you will, none ever growled so fierce as Brown Bernarr. I was warm, though. Some dogs crawled atop me during the night. My cloak was almost dry when one of them pissed in it. Or perhaps it was Brown Bernarr. Have you noticed that the rain stopped the instant I had a roof above me? It will start again now that I'm back out. Gods and dogs alike delight to piss on me."

"I'd best go see to Lord Mormont," said Jon.

The rain might have stopped, but the compound was still a morass of shallow lakes and slippery mud. Black brothers were folding their tents, feeding their horses, and chewing on strips of salt beef. Jarman Buckwell's scouts were tightening the girths on their saddles before setting out. "Jon," Buckwell greeted him from horseback. "Keep a good edge on that bastard sword of yours. We'll be needing it soon enough."

Craster's hall was dim after daylight. Inside, the night's torches had burned low, and it was hard to know that the sun had risen. Lord Mormont's raven was the first to spy him enter. Three lazy flaps of its great black wings, and it perched atop Longclaw's hilt. "Corn!" It nipped at a strand of Jon's hair.

"Ignore that wretched beggar bird, Jon, it's just had half my bacon." The Old Bear sat at Craster's board, breaking his fast with the other officers on fried bread, bacon, and sheepgut sausage. Craster's new axe was on the table, its gold inlay gleaming faintly in the torchlight. Its owner was sprawled unconscious in the sleeping loft above, but the women were all up, moving about and serving. "What sort of day do we have?"

"Cold, but the rain has stopped."

"Very good. See that my horse is saddled and ready. I mean for us to ride within the hour. Have you eaten? Craster serves plain fare, but filling."

I will not eat Craster's food, he decided suddenly. "I broke my fast with the men, my lord." Jon shooed the raven off Longclaw. The bird hopped back to Mormont's shoulder, where it promptly shat. "You might have done that on Snow instead of saving it for me," the Old Bear grumbled. The raven *quorked*.

He found Sam behind the hall, standing with Gilly at the broken rabbit hutch. She was helping him back into his cloak, but when she saw Jon she stole away. Sam gave him a look of wounded reproach. "I thought you would help her."

"And how was I to do that?" Jon said sharply. "Take her with us, wrapped up in your cloak? We were commanded not to—"

"I know," said Sam guiltily, "but she was afraid. I know what it is to be afraid. I told her . . ." He swallowed.

"What! That we'd take her with us?"

Sam's fat face blushed a deep red. "On the way home." He could not meet Jon's eyes. "She's going to have a baby."

"Sam, have you taken leave of all your sense? We may not even return this way. And if we do, do you think the Old Bear is going to let you pack off one of Craster's wives?"

"I thought . . . maybe by then I could think of a way . . ."

"I have no time for this, I have horses to groom and saddle." Jon walked away as confused as he was angry. Sam's heart was a big as the rest of him, but for all his reading he could be as thick as Grenn at times. It was impossible, and dishonorable besides. *So why do I feel so ashamed?*

Jon took his accustomed position at Mormont's side as the Night's Watch streamed out past the skulls on Craster's gate. They struck off north and west along a crooked game trail. Melting ice dripped down all about them, a slower sort of rain with its own soft music. North of the compound, the brook was in full spate, choked with leaves and bits of wood, but the scouts had found where the ford lay and the column was able to splash across. The water ran as high as a horse's belly. Ghost swam, emerging on the bank with his white fur dripping brown. When he shook, spraying mud and water in all directions, Mormont said nothing, but on his shoulder the raven screeched.

"My lord," Jon said quietly as the wood closed in around them once more. "Craster has no sheep. Nor any sons."

Mormont made no answer.

"At Winterfell one of the serving women told us stories," Jon went on. "She used to say that there were wildlings who would lay with the Others to birth half-human children."

"Hearth tales. Does Craster seem less than human to you?"

In half a hundred ways. "He gives his sons to the wood."

A long silence. Then: "Yes." And *"Yes,"* the raven muttered, strutting. *"Yes, yes, yes."*

"You knew?"

"Smallwood told me. Long ago. All the rangers know, though few will talk of it."

"Did my uncle know?"

"All the rangers," Mormont repeated. "You think I ought to stop him. Kill him if need be." The Old Bear sighed. "Were it only that he wished to rid himself of some mouths, I'd gladly send Yoren or Conwys to collect the boys. We could raise them to the black and the Watch would be that much the stronger. But the wildlings serve crueler gods than you or I. These boys are Craster's offerings. His prayers, if you will."

His wives must offer different prayers, Jon thought.

"How is it you came to know this?" the Old Bear asked him. "From one of Craster's wives?"

"Yes, my lord," Jon confessed. "I would sooner not tell you which. She was frightened and wanted help."

"The wide world is full of people wanting help, Jon. Would that some could find the courage to help themselves. Craster sprawls in his loft even now, stinking of wine and lost to sense. On his board below lies a sharp new axe. Were it me, I'd name it 'Answered Prayer' and make an end."

Yes. Jon thought of Gilly. She and her sisters. They were nineteen, and Craster was one, but . . .

"Yet it would be an ill day for us if Craster died. Your uncle could tell you of the times Craster's Keep made the difference between life and death for our rangers."

"My father . . ." He hesitated.

"Go on, Jon. Say what you would say."

"My father once told me that some men are not worth having," Jon finished. "A bannerman who is brutal or unjust dishonors his liege lord as well as himself."

"Craster is his own man. He has sworn us no vows. Nor is he subject to our laws. Your heart is noble, Jon, but learn a lesson here. We cannot set the world to rights. That is not our purpose. The Night's Watch has other wars to fight."

Other wars. Yes. I must remember. "Jarman Buckwell said I might have need of my sword soon."

"Did he?" Mormont did not seem pleased. "Craster said much and more last night, and confirmed enough of my fears to condemn me to a sleepless night on his floor. Mance Rayder is gathering his people together in the Frostfangs. That's why the villages are empty. It is the same tale that Ser Denys Mallister had from the wildling his men captured in the Gorge, but Craster has added the *where*, and that makes all the difference."

"Is he making a city, or an army?"

"Now, that is the question. How many wildlings are there? How many men of fighting age? No one knows with certainty. The Frostfangs are cruel, inhospitable, a wilderness of stone and ice. They will not long sustain any great number of people. I can see only one purpose in this gathering. Mance Rayder means to strike south, into the Seven Kingdoms."

"Wildlings have invaded the realm before." Jon had heard the tales from Old Nan and Maester Luwin both, back at Winterfell. "Raymun Redbeard led them south in the time of my grandfather's grandfather, and before him there was a king named Bael the Bard."

"Aye, and long before them came the Horned Lord and the brother kings Gendel and Gorne, and in ancient days Joramun, who blew the Horn of Winter and woke giants from the earth. Each man of them broke his strength on the Wall, or was broken by the power of Winterfell on the far side . . . but the Night's Watch is only a shadow of what we were, and who remains to oppose the wildlings besides us? The Lord of Winterfell is dead, and his heir has marched his strength south to fight the Lannisters. The wildlings may never again have such a chance as this. I knew Mance Rayder, Jon. He is an oathbreaker, yes . . . but he has eyes to see, and no man has ever dared to name him faintheart."

"What will we do?" asked Jon.

"Find him," said Mormont. "Fight him. Stop him."

Three hundred, thought Jon, *against the fury of the wild*. His fingers opened and closed.

THEON

She was undeniably a beauty. *But your first is always beautiful,* Theon Greyjoy thought.

"Now there's a pretty grin," a woman's voice said behind him. "The lordling likes the look of her, does he?"

Theon turned to give her an appraising glance. He liked what he saw. Ironborn, he knew at a glance; lean and long-legged, with black hair cut short, wind-chafed skin, strong sure hands, a dirk at her belt. Her nose was too big and too sharp for her thin face, but her smile made up for it. He judged her a few years older than he was, but no more than five-and-twenty. She moved as if she were used to a deck beneath her feet.

"Yes, she's a sweet sight," he told her, "though not half so sweet as you."

"Oho." She grinned. "I'd best be careful. This lordling has a honeyed tongue."

"Taste it and see."

"Is it that way, then?" she said, eyeing him boldly. There were women on the Iron Islands—not many, but a few—who crewed the longships along with their men, and it was said that salt and sea changed them, gave them a man's appetites. "Have you been that long at sea, lordling? Or were there no women where you came from?"

"Women enough, but none like you."

"And how would you know what I'm like?"

"My eyes can see your face. My ears can hear your laughter. And my cock's gone hard as a mast for you."

The woman stepped close and pressed a hand to the front of his breeches. "Well, you're no liar," she said, giving him a squeeze through the cloth. "How bad does it hurt?"

"Fiercely."

"Poor lordling." She released him and stepped back. "As it happens, I'm a woman wed, and new with child."

"The gods are good," Theon said. "No chance I'd give you a bastard that way."

"Even so, my man wouldn't thank you."

"No, but you might."

"And why would that be? I've had lords before. They're made the same as other men."

"Have you ever had a prince?" he asked her. "When you're wrinkled and grey and your teats hang past your belly, you can tell your children's children that once you loved a king."

"Oh, is it love we're talking now? And here I thought it was just cocks and cunts."

"Is it love you fancy?" He'd decided that he liked this wench, whoever she was; her sharp wit was a welcome respite from the damp gloom of Pyke. "Shall I name my longship after you, and play you the high harp, and keep you in a tower room in my castle with only jewels to wear, like a princess in a song?"

"You *ought* to name your ship after me," she said, ignoring all the rest. "It was me who built her."

"Sigrin built her. My lord father's shipwright."

"I'm Esgred. Ambrode's daughter, and wife to Sigrin."

He had not known that Ambrode had a daughter, or Sigrin a wife . . . but he'd met the younger shipwright only once, and the older one he scarce remembered. "You're wasted on Sigrin."

"Oho. Sigrin told me this sweet ship is wasted on you."

Theon bristled. "Do you know who I am?"

"Prince Theon of House Greyjoy. Who else? Tell me true, my lord, how well do you love her, this new maid of yours? Sigrin will want to know."

The longship was so new that she still smelled of pitch and resin. His uncle Aeron would bless her on the morrow, but Theon had ridden over from Pyke to get a look at her before she was launched. She was not so large as Lord Balon's own *Great Kraken* or his uncle Victarion's *Iron Victory*, but she looked swift and sweet, even sitting in her wooden cradle on the strand; lean black hull a hundred feet long, a single tall mast, fifty long oars, deck enough for a hundred men . . . and at the prow, the great iron ram in the shape of an arrowhead. "Sigrin did me good service," he admitted. "Is she as fast as she looks?"

"Faster—for a master that knows how to handle her."

"It has been a few years since I sailed a ship." *And I've never captained one, if truth be told.* "Still, I'm a Greyjoy, and an ironman. The sea is in my blood."

"And your blood will be in the sea, if you sail the way you talk," she told him.

"I would never mistreat such a fair maiden."

"Fair maiden?" She laughed. "She's a sea bitch, this one."

"There, and now you've named her. *Sea Bitch.*"

That amused her; he could see the sparkle in her dark eyes. "And you said you'd name her after me," she said in a voice of wounded reproach.

"I did." He caught her hand. "Help me, my lady. In the green lands, they believe a woman with child means good fortune for any man who beds her."

"And what would they know about ships in the green lands? Or women, for that matter? Besides, I think you made that up."

"If I confess, will you still love me?"

"Still? When have I ever loved you?"

"Never," he admitted, "but I am trying to repair that lack, my sweet Esgred. The wind is cold. Come aboard my ship and let me warm you. On the morrow my uncle Aeron will pour seawater over her prow and mumble a prayer to the Drowned God, but I'd sooner bless her with the milk of my loins, and yours."

"The Drowned God might not take that kindly."

"Bugger the Drowned God. If he troubles us, I'll drown him again. We're off to war within a fortnight. Would you send me into battle all sleepless with longing?"

"Gladly."

"A cruel maid. My ship is well named. If I steer her onto the rocks in my distraction, you'll have yourself to blame."

"Do you plan to steer with this?" Esgred brushed the front of his breeches once more, and smiled as a finger traced the iron outline of his manhood.

"Come back to Pyke with me," he said suddenly, thinking, *What will Lord Balon say? And why should I care? I am a man grown, if I want to bring a wench to bed it is no one's business but my own.*

"And what would I do in Pyke?" Her hand stayed where it was.

"My father will feast his captains tonight." He had them to feast every night, while he waited for the last stragglers to arrive, but Theon saw no need to tell all that.

"Would you make me your captain for the night, my lord prince?" She had the wickedest smile he'd ever seen on a woman.

"I might. If I knew you'd steer me safe into port."

"Well, I know which end of the oar goes in the sea, and there's no one better with ropes and knots." One-handed, she undid the lacing of his breeches, then grinned and stepped lightly away from him. "A pity I'm a woman wed, and new with child."

Flustered, Theon laced himself back up. "I need to start back to the castle. If you do not come with me, I may lose my way for grief, and all the islands would be poorer."

"We couldn't have that . . . but I have no horse, my lord."

"You could take my squire's mount."

"And leave your poor squire to walk all the way to Pyke?"

"Share mine, then."

"You'd like that well enough." The smile again. "Now, would I be behind you, or in front?"

"You would be wherever you liked."

"I like to be on top."

Where has this wench been all my life? "My father's hall is dim and dank. It needs Esgred to make the fires blaze."

"The lordling has a honeyed tongue."

"Isn't that where we began?"

She threw up her hands. "And where we end. Esgred is yours, sweet prince. Take me to your castle. Let me see your proud towers rising from the sea."

"I left my horse at the inn. Come." They walked down the strand together, and when Theon took her arm, she did not pull away. He liked the way she walked; there was a boldness to it, part saunter and part sway, that suggested she would be just as bold beneath the blankets.

Lordsport was as crowded as he'd ever seen it, swarming with the crews of the longships that lined the pebbled shore and rode at anchor well out past the breakwater. Ironmen did not bend their knees often nor easily, but Theon noted that oarsmen and townfolk alike grew quiet as they passed, and acknowledged him with respectful bows of the head. *They have finally learned who I am*, he thought. *And past time too.*

Lord Goodbrother of Great Wyk had come in the night before with his main strength, near forty longships. His men were everywhere, conspicuous in their striped goat's hair sashes. It was said about the inn that Otter Gimpknee's whores were being fucked bowlegged by beardless boys in sashes. The boys were welcome to them so far as Theon was concerned. A poxier den of slatterns he hoped he'd never see. His present companion was more to his taste. That she was wed to his father's shipwright and pregnant to boot only made her more intriguing.

"Has my lord prince begun choosing his crew?" Esgred asked as they made their way toward the stable. "Ho, Bluetooth," she shouted to a passing seafarer, a tall man in bearskin vest and raven-winged helm. "How fares your bride?"

"Fat with child, and talking of twins."

"So soon?" Esgred smiled that wicked smile. "You got your oar in the water quickly."

"Aye, and stroked and stroked and *stroked*," roared the man.

"A big man," Theon observed. "Bluetooth, was it? Should I choose him for my *Sea Bitch*?"

"Only if you mean to insult him. Bluetooth has a sweet ship of his own."

"I have been too long away to know one man from another," Theon admitted. He'd looked for a few of the friends he'd played with as a boy, but they were gone, dead, or grown into strangers. "My uncle Victarion has loaned me his own steersman."

"Rymolf Stormdrunk? A good man, so long as he's sober." She saw more faces she knew, and called out to a passing trio, "Uller, Qarl. Where's your brother, Skyte?"

"The Drowned God needed a strong oarsman, I fear," replied the stocky man with the white streak in his beard.

"What he means is, Eldiss drank too much wine and his fat belly burst," said the pink-cheeked youth beside him.

"What's dead may never die," Esgred said.

"What's dead may never die."

Theon muttered the words with them. "You seem well known," he said to the woman when the men had passed on.

"Every man loves the shipwright's wife. He had better, lest he wants his ship to sink. If you need men to pull your oars, you could do worse than those three."

"Lordsport has no lack of strong arms." Theon had given the matter no little thought. It was fighters he wanted, and men who would be loyal to *him*, not to his lord father or his uncles. He was playing the part of a dutiful young prince for the moment, while he waited for Lord Balon to reveal the fullness of his plans. If it turned out that he did not like those plans or his part in them, however, well . . .

"Strength is not enough. A longship's oars must move as one if you would have her best speed. Choose men who have rowed together before, if you're wise."

"Sage counsel. Perhaps you'd help me choose them." *Let her believe I want her wisdom, women fancy that.*

"I may. If you treat me kindly."

"How else?"

Theon quickened his stride as they neared the *Myraham*, rocking high and empty by the quay. Her captain had tried to sail a fortnight past, but Lord Balon would not permit it. None of the merchantmen that called at Lordsport had been allowed to depart again; his father wanted no word of the hosting to reach the mainland before he was ready to strike.

"Milord," a plaintive voice called down from the forecastle of the merchanter. The captain's daughter leaned over the rail, gazing after him. Her father had forbidden her to come ashore, but whenever Theon came to Lordsport he spied her wandering forlornly about the deck. "Milord, a moment," she called after him. "As it please milord . . ."

"Did she?" Esgred asked as Theon hurried her past the cog. "Please milord?"

He saw no sense in being coy with this one. "For a time. Now she wants to be my salt wife."

"Oho. Well, she'd profit from some salting, no doubt. Too soft and bland, that one. Or am I wrong?"

"You're not wrong." *Soft and bland. Precisely. How had she known?*

He had told Wex to wait at the inn. The common room was so crowded that Theon had to push his way through the door. Not a seat was to be had at bench nor table. Nor did he see his squire. *"Wex,"* he shouted over the din and clatter. *If he's up with one of those poxy whores, I'll strip the hide off him,* he was thinking when he finally spied the boy, dicing near the hearth . . . and winning too, by the look of the pile of coins before him.

"Time to go," Theon announced. When the boy paid him no mind, he seized him by the ear and pulled him from the game. Wex grabbed up a fistful of coppers and came along without a word. That was one of the things Theon liked best about him. Most squires have loose tongues, but Wex had been born dumb . . . which didn't seem to keep him from being clever as any twelve-year-old had a right to be. He was a baseborn son of one of Lord Botley's half brothers. Taking him as squire had been part of the price Theon had paid for his horse.

When Wex saw Esgred, his eyes went round. *You'd think he'd never seen a woman before,* Theon thought. "Esgred will be riding with me back to Pyke. Saddle the horses, and be quick about it."

The boy had ridden in on a scrawny little garron from Lord Balon's stable, but Theon's mount was quite another sort of beast. "Where did you find that hellhorse?" Esgred asked when she saw him, but from the way she laughed he knew she was impressed.

"Lord Botley bought him in Lannisport a year past, but he proved to be too much horse for him, so Botley was pleased to sell." The Iron Islands were too sparse and rocky for breeding good horses. Most of the islanders were indifferent riders at best, more comfortable on the deck of a longship than in the saddle. Even the lords rode garrons or shaggy Harlaw ponies, and ox carts were more common than drays. The smallfolk too poor to own either one pulled their own plows through the thin, stony soil.

But Theon had spent ten years in Winterfell, and did not intend to go to war without a good mount beneath him. Lord Botley's misjudgment was his good fortune: a stallion with a temper as black as his hide, larger than a courser if not quite so big as most destriers. As Theon was not quite so big as most knights, that suited him admirably. The animal had fire in his eyes. When he'd met his new owner, he'd pulled back his lips and tried to bite off his face.

"Does he have a name?" Esgred asked Theon as he mounted.

"Smiler." He gave her a hand, and pulled her up in front of him, where he could put his arms around her as they rode. "I knew a man once who told me that I smiled at the wrong things."

"Do you?"

"Only by the lights of those who smile at nothing." He thought of his father and his uncle Aeron.

"Are you smiling now, my lord prince?"

"Oh, yes." Theon reached around her to take the reins. She was almost of a height with him. Her hair could have used a wash and she had a faded pink scar on her pretty neck, but he liked the smell of her, salt and sweat and woman.

The ride back to Pyke promised to be a good deal more interesting than the ride down had been.

When they were well beyond Lordsport, Theon put a hand on her breast. Esgred reached up and plucked it away. "I'd keep both hands on the reins, or this black beast of yours is like to fling us both off and kick us to death."

"I broke him of that." Amused, Theon behaved himself for a while, chatting amiably of the weather (grey and overcast, as it had been since he arrived, with frequent rains) and telling her of the men he'd killed in the Whispering Wood. When he reached the part about coming *that* close to the Kingslayer himself, he slid his hand back up to where it had been. Her breasts were small, but he liked the firmness of them.

"You don't want to do that, my lord prince."

"Oh, but I do." Theon gave her a squeeze.

"Your squire is watching you."

"Let him. He'll never speak of it, I swear."

Esgred pried his fingers off her breast. This time she kept him firmly prisoned. She had strong hands.

"I like a woman with a good tight grip."

She snorted. "I'd not have thought it, by that wench on the waterfront."

"You must not judge me by her. She was the only woman on the ship."

"Tell me of your father. Will he welcome me kindly to his castle?"

"Why should he? He scarcely welcomed *me*, his own blood, the heir to Pyke and the Iron Islands."

"Are you?" she asked mildly. "It's said that you have uncles, brothers, a sister."

"My brothers are long dead, and my sister . . . well, they say Asha's favorite gown is a chainmail hauberk that hangs down past her knees, with boiled leather smallclothes beneath. Men's garb won't make her a man, though. I'll make a good marriage alliance with her once we've won the war, if I can find a man to take her. As I recall, she had a nose like a vulture's beak, a ripe crop of pimples, and no more chest than a boy."

"You can marry off your sister," Esgred observed, "but not your uncles."

"My uncles . . ." Theon's claim took precedence over those of his father's three brothers, but the woman had touched on a sore point nonetheless. In the islands it was scarce unheard of for a strong, ambitious uncle to dispossess a weak nephew of his rights, and usually murder him in the bargain. *But I am not weak*, Theon told himself, *and I mean to be stronger yet by the time my father dies.* "My uncles pose no threat to me," he declared. "Aeron is drunk on seawater and sanctity. He lives only for his god—"

"*His* god? Not yours?"

"Mine as well. What is dead can never die." He smiled thinly. "If I make pious noises as required, Damphair will give me no trouble. And my uncle Victarion—"

"Lord Captain of the Iron Fleet, and a fearsome warrior. I have heard them sing of him in the alehouses."

"During my lord father's rebellion, he sailed into Lannisport with my uncle Euron and burned the Lannister fleet where it lay at anchor," Theon recalled. "The plan was Euron's, though. Victarion is like some great grey bullock, strong and tireless and dutiful, but not like to win any races. No doubt, he'll serve me as loyally as he has served my lord father. He has neither the wits nor the ambition to plot betrayal."

"Euron Croweye has no lack of cunning, though. I've heard men say terrible things of that one."

Theon shifted his seat. "My uncle Euron has not been seen in the islands for close on two years. He may be dead." If so, it might be for the best. Lord Balon's eldest brother had never given up the Old Way, even for a day. His *Silence*, with its black sails and dark red hull, was infamous in every port from Ibben to Asshai, it was said.

"He may be dead," Esgred agreed, "and if he lives, why, he has spent so long at sea, he'd be half a stranger here. The ironborn would never seat a stranger in the Seastone Chair."

"I suppose not," Theon replied, before it occurred to him that some would call *him* a stranger as well. The thought made him frown. *Ten years is a long while, but I am back now, and my father is far from dead. I have time to prove myself.*

He considered fondling Esgred's breast again, but she would probably only take his hand away, and all this talk of his uncles had dampened his ardor somewhat. Time enough for such play at the castle, in the privacy of his chambers. "I will speak to Helya when we reach Pyke, and see that you have an honored place at the feast," he said. "I must sit on the dais, at my father's right hand, but I will come down and join you when he leaves the hall. He seldom lingers long. He has no belly for drink these days."

"A grievous thing when a great man grows old."

"Lord Balon is but the *father* of a great man."

"A modest lordling."

"Only a fool humbles himself when the world is so full of men eager to do that job for him." He kissed her lightly on the nape of her neck.

"What shall I wear to this great feast?" She reached back and pushed his face away.

"I'll ask Helya to garb you. One of my lady mother's gowns might do. She is off on Harlaw, and not expected to return."

"The cold winds have worn her away, I hear. Will you not go see her? Harlaw is only a day's sail, and surely Lady Greyjoy yearns for a last sight of her son."

"Would that I could. I am kept too busy here. My father relies on me, now that I am returned. Come peace, perhaps . . ."

"Your coming might bring *her* peace."

"Now you sound a woman," Theon complained.

"I confess, I am . . . and new with child."

Somehow that thought excited him. "So you say, but your body shows no signs of it. How shall it be proven? Before I believe you, I shall need to see your breasts grow ripe, and taste your mother's milk."

"And what will my husband say to this? Your father's own sworn man and servant?"

"We'll give him so many ships to build, he'll never know you've left him."

She laughed. "It's a cruel lordling who's seized me. If I promise you that one day you may watch my babe get suck, will you tell me more of your war, Theon of House Greyjoy? There are miles and mountains still ahead of us, and I would hear of this wolf king you served, and the golden lions he fights."

Ever anxious to please her, Theon obliged. The rest of the long ride passed swiftly as he filled her pretty head with tales of Winterfell and war. Some of the things he said astonished him. *She is easy to talk to, gods praise her,* he reflected. *I feel as though I've known her for years. If the wench's pillow play is half the equal of her wit, I'll need to keep her . . .* He thought of Sigrin the Shipwright, a thick-bodied, thick-witted man, flaxen hair already receding from a pimpled brow, and shook his head. *A waste. A most tragic waste.*

It seemed scarcely any time at all before the great curtain wall of Pyke loomed up before them.

The gates were open. Theon put his heels into Smiler and rode through at a brisk trot. The hounds were barking wildly as he helped Esgred dismount. Several came bounding up, tails wagging. They shot straight past him and almost bowled the woman over, leaping all around her, yapping and licking. *"Off,"* Theon shouted, aiming an ineffectual kick at one big brown bitch, but Esgred was laughing and wrestling with them.

A stableman came pounding up after the dogs. "Take the horse," Theon commanded him, "and get these damn dogs away—"

The lout paid him no mind. His face broke into a huge gap-toothed smile and he said, "Lady Asha. You're back."

"Last night," she said. "I sailed from Great Wyk with Lord Goodbrother, and spent the night at the inn. My little brother was kind enough to let me ride with him from Lordsport." She kissed one of the dogs on the nose and grinned at Theon.

All he could do was stand and gape at her. *Asha. No. She cannot be Asha.* He realized suddenly that there were two Ashas in his head. One was the little girl he had known. The other, more vaguely imagined, looked something like her mother. Neither looked a bit like this . . . this . . . this . . .

"The pimples went when the breasts came," she explained while she tussled with a dog, "but I kept the vulture's beak."

Theon found his voice. *"Why didn't you tell me?"*

Asha let go of the hound and straightened. "I wanted to see who you were first. And I did." She gave him a mocking half bow. "And now, little brother, pray excuse me. I need to bathe and dress for the feast. I wonder if I still have that chainmail gown I like to wear over my boiled leather smallclothes?" She gave him that evil grin, and crossed the bridge with that walk he'd liked so well, half saunter and half sway.

When Theon turned away, Wex was smirking at him. He gave the boy a clout on the ear. "That's for enjoying this so much." And another, harder. "And that's for not warning me. Next time, grow a tongue."

His own chambers in the Guest Keep had never seemed so chilly, though the thralls had left a brazier burning. Theon kicked his boots off, let his cloak fall to the floor, and poured himself a cup of wine, remembering a gawky girl with knob knees and pimples. *She unlaced my breeches*, he thought, outraged, *and she said . . . oh, gods, and I said . . .* He groaned. He could not possibly have made a more appalling fool of himself.

No, he thought then. *She was the one who made me a fool. The evil bitch must have enjoyed every moment of it. And the way she kept reaching for my cock . . .*

He took his cup and went to the window seat, where he sat drinking and watching the sea while the sun darkened over Pyke. *I have no place here*, he thought, *and Asha is the reason, may the Others take her!* The water below turned from green to grey to black. By then he could hear distant music, and he knew it was time to change for the feast.

Theon chose plain boots and plainer clothes, somber shades of black and grey to fit his mood. No ornament; he had nothing bought with iron. *I might have taken something off that wildling I killed to save Bran Stark, but he had nothing worth the taking. That's my cursed luck, I kill the poor.*

The long smoky hall was crowded with his father's lords and captains when Theon entered, near four hundred of them. Dagmer Cleftjaw had not yet returned from Old Wyk with the Stonehouses and Drumms, but all the rest were there—Harlaws from Harlaw, Blacktydes from Blacktyde, Sparrs, Merlyns, and Goodbrothers from Great Wyk, Saltcliffes and Sunderlies from Saltcliffe, and Botleys and Wynches from the other side of Pyke. The thralls were pouring ale, and there was music, fiddles and skins and drums. Three burly men were doing the finger dance, spinning short-hafted axes at each other. The trick was to catch the axe or leap over it without missing a step. It was called the finger dance because it usually ended when one of the dancers lost one . . . or two, or five.

Neither the dancers nor the drinkers took much note of Theon Greyjoy as he strode to the dais. Lord Balon occupied the Seastone Chair, carved in the shape of a great kraken from an immense block of oily black stone. Legend said that the First Men had found it standing on the shore of Old Wyk when they came to the Iron Islands. To the left of the high seat were Theon's uncles. Asha was ensconced at his right hand, in the place of honor. "You come late, Theon," Lord Balon observed.

"I ask your pardon." Theon took the empty seat beside Asha. Leaning close, he hissed in her ear, "You're in my place."

She turned to him with innocent eyes. "Brother, surely you are mistaken. Your place is at Winterfell." Her smile cut. "And where are all your pretty clothes? I heard you fancied silk and velvet against your skin." She was in soft green wool herself, simply cut, the fabric clinging to the slender lines of her body.

"Your hauberk must have rusted away, sister," he threw back. "A great pity. I'd like to see you all in iron."

Asha only laughed. "You may yet, little brother . . . if you think your *Sea Bitch* can keep up with my *Black Wind*." One of their father's thralls came near, bearing a flagon of wine. "Are you drinking ale or wine tonight, Theon?" She leaned over close. "Or is it still a taste of my mother's milk you thirst for?"

He flushed. "Wine," he told the thrall. Asha turned away and banged on the table, shouting for ale.

Theon hacked a loaf of bread in half, hollowed out a trencher, and summoned a cook to fill it with fish stew. The smell of the thick cream made him a little ill, but he forced himself to eat some. He'd drunk enough wine to float him through two meals. *If I retch, it will be on her.* "Does Father know that you've married his shipwright?" he asked his sister.

"No more than Sigrin does." She gave a shrug. "*Esgred* was the first ship he built. He named her after his mother. I would be hard-pressed to say which he loves best."

"Every word you spoke to me was a lie."

"Not *every* word. Remember when I told you I like to be on top?" Asha grinned.

That only made him angrier. "All that about being a woman wed, and new with child . . ."

"Oh, that part was true enough." Asha leapt to her feet. "*Rolfe, here,*" she shouted down at one of the finger dancers, holding up a hand. He saw her, spun, and suddenly an axe came flying from his hand, the blade gleaming as it tumbled end over end through the torchlight. Theon had time for a choked gasp before Asha snatched the axe from the air and slammed it down into the table, splitting his trencher in two and splattering his mantle with drippings. "There's my lord husband." His sister reached down inside her gown and drew a dirk from between her breasts. "And here's my sweet suckling babe."

He could not imagine how he looked at that moment, but suddenly Theon Greyjoy realized that the Great Hall was ringing with laughter, all of it at him. Even his father was smiling, gods be damned, and his uncle Victarion chuckled aloud. The best response he could summon was a queasy grin. *We shall see who is laughing when all this is done, bitch.*

Asha wrenched the axe out of the table and flung it back down at the dancers, to whistles and loud cheers. "You'd do well to heed what I told you about choosing a crew." A thrall offered them a platter, and she stabbed a salted fish and ate it off the end of her dirk. "If you had troubled to learn the first thing of Sigrin, I could never have fooled you. Ten years a wolf, and you land here and think to prince about the islands, but you know nothing and no one. Why should men fight and die for you?"

"I am their lawful prince," Theon said stiffly.

"By the laws of the green lands, you might be. But we make our own laws here, or have you forgotten?"

Scowling, Theon turned to contemplate the leaking trencher before him. He would have stew in his lap before long. He shouted for a thrall to clean it up. *Half my life I have waited to come home, and for what? Mockery and disregard!* This was not the Pyke he remembered. Or *did* he remember? He had been so young when they took him away to hold hostage.

The feast was a meager enough thing, a succession of fish stews, black bread, and spiceless goat. The tastiest thing Theon found to eat was an onion pie. Ale and wine continued to flow well after the last of the courses had been cleared away.

Lord Balon Greyjoy rose from the Seastone Chair. "Have done with your drink and come to my solar," he commanded his companions on the dais. "We have plans to lay." He left them with no other word, flanked by two of his guards. His brothers followed in short order. Theon rose to go after them.

"My little brother is in a rush to be off." Asha raised her drinking horn and beckoned for more ale.

"Our lord father is waiting."

"And has, for many a year. It will do him no harm to wait a little longer . . . but if you fear his wrath, scurry after him by all means. You ought to have no trouble catching our uncles." She smiled. "One is drunk on seawater, after all, and the other is a great grey bullock so dim he'll probably get lost."

Theon sat back down, annoyed. "I run after no man."

"No man, but every woman?"

"It was not me who grabbed your cock."

"I don't have one, remember? You grabbed every other bit of me quick enough."

He could feel the flush creeping up his cheeks. "I'm a man with a man's hungers. What sort of unnatural creature are you?"

"Only a shy maid." Asha's hand darted out under the table to give his cock a squeeze. Theon nearly jumped from his chair. "What, don't you want me to steer you into port, brother?"

"Marriage is not for you," Theon decided. "When I rule, I believe I will pack you off to the silent sisters." He lurched to his feet and strode off unsteadily to find his father.

Rain was falling by the time he reached the swaying bridge out to the Sea Tower. His stomach was crashing and churning like the waves below, and wine had unsteadied his feet. Theon gritted his teeth and gripped the rope tightly as he made his way across, pretending that it was Asha's neck he was clutching.

The solar was as damp and drafty as ever. Buried under his sealskin robes, his father sat before the brazier with his brothers on either side of him. Victarion was talking of tides and winds when Theon entered, but Lord Balon waved him silent. "I have made my plans. It is time you heard them."

"I have some suggestions—"

"When I require your counsel I shall ask for it," his father said. "We have had a bird from Old Wyk. Dagmer is bringing the Drumms and Stonehouses. If the god grants us good winds, we will sail when they arrive . . . or *you* will. I mean for you to strike the first blow, Theon. You shall take eight longships north—"

"*Eight?*" His face reddened. "What can I hope to accomplish with only eight longships?"

"You are to harry the Stony Shore, raiding the fishing villages and. sinking any ships you chance to meet. It may be that you will draw some of the northern lords out from behind their stone walls. Aeron will accompany you, and Dagmer Cleftjaw."

"May the Drowned God bless our swords," the priest said.

Theon felt as if he'd been slapped. He was being sent to do reaver's work, burning fishermen out of their hovels and raping their ugly daughters, and yet it seemed Lord Balon did not trust him sufficiently to do even that much. Bad enough to have to suffer the Damphair's scowls and chidings. With Dagmer Cleftjaw along as well, his command would be purely nominal.

"Asha my daughter," Lord Balon went on, and Theon turned to see that his sister had slipped in silently, "you shall take thirty longships of picked men round Sea Dragon Point. Land upon the tidal flats north of Deepwood Motte. March quickly, and the castle may fall before they even know you are upon them."

Asha smiled like a cat in cream. "I've always wanted a castle," she said sweetly.

"Then take one."

Theon had to bite his tongue. Deepwood Motte was the stronghold of the Glovers. With both Robett and Galbart warring in the south, it would be lightly held, and once the castle fell the ironmen would have a secure base in the heart of the north. *I should be the one sent to take Deepwood.* He *knew* Deepwood Motte, he had visited the Glovers several times with Eddard Stark.

"Victarion," Lord Balon said to his brother, "the main thrust shall fall to you. When my sons have struck their blows, Winterfell must respond. You should meet small opposition as you sail up Saltspear and the Fever River. At the headwaters, you will be less than twenty miles from Moat Cailin. The Neck is the key to the kingdom. Already we command the western seas. Once we hold Moat Cailin, the pup will not be able to win back to the north . . . and if he is fool enough to try, his enemies will seal the south end of the causeway behind him, and Robb the boy will find himself caught like a rat in a bottle."

Theon could keep silent no longer. "A bold plan, Father, but the lords in their castles—"

Lord Balon rode over him. "The lords are gone south with the pup. Those who remained behind are the cravens, old men, and green boys. They will yield or fall, one by one. Winterfell may defy us for a year, but what of it? The rest shall be ours, forest and field and hall, and we shall make the folk our thralls and salt wives."

Aeron Damphair raised his arms. "And the waters of wrath will rise high, and the Drowned God will spread his dominion across the green lands!"

"What is dead can never die," Victarion intoned. Lord Balon and Asha echoed his words, and Theon had no choice but to mumble along with them. And then it was done.

Outside the rain was falling harder than ever. The rope bridge twisted and writhed under his feet. Theon Greyjoy stopped in the center of the span and contemplated the rocks below. The sound of the waves was a crashing roar, and he could taste the salt spray on his lips. A sudden gust of wind made him lose his footing, and he stumbled to his knees.

Asha helped him rise. "You can't hold your wine either, brother."

Theon leaned on her shoulder and let her guide him across the rain-slick boards. "I liked you better when you were Esgred," he told her accusingly.

She laughed. "That's fair. I liked *you* better when you were nine."

TYRION

Through the door came the soft sound of the high harp, mingled with a trilling of pipes. The singer's voice was muffled by the thick walls, yet Tyrion knew the verse. *I loved a maid as fair as summer*, he remembered, *with sunlight in her hair . . .*

Ser Meryn Trant guarded the queen's door this night. His muttered "My lord" struck Tyrion as a tad grudging, but he opened the door nonetheless. The song broke off abruptly as he strode into his sister's bedchamber.

Cersei was reclining on a pile of cushions. Her feet were bare, her golden hair artfully tousled, her robe a green-and-gold samite that caught the light of the candles and shimmered as she looked up. "Sweet sister," Tyrion said, "how beautiful you look tonight." He turned to the singer. "And you as well, cousin. I had no notion you had such a lovely voice."

The compliment made Ser Lancel sulky; perhaps he thought he was being mocked. It seemed to Tyrion that the lad had grown three inches since being knighted. Lancel had thick sandy hair, green Lannister eyes, and a line of soft blond fuzz on his upper lip. At sixteen, he was cursed with all the certainty of youth, unleavened by any trace of humor or self-doubt, and wed to the arrogance that came so naturally to those born blond and strong and handsome. His recent elevation had only made him worse. "Did Her Grace send for you?" the boy demanded.

"Not that I recall," Tyrion admitted. "It grieves me to disturb your revels, Lancel, but as it happens, I have matters of import to discuss with my sister."

Cersei regarded him suspiciously. "If you are here about those begging brothers, Tyrion, spare me your reproaches. I won't have them spreading their filthy treasons in the streets. They can preach to each other in the dungeons."

"And count themselves lucky that they have such a gentle queen," added Lancel. "I would have had their tongues out."

"One even dared to say that the gods were punishing us because Jaime murdered the rightful king," Cersei declared. "It will not be borne, Tyrion. I gave you ample opportunity to deal with these lice, but you and your Ser Jacelyn did nothing, so I commanded Vylarr to attend to the matter."

"And so he did." Tyrion *had* been annoyed when the red cloaks had dragged a half dozen of the scabrous prophets down to the dungeons without consulting him, but they were not important enough to battle over. "No doubt we will all be better off for a little quiet in the streets. That is not why I came. I have tidings I know you will be anxious to hear, sweet sister, but they are best spoken of privily."

"Very well." The harpist and the piper bowed and hurried out, while Cersei kissed her cousin chastely on the cheek. "Leave us, Lancel. My brother's harmless when he's alone. If he'd brought his pets, we'd smell them."

The young knight gave his cousin a baleful glance and pulled the door shut forcefully behind him. "I'll have you know I make Shagga bathe once a fortnight," Tyrion said when he was gone.

"You're very pleased with yourself, aren't you? Why?"

"Why not?" Tyrion said. Every day, every night, hammers rang along the Street of Steel, and the great chain grew longer. He hopped up onto the great canopied bed. "Is this the bed where Robert died? I'm surprised you kept it."

"It gives me sweet dreams," she said. "Now spit out your business and waddle away, Imp."

Tyrion smiled. "Lord Stannis has sailed from Dragonstone."

Cersei bolted to her feet. "And yet you sit there grinning like a harvest-day pumpkin? Has Bywater called out the City Watch? We must send a bird to Harrenhal at once." He was laughing by then. She seized him by the shoulders and shook him. "Stop it. Are you mad, or drunk? *Stop it!*"

It was all he could do to get out the words. "I can't," he gasped. "It's too . . . gods, too funny . . . Stannis . . ."

"*What?*"

"He hasn't sailed against us," Tyrion managed. "He's laid siege to Storm's End. Renly is riding to meet him."

His sister's nails dug painfully into his arms. For a moment she stared incredulous, as if he had begun to gibber in an unknown tongue. "Stannis and Renly are fighting *each other?*" When he nodded, Cersei began to chuckle. "Gods be good," she gasped, "I'm starting to believe that Robert was the *clever* one."

Tyrion threw back his head and roared. They laughed together. Cersei pulled him off the bed and whirled him around and even hugged him, for a moment as giddy as a girl. By the time she let go of him, Tyrion was breathless and dizzy. He staggered to her sideboard and put out a hand to steady himself.

"Do you think it will truly come to battle between them? If they should come to some accord—"

"They won't," Tyrion said. "They are too different and yet too much alike, and neither could ever stomach the other."

"And Stannis has always felt he was cheated of Storm's End," Cersei said thoughtfully. "The ancestral seat of House Baratheon, his by rights . . . if you knew how many times he came to Robert singing that same dull song in that gloomy aggrieved tone he has. When Robert gave the place to Renly, Stannis clenched his jaw so tight I thought his teeth would shatter."

"He took it as a slight."

"It was meant as a slight," Cersei said.

"Shall we raise a cup to brotherly love?"

"Yes," she answered, breathless. "Oh, gods, yes."

His back was to her as he filled two cups with sweet Arbor red. It was the easiest thing in the world to sprinkle a pinch of fine powder into hers. "To Stannis!" he said as he handed her the wine. *Harmless when I'm alone, am I?*

"To Renly!" she replied, laughing. "May they battle long and hard, and the Others take them both!"

Is this the Cersei that Jaime sees? When she smiled, you saw how beautiful she was, truly. *I loved a maid as fair as summer, with sunlight in her hair.* He almost felt sorry for poisoning her.

It was the next morning as he broke his fast that her messenger arrived. The queen was indisposed and would not be able to leave her chambers. *Not able to leave her privy, more like.* Tyrion made the proper sympathetic noises and sent word to Cersei to rest easy, he would treat with Ser Cleos as they'd planned.

The Iron Throne of Aegon the Conqueror was a tangle of nasty barbs and jagged metal teeth waiting for any fool who tried to sit too comfortably, and the steps made his stunted legs cramp as he climbed up to it, all too aware of what an absurd spectacle he must be. Yet there was one thing to be said for it. It was *high*.

Lannister guardsmen stood silent in their crimson cloaks and lion-crested halfhelms. Ser Jacelyn's gold cloaks faced them across the hall. The steps to the throne were flanked by Bronn and Ser Preston of the Kingsguard. Courtiers filled the gallery while supplicants clustered near the towering oak-and-bronze doors. Sansa Stark looked especially lovely this morning, though her face was as pale as milk. Lord Gyles stood coughing, while poor cousin Tyrek wore his bridegroom's mantle of miniver and velvet. Since his marriage to little Lady Ermesande three days past, the other squires had taken to calling him "Wet Nurse" and asking him what sort of swaddling clothes his bride wore on their wedding night.

Tyrion looked down on them all, and found he liked it. "Call forth Ser Cleos Frey." His voice rang off the stone walls and down the length of the hall. He liked that too. *A pity Shae could not be here to see this*, he reflected. She'd asked to come, but it was impossible.

Ser Cleos made the long walk between the gold cloaks and the crimson, looking neither right nor left. As he knelt, Tyrion observed that his cousin was losing his hair.

"Ser Cleos," Littlefinger said from the council table, "you have our thanks for bringing us this peace offer from Lord Stark."

Grand Maester Pycelle cleared his throat. "The Queen Regent, the King's Hand, and the small council have considered the terms offered by this self-styled King in the North. Sad to say, they will not do, and you must tell these northmen so, ser."

"Here are *our* terms," said Tyrion. "Robb Stark must lay down his sword, swear fealty, and return to Winterfell. He must free my brother unharmed, and place his host under Jaime's command, to march against the rebels Renly and Stannis Baratheon. Each of Stark's bannermen must send us a son as hostage. A daughter will suffice where there is no son. They shall be treated gently and given high places here at court, so long as their fathers commit no new treasons."

Cleos Frey looked ill. "My lord Hand," he said, "Lord Stark will never consent to these terms."

We never expected he would, Cleos. "Tell him that we have raised another great host at Casterly Rock, that soon it will march on him from the west while my lord father advar ces from the east. Tell him that he stands alone, without hope of allies. Stannis and Renly Baratheon war against each other, and the Prince of Dorne has consented to wed his son Trystane to the Princess Myrcella." Murmurs of delight and consternation alike arose from the gallery and the back of the hall.

"As to this of my cousins," Tyrion went on, "we offer Harrion Karstark and Ser Wylis Manderly for Willem Lannister, and Lord Cerwyn and Ser Donnel Locke for your brother Tion. Tell Stark that two Lannisters are worth four northmen in any season." He waited for the laughter to die. "His father's bones he shall have, as a gesture of Joffrey's good faith."

"Lord Stark asked for his sisters and his father's sword as well," Ser Cleos reminded him.

Ser Ilyn Payne stood mute, the hilt of Eddard Stark's greatsword rising over one shoulder. "Ice," said Tyrion. "He'll have that when he makes his peace with us, not before."

"As you say. And his sisters?"

Tyrion glanced toward Sansa, and felt a stab of pity as he said, "Until such time as he frees my brother Jaime, unharmed, they shall remain here as hostages. How well they are treated depends on him." *And if the gods are good, Bywater will find Arya alive, before Robb learns she's gone missing.*

"I shall bring him your message, my lord."

Tyrion plucked at one of the twisted blades that sprang from the arm of the throne. *And now the thrust.* "Vylarr," he called.

"My lord."

"The men Stark sent are sufficient to protect Lord Eddard's bones, but a Lannister should have a Lannister escort," Tyrion declared. "Ser Cleos is the queen's cousin, and mine. We shall sleep more easily if you would see him safely back to Riverrun."

"As you command. How many men should I take?"

"Why, all of them."

Vylarr stood like a man made of stone. It was Grand Maester Pycelle who rose, gasping, "My lord Hand, that cannot . . . your father, Lord Tywin himself, he sent these good men to our city to protect Queen Cersei and her children . . ."

"The Kingsguard and the City Watch protect them well enough. The gods speed you on your way, Vylarr."

At the council table Varys smiled knowingly, Littlefinger sat feigning boredom, and Pycelle gaped like a fish, pale and confused. A herald stepped forward. "If any man has other matters to set before the King's Hand, let him speak now or go forth and hold his silence."

"*I* will be heard." A slender man all in black pushed his way between the Redwyne twins.

"Ser *Alliser!*" Tyrion exclaimed. "Why, I had no notion that you'd come to court. You should have sent me word."

"I have, as well you know." Thorne was as prickly as his name, a spare, sharp-featured man of fifty, hard-eyed and hard-handed, his black hair streaked with grey. "I have been shunned, ignored, and left to wait like some baseborn servant."

"Truly? Bronn, this was not well done. Ser Alliser and I are old friends. We walked the Wall together."

"Sweet Ser Alliser," murmured Varys, "you must not think too harshly of us. So many seek our Joffrey's grace, in these troubled and tumultuous times."

"More troubled than you know, eunuch."

"To his face we call him *Lord* Eunuch," quipped Littlefinger.

"How may we be of help to you, good brother?" Grand Maester Pycelle asked in soothing tones.

"The Lord Commander sent me to His Grace the king," Thorne answered. "The matter is too grave to be left to servants."

"The king is playing with his new crossbow," Tyrion said. Ridding himself of Joffrey had required only an ungainly Myrish crossbow that threw three quarrels at a time, and nothing would do but that he try it at once. "You can speak to servants or hold your silence."

"As you will," Ser Alliser said, displeasure in every word. "I am sent to tell you that we found two rangers, long missing. They were dead, yet when we brought the corpses back to the Wall they rose again in the night. One slew Ser Jaremy Rykker, while the second tried to murder the Lord Commander."

Distantly, Tyrion heard someone snigger. *Does he mean to mock me with this folly?* He shifted uneasily and glanced down at Varys, Littlefinger, and Pycelle, wondering if one of them had a role in this. A dwarf enjoyed at best a tenuous hold on dignity. Once the court and kingdom started to laugh at him, he was doomed. And yet . . . and yet . . .

Tyrion remembered a cold night under the stars when he'd stood beside the boy Jon Snow and a great white wolf atop the Wall at the end of the world, gazing out at the trackless dark beyond. He had felt—what?— *something*, to be sure, a dread that had cut like that frigid northern wind. A wolf had howled off in the night, and the sound had sent a shiver through him.

Don't be a fool, he told himself. *A wolf, a wind, a dark forest, it meant nothing. And yet* . . . He had come to have a liking for old Jeor Mormont during his time at Castle Black. "I trust that the Old Bear survived this attack?"

"He did."

"And that your brothers killed these, ah, dead men?"

"We did."

"You're certain that they are dead this time?" Tyrion asked mildly. When Bronn choked on a snort of laughter, he knew how he must proceed. "Truly truly dead?"

"They were dead the first time," Ser Alliser snapped. "Pale and cold, with black hands and feet. I brought Jared's hand, torn from his corpse by the bastard's wolf."

Littlefinger stirred. "And where is this charming token?"

Ser Alliser frowned uncomfortably. "It . . . rotted to pieces while I waited, unheard. There's naught left to show but bones."

Titters echoed through the hall. "Lord Baelish," Tyrion called down to Littlefinger, "buy our brave Ser Alliser a hundred spades to take back to the Wall with him."

"Spades?" Ser Alliser narrowed his eyes suspiciously.

"If you *bury* your dead, they won't come walking," Tyrion told him, and the court laughed openly. "Spades will end your troubles, with some strong backs to wield them. Ser Jacelyn, see that the good brother has his pick of the city dungeons."

Ser Jacelyn Bywater said, "As you will, my lord, but the cells are near empty. Yoren took all the likely men."

"Arrest some more, then," Tyrion told him. "Or spread the word that there's bread and turnips on the Wall, and they'll go of their own accord." The city had too many mouths to feed, and the Night's Watch a perpetual need of men. At Tyrion's signal, the herald cried an end, and the hall began to empty.

Ser Alliser Thorne was not so easily dismissed. He was waiting at the foot of the Iron Throne when Tyrion descended. "Do you think I sailed all the way from Eastwatch-by-the-Sea to be mocked by the likes of you?" he fumed, blocking the way. "This is no jape. I saw it with my own eyes. I tell you, the dead walk."

"You should try to kill them more thoroughly." Tyrion pushed past. Ser Alliser made to grab his sleeve, but Preston Greenfield thrust him back. "No closer, ser."

Thorne knew better than to challenge a knight of the Kingsguard. "You are a fool, Imp," he shouted at Tyrion's back.

The dwarf turned to face him. "Me? Truly? Then why were they laughing at you, I wonder?" He smiled wanly. "You came for men, did you not?"

"The cold winds are rising. The Wall must be held."

"And to hold it you need men, which I've given you . . . as you might have noted, if your ears heard anything but insults. Take them, thank me, and begone before I'm forced to take a crab fork to you again. Give my warm regards to Lord Mormont . . . and to Jon Snow as well." Bronn seized Ser Alliser by the elbow and marched him forcefully from the hall.

Grand Maester Pycelle had already scuttled off, but Varys and Littlefinger had watched it all, start to finish. "I grow ever more admiring of you, my lord," confessed the eunuch. "You appease the Stark boy with his father's bones and strip your sister of her protectors in one swift stroke. You give that black brother the men he seeks, rid the city of some hungry mouths, yet make it all seem mockery so none may say that the dwarf fears snarks and grumkins. Oh, deftly done." .

Littlefinger stroked his beard. "Do you truly mean to send away all your guards, Lannister?"

"No, I mean to send away all my *sister's* guards."

"The queen will never allow that."

"Oh, I think she may. I *am* her brother, and when you've known me longer, you'll learn that I mean everything I say."

"Even the lies?"

"*Especially* the lies. Lord Petyr, I sense that you are unhappy with me."

"I love you as much as I ever have, my lord. Though I do not relish being played for a fool. If Myrcella weds Trystane Martell, she can scarcely wed Robert Arryn, can she?"

"Not without causing a great scandal," he admitted. "I regret my little ruse, Lord Petyr, but when we spoke, I could not know the Dornishmen would accept my offer."

Littlefinger was not appeased. "I do not like being lied to, my lord. Leave me out of your next deception."

Only if you'll do the same for me, Tyrion thought, glancing at the dagger sheathed at Littlefinger's hip. "If I have given offense, I am deeply sorry. All men know how much we love you, my lord. And how much we need you."

"Try and remember that." With that Littlefinger left them.

"Walk with me, Varys," said Tyrion. They left through the king's door behind the throne, the eunuch's slippers whisking lightly over the stone.

"Lord Baelish has the truth of it, you know. The queen will never permit you to send away her guard."

"She will. You'll see to that."

A smile flickered across Varys's plump lips. "Will I?"

"Oh, for a certainty. You'll tell her it is part of my scheme to free Jaime."

Varys stroked a powdered cheek. "This would doubtless involve the four men your man Bronn searched for so diligently in all the low places of King's Landing. A thief, a poisoner, a mummer, and a murderer."

"Put them in crimson cloaks and 'ion helms, they'll look no different from any other guardsmen. I searched for some time for a ruse that might get them into Riverrun before I thought to hide them in plain sight. They'll ride in by the main gate, flying Lannister banners and escorting Lord Eddard's bones." He smiled crookedly. "Four men alone would be watched vigilantly. Four among a hundred can lose themselves. So I must send the true guardsmen as well as the false . . . as you'll tell my sister."

"And for the sake of her beloved brother, she will consent, despite her misgivings." They made their way down a deserted colonnade. "Still, the loss of her red cloaks will surely make her uneasy."

"I like her uneasy," said Tyrion.

Ser Cleos Frey left that very afternoon, escorted by Vylarr and a hundred red-cloaked Lannister guardsmen. The men Robb Stark had sent joined them at the King's Gate for the long ride west.

Tyrion found Timett dicing with his Burned Men in the barracks. "Come to my solar at midnight." Timett gave him a hard one-eyed stare, a curt nod. He was not one for long speeches.

That night he feasted with the Stone Crows and Moon Brothers in the Small Hall, though he shunned the wine for once. He wanted all his wits about him. "Shagga, what moon is this?"

Shagga's frown was a fierce thing. "Black, I think."

"In the west, they call that a traitor's moon. Try not to get too drunk tonight, and see that your axe is sharp."

"A Stone Crow's axe is always sharp, and Shagga's axes are sharpest of all. Once I cut off a man's head, but he did not know it until he tried to brush his hair. Then it fell off."

"Is that why you never brush yours?" The Stone Crows roared and stamped their feet, Shagga hooting loudest of all.

By midnight, the castle was silent and dark. Doubtless a few gold cloaks on the walls spied them leaving the Tower of the Hand, but no one raised a voice. He was the Hand of the King, and where he went was his own affair.

The thin wooden door split with a thunderous *crack* beneath the heel of Shagga's boot. Pieces went flying inward, and Tyrion heard a woman's gasp of fear. Shagga hacked the door apart with three great blows of his axe and kicked his way through the ruins. Timett followed, and then Tyrion, stepping gingerly over the splinters. The fire had burned down a few glowing embers, and shadows lay thick across the bedchamber. When Timett ripped the heavy curtains off the bed, the naked serving girl stared up with wide white eyes. "Please, my lords," she pleaded, "don't hurt me." She cringed away from Shagga, flushed and fearful, trying to cover her charms with her hands and coming up a hand short.

"Go," Tyrion told her. "It's not you we want."

"Shagga wants this woman."

"Shagga wants every whore in this city of whores," complained Timett son of Timett.

"Yes," Shagga said, unabashed. "Shagga would give her a strong child."

"If she wants a strong child, she'll know whom to seek," Tyrion said. "Timett, see her out . . . gently, if you would."

The Burned Man pulled the girl from the bed and half marched, half dragged her across the chamber. Shagga watched them go, mournful as a puppy. The girl stumbled over the shattered door and out into the hall, helped along by a firm shove from Timett. Above their heads, the ravens were screeching.

Tyrion dragged the soft blanket off the bed, uncovering Grand Maester Pycelle beneath. "Tell me, does the Citadel approve of you bedding the serving wenches, Maester?"

The old man was as naked as the girl, though he made a markedly less attractive sight. For once, his heavy-lidded eyes were open wide. "W-what is the meaning of this? I am an old man, your loyal servant . . ."

Tyrion hoisted himself onto the bed. "So loyal that you sent only one of my letters to Doran Martell. The other you gave to my sister."

"N-no," squealed Pycelle. "No, a falsehood, I swear it, it was not me. Varys, it was Varys, the Spider, I warned you—"

"Do all maesters lie so poorly? I told Varys that I was giving Prince Doran my nephew Tommen to foster. I told Littlefinger that I planned to wed Myrcella to Lord Robert of the Eyrie. I told no one that I had offered Myrcella to the Dornish . . . that truth was only in the letter I entrusted to *you.*"

Pycelle clutched for a corner of the blanket. "Birds are lost, messages stolen or sold . . . it was Varys, there are things I might tell you of that eunuch that would chill your blood . . ."

"My lady prefers my blood hot."

"Make no mistake, for every secret the eunuch whispers in your ear, he holds seven back. And Littlefinger, that one . . ."

"I know all about Lord Petyr. He's almost as untrustworthy as you. Shagga, cut off his manhood and feed it to the goats."

Shagga hefted the huge double-bladed axe. "There are no goats, Halfman."

"Make do."

Roaring, Shagga leapt forward. Pycelle shrieked and wet the bed, urine spraying in all directions as he tried to scramble back out of reach. The wildling caught him by the end of his billowy white beard and hacked off three-quarters of it with a single slash of the axe.

"Timett, do you suppose our friend will be more forthcoming without those whiskers to hide behind?" Tyrion used a bit of the sheet to wipe the piss off his boots.

"He will tell the truth soon." Darkness pooled in the empty pit of Timett's burned eye. "I can smell the stink of his fear."

Shagga tossed a handful of hair down to the rushes, and seized what beard was left. "Hold still, Maester," urged Tyrion. "When Shagga gets angry, his hands shake."

"Shagga's hands never shake," the huge man said indignantly, pressing the great crescent blade under Pycelle's quivering chin and sawing through another tangle of beard.

"How long have you been spying for my sister?" Tyrion asked.

Pycelle's breathing was rapid and shallow. "All I did, I did for House Lannister." A sheen of sweat covered the broad dome of the old man's brow, and wisps of white hair clung to his wrinkled skin. "Always . . . for years . . . your lord father, ask him, I was ever his true servant . . . 'twas I who bid Aerys open his gates . . ."

That took Tyrion by surprise. He had been no more than an ugly boy at Casterly Rock when the city fell. "So the Sack of King's Landing was your work as well?"

"For the realm! Once Rhaegar died, the war was done. Aerys was mad, Viserys too young, Prince Aegon a babe at the breast, but the realm needed a king . . . I prayed it should be your good father, but Robert was too strong, and Lord Stark moved too swiftly . . ."

"How many have you betrayed, I wonder? Aerys, Eddard Stark, me . . . King Robert as well? Lord Arryn, Prince Rhaegar? Where does it begin, Pycelle?" He *knew* where it ended.

The axe scratched at the apple of Pycelle's throat and stroked the soft wobbly skin under his jaw, scraping away the last hairs. "You . . . were not here," he gasped when the blade moved upward to his cheeks. "Robert . . . his wounds . . . if you had seen them, smelled them, you would have no doubt . . ."

"Oh, I know the boar did your work for you . . . but if he'd left the job half done, doubtless you would have finished it."

"He was a wretched king . . . vain, drunken, lecherous . . . he would have set your sister aside, his own queen . . . please . . . Renly was plotting to bring the Highgarden maid to court, to entice his brother . . . it is the gods' own truth . . ."

"And what was Lord Arryn plotting?"

"He *knew*," Pycelle said. "About . . . about . . ."

"I know what he knew about," snapped Tyrion, who was not anxious for Shagga and Timett to know as well.

"He was sending his wife back to the Eyrie, and his son to be fostered on Dragonstone . . . he meant to act . . ."

"So you poisoned him first."

"No." Pycelle struggled feebly. Shagga growled and grabbed his head. The clansman's hand was so big he could have crushed the maester's skull like an eggshell had he squeezed.

Tyrion *tsked* at him. "I saw the tears of Lys among your potions. And you sent away Lord Arryn's own maester and tended him yourself, so you could make certain that he died."

"A falsehood!"

"Shave him closer," Tyrion suggested. "The throat again."

The axe swept back down, rasping over the skin. A thin film of spit bubbled on Pycelle's lips as his mouth trembled. "I tried to save Lord Arryn. I vow—"

"Careful now, Shagga, you've cut him."

Shagga growled. "Dolf fathered warriors, not barbers."

When he felt the blood trickling down his neck and onto his chest, the old man shuddered, and the last strength went out of him. He looked shrunken, both smaller and frailer than he had been when they burst in on him. "Yes," he wimpered, *"yes,* Colemon was purging, so I sent him away. The queen needed Lord Arryn dead, she did not say so, could not, Varys was listening, always listening, but when I looked at her I knew. It was not me who gave him the poison, though, I swear it." The old man wept. "Varys will tell you, it was the boy, his squire, Hugh he was called, he must surely have done it, ask your sister, ask her."

Tyrion was disgusted. "Bind him and take him away," he commanded. "Throw him down in one of the black cells."

They dragged him out the splintered door. "Lannister," he moaned, "all I've done has been for Lannister . . ."

When he was gone, Tyrion made a leisurely search of the quarters and collected a few more small jars from his shelves. The ravens muttered above his head as he worked, a strangely peaceful noise. He would need to find someone to tend the birds until the Citadel sent a man to replace Pycelle.

He was the one I'd hoped to trust. Varys and Littlefinger were no more loyal, he suspected . . . only more subtle, and thus more dangerous. Perhaps his father's way would have been best: summon Ilyn Payne, mount three heads above the gates, and have done. *And wouldn't that be a pretty sight,* he thought.

ARYA

Fear cuts deeper than swords, Arya would tell herself, but that did not make the fear go away. It was as much a part of her days as stale bread and the blisters on her toes after a long day of walking the hard, rutted road.

She had thought she had known what it meant to be afraid, but she learned better in that storehouse beside the Gods Eye. Eight days she had lingered there before the Mountain gave the command to march, and every day she had seen someone die.

The Mountain would come into the storehouse after he had broken his fast and pick one of the prisoners for questioning. The village folk would never look at him. Maybe they thought that if they did not notice him, he would not notice them . . . but he saw them anyway and picked whom he liked. There was no place to hide, no tricks to play, no way to be safe.

One girl shared a soldier's bed three nights running; the Mountain picked her on the fourth day, and the soldier said nothing.

A smiley old man mended their clothing and babbled about his son, off serving in the gold cloaks at King's Landing. "A king's man, he is," he would say, "a good king's man like me, all for Joffrey." He said it so often the other captives began to call him All-for-Joffrey whenever the guards weren't listening. All-for-Joffrey was picked on the fifth day.

A young mother with a pox-scarred face offered to freely tell them all she knew if they'd promise not to hurt her daughter. The Mountain heard her out; the next morning he picked her daughter, to be certain she'd held nothing back.

The ones chosen were questioned in full view of the other captives, so they could see the fate of rebels and traitors. A man the others called the Tickler asked the questions. His face was so ordinary and his garb so plain that Arya might have thought him one of the villagers before she had seen him at his work. "Tickler makes them howl so hard they piss themselves," old stoop-shoulder Chiswyck told them. He was the man she'd tried to bite, who'd called her a fierce little thing and smashed her head with a mailed fist. Sometimes he helped the Tickler. Sometimes others did that. Ser Gregor Clegane himself would stand motionless, watching and listening, until the victim died.

The questions were always the same. Was there gold hidden in the village? Silver, gems? Was there more food? Where was Lord Beric Dondarrion? Which of the village folk had aided him? When he rode off, where did he go? How many men were with them? How many knights, how many bowmen, how many men-at-arms? How were they armed? How many were horsed? How many were wounded? What other enemy had they seen? How many? When? What banners did they fly? Where did they go? Was there gold hidden in the village? Silver, gems? Where was Lord Beric Dondarrion? How many men were with him? By the third day, Arya could have asked the questions herself.

They found a little gold, a little silver, a great sack of copper pennies, and a dented goblet set with garnets that two soldiers almost came to blows over. They learned that Lord Beric had ten starvelings with him, or else a hundred mounted knights; that he had ridden west, or north, or south; that he had crossed the lake in a boat; that he was strong as an aurochs or weak from the bloody flux. No one ever survived the Tickler's questioning; no man, no woman, no child. The strongest lasted past evenfall. Their bodies were hung beyond the fires for the wolves.

By the time they marched, Arya knew she was no water dancer. Syrio Forel would never have let them knock him down and take his sword away, nor stood by when they killed Lommy Greenhands. Syrio would never have sat silent in that storehouse nor shuffled along meekly among the other captives. The direwolf was the sigil of the Starks, but Arya felt more a lamb, surrounded by a herd of other sheep. She hated the villagers for their sheepishness, almost as much as she hated herself.

The Lannisters had taken everything: father, friends, home, hope, courage. One had taken Needle, while another had broken her wooden stick sword over his knee. They had even taken her stupid secret. The storehouse had been big enough for her to creep off and make her water in some corner when no one was looking, but it was different on the road. She held it as long as she could, but finally she had to squat by a bush and skin down her breeches in front of all of them. It was that or wet herself. Hot Pie gaped at her with big moon eyes, but no one else even troubled to look. Girl sheep or boy sheep, Ser Gregor and his men did not seem to care.

Their captors permitted no chatter. A broken lip taught Arya to hold her tongue. Others never learned at all. One boy of three would not stop calling for his father, so they smashed his face in with a spiked mace. Then the boy's mother started screaming and Raff the Sweetling killed her as well.

Arya watched them die and did nothing. What good did it do you to be brave? One of the women picked for questioning had tried to be brave, but she had died screaming like all the rest. There were no brave people on that march, only scared and hungry ones. Most were women and children. The few men were very old or very young; the rest had been chained to that gibbet and left for the wolves and the crows. Gendry was only spared because he'd admitted to forging the horned helm himself; smiths, even apprentice smiths, were too valuable to kill.

They were being taken to serve Lord Tywin Lannister at Harrenhal, the Mountain told them. "You're traitors and rebels, so thank your gods that Lord Tywin's giving you this chance. It's more than you'd get from the outlaws. Obey, serve, and live."

"It's not just, it's not," she heard one wizened old woman complain to another when they had bedded down for the night. "We never did no treason, the others come in and took what they wanted, same as this bunch."

"Lord Beric did us no hurt, though," her friend whispered. "And that red priest with him, he paid for all they took."

"Paid? He took two of my chickens and gave me a bit of paper with a mark on it. Can I eat a bit of raggy old paper, I ask you? Will it give me eggs?" She looked about to see that no guards were near, and spat three times. "There's for the Tullys and there's for the Lannisters and there's for the Starks."

"It's a sin and a shame," an old man hissed. "When the old king was still alive, he'd not have stood for this."

"King Robert?" Arya asked, forgetting herself.

"King *Aerys*, gods grace him," the old man said, too loudly. A guard came sauntering over to shut them up. The old man lost both his teeth, and there was no more talk that night.

Besides his captives, Ser Gregor was bringing back a dozen pigs, a cage of chickens, a scrawny milk cow, and nine wagons of salt fish. The Mountain and his men had horses, but the captives were all afoot, and those too weak to keep up were killed out of hand, along with anyone foolish enough to flee. The guards took women off into the bushes at night, and most seemed to expect it and went along meekly enough. One girl, prettier than the others, was made to go with four or five different men every night, until finally she hit one with a rock. Ser Gregor made everyone watch while he took off her head with a sweep of his massive two-handed greatsword. "Leave the body for the wolves," he commanded when the deed was done, handing the sword to his squire to be cleaned.

Arya glanced sidelong at Needle, sheathed at the hip of a black-bearded, balding man-at-arms called Polliver. *It's good that they took it away*, she thought. Otherwise she would have tried to stab Ser Gregor, and he would have cut her right in half, and the wolves would eat her too.

Polliver was not so bad as some of the others, even though he'd stolen Needle. The night she was caught, the Lannister men had been nameless strangers with faces as alike as their nasal helms, but she'd come to know them all. You had to know who was lazy and who was cruel, who was smart and who was stupid. You had to learn that even though the one they called Shitmouth had the foulest tongue she'd ever heard, he'd give you an extra piece of bread if you asked, while jolly old Chiswyck and soft-spoken Raff would just give you the back of their hand.

Arya watched and listened and polished her hates the way Gendry had once polished his horned helm. Dunsen wore those bull's horns now, and she hated him for it. She hated Polliver for Needle, and she hated old Chiswyck who thought he was funny. And Raff the Sweetling, who'd driven his spear through Lommy's throat, she hated even more. She hated Ser Amory Lorch for Yoren, and she hated Ser Meryn Trant for Syrio, the Hound for killing the butcher's boy Mycah, and Ser Ilyn and Prince Joffrey and the queen for the sake of her father and Fat Tom and Desmond and the rest, and even for Lady, Sansa's wolf. The Tickler was almost too scary to hate. At times she could almost forget he was still with them; when he was not asking questions, he was just another soldier, quieter than most, with a face like a thousand other men.

Every night Arya would say their names. "Ser Gregor," she'd whisper to her stone pillow. "Dunsen, Polliver, Chiswyck, Raff the Sweetling. The Tickler and the Hound. Ser Amory, Ser Ilyn, Ser Meryn, King Joffrey, Queen Cersei." Back in Winterfell, Arya had prayed with her mother in the sept and with her father in the godswood, but there were no gods on the road to Harrenhal, and her names were the only prayer she cared to remember.

Every day they marched, and every night she said her names, until finally the trees thinned and gave way to a patchwork landscape of rolling hills, meandering streams, and sunlit fields, where the husks of burnt holdfasts thrust up black as rotten teeth. It was another long day's march before they glimpsed the towers of Harrenhal in the distance, hard beside the blue waters of the lake.

It would be better once they got to Harrenhal, the captives told each other, but Arya was not so certain. She remembered Old Nan's stories of the castle built on fear. Harren the Black had mixed human blood in the mortar, Nan used to say, dropping her voice so the children would need to lean close to hear, but Aegon's dragons had roasted Harren and all his sons within their great walls of stone. Arya chewed her lip as she walked along on feet grown hard with callus. It would not be much longer, she told herself; those towers could not be more than a few miles off.

Yet they walked all that day and most of the next before at last they reached the fringes of Lord Tywin's army, encamped west of the castle amidst the scorched remains of a town. Harrenhal was deceptive from afar, because it was so *huge*. Its colossal curtain walls rose beside the lake, sheer and sudden as mountain cliffs, while atop their battlements the rows of wood-and-iron scorpions looked as small as the bugs for which they were named.

The stink of the Lannister host reached Arya well before she could make out the devices on the banners that sprouted along the lakeshore, atop the pavilions of the westermen. From the smell, Arya could tell that Lord Tywin had been here some time. The latrines that ringed the encampment were overflowing and swarming with flies, and she saw faint greenish fuzz on many of the sharpened stakes that protected the perimeters.

Harrenhal's gatehouse, itself as large as Winterfell's Great Keep, was as scarred as it was massive, its stones fissured and discolored. From outside, only the tops of five immense towers could be seen beyond the walls. The shortest of them was half again as tall as the highest tower in Winterfell, but they did not soar the way a proper tower did. Arya thought they looked like some old man's gnarled, knuckly fingers groping after a passing cloud. She remembered Nan telling how the stone had melted and flowed like candlewax down the steps and in the windows, glowing a sullen searing red as it sought out Harren where he hid. Arya could believe every word; each tower was more grotesque and misshapen than the last, lumpy and runneled and cracked.

"I don't want to go there," Hot Pie squeaked as Harrenhal opened its gates to them. "There's ghosts in there."

Chiswyck heard him, but for once he only smiled. "Baker boy, here's your choice. Come join the ghosts, or be one."

Hot Pie went in with the rest of them.

In the echoing stone-and-timber bathhouse, the captives were stripped and made to scrub and scrape themselves raw in tubs of scalding hot water. Two fierce old women supervised the process, discussing them as bluntly as if they were newly acquired donkeys. When Arya's turn came round, Goodwife Amabel clucked in dismay at the sight of her feet, while Goodwife Harra felt the callus on her fingers that long hours of practice with Needle had earned her. "Got those churning butter, I'll wager," she said. "Some farmer's whelp, are you? Well, never you mind, girl, you have a chance to win a higher place in this world if you work hard. If you won't work hard, you'll be beaten. And what do they call you?"

Arya dared not say her true name, but Arry was no good either, it was a boy's name and they could see she was no boy. "Weasel," she said, naming the first girl she could think of. "Lommy called me Weasel."

"I can see why," sniffed Goodwife Amabel. "That hair is a fright and a nest for lice as well. We'll have it off, and then you're for the kitchens."

"I'd sooner tend the horses." Arya liked horses, and maybe if she was in the stables she'd be able to steal one and escape.

Goodwife Harra slapped her so hard that her swollen lip broke open all over again. "And keep that tongue to yourself or you'll get worse. No one asked your views."

The blood in her mouth had a salty metal tang to it. Arya dropped her gaze and said nothing. *If I still had Needle, she wouldn't dare hit me,* she thought sullenly.

"Lord Tywin and his knights have grooms and squires to tend their horses, they don't need the likes of you," Goodwife Amabel said. "The kitchens are snug and clean, and there's always a warm fire to sleep by and plenty to eat. You might have done well there, but I can see you're not a clever girl. Harra, I believe we should give this one to Weese."

"If you think so, Amabel." They gave her a shift of grey roughspun wool and a pair of ill-fitting shoes, and sent her off.

Weese was understeward for the Wailing Tower, a squat man with a fleshy carbuncle of a nose and a nest of angry red boils near one corner of his plump lips. Arya was one of six sent to him. He looked them all over with a gimlet eye. "The Lannisters are generous to those as serve them well, an honor none of your sort deserve, but in war a man makes do with what's to hand. Work hard and mind your place and might be one day you'll rise as high as me. If you think to presume on his lordship's kindness, though, you'll find *me* waiting after m'lord has gone, y'see." He strutted up and down before them, telling them how they must never look the highborn in the eye, nor speak until spoken to, nor get in his lordship's way. "My nose never lies," he boasted. "I can smell defiance, I can smell pride, I can smell disobedience. I catch a whiff of any such stinks, you'll answer for it. When I sniff you, all I want to smell is fear."

DAENERYS

On the walls of Qarth, men beat gongs to herald her coming, while others blew curious horns that encircled their bodies like great bronze snakes. A column of camelry emerged from the city as her honor guards. The riders wore scaled copper armor and snouted helms with copper tusks and long black silk plumes, and sat high on saddles inlaid with rubies and garnets. Their camels were dressed in blankets of a hundred different hues.

"Qarth is the greatest city that ever was or ever will be," Pyat Pree had told her, back amongst the bones of Vaes Tolorro. "It is the center of the world, the gate between north and south, the bridge between east and west, ancient beyond memory of man and so magnificent that Saathos the Wise put out his eyes after gazing upon Qarth for the first time, because he knew that all he saw thereafter should look squalid and ugly by comparison."

Dany took the warlock's words well salted, but the magnificence of the great city was not to be denied. Three thick walls encircled Qarth, elaborately carved. The outer was red sandstone, thirty feet high and decorated with animals: snakes slithering, kites flying, fish swimming, intermingled with wolves of the red waste and striped zorses and monstrous elephants. The middle wall, forty feet high, was grey granite alive with scenes of war: the clash of sword and shield and spear, arrows in flight, heroes at battle and babes being butchered, pyres of the dead. The innermost wall was fifty feet of black marble, with carvings that made

Dany blush until she told herself that she was being a fool. She was no maid; if she could look on the grey wall's scenes of slaughter, why should she avert her eyes from the sight of men and women giving pleasure to one another?

The outer gates were banded with copper, the middle with iron; the innermost were studded with golden eyes. All opened at Dany's approach. As she rode her silver into the city, small children rushed out to scatter flowers in her path. They wore golden sandals and bright paint, no more.

All the colors that had been missing from Vaes Tolorro had found their way to Qarth; buildings crowded about her fantastical as a fever dream in shades of rose, violet, and umber. She passed under a bronze arch fashioned in the likeness of two snakes mating, their scales delicate flakes of jade, obsidian, and lapis lazuli. Slim towers stood taller than any Dany had ever seen, and elaborate fountains filled every square, wrought in the shapes of griffins and dragons and manticores.

The Qartheen lined the streets and watched from delicate balconies that looked too frail to support their weight. They were tall pale folk in linen and samite and tiger fur, every one a lord or lady to her eyes. The women wore gowns that left one breast bare, while the men favored beaded silk skirts. Dany felt shabby and barbaric as she rode past them in her lionskin robe with black Drogon on one shoulder. Her Dothraki called the Qartheen "Milk Men" for their paleness, and Khal Drogo had dreamed of the day when he might sack the great cities of the east. She glanced at her bloodriders, their dark almond-shaped eyes giving no hint of their thoughts. *Is it only the plunder they see?* she wondered. *How savage we must seem to these Qartheen.*

Pyat Pree conducted her little *khalasar* down the center of a great arcade where the city's ancient heroes stood thrice life-size on columns of white and green marble. They passed through a bazaar in a cavernous building whose latticework ceiling was home to a thousand gaily colored birds. Trees and flowers bloomed on the terraced walls above the stalls, while below it seemed as if everything the gods had put into the world was for sale.

Her silver shied as the merchant prince Xaro Xhoan Daxos rode up to her; the horses could not abide the close presence of camels, she had found. "If you see here anything that you would desire, O most beautiful of women, you have only to speak and it is yours," Xaro called down from his ornate horned saddle.

"Qarth itself is hers, she has no need of baubles," blue-lipped Pyat Pree sang out from her other side. "It shall be as I promised, *Khaleesi.* Come with me to the House of the Undying, and you shall drink of truth and wisdom."

"Why should she need your Palace of Dust, when I can give her sunlight and sweet water and silks to sleep in?" Xaro said to the warlock. "The Thirteen shall set a crown of black jade and fire opals upon her lovely head."

"The only palace I desire is the red castle at King's Landing, my lord Pyat." Dany was wary of the warlock; the *maegi* Mirri Maz Duur had soured her on those who played at sorcery. "And if the great of Qarth would give me gifts, Xaro, let them give me ships and swords to win back what is rightfully mine."

Pyat's blue lips curled upward in a gracious smile. "It shall be as you command, *Khaleesi.*" He moved away, swaying with his camel's motion, his long beaded robes trailing behind.

"The young queen is wise beyond her years," Xaro Xhoan Daxos murmured down at her from his high saddle. "There is a saying in Qarth. A warlock's house is built of bones and lies."

"Then why do men lower their voices when they speak of the warlocks of Qarth? All across the east, their power and wisdom are revered."

"Once they were mighty," Xaro agreed, "but now they are as ludicrous as those feeble old soldiers who boast of their prowess long after strength and skill have left them. They read their crumbling scrolls, drink shade-of-the-evening until their lips turn blue, and hint of dread powers, but they are hollow husks compared to those who went before. Pyat Pree's gifts will turn to dust in your hands, I warn you." He gave his camel a lick of his whip and sped away.

"The crow calls the raven black," muttered Ser Jorah in the Common Tongue of Westeros. The exile knight rode at her right hand, as ever. For their entrance into Qarth, he had put away his Dothraki garb and donned again the plate and mail and wool of the Seven Kingdoms half a world away. "You would do well to avoid both those men, Your Grace."

"Those men will help me to my crown," she said. "Xaro has vast wealth, and Pyat Pree—"

"—pretends to power," the knight said brusquely. On his dark green surcoat, the bear of House Mormont stood on its hind legs, black and fierce. Jorah looked no less ferocious as he scowled at the crowd that filled the bazaar. "I would not linger here long, my queen. I mislike the very smell of this place."

Dany smiled. "Perhaps it's the camels you're smelling. The Qartheen themselves seem sweet enough to my nose."

"Sweet smells are sometimes used to cover foul ones."

My great bear, Dany thought. *I am his queen, but I will always be his cub as well, and he will always guard me.* It made her feel safe, but sad as well. She wished she could love him better than she did.

Xaro Xhoan Daxos had offered Dany the hospitality of his home while

she was in the city. She had expected something grand. She had not
expected a palace larger than many a market town. *It makes Magister
Illyrio's manse in Pentos look like a swineherd's hovel,* she thought.
Xaro swore that his home could comfortably house all of her people and
their horses besides; indeed, it swallowed them. An entire wing was
given over to her. She would have her own gardens, a marble bathing
pool, a scrying tower and warlock's maze. Slaves would tend her every
need. In her private chambers, the floors were green marble, the walls
draped with colorful silk hangings that shimmered with every breath of
air. "You are too generous," she told Xaro Xhoan Daxos.

"For the Mother of Dragons, no gift is too great." Xaro was a languid,
elegant man with a bald head and a great beak of a nose crusted with
rubies, opals, and flakes of jade. "On the morrow, you shall feast upon
peacock and lark's tongue, and hear music worthy of the most beautiful
of women. The Thirteen will come to do you homage, and all the great of
Qarth."

All the great of Qarth will come to see my dragons, Dany thought, yet
she thanked Xaro for his kindness before she sent him on his way. Pyat
Pree took his leave as well, vowing to petition the Undying Ones for an
audience. "A honor rare as summer snows." Before he left he kissed her
bare feet with his pale blue lips and pressed on her a gift, a jar of oint-
ment that he swore would let her see the spirits of the air. Last of the
three seekers to depart was Quaithe the shadowbinder. From her Dany
received only a warning. "Beware," the woman in the red lacquer mask
said.

"Of whom?"

"Of all. They shall come day and night to see the wonder that has
been born again into the world, and when they see they shall lust. For
dragons are fire made flesh, and fire is power."

When Quaithe too was gone, Ser Jorah said, "She speaks truly, my
queen . . . though I like her no more than the others."

"I do not understand her." Pyat and Xaro had showered Dany with
promises from the moment they first glimpsed her dragons, declaring
themselves her loyal servants in all things, but from Quaithe she had
gotten only the rare cryptic word. And it disturbed her that she had never
seen the woman's face. *Remember Mirri Maz Duur,* she told herself.
Remember treachery. She turned to her bloodriders. "We will keep our
own watch so long as we are here. See that no one enters this wing of the
palace without my leave, and take care that the dragons are always well
guarded."

"It shall be done, *Khaleesi,*" Aggo said.

"We have seen only the parts of Qarth that Pyat Pree wished us to see," she went on. "Rakharo, go forth and look on the rest, and tell me what you find. Take good men with you—and women, to go places where men are forbidden."

"As you say, I do, blood of my blood," said Rakharo.

"Ser Jorah, find the docks and see what manner of ships lay at anchor. It has been half a year since I last heard tidings from the Seven Kingdoms. Perhaps the gods will have blown some good captain here from Westeros with a ship to carry us home."

The knight frowned. "That would be no kindness. The Usurper will kill you, sure as sunrise." Mormont hooked his thumbs through his swordbelt. "My place is here at your side."

"Jhogo can guard me as well. You have more languages than my blood-riders, and the Dothraki mistrust the sea and those who sail her. Only you can serve me in this. Go among the ships and speak to the crews, learn where they are from and where they are bound and what manner of men command them."

Reluctantly, the exile nodded. "As you say, my queen."

When all the men had gone, her handmaids stripped off the travel-stained silks she wore, and Dany padded out to where the marble pool sat in the shade of a portico. The water was deliciously cool, and the pool was stocked with tiny golden fish that nibbled curiously at her skin and made her giggle. It felt good to close her eyes and float, knowing she could rest as long as she liked. She wondered whether Aegon's Red Keep had a pool like this, and fragrant gardens full of lavender and mint. *It must, surely. Viserys always said the Seven Kingdoms were more beautiful than any other place in the world.*

The thought of home disquieted her. If her sun-and-stars had lived, he would have led his *khalasar* across the poison water and swept away her enemies, but his strength had left the world. Her bloodriders remained, sworn to her for life and skilled in slaughter, but only in the ways of the horselords. The Dothraki sacked cities and plundered kingdoms, they did not rule them. Dany had no wish to reduce King's Landing to a black-ened ruin full of unquiet ghosts. She had supped enough on tears. *I want to make my kingdom beautiful, to fill it with fat men and pretty maids and laughing children. I want my people to smile when they see me ride by, the way Viserys said they smiled for my father.*

But before she could do that she must conquer.

The Usurper will kill you, sure as sunrise, Mormont had said. Robert had slain her gallant brother Rhaegar, and one of his creatures had crossed the Dothraki sea to poison her and her unborn son. They said Robert Baratheon was strong as a bull and fearless in battle, a man who loved nothing better than war. And with him stood the great lords her brother had named the Usurper's dogs, cold-eyed Eddard Stark with his frozen heart, and the golden Lannisters, father and son, so rich, so powerful, so treacherous.

How could she hope to overthrow such men? When Khal Drogo had lived, men trembled and made him gifts to stay his wrath. If they did not, he took their cities, wealth and wives and all. But his *khalasar* had been vast, while hers was meager. Her people had followed her across the red waste as she chased her comet, and would follow her across the poison water too, but they would not be enough. Even her dragons might not be enough. Viserys had believed that the realm would rise for its rightful king . . . but Viserys had been a fool, and fools believe in foolish things.

Her doubts made her shiver. Suddenly the water felt cold to her, and the little fish prickling at her skin annoying. Dany stood and climbed from the pool. "Irri," she called, "Jhiqui."

As the handmaids toweled her dry and wrapped her in a sandsilk robe, Dany's thoughts went to the three who had sought her out in the City of Bones. *The Bleeding Star led me to Qarth for a purpose. Here I will find what I need, if I have the strength to take what is offered, and the wisdom to avoid the traps and snares. If the gods mean for me to conquer, they will provide, they will send me a sign, and if not . . . if not . . .*

It was near evenfall and Dany was feeding her dragons when Irri stepped through the silken curtains to tell her that Ser Jorah had returned from the docks . . . and not alone. "Send him in, with whomever he has brought," she said, curious.

When they entered, she was seated on a mound of cushions, her dragons all about her. The man he brought with him wore a cloak of green and yellow feathers and had skin as black as polished jet. "Your Grace," the knight said, "I bring you Quhuru Mo, captain of the *Cinnamon Wind* out of Tall Trees Town."

The black man knelt. "I am greatly honored, my queen," he said, not in the tongue of the Summer Isles, which Dany did not know, but in the liquid Valyrian of the Nine Free Cities.

"The honor is mine, Quhuru Mo," said Dany in the same language. "Have you come from the Summer Isles?"

"This is so, Your Grace, but before, not half a year past, we called at Oldtown. From there I bring you a wondrous gift."

"A gift?"

"A gift of news. Dragonmother, Stormborn, I tell you true, Robert Baratheon is dead."

Outside her walls, dusk was settling over Qarth, but a sun had risen in Dany's heart. "Dead?" she repeated. In her lap, black Drogon *hissed*, and pale smoke rose before her face like a veil. "You are certain? The Usurper is dead?"

"So it is said in Oldtown, and Dorne, and Lys, and all the other ports where we have called."

He sent me poisoned wine, yet I live and he is gone. "What was the manner of his death?" On her shoulder, pale Viserion flapped wings the color of cream, stirring the air.

"Torn by a monstrous boar whilst hunting in his kingswood, or so I heard in Oldtown. Others say his queen betrayed him, or his brother, or Lord Stark who was his Hand. Yet all the tales agree in this: King Robert is dead and in his grave."

Dany had never looked upon the Usurper's face, yet seldom a day had passed when she had not thought of him. His great shadow had lain across her since the hour of her birth, when she came forth amidst blood and storm into a world where she no longer had a place. And now this ebony stranger had lifted that shadow.

"The boy sits the Iron Throne now," Ser Jorah said.

"King Joffrey reigns," Quhuru Mo agreed, "but the Lannisters rule. Robert's brothers have fled King's Landing. The talk is, they mean to claim the crown. And the Hand has fallen, Lord Stark who was King Robert's friend. He has been seized for treason."

"Ned Stark a traitor?" Ser Jorah snorted. "Not bloody likely. The Long Summer will come again before that one would besmirch his precious honor."

"What honor could he have?" Dany said. "He was a traitor to his true king, as were these Lannisters." It pleased her to hear that the Usurper's dogs were fighting amongst themselves, though she was unsurprised. The same thing happened when her Drogo died, and his great *khalasar* tore itself to pieces. "My brother is dead as well, Viserys who was the true king," she told the Summer Islander. "Khal Drogo my lord husband killed him with a crown of molten gold." Would her brother have been any wiser, had he known that the vengeance he had prayed for was so close at hand?

"Then I grieve for you, Dragonmother, and for bleeding Westeros, bereft of its rightful king."

Beneath Dany's gentle fingers, green Rhaegal stared at the stranger with eyes of molten gold. When his mouth opened, his teeth gleamed like black needles. "When does your ship return to Westeros, Captain?"

"Not for a year or more, I fear. From here the *Cinnamon Wind* sails east, to make the trader's circle round the Jade Sea."

"I see," said Dany, disappointed. "I wish you fair winds and good trading, then. You have brought me a precious gift."

"I have been amply repaid, great queen."

She puzzled at that. "How so?"

His eyes gleamed. "I have seen dragons."

Dany laughed. "And will see more of them one day, I hope. Come to me in King's Landing when I am on my father's throne, and you shall have a great reward."

The Summer Islander promised he would do so, and kissed her lightly on the fingers as he took his leave. Jhiqui showed him out, while Ser Jorah Mormont remained.

"*Khaleesi*," the knight said when they were alone, "I should not speak so freely of your plans, if I were you. This man will spread the tale wherever he goes now."

"Let him," she said. "Let the whole world know my purpose. The Usurper is dead, what does it matter?"

"Not every sailor's tale is true," Ser Jorah cautioned, "and even if Robert be truly dead, his son rules in his place. This changes nothing, truly."

"This changes *everything*." Dany rose abruptly. Screeching, her dragons uncoiled and spread their wings. Drogon flapped and clawed up to the lintel over the archway. The others skittered across the floor, wingtips scrabbling on the marble. "Before, the Seven Kingdoms were like my Drogo's *khalasar*, a hundred thousand made as one by his strength. Now they fly to pieces, even as the *khalasar* did after my *khal* lay dead."

"The high lords have always fought. Tell me who's won and I'll tell you what it means. *Khaleesi*, the Seven Kingdoms are not going to fall into your hands like so many ripe peaches. You will need a fleet, gold, armies, alliances—"

"All this I know." She took his hands in hers and looked up into his dark suspicious eyes. *Sometimes he thinks of me as a child he must protect, and sometimes as a woman he would like to bed, but does he ever truly see me as his queen?* "I am not the frightened girl you met in Pentos. I have counted only fifteen name days, true . . . but I am as old as the crones in the *dosh khaleen* and as young as my dragons, Jorah. I have borne a child, burned a *khal*, and crossed the red waste and the Dothraki sea. Mine is the blood of the dragon."

"As was your brother's," he said stubbornly.

"I am not Viserys."

"No," he admitted. "There is more of Rhaegar in you, I think, but even Rhaegar could be slain. Robert proved that on the Trident, with no more than a warhammer. Even dragons can die."

"Dragons die." She stood on her toes to kiss him lightly on an unshaven cheek. "But so do dragonslayers."

BRAN

Meera moved in a wary circle, her net dangling loose in her left hand, the slender three-pronged frog spear poised in her right. Summer followed her with his golden eyes, turning, his tail held stiff and tall. Watching, watching . . .

"Yai!" the girl shouted, the spear darting out. The wolf slid to the left and leapt before she could draw back the spear. Meera cast her net, the tangles unfolding in the air before her. Summer's leap carried him into it. He dragged it with him as he slammed into her chest and knocked her over backward. Her spear went spinning away. The damp grass cushioned her fall but the breath went out of her in an "Oof." The wolf crouched atop her.

Bran hooted. "You lose."

"She wins," her brother Jojen said. "Summer's snared."

He was right, Bran saw. Thrashing and growling at the net, trying to rip free, Summer was only ensnaring himself worse. Nor could he bite through. "Let him out."

Laughing, the Reed girl threw her arms around the tangled wolf and rolled them both. Summer gave a piteous whine, his legs kicking against the cords that bound them. Meera knelt, undid a twist, pulled at a corner, tugged deftly here and there, and suddenly the direwolf was bounding free.

"Summer, to me." Bran spread his arms. "Watch," he said, an instant before the wolf bowled into him. He clung with all his strength as the wolf dragged him bumping through the grass. They wrestled and rolled and clung to each other, one snarling and yapping, the other laughing. In the end it was Bran sprawled on top, the mud-spattered direwolf under him. "Good wolf," he panted. Summer licked him across the ear.

Meera shook her head. "Does he never grow angry?"

"Not with me." Bran grabbed the wolf by his ears and Summer snapped at him fiercely, but it was all in play. "Sometimes he tears my garb but he's never drawn blood."

"*Your* blood, you mean. If he'd gotten past my net . . ."

"He wouldn't hurt you. He knows I like you." All of the other lords and knights had departed within a day or two of the harvest feast, but the Reeds had stayed to become Bran's constant companions. Jojen was so solemn that Old Nan called him "little grandfather," but Meera reminded Bran of his sister Arya. She wasn't scared to get dirty, and she could run and fight and throw as good as a boy. She was older than Arya, though; almost sixteen, a woman grown. They were both older than Bran, even though his ninth name day had finally come and gone, but they never treated him like a child.

"I wish you were our wards instead of the Walders." He began to struggle toward the nearest tree. His dragging and wriggling was unseemly to watch, but when Meera moved to lift him he said, "No, don't help me." He rolled clumsily and pushed and squirmed backward, using the strength of his arms, until he was sitting with his back to the trunk of a tall ash. "See, I told you." Summer lay down with his head in Bran's lap. "I never knew anyone who fought with a net before," he told Meera while he scratched the direwolf between the ears. "Did your master-at-arms teach you net-fighting?"

"My father taught me. We have no knights at Greywater. No master-at-arms, and no maester."

"Who keeps your ravens?"

She smiled. "Ravens can't find Greywater Watch, no more than our enemies can."

"Why not?"

"Because it moves," she told him.

Bran had never heard of a moving castle before. He looked at her uncertainly, but he couldn't tell whether she was teasing him or not. "I wish I could see it. Do you think your lord father would let me come visit when the war is over?"

"You would be most welcome, my prince. Then or now."

"*Now?*" Bran had spent his whole life at Winterfell. He yearned to see far places. "I could ask Ser Rodrik when he returns." The old knight was off east, trying to set to rights the trouble there. Roose Bolton's bastard had started it by seizing Lady Hornwood as she returned from the harvest feast, marrying her that very night even though he was young enough to be her son. Then Lord Manderly had taken her castle. To protect the Hornwood holdings from the Boltons, he had written, but Ser Rodrik had been almost as angry with him as with the bastard. "Ser Rodrik might let me go. Maester Luwin never would."

Sitting cross-legged under the weirwood, Jojen Reed regarded him solemnly. "It would be good if you left Winterfell, Bran."

"It would?"

"Yes. And sooner rather than later."

"My brother has the greensight," said Meera. "He dreams things that haven't happened, but sometimes they do."

"There is no *sometimes*, Meera." A look passed between them; him sad, her defiant.

"Tell me what's going to happen," Bran said.

"I will," said Jojen, "if you'll tell me about your dreams."

The godswood grew quiet. Bran could hear leaves rustling, and Hodor's distant splashing from the hot pools. He thought of the golden man and the three-eyed crow, remembered the crunch of bones between his jaws and the coppery taste of blood. "I don't have dreams. Maester Luwin gives me sleeping draughts."

"Do they help?"

"Sometimes."

Meera said, "All of Winterfell knows you wake at night shouting and sweating, Bran. The women talk of it at the well, and the guards in their hall."

"Tell us what frightens you so much," said Jojen.

"I don't want to. Anyway, it's only dreams. Maester Luwin says dreams might mean anything or nothing."

"My brother dreams as other boys do, and those dreams might mean anything," Meera said, "but the green dreams are different."

Jojen's eyes were the color of moss, and sometimes when he looked at you he seemed to be seeing something else. Like now. "I dreamed of a winged wolf bound to earth with grey stone chains," he said. "It was a green dream, so I knew it was true. A crow was trying to peck through the chains, but the stone was too hard and his beak could only chip at them."

"Did the crow have three eyes?"

Jojen nodded.

Summer raised his head from Bran's lap, and gazed at the mudman with his dark golden eyes.

"When I was little I almost died of greywater fever. That was when the crow came to me."

"He came to me after I fell," Bran blurted. "I was asleep for a long time. He said I had to fly or die, and I woke up, only I was broken and I couldn't fly after all."

"You can if you want to." Picking up her net, Meera shook out the last tangles and began arranging it in loose folds.

"*You* are the winged wolf, Bran," said Jojen. "I wasn't sure when we first came, but now I am. The crow sent us here to break your chains."

"Is the crow at Greywater?"

"No. The crow is in the north."

"At the Wall?" Bran had always wanted to see the Wall. His bastard brother Jon was there now, a man of the Night's Watch.

"Beyond the Wall." Meera Reed hung the net from her belt. "When Jojen told our lord father what he'd dreamed, he sent us to Winterfell."

"How would I break the chains, Jojen?" Bran asked.

"Open your eye."

"They *are* open Can't you *see*?"

"Two are open." Jojen pointed. "One, two."

"I only *have* two."

"You have three. The crow gave you the third, but you will not open it." He had a slow soft way of speaking. "With two eyes you see my face. With three you could see my heart. With two you can see that oak tree there. With three you could see the acorn the oak grew from and the stump that it will one day become. With two you see no farther than your walls. With three you would gaze south to the Summer Sea and north beyond the Wall."

Summer got to his feet. "I don't need to see so far." Bran made a nervous smile. "I'm tired of talking about crows. Let's talk about wolves. Or lizard-lions. Have you ever hunted one, Meera? We don't have them here."

Meera plucked her frog spear out of the bushes. "They live in the water. In slow streams and deep swamps—"

Her brother interrupted. "Did you dream of a lizard-lion?"

"No," said Bran. "I told you, I don't want—"

"Did you dream of a wolf?"

He was making Bran angry. "I don't have to tell you my dreams. I'm the prince. I'm the Stark in Winterfell."

"Was it Summer?"

"You be quiet."

"The night of the harvest feast, you dreamed you were Summer in the godswood, didn't you?"

"*Stop it!*" Bran shouted. Summer slid toward the weirwood, his white teeth bared.

Jojen Reed took no mind. "When I touched Summer, I felt you in him. Just as you are in him now."

"You couldn't have. I was in bed. I was sleeping."

"You were in the godswood, all in grey."

"It was only a bad dream . . ."

Jojen stood. "I felt you. I felt you fall. Is that what scares you, the falling?"

The falling, Bran thought, *and the golden man, the queen's brother, he scares me too, but mostly the falling.* He did not say it, though. How could he? He had not been able to tell Ser Rodrik or Maester Luwin, and he could not tell the Reeds either. If he didn't talk about it, maybe he would forget. He had never wanted to remember. It might not even be a true remembering.

"Do you fall every night, Bran?" Jojen asked quietly.

A low rumbling growl rose from Summer's throat, and there was no play in it. He stalked forward, all teeth and hot eyes. Meera stepped between the wolf and her brother, spear in hand. "Keep him back, Bran."

"Jojen is making him angry."

Meera shook out her net.

"It's your anger, Bran," her brother said. "Your fear."

"It isn't. I'm not a wolf." Yet he'd howled with them in the night, and tasted blood in his wolf dreams.

"Part of you is Summer, and part of Summer is you. You know that, Bran."

Summer rushed forward, but Meera blocked him, jabbing with the three-pronged spear. The wolf twisted aside, circling, stalking. Meera turned to face him. "Call him back, Bran."

"Summer!" Bran shouted. "To me, Summer!" He slapped an open palm down on the meat of his thigh. His hand tingled, though his dead leg felt nothing.

The direwolf lunged again, and again Meera's spear darted out. Summer dodged, circled back. The bushes rustled, and a lean black shape came padding from behind the weirwood, teeth bared. The scent was strong; his brother had smelled his rage. Bran felt hairs rise on the back of his neck. Meera stood beside her brother, with wolves to either side. "Bran, call them off."

"I *can't!*"

"Jojen, up the tree."

"There's no need. Today is not the day I die."

"*Do it!*" she screamed, and her brother scrambled up the trunk of the weirwood, using the face for his handholds. The direwolves closed. Meera abandoned spear and net, jumped up, and grabbed the branch above her head. Shaggy's jaws snapped shut beneath her ankle as she swung up and over the limb. Summer sat back on his haunches and howled, while Shaggydog worried the net, shaking it in his teeth.

Only then did Bran remember that they were not alone. He cupped hands around his mouth. "Hodor!" he shouted. *"Hodor! Hodor!"* He was badly frightened and somehow ashamed. "They won't hurt Hodor," he assured his treed friends.

A few moments passed before they heard a tuneless humming. Hodor arrived half-dressed and mud-spattered from his visit to the hot pools, but Bran had never been so glad to see him. "Hodor, help me. Chase off the wolves. Chase them off."

Hodor went to it gleefully, waving his arms and stamping his huge feet, shouting "Hodor, Hodor," running first at one wolf and then the other. Shaggydog was the first to flee, slinking back into the foliage with a final snarl. When Summer had enough, he came back to Bran and lay down beside him.

No sooner did Meera touch ground than she snatched up her spear and net again. Jojen never took his eyes off Summer. "We will talk again," he promised Bran.

It was the wolves, it wasn't me. He did not understand why they'd gotten so wild. *Maybe Maester Luwin was right to lock them in the godswood.* "Hodor," he said, "bring me to Maester Luwin."

The maester's turret below the rookery was one of Bran's favorite places. Luwin was hopelessly untidy, but his clutter of books and scrolls and bottles was as familiar and comforting to Bran as his bald spot and the flapping sleeves of his loose grey robes. He liked the ravens too.

He found Luwin perched on a high stool, writing. With Ser Rodrik gone, all of the governance of the castle had fallen on his shoulders. "My prince," he said when Hodor entered, "you're early for lessons today." The maester spent several hours every afternoon tutoring Bran, Rickon, and the Walder Freys.

"Hodor, stand still." Bran grasped a wall sconce with both hands and used it to pull himself up and out of the basket. He hung for a moment by his arms until Hodor carried him to a chair. "Meera says her brother has the greensight."

Maester Luwin scratched at the side of his nose with his writing quill. "Does she now?"

He nodded. "You told me that the children of the forest had the greensight. I remember."

"Some claimed to have that power. Their wise men were called *greenseers.*"

"Was it magic?"

"Call it that for want of a better word, if you must. At heart it was only a different sort of knowledge."

"What was it?"

Luwin set down his quill. "No one truly knows, Bran. The children are gone from the world, and their wisdom with them. It had to do with the faces in the trees, we think. The First Men believed that the green-seers could see through the eyes of the weirwoods. That was why they cut down the trees whenever they warred upon the children. Supposedly the greenseers also had power over the beasts of the wood and the birds in the trees. Even fish. Does the Reed boy claim such powers?"

"No. I don't think. But he has dreams that come true sometimes, Meera says."

"All of us have dreams that come true sometimes. You dreamed of your lord father in the crypts before we knew he was dead, remember?"

"Rickon did too. We dreamed the same dream."

"Call it greensight, if you wish . . . but remember as well all those tens of thousands of dreams that you and Rickon have dreamed that did *not* come true. Do you perchance recall what I taught you about the chain collar that every maester wears?"

Bran thought for a moment, trying to remember. "A maester forges his chain in the Citadel of Oldtown. It's a chain because you swear to serve, and it's made of different metals because you serve the realm and the realm has different sorts of people. Every time you learn something you get another link. Black iron is for ravenry, silver for healing, gold for sums and numbers. I don't remember them all."

Luwin slid a finger up under his collar and began to turn it, inch by inch. He had a thick neck for a small man, and the chain was tight, but a few pulls had it all the way around. "This is Valyrian steel," he said when the link of dark grey metal lay against the apple of his throat. "Only one maester in a hundred wears such a link. This signifies that I have studied what the Citadel calls *the higher mysteries*—magic, for want of a better word. A fascinating pursuit, but of small use, which is why so few maesters trouble themselves with it.

"All those who study the higher mysteries try their own hand at spells, soon or late. I yielded to the temptation too, I must confess it. Well, I was a boy, and what boy does not secretly wish to find hidden powers in himself? I got no more for my efforts than a thousand boys before me, and a thousand since. Sad to say, magic does not work."

"Sometimes it does," Bran protested. "I had that dream, and Rickon did too. And there are mages and warlocks in the east . . ."

"There are men who *call* themselves mages and warlocks," Maester Luwin said. "I had a friend at the Citadel who could pull a rose out of your ear, but he was no more magical than I was. Oh, to be sure, there is much we do not understand. The years pass in their hundreds and their thousands, and what does any man see of life but a few summers, a few winters? We look at mountains and call them eternal, and so they seem . . . but in the course of time, mountains rise and fall, rivers change their courses, stars fall from the sky, and great cities sink beneath the sea. Even gods die, we think. Everything changes.

"Perhaps magic was once a mighty force in the world, but no longer. What little remains is no more than the wisp of smoke that lingers in the air after a great fire has burned out, and even that is fading. Valyria was the last ember, and Valyria is gone. The dragons are no more, the giants are dead, the children of the forest forgotten with all their lore.

"No, my prince. Jojen Reed may have had a dream or two that he believes came true, but he does not have the greensight. No living man has that power."

Bran said as much to Meera Reed when she came to him at dusk as he sat in his window seat watching the lights flicker to life. "I'm sorry for what happened with the wolves. Summer shouldn't have tried to hurt Jojen, but Jojen shouldn't have said all that about my dreams. The crow lied when he said I could fly, and your brother lied too."

"Or perhaps your maester is wrong."

"He isn't. Even my father relied on his counsel."

"Your father listened, I have no doubt. But in the end, he decided for himself. Bran, will you let me tell you about a dream Jojen dreamed of you and your fosterling brothers?"

"The Walders aren't my brothers."

She paid that no heed. "You were sitting at supper, but instead of a servant, Maester Luwin brought you your food. He served you the king's cut off the roast, the meat rare and bloody, but with a savory smell that made everyone's mouth water. The meat he served the Freys was old and grey and dead. Yet they liked their supper better than you liked yours."

"I don't understand."

"You will, my brother says. When you do, we'll talk again."

Bran was almost afraid to sit to supper that night, but when he did, it was pigeon pie they set before him. Everyone else was served the same, and he couldn't see that anything was wrong with the food they served the Walders. *Maester Luwin has the truth of it*, he told himself. Nothing bad was coming to Winterfell, no matter what Jojen said. Bran was relieved . . . but disappointed too. So long as there was magic, anything could happen. Ghosts could walk, trees could talk, and broken boys could grow up to be knights. "But there isn't," he said aloud in the darkness of his bed. "There's no magic, and the stories are just stories."

And he would never walk, nor fly, nor be a knight.

TYRION

The rushes were scratchy under the soles of his bare feet. "My cousin chooses a queer hour to come visiting," Tyrion told a sleep-befuddled Podrick Payne, who'd doubtless expected to be well roasted for waking him. "See him to my solar and tell him I'll be down shortly."

It was well past midnight, he judged from the black outside the window. *Does Lancel think to find me drowsy and slow of wit at this hour?* he wondered. *No, Lancel scarce thinks at all, this is Cersei's doing.* His sister would be disappointed. Even abed, he worked well into the morning—reading by the flickering light of a candle, scrutinizing the reports of Varys's whisperers, and poring over Littlefinger's books of accounts until the columns blurred and his eyes ached.

He splashed some tepid water on his face from the basin beside his bed and took his time squatting in the garderobe, the night air cold on his bare skin. Ser Lancel was sixteen, and not known for his patience. Let him wait, and grow more anxious in the waiting. When his bowels were empty, Tyrion slipped on a bedrobe and roughed his thin flaxen hair with his fingers, all the more to look as if he had wakened from sleep.

Lancel was pacing before the ashes of the hearth, garbed in slashed red velvet with black silk undersleeves, a jeweled dagger and a gilded scabbard hanging from his swordbelt. "Cousin," Tyrion greeted him. "Your visits are too few. To what do I owe this undeserved pleasure?"

"Her Grace the Queen Regent has sent me to command you to release

Grand Maester Pycelle." Ser Lancel showed Tyrion a crimson ribbon, bearing Cersei's lion seal impressed in golden wax. "Here is her warrant."

"So it is." Tyrion waved it away. "I hope my sister is not overtaxing her strength, so soon after her illness. It would be a great pity if she were to suffer a relapse."

"Her Grace is quite recovered," Ser Lancel said curtly.

"Music to my ears." *Though not a tune I'm fond of. I should have given her a larger dose.* Tyrion had hoped for a few more days without Cersei's interference, but he was not too terribly surprised by her return to health. She was Jaime's twin, after all. He made himself smile pleasantly. "Pod, build us a fire, the air is too chilly for my taste. Will you take a cup with me, Lancel? I find that mulled wine helps me sleep."

"I need no help sleeping," Ser Lancel said. "I am come at Her Grace's behest, not to drink with you, Imp."

Knighthood had made the boy bolder, Tyrion reflected—that, and the sorry part he had played in murdering King Robert. "Wine does have its dangers." He smiled as he poured. "As to Grand Maester Pycelle . . . if my sweet sister is so concerned for him, I would have thought she'd come herself. Instead she sends you. What am I to make of that?"

"Make of it what you will, so long as you release your prisoner. The Grand Maester is a staunch friend to the Queen Regent, and under her personal protection." A hint of a sneer played about the lad's lips; he was enjoying this. *He takes his lessons from Cersei.* "Her Grace will never consent to this outrage. She reminds you that *she* is Joffrey's regent."

"As I am Joffrey's Hand."

"The Hand serves," the young knight informed him airily. "The regent *rules* until the king is of age."

"Perhaps you ought write that down so I'll remember it better." The fire was crackling merrily. "You may leave us, Pod," Tyrion told his squire. Only when the boy was gone did he turn back to Lancel. "There is more?"

"Yes. Her Grace bids me inform you that Ser Jacelyn Bywater defied a command issued in the king's own name."

Which means that Cersei has already ordered Bywater to release Pycelle, and been rebuffed. "I see."

"She insists that the man be removed from his office and placed under arrest for treason. I warn you—"

He set aside his wine cup. "I'll h ar no warnings from you, boy."

"*Ser,*" Lancel said stiffly. He touched his sword, perhaps to remind Tyrion that he wore one. "Have a care how you speak to me, Imp." Doubtless he meant to sound threatening, but that absurd wisp of a mustache ruined the effect.

"Oh, unhand your sword. One cry from me and Shagga will burst in and kill you. With an axe, not a wineskin."

Lancel reddened; was he such a fool as to believe his part in Robert's death had gone unnoted? "I am a knight—"

"So I've noted. Tell me—did Cersei have you knighted before or after she took you into her bed?"

The flicker in Lancel's green eyes was all the admission Tyrion needed. So Varys told it true. *Well, no one can ever claim that my sister does not love her family.* "What, nothing to say? No more warnings for me, *ser*?"

"You will withdraw these filthy accusations or—"

"Please. Have you given any thought to what Joffrey will do when I tell him you murdered his father to bed his mother?"

"It was not like that!" Lancel protested, horrified.

"No? What *was* it like, pray?"

"The queen gave me the strongwine! Your own father Lord Tywin, when I was named the king's squire, he told me to obey her in everything."

"Did he tell you to fuck her too?" *Look at him. Not quite so tall, his features not so fine, and his hair is sand instead of spun gold, yet still . . . even a poor copy of Jaime is sweeter than an empty bed, I suppose.* "No, I thought not."

"I never meant . . . I only did as I was bid, I . . ."

". . . hated every instant of it, is that what you would have me believe? A high place at court, knighthood, my sister's legs opening for you at night, oh, yes, it must have been terrible for you." Tyrion pushed himself to his feet. "Wait here. His Grace will want to hear this."

The defiance went from Lancel all at once. The young knight fell to his knees a frightened boy. "Mercy, my lord, I beg you."

"Save it for Joffrey. He likes a good beg."

"My lord, it was your sister's bidding, the queen, as you said, but His Grace . . . he'd never understand . . ."

"Would you have me keep the truth from the king?"

"For my father's sake! I'll leave the city, it will be as if it never happened! I swear, I will end it . . ."

It was hard not to laugh. "I think not."

Now the lad looked lost. "My lord?"

"You heard me. My father told you to obey my sister? Very well, obey her. Stay close to her side, keep her trust, pleasure her as often as she requires it. No one need ever know . . . so long as you keep faith with me. I want to know what Cersei is doing. Where she goes, who she sees, what they talk of, what plans she is hatching. All. And you will be the one to tell me, won't you?"

"Yes, my lord." Lancel spoke without a moment's hesitation. Tyrion liked that. "I will. I swear it. As you command."

"Rise." Tyrion filled the second cup and pressed it on him. "Drink to our understanding. I promise, there are no boars in the castle that I know of." Lancel lifted the cup and drank, albeit stiffly. "Smile, cousin. My sister is a beautiful woman, and it's all for the good of the realm. You could do well out of this. Knighthood is nothing. If you're clever, you'll have a lordship from me before you're done." Tyrion swirled the wine in his cup. "We want Cersei to have every faith in you. Go back and tell her I beg her forgiveness. Tell her that you frightened me, that I want no conflict between us, that henceforth I shall do nothing without her consent."

"But . . . her demands . . ."

"Oh, I'll give her Pycelle."

"You will?" Lancel seemed astonished.

Tyrion smiled. "I'll release him on the morrow. I could swear that I hadn't harmed a hair on his head, but it wouldn't be strictly true. In any case, he's well enough, though I won't vouch for his vigor. The black cells are not a healthy place for a man his age. Cersei can keep him as a pet or send him to the Wall, I don't care which, but I won't have him on the council."

"And Ser Jacelyn?"

"Tell my sister you believe you can win him away from me, given time. That ought to content her for a while."

"As you say." Lancel finished his wine.

"One last thing. With King Robert dead, it would be most embarrassing should his grieving widow suddenly grow great with child."

"My lord, I . . . we . . . the queen has commanded me not to . . ." His ears had turned Lannister crimson. "I spill my seed on her belly, my lord."

"A lovely belly, I have no doubt. Moisten it as often as you wish . . . but see that your dew falls nowhere else. I want no more nephews, is that clear?"

Ser Lancel made a stiff bow and took his leave.

Tyrion allowed himself a moment to feel sorry for the boy. *Another fool, and a weakling as well, but he does not deserve what Cersei and I are doing to him.* It was a kindness that his uncle Kevan had two other sons; this one was unlikely to live out the year. Cersei would have him killed out of hand if she learned he was betraying her, and if by some grace of the gods she did not, Lancel would never survive the day Jaime Lannister returned to King's Landing. The only question would be whether Jaime cut him down in a jealous rage, or Cersei murdered him first to keep Jaime from finding out. Tyrion's silver was on Cersei.

A restlessness was on him, and Tyrion knew full well he would not get back to sleep tonight. *Not here, in any case.* He found Podrick Payne asleep in a chair outside the door of the solar, and shook him by the shoulder. "Summon Bronn, and then run down to the stables and have two horses saddled."

The squire's eyes were cloudy with sleep. "Horses."

"Those big brown animals that love apples, I'm sure you've seen them. Four legs and a tail. But Bronn first."

The sellsword was not long in appearing. "Who pissed in your soup?" he demanded.

"Cersei, as ever. You'd think I'd be used to the taste by now, but never mind. My gentle sister seems to have mistaken me for Ned Stark."

"I hear he was taller."

"Not after Joff took off his head. You ought to have dressed more warmly, the night is chill."

"Are we going somewhere?"

"Are all sellswords as clever as you?"

The city streets were dangerous, but with Bronn beside him Tyrion felt safe enough. The guards let him out a postern gate in the north wall, and they rode down Shadowblack Lane to the foot of Aegon's High Hill, and thence onto Pigrun Alley, past rows of shuttered windows and tall timber-and-stone buildings whose upper stories leaned out so far over the street they almost kissed. The moon seemed to follow them as they went, playing peek-and-sneak among the chimneys. They encountered no one but a lone old crone, carrying a dead cat by the tail. She gave them a fearful look, as if she were afraid they might try to steal her dinner, and slunk off into the shadows without a word.

Tyrion reflected on the men who had been Hand before him, who had proved no match for his sister's wiles. *How could they be? Men like that . . . too honest to live, too noble to shit, Cersei devours such fools every morning when she breaks her fast. The only way to defeat my sister is to play her own game, and that was something the Lords Stark and Arryn would never do.* Small wonder that both of them were dead, while Tyrion Lannister had never felt more alive. His stunted legs might make him a comic grotesque at a harvest ball, but *this* dance he knew.

Despite the hour, the brothel was crowded. Chataya greeted them pleasantly and escorted them to the common room. Bronn went upstairs with a dark-eyed girl from Dorne, but Alayaya was busy entertaining. "She will be so pleased to know you've come," said Chataya. "I will see that the turret room is made ready for you. Will my lord take a cup of wine while he waits?"

"I will," he said.

The wine was poor stuff compared to the vintages from the Arbor the house normally served. "You must forgive us, my lord," Chataya said. "I cannot find good wine at any price of late."

"You are not alone in that, I fear."

Chataya commiserated with him a moment, then excused herself and glided off. *A handsome woman,* Tyrion reflected as he watched her go. He had seldom seen such elegance and dignity in a whore. Though to be sure, she saw herself more as a kind of priestess. *Perhaps that is the secret. It is not what we do, so much as why we do it.* Somehow that thought comforted him.

A few of the other patrons were giving him sideways looks. The last time he ventured out, a man had spit on him . . . well, had tried to. Instead he'd spit on Bronn, and in future would do his spitting without teeth.

"Is milord feeling unloved?" Dancy slid into his lap and nibbled at his ear. "I have a cure for that."

Smiling, Tyrion shook his head. "You are too beautiful for words, sweetling, but I've grown fond of Alayaya's remedy."

"You've never *tried* mine. Milord never chooses anyone but 'Yaya. She's good but I'm better, don't you want to see?"

"Next time, perhaps." Tyrion had no doubt that Dancy would be a lively handful. She was pug-nosed and bouncy, with freckles and a mane of thick red hair that tumbled down past her waist. But he had Shae waiting for him at the manse.

Giggling, she put her hand between his thighs and squeezed him through his breeches. "I don't think *he* wants to wait till next time," she announced. "He wants to come out and count all my freckles, I think."

"Dancy." Alayaya stood in the doorway, dark and cool in gauzy green silk. "His lordship is come to visit me."

Tyrion gently disentangled himself from the other girl and stood. Dancy did not seem to mind. "Next time," she reminded him. She put a finger in her mouth and sucked it.

As the black-skinned girl led him up the stairs, she said, "Poor Dancy. She has a fortnight to get my lord to choose her. Elsewise she loses her black pearls to Marei."

Marei was a cool, pale, delicate girl Tyrion had noticed once or twice. Green eyes and porcelain skin, long straight silvery hair, very lovely, but too solemn by half. "I'd hate to have the poor child lose her pearls on account of me."

"Then take her upstairs next time."

"Maybe I will."

She smiled. "I think not, my lord."

She's right, Tyrion thought, *I won't. Shae may be only a whore, but I am faithful to her after my fashion.*

In the turret room, as he opened the door of the wardrobe, he looked at Alayaya curiously. "What do you do while I'm gone?"

She raised her arms and stretched like some sleek black cat. "Sleep. I am much better rested since you began to visit us, my lord. And Marei is teaching us to read, perhaps soon I will be able to pass the time with a book."

"Sleep is good," he said. "And books are better." He gave her a quick kiss on the cheek. Then it was down the shaft and through the tunnel.

As he left the stable on his piebald gelding, Tyrion heard the sound of music drifting over the rooftops. It was pleasant to think that men still sang, even in the midst of butchery and famine. Remembered notes filled his head, and for a moment he could almost hear Tysha as she'd sung to him half a lifetime ago. He reined up to listen. The tune was wrong, the words too faint to hear. A different song then, and why not? His sweet innocent Tysha had been a lie start to finish, only a whore his brother Jaime had hired to make him a man.

I'm free of Tysha now, he thought. *She's haunted me half my life, but I don't need her anymore, no more than I need Alayaya or Dancy or Marei, or the hundreds like them I've bedded with over the years. I have Shae now. Shae.*

The gates of the manse were closed and barred. Tyrion pounded until the ornate bronze eye clacked open. "It's me." The man who admitted him was one of Varys's prettier finds, a Braavosi daggerman with a harelip and a lazy eye. Tyrion had wanted no handsome young guardsmen loitering about Shae day after day. "Find me old, ugly, scarred men, preferably impotent," he had told the eunuch. "Men who prefer boys. Or men who prefer sheep, for that matter." Varys had not managed to come up with any sheeplovers, but he did find a eunuch strangler and a pair of foul-smelling Ibbenese who were as fond of axes as they were of each other. The others were as choice a lot of mercenaries as ever graced a dungeon, each uglier than the last. When Varys had paraded them before him, Tyrion had been afraid he'd gone too far, but Shae had never uttered a word of complaint. *And why would she? She has never complained of me, and I'm more hideous than all her guards together. Perhaps she does not even see ugliness.*

Even so, Tyrion would sooner have used some of his mountain clansmen to guard the manse; Chella's Black Ears perhaps, or the Moon Brothers. He had more faith in their iron loyalties and sense of honor than in the greed of sellswords. The risk was too great, however. All King's Landing knew the wildlings were his. If he sent the Black Ears here, it would only be a matter of time until the whole city knew the King's Hand was keeping a concubine.

One of the Ibbenese took his horse. "Have you woken her?" Tyrion asked him.

"No, m'lord."

"Good."

The fire in the bedchamber had burned down to embers, but the room was still warm. Shae had kicked off her blankets and sheets as she slept. She lay nude atop the featherbed, the soft curves of her young body limned in the faint glow from the hearth. Tyrion stood in the door and drank in the sight of her. *Younger than Marei, sweeter than Dancy, more beautiful than Alayaya, she's all I need and more.* How could a whore look so clean and sweet and innocent, he wondered?

He had not intended to disturb her, but the sight of her was enough to make him hard. He let his garments fall to the floor, then crawled onto the bed and gently pushed her legs apart and kissed her between the thighs. Shae murmured in her sleep. He kissed her again, and licked at her secret sweetness, on and on until his beard and her cunt were both soaked. When she gave a soft moan and shuddered, he climbed up and thrust himself inside her and exploded almost at once.

Her eyes were open. She smiled and stroked his head and whispered, "I just had the sweetest dream, m'lord."

Tyrion nipped at her small hard nipple and nestled his head on her shoulder. He did not pull out of her; would that he never had to pull out of her. "This is no dream," he promised her. *It is real, all of it,* he thought, *the wars, the intrigues, the great bloody game, and me in the center of it . . . me, the dwarf, the monster, the one they scorned and laughed at, but now I hold it all, the power, the city, the girl. This was what I was made for, and gods forgive me, but I do love it . . .*

And her. And her.

ARYA

Whatever names Harren the Black had meant to give his towers were long forgotten. They were called the Tower of Dread, the Widow's Tower, the Wailing Tower, the Tower of Ghosts, and Kingspyre Tower. Arya slept in a shallow niche in the cavernous vaults beneath the Wailing Tower, on a bed of straw. She had water to wash in whenever she liked, a chunk of soap. The work was hard, but no harder than walking miles every day. Weasel did not need to find worms and bugs to eat, as Arry had; there was bread every day, and barley stews with bits of carrot and turnip, and once a fortnight even a bite of meat.

Hot Pie ate even better; he was where he belonged, in the kitchens, a round stone building with a domed roof that was a world unto itself. Arya took her meals at a trestle table in the undercroft with Weese and his other charges, but sometimes she would be chosen to help fetch their food, and she and Hot Pie could steal a moment to talk. He could never remember that she was now Weasel and kept calling her Arry, even though he knew she was a girl. Once he tried to slip her a hot apple tart, but he made such a clumsy job of it that two of the cooks saw. They took the tart away and beat him with a big wooden spoon.

Gendry had been sent to the forge; Arya seldom saw him. As for those she served with, she did not even want to know their names. That only made it hurt worse when they died. Most of them were older than she was and content to let her alone.

Harrenhal was vast, much of it far gone in decay. Lady Whent had held the castle as bannerman to House Tully, but she'd used only the lower thirds of two of the five towers, and let the rest go to ruin. Now she was fled, and the small household she'd left could not begin to tend the needs of all the knights, lords, and highborn prisoners Lord Tywin had brought, so the Lannisters must forage for servants as well as for plunder and provender. The talk was that Lord Tywin planned to restore Harrenhal to glory, and make it his new seat once the war was done.

Weese used Arya to run messages, draw water, and fetch food, and sometimes to serve at table in the Barracks Hall above the armory, where the men-at-arms took their meals. But most of her work was cleaning. The ground floor of the Wailing Tower was given over to store-rooms and granaries, and two floors above housed part of the garrison, but the upper stories had not been occupied for eighty years. Now Lord Tywin had commanded that they be made fit for habitation again. There were floors to be scrubbed, grime to be washed off windows, broken chairs and rotted beds to be carried off. The topmost story was infested with nests of the huge black bats that House Whent had used for its sigil, and there were rats in the cellars as well . . . and ghosts, some said, the spirits of Harren the Black and his sons.

Arya thought that was stupid. Harren and his sons had died in Kings-pyre Tower, that was why it had that name, so why should they cross the yard to haunt her? The Wailing Tower only wailed when the wind blew from the north, and that was just the sound the air made blowing through the cracks in the stones where they had fissured from the heat. If there *were* ghosts in Harrenhal, they never troubled her. It was the living men she feared, Weese and Ser Gregor Clegane and Lord Tywin Lannister himself, who kept his apartments in Kingspyre Tower, still the tallest and mightiest of all, though lopsided beneath the weight of the slagged stone that made it look like some giant half-melted black candle.

She wondered what Lord Tywin would do if she marched up to him and confessed to being Arya Stark, but she knew she'd never get near enough to talk to him, and anyhow he'd never believe her if she did, and afterward Weese would beat her bloody.

In his own small strutting way, Weese was nearly as scary as Ser Gregor. The Mountain swatted men like flies, but most of the time he did not even seem to know the fly was there. Weese *always* knew you were there, and what you were doing, and sometimes what you were thinking. He would hit at the slightest provocation, and he had a dog who was near as bad as he was, an ugly spotted bitch that smelled worse than any dog Arya had ever known. Once she saw him set the dog on a latrine boy who'd annoyed him. She tore a big chunk out of the boy's calf while Weese laughed.

It took him only three days to earn the place of honor in her nightly prayers. "Weese," she would whisper, first of all. "Dunsen, Chiswyck, Polliver, Raff the Sweetling. The Tickler and the Hound. Ser Gregor, Ser Amory, Ser Ilyn, Ser Meryn, King Joffrey, Queen Cersei." If she let herself forget even one of them, how would she ever find him again to kill him?

On the road Arya had felt like a sheep, but Harrenhal turned her into a mouse. She was grey as a mouse in her scratchy wool shift, and like a mouse she kept to the crannies and crevices and dark holes of the castle, scurrying out of the way of the mighty.

Sometimes she thought they were *all* mice within those thick walls, even the knights and the great lords. The size of the castle made even Gregor Clegane seem small. Harrenhal covered thrice as much ground as Winterfell, and its buildings were so much larger they could scarcely be compared. Its stables housed a thousand horses, its godswood covered twenty acres, its kitchens were as large as Winterfell's Great Hall, and its own great hall, grandly named the Hall of a Hundred Hearths even though it only had thirty and some (Arya had tried to count them, twice, but she came up with thirty-three once and thirty-five the other time) was so cavernous that Lord Tywin could have feasted his entire host, though he never did. Walls, doors, halls, steps, everything was built to an inhuman scale that made Arya remember the stories Old Nan used to tell of the giants who lived beyond the Wall.

And as lords and ladies never notice the little grey mice under their feet, Arya heard all sorts of secrets just by keeping her ears open as she went about her duties. Pretty Pia from the buttery was a slut who was working her way through every knight in the castle. The wife of the gaoler was with child, but the real father was either Ser Alyn Stackspear or a singer called Whitesmile Wat. Lord Lefford made mock of ghosts at table, but always kept a candle burning by his bed. Ser Dunaver's squire Jodge could not hold his water when he slept. The cooks despised Ser Harys Swyft and spit in all his food. Once she even overheard Maester Tothmure's serving girl confiding to her brother about some message that said Joffrey was a bastard and not the rightful king at all. "Lord Tywin told him to burn the letter and never speak such filth again," the girl whispered.

King Robert's brothers Stannis and Renly had joined the fighting, she heard. "And both of them kings now," Weese said. "Realm's got more kings than a castle's got rats." Even Lannister men questioned how long Joffrey would hold the Iron Throne. "The lad's got no army but them gold cloaks, and he's ruled by a eunuch, a dwarf, and a woman," she heard a lordling mutter in his cups. "What good will the likes of them be if it comes to battle?" There was always talk of Beric Dondarrion. A fat archer once said the Bloody Mummers had slain him, but the others only laughed. "Lorch killed the man at Rushing Falls, and the Mountain's slain him twice. Got me a silver stag says he don't stay dead this time neither."

Arya did not know who Bloody Mummers were until a fortnight later, when the queerest company of men she'd ever seen arrived at Harrenhal. Beneath the standard of a black goat with bloody horns rode copper men with bells in their braids; lancers astride striped black-and-white horses; bowmen with powdered cheeks; squat hairy men with shaggy shields; brown-skinned men in feathered cloaks; a wispy fool in green-and-pink motley; swordsmen with fantastic forked beards dyed green and purple and silver; spearmen with colored scars that covered their cheeks; a slender man in septon's robes, a fatherly one in maester's grey, and a sickly one whose leather cloak was fringed with long blond hair.

At their head was a man stick-thin and very tall, with a drawn emaciated face made even longer by the ropy black beard that grew from his pointed chin nearly to his waist. The helm that hung from his saddle horn was black steel, fashioned in the shape of a goat's head. About his neck he wore a chain made of linked coins of many different sizes, shapes, and metals, and his horse was one of the strange black-and-white ones.

"You don't want to know that lot, Weasel," Weese said when he saw her looking at the goat-helmed man. Two of his drinking friends were with him, men-at-arms in service to Lord Lefford.

"Who are they?" she asked.

One of the soldiers laughed. "The Footmen, girl. Toes of the Goat. Lord Tywin's Bloody Mummers."

"Pease for wits. You get her flayed, *you* can scrub the bloody steps," said Weese. "They're sellswords, Weasel girl. Call themselves the Brave Companions. Don't use them other names where they can hear, or they'll hurt you bad. The goat-helm's their captain, Lord Vargo Hoat."

"He's no fucking lord," said the second soldier. "I heard Ser Amory say so. He's just some sellsword with a mouth full of slobber and a high opinion of hisself."

"Aye," said Weese, "but she better *call* him lord if she wants to keep all her parts."

Arya looked at Vargo Hoat again. *How many monsters does Lord Tywin have?*

The Brave Companions were housed in the Widow's Tower, so Arya need not serve them. She was glad of that; on the very night they arrived, fighting broke out between the sellswords and some Lannister men. Ser Harys Swyft's squire was stabbed to death and two of the Bloody

Mummers were wounded. The next morning Lord Tywin hanged them both from the gatehouse walls, along with one of Lord Lydden's archers. Weese said the archer had started all the trouble by taunting the sellswords over Beric Dondarrion. After the hanged men had stopped kicking, Vargo Hoat and Ser Harys embraced and kissed and swore to love each other always as Lord Tywin looked on. Arya thought it was funny the way Vargo Hoat lisped and slobbered, but she knew better than to laugh.

The Bloody Mummers did not linger long at Harrenhal, but before they rode out again, Arya heard one of them saying how a northern army under Roose Bolton had occupied the ruby ford of the Trident. "If he crosses, Lord Tywin will smash him again like he did on the Green Fork," a Lannister bowmen said, but his fellows jeered him down. "Bolton'll never cross, not till the Young Wolf marches from Riverrun with his wild northmen and all them wolves."

Arya had not known her brother was so near. Riverrun was much closer than Winterfell, though she was not certain where it lay in relation to Harrenhal. *I could find out somehow, I know I could, if only I could get away.* When she thought of seeing Robb's face again Arya had to bite her lip. *And I want to see Jon too, and Bran and Rickon, and Mother. Even Sansa . . . I'll kiss her and beg her pardons like a proper lady, she'll like that.*

From the courtyard talk she'd learned that the upper chambers of the Tower of Dread housed three dozen captives taken during some battle on the Green Fork of the Trident. Most had been given freedom of the castle in return for their pledge not to attempt escape. *They vowed not to escape,* Arya told herself, *but they never swore not to help me escape.*

The captives ate at their own table in the Hall of a Hundred Hearths, and could often be seen about the grounds. Four brothers took their exercise together every day, fighting with staves and wooden shields in the Flowstone Yard. Three of them were Freys of the Crossing, the fourth their bastard brother. They were only there a short time, though; one morning two other brothers arrived under a peace banner with a chest of gold, and ransomed them from the knights who'd captured them. The six Freys all left together.

No one ransomed the northmen, though. One fat lordling haunted the kitchens, Hot Pie told her, always looking for a morsel. His mustache was so bushy that it covered his mouth, and the clasp that held his cloak was a silver-and-sapphire trident. He belonged to Lord Tywin, but the fierce, bearded young man who liked to walk the battlements alone in a black cloak patterned with white suns had been taken by some hedge knight who meant to get rich off him. Sansa would have known who he was, and the fat one too, but Arya had never taken much interest in titles and sigils. Whenever Septa Mordane had gone on about the history of this house and that house, she was inclined to drift and dream and wonder when the lesson would be done.

She *did* remember Lord Cerwyn, though. His lands had been close to Winterfell, so he and his son Cley had often visited. Yet as fate would have it, he was the only captive who was never seen; he was abed in a tower cell, recovering from a wound. For days and days Arya tried to work out how she might steal past the door guards to see him. If he knew her, he would be honor bound to help her. A lord would have gold for a certainty, they all did; perhaps he would pay some of Lord Tywin's own sellswords to take her to Riverrun. Father had always said that most sellswords would betray anyone for enough gold.

Then one morning she spied three women in the cowled grey robes of the silent sisters loading a corpse into their wagon. The body was sewn into a cloak of the finest silk, decorated with a battle-axe sigil. When Arya asked who it was, one of the guards told her that Lord Cerwyn had died. The words felt like a kick in the belly. *He could never have helped you anyway,* she thought as the sisters drove the wagon through the gate. *He couldn't even help himself, you stupid mouse.*

After that it was back to scrubbing and scurrying and listening at doors. Lord Tywin would soon march on Riverrun, she heard. Or he would drive south to Highgarden, no one would ever expect that. No, he must defend King's Landing, Stannis was the greatest threat. He'd sent Gregor Clegane and Vargo Hoat to destroy Roose Bolton and remove the dagger from his back. He'd sent ravens to the Eyrie, he meant to wed the Lady Lysa Arryn and win the Vale. He'd bought a ton of silver to forge magic swords that would slay the Stark wargs. He was writing Lady Stark to make a peace, the Kingslayer would soon be freed.

Though ravens came and went every day, Lord Tywin himself spent most of his days behind closed doors with his war council. Arya caught glimpses of him, but always from afar—once walking the walls in the company of three maesters and the fat captive with the bushy mustache, once riding out with his lords bannermen to visit the encampments, but most often standing in an arch of the covered gallery watching men at practice in the yard below. He stood with his hands locked together on the gold pommel of his longsword. They said Lord Tywin loved gold most of all; he even *shit* gold, she heard one squire jest. The Lannister lord was strong-looking for an old man, with stiff golden whiskers and a bald head. There was something in his face that reminded Arya of her own father, even though they looked nothing alike. *He has a lord's face, that's all,* she told herself. She remembered hearing her lady mother tell Father to put on his lord's face and go deal with some matter. Father had laughed at that. She could not imagine Lord Tywin ever laughing at anything.

One afternoon, while she was waiting her turn to draw a pail of water from the well, she heard the hinges of the east gate groaning. A party of men rode under the portcullis at a walk. When she spied the manticore crawling across the shield of their leader, a stab of hate shot through her.

In the light of day, Ser Amory Lorch looked less frightening than he had by torchlight, but he still had the pig's eyes she recalled. One of the women said that his men had ridden all the way around the lake chasing Beric Dondarrion and slaying rebels. *We weren't rebels,* Arya thought. *We were the Night's Watch; the Night's Watch takes no side.* Ser Amory had fewer men than she remembered, though, and many wounded. *I hope their wounds fester. I hope they all die.*

Then she saw the three near the end of the column.

Rorge had donned a black halfhelm with a broad iron nasal that made it hard to see that he did not have a nose. Biter rode ponderously beside him on a destrier that looked ready to collapse under his weight. Half-healed burns covered his body, making him even more hideous than before.

But Jaqen H'ghar still smiled. His garb was still ragged and filthy, but he had found time to wash and brush his hair. It streamed down across his shoulders, red and white and shiny, and Arya heard the girls giggling to each other in admiration.

I should have let the fire have them. Gendry said to, I should have listened. If she hadn't thrown them that axe they'd all be dead. For a moment she was afraid, but they rode past her without a flicker of interest. Only Jaqen H'ghar so much as glanced in her direction, and his eyes passed right over her. *He does not know me,* she thought. *Arry was a fierce little boy with a sword, and I'm just a grey mouse girl with a pail.*

She spent the rest of that day scrubbing steps inside the Wailing Tower. By evenfall her hands were raw and bleeding and her arms so sore they trembled when she lugged the pail back to the cellar. Too tired even for food, Arya begged Weese's pardons and crawled into her straw to sleep. "Weese," she yawned. "Dunsen, Chiswyck, Polliver, Raff the Sweetling. The Tickler and the Hound. Ser Gregor, Ser Amory, Ser Ilyn, Ser Meryn, King Joffrey, Queen Cersei." She thought she might add three more names to her prayer, but she was too tired to decide tonight.

Arya was dreaming of wolves running wild through the wood when a strong hand clamped down over her mouth like smooth warm stone, solid and unyielding. She woke at once, squirming and struggling. "A girl says nothing," a voice whispered close behind her ear. "A girl keeps her lips closed, no one hears, and friends may talk in secret. Yes?"

Heart pounding, Arya managed the tiniest of nods.

Jaqen H'ghar took his hand away. The cellar was black as pitch and she could not see his face, even inches away. She could *smell* him, though; his skin smelled clean and soapy, and he had scented his hair. "A boy becomes a girl," he murmured.

"I was *always* a girl. I didn't think you saw me."

"A man sees. A man knows."

She remembered that she hated him. "You scared me. You're one of *them* now, I should have let you burn. What are you doing here? Go away or I'll yell for Weese."

"A man pays his debts. A man owes three."

"Three?"

"The Red God has his due, sweet girl, and only death may pay for life. This girl took three that were his. This girl must give three in their places. Speak the names, and a man will do the rest."

He wants to help me, Arya realized with a rush of hope that made her dizzy. "Take me to Riverrun, it's not far, if we stole some horses we could—"

He laid a finger on her lips. "Three lives you shall have of me. No more, no less. Three and we are done. So a girl must ponder." He kissed her hair softly. "But not too long."

By the time Arya lit her stub of a candle, only a faint smell remained of him, a whiff of ginger and cloves lingering in the air. The woman in the next niche rolled over on her straw and complained of the light, so Arya blew it out. When she closed her eyes, she saw faces swimming before her. Joffrey and his mother, Ilyn Payne and Meryn Trant and Sandor Clegane . . . but they were in King's Landing hundreds of miles away, and Ser Gregor had lingered only a few nights before departing again for more foraging, taking Raff and Chiswyck and the Tickler with him. Ser Amory Lorch was here, though, and she hated him almost as much. Didn't she? She wasn't certain. And there was always Weese.

She thought of him again the next morning, when lack of sleep made her yawn. "Weasel," Weese purred, "next time I see that mouth droop open, I'll pull out your tongue and feed it to my bitch." He twisted her ear between his fingers to make certain she'd heard, and told her to get back to those steps, he wanted them clean down to the third landing by nightfall.

As she worked, Arya thought about the people she wanted dead. She pretended she could see their faces on the steps, and scrubbed harder to wipe them away. The Starks were at war with the Lannisters and she was a Stark, so she should kill as many Lannisters as she could, that was what you did in wars. But she didn't think she should trust Jaqen. *I should kill them myself*. Whenever her father had condemned a man to death, he did the deed himself with Ice, his greatsword. "If you would take a man's life, you owe it to him to look him in the face and hear his last words," she'd heard him tell Robb and Jon once.

The next day she avoided Jaqen H'ghar, and the day after that. It was not hard. She was very small and Harrenhal was very large, full of places where a mouse could hide.

And then Ser Gregor returned, earlier than expected, driving a herd of goats this time in place of a herd of prisoners. She heard he'd lost four men in one of Lord Beric's night raids, but those Arya hated returned unscathed and took up residence on the second floor of the Wailing Tower. Weese saw that they were well supplied with drink. "They always have a good thirst, that lot," he grumbled. "Weasel, go up and ask if they've got any clothes that need mending, I'll have the women see to it."

Arya ran up her well-scrubbed steps. No one paid her any mind when she entered. Chiswyck was seated by the fire with a horn of ale to hand, telling one of his funny stories. She dared not interrupt, unless she wanted a bloody lip.

"After the Hand's tourney, it were, before the war come," Chiswyck was saying. "We were on our ways back west, seven of us with Ser Gregor. Raff was with me, and young Joss Stilwood, he'd squired for Ser in the lists. Well, we come on this pisswater river, running high on account there'd been rains. No way to ford, but there's an alehouse near, so there we repair. Ser rousts the brewer and tells him to keep our horns full till the waters fall, and you should see the man's pig eyes shine at the sight o' silver. So he's fetching us ale, him and his daughter, and poor thin stuff it is, no more'n brown piss, which don't make me any happier, nor Ser neither. And all the time this brewer's saying how glad he is to have us, custom being slow on account o' them rains. The fool won't shut his yap, not him, though Ser is saying not a word, just brooding on the Knight o' Pansies and that bugger's trick he played. You can see how tight his mouth sits, so me and the other lads we know better'n to say a squeak to him, but this brewer he's got to talk, he even asks how m'lord fared in the jousting. Ser just gave him this look." Chiswyck cackled, quaffed his ale, and wiped the foam away with the back of his hand. "Meanwhile, this daughter of his has been fetching and pouring, a fat little thing, eighteen or so—"

"Thirteen, more like," Raff the Sweetling drawled.

"Well, be that as it may, she's not much to look at, but Eggon's been drinking and gets to touching her, and might be I did a little touching meself, and Raff's telling young Stilwood that he ought t' drag the girl upstairs and make hisself a man, giving the lad courage as it were. Finally Joss reaches up under her skirt, and she shrieks and drops her flagon and goes running off to the kitchen. Well, it would have ended right there, only what does the old fool do but he goes to *Ser* and asks him to make us leave the girl alone, him being an anointed knight and all such.

"Ser Gregor, he wasn't paying no mind to none of our fun, but now he *looks,* you know how he does, and he commands that the girl be brought before him. Now the old man has to drag her out of the kitchen, and no one to blame but hisself. Ser looks her over and says, 'So this is the whore you're so concerned for,' and this besotted old fool says, 'My Layna's no whore, ser,' right to Gregor's face. Ser, he never blinks, just says, 'She is now,' tosses the old man another silver, rips the dress off the wench, and takes her right there on the table in front of her da, her flopping and wiggling like a rabbit and making these noises. The look on the old man's face, I laughed so hard ale was coming out me nose. Then this boy hears the noise, the son I figure, and comes rushing up from the cellar, so Raff has to stick a dirk in his belly. By then Ser's done, so he goes back to his drinking and we all have a turn. Tobbot, you know how he is, he flops her over and goes in the back way. The girl was done fighting by the time I had her, maybe she'd decided she liked it after all, though to tell the truth I wouldn't have minded a little wiggling. And now here's the best bit . . . when it's all done, Ser tells the old man that he wants his change. The girl wasn't worth a silver, he says . . . and damned if that old man didn't fetch a fistful of coppers, beg m'lord's pardon, and *thank him for the custom!*"

The men all roared, none louder than Chiswyck himself, who laughed so hard at his own story that snot dribbled from his nose down into his scraggy grey beard. Arya stood in the shadows of the stairwell and watched him. She crept back down to the cellars without saying a word. When Weese found that she hadn't asked about the clothes, he yanked down her breeches and caned her until blood ran down her thighs, but Arya closed her eyes and thought of all the sayings Syrio had taught her, so she scarcely felt it.

Two nights later, he sent her to the Barracks Hall to serve at table. She was carrying a flagon of wine and pouring when she glimpsed Jaqen H'ghar at his trencher across the aisle. Chewing her lip, Arya glanced around warily to make certain Weese was not in sight. *Fear cuts deeper than swords,* she told herself.

She took a step, and another, and with each she felt less a mouse. She worked her way down the bench, filling wine cups. Rorge sat to Jaqen's right, deep drunk, but he took no note of her. Arya leaned close and whispered, "Chiswyck," right in Jaqen's ear. The Lorathi gave no sign that he had heard.

When her flagon was empty, Arya hurried down to the cellars to refill it from the cask, and quickly returned to her pouring. No one had died of thirst while she was gone, nor even noted her brief absence.

Nothing happened the next day, nor the day after, but on the third day Arya went to the kitchens with Weese to fetch their dinner. "One of the Mountain's men fell off a wallwalk last night and broke his fool neck," she heard Weese tell a cook.

"Drunk?" the woman asked.

"No more'n usual. Some are saying it was Harren's ghost flung him down." He snorted to show what *he* thought of such notions.

It wasn't Harren, Arya wanted to say, *it was me.* She had killed Chiswyck with a whisper, and she would kill two more before she was through. *I'm the ghost in Harrenhal,* she thought. And that night, there was one less name to hate.

CATELYN

The meeting place was a grassy sward dotted with pale grey mushrooms and the raw stumps of felled trees.

"We are the first, my lady," Hallis Mollen said as they reined up amidst the stumps, alone between the armies. The direwolf banner of House Stark flapped and fluttered atop the lance he bore. Catelyn could not see the sea from here, but she could feel how close it was. The smell of salt was heavy on the wind gusting from the east.

Stannis Baratheon's foragers had cut the trees down for his siege towers and catapults. Catelyn wondered how long the grove had stood, and whether Ned had rested here when he led his host south to lift the last siege of Storm's End. He had won a great victory that day, all the greater for being bloodless.

Gods grant that I shall do the same, Catelyn prayed. Her own liege men thought she was mad even to come. "This is no fight of ours, my lady," Ser Wendel Manderly had said. "I know the king would not wish his mother to put herself at risk."

"We are all at risk," she told him, perhaps too sharply. "Do you think I wish to be here, ser?" *I belong at Riverrun with my dying father, at Winterfell with my sons.* "Robb sent me south to speak for him, and speak for him I shall." It would be no easy thing to forge a peace between these brothers, Catelyn knew, yet for the good of the realm, it must be tried.

Across rain-sodden fields and stony ridges, she could see the great castle of Storm's End rearing up against the sky, its back to the unseen sea. Beneath that mass of pale grey stone, the encircling army of Lord Stannis Baratheon looked as small and insignificant as mice with banners.

The songs said that Storm's End had been raised in ancient days by Durran, the first Storm King, who had won the love of the fair Elenei, daughter of the sea god and the goddess of the wind. On the night of their wedding, Elenei had yielded her maidenhood to a mortal's love and thus doomed herself to a mortal's death, and her grieving parents had unleashed their wrath and sent the winds and waters to batter down Durran's hold. His friends and brothers and wedding guests were crushed beneath collapsing walls or blown out to sea, but Elenei sheltered Durran within her arms so he took no harm, and when the dawn came at last he declared war upon the gods and vowed to rebuild.

Five more castles he built, each larger and stronger than the last, only to see them smashed asunder when the gale winds came howling up Shipbreaker Bay, driving great walls of water before them. His lords pleaded with him to build inland; his priests told him he must placate the gods by giving Elenei back to the sea; even his smallfolk begged him to relent. Durran would have none of it. A seventh castle he raised, most massive of all. Some said the children of the forest helped him build it, shaping the stones with magic; others claimed that a small boy told him what he must do, a boy who would grow to be Bran the Builder. No matter how the tale was told, the end was the same. Though the angry gods threw storm after storm against it, the seventh castle stood defiant, and Durran Godsgrief and fair Elenei dwelt there together until the end of their days.

Gods do not forget, and still the gales came raging up the narrow sea. Yet Storm's End endured, through centuries and tens of centuries, a castle like no other. Its great curtain wall was a hundred feet high, unbroken by arrow slit or postern, everywhere rounded, curving, *smooth*, its stones fit so cunningly together that nowhere was crevice nor angle nor gap by which the wind might enter. That wall was said to be forty feet thick at its narrowest, and near eighty on the seaward face, a double course of stones with an inner core of sand and rubble. Within that mighty bulwark, the kitchens and stables and yards sheltered safe from wind and wave. Of towers, there was but one, a colossal drum tower, windowless where it faced the sea, so large that it was granary and barracks and feast hall and lord's dwelling all in one, crowned by massive battlements that made it look from afar like a spiked fist atop an upthrust arm.

"My lady," Hal Mollen called. Two riders had emerged from the tidy little camp beneath the castle, and were coming toward them at a slow walk. "That will be King Stannis."

"No doubt." Catelyn watched them come. *Stannis it must be, yet that is not the Baratheon banner.* It was a bright yellow, not the rich gold of Renly's standards, and the device it bore was red, though she could not make out its shape.

Renly would be last to arrive. He had told her as much when she set out. He did not propose to mount his horse until he saw his brother well on his way. The first to arrive must wait on the other, and Renly would do no waiting. *It is a sort of game kings play,* she told herself. Well, she was no king, so she need not play it. Catelyn was practiced at waiting.

As he neared, she saw that Stannis wore a crown of red gold with points fashioned in the shape of flames. His belt was studded with garnets and yellow topaz, and a great square-cut ruby was set in the hilt of the sword he wore. Otherwise his dress was plain: studded leather jerkin over quilted doublet, worn boots, breeches of brown roughspun. The device on his sun-yellow banner showed a red heart surrounded by a blaze of orange fire. The crowned stag was there, yes . . . shrunken and enclosed within the heart. Even more curious was his standard bearer—a woman, garbed all in reds, face shadowed within the deep hood of her scarlet cloak. *A red priestess,* Catelyn thought, wondering. The sect was numerous and powerful in the Free Cities and the distant east, but there were few in the Seven Kingdoms.

"Lady Stark," Stannis Baratheon said with chill courtesy as he reined up. He inclined his head, balder than she remembered.

"Lord Stannis," she returned.

Beneath the tight-trimmed beard his heavy jaw clenched hard, yet he did not hector her about titles. For that she was duly grateful. "I had not thought to find you at Storm's End."

"I had not thought to be here."

His deepset eyes regarded her uncomfortably. This was not a man made for easy courtesies. "I am sorry for your lord's death," he said, "though Eddard Stark was no friend to me."

"He was never your enemy, my lord. When the Lords Tyrell and Redwyne held you prisoned in that castle, starving, it was Eddard Stark who broke the siege."

"At my brother's command, not for love of me," Stannis answered. "Lord Eddard did his duty, I will not deny it. Did I ever do less? *I* should have been Robert's Hand."

"That was your brother's will. Ned never wanted it."

"Yet he took it. That which should have been mine. Still, I give you my word, you shall have justice for his murder."

How they loved to promise heads, these men who would be king. "Your brother promised me the same. But if truth be told, I would sooner have my daughters back, and leave justice to the gods. Cersei still holds my Sansa, and of Arya there has been no word since the day of Robert's death."

"If your children are found when I take the city, they shall be sent to you." *Alive or dead,* his tone implied.

"And when shall that be, Lord Stannis? King's Landing is close to your Dragonstone, but I find you here instead."

"You are frank, Lady Stark. Very well, I'll answer you frankly. To take the city, I need the power of these southron lords I see across the field. My brother has them. I must needs take them from him."

"Men give their allegiance where they will, my lord. These lords swore fealty to Robert and House Baratheon. If you and your brother were to put aside your quarrel—"

"I have no quarrel with Renly, should he prove dutiful. I am his elder, and his king. I want only what is mine by rights. Renly owes me loyalty and obedience. I mean to have it. From him, and from these other lords." Stannis studied her face. "And what cause brings you to this field, my lady? Has House Stark cast its lot with my brother, is that the way of it?"

This one will never bend, she thought, yet she must try nonetheless. Too much was at stake. "My son reigns as King in the North, by the will of our lords and people. He bends the knee to no man, but holds out the hand of friendship to all."

"Kings have no friends," Stannis said bluntly, "only subjects and enemies."

"And brothers," a cheerful voice called out behind her. Catelyn glanced over her shoulder as Lord Renly's palfrey picked her way through the stumps. The younger Baratheon was splendid in his green velvet doublet and satin cloak trimmed in vair. The crown of golden roses girded his temples, jade stag's head rising over his forehead, long black hair spilling out beneath. Jagged chunks of black diamond studded his swordbelt, and a chain of gold and emeralds looped around his neck.

Renly had chosen a woman to carry his banner as well, though Brienne hid face and form behind plate armor that gave no hint of her sex. Atop her twelve-foot lance, the crowned stag pranced black-on-gold as the wind off the sea rippled the cloth.

His brother's greeting was curt. "Lord Renly."

"*King* Renly. Can that truly be you, Stannis?"

Stannis frowned. "Who else should it be?"

Renly gave an easy shrug. "When I saw that standard, I could not be certain. Whose banner do you bear?"

"Mine own."

The red-clad priestess spoke up. "The king has taken for his sigil the fiery heart of the Lord of Light."

Renly seemed amused by that. "All for the good. If we both use the same banner, the battle will be terribly confused."

Catelyn said, "Let us hope there will be no battle. We three share a common foe who would destroy us all."

Stannis studied her, unsmiling. "The Iron Throne is mine by rights. All those who deny that are my foes."

"The whole of the realm denies it, brother," said Renly. "Old men deny it with their death rattle, and unborn children deny it in their mothers' wombs. They deny it in Dorne and they deny it on the Wall. No one wants you for their king. Sorry."

Stannis clenched his jaw, his face taut. "I swore I would never treat with you while you wore your traitor's crown. Would that I had kept to that vow."

"This is folly," Catelyn said sharply. "Lord Tywin sits at Harrenhal with twenty thousand swords. The remnants of the Kingslayer's army have regrouped at the Golden Tooth, another Lannister host gathers beneath the shadow of Casterly Rock, and Cersei and her son hold King's Landing and your precious Iron Throne. You each name yourself *king*, yet the kingdom bleeds, and no one lifts a sword to defend it but my son."

Renly shrugged. "Your son has won a few battles. I shall win the war. The Lannisters can wait my pleasure."

"If you have proposals to make, make them," Stannis said brusquely, "or I will be gone."

"Very well," said Renly. "I propose that you dismount, bend your knee, and swear me your allegiance."

Stannis choked back rage. "That you shall never have."

"You served Robert, why not me?"

"Robert was my elder brother. You are the younger."

"Younger, bolder, and *far* more comely . . ."

". . . and a thief and a usurper besides."

Renly shrugged. "The Targaryens called Robert usurper. He seemed to be able to bear the shame. So shall I."

This will not do. "Listen to yourselves! If you were sons of mine, I would bang your heads together and lock you in a bedchamber until you remembered that you were brothers."

Stannis frowned at her. "You presume too much, Lady Stark. I am the rightful king, and your son no less a traitor than my brother here. His day will come as well."

The naked threat fanned her fury. "You are very free to name others traitor and usurper, my lord, yet how are you any different? You say you alone are the rightful king, yet it seems to me that Robert had two sons. By all the laws of the Seven Kingdoms, Prince Joffrey is his rightful heir, and Tommen after him . . . and we are *all* traitors, however good our reasons."

Renly laughed. "You must forgive Lady Catelyn, Stannis. She's come all the way down from Riverrun, a long way ahorse. I fear she never saw your little letter."

"Joffrey is not my brother's seed," Stannis said bluntly. "Nor is Tommen. They are bastards. The girl as well. All three of them abominations born of incest."

Would even Cersei be so mad? Catelyn was speechless.

"Isn't that a sweet story, my lady?" Renly asked. "I was camped at Horn Hill when Lord Tarly received his letter, and I must say, it took my breath away." He smiled at his brother. "I had never suspected you were so clever, Stannis. Were it only true, you would indeed be Robert's heir."

"*Were* it true? Do you name me a liar?"

"Can you prove any word of this fable?"

Stannis ground his teeth.

Robert could never have known, Catelyn thought, *or Cersei would have lost her head in an instant.* "Lord Stannis," she asked, "if you knew the queen to be guilty of such monstrous crimes, why did you keep silent?"

"I did not keep silent," Stannis declared. "I brought my suspicions to Jon Arryn."

"Rather than your own brother?"

"My brother's regard for me was never more than dutiful," said Stannis. "From me, such accusations would have seemed peevish and self-serving, a means of placing myself first in the line of succession. I believed Robert would be more disposed to listen if the charges came from Lord Arryn, whom he loved."

"Ah," said Renly. "So we have the word of a dead man."

"Do you think he died by happenstance, you purblind fool? Cersei had him poisoned, for fear he would reveal her. Lord Jon had been gathering certain proofs—"

"—which doubtless died with him. How inconvenient."

Catelyn was remembering, fitting pieces together. "My sister Lysa accused the queen of killing her husband in a letter she sent me at Winterfell," she admitted. "Later, in the Eyrie, she laid the murder at the feet of the queen's brother Tyrion."

Stannis snorted. "If you step in a nest of snakes, does it matter which one bites you first?"

"All this of snakes and incest is droll, but it changes nothing. You may

well have the better claim, Stannis, but I still have the larger army."
Renly's hand slid inside his cloak. Stannis saw, and reached at once for
the hilt of his sword, but before he could draw steel his brother pro-
duced . . . a peach. "Would you like one, brother?" Renly asked, smiling. "From Highgarden. You've never tasted anything so sweet, I promise
you." He took a bite. Juice ran from the corner of his mouth.

"I did not come here to eat fruit." Stannis was fuming.

"My lords!" Catelyn said. "We ought to be hammering out the terms
of an alliance, not trading taunts."

"A man should never refuse to taste a peach," Renly said as he tossed
the stone away. "He may never get the chance again. Life is short, Stannis. Remember what the Starks say. Winter is coming." He wiped his
mouth with the back of his hand.

"I did not come here to be threatened, either."

"Nor were you," Renly snapped back. "When I make threats, you'll
know it. If truth be told, I've never liked you, Stannis, but you *are* my
own blood, and I have no wish to slay you. So if it is Storm's End you
want, take it . . . as a brother's gift. As Robert once gave it to me, I give
it to you."

"It is not yours to give. It is mine by rights."

Sighing, Renly half turned in the saddle. "What am I to do with this
brother of mine, Brienne? He refuses my peach, he refuses my castle, he
even shunned my wedding . . ."

"We both know your wedding was a mummer's farce. A year ago you
were scheming to make the girl one of Robert's whores."

"A year ago I was scheming to make the girl Robert's queen," Renly
said, "but what does it matter? The boar got Robert and I got Margaery.
You'll be pleased to know she came to me a maid."

"In your bed she's like to die that way."

"Oh, I expect I'll get a son on her within the year. Pray, how many
sons do you have, Stannis? Oh, yes—none." Renly smiled innocently.
"As to your daughter, I understand. If my wife looked like yours, I'd send
my fool to service her as well."

"Enough!" Stannis roared. "I will not be mocked to my face, do you
hear me? *I will not!"* He yanked his longsword from its scabbard. The
steel gleamed strangely bright in the wan sunlight, now red, now yellow,
now blazing white. The air around it seemed to shimmer, as if from heat.

Catelyn's horse whinnied and backed away a step, but Brienne moved
between the brothers, her own blade in hand. "Put up your steel!" she
shouted at Stannis.

Cersei Lannister is laughing herself breathless, Catelyn thought wearily.

Stannis pointed his shining sword at his brother. "I am not without mercy," thundered he who was notoriously without mercy. "Nor do I wish to sully Lightbringer with a brother's blood. For the sake of the mother who bore us both, I will give you this night to rethink your folly, Renly. Strike your banners and come to me before dawn, and I will grant you Storm's End and your old seat on the council and even name you my heir until a son is born to me. Otherwise, I shall destroy you."

Renly laughed. "Stannis, that's a very pretty sword, I'll grant you, but I think the glow off it has ruined your eyes. Look across the fields, brother. Can you see all those banners?"

"Do you think a few bolts of cloth will make you king?"

"Tyrell swords will make me king. Rowan and Tarly and Caron will make me king, with axe and mace and warhammer. Tarth arrows and Penrose lances, Fossoway, Cuy, Mullendore, Estermont, Selmy, Hightower, Oakheart, Crane, Caswell, Blackbar, Morrigen, Beesbury, Shermer, Dunn, Footly . . . even House Florent, your own wife's brothers and uncles, they will make me king. All the chivalry of the south rides with me, and that is the least part of my power. My foot is coming behind, a hundred thousand swords and spears and pikes. And you will *destroy* me? With what, pray? That paltry rabble I see there huddled under the castle walls? I'll call them five thousand and be generous, codfish lords and onion knights and sellswords. Half of them are like to come over to me before the battle starts. You have fewer than four hundred horse, my scouts tell me—freeriders in boiled leather who will not stand an instant against armored lances. I do not care how seasoned a warrior you think you are, Stannis, that host of yours won't survive the first charge of my vanguard."

"We shall see, brother." Some of the light seemed to go out of the world when Stannis slid his sword back into its scabbard. "Come the dawn, we shall see."

"I hope your new god's a merciful one, brother."

Stannis snorted and galloped away, disdainful. The red priestess lingered a moment behind. "Look to your own sins, Lord Renly," she said as she wheeled her horse around.

Catelyn and Lord Renly returned together to the camp where his thousands and her few waited their return. "That was amusing, if not terribly profitable," he commented. "I wonder where I can get a sword like that? Well, doubtless Loras will make me a gift of it after the battle. It grieves me that it must come to this."

"You have a cheerful way of grieving," said Catelyn, whose distress was not feigned.

"Do I?" Renly shrugged. "So be it. Stannis was never the most cherished of brothers, I confess. Do you suppose this tale of his is true? If Joffrey is the Kingslayer's get—"

"—your brother is the lawful heir."

"While he lives," Renly admitted. "Though it's a fool's law, wouldn't you agree? Why the oldest son, and not the best-fitted? The crown will suit me, as it never suited Robert and would not suit Stannis. I have it in me to be a great king, strong yet generous, clever, just, diligent, loyal to my friends and terrible to my enemies, yet capable of forgiveness, patient—"

"—humble?" Catelyn supplied.

Renly laughed. "You must allow a king *some* flaws, my lady."

Catelyn felt very tired. It had all been for nothing. The Baratheon brothers would drown each other in blood while her son faced the Lannisters alone, and nothing she could say or do would stop it. *It is past time I went back to Riverrun to close my father's eyes,* she thought. *That much at least I can do. I may be a poor envoy, but I am a good mourner, gods save me.*

Their camp was well sited atop a low stony ridge that ran from north to south. It was far more orderly than the sprawling encampment on the Mander, though only a quarter as large. When he'd learned of his brother's assault on Storm's End, Renly had split his forces, much as Robb had done at the Twins. His great mass of foot he had left behind at Bitterbridge with his young queen, his wagons, carts, draft animals, and all his cumbersome siege machinery, while Renly himself led his knights and freeriders in a swift dash east.

How like his brother Robert he was, even in that . . . only Robert had always had Eddard Stark to temper his boldness with caution. Ned would surely have prevailed upon Robert to bring up his *whole* force, to encircle Stannis and besiege the besiegers. That choice Renly had denied himself in his headlong rush to come to grips with his brother. He had outdistanced his supply lines, left food and forage days behind with all his wagons and mules and oxen. He *must* come to battle soon, or starve.

Catelyn sent Hal Mollen to tend to their horses while she accompanied Renly back to the royal pavilion at the heart of the encampment. Inside the walls of green silk, his captains and lords bannermen were waiting to hear word of the parley. "My brother has not changed," their young king told them as Brienne unfastened his cloak and lifted the gold-and-jade crown from his brow. "Castles and courtesies will not appease him, he must have blood. Well, I am of a mind to grant his wish."

"Your Grace, I see no need for battle here," Lord Mathis Rowan put in. "The castle is strongly garrisoned and well provisioned, Ser Cortnay Penrose is a seasoned commander, and the trebuchet has not been built that could breach the walls of Storm's End. Let Lord Stannis have his siege. He will find no joy in it, and whilst he sits cold and hungry and profitless, we will take King's Landing."

"And have men say I feared to face Stannis?"

"Only fools will say that," Lord Mathis argued.

Renly looked to the others. "What say you all?"

"I say that Stannis is a danger to you," Lord Randyll Tarly declared. "Leave him unblooded and he will only grow stronger, while your own power is diminished by battle. The Lannisters will not be beaten in a day. By the time you are done with them, Lord Stannis may be as strong as you . . . or stronger."

Others chorused their agreement. The king looked pleased. "We shall fight, then."

I have failed Robb as I failed Ned, Catelyn thought. "My lord," she announced. "If you are set on battle, my purpose here is done. I ask your leave to return to Riverrun."

"You do not have it." Renly seated himself on a camp chair.

She stiffened. "I had hoped to help you make a peace, my lord. I will not help you make a war."

Renly gave a shrug. "I daresay we'll prevail without your five-and-twenty, my lady. I do not mean for you to take part in the battle, only to watch it."

"I was at the Whispering Wood, my lord. I have seen enough butchery. I came here an envoy—"

"And an envoy you shall leave," Renly said, "but wiser than you came. You shall see what befalls rebels with your own eyes, so your son can hear it from your own lips. We'll keep you safe, never fear." He turned away to make his dispositions. "Lord Mathis, you shall lead the center of my main battle. Bryce, you'll have the left. The right is mine. Lord Estermont, you shall command the reserve."

"I shall not fail you, Your Grace," Lord Estermont replied.

Lord Mathis Rowan spoke up. "Who shall have the van?"

"Your Grace," said Ser Jon Fossoway, "I beg the honor."

"Beg all you like," said Ser Guyard the Green, "by rights it should be one of the seven who strikes the first blow."

"It takes more than a pretty cloak to charge a shield wall," Randyll Tarly announced. "I was leading Mace Tyrell's van when you were still sucking on your mother's teat, Guyard."

A clamor filled the pavilion, as other men loudly set forth their claims. *The knights of summer,* Catelyn thought. Renly raised a hand. "Enough, my lords. If I had a dozen vans, all of you should have one, but the greatest glory by rights belongs to the greatest knight. Ser Loras shall strike the first blow."

"With a glad heart, Your Grace." The Knight of Flowers knelt before the king. "Grant me your blessing, and a knight to ride beside me with your banner. Let the stag and rose go to battle side by side."

Renly glanced about him. "Brienne."

"Your Grace?" She was still armored in her blue steel, though she had taken off her helm. The crowded tent was hot, and sweat plastered limp yellow hair to her broad, homely face. "My place is at your side. I am your sworn shield . . ."

"One of seven," the king reminded her. "Never fear, four of your fellows will be with me in the fight."

Brienne dropped to her knees. "If I must part from Your Grace, grant me the honor of arming you for battle."

Catelyn heard someone snigger behind her. *She loves him, poor thing,* she thought sadly. *She'd play his squire just to touch him, and never care how great a fool they think her.*

"Granted," Renly said. "Now leave me, all of you. Even kings must rest before a battle."

"My lord," Catelyn said, "there was a small sept in the last village we passed. If you will not permit me to depart for Riverrun, grant me leave to go there and pray."

"As you will. Ser Robar, give Lady Stark safe escort to this sept . . . but see that she returns to us by dawn."

"You might do well to pray yourself," Catelyn added.

"For victory?"

"For wisdom."

Renly laughed. "Loras, stay and help me pray. It's been so long I've quite forgotten how. As to the rest of you, I want every man in place by first light, armed, armored, and horsed. We shall give Stannis a dawn he will not soon forget."

Dusk was falling when Catelyn left the pavilion. Ser Robar Royce fell in beside her. She knew him slightly—one of Bronze Yohn's sons, comely in a rough-hewn way, a tourney warrior of some renown. Renly had gifted him with a rainbow cloak and a suit of blood red armor, and named him one of his seven. "You are a long way from the Vale, ser," she told him.

"And you far from Winterfell, my lady."

"I know what brought me here, but why have you come? This is not your battle, no more than it is mine."

"I made it my battle when I made Renly my king."

"The Royces are bannermen to House Arryn."

"My lord father owes Lady Lysa fealty, as does his heir. A second son must find glory where he can." Ser Robar shrugged. "A man grows weary of tourneys."

He could not be older than one-and-twenty, Catelyn thought, of an age with his king . . . but *her* king, her Robb, had more wisdom at fifteen than this youth had ever learned. Or so she prayed.

In Catelyn's small corner of the camp, Shadd was slicing carrots into a kettle, Hal Mollen was dicing with three of his Winterfell men, and Lucas Blackwood sat sharpening his dagger. "Lady Stark," Lucas said when he saw her, "Mollen says it is to be battle at dawn."

"Hal has the truth of it," she answered. *And a loose tongue as well, it would seem.*

"Do we fight or flee?"

"We pray, Lucas," she answered him. "We pray."

SANSA

The longer you keep him waiting, the worse it will go for you," Sandor Clegane warned her.

Sansa tried to hurry, but her fingers fumbled at buttons and knots. The Hound was always rough-tongued, but something in the way he had looked at her filled her with dread. Had Joffrey found out about her meetings with Ser Dontos? *Please no,* she thought as she brushed out her hair. Ser Dontos was her only hope. *I have to look pretty, Joff likes me to look pretty, he's always liked me in this gown, this color.* She smoothed the cloth down. The fabric was tight across her chest.

When she emerged, Sansa walked on the Hound's left, away from the burned side of his face. "Tell me what I've done."

"Not you. Your kingly brother."

"Robb's a traitor." Sansa knew the words by rote. "I had no part in whatever he did." *Gods be good, don't let it be the Kingslayer.* If Robb had harmed Jaime Lannister, it would mean her life. She thought of Ser Ilyn, and how those terrible pale eyes staring pitilessly out of that gaunt pockmarked face.

The Hound snorted. "They trained you well, little bird." He conducted her to the lower bailey, where a crowd had gathered around the archery butts. Men moved aside to let them through. She could hear Lord Gyles coughing. Loitering stablehands eyed her insolently, but Ser Horas Redwyne averted his gaze as she passed, and his brother Hobber pretended not to see her. A yellow cat was dying on the ground, mewling piteously, a crossbow quarrel through its ribs. Sansa stepped around it, feeling ill.

Ser Dontos approached on his broomstick horse; since he'd been too drunk to mount his destrier at the tourney, the king had decreed that henceforth he must always go horsed. "Be brave," he whispered, squeezing her arm.

Joffrey stood in the center of the throng, winding an ornate crossbow. Ser Boros and Ser Meryn were with him. The sight of them was enough to tie her insides in knots.

"Your Grace." She fell to her knees.

"Kneeling won't save you now," the king said. "Stand up. You're here to answer for your brother's latest treasons."

"Your Grace, whatever my traitor brother has done, I had no part. You know that, I beg you, please—"

"*Get her up!*"

The Hound pulled her to her feet, not ungently.

"Ser Lancel," Joff said, "tell her of this outrage."

Sansa had always thought Lancel Lannister comely and well spoken, but there was neither pity nor kindness in the look he gave her. "Using some vile sorcery, your brother fell upon Ser Stafford Lannister with an army of wargs, not three days ride from Lannisport. Thousands of good men were butchered as they slept, without the chance to lift sword. After the slaughter, the northmen feasted on the flesh of the slain."

Horror coiled cold hands around Sansa's throat.

"You have nothing to say?" asked Joffrey.

"Your Grace, the poor child is shocked witless," murmured Ser Dontos.

"Silence, fool." Joffrey lifted his crossbow and pointed it at her face. "You Starks are as unnatural as those wolves of yours. I've not forgotten how your monster savaged me."

"That was Arya's wolf," she said. "Lady never hurt you, but you killed her anyway."

"No, your father did," Joff said, "but I killed your father. I wish I'd done it myself. I killed a man last night who was bigger than your father. They came to the gate shouting my name and calling for bread like I was some *baker*, but I taught them better. I shot the loudest one right through the throat."

"And he died?" With the ugly iron head of the quarrel staring her in the face, it was hard to think what else to say.

"Of course he died, he had my quarrel in his throat. There was a woman throwing rocks, I got her as well, but only in the arm." Frowning, he lowered the crossbow. "I'd shoot you too, but if I do Mother says they'd kill my uncle Jaime. Instead you'll just be punished and we'll send word to your brother about what will happen to you if, he doesn't yield. Dog, hit her."

"Let me beat her!" Ser Dontos shoved forward, tin armor clattering. He was armed with a "morningstar" whose head was a melon. *My Florian.* She could have kissed him, blotchy skin and broken veins and all. He trotted his broomstick around her, shouting "Traitor, traitor" and whacking her over the head with the melon. Sansa covered herself with her hands, staggering every time the fruit pounded her, her hair sticky by the second blow. People were laughing. The melon flew to pieces. *Laugh, Joffrey,* she prayed as the juice ran down her face and the front of her blue silk gown. *Laugh and be satisfied.*

Joffrey did not so much as snigger. "Boros. Meryn."

Ser Meryn Trant seized Dontos by the arm and flung him brusquely away. The red-faced fool went sprawling, broomstick, melon, and all. Ser Boros seized Sansa.

"Leave her face," Joffrey commanded. "I like her pretty."

Boros slammed a fist into Sansa's belly, driving the air out of her. When she doubled over, the knight grabbed her hair and drew his sword, and for one hideous instant she was certain he meant to open her throat. As he laid the flat of the blade across her thighs, she thought her legs might break from the force of the blow. Sansa screamed. Tears welled in her eyes. *It will be over soon.* She soon lost count of the blows.

"Enough," she heard the Hound rasp.

"No it isn't," the king replied. "Boros, make her naked."

Boros shoved a meaty hand down the front of Sansa's bodice and gave a hard yank. The silk came tearing away, baring her to the waist. Sansa covered her breasts with her hands. She could hear sniggers, far off and cruel. "Beat her bloody," Joffrey said, "we'll see how her brother fancies—"

"What is the meaning of this?"

The Imp's voice cracked like a whip, and suddenly Sansa was free. She stumbled to her knees, arms crossed over her chest, her breath ragged. "Is this your notion of chivalry, Ser Boros?" Tyrion Lannister demanded angrily. His pet sellsword stood with him, and one of his wildlings, the one with the burned eye. "What sort of knight beats helpless maids?"

"The sort who serves his king, Imp." Ser Boros raised his sword, and Ser Meryn stepped up beside him, his blade scraping clear of its scabbard.

"Careful with those," warned the dwarf's sellsword. "You don't want to get blood all over those pretty white cloaks."

"Someone give the girl something to cover herself with," the Imp said.

Sandor Clegane unfastened his cloak and tossed it at her. Sansa clutched it against her chest, fists bunched hard in the white wool. The coarse weave was scratchy against her skin, but no velvet had ever felt so fine.

"This girl's to be your queen," the Imp told Joffrey. "Have you no regard for her honor?"

"I'm punishing her."

"For what crime? She did not fight her brother's battle."

"She has the blood of a wolf."

"And you have the wits of a goose."

"You can't talk to me that way. The king can do as he likes."

"Aerys Targaryen did as he liked. Has your mother ever told you what happened to him?"

Ser Boros Blount *harrumphed*. "No man threatens His Grace in the presence of the Kingsguard." ·

Tyrion Lannister raised an eyebrow. "I am not threatening the king, ser, I am educating my nephew. Bronn, Timett, the next time Ser Boros opens his mouth, kill him." The dwarf smiled. "Now *that* was a threat, ser. See the difference?"

Ser Boros turned a dark shade of red. "The queen will hear of this!"

"No doubt she will. And why wait? Joffrey, shall we send for your mother?"

The king flushed.

"Nothing to say, Your Grace?" his uncle went on. "Good. Learn to use your ears more and your mouth less, or your reign will be shorter than I am. Wanton brutality is no way to win your people's love . . . or your queen's."

"Fear is better than love, Mother says." Joffrey pointed at Sansa. "*She* fears me."

The Imp sighed. "Yes, I see. A pity Stannis and Renly aren't twelve-year-old girls as well. Bronn, Timett, bring her."

Sansa moved as if in a dream. She thought the Imp's men would take her back to her bedchamber in Maegor's Holdfast, but instead they conducted her to the Tower of the Hand. She had not set foot inside that place since the day her father fell from grace, and it made her feel faint to climb those steps again.

Some serving girls took charge of her, mouthing meaningless comforts to stop her shaking. One stripped off the ruins of her gown and small-clothes, and another bathed her and washed the sticky juice from her face and her hair. As they scrubbed her down with soap and sluiced warm water over her head, all she could see were the faces from the bailey. *Knights are sworn to defend the weak, protect women, and fight for the right, but none of them did a thing.* Only Ser Dontos had tried to help, and he was no longer a knight, no more than the Imp was, nor the Hound . . . the Hound hated knights . . . *I hate them too*, Sansa thought. *They are no true knights, not one of them.*

After she was clean, plump ginger-headed Maester Frenken came to see her. He bid her lie facedown on the mattress while he spread a salve across the angry red welts that covered the backs of her legs. Afterward he mixed her a draught of dreamwine, with some honey so it might go down easier. "Sleep a bit, child. When you wake, all this will seem a bad dream."

No it won't, you stupid man, Sansa thought, but she drank the dreamwine anyway, and slept.

It was dark when she woke again, not quite knowing where she was, the room both strange and strangely familiar. As she rose, a stab of pain went through her legs and brought it all back. Tears filled her eyes. Someone had laid out a robe for her beside the bed. Sansa slipped it on and opened the door. Outside stood a hard-faced woman with leathery brown skin, three necklaces looped about her scrawny neck. One was gold and one was silver and one was made of human ears. "Where does she think she's going?" the woman asked, leaning on a tall spear.

"The godswood." She had to find Ser Dontos, beg him to take her home *now* before it was too late.

"The halfman said you're not to leave," the woman said. "Pray here, the gods will hear."

Meekly, Sansa dropped her eyes and retreated back inside. She realized suddenly why this place seemed so familiar. *They've put me in Arya's old bedchamber, from when Father was the Hand of the King. All her things are gone and the furnishings have been moved around, but it's the same . . .*

A short time later, a serving girl brought a platter of cheese and bread and olives, with a flagon of cold water. "Take it away," Sansa commanded, but the girl left the food on a table. She *was* thirsty, she realized. Every step sent knives through her thighs, but she made herself cross the room. She drank two cups of water, and was nibbling on an olive when the knock came.

Anxiously, she turned toward the door, smoothed down the folds of her robe. "Yes?"

The door opened, and Tyrion Lannister stepped inside. "My lady. I trust I am not disturbing you?"

"Am I your prisoner?"

"My guest." He was wearing his chain of office, a necklace of linked golden hands. "I thought we might talk."

"As my lord commands." Sansa found it hard not to stare; his face was so ugly it held a queer fascination for her.

"The food and garments are to your satisfaction?" he asked. "If there is anything else you need, you have only to ask."

"You are most kind. And this morning . . . it was very good of you to help me."

"You have a right to know why Joffrey was so wroth. Six nights gone, your brother fell upon my uncle Stafford, encamped with his host at a village called Oxcross not three days ride from Casterly Rock. Your northerners won a crushing victory. We received word only this morning."

Robb will kill you all, she thought, exulting. "It's . . . terrible, my lord. My brother is a vile traitor."

The dwarf smiled wanly. "Well, he's no fawn, he's made that clear enough."

"Ser Lancel said Robb led an army of wargs . . ."

The Imp gave a disdainful bark of laughter. "Ser Lancel's a wineskin warrior who wouldn't know a warg from a wart. Your brother had his direwolf with him, but I suspect that's as far as it went. The northmen crept into my uncle's camp and cut his horse lines, and Lord Stark sent his wolf among them. Even war-trained destriers went mad. Knights were trampled to death in their pavilions, and the rabble woke in terror and fled, casting aside their weapons to run the faster. Ser Stafford was slain as he chased after a horse. Lord Rickard Karstark drove a lance through his chest. Ser Rubert Brax is also dead, along with Ser Lymond Vikary, Lord Crakehall, and Lord Jast. Half a hundred more have been taken captive, including Jast's sons and my nephew Martyn Lannister. Those who survived are spreading wild tales and swearing that the old gods of the north march with your brother."

"Then . . . there was no sorcery?"

Lannister snorted. "Sorcery is the sauce fools spoon over failure to hide the flavor of their own incompetence. My mutton-headed uncle had not even troubled to post sentries, it would seem. His host was raw—apprentice boys, miners, fieldhands, fisherfolk, the sweepings of Lannisport. The only mystery is how your brother reached him. Our forces still hold the stronghold at the Golden Tooth, and they swear he did not pass." The dwarf gave an irritated shrug. "Well, Robb Stark is my father's bane. Joffrey is mine. Tell me, what do you feel for my kingly nephew?"

"I love him with all my heart," Sansa said at once.

"Truly?" He did not sound convinced. "Even now?"

"My love for His Grace is greater than it has ever been."

The Imp laughed aloud. "Well, someone has taught you to lie well. You may be grateful for that one day, child. You *are* a child still, are you not? Or have you flowered?"

Sansa blushed. It was a rude question, but the shame of being stripped before half the castle made it seem like nothing. "No, my lord."

"That's all to the good. If it gives you any solace, I do not intend that you ever wed Joffrey. No marriage will reconcile Stark and Lannister after all that has happened, I fear. More's the pity. The match was one of King Robert's better notions, if Joffrey hadn't mucked it up."

She knew she ought to say something, but the words caught in her throat.

"You grow very quiet," Tyrion Lannister observed. "Is this what you want? An end to your betrothal?"

"I . . ." Sansa did not know what to say. *Is it a trick? Will he punish me if I tell the truth?* She stared at the dwarf's brutal bulging brow, the hard black eye and the shrewd green one, the crooked teeth and wiry beard. "I only want to be loyal."

"Loyal," the dwarf mused, "and far from any Lannisters. I can scarce blame you for that. When I was your age, I wanted the same thing." He smiled. "They tell me you visit the godswood every day. What do you pray for, Sansa?"

I pray for Robb's victory and Joffrey's death . . . and for home. For Winterfell. "I pray for an end to the fighting."

"We'll have that soon enough. There will be another battle, between your brother Robb and my lord father, and that will settle the issue."

Robb will beat him, Sansa thought. *He beat your uncle and your brother Jaime, he'll beat your father too.*

It was as if her face were an open book, so easily did the dwarf read her hopes. "Do not take Oxcross too much to heart, my lady," he told her, not unkindly. "A battle is not a war, and my lord father is assuredly not my uncle Stafford. The next time you visit the godswood, pray that your brother has the wisdom to bend the knee. Once the north returns to the king's peace, I mean to send you home." He hopped down off the window seat and said, "You may sleep here tonight. I'll give you some of my own men as a guard, some Stone Crows perhaps—"

"No," Sansa blurted out, aghast. If she was locked in the Tower of the Hand, guarded by the dwarf's men, how would Ser Dontos ever spirit her away to freedom?

"Would you prefer Black Ears? I'll give you Chella if a woman would make you more at ease."

"Please, no, my lord, the wildlings frighten me."

He grinned. "Me as well. But more to the point, they frighten Joffrey and that nest of sly vipers and lickspittle dogs he calls a Kingsguard. With Chella or Timett by your side, no one would dare offer you harm."

"I would sooner return to my own bed." A lie came to her suddenly, but it seemed so *right* that she blurted it out at once. "This tower was where my father's men were slain. Their ghosts would give me terrible dreams, and I would see their blood wherever I looked."

Tyrion Lannister studied her face. "I am no stranger to nightmares, Sansa. Perhaps you are wiser than I knew. Permit me at least to escort you safely back to your own chambers."

CATELYN

It was full dark before they found the village. Catelyn found herself wondering if the place had a name. If so, its people had taken that knowledge with them when they fled, along with all they owned, down to the candles in the sept. Ser Wendel lit a torch and led her through the low door.

Within, the seven walls were cracked and crooked. *God is one*, Septon Osmynd had taught her when she was a girl, *with seven aspects, as the sept is a single building, with seven walls*. The wealthy septs of the cities had statues of the Seven and an altar to each. In Winterfell, Septon Chayle hung carved masks from each wall. Here Catelyn found only rough charcoal drawings. Ser Wendel set the torch in a sconce near the door, and left to wait outside with Robar Royce.

Catelyn studied the faces. The Father was bearded, as ever. The Mother smiled, loving and protective. The Warrior had his sword sketched in beneath his face, the Smith his hammer. The Maid was beautiful, the Crone wizened and wise.

And the seventh face . . . the Stranger was neither male nor female, yet both, ever the outcast, the wanderer from far places, less and more than human, unknown and unknowable. Here the face was a black oval, a shadow with stars for eyes. It made Catelyn uneasy. She would get scant comfort there.

She knelt before the Mother. "My lady, look down on this battle with a mother's eyes. They are all sons, every one. Spare them if you can, and spare my own sons as well. Watch over Robb and Bran and Rickon. Would that I were with them."

A crack ran down through the Mother's left eye. It made her look as if she were crying. Catelyn could hear Ser Wendel's booming voice, and now and again Ser Robar's quiet answers, as they talked of the coming battle. Otherwise the night was still. Not even a cricket could be heard, and the gods kept their silence. *Did your old gods ever answer you, Ned?* she wondered. *When you knelt before your heart tree, did they hear you?*

Flickering torchlight danced across the walls, making the faces seem half-alive, twisting them, changing them. The statues in the great septs of the cities wore the faces the stonemasons had given them, but these charcoal scratchings were so crude they might be anyone. The Father's face made her think of her own father, dying in his bed at Riverrun. The Warrior was Renly and Stannis, Robb and Robert, Jaime Lannister and Jon Snow. She even glimpsed Arya in those lines, just for an instant. Then a gust of wind through the door made the torch sputter, and the semblance was gone, washed away in orange glare.

The smoke was making her eyes burn. She rubbed at them with the heels of her scarred hands. When she looked up at the Mother again, it was her own mother she saw. Lady Minisa Tully had died in childbed, trying to give Lord Hoster a second son. The baby had perished with her, and afterward some of the life had gone out of Father. *She was always so calm,* Catelyn thought, remembering her mother's soft hands, her warm smile. *If she had lived, how different our lives might have been.* She wondered what Lady Minisa would make of her eldest daughter, kneeling here before her. *I have come so many thousands of leagues, and for what? Who have I served? I have lost my daughters, Robb does not want me, and Bran and Rickon must surely think me a cold and unnatural mother. I was not even with Ned when he died . . .*

Her head swam, and the sept seemed to move around her. The shadows swayed and shifted, furtive animals racing across the cracked white walls. Catelyn had not eaten today. Perhaps that had been unwise. She told herself that there had been no time, but the truth was that food had lost its savor in a world without Ned. *When they took his head off, they killed me too.*

Behind her the torch spit, and suddenly it seemed to her that it was her sister's face on the wall, though the eyes were harder than she recalled, not Lysa's eyes but Cersei's. *Cersei is a mother too. No matter who fathered those children, she felt them kick inside her, brought them forth with her pain and blood, nursed them at her breast. If they are truly Jaime's . . .*

"Does Cersei pray to you too, my lady?" Catelyn asked the Mother. She could see the proud, cold, lovely features of the Lannister queen etched upon the wall. The crack was still there; even Cersei could weep for her children. "Each of the Seven embodies all of the Seven," Septon Osmynd had told her once. There was as much beauty in the Crone as in the Maiden, and the Mother could be fiercer than the Warrior when her children were in danger. *Yes* . . .

She had seen enough of Robert Baratheon at Winterfell to know that the king did not regard Joffrey with any great warmth. If the boy was truly Jaime's seed, Robert would have put him to death along with his mother, and few would have condemned him. Bastards were common enough, but incest was a monstrous sin to both old gods and new, and the children of such wickedness were named abominations in sept and godswood alike. The dragon kings had wed brother to sister, but they were the blood of old Valyria where such practices had been common, and like their dragons the Targaryens answered to neither gods nor men.

Ned must have known, and Lord Arryn before him. Small wonder that the queen had killed them both. *Would I do any less for my own?* Catelyn clenched her hands, feeling the tightness in her scarred fingers where the assassin's steel had cut to the bone as she fought to save her son. "Bran knows too," she whispered, lowering her head. *Gods be good, he must have seen something, heard something, that was why they tried to kill him in his bed.*

Lost and weary, Catelyn Stark gave herself over to her gods. She knelt before the Smith, who fixed things that were broken, and asked that he give her sweet Bran his protection. She went to the Maid and beseeched her to lend her courage to Arya and Sansa, to guard them in their innocence. To the Father, she prayed for justice, the strength to seek it and the wisdom to know it, and she asked the Warrior to keep Robb strong and shield him in his battles. Lastly she turned to the Crone, whose statues often showed her with a lamp in one hand. "Guide me, wise lady," she prayed. "Show me the path I must walk, and do not let me stumble in the dark places that lie ahead."

Finally there were footsteps behind her, and a noise at the door. "My lady," Ser Robar said gently, "pardon, but our time is at an end. We must be back before the dawn breaks."

Catelyn rose stiffly. Her knees ached, and she would have given much for a featherbed and a pillow just then. "Thank you, ser. I am ready."

They rode in silence through sparse woodland where the trees leaned drunkenly away from the sea. The nervous whinny of horses and the clank of steel guided them back to Renly's camp. The long ranks of man and horse were armored in darkness, as black as if the Smith had hammered night itself into steel. There were banners to her right, banners to her left, and rank on rank of banners before her, but in the predawn gloom, neither colors nor sigils could be discerned. *A grey army*, Catelyn thought. *Grey men on grey horses beneath grey banners.* As they sat their horses waiting, Renly's shadow knights pointed their lances upward, so she rode through a forest of tall naked trees, bereft of leaves and life. Where Storm's End stood was only a deeper darkness, a wall of black through which no stars could shine, but she could see torches moving across the fields where Lord Stannis had made his camp.

The candles within Renly's pavilion made the shimmering silken walls seem to glow, transforming the great tent into a magical castle alive with emerald light. Two of the Rainbow Guard stood sentry at the door to the royal pavilion. The green light shone strangely against the purple plums of Ser Parmen's surcoat, and gave a sickly hue to the sunflowers that covered every inch of Ser Emmon's enameled yellow plate. Long silken plumes flew from their helms, and rainbow cloaks draped their shoulders.

Within, Catelyn found Brienne armoring the king for battle while the Lords Tarly and Rowan spoke of dispositions and tactics. It was pleasantly warm inside, the heat shimmering off the coals in a dozen small iron braziers. "I must speak with you, Your Grace," she said, granting him a king's style for once, anything to make him heed her.

"In a moment, Lady Catelyn," Renly replied. Brienne fit backplate to breastplate over his quilted tunic. The king's armor was a deep green, the green of leaves in a summer wood, so dark it drank the candlelight. Gold highlights gleamed from inlay and fastenings like distant fires in that wood, winking every time he moved. "Pray continue, Lord Mathis."

"Your Grace," Mathis Rowan said with a sideways glance at Catelyn. "As I was saying, our battles are well drawn up. Why wait for daybreak? Sound the advance."

"And have it said that I won by treachery, with an unchivalrous attack? Dawn was the chosen hour."

"Chosen by Stannis," Randyll Tarly pointed out. "He'd have us charge into the teeth of the rising sun. We'll be half-blind."

"Only until first shock," Renly said confidently. "Ser Loras will break them, and after that it will be chaos." Brienne tightened green leather straps and buckled golden buckles. "When my brother falls, see that no insult is done to his corpse. He is my own blood, I will not have his head paraded about on a spear."

"And if he yields?" Lord Tarly asked.

"Yields?" Lord Rowan laughed. "When Mace Tyrell laid siege to Storm's End, Stannis ate rats rather than open his gates."

"Well I remember." Renly lifted his chin to allow Brienne to fasten his gorget in place. "Near the end, Ser Gawen Wylde and three of his knights tried to steal out a postern gate to surrender. Stannis caught them and ordered them flung from the walls with catapults. I can still see Gawen's face as they strapped him down. He had been our master-at-arms."

Lord Rowan appeared puzzled. "No men were hurled from the walls. I would surely remember that."

"Maester Cressen told Stannis that we might be forced to eat our dead, and there was no gain in flinging away good meat." Renly pushed back his hair. Brienne bound it with a velvet tie and pulled a padded cap down over his ears, to cushion the weight of his helm. "Thanks to the Onion Knight we were never reduced to dining on corpses, but it was a close thing. Too close for Ser Gawen, who died in his cell."

"Your Grace." Catelyn had waited patiently, but time grew short. "You promised me a word."

Renly nodded. "See to your battles, my lords . . . oh, and if Barristan Selmy is at my brother's side, I want him spared."

"There's been no word of Ser Barristan since Joffrey cast him out," Lord Rowan objected.

"I know that old man. He needs a king to guard, or who is he? Yet he never came to me, and Lady Catelyn says he is not with Robb Stark at Riverrun. Where else but with Stannis?"

"As you say, Your Grace. No harm will come to him." The lords bowed deeply and departed.

"Say your say, Lady Stark," Renly said. Brienne swept his cloak over his broad shoulders. It was cloth-of-gold, heavy, with the crowned stag of Baratheon picked out in flakes of jet.

"The Lannisters tried to kill my son Bran. A thousand times I have asked myself why. Your brother gave me my answer. There was a hunt the day he fell. Robert and Ned and most of the other men rode out after boar, but Jaime Lannister remained at Winterfell, as did the queen."

Renly was not slow to take the implication. "So you believe the boy caught them at their incest . . ."

"I beg you, my lord, grant me leave to go to your brother Stannis and tell him what I suspect."

"To what end?"

"Robb will set aside his crown if you and your brother will do the same," she said, hoping it was true. She would *make* it true if she must; Robb would listen to her, even if his lords would not. "Let the three of you call for a Great Council, such as the realm has not seen for a hundred years. We will send to Winterfell, so Bran may tell his tale and all men may know the Lannisters for the true usurpers. Let the assembled lords of the Seven Kingdoms choose who shall rule them."

Renly laughed. "Tell me, my lady, do direwolves vote on who should lead the pack?" Brienne brought the king's gauntlets and greathelm, crowned with golden antlers that would add a foot and a half to his height. "The time for talk is done. Now we see who is stronger." Renly pulled a lobstered green-and-gold gauntlet over his left hand, while Brienne knelt to buckle on his belt, heavy with the weight of longsword and dagger.

"I beg you in the name of the Mother," Catelyn began when a sudden gust of wind flung open the door of the tent. She thought she glimpsed movement, but when she turned her head, it was only the king's shadow shifting against the silken walls. She heard Renly begin a jest, his shadow moving, lifting its sword, black on green, candles guttering, shivering, something was queer, wrong, and then she saw Renly's sword still in its scabbard, sheathed still, but the shadowsword . . .

"Cold," said Renly in a small puzzled voice, a heartbeat before the steel of his gorget parted like cheesecloth beneath the shadow of a blade that was not there. He had time to make a small thick gasp before the blood came gushing out of his throat.

"Your Gr—*no!*" cried Brienne the Blue when she saw that evil flow, sounding as scared as any little girl. The king stumbled into her arms, a sheet of blood creeping down the front of his armor, a dark red tide that drowned his green and gold. More candles guttered out. Renly tried to speak, but he was choking on his own blood. His legs collapsed, and only Brienne's strength held him up. She threw back her head and screamed, wordless in her anguish.

The shadow. Something dark and evil had happened here, she knew, something that she could not begin to understand. *Renly never cast that shadow. Death came in that door and blew the life out of him as swift as the wind snuffed out his candles.*

Only a few instants passed before Robar Royce and Emmon Cuy came bursting in, though it felt like half the night. A pair of men-at-arms crowded in behind with torches. When they saw Renly in Brienne's arms, and her drenched with the king's blood, Ser Robar gave a cry of horror. "Wicked woman!" screamed Ser Emmon, he of the sunflowered steel. "Away from him, you vile creature!"

"Gods be good, Brienne, *why?*" asked Ser Robar.

Brienne looked up from her king's body. The rainbow cloak that hung from her shoulders had turned red where the king's blood had soaked into the cloth. "I . . . I . . ."

"You'll die for this." Ser Emmon snatched up a long-handled battle-axe from the weapons piled near the door. "You'll pay for the king's life with your own!"

"*NO!*" Catelyn Stark screamed, finding her voice at last, but it was too late, the blood madness was on them, and they rushed forward with shouts that drowned her softer words.

Brienne moved faster than Catelyn would have believed. Her own sword was not to hand, so she snatched Renly's from its scabbard and raised it to catch Emmon's axe on the downswing. A spark flashed blue-white as steel met steel with a rending crash, and Brienne sprang to her feet, the body of the dead king thrust rudely aside. Ser Emmon stumbled over it as he tried to close, and Brienne's blade sheared through the wooden haft to send his axehead spinning. Another man thrust a flaming torch at her back, but the rainbow cloak was too sodden with blood to burn. Brienne spun and cut, and torch and hand went flying. Flames crept across the carpet. The maimed man began to scream. Ser Emmon dropped the axe and fumbled for his sword. The second man-at-arms lunged, Brienne parried, and their swords danced and clanged against each other. When Emmon Cuy came wading back in, Brienne was forced to retreat, yet somehow she held them both at bay. On the ground, Renly's head rolled sickeningly to one side, and a second mouth yawned wide, the blood coming from him now in slow pulses.

Ser Robar had hung back, uncertain, but now he was reaching for his hilt. "Robar, no, listen." Catelyn seized his arm. "You do her wrong, it was not her. *Help her!* Hear me, it was Stannis." The name was on her lips before she could think how it got there, but as she said it, she knew that it was true. "I swear it, you know me, it was *Stannis* killed him."

The young rainbow knight stared at this madwoman with pale and frightened eyes. "Stannis? How?"

"I do not know. Sorcery, some dark magic, there was a shadow, a *shadow.*" Her own voice sounded wild and crazed to her, but the words poured out in a rush as the blades continued to clash behind her. "A shadow with a sword, I swear it, I saw. Are you blind, the girl *loved* him! *Help her!*" She glanced back, saw the second guardsman fall, his blade dropping from limp fingers. Outside there was shouting. More angry men would be bursting in on them any instant, she knew. "She is innocent, Robar. You have my word, on my husband's grave and my honor as a Stark!"

That resolved him. "I will hold them," Ser Robar said. "Get her away." He turned and went out.

The fire had reached the wall and was creeping up the side of the tent. Ser Emmon was pressing Brienne hard, him in his enameled yellow steel and her in wool. He had forgotten Catelyn, until the iron brazier came crashing into the back of his head. Helmed as he was, the blow did no lasting harm, but it sent him to his knees. "Brienne, with me," Catelyn commanded. The girl was not slow to see the chance. A slash, and the green silk parted. They stepped out into darkness and the chill of dawn. Loud voices came from the other side of the pavilion. "This way," Catelyn urged, "and slowly. We must not run, or they will ask why. Walk easy, as if nothing were amiss."

Brienne thrust her sword blade through her belt and fell in beside Catelyn. The night air smelled of rain. Behind them, the king's pavilion was well ablaze, flames rising high against the dark. No one made any move to stop them. Men rushed past them, shouting of fire and murder and sorcery. Others stood in small groups and spoke in low voices. A few were praying, and one young squire was on his knees, sobbing openly.

Renly's battles were already coming apart as the rumors spread from mouth to mouth. The nightfires had burned low, and as the east began to lighten the immense mass of Storm's End emerged like a dream of stone while wisps of pale mist raced across the field, flying from the sun on wings of wind. *Morning ghosts,* she had heard Old Nan call them once, spirits returning to their graves. And Renly one of them now, gone like his brother Robert, like her own dear Ned.

"I never held him but as he died," Brienne said quietly as they walked through the spreading chaos. Her voice sounded as if she might break at any instant. "He was laughing one moment, and suddenly the blood was everywhere . . . my lady, I do not understand. Did you see, did you . . . ?"

"I saw a shadow. I thought it was Renly's shadow at the first, but it was his brother's."

"Lord Stannis?"

"I *felt* him. It makes no sense, I know . . ."

It made sense enough for Brienne. "I will kill him," the tall homely girl declared. "With my lord's own sword, I will kill him. I swear it. I swear it. I swear it."

Hal Mollen and the rest of her escort were waiting with the horses. Ser Wendel Manderly was all in a lather to know what was happening. "My lady, the camp has gone mad," he blurted when he saw them. "Lord Renly, is he—" He stopped suddenly, staring at Brienne and the blood that drenched her.

"Dead, but not by our hands."

"The battle—" Hal Mollen began.

"There will be no battle." Catelyn mounted, and her escort formed up about her, with Ser Wendel to her left and Ser Perwyn Frey on her right. "Brienne, we brought mounts enough for twice our number. Choose one, and come with us."

"I have my own horse, my lady. And my armor—"

"Leave them. We must be well away before they think to look for us. We were both with the king when he was killed. That will not be forgotten." Wordless, Brienne turned and did as she was bid. "Ride," Catelyn commanded her escort when they were all ahorse. "If any man tries to stop us, cut him down."

As the long fingers of dawn fanned across the fields, color was returning to the world. Where grey men had sat grey horses armed with shadow spears, the points of ten thousand lances now glinted silvery cold, and on the myriad flapping banners Catelyn saw the blush of red and pink and orange, the richness of blues and browns, the blaze of gold and yellow. All the power of Storm's End and Highgarden, the power that had been Renly's an hour ago. *They belong to Stannis now,* she realized, *even if they do not know it themselves yet. Where else are they to turn, if not to the last Baratheon? Stannis has won all with a single evil stroke.*

I am the rightful king, he had declared, his jaw clenched hard as iron, *and your son no less a traitor than my brother here. His day will come as well.*

A chill went through her.

JON

The hill jutted above the dense tangle of forest, rising solitary and sudden, its windswept heights visible from miles off. The wildlings called it the Fist of the First Men, rangers said. It *did* look like a fist, Jon Snow thought, punching up through earth and wood, its bare brown slopes knuckled with stone.

He rode to the top with Lord Mormont and the officers, leaving Ghost below under the trees. The direwolf had run off three times as they climbed, twice returning reluctantly to Jon's whistle. The third time, the Lord Commander lost patience and snapped, "Let him go, boy. I want to reach the crest before dusk. Find the wolf later."

The way up was steep and stony, the summit crowned by a chest-high wall of tumbled rocks. They had to circle some distance west before they found a gap large enough to admit the horses. "This is good ground, Thoren," the Old Bear proclaimed when at last they attained the top. "We could scarce hope for better. We'll make our camp here to await Halfhand." The Lord Commander swung down off his saddle, dislodging the raven from his shoulder. Complaining loudly, the bird took to the air.

The views atop the hill were bracing, yet it was the ringwall that drew Jon's eye, the weathered grey stones with their white patches of lichen, their beards of green moss. It was said that the Fist had been a ringfort of the First Men in the Dawn Age. "An old place, and strong," Thoren Smallwood said.

"*Old*," Mormont's raven screamed as it flapped in noisy circles about their heads. "*Old, old, old.*"

"Quiet," Mormont growled up at the bird. The Old Bear was too proud to admit to weakness, but Jon was not deceived. The strain of keeping up with younger men was taking its toll.

"These heights will be easy to defend, if need be," Thoren pointed out as he walked his horse along the ring of stones, his sable-trimmed cloak stirring in the wind.

"Yes, this place will do." The Old Bear lifted a hand to the wind, and raven landed on his forearm, claws scrabbling against his black ringmail.

"What about water, my lord?" Jon wondered.

"We crossed a brook at the foot of the hill."

"A long climb for a drink," Jon pointed out, "and outside the ring of stones."

Thoren said, "Are you too lazy to climb a hill, boy?"

When Lord Mormont said, "We're not like to find another place as strong. We'll carry water, and make certain we are well supplied," Jon knew better than to argue. So the command was given, and the brothers of the Night's Watch raised their camp behind the stone ring the First Men had made. Black tents sprouted like mushrooms after a rain, and blankets and bedrolls covered the bare ground. Stewards tethered the garrons in long lines, and saw them fed and watered. Foresters took their axes to the trees in the waning afternoon light to harvest enough wood to see them through the night. A score of builders set to clearing brush, digging latrines, and untying their bundles of fire-hardened stakes. "I will have every opening in the ringwall ditched and staked before dark," the Old Bear had commanded.

Once he'd put up the Lord Commander's tent and seen to their horses, Jon Snow descended the hill in search of Ghost. The direwolf came at once, all in silence. One moment Jon was striding beneath the trees, whistling and shouting, alone in the green, pinecones and fallen leaves under his feet; the next, the great white direwolf was walking beside him, pale as morning mist.

But when they reached the ringfort, Ghost balked again. He padded forward warily to sniff at the gap in the stones, and then retreated, as if he did not like what he'd smelled. Jon tried to grab him by the scruff of his neck and haul him bodily inside the ring, no easy task; the wolf weighed as much as he did, and was stronger by far. "Ghost, what's *wrong* with you?" It was not like him to be so unsettled. In the end Jon had to give it up. "As you will," he told the wolf. "Go, hunt." The red eyes watched him as he made his way back through the mossy stones.

They ought to be safe here. The hill offered commanding views, and the slopes were precipitous to the north and west and only slightly more gentle to the east. Yet as the dusk deepened and darkness seeped into the hollows between the trees, Jon's sense of foreboding grew. *This is the haunted forest,* he told himself. *Maybe there are ghosts here, the spirits of the First Men. This was their place, once.*

"Stop acting the boy," he told himself. Clambering atop the piled rocks, Jon gazed off toward the setting sun. He could see the light shimmering like hammered gold off the surface of the Milkwater as it curved away to the south. Upriver the land was more rugged, the dense forest giving way to a series of bare stony hills that rose high and wild to the north and west. On the horizon stood the mountains like a great shadow, range on range of them receding into the blue-grey distance, their jagged peaks sheathed eternally in snow. Even from afar they looked vast and cold and inhospitable.

Closer at hand, it was the trees that ruled. To south and east the wood went on as far as Jon could see, a vast tangle of root and limb painted in a thousand shades of green, with here and there a patch of red where a weirwood shouldered through the pines and sentinels, or a blush of yellow where some broadleafs had begun to turn. When the wind blew, he could hear the creak and groan of branches older than he was. A thousand leaves fluttered, and for a moment the forest seemed a deep green sea, storm-tossed and heaving, eternal and unknowable.

Ghost was not like to be alone down there, he thought. Anything could be moving under that sea, creeping toward the ringfort through the dark of the wood, concealed beneath those trees. *Anything.* How would they ever know? He stood there for a long time, until the sun vanished behind the saw-toothed mountains and darkness began to creep through the forest.

"Jon?" Samwell Tarly called up. "I thought it looked like you. Are you well?"

"Well enough." Jon hopped down. "How did you fare today?"

"Well. I fared well. Truly."

Jon was not about to share his disquiet with his friend, not when Samwell Tarly was at last beginning to find his courage. "The Old Bear means to wait here for Qhorin Halfhand and the men from the Shadow Tower."

"It seems a strong place," said Sam. "A ringfort of the First Men. Do you think there were battles fought here?"

"No doubt. You'd best get a bird ready. Mormont will want to send back word."

"I wish I could send them all. They hate being caged."

"You would too, if you could fly."

"If I could fly, I'd be back at Castle Black eating a pork pie," said Sam. Jon clapped him on the shoulder with his burned hand. They walked back through the camp together. Cookfires were being lit all around them. Overhead, the stars were coming out. The long red tail of Mormont's Torch burned as bright as the moon. Jon heard the ravens before he saw them. Some were calling his name. The birds were not shy when it came to making noise.

They feel it too. "I'd best see to the Old Bear," he said. "He gets noisy when he isn't fed as well."

He found Mormont talking with Thoren Smallwood and half a dozen other officers. "There you are," the old man said gruffly. "Bring us some hot wine, if you would. The night is chilly."

"Yes, my lord." Jon built a cookfire, claimed a small cask of Mormont's favorite robust red from stores, and poured it into a kettle. He hung the kettle above the flames while he gathered the rest of his ingredients. The Old Bear was particular about his hot spiced wine. So much cinnamon and so much nutmeg and so much honey, not a drop more. Raisins and nuts and dried berries, but no lemon, that was the rankest sort of southron heresy—which was queer, since he always took lemon in his morning beer. The drink must be hot to warm a man properly, the Lord Commander insisted, but the wine must never be allowed to come to a boil. Jon kept a careful eye on the kettle.

As he worked, he could hear the voices from inside the tent. Jarman Buckwell said, "The easiest road up into the Frostfangs is to follow the Milkwater back to its source. Yet if we go that path, Rayder will know of our approach, certain as sunrise."

"The Giant's Stair might serve," said Ser Mallador Locke, "or the Skirling Pass, if it's clear."

The wine was steaming. Jon lifted the kettle off the fire, filled eight cups, and carried them into the tent. The Old Bear was peering at the crude map Sam had drawn him that night back in Craster's Keep. He took a cup from Jon's tray, tried a swallow of wine, and gave a brusque nod of approval. His raven hopped down his arm. *"Corn,"* it said. *"Corn. Corn."*

Ser Ottyn Wythers waved the wine away. "I would not go into the mountains at all," he said in a thin, tired voice. "The Frostfangs have a cruel bite even in summer, and now . . . if we should be caught by a storm . . ."

"I do not mean to risk the Frostfangs unless I must," said Mormont. "Wildlings can no more live on snow and stone than we can. They will emerge from the heights soon, and for a host of any size, the only route is along the Milkwater. If so, we are strongly placed here. They cannot hope to slip by us."

"They may not wish to. They are thousands, and we will be three hundred when the Halfhand reaches us." Ser Mallador accepted a cup from Jon.

"If it comes to battle, we could not hope for better ground than here," declared Mormont. "We'll strengthen the defenses. Pits and spikes, caltrops scattered on the slopes, every breach mended. Jarman, I'll want your sharpest eyes as watchers. A ring of them, all around us and along the river, to warn of any approach. Hide them up in trees. And we had best start bringing up water too, more than we need. We'll dig cisterns. It will keep the men occupied, and may prove needful later."

"My rangers—" started Thoren Smallwood.

"Your rangers will limit their ranging to this side of the river until the Halfhand reaches us. After that, we'll see. I will not lose more of my men."

"Mance Rayder might be massing his host a day's ride from here, and we'd never know," Smallwood complained.

"We know where the wildlings are massing," Mormont came back. "We had it from Craster. I mislike the man, but I do not think he lied to us in this."

"As you say." Smallwood took a sullen leave. The others finished their wine and followed, more courteously.

"Shall I bring you supper, my lord?" Jon asked.

"Corn," the raven cried. Mormont did not answer at once. When he did he said only, "Did your wolf find game today?"

"He's not back yet."

"We could do with fresh meat." Mormont dug into a sack and offered his raven a handful of corn. "You think I'm wrong to keep the rangers close?"

"That's not for me to say, my lord."

"It is if you're asked."

"If the rangers must stay in sight of the Fist, I don't see how they can hope to find my uncle," Jon admitted.

"They can't." The raven pecked at the kernels in the Old Bear's palm. "Two hundred men or ten thousand, the country is too vast." The corn gone, Mormont turned his hand over.

"You would not give up the search?"

"Maester Aemon thinks you clever." Mormont moved the raven to his shoulder. The bird tilted its head to one side, little eyes a-glitter.

The answer was there. "Is it . . . it seems to me that it might be easier for one man to find two hundred than for two hundred to find one."

The raven gave a cackling scream, but the Old Bear smiled through the grey of his beard. "This many men and horses leave a trail even

Aemon could follow. On this hill, our fires ought to be visible as far off as the foothills of the Frostfangs. If Ben Stark is alive and free, he will come to us, I have no doubt."

"Yes," said Jon, "but . . . what if . . ."

". . . he's dead?" Mormont asked, not unkindly.

Jon nodded, reluctantly.

"*Dead,*" the raven said. "*Dead. Dead.*"

"He may come to us anyway," the Old Bear said. "As Othor did, and Jafer Flowers. I dread that as much as you, Jon, but we must admit the possibility."

"*Dead,*" his raven cawed, ruffling its wings. Its voice grew louder and more shrill. "*Dead.*"

Mormont stroked the bird's black feathers, and stifled a sudden yawn with the back of his hand. "I will forsake supper, I believe. Rest will serve me better. Wake me at first light."

"Sleep well, my lord." Jon gathered up the empty cups and stepped outside. He heard distant laughter, the plaintive sound of pipes. A great blaze was crackling in the center of the camp, and he could smell stew cooking. The Old Bear might not be hungry, but Jon was. He drifted over toward the fire.

Dywen was holding forth, spoon in hand. "I know this wood as well as any man alive, and I tell you, I wouldn't care to ride through it alone tonight. Can't you smell it?"

Grenn was staring at him with wide eyes, but Dolorous Edd said, "All I smell is the shit of two hundred horses. And this stew. Which has a similar aroma, now that I come to sniff it."

"I've got your *similar aroma* right here." Hake patted his dirk. Grumbling, he filled Jon's bowl from the kettle.

The stew was thick with barley, carrot, and onion, with here and there a ragged shred of salt beef, softened in the cooking.

"What is it you smell, Dywen?" asked Grenn.

The forester sucked on his spoon a moment. He had taken out his teeth. His face was leathery and wrinkled, his hands gnarled as old roots. "Seems to me like it smells . . . well . . . *cold.*"

"Your head's as wooden as your teeth," Hake told him. "There's no smell to cold."

There is, thought Jon, remembering the night in the Lord Commander's chambers. *It smells like death.* Suddenly he was not hungry anymore. He gave his stew to Grenn, who looked in need of an extra supper to warm him against the night.

The wind was blowing briskly when he left. By morning, frost would cover the ground, and the tent ropes would be stiff and frozen. A few fingers of spiced wine sloshed in the bottom of the kettle. Jon fed fresh wood to the fire and put the kettle over the flames to reheat. He flexed his fingers as he waited, squeezing and spreading until the hand tingled. The first watch had taken up their stations around the perimeter of the camp. Torches flickered all along the ringwall. The night was moonless, but a thousand stars shone overhead.

A sound rose out of the darkness, faint and distant, but unmistakable: the howling of wolves. Their voices rose and fell, a chilly song, and lonely. It made the hairs rise along the back of his neck. Across the fire, a pair of red eyes regarded him from the shadows. The light of the flames made them glow.

"Ghost," Jon breathed, surprised. "So you came inside after all, eh?" The white wolf often hunted all night; he had not expected to see him again till daybreak. "Was the hunting so bad?" he asked. "Here. To me, Ghost."

The direwolf circled the fire, sniffing Jon, sniffing the wind, never still. It did not seem as if he were after meat right now. *When the dead came walking, Ghost knew. He woke me, warned me.* Alarmed, he got to his feet. "Is something out there? Ghost, do you have a scent?" *Dywen said he smelled cold.*

The direwolf loped off, stopped, looked back. *He wants me to follow.* Pulling up the hood of his cloak, Jon walked away from the tents, away from the warmth of his fire, past the lines of shaggy little garrons. One of the horses whickered nervously when Ghost padded by. Jon soothed him with a word and paused to stroke his muzzle. He could hear the wind whistling through cracks in the rocks as they neared the ringwall. A voice called out a challenge. Jon stepped into the torchlight. "I need to fetch water for the Lord Commander."

"Go on, then," the guard said. "Be quick about it." Huddled beneath his black cloak, with his hood drawn up against the wind, the man never even looked to see if he had a bucket.

Jon slipped sideways between two sharpened stakes while Ghost slid beneath them. A torch had been thrust down into a crevice, its flames flying pale orange banners when the gusts came. He snatched it up as he squeezed through the gap between the stones. Ghost went racing down the hill. Jon followed more slowly, the torch thrust out before him as he made his descent. The camp sounds faded behind him. The night was black, the slope steep, stony, and uneven. A moment's inattention would be a sure way to break an ankle . . . or his neck. *What am I doing?* he asked himself as he picked his way down.

The trees stood beneath him, warriors armored in bark and leaf, deployed in their silent ranks awaiting the command to storm the hill. Black, they seemed . . . it was only when his torchlight brushed against them that Jon glimpsed a flash of green. Faintly, he heard the sound of water flowing over rocks. Ghost vanished in the underbrush. Jon struggled after him, listening to the call of the brook, to the leaves sighing in the wind. Branches clutched at his cloak, while overhead thick limbs twined together and shut out the stars.

He found Ghost lapping from the stream. *"Ghost,"* he called, "to me. *Now."* When the direwolf raised his head, his eyes glowed red and baleful, and water streamed down from his jaws like slaver. There was something fierce and terrible about him in that instant. And then he was off, bounding past Jon, racing through the trees. "Ghost, *no,* stay," he shouted, but the wolf paid no heed. The lean white shape was swallowed by the dark, and Jon had only two choices—to climb the hill again, alone, or to follow.

He followed, angry, holding the torch out low so he could see the rocks that threatened to trip him with every step, the thick roots that seemed to grab as his feet, the holes where a man could twist an ankle. Every few feet he called again for Ghost, but the night wind was swirling amongst the trees and it drank the words. *This is madness,* he thought as he plunged deeper into the trees. He was about to turn back when he glimpsed a flash of white off ahead and to the right, back toward the hill. He jogged after it, cursing under his breath.

A quarter way around the Fist he chased the wolf before he lost him again. Finally he stopped to catch his breath amidst the scrub, thorns, and tumbled rocks at the base of the hill. Beyond the torchlight, the dark pressed close.

A soft scrabbling noise made him turn. Jon moved toward the sound, stepping carefully among boulders and thornbushes. Behind a fallen tree, he came on Ghost again. The direwolf was digging furiously, kicking up dirt.

"What have you found?" Jon lowered the torch, revealing a rounded mound of soft earth. *A grave,* he thought. *But whose!*

He knelt, jammed the torch into the ground beside him. The soil was loose, sandy. Jon pulled it out by the fistful. There were no stones, no roots. Whatever was here had been put here recently. Two feet down, his fingers touched cloth. He had been expecting a corpse, fearing a corpse, but this was something else. He pushed against the fabric and felt small, hard shapes beneath, unyielding. There was no smell, no sign of graveworms. Ghost backed off and sat on his haunches, watching.

Jon brushed the loose soil away to reveal a rounded bundle perhaps two feet across. He jammed his fingers down around the edges and worked it loose. When he pulled it free, whatever was inside shifted and clinked. *Treasure,* he thought, but the shapes were wrong to be coins, and the *sound* was wrong for metal.

A length of frayed rope bound the bundle together. Jon unsheathed his dagger and cut it, groped for the edges of the cloth, and pulled. The bundle turned, and its contents spilled out onto the ground, glittering dark and bright. He saw a dozen knives, leaf-shaped spearheads, numerous arrowheads. Jon picked up a dagger blade, featherlight and shiny black, hiltless. Torchlight ran along its edge, a thin orange line that spoke of razor sharpness. *Dragonglass. What the maesters call obsidian.* Had Ghost uncovered some ancient cache of the children of the forest, buried here for thousands of years? The Fist of the First Men was an old place, only . . .

Beneath the dragonglass was an old warhorn, made from an auroch's horn and banded in bronze. Jon shook the dirt from inside it, and a stream of arrowheads fell out. He let them fall, and pulled up a corner of the cloth the weapons had been wrapped in, rubbing it between his fingers. *Good wool, thick, a double weave, damp but not rotted.* It could not have been long in the ground. And it was *dark.* He seized a handful and pulled it close to the torch. *Not dark. Black.*

Even before Jon stood and shook it out, he knew what he had: the black cloak of a Sworn Brother of the Night's Watch.

BRAN

Alebelly found him in the forge, working the bellows for Mikken. "Maester wants you in the turret, m'lord prince. There's been a bird from the king."

"From Robb?" Excited, Bran did not wait for Hodor, but let Alebelly carry him up the steps. He was a big man, though not so big as Hodor and nowhere near as strong. By the time they reached the maester's turret he was red-faced and puffing. Rickon was there before them, and both Walder Freys as well.

Maester Luwin sent Alebelly away and closed his door. "My lords," he said gravely, "we have had a message from His Grace, with both good news and ill. He has won a great victory in the west, shattering a Lannister army at a place named Oxcross, and has taken several castles as well. He writes us from Ashemark, formerly the stronghold of House Marbrand."

Rickon tugged at the maester's robe. "Is Robb coming home?"

"Not just yet, I fear. There are battles yet to fight."

"Was it Lord Tywin he defeated?" asked Bran.

"No," said the maester. "Ser Stafford Lannister commanded the enemy host. He was slain in the battle."

Bran had never even heard of Ser Stafford Lannister. He found himself agreeing with Big Walder when he said, "Lord Tywin is the only one who matters."

"Tell Robb I want him to come home," said Rickon. "He can bring his wolf home too, and Mother and Father." Though he knew Lord Eddard was dead, sometimes Rickon forgot . . . willfully, Bran suspected. His little brother was stubborn as only a boy of four can be.

Bran was glad for Robb's victory, but disquieted as well. He remembered what Osha had said the day that his brother had led his army out of Winterfell. *He's marching the wrong way*, the wildling woman had insisted.

"Sadly, no victory is without cost." Maester Luwin turned to the Walders. "My lords, your uncle Ser Stevron Frey was among those who lost their lives at Oxcross. He took a wound in the battle, Robb writes. It was not thought to be serious, but three days later he died in his tent, asleep."

Big Walder shrugged. "He was very old. Five-and-sixty, I think. Too old for battles. He was always saying he was tired."

Little Walder hooted. "Tired of waiting for our grandfather to die, you mean. Does this mean Ser Emmon's the heir now?"

"Don't be stupid," his cousin said. "The sons of the first son come before the second son. Ser Ryman is next in line, and then Edwyn and Black Walder and Petyr Pimple. And then Aegon and all *his* sons."

"Ryman is old too," said Little Walder. "Past forty, I bet. And he has a bad belly. Do you think he'll be lord?"

"*I'll* be lord. I don't care if he is."

Maester Luwin cut in sharply. "You ought to be ashamed of such talk, my lords. Where is your grief? Your uncle is dead."

"Yes," said Little Walder. "We're very sad."

They weren't, though. Bran got a sick feeling in his belly. *They like the taste of this dish better than I do.* He asked Maester Luwin to be excused.

"Very well." The maester rang for help. Hodor must have been busy in the stables. It was Osha who came. She was stronger than Alebelly, though, and had no trouble lifting Bran in her arms and carrying him down the steps.

"Osha," Bran asked as they crossed the yard. "Do you know the way north? To the Wall and . . . and even past?"

"The way's easy. Look for the Ice Dragon, and chase the blue star in the rider's eye." She backed through a door and started up the winding steps.

"And there are still giants there, and . . . the rest . . . the Others, and the children of the forest too?"

"The giants I've seen, the children I've heard tell of, and the white walkers . . . why do you want to know?"

"Did you ever see a three-eyed crow?"

"No." She laughed. "And I can't say I'd want to." Osha kicked open the door to his bedchamber and set him in his window seat, where he could watch the yard below.

It seemed only a few heartbeats after she took her leave that the door opened again, and Jojen Reed entered unbidden, with his sister Meera behind him. "You heard about the bird?" Bran asked. The other boy nodded. "It wasn't a supper like you said. It was a letter from Robb, and we didn't eat it, but—"

"The green dreams take strange shapes sometimes," Jojen admitted. "The truth of them is not always easy to understand."

"Tell me the bad thing you dreamed," Bran said. "The bad thing that is coming to Winterfell."

"Does my lord prince believe me now? Will he trust my words, no matter how queer they sound in his ears?"

Bran nodded.

"It is the sea that comes."

"The *sea?*"

"I dreamed that the sea was lapping all around Winterfell. I saw black waves crashing against the gates and towers, and then the salt water came flowing over the walls and filled the castle. Drowned men were floating in the yard. When I first dreamed the dream, back at Greywater, I didn't know their faces, but now I do. That Alebelly is one, the guard who called our names at the feast. Your septon's another. Your smith as well."

"Mikken?" Bran was as confused as he was dismayed. "But the sea is hundreds and hundreds of leagues away, and Winterfell's walls are so high the water couldn't get in even if it did come."

"In the dark of night the salt sea will flow over these walls," said Jojen. "I saw the dead, bloated and drowned."

"We have to tell them," Bran said. "Alebelly and Mikken, and Septon Chayle. Tell them not to drown."

"It will not save them," replied the boy in green.

Meera came to the window seat and put a hand on his shoulder. "They will not believe, Bran. No more than you did."

Jojen sat on Bran's bed. "Tell me what *you* dream."

He was scared, even then, but he had sworn to trust them, and a Stark of Winterfell keeps his sworn word. "There's different kinds," he said slowly. "There's the wolf dreams, those aren't so bad as the others. I run and hunt and kill squirrels. And there's dreams where the crow comes and tells me to fly. Sometimes the tree is in those dreams too, calling my name. That frightens me. But the worst dreams are when I fall." He looked down into the yard, feeling miserable. "I never used to fall before. When I climbed. I went everyplace, up on the roofs and along the walls, I used to feed the crows in the Burned Tower. Mother was afraid that I would fall but I knew I never would. Only I did, and now when I sleep I fall all the time."

Meera gave his shoulder a squeeze. "Is that all?"

"I guess."

"Warg," said Jojen Reed.

Bran looked at him, his eyes wide. "What?"

"Warg. Shapechanger. Beastling. That is what they will call you, if they should ever hear of your wolf dreams."

The names made him afraid again. *"Who* will call me?"

"Your own folk. In fear. Some will hate you if they know what you are. Some will even try to kill you."

Old Nan told scary stories of beastlings and shapechangers sometimes. In the stories they were always evil. "I'm not like that," Bran said. "I'm *not*. It's only dreams."

"The wolf dreams are no true dreams. You have your eye closed tight whenever you're awake, but as you drift off it flutters open and your soul seeks out its other half. The power is strong in you."

"I don't want it. I want to be a *knight*."

"A knight is what you want. A warg is what you are. You can't change that, Bran, you can't deny it or push it away. You are the winged wolf, but you will never fly." Jojen got up and walked to the window. "Unless you *open your eye*." He put two fingers together and poked Bran in the forehead, hard.

When he raised his hand to the spot, Bran felt only the smooth unbroken skin. There was no eye, not even a closed one. "How can I open it if it's not there?"

"You will never find the eye with your fingers, Bran. You must search with your heart." Jojen studied Bran's face with those strange green eyes. "Or are you afraid?"

"Maester Luwin says there's nothing in dreams that a man need fear."

"There is," said Jojen.

"What?"

"The past. The future. The truth."

They left him more muddled than ever. When he was alone, Bran tried to open his third eye, but he didn't know how. No matter how he wrinkled his forehead and poked at it, he couldn't see any different than he'd done before. In the days that followed, he tried to warn others about what Jojen had seen, but it didn't go as he wanted. Mikken thought it was funny. "The sea, is it? Happens I always wanted to see the sea. Never got where I could go to it, though. So now it's coming to me, is it? The gods are good, to take such trouble for a poor smith."

"The gods will take me when they see fit," Septon Chayle said quietly, "though I scarcely think it likely that I'll drown, Bran. I grew up on the banks of the White Knife, you know. I'm quite the strong swimmer."

Alebelly was the only one who paid the warning any heed. He went to talk to Jojen himself, and afterward stopped bathing and refused to go near the well. Finally he stank so bad that six of the other guards threw him into a tub of scalding water and scrubbed him raw while he screamed that they were going to drown him like the frogboy had said. Thereafter he scowled whenever he saw Bran or Jojen about the castle, and muttered under his breath.

It was a few days after Alebelly's bath that Ser Rodrik returned to Winterfell with his prisoner, a fleshy young man with fat moist lips and long hair who smelled like a privy, even worse than Alebelly had. "Reek, he's called," Hayhead said when Bran asked who it was. "I never heard his true name. He served the Bastard of Bolton and helped him murder Lady Hornwood, they say."

The Bastard himself was dead, Bran learned that evening over supper. Ser Rodrik's men had caught him on Hornwood land doing something horrible (Bran wasn't quite sure what, but it seemed to be something you did without your clothes) and shot him down with arrows as he tried to ride away. They came too late for poor Lady Hornwood, though. After their wedding, the Bastard had locked her in a tower and neglected to feed her. Bran had heard men saying that when Ser Rodrik had smashed down the door he found her with her mouth all bloody and her fingers chewed off.

"The monster has tied us a thorny knot," the old knight told Maester Luwin. "Like it or no, Lady Hornwood was his wife. He made her say the vows before both septon and heart tree, and bedded her that very night before witnesses. She signed a will naming him as heir and fixed her seal to it."

"Vows made at sword point are not valid," the maester argued.

"Roose Bolton may not agree. Not with land at issue." Ser Rodrik looked unhappy. "Would that I could take this serving man's head off as well, he's as bad as his master. But I fear I must keep him alive until Robb returns from his wars. He is the only witness to the worst of the Bastard's crimes. Perhaps when Lord Bolton hears his tale, he will abandon his claim, but meantime we have Manderly knights and Dreadfort men killing one another in Hornwood forests, and I lack the strength to stop them." The old knight turned in his seat and gave Bran a stern look. "And what have you been about while I've been away, my lord prince? Commanding our guardsmen not to wash? Do you want them smelling like this Reek, is that it?"

"The sea is coming here," Bran said. "Jojen saw it in a green dream. Alebelly is going to drown."

Maester Luwin tugged at his chain collar. "The Reed boy believes he sees the future in his dreams, Ser Rodrik. I've spoken to Bran about the uncertainty of such prophecies, but if truth be told, there *is* trouble along the Stony Shore. Raiders in longships, plundering fishing villages. Raping and burning. Leobald Tallhart has sent his nephew Benfred to deal with them, but I expect they'll take to their ships and flee at the first sight of armed men."

"Aye, and strike somewhere else. The Others take all such cowards. They would never dare, no more than the Bastard of Bolton, if our main strength were not a thousand leagues south." Ser Rodrik looked at Bran. "What else did the lad tell you?"

"He said the water would flow over our walls. He saw Alebelly drowned, and Mikken and Septon Chayle too."

Ser Rodrik frowned. "Well, should it happen that I need to ride against these raiders myself, I shan't take Alebelly, then. He didn't see *me* drowned, did he? No? Good."

It heartened Bran to hear that. *Maybe they won't drown, then*, he thought. *If they stay away from the sea.*

Meera thought so too, later that night when she and Jojen met Bran in his room to play a three-sided game of tiles, but her brother shook his head. "The things I see in green dreams can't be changed."

That made his sister angry. "Why would the gods send a warning if we can't heed it and change what's to come?"

"I don't know," Jojen said sadly.

"If you were Alebelly, you'd probably jump into the well to have done with it! He should *fight*, and Bran should too."

"Me?" Bran felt suddenly afraid. "What should I fight? Am I going to drown too?"

Meera looked at him guiltily. "I shouldn't have said . . ."

He could tell that she was hiding something. "Did you see me in a green dream?" he asked Jojen nervously. "Was I drowned?"

"Not drowned." Jojen spoke as if every word pained him. "I dreamed of the man who came today, the one they call Reek. You and your brother lay dead at his feet, and he was skinning off your faces with a long red blade."

Meera rose to her feet. "If I went to the dungeon, I could drive a spear right through his heart. How could he murder Bran if he was dead?"

"The gaolers will stop you," Jojen said. "The guards. And if you tell them why you want him dead, they'll never believe."

"I have guards too," Bran reminded them. "Alebelly and Poxy Tym and Hayhead and the rest."

Jojen's mossy eyes were full of pity. "They won't be able to stop him, Bran. I couldn't see why, but I saw the end of it. I saw you and Rickon in your crypts, down in the dark with all the dead kings and their stone wolves."

No, Bran thought. *No.* "If I went away . . . to Greywater, or to the crow, someplace far where they couldn't find me . . ."

"It will not matter. The dream was green, Bran, and the green dreams do not lie."

TYRION

Varys stood over the brazier, warming his soft hands. "It would appear Renly was murdered most fearfully in the very midst of his army. His throat was opened from ear to ear by a blade that passed through steel and bone as if they were soft cheese."

"Murdered by whose hand?" Cersei demanded.

"Have you ever considered that too many answers are the same as no answer at all? My informers are not always as highly placed as we might like. When a king dies, fancies sprout like mushrooms in the dark. A groom says that Renly was slain by a knight of his own Rainbow Guard. A washerwoman claims Stannis stole through the heart of his brother's army with his magic sword. Several men-at-arms believe a woman did the fell deed, but cannot agree on *which* woman. A maid that Renly had spurned, claims one. A camp follower brought in to serve his pleasure on the eve of battle, says a second. The third ventures that it might have been the Lady Catelyn Stark."

The queen was not pleased. "Must you waste our time with every rumor the fools care to tell?"

"You pay me well for these rumors, my gracious queen."

"We pay you for the truth, Lord Varys. Remember that, or this small council may grow smaller still."

Varys tittered nervously. "You and your noble brother will leave His Grace with no council at all if you continue."

"I daresay, the realm could survive a few less councillors," said Littlefinger with a smile.

"Dear dear Petyr," said Varys, "are you not concerned that yours might be the next name on the Hand's little list?"

"Before you, Varys? I should never dream of it."

"Mayhaps we will be brothers on the Wall together, you and I." Varys giggled again.

"Sooner than you'd like, if the next words out of your mouth are not something useful, eunuch." From the look of her eyes, Cersei was prepared to castrate Varys all over again.

"Might this be some ruse?" asked Littlefinger.

"If so, it is a ruse of surpassing cleverness," said Varys. "It has certainly hoodwinked me."

Tyrion had heard enough. "Joff will be so disappointed," he said. "He was saving such a nice spike for Renly's head. But whoever did the deed, we must assume Stannis was behind it. The gain is clearly his." He did not like this news; he had counted on the brothers Baratheon decimating each other in bloody battle. He could feel his elbow throbbing where the morningstar had laid it open. It did that sometimes in the damp. He squeezed it uselessly in his hand and asked, "What of Renly's host?"

"The greater part of his foot remains at Bitterbridge." Varys abandoned the brazier to take his seat at the table. "Most of the lords who rode with Lord Renly to Storm's End have gone over banner-and-blade to Stannis, with all their chivalry."

"Led by the Florents, I'd wager," said Littlefinger.

Varys gave him a simpering smile. "You would win, my lord. Lord Alester was indeed the first to bend the knee. Many others followed."

"Many," Tyrion said pointedly, "but not all?"

"Not all," agreed the eunuch. "Not Loras Tyrell, nor Randyll Tarly, nor Mathis Rowan. And Storm's End itself has not yielded. Ser Cortnay Penrose holds the castle in Renly's name, and will not believe his liege is dead. He demands to see the mortal remains before he opens his gates, but it seems that Renly's corpse has unaccountably vanished. Carried away, most likely. A fifth of Renly's knights departed with Ser Loras rather than bend the knee to Stannis. It's said the Knight of Flowers went mad when he saw his king's body, and slew three of Renly's guards in his wrath, among them Emmon Cuy and Robar Royce."

A pity he stopped at three, thought Tyrion.

"Ser Loras is likely making for Bitterbridge," Varys went on. "His sister is there, Renly's queen, as well as a great many soldiers who suddenly find themselves kingless. Which side will they take now? A ticklish question. Many serve the lords who remained at Storm's End, and those lords now belong to Stannis."

Tyrion leaned forward. "There is a chance here, it seems to me. Win Loras Tyrell to our cause and Lord Mace Tyrell and his bannermen might join us as well. They may have sworn their swords to Stannis for the moment, yet they cannot love the man, or they would have been his from the start."

"Is their love for us any greater?" asked Cersei.

"Scarcely," said Tyrion. "They loved Renly, clearly, but Renly is slain. Perhaps we can give them good and sufficient reasons to prefer Joffrey to Stannis . . . *if* we move quickly."

"What sort of reasons do you mean to give them?"

"Gold reasons," Littlefinger suggested at once.

Varys made a *tsk*ing sound. "Sweet Petyr, surely you do not mean to suggest that these puissant lords and noble knights could be *bought* like so many chickens in the market."

"Have you been to our markets of late, Lord Varys?" asked Littlefinger. "You'd find it easier to buy a lord than a chicken, I daresay. Of course, lords cluck prouder than chickens, and take it ill if you offer them coin like a tradesman, but they are seldom adverse to taking gifts . . . honors, lands, castles . . ."

"Bribes might sway some of the lesser lords," Tyrion said, "but never Highgarden."

"True," Littlefinger admitted. "The Knight of Flowers is the key there. Mace Tyrell has two older sons, but Loras has always been his favorite. Win him, and Highgarden will be yours."

Yes, Tyrion thought. "It seems to me we should take a lesson from the late Lord Renly. We can win the Tyrell alliance as he did. With a marriage."

Varys understood the quickest. "You think to wed King Joffrey to Margaery Tyrell."

"I do." Renly's young queen was no more than fifteen, sixteen, he seemed to recall . . . older than Joffrey, but a few years were nothing, it was so neat and sweet he could taste it.

"Joffrey is betrothed to Sansa Stark," Cersei objected.

"Marriage contracts can be broken. What advantage is there in wedding the king to the daughter of a dead traitor?"

Littlefinger spoke up. "You might point out to His Grace that the Tyrells are much wealthier than the Starks, and that Margaery is said to be lovely . . . and beddable besides."

"Yes," said Tyrion, "Joff ought to like that well enough."

"My son is too young to care about such things."

"You think so?" asked Tyrion. "He's thirteen, Cersei. The same age at which I married."

"You shamed us all with that sorry episode. Joffrey is made of finer stuff."

"So fine that he had Ser Boros rip off Sansa's gown."

"He was angry with the girl."

"He was angry with that cook's boy who spilled the soup last night as well, but he didn't strip him naked."

"This was not a matter of some spilled soup—"

No, it was a matter of some pretty teats. After that business in the yard, Tyrion had spoken with Varys about how they might arrange for Joffrey to visit Chataya's. A taste of honey might sweeten the boy, he hoped. He might even be *grateful,* gods forbid, and Tyrion could do with a shade more gratitude from his sovereign. It would need to be done secretly, of course. The tricky bit would be parting him from the Hound. "The dog is never far from his master's heels," he'd observed to Varys, "but all men sleep. And some gamble and whore and visit winesinks as well."

"The Hound does all these things, if that is your question."

"No," said Tyrion. "My question is *when.*"

Varys had laid a finger on his cheek, smiling enigmatically. "My lord, a suspicious man might think you wished to find a time when Sandor Clegane was not protecting King Joffrey, the better to do the boy some harm."

"Surely you know me better than that, Lord Varys," Tyrion said. "Why, all I want is for Joffrey to love me."

The eunuch had promised to look into the matter. The war made its own demands, though; Joffrey's initiation into manhood would need to wait. "Doubtless you know your son better than I do," he made himself tell Cersei, "but regardless, there's still much to be said for a Tyrell marriage. It may be the only way that Joffrey lives long enough to reach his wedding night."

Littlefinger agreed. "The Stark girl brings Joffrey nothing but her body, sweet as that may be. Margaery Tyrell brings fifty thousand swords and all the strength of Highgarden."

"Indeed." Varys laid a soft hand on the queen's sleeve. "You have a mother's heart, and I know His Grace loves his little sweetling. Yet kings must learn to put the needs of the realm before their own desires. I say this offer must be made."

The queen pulled free of the eunuch's touch. "You would not speak so if you were women. Say what you will, my lords, but Joffrey is too proud to settle for Renly's leavings. He will never consent."

Tyrion shrugged. "When the king comes of age in three years, he may give or withhold his consent as he pleases. Until then, you are his regent and I am his Hand, and he will marry whomever we tell him to marry. Leavings or no."

Cersei's quiver was empty. "Make your offer then, but gods save you all if Joff does not like this girl."

"I'm so pleased we can agree," Tyrion said. "Now, which of us shall go to Bitterbridge? We must reach Ser Loras with our offer before his blood can cool."

"You mean to send one of the council?"

"I can scarcely expect the Knight of Flowers to treat with Bronn or Shagga, can I? The Tyrells are proud."

His sister wasted no time trying to twist the situation to her advantage. "Ser Jacelyn Bywater is nobly born. Send him."

Tyrion shook his head. "We need someone who can do more than repeat our words and fetch back a reply. Our envoy must speak for king and council and settle the matter quickly."

"The Hand speaks with the king's voice." Candlelight gleamed green as wildfire in Cersei's eyes. "If we send you, Tyrion, it will be as if Joffrey went himself. And who better? You wield words as skillfully as Jaime wields a sword."

Are you that eager to get me out of the city, Cersei? "You are too kind, sister, but it seems to me that a boy's mother is better fitted to arrange his marriage than any uncle. And you have a gift for winning friends that I could never hope to match."

Her eyes narrowed. "Joff needs me at his side."

"Your Grace, my lord Hand," said Littlefinger, "the king needs both of you here. Let me go in your stead."

"You?" *What gain does he see in this?* Tyrion wondered.

"I am of the king's council, yet not the king's blood, so I would make a poor hostage. I knew Ser Loras passing well when he was here at court, and gave him no cause to mislike me. Mace Tyrell bears me no enmity that I know of, and I flatter myself that I am not unskilled in negotiation."

He has us. Tyrion did not trust Petyr Baelish, nor did he want the man out of his sight, yet what other choice was left him? It must be Littlefinger or Tyrion himself, and he knew full well that if he left King's Landing for any length of time, all that he had managed to accomplish would be undone. "There is fighting between here and Bitterbridge," he said cautiously. "And you can be past certain that Lord Stannis will be dispatching his own shepherds to gather in his brother's wayward lambs."

"I've never been frightened of shepherds. It's the sheep who trouble me. Still, I suppose an escort might be in order."

"I can spare a hundred gold cloaks," Tyrion said.

"Five hundred."

"Three hundred."

"And forty more—twenty knights with as many squires. If I arrive without a knightly tail, the Tyrells will think me of small account."

That was true enough. "Agreed."

"I'll include Horror and Slobber in my party, and send them on to their lord father afterward. A gesture of goodwill. We need Paxter Redwyne, he's Mace Tyrell's oldest friend, and a great power in his own right."

"And a traitor," the queen said, balking. "The Arbor would have declared for Renly with all the rest, except that Redwyne knew full well his whelps would suffer for it."

"Renly is dead, Your Grace," Littlefinger pointed out, "and neither Stannis nor Lord Paxter will have forgotten how Redwyne galleys closed the sea during the siege of Storm's End. Restore the twins and perchance we may win Redwyne's love."

Cersei remained unconvinced. "The Others can keep his love, I want his swords and sails. Holding tight to those twins is the best way to make certain that we'll have them."

Tyrion had the answer. "Then let us send Ser Hobber back to the Arbor and keep Ser Horas here. Lord Paxter ought to be clever enough to riddle out the meaning of that, I should think."

The suggestion was carried without protest, but Littlefinger was not done. "We'll want horses. Swift and strong. The fighting will make remounts hard to come by. A goodly supply of gold will also be needed, for those gifts we spoke of earlier."

"Take as much as you require. If the city falls, Stannis will steal it all anyway."

"I'll want my commission in writing. A document that will leave Mace Tyrell in no doubt as to my authority, granting me full power to treat with him concerning this match and any other arrangements that might be required, and to make binding pledges in the king's name. It should be signed by Joffrey and every member of this council, and bear all our seals."

Tyrion shifted uncomfortably. "Done. Will that be all? I remind you, there's a long road between here and Bitterbridge."

"I'll be riding it before dawn breaks." Littlefinger rose. "I trust that on my return, the king will see that I am suitably rewarded for my valiant efforts in his cause?"

Varys giggled. "Joffrey is such a grateful sovereign, I'm certain you will have no cause to complain, my good brave lord."

The queen was more direct. "What do you want, Petyr?"

Littlefinger glanced at Tyrion with a sly smile. "I shall need to give that some consideration. No doubt I'll think of something." He sketched an airy bow and took his leave, as casual as if he were off to one of his brothels.

Tyrion glanced out the window. The fog was so thick that he could not even see the curtain wall across the yard. A few dim lights shone indistinct through that greyness. *A foul day for travel,* he thought. He did not envy Petyr Baelish. "We had best see to drawing up those documents. Lord Varys, send for parchment and quill. And someone will need to wake Joffrey."

It was still grey and dark when the meeting finally ended. Varys scurried off alone, his soft slippers whisking along the floor. The Lannisters lingered a moment by the door. "How comes your chain, brother?" the queen asked as Ser Preston fastened a vair-lined cloth-of-silver cloak about her shoulders.

"Link by link, it grows longer. We should thank the gods that Ser Cortnay Penrose is as stubborn as he is. Stannis will never march north with Storm's End untaken in his rear."

"Tyrion, I know we do not always agree on policy, but it seems to me that I was wrong about you. You are not so big a fool as I imagined. In truth, I realize now that you have been a great help. For that I thank you. You must forgive me if I have spoken to you harshly in the past."

"Must I?" He gave her a shrug, a smile. "Sweet sister, you have said nothing that requires forgiveness."

"Today, you mean?" They both laughed . . . and Cersei leaned over and planted a quick, soft kiss on his brow.

Too astonished for words, Tyrion could only watch her stride off down the hall, Ser Preston at her side. "Have I lost my wits, or did my sister just kiss me?" he asked Bronn when she was gone.

"Was it so sweet?"

"It was . . . unanticipated." Cersei had been behaving queerly of late. Tyrion found it very unsettling. "I am trying to recall the last time she kissed me. I could not have been more than six or seven. Jaime had dared her to do it."

"The woman's finally taken note of your charms."

"No," Tyrion said. "No, the woman is hatching something. Best find out what, Bronn. You know I hate surprises."

THEON

Theon wiped the spittle off his cheek with the back of his hand. "Robb will gut you, Greyjoy," Benfred Tallheart screamed. "He'll feed your turncloak's heart to his wolf, you piece of sheep dung."

Aeron Damphair's voice cut through the insults like a sword through cheese. "Now you must kill him."

"I have questions for him first," said Theon.

"*Fuck* your questions." Benfred hung bleeding and helpless between Stygg and Werlag. "You'll choke on them before you get any answers from me, craven. Turncloak."

Uncle Aeron was relentless. "When he spits on you, he spits on all of us. He spits on the Drowned God. He must die."

"My father gave *me* the command here, Uncle."

"And sent me to counsel you."

And to watch me. Theon dare not push matters too far with his uncle. The command was his, yes, but his men had a faith in the Drowned God that they did not have in him, and they were terrified of Aeron Damphair. *I cannot fault them for that.*

"You'll lose your head for this, Greyjoy. The crows will eat the jelly of your eyes." Benfred tried to spit again, but only managed a little blood. "The Others bugger your wet god."

Tallhart, you've spit away your life, Theon thought. "Stygg, silence him," he said.

They forced Benfred to his knees. Werlag tore the rabbitskin off his belt and jammed it between his teeth to stop his shouting. Stygg unlimbered his axe.

"No," Aeron Damphair declared. "He must be given to the god. The old way."

What does it matter? Dead is dead. "Take him, then."

"You will come as well. You command here. The offering should come from you."

That was more than Theon could stomach. "You are the priest, Uncle, I leave the god to you. Do me the same kindness and leave the battles to me." He waved his hand, and Werlag and Stygg began to drag their captive off toward the shore. Aeron Damphair gave his nephew a reproachful look, then followed. Down to the pebbled beach they would go, to drown Benfred Tallhart in salt water. The old way.

Perhaps it's a kindness, Theon told himself as he stalked off in the other direction. Stygg was hardly the most expert of headsmen, and Benfred had a neck thick as a boar's, heavy with muscle and fat. *I used to mock him for it, just to see how angry I could make him,* he remembered. That had been, what, three years past? When Ned Stark had ridden to Torrhen's Square to see Ser Helman, Theon had accompanied him and spent a fortnight in Benfred's company.

He could hear the rough noises of victory from the crook in the road where the battle had been fought . . . if you'd go so far as to call it a battle. *More like slaughtering sheep, if truth be told. Sheep fleeced in steel, but sheep nonetheless.*

Climbing a jumble of stone, Theon looked down on the dead men and dying horses. The horses had deserved better. Tymor and his brothers had gathered up what mounts had come through the fight unhurt, while Urzen and Black Lorren silenced the animals too badly wounded to be saved. The rest of his men were looting the corpses. Gevin Harlaw knelt on a dead man's chest, sawing off his finger to get at a ring. *Paying the iron price. My lord father would approve.* Theon thought of seeking out the bodies of the two men he'd slain himself to see if they had any jewelry worth the taking, but the notion left a bitter taste in his mouth. He could imagine what Eddard Stark would have said. Yet that thought made him angry too. *Stark is dead and rotting, and naught to me,* he reminded himself.

Old Botley, who was called Fishwhiskers, sat scowling by his pile of plunder while his three sons added to it. One of them was in a shoving match with a fat man named Todric, who was reeling among the slain with a horn of ale in one hand and an axe in the other, clad in a cloak of white foxfur only slightly stained by the blood of its previous owner.

Drunk, Theon decided, watching him bellow. It was said that the ironmen of old had oft been blood-drunk in battle, so berserk that they felt no pain and feared no foe, but this was a common ale-drunk.

"Wex, my bow and quiver." The boy ran and fetched them. Theon bent the bow and slipped the string into its notches as Todric knocked down the Botley boy and flung ale into his eyes. Fishwhiskers leapt up cursing, but Theon was quicker. He drew on the hand that clutched the drinking horn, figuring to give them a shot to talk about, but Todric spoiled it by lurching to one side just as he loosed. The arrow took him through the belly.

The looters stopped to gape. Theon lowered his bow. "No drunkards, I said, and no squabbles over plunder." On his knees, Todric was dying noisily. "Botley, silence him." Fishwhiskers and his sons were quick to obey. They slit Todric's throat as he kicked feebly, and were stripping him of cloak and rings and weapons before he was even dead.

Now they know I mean what I say. Lord Balon might have given him the command, but Theon knew that some of his men saw only a soft boy from the green lands when they looked at him. "Anyone else have a thirst?" No one replied. "Good." He kicked at Benfred's fallen banner, clutched in the dead hand of the squire who'd borne it. A rabbitskin had been tied below the flag. *Why rabbitskins?* he had meant to ask, but being spat on had made him forget his questions. He tossed his bow back to Wex and strode off, remembering how elated he'd felt after the Whispering Wood, and wondering why this did not taste as sweet. *Tallhart, you bloody overproud fool, you never even sent out a scout.*

They'd been joking and even *singing* as they'd come on, the three trees of Tallhart streaming above them while rabbitskins flapped stupidly from the points of their lances. The archers concealed behind the gorse had spoiled the song with a rain of arrows, and Theon himself had led his men-at-arms out to finish the butcher's work with dagger, axe, and warhammer. He had ordered their leader spared for questioning.

Only he had not expected it to be Benfred Tallhart.

His limp body was being dragged from the surf when Theon returned to his *Sea Bitch.* The masts of his longships stood outlined against the sky along the pebbled beach. Of the fishing village, nothing remained but cold ashes that stank when it rained. The men had been put to the sword, all but a handful that Theon had allowed to flee to bring the word to Torrhen's Square. Their wives and daughters had been claimed for salt wives, those who were young enough and fair. The crones and the ugly ones had simply been raped and killed, or taken for thralls if they had useful skills and did not seem likely to cause trouble.

Theon had planned that attack as well, bringing his ships up to the shore in the chill darkness before the dawn and leaping from the prow with a longaxe in his hand to lead his men into the sleeping village. He did not like the taste of any of this, but what choice did he have?

His thrice-damned sister was sailing her *Black Wind* north even now, sure to win a castle of her own. Lord Balon had let no word of the hosting escape the Iron Islands, and Theon's bloody work along the Stony Shore would be put down to sea raiders out for plunder. The northmen would not realize their true peril, not until the hammers fell on Deepwood Motte and Moat Cailin. *And after all is done and won, they will make songs for that bitch Asha, and forget that I was even here.* That is, if he allowed it.

Dagmer Cleftjaw stood by the high carved prow of his longship, *Foamdrinker*. Theon had assigned him the task of guarding the ships; otherwise men would have called it Dagmer's victory, not his. A more prickly man might have taken that for a slight, but the Cleftjaw had only laughed.

"The day is won," Dagmer called down. "And yet you do not smile, boy. The living should smile, for the dead cannot." He smiled himself to show how it was done. It made for a hideous sight. Under a snowy white mane of hair, Dagmer Cleftjaw had the most gut-churning scar Theon had ever seen, the legacy of the longaxe that had near killed him as a boy. The blow had splintered his jaw, shattered his front teeth, and left him four lips where other men had but two. A shaggy beard covered his cheeks and neck, but the hair would not grow over the scar, so a shiny seam of puckered, twisted flesh divided his face like a crevasse through a snowfield. "We could hear them singing," the old warrior said. "It was a good song, and they sang it bravely."

"They sang better than they fought. Harps would have done them as much good as their lances did."

"How many men are lost?"

"Of ours?" Theon shrugged. "Todric. I killed him for getting drunk and fighting over loot."

"Some men are born to be killed." A lesser man might have been afraid to show a smile as frightening as his, yet Dagmer grinned more often and more broadly than Lord Balon ever had.

Ugly as it was, that smile brought back a hundred memories. Theon had seen it often as a boy, when he'd jumped a horse over a mossy wall, or flung an axe and split a target square. He'd seen it when he blocked a blow from Dagmer's sword, when he put an arrow through a seagull on the wing, when he took the tiller in hand and guided a longship safely through a snarl of foaming rocks. *He gave me more smiles than my father and Eddard Stark together.* Even Robb . . . he ought to have won a smile the day he'd saved Bran from that wildling, but instead he'd gotten a scolding, as if he were some cook who'd burned the stew.

"You and I must talk, Uncle," Theon said. Dagmer was no true uncle, only a sworn man with perhaps a pinch of Greyjoy blood four or five lives back, and that from the wrong side of the blanket. Yet Theon had always called him uncle nonetheless.

"Come onto my deck, then." There were no *m'lords* from Dagmer, not when he stood on his own deck. On the Iron Islands, every captain was a king aboard his own ship.

He climbed the plank to the deck of the *Foamdrinker* in four long strides, and Dagmer led him back to the cramped aft cabin, where the old man poured a horn of sour ale and offered Theon the same. He declined. "We did not capture enough horses. A few, but . . . well, I'll make do with what I have, I suppose. Fewer men means more glory."

"What need do we have of horses?" Like most ironmen, Dagmer preferred to fight on foot or from the deck of a ship. "Horses will only shit on our decks and get in our way."

"If we sailed, yes," Theon admitted. "I have another plan." He watched the other carefully to see how he would take that. Without the Cleftjaw he could not hope to succeed. Command or no, the men would never follow him if both Aeron and Dagmer opposed him, and he had no hope of winning over the sour-faced priest.

"Your lord father commanded us to harry the coast, no more." Eyes pale as sea foam watched Theon from under those shaggy white eyebrows. Was it disapproval he saw there, or a spark of interest? The latter, he thought . . . hoped . . .

"You are my father's man."

"His *best* man, and always have been."

Pride, Theon thought. *He is proud, I must use that, his pride will be the key.* "There is no man in the Iron Islands half so skilled with spear or sword."

"You have been too long away, boy. When you left, it was as you say, but I am grown old in Lord Greyjoy's service. The singers call Andrik best now. Andrik the Unsmiling, they name him. A giant of a man. He serves Lord Drumm of Old Wyk. And Black Lorren and Qarl the Maid are near as dread."

"This Andrik may be a great fighter, but men do not fear him as they fear you."

"Aye, that's so," Dagmer said. The fingers curled around the drinking horn were heavy with rings, gold and silver and bronze, set with chunks of sapphire and garnet and dragonglass. He had paid the iron price for every one, Theon knew.

"If I had a man like you in my service, I should not waste him on this child's business of harrying and burning. This is no work for Lord Balon's best man . . ."

Dagmer's grin twisted his lips apart and showed the brown splinters of his teeth. "Nor for his trueborn son?" He hooted. "I know you too well, Theon. I saw you take your first step, helped you bend your first bow. 'Tis not me who feels wasted."

"By rights I should have my sister's command," he admitted, uncomfortably aware of how peevish that sounded.

"You take this business too hard, boy. It is only that your lord father does not know you. With your brothers dead and you taken by the wolves, your sister was his solace. He learned to rely on her, and she has never failed him."

"Nor have I. The Starks knew my worth. I was one of Brynden Blackfish's picked scouts, and I charged with the first wave in the Whispering Wood. I was *that* close to crossing swords with the Kingslayer himself." Theon held his hands two feet apart. "Daryn Hornwood came between us, and died for it."

"Why do you tell me this?" Dagmer asked. "It was me who put your first sword in your hand. I know you are no craven."

"Does my father?"

The hoary old warrior looked as if he had bitten into something he did not like the taste of. "It is only . . . Theon, the Boy Wolf is your friend, and these Starks had you for ten years."

"I am no Stark." *Lord Eddard saw to that.* "I am a Greyjoy, and I mean to be my father's heir. How can I do that unless I prove myself with some great deed?"

"You are young. Other wars will come, and you shall do your great deeds. For now, we are commanded to harry the Stony Shore."

"Let my uncle Aeron see to it. I'll give him six ships, all but *Foamdrinker* and *Sea Bitch*, and he can burn and drown to his god's surfeit."

"The command was given you, not Aeron Damphair."

"So long as the harrying is done, what does it matter? No priest could do what I mean to, nor what I ask of you. I have a task that only Dagmer Cleftjaw can accomplish."

Dagmer took a long draught from his horn. "Tell me."

He is tempted, Theon thought. *He likes this reaver's work no better than I do.* "If my sister can take a castle, so can I."

"Asha has four or five times the men we do."

Theon allowed himself a sly smile. "But we have four times the wits, and five times the courage."

"Your father—"

"—will thank me, when I hand him his kingdom. I mean to do a deed that the harpers will sing of for a thousand years."

He knew that would give Dagmer pause. A singer had made a song about the axe that cracked his jaw in half, and the old man loved to hear it. Whenever he was in his cups he would call for a reaving song, something loud and stormy that told of dead heroes and deeds of wild valor. *His hair is white and his teeth are rotten, but he still has a taste for glory.*

"What would my part be in this scheme of yours, boy?" Dagmer Cleftjaw asked after a long silence, and Theon knew he had won.

"To strike terror into the heart of the foe, as only one of your name could do. You'll take the great part of our force and march on Torrhen's Square. Helman Tallhart took his best men south, and Benfred died here with their sons. His uncle Leobald will remain, with some small garrison." *If I had been able to question Benfred, I would know just how small.* "Make no secret of your approach. Sing all the brave songs you like. I want them to close their gates."

"Is this Torrhen's Square a strong keep?"

"Strong enough. The walls are stone, thirty feet high, with square towers at each corner and a square keep within."

"Stone walls cannot be fired. How are we to take them? We do not have the numbers to storm even a small castle."

"You will make camp outside their walls and set to building catapults and siege engines."

"That is not the Old Way. Have you forgotten? Ironmen fight with swords and axes, not by flinging rocks. There is no glory in starving out a foeman."

"Leobald will not know that. When he sees you raising siege towers, his old woman's blood will run cold, and he will bleat for help. Stay your archers, Uncle, and let the raven fly. The castellan at Winterfell is a brave man, but age has stiffened his wits as well as his limbs. When he learns that one of his king's bannermen is under attack by the fearsome Dagmer Cleftjaw, he will summon his strength and ride to Tallhart's aid. It is his duty. Ser Rodrik is nothing if not dutiful."

"Any force he summons will be larger than mine," Dagmer said, "and these old knights are more cunning than you think, or they would never have lived to see their first grey hair. You set us a battle we cannot hope to win, Theon. This Torrhen's Square will never fall."

Theon smiled. "It's not Torrhen's Square I mean to take."

ARYA

Confusion and clangor ruled the castle. Men stood on the beds of wagons loading casks of wine, sacks of flour, and bundles of new-fletched arrows. Smiths straightened swords, knocked dents from breastplates, and shoed destriers and pack mules alike. Mail shirts were tossed in barrels of sand and rolled across the lumpy surface of the Flowstone Yard to scour them clean. Weese's women had twenty cloaks to mend, a hundred more to wash. The high and humble crowded into the sept together to pray. Outside the walls, tents and pavilions were coming down. Squires tossed pails of water over cookfires, while soldiers took out their oilstones to give their blades one last good lick. The noise was a swelling tide: horses blowing and whickering, lords shouting commands, men-at-arms trading curses, camp followers squabbling.

Lord Tywin Lannister was marching at last.

Ser Addam Marbrand was the first of the captains to depart, a day before the rest. He made a gallant show of it, riding a spirited red courser whose mane was the same copper color as the long hair that streamed past Ser Addam's shoulders. The horse was barded in bronze-colored trappings dyed to match the rider's cloak and emblazoned with the burning tree. Some of the castle women sobbed to see him go. Weese said he was a great horseman and sword fighter, Lord Tywin's most daring commander.

I hope he dies, Arya thought as she watched him ride out the gate, his men streaming after him in a double column. *I hope they all die.* They were going to fight Robb, she knew. Listening to the talk as she went about her work, Arya had learned that Robb had won some great victory in the west. He'd burned Lannisport, some said, or else he meant to burn it. He'd captured Casterly Rock and put everyone to the sword, or he was besieging the Golden Tooth . . . but *something* had happened, that much was certain.

Weese had her running messages from dawn to dusk. Some of them even took her beyond the castle walls, out into the mud and madness of the camp. *I could flee,* she thought as a wagon rumbled past her. *I could hop on the back of a wagon and hide, or fall in with the camp followers, no one would stop me.* She might have done it if not for Weese. He'd told them more than once what he'd do to anyone who tried to run off on him. "It won't be no beating, oh, no. I won't lay a finger on you. I'll just save you for the Qohorik, yes I will, I'll save you for the Crippler. Vargo Hoat his name is, and when he gets back he'll cut off your feet." *Maybe if Weese were dead,* Arya thought . . . but not when she was with him. He could look at you and smell what you were thinking, he always said so.

Weese never imagined she could read, though, so he never bothered to seal the messages he gave her. Arya peeked at them all, but they were never anything good, just stupid stuff sending this cart to the granary and that one to the armory. One was a demand for payment on a gambling debt, but the knight she gave it to couldn't read. When she told him what it said he tried to hit her, but Arya ducked under the blow, snatched a silver-banded drinking horn off his saddle, and darted away. The knight roared and came after her, but she slid between two wayns, wove through a crowd of archers, and jumped a latrine trench. In his mail he couldn't keep up. When she gave the horn to Weese, he told her that a smart little Weasel like her deserved a reward. "I've got my eye on a plump crisp capon to sup on tonight. We'll share it, me and you. You'll like that."

Everywhere she went, Arya searched for Jaqen H'ghar, wanting to whisper another name to him before those she hated were all gone out of her reach, but amidst the chaos and confusion the Lorathi sellsword was not to be found. He still owed her two deaths, and she was worried she would never get them if he rode off to battle with the rest. Finally she worked up the courage to ask one of the gate guards if he'd gone. "One of Lorch's men, is he?" the man said. "He won't be going, then. His lordship's named Ser Amory castellan of Harrenhal. That whole lot's staying right here, to hold the castle. The Bloody Mummers will be left as well, to do the foraging. That goat Vargo Hoat is like to spit, him and Lorch have always hated each other."

The Mountain would be leaving with Lord Tywin, though. He would command the van in battle, which meant that Dunsen, Polliver, and Raff would all slip between her fingers unless she could find Jaqen and have him kill one of them before they left.

"Weasel," Weese said that afternoon. "Get to the armory and tell Lucan that Ser Lyonel notched his sword in practice and needs a new one. Here's his mark." He handed her a square of paper. "Be quick about it now, he's to ride with Ser Kevan Lannister."

Arya took the paper and ran. The armory adjoined the castle smithy, a long high-roofed tunnel of a building with twenty forges built into its walls and long stone water troughs for tempering the steel. Half of the forges were at work when she entered. The walls rang with the sound of hammers, and burly men in leather aprons stood sweating in the sullen heat as they bent over bellows and anvils. When she spied Gendry, his bare chest was slick with sweat, but the blue eyes under the heavy black hair had the stubborn look she remembered. Arya didn't know that she even wanted to talk to him. It was his fault they'd all been caught. "Which one is Lucan?" She thrust out the paper. "I'm to get a new sword for Ser Lyonel."

"Never mind about Ser Lyonel." He drew her aside by the arm. "Last night Hot Pie asked me if I heard you yell *Winterfell* back at the holdfast, when we were all fighting on the wall."

"I never did!"

"Yes you did. I heard you too."

"Everyone was yelling stuff," Arya said defensively. "Hot Pie yelled *hot pie*. He must have yelled it a hundred times."

"It's what *you* yelled that matters. I told Hot Pie he should clean the wax out of his ears, that all you yelled was *Go to hell!* If he asks you, you better say the same."

"I will," she said, even though she thought *go to hell* was a stupid thing to yell. She didn't dare tell Hot Pie who she really was. *Maybe I should say Hot Pie's name to Jaqen.*

"I'll get Lucan," Gendry said.

Lucan grunted at the writing (though Arya did not think he could read it), and pulled down a heavy longsword. "This is too good for that oaf, and you tell him I said so," he said as he gave her the blade.

"I will," she lied. If she did any such thing, Weese would beat her bloody. Lucan could deliver his own insults.

The longsword was a lot heavier than Needle had been, but Arya liked the feel of it. The weight of steel in her hands made her feel stronger. *Maybe I'm not a water dancer yet, but I'm not a mouse either. A mouse couldn't use a sword but I can.* The gates were open, soldiers coming and going, drays rolling in empty and going out creaking and swaying under their loads. She thought about going to the stables and telling them that Ser Lyonel wanted a new horse. She had the paper, the stableboys wouldn't be able to read it any better than Lucan had. *I could take the horse and the sword and just ride out. If the guards tried to stop me I'd show them the paper and say I was bringing everything to Ser Lyonel.* She had no notion what Ser Lyonel looked like or where to find him, though. If they questioned her, they'd know, and then Weese . . . Weese . . .

As she chewed her lip, trying not to think about how it would feel to have her feet cut off, a group of archers in leather jerkins and iron helms went past, their bows slung across their shoulders. Arya heard snatches of their talk.

". . . giants I tell you, he's got *giants* twenty foot tall come down from beyond the Wall, follow him like dogs . . ."

". . . not natural, coming on them so fast, in the night and all. He's more wolf than man, all them Starks are . . ."

". . . shit on your wolves and giants, the boy'd piss his pants if he knew we was coming. He wasn't man enough to march on Harrenhal, was he? Ran t'other way, didn't he? He'd run now if he knew what was best for him."

"So you say, but might be the boy knows something we don't, maybe it's *us* ought to be run . . ."

Yes, Arya thought. *Yes, it's you who ought to run, you and Lord Tywin and the Mountain and Ser Addam and Ser Amory and stupid Ser Lyonel whoever he is, all of you better run or my brother will kill you, he's a Stark, he's more wolf than man, and so am I.*

"Weasel." Weese's voice cracked like a whip. She never saw where he came from, but suddenly he was right in front of her. "Give me that. Took you long enough." He snatched the sword from her fingers, and dealt her a stinging slap with the back of his hand. "Next time be quicker about it."

For a moment she had been a wolf again, but Weese's slap took it all away and left her with nothing but the taste of her own blood in her mouth. She'd bitten her tongue when he hit her. She hated him for that.

"You want another?" Weese demanded. "You'll get it too. I'll have none of your insolent looks. Get down to the brewhouse and tell Tuf-fleberry that I have two dozen barrels for him, but he better send his lads to fetch them or I'll find someone wants 'em worse." Arya started off, but not quick enough for Weese. "You *run* if you want to eat tonight," he shouted, his promises of a plump crisp capon already forgotten. "And don't be getting lost again, or I swear I'll beat you bloody."

You won't, Arya thought. *You won't ever again.* But she ran. The old gods of the north must have been guiding her steps. Halfway to the brewhouse, as she passing under the stone bridge that arched between Widow's Tower and Kingspyre, she heard harsh, growling laughter. Rorge came around a corner with three other men, the manticore badge of Ser Amory sewn over their hearts. When he saw her, he stopped and grinned, showing a mouthful of crooked brown teeth under the leather flap he wore sometimes to cover the hole in his face. "Yoren's little cunt," he called her. "Guess we know why that black bastard wanted *you* on the Wall, don't we?" He laughed again, and the others laughed with him. "Where's your stick now?" Rorge demanded suddenly, the smile gone as quick as it had come. "Seems to me I promised to fuck you with it." He took a step toward her. Arya edged backward. "Not so brave now that I'm not in chains, are you?"

"I *saved* you." She kept a good yard between them, ready to run quick as a snake if he made a grab for her.

"Owe you another fucking for that, seems like. Did Yoren pump your cunny, or did he like that tight little ass better?"

"I'm looking for Jaqen," she said. "There's a message."

Rorge halted. Something in his eyes . . . could it be that he was *scared* of Jaqen H'ghar? "The bathhouse. Get out of my way."

Arya whirled and ran, swift as a deer, her feet flying over the cobbles all the way to the bathhouse. She found Jaqen soaking in a tub, steam rising around him as a serving girl sluiced hot water over his head. His long hair, red on one side and white on the other, fell down across his shoulders, wet and heavy.

She crept up quiet as a shadow, but he opened his eyes all the same. "She steals in on little mice feet, but a man hears," he said. *How could he hear me?* she wondered, and it seemed as if he heard that as well. "The scuff of leather on stone sings loud as warhorns to a man with open ears. Clever girls go barefoot."

"I have a message." Arya eyed the serving girl uncertainly. When she did not seem likely to go away, she leaned in until her mouth was almost touching his ear. "Weese," she whispered.

Jaqen H'ghar closed his eyes again, floating languid, half-asleep. "Tell his lordship a man shall attend him at his leisure." His hand moved suddenly, splashing hot water at her, and Arya had to leap back to keep from getting drenched.

When she told Tuffleberry what Weese had said, the brewer cursed loudly. "You tell Weese my lads got duties to attend to, and you tell him he's a pox-ridden bastard too, and the seven hells will freeze over before he gets another horn of my ale. I'll have them barrels within the hour or Lord Tywin will hear of it, see if he don't."

Weese cursed too when Arya brought back that message, even though she left out the pox-ridden bastard part. He fumed and threatened, but in the end he rounded up six men and sent them off grumbling to fetch the barrels down to the brewhouse.

Supper that evening was a thin stew of barley, onion, and carrots, with a wedge of stale brown bread. One of the women had taken to sleeping in Weese's bed, and she got a piece of ripe blue cheese as well, and a wing off the capon that Weese had spoken of that morning. He ate the rest himself, the grease running down in a shiny line through the boils that festered at the corner of his mouth. The bird was almost gone when he glanced up from his trencher and saw Arya staring. "Weasel, come here."

A few mouthfuls of dark meat still clung to one thigh. *He forgot, but now he's remembered*, Arya thought. It made her feel bad for telling Jaqen to kill him. She got off the bench and went to the head of the table.

"I saw you looking at me." Weese wiped his fingers on the front of her shift. Then he grabbed her throat with one hand and slapped her with the other. "What did I tell you?" He slapped her again, backhand. "Keep those eyes to yourself, or next time I'll spoon one out and feed it to my bitch." A shove sent her stumbling to the floor. Her hem caught on a loose nail in the splintered wooden bench and ripped as she fell. "You'll mend that before you sleep," Weese announced as he pulled the last bit of meat off the capon. When he was finished he sucked his fingers noisily, and threw the bones to his ugly spotted dog.

"Weese," Arya whispered that night as she bent over the tear in her shift. "Dunsen, Polliver, Raff the Sweetling," she said, calling a name every time she pushed the bone needle through the undyed wool. "The Tickler and the Hound. Ser Gregor, Ser Amory, Ser Ilyn, Ser Meryn, King Joffrey, Queen Cersei." She wondered how much longer she would have to include Weese in her prayer, and drifted off to sleep dreaming that on the morrow, when she woke, he'd be dead.

But it was the sharp toe of Weese's boot that woke her, as ever. The main strength of Lord Tywin's host would ride this day, he told them as they broke their fast on oatcakes. "Don't none of you be thinking how easy it'll be here once m'lord of Lannister is gone," he warned. "The castle won't grow no smaller, I promise you that, only now there'll be fewer hands to tend to it. You lot of slugabeds are going to learn what work is now, yes you are."

Not from you. Arya picked at her oaten cake. Weese frowned at her, as if he smelled her secret. Quickly she dropped her gaze to her food, and dared not raise her eyes again.

Pale light filled the yard when Lord Tywin Lannister took his leave of Harrenhal. Arya watched from an arched window halfway up the Wailing Tower. His charger wore a blanket of enameled crimson scales and gilded crinet and chamfron, while Lord Tywin himself sported a thick ermine cloak. His brother Ser Kevan looked near as splendid. No less than four standard-bearers went before them, carrying huge crimson banners emblazoned with the golden lion. Behind the Lannisters came their great lords and captains. Their banners flared and flapped, a pageant of color: red ox and golden mountain, purple unicorn and bantam rooster, brindled boar and badger, a silver ferret and a juggler in motley, stars and sunbursts, peacock and panther, chevron and dagger, black hood and blue beetle and green arrow.

Last of all came Ser Gregor Clegane in his grey plate steel, astride a stallion as bad-tempered as his rider. Polliver rode beside him, with the black dog standard in his hand and Gendry's horned helm on his head. He was a tall man, but he looked no more than a half-grown boy when he rode in his master's shadow.

A shiver crept up Arya's spine as she watched them pass under the great iron portcullis of Harrenhal. Suddenly she knew that she had made a terrible mistake. *I'm so stupid*, she thought. Weese did not matter, no more than Chiswyck had. *These* were the men who mattered, the ones she ought to have killed. Last night she could have whispered any of them dead, if only she hadn't been so mad at Weese for hitting her and lying about the capon. *Lord Tywin, why didn't I say Lord Tywin?*

Perhaps it was not too late to change her mind. Weese was not killed yet. If she could find Jaqen, tell him . . .

Hurriedly, Arya ran down the twisting steps, her chores forgotten. She heard the rattle of chains as the portcullis was slowly lowered, its spikes sinking deep into the ground . . . and then another sound, a shriek of pain and fear.

A dozen people got there before her, though none was coming any too close. Arya squirmed between them. Weese was sprawled across the cobbles, his throat a red ruin, eyes gaping sightlessly up at a bank of grey cloud. His ugly spotted dog stood on his chest, lapping at the blood pulsing from his neck, and every so often ripping a mouthful of flesh out of the dead man's face.

Finally someone brought a crossbow and shot the spotted dog dead while she was worrying at one of Weese's ears.

"Damnedest thing," she heard a man say. "He had that bitch dog since she was a pup."

"This place is cursed," the man with the crossbow said.

"It's Harren's ghost, that's what it is," said Goodwife Amabel. "I'll not sleep here another night, I swear it."

Arya lifted her gaze from the dead man and his dead dog. Jaqen H'ghar was leaning up against the side of the Wailing Tower. When he saw her looking, he lifted a hand to his face and laid two fingers casually against his cheek.

CATELYN

Two days ride from Riverrun, a scout spied them watering their horses beside a muddy steam. Catelyn had never been so glad to see the twin tower badge of House Frey.

When she asked him to lead them to her uncle, he said, "The Blackfish is gone west with the king, my lady. Martyn Rivers commands the outriders in his stead."

"I see." She had met Rivers at the Twins; a baseborn son of Lord Walder Frey, half brother to Ser Perwyn. It did not surprise her to learn that Robb had struck at the heart of Lannister power; clearly he had been contemplating just that when he sent her away to treat with Renly. "Where is Rivers now?"

"His camp is two hours ride, my lady."

"Take us to him," she commanded. Brienne helped her back into her saddle, and they set out at once.

"Have you come from Bitterbridge, my lady?" the scout asked.

"No." She had not dared. With Renly dead, Catelyn had been uncertain of the reception she might receive from his young widow and her protectors. Instead she had ridden through the heart of the war, through fertile riverlands turned to blackened desert by the fury of the Lannisters, and each night her scouts brought back tales that made her ill. "Lord Renly is slain," she added.

"We'd hoped that tale was some Lannister lie, or—"

"Would that it were. My brother commands in Riverrun?"

"Yes, my lady. His Grace left Ser Edmure to hold Riverrun and guard his rear."

Gods grant him the strength to do so, Catelyn thought. *And the wisdom as well.* "Is there word from Robb in the west?"

"You have not heard?" The man seemed surprised. "His Grace won a great victory at Oxcross. Ser Stafford Lannister is dead, his host scattered."

Ser Wendel Manderly gave a *whoop* of pleasure, but Catelyn only nodded. Tomorrow's trials concerned her more than yesterday's triumphs.

Martyn Rivers had made his camp in the shell of a shattered holdfast, beside a roofless stable and a hundred fresh graves. He went to one knee when Catelyn dismounted. "Well met, my lady. Your brother charged us to keep an eye out for your party, and escort you back to Riverrun in all haste should we come upon you."

Catelyn scarce liked the sound of that. "Is it my father?"

"No, my lady. Lord Hoster is unchanged." Rivers was a ruddy man with scant resemblance to his half brothers. "It is only that we feared you might chance upon Lannister scouts. Lord Tywin has left Harrenhal and marches west with all his power."

"Rise," she told Rivers, frowning. Stannis Baratheon would soon be on the march as well, gods help them all. "How long until Lord Tywin is upon us?"

"Three days, perhaps four, it is hard to know. We have eyes out along all the roads, but it would be best not to linger."

Nor did they. Rivers broke his camp quickly and saddled up beside her, and they set off again, near fifty strong now, flying beneath the direwolf, the leaping trout, the twin towers.

Her men wanted to hear more of Robb's victory at Oxcross, and Rivers obliged. "There's a singer come to Riverrun, calls himself Rymund the Rhymer, he's made a song of the fight. Doubtless you'll hear it sung tonight, my lady. 'Wolf in the Night,' this Rymund calls it." He went on to tell how the remnants of Ser Stafford's host had fallen back on Lannisport. Without siege engines there was no way to storm Casterly Rock, so the Young Wolf was paying the Lannisters back in kind for the devastation they'd inflicted on the riverlands. Lords Karstark and Glover were raiding along the coast, Lady Mormont had captured thousands of cattle and was driving them back toward Riverrun, while the Greatjon had seized the gold mines at Castamere, Nunn's Deep, and the Pendric Hills. Ser Wendel laughed. "Nothing's more like to bring a Lannister running than a threat to his gold."

"How did the king ever take the Tooth?" Ser Perwyn Frey asked his bastard brother. "That's a hard strong keep, and it commands the hill road."

"He never took it. He slipped around it in the night. It's said the direwolf showed him the way, that Grey Wind of his. The beast sniffed out a goat track that wound down a defile and up along beneath a ridge, a crooked and stony way, yet wide enough for men riding single file. The Lannisters in their watchtowers got not so much a glimpse of them." Rivers lowered his voice. "There's some say that after the battle, the king cut out Stafford Lannister's heart and fed it to the wolf."

"I would not believe such tales," Catelyn said sharply. "My son is no savage."

"As you say, my lady. Still, it's no more than the beast deserved. That is no common wolf, that one. The Greatjon's been heard to say that the old gods of the north sent those direwolves to your children."

Catelyn remembered the day when her boys had found the pups in the late summer snows. There had been five, three male and two female for the five trueborn children of House Stark . . . and a sixth, white of fur and red of eye, for Ned's bastard son Jon Snow. *No common wolves*, she thought. *No indeed.*

That night as they made their camp, Brienne sought out her tent. "My lady, you are safely back among your own now, a day's ride from your brother's castle. Give me leave to go."

Catelyn should not have been surprised. The homely young woman had kept to herself all through their journey, spending most of her time with the horses, brushing out their coats and pulling stones from their shoes. She had helped Shadd cook and clean game as well, and soon proved that she could hunt as well as any. Any task Catelyn asked her to turn her hand to, Brienne had performed deftly and without complaint, and when she was spoken to she answered politely, but she never chattered, nor wept, nor laughed. She had ridden with them every day and slept among them every night without ever truly becoming one of them.

It was the same when she was with Renly, Catelyn thought. *At the feast, in the melee, even in Renly's pavilion with her brothers of the Rainbow Guard. There are walls around this one higher than Winterfell's.*

"If you left us, where would you go?" Catelyn asked her.

"Back," Brienne said. "To Storm's End."

"Alone." It was not a question.

The broad face was a pool of still water, giving no hint of what might live in the depths below. "Yes."

"You mean to kill Stannis."

Brienne closed her thick callused fingers around the hilt of her sword.

The sword that had been his. "I swore a vow. Three times I swore. You heard me."

"I did," Catelyn admitted. The girl had kept the rainbow cloak when she discarded the rest of her bloodstained clothing, she knew. Brienne's own things had been left behind during their flight, and she had been forced to clothe herself in odd bits of Ser Wendel's spare garb, since no one else in their party had garments large enough to fit her. "Vows should be kept, I agree, but Stannis has a great host around him, and his own guards sworn to keep him safe."

"I am not afraid of his guards. I am as good as any of them. I should never have fled."

"Is that what troubles you, that some fool might call you craven?" She sighed. "Renly's death was no fault of yours. You served him valiantly, but when you seek to follow him into the earth, you serve no one." She stretched out a hand, to give what comfort a touch could give. "I know how hard it is—"

Brienne shook off her hand. "No one knows."

"You're wrong," Catelyn said sharply. "Every morning, when I wake, I remember that Ned is gone. I have no skill with swords, but that does not mean that I do not dream of riding to King's Landing and wrapping my hands around Cersei Lannister's white throat and squeezing until her face turns black."

The Beauty raised her eyes, the only part of her that was truly beautiful. "If you dream that, why would you seek to hold me back? Is it because of what Stannis said at the parley?"

Was it? Catelyn glanced across the camp. Two men were walking sentry, spears in hand. "I was taught that good men must fight evil in this world, and Renly's death was evil beyond all doubt. Yet I was also taught that the gods make kings, not the swords of men. If Stannis is our rightful king—"

"He's not. Robert was never the rightful king either, even Renly said as much. Jaime Lannister *murdered* the rightful king, after Robert killed his lawful heir on the Trident. Where were the gods then? The gods don't care about men, no more than kings care about peasants."

"A good king does care."

"Lord Renly . . . His Grace, he . . . he would have been the *best* king, my lady, he was so good, he . . ."

"He is gone, Brienne," she said, as gently as she could. "Stannis and Joffrey remain . . . and so does my son."

"He wouldn't . . . you'd never make a *peace* with Stannis, would you? Bend the knee? You wouldn't . . ."

"I will tell you true, Brienne. I do not know. My son may be a king, but I am no queen . . . only a mother who would keep her children safe, however she could."

"I am not made to be a mother. I need to fight."

"Then fight . . . but for the living, not the dead. Renly's enemies are Robb's enemies as well."

Brienne stared at the ground and shuffled her feet. "I do not know your son, my lady." She looked up. "I could serve you. If you would have me."

Catelyn was startled. "Why me?"

The question seemed to trouble Brienne. "You helped me. In the pavilion . . . when they thought that I had . . . that I had . . ."

"You were innocent."

"Even so, you did not have to do that. You could have let them kill me. I was nothing to you."

Perhaps I did not want to be the only one who knew the dark truth of what had happened there, Catelyn thought. "Brienne, I have taken many wellborn ladies into my service over the years, but never one like you. I am no battle commander."

"No, but you have courage. Not battle courage perhaps but . . . I don't know . . . a kind of *woman's* courage. And I think, when the time comes, you will not try and hold me back. Promise me that. That you will not hold me back from Stannis."

Catelyn could still hear Stannis saying that Robb's turn too would come in time. It was like a cold breath on the back of her neck. "When the time comes, I will not hold you back."

The tall girl knelt awkwardly, unsheathed Renly's longsword, and laid it at her feet. "Then I am yours, my lady. Your liege man, or . . . whatever you would have me be. I will shield your back and keep your counsel and give my life for yours, if need be. I swear it by the old gods and the new."

"And I vow that you shall always have a place by my hearth and meat and mead at my table, and pledge to ask no service of you that might bring you into dishonor. I swear it by the old gods and the new. Arise." As she clasped the other woman's hands between her own, Catelyn could not help but smile. *How many times did I watch Ned accept a man's oath of service?* She wondered what he would think if he could see her now.

They forded the Red Fork late the next day, upstream of Riverrun where the river made a wide loop and the waters grew muddy and shallow. The crossing was guarded by a mixed force of archers and pikemen wearing the eagle badge of the Mallisters. When they saw Catelyn's banners, they emerged from behind their sharpened stakes and sent a man over from the far bank to lead her party across. "Slow and careful like, milady," he warned as he took the bridle of her horse. "We've planted iron spikes under the water, y'see, and there's caltrops scattered among them rocks there. It's the same on all the fords, by your brother's command."

Edmure thinks to fight here. The realization gave her a queasy feeling in the bowels, but she held her tongue.

Between the Red Fork and the Tumblestone, they joined a stream of smallfolk making for the safety of Riverrun. Some were driving animals before them, others pulling wayns, but they made way as Catelyn rode past, and cheered her with cries of "Tully!" or "Stark!" Half a mile from the castle, she passed through a large encampment where the scarlet banner of the Blackwoods waved above the lord's tent. Lucas took his leave of her there, to seek out his father, Lord Tytos. The rest rode on.

Catelyn spied a second camp strung out along the bank north of the Tumblestone, familiar standards flapping in the wind—Marq Piper's dancing maiden, Darry's plowman, the twining red-and-white snakes of the Paeges. They were all her father's bannermen, lords of the Trident. Most had left Riverrun before she had, to defend their own lands. If they were here again, it could only mean that Edmure had called them back. *Gods save us, it's true, he means to offer battle to Lord Tywin.*

Something dark was dangling against the walls of Riverrun, Catelyn saw from a distance. When she rode close, she saw dead men hanging from the battlements, slumped at the ends of long ropes with hempen nooses tight around their necks, their faces swollen and black. The crows had been at them, but their crimson cloaks still showed bright against the sandstone walls.

"They have hanged some Lannisters," Hal Mollen observed.

"A pretty sight," Ser Wendel Manderly said cheerfully.

"Our friends have begun without us," Perwyn Frey jested. The others laughed, all but Brienne, who gazed up at the row of bodies unblinking, and neither spoke nor smiled.

If they have slain the Kingslayer, then my daughters are dead as well. Catelyn spurred her horse to a canter. Hal Mollen and Robin Flint raced past at a gallop, halooing to the gatehouse. The guards on the walls had doubtless spied her banners some time ago, for the portcullis was up as they approached.

Edmure rode out from the castle to meet her, surrounded by three of her father's sworn men—great-bellied Ser Desmond Grell the master-at-arms, Utherydes Wayn the steward, and Ser Robin Ryger, Riverrun's big bald captain of guards. They were all three of an age with Lord Hoster, men who had spent their lives in her father's service. *Old men*, Catelyn realized.

Edmure wore a blue-and-red cloak over a tunic embroidered with silver fish. From the look of him, he had not shaved since she rode south;

his beard was a fiery bush. "Cat, it is good to have you safely back. When we heard of Renly's death, we feared for your life. And Lord Tywin is on the march as well."

"So I am told. How fares our father?"

"One day he seems stronger, the next . . ." He shook his head. "He's asked for you. I did not know what to tell him."

"I will go to him soon," she vowed. "Has there been word from Storm's End since Renly died? Or from Bitterbridge?" No ravens came to men on the road, and Catelyn was anxious to know what had happened behind her.

"Nothing from Bitterbridge. From Storm's End, three birds from the castellan, Ser Cortnay Penrose, all carrying the same plea. Stannis has him surrounded by land and sea. He offers his allegiance to whatsoever king will break the siege. He fears for the boy, he says. What boy would that be, do you know?"

"Edric Storm," Brienne told them. "Robert's bastard son."

Edmure looked at her curiously. "Stannis has sworn that the garrison might go free, unharmed, provided they yield the castle within the fortnight and deliver the boy into his hands, but Ser Cortnay will not consent."

He risks all for a baseborn boy whose blood is not even his own, Catelyn thought. "Did you send him an answer?"

Edmure shook his head. "Why, when we have neither help nor hope to offer? And Stannis is no enemy of ours."

Ser Robin Ryger spoke. "My lady, can you tell us the manner of Lord Renly's death? The tales we've heard have been queer."

"Cat," her brother said, "some say *you* killed Renly. Others claim it was some southron woman." His glance lingered on Brienne.

"My king was murdered," the girl said quietly, "and not by Lady Catelyn. I swear it on my sword, by the gods old and new."

"This is Brienne of Tarth, the daughter of Lord Selwyn the Evenstar, who served in Renly's Rainbow Guard," Catelyn told them. "Brienne, I am honored to acquaint you with my brother Ser Edmure Tully, heir to Riverrun. His steward Utherydes Wayn. Ser Robin Ryger and Ser Desmond Grell."

"Honored," said Ser Desmond. The others echoed him. The girl flushed, embarrassed even at this commonplace courtesy. If Edmure thought her a curious sort of lady, at least he had the grace not to say so.

"Brienne was with Renly when he was killed, as was I," said Catelyn, "but we had no part in his death." She did not care to speak of the shadow, here in the open with men all around, so she waved a hand at the bodies. "Who are these men you've hanged?"

Edmure glanced up uncomfortably. "They came with Ser Cleos when he brought the queen's answer to our peace offer."

Catelyn was shocked. "You've killed *envoys?*"

"False envoys," Edmure declared. "They pledged me their peace and surrendered their weapons, so I allowed them freedom of the castle, and for three nights they ate my meat and drank my mead whilst I talked with Ser Cleos. On the fourth night, they tried to free the Kingslayer." He pointed up. "That big brute killed two guards with naught but those ham hands of his, caught them by the throats and smashed their skulls together while that skinny lad beside him was opening Lannister's cell with a bit of wire, gods curse him. The one on the end was some sort of damned mummer. He used my own voice to command that the River Gate be opened. The guardsmen swear to it, Enger and Delp and Long Lew, all three. If you ask me, the man sounded nothing like me, and yet the oafs were raising the portcullis all the same."

This was the Imp's work, Catelyn suspected; it stank of the same sort of cunning he had displayed at the Eyrie. Once, she would have named Tyrion the least dangerous of the Lannisters. Now she was not so certain. "How is it you caught them?"

"Ah, as it happened, I was not in the castle. I'd crossed the Tumblestone to, ah . . ."

"You were whoring or wenching. Get on with the tale."

Edmure's cheeks flamed as red as his beard. "It was the hour before dawn, and I was only then returning. When Long Lew saw my boat and recognized me, he finally thought to wonder who was standing below barking commands, and raised a cry."

"Tell me the Kingslayer was retaken."

"Yes, though not easily. Jaime got hold of a sword, slew Poul Pemford and Ser Desmond's squire Myles, and wounded Delp so badly that Maester Vyman fears he'll soon die as well. It was a bloody mess. At the sound of steel, some of the other red cloaks rushed to join him, barehand or no. I hanged those beside the four who freed him, and threw the rest in the dungeons. Jaime too. We'll have no more escapes from that one. He's down in the dark this time, chained hand and foot and bolted to the wall."

"And Cleos Frey?"

"He swears he knew naught of the plot. Who can say? The man is half Lannister, half Frey, and all liar. I put him in Jaime's old tower cell."

"You say he brought terms?"

"If you can call them that. You'll like them no more than I did, I promise."

"Can we hope for no help from the south, Lady Stark?" asked

Utherydes Wayn, her father's steward. "This charge of incest . . . Lord Tywin does not suffer such slights lightly. He will seek to wash the stain from his daughter's name with the blood of her accuser, Lord Stannis must see that. He has no choice but to make common cause with us."

Stannis has made common cause with a power greater and darker. "Let us speak of these matters later." Catelyn trotted over the drawbridge, putting the grisly row of dead Lannisters behind her. Her brother kept pace. As they rode out into the bustle of Riverrun's upper bailey, a naked toddler ran in front of the horses. Catelyn jerked her reins hard to avoid him, glancing about in dismay. Hundreds of smallfolk had been admitted to the castle, and allowed to erect crude shelters against the walls. Their children were everywhere underfoot, and the yard teemed with their cows, sheep, and chickens. "Who are all these folk?"

"My people," Edmure answered. "They were afraid."

Only my sweet brother would crowd all these useless mouths into a castle that might soon be under siege. Catelyn knew that Edmure had a soft heart; sometimes she thought his head was even softer. She loved him for it, yet still . . .

"Can Robb be reached by raven?"

"He's in the field, my lady," Ser Desmond replied. "The bird would have no way to find him."

Utherydes Wayn coughed. "Before he left us, the young king instructed us to send you on to the Twins upon your return, Lady Stark. He asks that you learn more of Lord Walder's daughters, to help him select his bride when the time comes."

"We'll provide you with fresh mounts and provisions," her brother promised. "You'll want to refresh yourself before—"

"I'll want to stay," Catelyn said, dismounting. She had no intention of leaving Riverrun and her dying father to pick Robb's wife for him. *Robb wants me safe, I cannot fault him for that, but his pretext is growing threadbare.* "Boy," she called, and an urchin from the stables ran out to take the reins of her horse.

Edmure swung down from his saddle. He was a head taller than she was, but he would always be her little brother. "Cat," he said unhappily, "Lord Tywin is coming—"

"He is making for the west, to defend his own lands. If we close our gates and shelter behind the walls, we can watch him pass with safety."

"This is Tully land," Edmure declared. "If Tywin Lannister thinks to cross it unbloodied, I mean to teach him a hard lesson."

The same lesson you taught his son? Her brother could be stubborn as river rock when his pride was touched, but neither of them was likely to forget how Ser Jaime had cut Edmure's host to bloody pieces the last time he had offered battle. "We have nothing to gain and everything to lose by meeting Lord Tywin in the field," Catelyn said tactfully.

"The yard is not the place to discuss my battle plans."

"As you will. Where shall we go?"

Her brother's face darkened. For a moment she thought he was about to lose his temper with her, but finally he snapped, "The godswood. If you will insist."

She followed him along a gallery to the godswood gate. Edmure's anger had always been a sulky, sullen thing. Catelyn was sorry she had wounded him, but the matter was too important for her to concern herself with his pride. When they were alone beneath the trees, Edmure turned to face her.

"You do not have the strength to meet the Lannisters in the field," she said bluntly.

"When all my strength is marshaled, I should have eight thousand foot and three thousand horse," Edmure said.

"Which means Lord Tywin will have near twice your numbers."

"Robb's won his battles against worse odds," Edmure replied, "and I have a plan. You've forgotten Roose Bolton. Lord Tywin defeated him on the Green Fork, but failed to pursue. When Lord Tywin went to Harrenhal, Bolton took the ruby ford and the crossroads. He has ten thousand men. I've sent word to Helman Tallhart to join him with the garrison Robb left at the Twins—"

"Edmure, Robb left those men to *hold* the Twins and make certain Lord Walder keeps faith with us."

"He has," Edmure said stubbornly. "The Freys fought bravely in the Whispering Wood, and old Ser Stevron died at Oxcross, we hear. Ser Ryman and Black Walder and the rest are with Robb in the west, Martyn has been of great service scouting, and Ser Perwyn helped see you safe to Renly. Gods be good, how much more can we ask of them? Robb's betrothed to one of Lord Walder's daughters, and Roose Bolton wed another, I hear. And haven't you taken two of his grandsons to be fostered at Winterfell?"

"A ward can easily become a hostage, if need be." She had not known that Ser Stevron was dead, nor of Bolton's marriage.

"If we're two hostages to the good, all the more reason Lord Walder dare not play us false. Bolton needs Frey's men, and Ser Helman's as well. I've commanded him to retake Harrenhal."

"That's like to be a bloody business."

"Yes, but once the castle falls, Lord Tywin will have no safe retreat. My own levies will defend the fords of Red Fork against his crossing. If he attacks across the river, he'll end as Rhaegar did when he tried to cross the Trident. If he holds back, he'll be caught between Riverrun and Harrenhal, and when Robb returns from the west we can finish him for good and all."

Her brother's voice was full of brusque confidence, but Catelyn found herself wishing that Robb had not taken her uncle Brynden west with him. The Blackfish was the veteran of half a hundred battles; Edmure was the veteran of one, and that one lost.

"The plan's a good one," he concluded. "Lord Tytos says so, and Lord Jonos as well. When did Blackwood and Bracken agree about *anything* that was not certain, I ask you?"

"Be that as it may." She was suddenly weary. Perhaps she was wrong to oppose him. Perhaps it was a splendid plan, and her misgivings only a woman's fears. She wished Ned were here, or her uncle Brynden, or . . . "Have you asked Father about this?"

"Father is in no state to weigh strategies. Two days ago he was making plans for your marriage to Brandon Stark! Go see him yourself if you do not believe me. This plan will work, Cat, you'll see."

"I hope so, Edmure. I truly do." She kissed him on the cheek, to let him know she meant it, and went to find her father.

Lord Hoster Tully was much as she had left him—abed, haggard, flesh pale and clammy. The room smelled of sickness, a cloying odor made up in equal parts of stale sweat and medicine. When she pulled back the drapes, her father gave a low moan, and his eyes fluttered open. He stared at her as if he could not comprehend who she was or what she wanted.

"Father." She kissed him. "I am returned."

He seemed to know her then. "You've come," he whispered faintly, lips barely moving.

"Yes," she said. "Robb sent me south, but I hurried back."

"South . . . where . . . is the Eyrie south, sweetling? I don't re-call . . . oh, dear heart, I was afraid . . . have you forgiven me, child?" Tears ran down his cheeks.

"You've done nothing that needs forgiveness, Father." She stroked his limp white hair and felt his brow. The fever still burned him from within, despite all the maester's potions.

"It was best," her father whispered. "Jon's a good man, good . . . strong, kind . . . take care of you . . . he will . . . and well born, lis-ten to me, you must, I'm your father . . . your father . . . you'll wed when Cat does, yes you *will* . . ."

He thinks I'm Lysa, Catelyn realized. *Gods be good, he talks as if we were not married yet.*

Her father's hands clutched at hers, fluttering like two frightened white birds. "That stripling . . . wretched boy . . . not speak that name to me, your duty . . . your mother, she would . . ." Lord Hoster cried as a spasm of pain washed over him. "Oh, gods forgive me, forgive me, *forgive* me. My medicine . . ."

And then Maester Vyman was there, holding a cup to his lips. Lord Hoster sucked at the thick white potion as eager as a babe at the breast, and Catelyn could see peace settle over him once more. "He'll sleep now, my lady," the maester said when the cup was empty. The milk of the poppy had left a thick white film around her father's mouth. Maester Vyman wiped it away with a sleeve.

Catelyn could watch no more. Hoster Tully had been a strong man, and proud. It hurt her to see him reduced to this. She went out to the terrace. The yard below was crowded with refugees and chaotic with their noises, but beyond the walls the rivers flowed clean and pure and endless. *Those are his rivers, and soon he will return to them for his last voyage.*

Maester Vyman had followed her out. "My lady," he said softly, "I cannot keep the end at bay much longer. We ought send a rider after his brother. Ser Brynden would wish to be here."

"Yes," Catelyn said, her voice thick with her grief.

"And the Lady Lysa as well, perhaps?"

"Lysa will not come."

"If you wrote her yourself, perhaps . . ."

"I will put some words to paper, if that please you." She wondered who Lysa's "wretched stripling" had been. Some young squire or hedge knight, like as not . . . though by the vehemence with which Lord Hoster had opposed him, he might have been a tradesman's son or base-born apprentice, even a singer. Lysa had always been too fond of singers. *I must not blame her. Jon Arryn was twenty years older than our father, however noble.*

The tower her brother had set aside for her use was the very same that she and Lysa had shared as maids. It would feel good to sleep on a feather-erbed again, with a warm fire in the hearth; when she was rested the world would seem less bleak.

But outside her chambers she found Utherydes Wayn waiting with two women clad in grey, their faces cowled save for their eyes. Catelyn knew at once why they were here. *"Ned?"*

The sisters lowered their gaze. Utherydes said, "Ser Cleos brought him from King's Landing, my lady."

"Take me to him," she commanded.

They had laid him out on a trestle table and covered him with a banner, the white banner of House Stark with its grey direwolf sigil. "I would look on him," Catelyn said.

"Only the bones remain, my lady."

"I would look on him," she repeated.

One of the silent sisters turned down the banner.

Bones, Catelyn thought. *This is not Ned, this is not the man I loved, the father of my children.* His hands were clasped together over his chest, skeletal fingers curled about the hilt of some longsword, but they were not Ned's hands, so strong and full of life. They had dressed the bones in Ned's surcoat, the fine white velvet with the direwolf badge over the heart, but nothing remained of the warm flesh that had pillowed her head so many nights, the arms that had held her. The head had been rejoined to the body with fine silver wire, but one skull looks much like another, and in those empty hollows she found no trace of her lord's dark grey eyes, eyes that could be soft as a fog or hard as stone. *They gave his eyes to crows*, she remembered.

Catelyn turned away. "That is not his sword."

"Ice was not returned to us, my lady," Utherydes said. "Only Lord Eddard's bones."

"I suppose I must thank the queen for even that much."

"Thank the Imp, my lady. It was his doing."

One day I will thank them all. "I am grateful for your service, sisters," Catelyn said, "but I must lay another task upon you. Lord Eddard was a Stark, and his bones must be laid to rest beneath Winterfell." *They will make a statue of him, a stone likeness that will sit in the dark with a direwolf at his feet and a sword across his knees.* "Make certain the sisters have fresh horses, and aught else they need for the journey," she told Utherydes Wayn. "Hal Mollen will escort them back to Winterfell, it is his place as captain of guards." She gazed down at the bones that were all that remained of her lord and love. "Now leave me, all of you. I would be alone with Ned tonight."

The women in grey bowed their heads. *The silent sisters do not speak to the living*, Catelyn remembered dully, *but some say they can talk to the dead.* And how she envied that . . .

DAENERYS

The drapes kept out the dust and heat of the streets, but they could not keep out disappointment. Dany climbed inside wearily, glad for the refuge from the sea of Qartheen eyes. "Make way," Jhogo shouted at the crowd from horseback, snapping his whip, "make way, make way for the Mother of Dragons."

Reclining on cool satin cushions, Xaro Xhoan Daxos poured ruby-red wine into matched goblets of jade and gold, his hands sure and steady despite the sway of the palanquin. "I see a deep sadness written upon your face, my light of love." He offered her a goblet. "Could it be the sadness of a lost dream?"

"A dream delayed, no more." Dany's tight silver collar was chafing against her throat. She unfastened it and flung it aside. The collar was set with an enchanted amethyst that Xaro swore would ward her against all poisons. The Pureborn were notorious for offering poisoned wine to those they thought dangerous, but they had not given Dany so much as a cup of water. *They never saw me for a queen,* she thought bitterly. *I was only an afternoon's amusement, a horse girl with a curious pet.*

Rhaegal hissed and dug sharp black claws into her bare shoulder as Dany stretched out a hand for the wine. Wincing, she shifted him to her other shoulder, where he could claw her gown instead of her skin. She was garbed after the Qartheen fashion. Xaro had warned her that the Enthroned would never listen to a Dothraki, so she had taken care to go before them in flowing green samite with one breast bared, silvered sandals on her feet, with a belt of black-and-white pearls about her waist. *For all the help they offered, I could have gone naked. Perhaps I should have.* She drank deep.

Descendants of the ancient kings and queens of Qarth, the Pureborn commanded the Civic Guard and the fleet of ornate galleys that ruled the straits between the seas. Daenerys Targaryen had wanted that fleet, or part of it, and some of their soldiers as well. She made the traditional sacrifice in the Temple of Memory, offered the traditional bribe to the Keeper of the Long List, sent the traditional persimmon to the Opener of the Door, and finally received the traditional blue silk slippers summoning her to the Hall of a Thousand Thrones.

The Pureborn heard her pleas from the great wooden seats of their ancestors, rising in curved tiers from a marble floor to a high-domed ceiling painted with scenes of Qarth's vanished glory. The chairs were immense, fantastically carved, bright with goldwork and studded with amber, onyx, lapis, and jade, each one different from all the others, and each striving to be the most fabulous. Yet the men who sat in them seemed so listless and world-weary that they might have been asleep. *They listened, but they did not hear, or care,* she thought. *They are Milk Men indeed. They never meant to help me. They came because they were curious. They came because they were bored, and the dragon on my shoulder interested them more than I did.*

"Tell me the words of the Pureborn," prompted Xaro Xhoan Daxos. "Tell me what they said to sadden the queen of my heart."

"They said no." The wine tasted of pomegranates and hot summer days. "They said it with great courtesy, to be sure, but under all the lovely words, it was still no."

"Did you flatter them?"

"Shamelessly."

"Did you weep?"

"The blood of the dragon does not weep," she said testily.

Xaro sighed. "You ought to have wept." The Qartheen wept often and easily; it was considered a mark of the civilized man. "The men we bought, what did they say?"

"Mathos said nothing. Wendello praised the way I spoke. The Exquisite refused me with the rest, but he wept afterward."

"Alas, that Qartheen should be so faithless." Xaro was not himself of the Pureborn, but he had told her whom to bribe and how much to offer. "Weep, weep, for the treachery of men."

Dany would sooner have wept for her gold. The bribes she'd tendered to Mathos Mallarawan, Wendello Qar Deeth, and Egon Emeros the Exquisite might have bought her a ship, or hired a score of sellswords. "Suppose I sent Ser Jorah to demand the return of my gifts?" she asked.

"Suppose a Sorrowful Man came to my palace one night and killed you as you slept," said Xaro. The Sorrowful Men were an ancient sacred guild of assassins, so named because they always whispered, "I am so sorry," to their victims before they killed them. The Qartheen were nothing if not polite. "It is wisely said that it is easier to milk the Stone Cow of Faros than to wring gold from the Pureborn."

Dany did not know where Faros was, but it seemed to her that Qarth was full of stone cows. The merchant princes, grown vastly rich off the trade between the seas, were divided into three jealous factions: the Ancient Guild of Spicers, the Tourmaline Brotherhood, and the Thirteen, to which Xaro belonged. Each vied with the others for dominance, and all three contended endlessly with the Pureborn. And brooding over all were the warlocks, with their blue lips and dread powers, seldom seen but much feared.

She would have been lost without Xaro. The gold that she had squandered to open the doors of the Hall of a Thousand Thrones was largely a product of the merchant's generosity and quick wits. As the rumor of living dragons had spread through the east, ever more seekers had come to learn if the tale was true—and Xaro Xhoan Daxos saw to it that the great and the humble alike offered some token to the Mother of Dragons.

The trickle he started soon swelled to a flood. Trader captains brought lace from Myr, chests of saffron from Yi Ti, amber and dragonglass out of Asshai. Merchants offered bags of coin, silversmiths rings and chains. Pipers piped for her, tumblers tumbled, and jugglers juggled, while dyers draped her in colors she had never known existed. A pair of Jogos Nhai presented her with one of their striped zorses, black and white and fierce. A widow brought the dried corpse of her husband, covered with a crust of silvered leaves; such remnants were believed to have great power, especially if the deceased had been a sorcerer, as this one had. And the Tourmaline Brotherhood pressed on her a crown wrought in the shape of a three-headed dragon; the coils were yellow gold, the wings silver, the heads carved from jade, ivory, and onyx.

The crown was the only offering she'd kept. The rest she sold, to gather the wealth she had wasted on the Pureborn. Xaro would have sold the crown too—the Thirteen would see that she had a much finer one, he swore—but Dany forbade it. "Viserys sold my mother's crown, and men called him a beggar. I shall keep this one, so men will call me a queen." And so she did, though the weight of it made her neck ache.

Yet even crowned, I am a beggar still, Dany thought. *I have become the most splendid beggar in the world, but a beggar all the same.* She hated it, as her brother must have. *All those years of running from city to city one step ahead of the Usurper's knives, pleading for help from archons and princes and magisters, buying our food with flattery. He must have known how they mocked him. Small wonder he turned so angry and bitter.* In the end it had driven him mad. *It will do the same to me if I let it.* Part of her would have liked nothing more than to lead her people back to Vaes Tolorro, and make the dead city bloom. *No, that is defeat. I have something Viserys never had. I have the dragons. The dragons are all the difference.*

She stroked Rhaegal. The green dragon closed his teeth around the meat of her hand and nipped hard. Outside, the great city murmured and thrummed and seethed, all its myriad voices blending into one low sound like the surge of the sea. "Make way, you Milk Men, make way for the Mother of Dragons," Jhogo cried, and the Qartheen moved aside, though perhaps the oxen had more to do with that than his voice. Through the swaying draperies, Dany caught glimpses of him astride his grey stallion. From time to time he gave one of the oxen a flick with the silver-handled whip she had given him. Aggo guarded on her other side, while Rakharo rode behind the procession, watching the faces in the crowd for any sign of danger. Ser Jorah she had left behind today, to guard her other dragons; the exile knight had been opposed to this folly from the start. *He distrusts everyone,* she reflected, *and perhaps for good reason.*

As Dany lifted her goblet to drink, Rhaegal sniffed at the wine and drew his head back, hissing. "Your dragon has a good nose." Xaro wiped his lips. "The wine is ordinary. It is said that across the Jade Sea they make a golden vintage so fine that one sip makes all other wines taste like vinegar. Let us take my pleasure barge and go in search of it, you and I."

"The Arbor makes the best wine in the world," Dany declared. Lord Redwyne had fought for her father against the Usurper, she remembered, one of the few to remain true to the last. *Will he fight for me as well?* There was no way to be certain after so many years. "Come with me to the Arbor, Xaro, and you'll have the finest vintages you ever tasted. But we'll need to go in a warship, not a pleasure barge."

"I have no warships. War is bad for trade. Many times I have told you, Xaro Xhoan Daxos is a man of peace."

Xaro Xhoan Daxos is a man of gold, she thought, *and gold will buy me all the ships and swords I need.* "I have not asked you to take up a sword, only to lend me your ships."

He smiled modestly. "Of trading ships I have a few, that is so. Who can say how many? One may be sinking even now, in some stormy corner of the Summer Sea. On the morrow, another will fall afoul of corsairs. The next day, one of my captains may look at the wealth in his hold and think, *All this should belong to me.* Such are the perils of trade.

Why, the longer we talk, the fewer ships I am likely to have. I grow poorer by the instant."

"Give me ships, and I will make you rich again."

"Marry me, bright light, and sail the ship of my heart. I cannot sleep at night for thinking of your beauty."

Dany smiled. Xaro's flowery protestations of passion amused her, but his manner was at odds with his words. While Ser Jorah had scarcely been able to keep his eyes from her bare breast when he'd helped her into the palanquin, Xaro hardly deigned to notice it, even in these close confines. And she had seen the beautiful boys who surrounded the merchant prince, flitting through his palace halls in wisps of silk. "You speak sweetly, Xaro, but under your words I hear another *no*."

"This Iron Throne you speak of sounds monstrous cold and hard. I cannot bear the thought of jagged barbs cutting your sweet skin." The jewels in Xaro's nose gave him the aspect of some strange glittery bird. His long, elegant fingers waved dismissal. "Let this be your kingdom, most exquisite of queens, and let me be your king. I will give you a throne of gold, if you like. When Qarth begins to pall, we can journey round Yi Ti and search for the dreaming city of the poets, to sip the wine of wisdom from a dead man's skull."

"I mean to sail to Westeros, and drink the wine of vengeance from the skull of the Usurper." She scratched Rhaegal under one eye, and his jade-green wings unfolded for a moment, stirring the still air in the palanquin.

A single perfect tear ran down the cheek of Xaro Xhoan Daxos. "Will nothing turn you from this madness?"

"Nothing," she said, wishing she was as certain as she sounded. "If each of the Thirteen would lend me ten ships—"

"You would have one hundred thirty ships, and no crew to sail them. The justice of your cause means naught to the common men of Qarth. Why should my sailors care who sits upon the throne of some kingdom at the edge of the world?"

"I will pay them to care."

"With what coin, sweet star of my heaven?"

"With the gold the seekers bring."

"That you may do," Xaro acknowledged, "but so much caring will cost dear. You will need to pay them far more than I do, and all of Qarth laughs at my ruinous generosity."

"If the Thirteen will not aid me, perhaps I should ask the Guild of Spicers or the Tourmaline Brotherhood?"

Xaro gave a languid shrug. "They will give you nothing but flattery and lies. The Spicers are dissemblers and braggarts and the Brotherhood is full of pirates."

"Then I must heed Pyat Pree, and go to the warlocks."

The merchant prince sat up sharply. "Pyat Pree has blue lips, and it is truly said that blue lips speak only lies. Heed the wisdom of one who loves you. Warlocks are bitter creatures who eat dust and drink of shadows. They will give you naught. They have naught to give."

"I would not need to seek sorcerous help if my friend Xaro Xhoan Daxos would give me what I ask."

"I have given you my home and heart, do they mean nothing to you? I have given you perfume and pomegranates, tumbling monkeys and spitting snakes, scrolls from lost Valyria, an idol's head and a serpent's foot. I have given you this palanquin of ebony and gold, and a matched set of bullocks to bear it, one white as ivory and one black as jet, with horns inlaid with jewels."

"Yes," Dany said. "But it was ships and soldiers I wanted."

"Did I not give you an army, sweetest of women? A thousand knights, each in shining armor."

The armor had been made of silver and gold, the knights of jade and beryl and onyx and tourmaline, of amber and opal and amethyst, each as tall as her little finger. "A thousand lovely knights," she said, "but not the sort my enemies need fear. And my bullocks cannot carry me across the water, I—why are we stopping?" The oxen had slowed notably.

"*Khaleesi*," Aggo called through the drapes as the palanquin jerked to a sudden halt. Dany rolled onto an elbow to lean out. They were on the fringes of the bazaar, the way ahead blocked by a solid wall of people. "What are they looking at?"

Jhogo rode back to her. "A firemage, *Khaleesi*."

"I want to see."

"Then you must." The Dothraki offered a hand down. When she took it, he pulled her up onto his horse and sat her in front of him, where she could see over the heads of the crowd. The firemage had conjured a ladder in the air, a crackling orange ladder of swirling flame that rose unsupported from the floor of the bazaar, reaching toward the high latticed roof.

Most of the spectators, she noticed, were not of the city: she saw sailors off trading ships, merchants come by caravan, dusty men out of the red waste, wandering soldiers, craftsmen, slavers. Jhogo slid one hand about her waist and leaned close. "The Milk Men shun him. *Khaleesi*, do you see the girl in the felt hat? There, behind the fat priest. She is a—"

"—cutpurse," finished Dany. She was no pampered lady, blind to such things. She had seen cutpurses aplenty in the streets of the Free Cities, during the years she'd spent with her brother, running from the Usurper's hired knives.

The mage was gesturing, urging the flames higher and higher with broad sweeps of his arms. As the watchers craned their necks upward, the cutpurses squirmed through the press, small blades hidden in their palms. They relieved the prosperous of their coin with one hand while pointing upward with the other.

When the fiery ladder stood forty feet high, the mage leapt forward and began to climb it, scrambling up hand over hand as quick as a monkey. Each rung he touched dissolved behind him, leaving no more than a wisp of silver smoke. When he reached the top, the ladder was gone and so was he.

"A fine trick," announced Jhogo with admiration.

"No trick," a woman said in the Common Tongue.

Dany had not noticed Quaithe in the crowd, yet there she stood, eyes wet and shiny behind the implacable red lacquer mask. "What mean you, my lady?"

"Half a year gone, that man could scarcely wake fire from dragonglass. He had some small skill with powders and wildfire, sufficient to entrance a crowd while his cutpurses did their work. He could walk across hot coals and make burning roses bloom in the air, but he could no more aspire to climb the fiery ladder than a common fisherman could hope to catch a kraken in his nets."

Dany looked uneasily at where the ladder had stood. Even the smoke was gone now, and the crowd was breaking up, each man going about his business. In a moment more than a few would find their purses flat and empty. "And now?"

"And now his powers grow, *Khaleesi.* And you are the cause of it."

"Me?" She laughed. "How could that be?"

The woman stepped closer and lay two fingers on Dany's wrist. "You are the Mother of Dragons, are you not?"

"She is, and no spawn of shadows may touch her." Jhogo brushed Quaithe's fingers away with the handle of his whip.

The woman took a step backward. "You must leave this city soon, Daenerys Targaryen, or you will never be permitted to leave it at all."

Dany's wrist still tingled where Quaithe had touched her. "Where would you have me go?" she asked.

"To go north, you must journey south. To reach the west, you must go east. To go forward you must go back, and to touch the light you must pass beneath the shadow."

Asshai, Dany thought. *She would have me go to Asshai.* "Will the Asshai'i give me an army?" she demanded. "Will there be gold for me in Asshai? Will there be ships? What is there in Asshai that I will not find in Qarth?"

"Truth," said the woman in the mask. And bowing, she faded back into the crowd.

Rakharo snorted contempt through his drooping black mustachios. *"Khaleesi,* better a man should swallow scorpions than trust in the spawn of shadows, who dare not show their face beneath the sun. It is known."

"It is known," Aggo agreed.

Xaro Xhoan Daxos had watched the whole exchange from his cushions. When Dany climbed back into the palanquin beside him, he said, "Your savages are wiser than they know. Such truths as the Asshai'i hoard are not like to make you smile." Then he pressed another cup of wine on her, and spoke of love and lust and other trifles all the way back to his manse.

In the quiet of her chambers, Dany stripped off her finery and donned a loose robe of purple silk. Her dragons were hungry, so she chopped up a snake and charred the pieces over a brazier. *They are growing,* she realized as she watched them snap and squabble over the blackened flesh. *They must weigh twice what they had in Vaes Tolorro.* Even so, it would be years before they were large enough to take to war. *And they must be trained as well, or they will lay my kingdom waste.* For all her Targaryen blood, Dany had not the least idea of how to train a dragon.

Ser Jorah Mormont came to her as the sun was going down. "The Pureborn refused you?"

"As you said they would. Come, sit, give me your counsel." Dany drew him down to the cushions beside her, and Jhiqui brought them a bowl of purple olives and onions drowned in wine.

"You will get no help in this city, *Khaleesi."* Ser Jorah took an onion between thumb and forefinger. "Each day I am more convinced of that than the day before. The Pureborn see no farther than the walls of Qarth, and Xaro . . ."

"He asked me to marry him again."

"Yes, and I know why." When the knight frowned, his heavy black brows joined together above his deep-set eyes.

"He dreams of me, day and night." She laughed.

"Forgive me, my queen, but it is your dragons he dreams of."

"Xaro assures me that in Qarth, man and woman each retain their own property after they are wed. The dragons are mine." She smiled as Drogon came hopping and flapping across the marble floor to crawl up on the cushion beside her.

"He tells it true as far as it goes, but there's one thing he failed to mention. The Qartheen have a curious wedding custom, my queen. On the day of their union, a wife may ask a token of love from her husband. Whatsoever she desires of his worldly goods, he must grant. And he may ask the same of her. One thing only may be asked, but whatever is named may not be denied."

"One thing," she repeated. "And it may not be denied?"

"With one dragon, Xaro Xhoan Daxos would rule this city, but one ship will further our cause but little."

Dany nibbled at an onion and reflected ruefully on the faithlessness of men. "We passed through the bazaar on our way back from the Hall of a Thousand Thrones," she told Ser Jorah. "Quaithe was there." She told him of the firemage and the fiery ladder, and what the woman in the red mask had told her.

"I would be glad to leave this city, if truth be told," the knight said when she was done. "But not for Asshai."

"Where, then?"

"East," he said.

"I am half a world away from my kingdom even here. If I go any farther east I may never find my way home to Westeros."

"If you go west, you risk your life."

"House Targaryen has friends in the Free Cities," she reminded him. "Truer friends than Xaro or the Pureborn."

"If you mean Illyrio Mopatis, I wonder. For sufficient gold, Illyrio would sell you as quickly as he would a slave."

"My brother and I were guests in Illyrio's manse for half a year. If he meant to sell us, he could have done it then."

"He did sell you," Ser Jorah said. "To Khal Drogo."

Dany flushed. He had the truth of it, but she did not like the sharpness with which he put it. "Illyrio protected us from the Usurper's knives, and he believed in my brother's cause."

"Illyrio believes in no cause but Illyrio. Gluttons are greedy men as a rule, and magisters are devious. Illyrio Mopatis is both. What do you truly know of him?"

"I know that he gave me my dragon eggs."

He snorted. "If he'd known they were like to hatch, he'd would have sat on them himself."

That made her smile despite herself. "Oh, I have no doubt of that, ser. I know Illyrio better than you think. I was a child when I left his manse in Pentos to wed my sun-and-stars, but I was neither deaf nor blind. And I am no child now."

"Even if Illyrio is the friend you think him," the knight said stubbornly, "he is not powerful enough to enthrone you by himself, no more than he could your brother."

"He is rich," she said. "Not so rich as Xaro, perhaps, but rich enough to hire ships for me, and men as well."

"Sellswords have their uses," Ser Jorah admitted, "but you will not win your father's throne with sweepings from the Free Cities. Nothing knits a broken realm together so quick as an invading army on its soil."

"I am their rightful queen," Dany protested.

"You are a stranger who means to land on their shores with an army of outlanders who cannot even speak the Common Tongue. The lords of Westeros do not know you, and have every reason to fear and mistrust you. You must win them over before you sail. A few at least."

"And how am I to do that, if I go east as you counsel?"

He ate an olive and spit out the pit into his palm. "I do not know, Your Grace," he admitted, "but I do know that the longer you remain in one place, the easier it will be for your enemies to find you. The name *Targaryen* still frightens them, so much so that they sent a man to murder you when they heard you were with child. What will they do when they learn of your dragons?"

Drogon was curled up beneath her arm, as hot as a stone that has soaked all day in the blazing sun. Rhaegal and Viserion were fighting over a scrap of meat, buffeting each other with their wings as smoke hissed from their nostrils. *My furious children*, she thought. *They must not come to harm.* "The comet led me to Qarth for a reason. I had hoped to find my army here, but it seems that will not be. What else remains, I ask myself?" *I am afraid*, she realized, *but I must be brave.* "Come the morrow, you must go to Pyat Pree."

TYRION

The girl never wept. Young as she was, Myrcella Baratheon was a princess born. *And a Lannister, despite her name,* Tyrion reminded himself, *as much Jaime's blood as Cersei's.*

To be sure, her smile was a shade tremulous when her brothers took their leave of her on the deck of the *Seaswift,* but the girl knew the proper words to say, and she said them with courage and dignity. When the time came to part, it was Prince Tommen who cried, and Myrcella who gave him comfort.

Tyrion looked down upon the farewells from the high deck of *King Robert's Hammer,* a great war galley of four hundred oars. *Rob's Hammer,* as her oarsmen called her, would form the main strength of Myrcella's escort. *Lionstar, Bold Wind,* and *Lady Lyanna* would sail with her as well.

It made Tyrion more than a little uneasy to detach so great a part of their already inadequate fleet, depleted as it was by the loss of all those ships that had sailed with Lord Stannis to Dragonstone and never returned, but Cersei would hear of nothing less. Perhaps she was wise. If the girl was captured before she reached Sunspear, the Dornish alliance would fall to pieces. So far Doran Martell had done no more than call his banners. Once Myrcella was safe in Braavos, he had pledged to move his strength to the high passes, where the threat might make some of the Marcher lords rethink their loyalties and give Stannis pause about marching north. It was purely a feint, however. The Martells would not commit to actual battle unless Dorne itself was attacked, and Stannis was not so great a fool. *Though some of his bannermen may be*, Tyrion reflected. *I should think on that.*

He cleared his throat. "You know your orders, Captain."

"I do, my lord. We are to follow the coast, staying always in sight of land, until we reach Crackclaw Point. From there we are to strike out across the narrow sea for Braavos. On no account are we to sail within sight of Dragonstone."

"And if our foes should chance upon you nonetheless?"

"If a single ship, we are to run them off or destroy them. If there are more, the *Bold Wind* will cleave to the *Seaswift* to protect her while the rest of the fleet does battle."

Tyrion nodded. If the worst happened, the little *Seaswift* ought to be able to outrun pursuit. A small ship with big sails, she was faster than any warship afloat, or so her captain had claimed. Once Myrcella reached Braavos, she ought to be safe. He was sending Ser Arys Oakheart as her sworn shield, and had engaged the Braavosi to bring her the rest of the way to Sunspear. Even Lord Stannis would hesitate to wake the anger of the greatest and most powerful of the Free Cities. Traveling from King's Landing to Dorne by way of Braavos was scarcely the most direct of routes, but it *was* the safest . . . or so he hoped.

If Lord Stannis knew of this sailing, he could not choose a better time to send his fleet against us. Tyrion glanced back to where the Rush emptied out into Blackwater Bay and was relieved to see no signs of sails on the wide green horizon. At last report, the Baratheon fleet still lay off Storm's End, where Ser Cortnay Penrose continued to defy the besiegers in dead Renly's name. Meanwhile, Tyrion's winch towers stood three-quarters complete. Even now men were hoisting heavy blocks of stone into place, no doubt cursing him for making them work through the festivities. Let them curse. *Another fortnight, Stannis, that's all I require. Another fortnight and it will be done.*

Tyrion watched his niece kneel before the High Septon to receive his blessing on her voyage. Sunlight caught in his crystal crown and spilled rainbows across Myrcella's upturned face. The noise from the riverside made it impossible to hear the prayers. He hoped the gods had sharper ears. The High Septon was as fat as a house, and more pompous and long of wind than even Pycelle. *Enough, old man, make an end to it*, Tyrion thought irritably. *The gods have better things to do than listen to you, and so do I.*

When at last the droning and mumbling was done, Tyrion took his farewell of the captain of *Rob's Hammer.* "Deliver my niece safely to Braavos, and there will be a knighthood waiting for you on your return," he promised.

As he made his way down the steep plank to the quay, Tyrion could feel unkind eyes upon him. The galley rocked gently and the movement underfoot made his waddle worse than ever. *I'll wager they'd love to snigger.* No one dared, not openly, though he heard mutterings mingled with the creak of wood and rope and the rush of the river around the pilings. *They do not love me,* he thought. *Well, small wonder. I'm well fed and ugly, and they are starving.*

Bronn escorted him through the crowd to join his sister and her sons. Cersei ignored him, preferring to lavish her smiles on their cousin. He watched her charming Lancel with eyes as green as the rope of emeralds around her slim white throat, and smiled a small sly smile to himself. *I know your secret, Cersei,* he thought. His sister had oft called upon the High Septon of late, to seek the blessings of the gods in their coming struggle with Lord Stannis . . . or so she would have him believe. In truth, after a brief call at the Great Sept of Baelor, Cersei would don a plain brown traveler's cloak and steal off to meet a certain hedge knight with the unlikely name of Ser Osmund Kettleblack, and his equally unsavory brothers Osney and Osfryd. Lancel had told him all about them. Cersei meant to use the Kettleblacks to buy her own force of sellswords.

Well, let her enjoy her plots. She was much sweeter when she thought she was outwitting him. The Kettleblacks would charm her, take her coin, and promise her anything she asked, and why not, when Bronn was matching every copper penny, coin for coin? Amiable rogues all three, the brothers were in truth much more skilled at deceit than they'd ever been at bloodletting. Cersei had managed to buy herself three hollow drums; they would make all the fierce booming sounds she required, but there was nothing inside. It amused Tyrion no end.

Horns blew fanfares as *Lionstar* and *Lady Lyanna* pushed out from shore, moving downriver to clear the way for *Seaswift*. A few cheers went up from the crush along the banks, as thin and ragged as the clouds scuttling overhead. Myrcella smiled and waved from the deck. Behind her stood Arys Oakheart, his white cloak streaming. The captain ordered lines cast off, and oars pushed the *Seaswift* out into the lusty current of the Blackwater Rush, where her sails blossomed in the wind—common white sails, as Tyrion had insisted, not sheets of Lannister crimson. Prince Tommen sobbed. "You mew like a suckling babe," his brother hissed at him. "Princes aren't supposed to cry."

"Prince Aemon the Dragonknight cried the day Princess Naerys wed his brother Aegon," Sansa Stark said, "and the twins Ser Arryk and Ser Erryk died with tears on their cheeks after each had given the other a mortal wound."

"Be quiet, or I'll have Ser Meryn give *you* a mortal wound," Joffrey told his betrothed. Tyrion glanced at his sister, but Cersei was engrossed in something Ser Balon Swann was telling her. *Can she truly be so blind as to what he is?* he wondered.

Out on the river, *Bold Wind* unshipped her oars and glided downstream in the wake of *Seaswift.* Last came *King Robert's Hammer*, the might of the royal fleet . . . or at least that portion that had not fled to Dragonstone last year with Stannis. Tyrion had chosen the ships with care, avoiding any whose captains might be of doubtful loyalty, according to Varys . . . but as Varys himself was of doubtful loyalty, a certain amount of apprehension remained. *I rely too much on Varys*, he reflected. *I need my own informers. Not that I'd trust them either.* Trust would get you killed.

He wondered again about Littlefinger. There had been no word from Petyr Baelish since he had ridden off for Bitterbridge. That might mean nothing—or everything. Even Varys could not say. The eunuch had suggested that perhaps Littlefinger had met some misfortune on the roads. He might even be slain. Tyrion had snorted in derision. "If Littlefinger is dead, then I'm a giant." More likely, the Tyrells were balking at the proposed marriage. Tyrion could scarcely blame them. *If I were Mace Tyrell, I would sooner have Joffrey's head on a pike than his cock in my daughter.*

The little fleet was well out into the bay when Cersei indicated that it was time to go. Bronn brought Tyrion's horse and helped him mount. That was Podrick Payne's task, but they had left Pod back at the Red Keep. The gaunt sellsword made for a much more reassuring presence than the boy would have.

The narrow streets were lined by men of the City Watch, holding back the crowd with the shafts of their spears. Ser Jacelyn Bywater went in front, heading a wedge of mounted lancers in black ringmail and golden cloaks. Behind him came Ser Aron Santagar and Ser Balon Swann, bearing the king's banners, the lion of Lannister and crowned stag of Baratheon.

King Joffrey followed on a tall grey palfrey, a golden crown set upon his golden curls. Sansa Stark rode a chestnut mare at his side, looking neither right nor left, her thick auburn hair flowing to her shoulders beneath a net of moonstones. Two of the Kingsguard flanked the couple, the Hound on the king's right hand and Ser Mandon Moore to the left of the Stark girl.

Next came Tommen, snuffling, with Ser Preston Greenfield in his white armor and cloak, and then Cersei, accompanied by Ser Lancel and protected by Meryn Trant and Boros Blount. Tyrion fell in with his sister. After them followed the High Septon in his litter, and a long tail of other courtiers—Ser Horas Redwyne, Lady Tanda and her daughter, Jalabhar

Xho, Lord Gyles Rosby, and the rest. A double column of guardsmen brought up the rear.

The unshaven and the unwashed stared at the riders with dull resentment from behind the line of spears. *I like this not one speck*, Tyrion thought. Bronn had a score of sellswords scattered through the crowd with orders to stop any trouble before it started. Perhaps Cersei had similarly disposed her Kettleblacks. Somehow Tyrion did not think it would help much. If the fire was too hot, you could hardly keep the pudding from scorching by tossing a handful of raisins in the pot.

They crossed Fishmonger's Square and rode along Muddy Way before turning onto the narrow, curving Hook to begin their climb up Aegon's High Hill. A few voices raised a cry of *"Joffrey! All hail, all hail!"* as the young king rode by, but for every man who picked up the shout, a hundred kept their silence. The Lannisters moved through a sea of ragged men and hungry women, breasting a tide of sullen eyes. Just ahead of him, Cersei was laughing at something Lancel had said, though he suspected her merriment was feigned. She could not be oblivious to the unrest around them, but his sister always believed in putting on the brave show.

Halfway along the route, a wailing woman forced her way between two watchmen and ran out into the street in front of the king and his companions, holding the corpse of her dead baby above her head. It was blue and swollen, grotesque, but the real horror was the mother's eyes. Joffrey looked for a moment as if he meant to ride her down, but Sansa Stark leaned over and said something to him. The king fumbled in his purse, and flung the woman a silver stag. The coin bounced off the child and rolled away, under the legs of the gold cloaks and into the crowd, where a dozen men began to fight for it. The mother never once blinked. Her skinny arms were trembling from the dead weight of her son.

"Leave her, Your Grace," Cersei called out to the king, "she's beyond our help, poor thing."

The mother heard her. Somehow the queen's voice cut through the woman's ravaged wits. Her slack face twisted in loathing. *"Whore!"* she shrieked. *"Kingslayer's whore! Brotherfucker!"* Her dead child dropped from her arms like a sack of flour as she pointed at Cersei. *"Brotherfucker brotherfucker brotherfucker."*

Tyrion never saw who threw the dung. He only heard Sansa's gasp and Joffrey's bellowed curse, and when he turned his head, the king was wiping brown filth from his cheek. There was more caked in his golden hair and spattered over Sansa's legs.

"Who threw that?" Joffrey screamed. He pushed his fingers into his hair, made a furious face, and flung away another handful of dung. "I want the man who threw that!" he shouted. "A hundred golden dragons to the man who gives him up."

"He was up there!" someone shouted from the crowd. The king wheeled his horse in a circle to survey the rooftops and open balconies above them. In the crowd people were pointing, shoving, cursing one another and the king.

"Please, Your Grace, let him go," Sansa pleaded.

The king paid her no heed. "Bring me the man who flung that filth!" Joffrey commanded. "He'll lick it off me or I'll have his head. Dog, you bring him here!"

Obedient, Sandor Clegane swung down from his saddle, but there was no way through that wall of flesh, let alone to the roof. Those closest to him began to squirm and shove to get away, while others pushed forward to see. Tyrion smelled disaster. "Clegane, leave off, the man is long fled."

"I *want* him!" Joffrey pointed at the roof. "He was up there! Dog, cut through them and bring—"

A tumult of sound drowned his last words, a rolling thunder of rage and fear and hatred that engulfed them from all sides. *"Bastard!"* someone screamed at Joffrey, *"bastard monster."* Other voices flung calls of *"Whore"* and *"Brotherfucker"* at the queen, while Tyrion was pelted with shouts of *"Freak"* and *"Halfman."* Mixed in with the abuse, he heard a few cries of *"Justice"* and *"Robb, King Robb, the Young Wolf,"* of *"Stannis!"* and even *"Renly!"* From both sides of the street, the crowd surged against the spear shafts while the gold cloaks struggled to hold the line. Stones and dung and fouler things whistled overhead. "Feed us!" a woman shrieked. "Bread!" boomed a man behind her. *"We want bread,* bastard!" In a heartbeat, a thousand voices took up the chant. King Joffrey and King Robb and King Stannis were forgotten, and King Bread ruled alone. *"Bread,"* they clamored. *"Bread, bread!"*

Tyrion spurred to his sister's side, yelling, "Back to the castle. *Now."* Cersei gave a curt nod, and Ser Lancel unsheathed his sword. Ahead of the column, Jacelyn Bywater was roaring commands. His riders lowered their lances and drove forward in a wedge. The king was wheeling his palfrey around in anxious circles while hands reached past the line of gold cloaks, grasping for him. One managed to get hold of his leg, but only for an instant. Ser Mandon's sword slashed down, parting hand from wrist. *"Ride!"* Tyrion shouted at his nephew, giving the horse a sharp *smack* on the rump. The animal reared, trumpeting, and plunged ahead, the press shattering before him.

Tyrion drove into the gap hard on the king's hooves. Bronn kept pace, sword in hand. A jagged rock flew past his head as he rode, and a rotten cabbage exploded against Ser Mandon's shield. To their left, three gold cloaks went down under the surge, and then the crowd was rushing forward, trampling the fallen men. The Hound had vanished behind, though his riderless horse galloped beside them. Tyrion saw Aron Santagar pulled from the saddle, the gold-and-black Baratheon stag torn from his grasp. Ser Balon Swann dropped the Lannister lion to draw his longsword. He slashed right and left as the fallen banner was ripped apart, the thousand ragged pieces swirling away like crimson leaves in a stormwind. In an instant they were gone. Someone staggered in front of Joffrey's horse and shrieked as the king rode him down. Whether it had been man, woman, or child Tyrion could not have said. Joffrey was galloping at his side, whey-faced, with Ser Mandon Moore a white shadow on his left.

And suddenly the madness was behind and they were clattering across the cobbled square that fronted on the castle barbican. A line of spearmen held the gates. Ser Jacelyn was wheeling his lances around for another charge. The spears parted to let the king's party pass under the portcullis. Pale red walls loomed up about them, reassuringly high and aswarm with crossbowmen.

Tyrion did not recall dismounting. Ser Mandon was helping the shaken king off his horse when Cersei, Tommen, and Lancel rode through the gates with Ser Meryn and Ser Boros close behind. Boros had blood smeared along his blade, while Meryn's white cloak had been torn from his back. Ser Balon Swann rode in helmetless, his mount lathered and bleeding at the mouth. Horas Redwyne brought in Lady Tanda, half-crazed with fear for her daughter Lollys, who had been knocked from the saddle and left behind. Lord Gyles, more grey of face than ever, stammered out a tale of seeing the High Septon spilled from his litter, screeching prayers as the crowd swept over him. Jalabhar Xho said he thought he'd seen Ser Preston Greenfield of the Kingsguard riding back toward the High Septon's overturned litter, but he was not certain.

Tyrion was dimly aware of a maester asking if he was injured. He pushed his way across the yard to where his nephew stood, his dung-encrusted crown askew. "Traitors," Joffrey was babbling excitedly, "I'll have all their heads, I'll—"

The dwarf slapped his flushed face so hard the crown flew from Joffrey's head. Then he shoved him with both hands and knocked him sprawling. "You blind bloody *fool.*"

"They were traitors," Joffrey squealed from the ground. "They called me names and attacked me!"

"You set your dog on them! What did you imagine they would do, bend the knee meekly while the Hound lopped off some limbs? You spoiled witless little *boy,* you've killed Clegane and gods know how

many more, and yet *you* come through unscratched. *Damn you!*" And he kicked him. It felt so good he might have done more, but Ser Mandon Moore pulled him off as Joffrey howled, and then Bronn was there to take him in hand. Cersei knelt over her son, while Ser Balon Swann restrained Ser Lancel. Tyrion wrenched free of Bronn's grip. "How many are still out there?" he shouted to no one and everyone.

"My daughter," cried Lady Tanda. "Please, someone must go back for Lollys . . ."

"Ser Preston is not returned," Ser Boros Blount reported, "nor Aron Santagar."

"Nor Wet Nurse," said Ser Horas Redwyne. That was the mocking name the other squires had hung on young Tyrek Lannister.

Tyrion glanced round the yard. "Where's the Stark girl?"

For a moment no one answered. Finally Joffrey said, "She was riding by me. I don't know where she went."

Tyrion pressed blunt fingers into his throbbing temples. If Sansa Stark had come to harm, Jaime was as good as dead. "Ser Mandon, you were her shield."

Ser Mandon Moore remained untroubled. "When they mobbed the Hound, I thought first of the king."

"And rightly so," Cersei put in. "Boros, Meryn, go back and find the girl."

"And my daughter," Lady Tanda sobbed. "Please, sers . . ."

Ser Boros did not look pleased at the prospect of leaving the safety of the castle. "Your Grace," he told the queen, "the sight of our white cloaks might enrage the mob."

Tyrion had stomached all he cared to. "The Others take your fucking cloaks! *Take them off* if you're afraid to wear them, you bloody oaf . . . but *find me Sansa Stark* or I swear, I'll have Shagga split that ugly head of yours in two to see if there's anything inside but black pudding."

Ser Boros went purple with rage. "You would call *me* ugly, *you!*" He started to raise the bloody sword still clutched in his mailed fist. Bronn shoved Tyrion unceremoniously behind him.

"*Stop it!*" Cersei snapped. "Boros, you'll do as you're bid, or we'll find someone else to wear that cloak. Your oath—"

"There she is!" Joffrey shouted, pointing.

Sandor Clegane cantered briskly through the gates astride Sansa's chestnut courser. The girl was seated behind, both arms tight around the Hound's chest.

Tyrion called to her. "Are you hurt, Lady Sansa?"

Blood was trickling down Sansa's brow from a deep gash on her scalp. "They . . . they were throwing things . . . rocks and filth, eggs . . . I tried to tell them, I had no bread to give them. A man tried to pull me from the saddle. The Hound killed him, I think . . . his arm . . ." Her eyes widened and she put a hand over her mouth. "He *cut off his arm.*"

Clegane lifted her to the ground. His white cloak was torn and stained, and blood seeped through a jagged tear in his left sleeve. "The little bird's bleeding. Someone take her back to her cage and see to that cut." Maester Frenken scurried forward to obey. "They did for Santagar," the Hound continued. "Four men held him down and took turns bashing at his head with a cobblestone. I gutted one, not that it did Ser Aron much good."

Lady Tanda approached him. "My daughter—"

"Never saw her." The Hound glanced around the yard, scowling. "Where's my horse? If anything's happened to that horse, someone's going to pay."

"He was running with us for a time," Tyrion said, "but I don't know what became of him after that."

"*Fire!*" a voice screamed down from atop the barbican. "My lords, there's smoke in the city. Flea Bottom's afire."

Tyrion was inutterably weary, but there was no *time* for despair. "Bronn, take as many men as you need and see that the water wagons are not molested." *Gods be good, the wildfire, if any blaze should reach that* . . . "We can lose all of Flea Bottom if we must, but on no account must the fire reach the Guildhall of the Alchemists, is that understood? Clegane, you'll go with him."

For half a heartbeat, Tyrion thought he glimpsed fear in the Hound's dark eyes. *Fire,* he realized. *The Others take me, of course he hates fire, he's tasted it too well.* The look was gone in an instant, replaced by Clegane's familiar scowl. "I'll go," he said, "though not by *your* command. I need to find that horse."

Tyrion turned to the three remaining knights of the Kingsguard. "Each of you will ride escort to a herald. Command the people to return to their homes. Any man found on the streets after the last peal of the evenfall bell will be killed."

"Our place is beside the king," Ser Meryn said, complacent.

Cersei reared up like a viper. "Your place is where my brother says it is," she spit. "The Hand speaks with the king's own voice, and disobedience is treason."

Boros and Meryn exchanged a look. "Should we wear our cloaks, Your Grace?" Ser Boros asked.

"Go naked for all I care. It might remind the mob that you're men. They're like to have forgotten after seeing the way you behaved out there in the street."

Tyrion let his sister rage. His head was throbbing. He thought he could smell smoke, though perhaps it was just the scent of his nerves fraying.

Two of the Stone Crows guarded the door of the Tower of the Hand. "Find me Timett son of Timett."

"Stone Crows do not run squeaking after Burned Men," one of the wildlings informed him haughtily.

For a moment Tyrion had forgotten who he was dealing with. "Then find me Shagga."

"Shagga sleeps."

It was an effort not to scream. "Wake. Him."

"It is no easy thing to wake Shagga son of Dolf," the man complained. "His wrath is fearsome." He went off grumbling.

The clansman wandered in yawning and scratching. "Half the city is rioting, the other half is burning, and Shagga lies snoring," Tyrion said.

"Shagga mislikes your muddy water here, so he must drink your weak ale and sour wine, and after his head hurts."

"I have Shae in a manse near the Iron Gate. I want you to go to her and keep her safe, whatever may come."

The huge man smiled, his teeth a yellow crevasse in the hairy wilderness of his beard. "Shagga will fetch her here."

"Just see that no harm comes to her. Tell her I will come to her as soon as I may. This very night, perhaps, or on the morrow for a certainty."

Yet by evenfall the city was still in turmoil, though Bronn reported that the fires were quenched and most of the roving mobs dispersed. Much as Tyrion yearned for the comfort of Shae's arms, he realized he would go nowhere that night.

Ser Jacelyn Bywater delivered the butcher's bill as he was supping on a cold capon and brown bread in the gloom of his solar. Dusk had faded to darkness by then, but when his servants came to light his candles and start a fire in the hearth, Tyrion had roared at them and sent them running. His mood was as black as the chamber, and Bywater said nothing to lighten it.

The list of the slain was topped by the High Septon, ripped apart as he squealed to his gods for mercy. *Starving men take a hard view of priests too fat to walk,* Tyrion reflected.

Ser Preston's corpse had been overlooked at first; the gold cloaks had been searching for a knight in white armor, and he had been stabbed and hacked so cruelly that he was red-brown from head to heel.

Ser Aron Santagar had been found in a gutter, his head a red pulp inside a crushed helm.

Lady Tanda's daughter had surrendered her maidenhood to half a hundred shouting men behind a tanner's shop. The gold cloaks found her wandering naked on Sowbelly Row.

Tyrek was still missing, as was the High Septon's crystal crown. Nine gold cloaks had been slain, two score wounded. No one had troubled to count how many of the mob had died.

"I want Tyrek found, alive or dead," Tyrion said curtly when Bywater was done. "He's no more than a boy. Son to my late uncle Tygett. His father was always kind to me."

"We'll find him. The septon's crown as well."

"The Others can bugger each other with the septon's crown, for all I care."

"When you named me to command the Watch, you told me you wanted plain truth, always."

"Somehow I have a feeling I am not going to like whatever you're about to say," Tyrion said gloomily.

"We held the city today, my lord, but I make no promises for the morrow. The kettle is close to boiling. So many thieves and murderers are abroad that no man's house is safe, the bloody flux is spreading in the stews along Pisswater Bend, there's no food to be had for copper nor silver. Where before you heard only mutterings from the gutter, now there's open talk of treason in guildhalls and markets."

"Do you need more men?"

"I do not trust half the men I have now. Slynt tripled the size of the Watch, but it takes more than a gold cloak to make a watchman. There are good men and loyal among the new recruits, but also more brutes, sots, cravens, and traitors than you'd care to know. They're half-trained and undisciplined, and what loyalty they have is to their own skins. If it comes to battle, they'll not hold, I fear."

"I never expected them to," said Tyrion. "Once our walls are breeched, we are lost, I've known that from the start."

"My men are largely drawn from the smallfolk. They walk the same streets, drink in the same winesinks, spoon down their bowls of brown in the same pot-shops. Your eunuch must have told you, there is small love for the Lannisters in King's Landing. Many still remember how your lord father sacked the city, when Aerys opened the gates to him. They whisper that the gods are punishing us for the sins of your House—for your brother's murder of King Aerys, for the butchery of Rhaegar's children, for the execution of Eddard Stark and the savagery of Joffrey's justice. Some talk openly of how much better things were when Robert was king, and hint that times would be better again with Stannis on the throne. In pot-shops and winesinks and brothels, you hear these things— and in the barracks and guardhalls as well, I fear."

"They hate my family, is that what you are telling me?"

"Aye . . . and will turn on them, if the chance comes."

"Me as well?"

"Ask your eunuch."

"I'm asking you."

Bywater's deep-set eyes met the dwarf's mismatched ones, and did not blink. "You most of all, my lord."

"*Most of all?*" The injustice was like to choke him. "It was Joffrey who told them to eat their dead, Joffrey who set his dog on them. How could they blame me?"

"His Grace is but a boy. In the streets, it is said that he has evil councillors. The queen has never been known as a friend to the commons, nor is Lord Varys called the Spider out of love . . . but it is you they blame most. Your sister and the eunuch were here when times were better under King Robert, but you were not. They say that you've filled the city with swaggering sellswords and unwashed savages, brutes who take what they want and follow no laws but their own. They say you exiled Janos Slynt because you found him too bluff and honest for your liking. They say you threw wise and gentle Pycelle into the dungeons when he dared raise his voice against you. Some even claim that you mean to seize the Iron Throne for your own."

"Yes, and I am a monster besides, hideous and misshapen, never forget that." His hand coiled into a fist. "I've heard enough. We both have work to attend to. Leave me."

Perhaps my lord father was right to despise me all these years, if this is the best I can achieve, Tyrion thought when he was alone. He stared down at the remains of his supper, his belly roiling at the sight of the cold greasy capon. Disgusted, he pushed it away, shouted for Pod, and sent the boy running to summon Varys and Bronn. *My most trusted advisers are a eunuch and a sellsword, and my lady's a whore. What does that say of me?*

Bronn complained of the gloom when he arrived, and insisted on a fire in the hearth. It was blazing by the time Varys made his appearance. "Where have you been?" Tyrion demanded.

"About the king's business, my sweet lord."

"Ah, yes, the *king*," Tyrion muttered. "My nephew is not fit to sit a privy, let alone the Iron Throne."

Varys shrugged. "An apprentice must be taught his trade."

"Half the 'prentices on Reeking Lane could rule better than this king of yours." Bronn seated himself across the table and pulled a wing off the capon.

Tyrion had made a practice of ignoring the sellsword's frequent insolences, but tonight he found it galling. "I don't recall giving you leave to finish my supper."

"You didn't look to be eating it," Bronn said through a mouthful of meat. "City's starving, it's a crime to waste food. You have any wine?"

Next he'll want me to pour it for him, Tyrion thought darkly. "You go too far," he warned.

"And you never go far enough." Bronn tossed the wingbone to the rushes. "Ever think how easy life would be if the other one had been born first?" He thrust his fingers inside the capon and tore off a handful of breast. "The weepy one, Tommen. Seems like he'd do whatever he was told, as a good king should."

A chill crept down Tyrion's spine as he realized what the sellsword was hinting at. *If Tommen was king . . .*

There was only one way Tommen would become king. No, he could not even think it. Joffrey was his own blood, and Jaime's son as much as Cersei's. "I could have your head off for saying that," he told Bronn, but the sellsword only laughed.

"Friends," said Varys, "quarreling will not serve us. I beg you both, take heart."

"Whose?" asked Tyrion sourly. He could think of several tempting choices.

DAVOS

Ser Cortnay Penrose wore no armor. He sat a sorrel stallion, his standard-bearer a dapple grey. Above them flapped Baratheon's crowned stag and the crossed quills of Penrose, white on a russet field. Ser Cortnay's spade-shaped beard was russet as well, though he'd gone wholly bald on top. If the size and splendor of the king's party impressed him, it did not show on that weathered face.

They trotted up with much clinking of chain and rattle of plate. Even Davos wore mail, though he could not have said why; his shoulders and lower back ached from the unaccustomed weight. It made him feel cumbered and foolish, and he wondered once more why he was here. *It is not for me to question the king's commands, and yet . . .*

Every man of the party was of better birth and higher station than Davos Seaworth, and the great lords glittered in the morning sun. Silvered steel and gold inlay brightened their armor, and their warhelms were crested in a riot of silken plumes, feathers, and cunningly wrought heraldic beasts with gemstone eyes. Stannis himself looked out of place in this rich and royal company. Like Davos, the king was plainly garbed in wool and boiled leather, though the circlet of red gold about his temples lent him a certain grandeur. Sunlight flashed off its flame-shaped points whenever he moved his head.

This was the closest Davos had come to His Grace in the eight days since *Black Betha* had joined the rest of the fleet off Storm's End. He'd sought an audience within an hour of his arrival, only to be told that the king was occupied. The king was often occupied, Davos learned from his son Devan, one of the royal squires. Now that Stannis Baratheon had come into his power, the lordlings buzzed around him like flies round a corpse. *He looks half a corpse too, years older than when I left Dragonstone.* Devan said the king scarcely slept of late. "Since Lord Renly died, he has been troubled by terrible nightmares," the boy had confided to his father. "Maester's potions do not touch them. Only the Lady Melisandre can soothe him to sleep."

Is that why she shares his pavilion now? Davos wondered. *To pray with him? Or does she have another way to soothe him to sleep?* It was an unworthy question, and one he dared not ask, even of his own son. Devan was a good boy, but he wore the flaming heart proudly on his doublet, and his father had seen him at the nightfires as dusk fell, beseeching the Lord of Light to bring the dawn. *He is the king's squire,* he told himself, *it is only to be expected that he would take the king's god.*

Davos had almost forgotten how high and thick the walls of Storm's End loomed up close. King Stannis halted beneath them, a few feet from Ser Cortnay and his standard-bearer. "Ser," he said with stiff courtesy. He made no move to dismount.

"My lord." That was less courteous, but not unexpected.

"It is customary to grant a king the style *Your Grace,*" announced Lord Florent. A red gold fox poked its shining snout out from his breastplate through a circle of lapis lazuli flowers. Very tall, very courtly, and very rich, the Lord of Brightwater Keep had been the first of Renly's bannermen to declare for Stannis, and the first to renounce his old gods and take up the Lord of Light. Stannis had left his queen on Dragonstone along with her uncle Axell, but the queen's men were more numerous and powerful than ever, and Alester Florent was the foremost.

Ser Cortnay Penrose ignored him, preferring to address Stannis. "This is a notable company. The great lords Estermont, Errol, and Varner. Ser Jon of the green-apple Fossoways and Ser Bryan of the red. Lord Caron and Ser Guyard of King Renly's Rainbow Guard . . . *and* the puissant Lord Alester Florent of Brightwater, to be sure. Is that your Onion Knight I spy to the rear? Well met, Ser Davos. I fear I do not know the lady."

"I am named Melisandre, ser." She alone came unarmored, but for her flowing red robes. At her throat the great ruby drank the daylight. "I serve your king, and the Lord of Light."

"I wish you well of them, my lady," Ser Cortnay answered, "but I bow to other gods, and a different king."

"There is but one true king, and one true god," announced Lord Florent.

"Are we here to dispute theology, my lord? Had I known, I would have brought a septon."

"You know full well why we are here," said Stannis. "You have had a fortnight to consider my offer. You sent your ravens. No help has come. Nor will it. Storm's End stands alone, and I am out of patience. One last time, ser, I command you to open your gates, and deliver me that which is mine by rights."

"And the terms?" asked Ser Cortnay.

"Remain as before," said Stannis. "I will pardon you for your treason, as I have pardoned these lords you see behind me. The men of your garrison will be free to enter my service or to return unmolested to their homes. You may keep your weapons and as much property as a man can carry. I will require your horses and pack animals, however."

"And what of Edric Storm?"

"My brother's bastard must be surrendered to me."

"Then my answer is still no, my lord."

The king clenched his jaw. He said nothing.

Melisandre spoke instead. "May the Lord of Light protect you in your darkness, Ser Cortnay."

"May the Others bugger your Lord of Light," Penrose spat back, "and wipe his arse with that rag you bear."

Lord Alester Florent cleared his throat. "Ser Cortnay, mind your tongue. His Grace means the boy no harm. The child is his own blood, and mine as well. My niece Delena was the mother, as all men know. If you will not trust to the king, trust to me. You know me for a man of honor—"

"I know you for a man of ambition," Ser Cortnay broke in. "A man who changes kings and gods the way I change my boots. As do these other turncloaks I see before me."

An angry clamor went up from the king's men. *He is not far wrong*, Davos thought. Only a short time before, the Fossoways, Guyard Morrigen, and the Lords Caron, Varner, Errol, and Estermont had all belonged to Renly. They had sat in his pavilion, helped him make his battle plans, plotted how Stannis might be brought low. And Lord Florent had been with them—he might be Queen Selyse's own uncle, but that had not kept the Lord of Brightwater from bending his knee to Renly when Renly's star was rising.

Bryce Caron walked his horse forward a few paces, his long rainbow-striped cloak twisting in the wind off the bay. "No man here is a turncloak, ser. My fealty belongs to Storm's End, and King Stannis is its rightful lord . . . *and* our true king. He is the last of House Baratheon, Robert's heir and Renly's."

"If that is so, why is the Knight of Flowers not among you? And where is Mathis Rowan? Randyll Tarly? Lady Oakheart? Why are they not here in your company, they who loved Renly best? *Where is Brienne of Tarth, I ask you?*"

"That one?" Ser Guyard Morrigen laughed harshly. "She ran. As well she might. Hers was the hand that slew the king."

"A lie," Ser Cortnay said. "I knew Brienne when she was no more than a girl playing at her father's feet in Evenfall Hall, and I knew her still better when the Evenstar sent her here to Storm's End. She loved Renly Baratheon from the first moment she laid eyes on him, a blind man could see it."

"To be sure," declared Lord Florent airily, "and she would scarcely be the first maid maddened to murder by a man who spurned her. Though for my own part, I believe it was Lady Stark who slew the king. She had journeyed all the way from Riverrun to plead for an alliance, and Renly had refused her. No doubt she saw him as a danger to her son, and so removed him."

"It was Brienne," insisted Lord Caron. "Ser Emmon Cuy swore as much before he died. You have my oath on that, Ser Cortnay."

Contempt thickened Ser Cortnay's voice. "And what is that worth? You wear your cloak of many colors, I see. The one Renly gave you when you swore your *oath* to protect him. If he is dead, how is it you are not?" He turned his scorn on Guyard Morrigen. "I might ask the same of you, ser. Guyard the Green, yes? Of the Rainbow Guard? Sworn to give his own life for his king's? If I had such a cloak, I would be ashamed to wear it."

Morrigen bristled. "Be glad this is a parley, Penrose, or I would have your tongue for those words."

"And cast it in the same fire where you left your manhood?"

"*Enough!*" Stannis said. "The Lord of Light willed that my brother die for his treason. Who did the deed matters not."

"Not to *you*, perhaps," said Ser Cortnay. "I have heard your proposal, Lord Stannis. Now here is mine." He pulled off his glove and flung it full in the king's face. "Single combat. Sword, lance, or any weapon you care to name. Or if you fear to hazard your magic sword and royal skin against an old man, name you a champion, and I shall do the same." He gave Guyard Morrigen and Bryce Caron a scathing look. "Either of these pups would do nicely, I should think."

Ser Guyard Morrigen grew dark with fury. "I will take up the gage, if it please the king."

"As would I." Bryce Caron looked to Stannis.

The king ground his teeth. "No."

Ser Cortnay did not seem surprised. "Is it the justice of your cause you doubt, my lord, or the strength of your arm? Are you afraid I'll piss on your burning sword and put it out?"

"Do you take me for an utter fool, ser?" asked Stannis. "I have twenty thousand men. You are besieged by land and sea. Why would I choose single combat when my eventual victory is certain?" The king pointed a finger at him. "I give you fair warning. If you force me to take my castle by storm, you may expect no mercy. I will hang you for traitors, every one of you."

"As the gods will it. Bring on your storm, my lord—and recall, if you do, the *name* of this castle." Ser Cortnay gave a pull on his reins and rode back toward the gate.

Stannis said no word, but turned his horse around and started back toward his camp. The others followed. "If we storm these walls thousands will die," fretted ancient Lord Estermont, who was the king's grandfather on his mother's side. "Better to hazard but a single life, surely? Our cause is righteous, so the gods must surely bless our champion's arms with victory."

God, old man, thought Davos. *You forget, we have only one now, Melisandre's Lord of Light.*

Ser Jon Fossoway said, "I would gladly take this challenge myself, though I'm not half the swordsman Lord Caron is, or Ser Guyard. Renly left no notable knights at Storm's End. Garrison duty is for old men and green boys."

Lord Caron agreed. "An easy victory, to be sure. And what glory, to win Storm's End with a single stroke!"

Stannis raked them all with a look. "You chatter like magpies, and with less sense. I will have quiet." The king's eyes fell on Davos. "Ser. Ride with me." He spurred his horse away from his followers. Only Melisandre kept pace, bearing the great standard of the fiery heart with the crowned stag within. *As if it had been swallowed whole.*

Davos saw the looks that passed between the lordlings as he rode past them to join the king. These were no onion knights, but proud men from houses whose names were old in honor. Somehow he knew that Renly had never chided them in such a fashion. The youngest of the Baratheons had been born with a gift for easy courtesy that his brother sadly lacked.

He eased back to a slow trot when his horse came up beside the king's. "Your Grace." Seen at close hand, Stannis looked worse than Davos had realized from afar. His face had grown haggard, and he had dark circles under his eyes.

"A smuggler must be a fair judge of men," the king said. "What do you make of this Ser Cortnay Penrose?"

"A stubborn man," said Davos carefully.

"Hungry for death, I call it. He throws my pardon in my face. Aye, and throws his life away in the bargain, and the lives of every man inside those walls. *Single combat?*" The king snorted in derision. "No doubt he mistook me for Robert."

"More like he was desperate. What other hope does he have?"

"None. The castle will fall. But how to do it quickly?" Stannis brooded on that for a moment. Under the steady *clop-clop* of hooves, Davos could hear the faint sound of the king grinding his teeth. "Lord Alester urges me to bring old Lord Penrose here. Ser Cortnay's father. You know the man, I believe?"

"When I came as your envoy, Lord Penrose received me more courteously than most," Davos said. "He is an old done man, sire. Sickly and failing."

"Florent would have him fail more visibly. In his son's sight, with a noose about his neck."

It was dangerous to oppose the queen's men, but Davos had vowed always to tell his king the truth. "I think that would be ill done, my liege. Ser Cortnay will watch his father die before he would ever betray his trust. It would gain us nothing, and bring dishonor to our cause."

"What dishonor?" Stannis bristled. "Would you have me spare the lives of traitors?"

"You have spared the lives of those behind us."

"Do you scold me for that, smuggler?"

"It is not my place." Davos feared he had said too much.

The king was relentless. "You esteem this Penrose more than you do my lords bannermen. Why?"

"He keeps faith."

"A misplaced faith in a dead usurper."

"Yes," Davos admitted, "but still, he keeps faith."

"As those behind us do not?"

Davos had come too far with Stannis to play coy now. "Last year they were Robert's men. A moon ago they were Renly's. This morning they are yours. Whose will they be on the morrow?"

And Stannis laughed. A sudden gust, rough and full of scorn. "I told you, Melisandre," he said to the red woman, "my Onion Knight tells me the truth."

"I see you know him well, Your Grace," the red woman said.

"Davos, I have missed you sorely," the king said. "Aye, I have a tail of traitors, your nose does not deceive you. My lords bannermen are inconstant even in their treasons. I need them, but you should know how it sickens me to pardon such as these when I have punished better men for lesser crimes. You have every right to reproach me, Ser Davos."

"You reproach yourself more than I ever could, Your Grace. You must have these great lords to win your throne—"

"Fingers and all, it seems." Stannis smiled grimly.

Unthinking, Davos raised his maimed hand to the pouch at his throat, and felt the fingerbones within. *Luck.*

The king saw the motion. "Are they still there, Onion Knight? You have not lost them?"

"No."

"Why do you keep them? I have often wondered."

"They remind me of what I was. Where I came from. They remind me of your justice, my liege."

"It *was* justice," Stannis said. "A good act does not wash out the bad, nor a bad act the good. Each should have its own reward. You were a hero *and* a smuggler." He glanced behind at Lord Florent and the others, rainbow knights and turncloaks, who were following at a distance. "These pardoned lords would do well to reflect on that. Good men and true will fight for Joffrey, wrongly believing him the true king. A northman might even say the same of Robb Stark. But these lords who flocked to my brother's banners *knew* him for a usurper. They turned their backs on their rightful king for no better reason than dreams of power and glory, and I have marked them for what they are. Pardoned them, yes. Forgiven. But not forgotten." He fell silent for a moment, brooding on his plans for justice. And then, abruptly, he said, "What do the smallfolk say of Renly's death?"

"They grieve. Your brother was well loved."

"Fools love a fool," grumbled Stannis, "but I grieve for him as well. For the boy he was, not the man he grew to be." He was silent for a time, and then he said, "How did the commons take the news of Cersei's incest?"

"While we were among them they shouted for King Stannis. I cannot speak for what they said once we had sailed."

"So you do not think they believed?"

"When I was smuggling, I learned that some men believe everything and some nothing. We met both sorts. And there is another tale being spread as well—"

"Yes." Stannis bit off the word. "Selyse has given me horns, and tied a fool's bells to the end of each. My daughter fathered by a halfwit jester! A tale as vile as it is absurd. Renly threw it in my teeth when we met to parley. You would need to be as mad as Patchface to believe such a thing."

"That may be so, my liege . . . but whether they believe the story or no, they delight to tell it." In many places it had come before them, poisoning the well for their own true tale.

"Robert could piss in a cup and men would call it wine, but I offer them pure cold water and they squint in suspicion and mutter to each other about how queer it tastes." Stannis ground his teeth. "If someone said I had magicked myself into a boar to kill Robert, likely they would believe that as well."

"You cannot stop them talking, my liege," Davos said, "but when you take your vengeance on your brothers' true killers, the realm will know such tales for lies."

Stannis only seemed to half hear him. "I have no doubt that Cersei had a hand in Robert's death. I will have justice for him. Aye, and for Ned Stark and Jon Arryn as well."

"And for Renly?" The words were out before Davos could stop to consider them.

For a long time the king did not speak. Then, very softly, he said, "I dream of it sometimes. Of Renly's dying. A green tent, candles, a woman screaming. And blood." Stannis looked down at his hands. "I was still abed when he died. Your Devan will tell you. He tried to wake me. Dawn was nigh and my lords were waiting, fretting. I should have been ahorse, armored. I knew Renly would attack at break of day. Devan says I thrashed and cried out, but what does it matter? It was a dream. I was in my tent when Renly died, and when I woke my hands were clean."

Ser Davos Seaworth could feel his phantom fingertips start to itch. *Something is wrong here*, the onetime smuggler thought. Yet he nodded and said, "I see."

"Renly offered me a peach. At our parley. Mocked me, defied me, threatened me, and offered me a peach. I thought he was drawing a blade and went for mine own. Was that his purpose, to make me show fear? Or was it one of his pointless jests? When he spoke of how sweet the peach was, did his words have some hidden meaning?" The king gave a shake of his head, like a dog shaking a rabbit to snap its neck. "Only Renly could vex me so with a piece of fruit. He brought his doom on himself with his treason, but I did love him, Davos. I know that now. I swear, I will go to my grave thinking of my brother's peach."

By then they were in amongst the camp, riding past the ordered rows of tents, the blowing banners, and the stacks of shields and spears. The stink of horse dung was heavy in the air, mingled with the woodsmoke and the smell of cooking meat. Stannis reined up long enough to bark a brusque dismissal to Lord Florent and the others, commanding them to attend him in his pavilion one hour hence for a council of war. They bowed their heads and dispersed, while Davos and Melisandre rode to the king's pavilion.

The tent had to be large, since it was there his lords bannermen came to council. Yet there was nothing grand about it. It was a soldier's tent of heavy canvas, dyed the dark yellow that sometimes passed for gold. Only the royal banner that streamed atop the center pole marked it as a king's. That, and the guards without; queen's men leaning on tall spears, with the badge of the fiery heart sewn over their own.

Grooms came up to help them dismount. One of the guards relieved Melisandre of her cumbersome standard, driving the staff deep into the soft ground. Devan stood to one side of the door, waiting to lift the flap for the king. An older squire waited beside him. Stannis took off his crown and handed it to Devan. "Cold water, cups for two. Davos, attend me. My lady, I shall send for you when I require you."

"As the king commands." Melisandre bowed.

After the brightness of the morning, the interior of the pavilion seemed cool and dim. Stannis seated himself on a plain wooden camp stool and waved Davos to another. "One day I may make you a lord, smuggler. If only to irk Celtigar and Florent. You will not thank me, though. It will mean you must suffer through these councils, and feign interest in the braying of mules."

"Why do you have them, if they serve no purpose?"

"The mules love the sound of their own braying, why else? And I need them to haul my cart. Oh, to be sure, once in a great while some useful notion is put forth. But not today, I think—ah, here's your son with our water."

Devan set the tray on the table and filled two clay cups. The king sprinkled a pinch of salt in his cup before he drank; Davos took his water straight, wishing it were wine. "You were speaking of your council?"

"Let me tell you how it will go. Lord Velaryon will urge me to storm the castle walls at first light, grapnels and scaling ladders against arrows and boiling oil. The young mules will think this a splendid notion. Estermont will favor settling down to starve them out, as Tyrell and Redwyne once tried with me. That might take a year, but old mules are patient. And Lord Caron and the others who like to kick will want to take up Ser Cortnay's gauntlet and hazard all upon a single combat. Each one imagining *he* will be my champion and win undying fame." The king finished his water. "What would *you* have me do, smuggler?"

Davos considered a moment before he answered. "Strike for King's Landing at once."

The king snorted. "And leave Storm's End untaken?"

"Ser Cortnay does not have the power to harm you. The Lannisters do. A siege would take too long, single combat is too chancy, and an assault would cost thousands of lives with no certainty of success. And there is no need. Once you dethrone Joffrey this castle must come to you with all the rest. It is said about the camp that Lord Tywin Lannister rushes west to rescue Lannisport from the vengeance of the northmen . . ."

"You have a passing clever father, Devan," the king told the boy standing by his elbow. "He makes me wish I had more smugglers in my service. And fewer lords. Though you are wrong in one respect, Davos. There *is* a need. If I leave Storm's End untaken in my rear, it will be said I was defeated here. And that I cannot permit. Men do not love me as they loved my brothers. They follow me because they fear me . . . and defeat is death to fear. The castle must fall." His jaw ground side to side. "Aye, and *quickly*. Doran Martell has called his banners and fortified the mountain passes. His Dornishmen are poised to sweep down onto the Marches. And Highgarden is far from spent. My brother left the greater part of his power at Bitterbridge, near sixty thousand foot. I sent my wife's brother Ser Errol with Ser Parmen Crane to take them under my command, but they have not returned. I fear that Ser Loras Tyrell reached Bitterbridge before my envoys, and took that host for his own."

"All the more reason to take King's Landing as soon as we may. Salladhor Saan told me—"

"Salladhor Saan thinks only of gold!" Stannis exploded. "His head is full of dreams of the treasure he fancies lies under the Red Keep, so let us hear no more of Salladhor Saan. The day I need military counsel from a Lysene brigand is the day I put off my crown and take the black." The king made a fist. "Are you here to serve me, smuggler? Or to vex me with arguments?"

"I am yours," Davos said.

"Then hear me. Ser Cortnay's lieutenant is cousin to the Fossoways. Lord Meadows, a green boy of twenty. Should some ill chance strike down Penrose, command of Storm's End would pass to this stripling, and his cousins believe he would accept my terms and yield up the castle."

"I remember another stripling who was given command of Storm's End. He could not have been much more than twenty."

"Lord Meadows is not as stonehead stubborn as I was."

"Stubborn or craven, what does it matter? Ser Cortnay Penrose seemed hale and hearty to me."

"So did my brother, the day before his death. The night is dark and full of terrors, Davos."

Davos Seaworth felt the small hairs rising on the back of his neck. "My lord, I do not understand you."

"I do not require your understanding. Only your service. Ser Cortnay will be dead within the day. Melisandre has seen it in the flames of the future. His death and the manner of it. He will not die in knightly combat, needless to say." Stannis held out his cup, and Devan filled it again from the flagon. "Her flames do not lie. She saw Renly's doom as well. On Dragonstone she saw it, and told Selyse. Lord Velaryon and your friend Salladhor Saan would have had me sail against Joffrey, but

Melisandre told me that if I went to Storm's End, I would win the best part of my brother's power, and she was right."

"B-but," Davos stammered, "Lord Renly only came here because you had laid siege to the castle. He was marching toward King's Landing before, against the Lannisters, he would have—"

Stannis shifted in his seat, frowning. "*Was, would have,* what is that? He did what he did. He came here with his banners and his peaches, to his doom . . . and it was well for me he did. Melisandre saw another day in her flames as well. A morrow where Renly rode out of the south in his green armor to smash my host beneath the walls of King's Landing. Had I met my brother there, it might have been me who died in place of him."

"Or you might have joined your strength to his to bring down the Lannisters," Davos protested. "Why not that? If she saw two futures, well . . . *both* cannot be true."

King Stannis pointed a finger. "There you err, Onion Knight. Some lights cast more than one shadow. Stand before the nightfire and you'll see for yourself. The flames shift and dance, never still. The shadows grow tall and short, and every man casts a dozen. Some are fainter than others, that's all. Well, men cast their shadows across the future as well. One shadow or many. Melisandre sees them all.

"You do not love the woman. I know that, Davos, I am not blind. My lords mislike her too. Estermont thinks the flaming heart ill-chosen and begs to fight beneath the crowned stag as of old. Ser Guyard says a woman should not be my standard-bearer. Others whisper that she has no place in my war councils, that I ought to send her back to Asshai, that it is sinful to keep her in my tent of a night. Aye, they whisper . . . while she serves."

"Serves how?" Davos asked, dreading the answer.

"As needed." The king looked at him. "And you?"

"I . . ." Davos licked his lips. "I am yours to command. What would you have me do?"

"Nothing you have not done before. Only land a boat beneath the castle, unseen, in the black of night. Can you do that?"

"Yes. Tonight?"

The king gave a curt nod. "You will need a small boat. Not *Black Betha.* No one must know what you do."

Davos wanted to protest. He was a knight now, no longer a smuggler, and he had never been an assassin. Yet when he opened his mouth, the words would not come. This was *Stannis,* his just lord, to whom he owed all he was. And he had his sons to consider as well. *Gods be good, what has she done to him?*

"You are quiet," Stannis observed.

And should remain so, Davos told himself, yet instead he said, "My liege, you must have the castle, I see that now, but surely there are other ways. *Cleaner* ways. Let Ser Cortnay keep the bastard boy and he may well yield."

"I must have the boy, Davos. *Must.* Melisandre has seen that in the flames as well."

Davos groped for some other answer. "Storm's End holds no knight who can match Ser Guyard or Lord Caron, or any of a hundred others sworn to your service. This single combat . . . could it be that Ser Cortnay seeks for a way to yield with honor? Even if it means his own life?"

A troubled look crossed the king's face like a passing cloud. "More like he plans some treachery. There will be no combat of champions. Ser Cortnay was dead before he ever threw that glove. The flames do not lie, Davos."

Yet they require me to make them true, he thought. It had been a long time since Davos Seaworth felt so sad.

And so it was that he found himself once more crossing Shipbreaker Bay in the dark of night, steering a tiny boat with a black sail. The sky was the same, and the sea. The same salt smell was in the air, and the water chuckling against the hull was just as he remembered it. A thousand flickering campfires burned around the castle, as the fires of the Tyrells and Redwynes had sixteen years before. But all the rest was different.

The last time it was life I brought to Storm's End, shaped to look like onions. This time it is death, in the shape of Melisandre of Asshai. Sixteen years ago, the sails had cracked and snapped with every shift of wind, until he'd pulled them down and gone on with muffled oars. Even so, his heart had been in his gullet. The men on the Redwyne galleys had grown lax after so long, however, and they had slipped through the cordon smooth as black satin. This time, the only ships in sight belonged to Stannis, and the only danger would come from watchers on the castle walls. Even so, Davos was taut as a bowstring.

Melisandre huddled upon a thwart, lost in the folds of a dark red cloak that covered her from head to heels, her face a paleness beneath the cowl. Davos loved the water. He slept best when he had a deck rocking beneath him, and the sighing of the wind in his rigging was a sweeter sound to him than any a singer could make with his harp strings. Even the sea brought him no comfort tonight, though. "I can smell the fear on you, ser knight," the red woman said softly.

"Someone once told me the night is dark and full of terrors. And tonight I am no knight. Tonight I am Davos the smuggler again. Would that you were an onion."

She laughed. "Is it me you fear? Or what we do?"

"What *you* do. I'll have no part of it."

"Your hand raised the sail. Your hand holds the tiller."

Silent, Davos tended to his course. The shore was a snarl of rocks, so he was taking them well out across the bay. He would wait for the tide to turn before coming about. Storm's End dwindled behind them, but the red woman seemed unconcerned. "Are you a good man, Davos Seaworth?" she asked.

Would a good man be doing this? "I am a man," he said. "I am kind to my wife, but I have known other women. I have tried to be a father to my sons, to help make them a place in this world. Aye, I've broken laws, but I never felt evil until tonight. I would say my parts are mixed, m'lady. Good *and* bad."

"A grey man," she said. "Neither white nor black, but partaking of both. Is that what you are, Ser Davos?"

"What if I am? It seems to me that most men are grey."

"If half of an onion is black with rot, it is a rotten onion. A man is good, or he is evil."

The fires behind them had melted into one vague glow against the black sky, and the land was almost out of sight. It was time to come about. "Watch your head, my lady." He pushed on the tiller, and the small boat threw up a curl of black water as she turned. Melisandre leaned under the swinging yard, one hand on the gunwale, calm as ever. Wood creaked, canvas cracked, and water splashed, so loudly a man might swear the castle was sure to hear. Davos knew better. The endless crash of wave on rock was the only sound that ever penetrated the massive seaward walls of Storm's End, and that but faintly.

A rippling wake spread out behind as they swung back toward the shore. "You speak of men and onions," Davos said to Melisandre. "What of women? Is it not the same for them? Are you good or evil, my lady?"

That made her chuckle. "Oh, good. I am a knight of sorts myself, sweet ser. A champion of light and life."

"Yet you mean to kill a man tonight," he said. "As you killed Maester Cressen."

"Your maester poisoned himself. He meant to poison me, but I was protected by a greater power and he was not."

"And Renly Baratheon? Who was it who killed him?"

Her head turned. Beneath the shadow of the cowl, her eyes burned like pale red candle flames. "Not I."

"Liar." Davos was certain now.

Melisandre laughed again. "You are lost in darkness and confusion, Ser Davos."

"And a good thing." Davos gestured at the distant lights flickering along the walls of Storm's End. "Feel how cold the wind is? The guards will huddle close to those torches. A little warmth, a little light, they're a comfort on a night like this. Yet that will blind them, so they will not see us pass." *I hope.* "The god of darkness protects us now, my lady. Even you."

The flames of her eyes seemed to burn a little brighter at that. "Speak not that name, ser. Lest you draw his black eye upon us. He protects no man, I promise you. He is the enemy of all that lives. It is the torches that hide us, you have said so yourself. Fire. The bright gift of the Lord of Light."

"Have it your way."

"His way, rather."

The wind was shifting, Davos could feel it, see it in the way the black canvas rippled. He reached for the halyards. "Help me bring in the sail. I'll row us the rest of the way."

Together they tied off the sail as the boat rocked beneath them. As Davos unshipped the oars and slid them into the choppy black water, he said, "Who rowed you to Renly?"

"There was no need," she said. "He was unprotected. But here . . . this Storm's End is an old place. There are spells woven into the stones. Dark walls that no shadow can pass—ancient, forgotten, yet still in place."

"Shadow?" Davos felt his flesh prickling. "A shadow is a thing of darkness."

"You are more ignorant than a child, ser knight. There are no shadows in the dark. Shadows are the servants of light, the children of fire. The brightest flame casts the darkest shadows."

Frowning, Davos hushed her then. They were coming close to shore once more, and voices carried across the water. He rowed, the faint sound of his oars lost in the rhythm of the waves. The seaward side of Storm's End perched upon a pale white cliff, the chalky stone sloping up steeply to half again the height of the massive curtain wall. A mouth yawned in the cliff, and it was that Davos steered for, as he had sixteen years before. The tunnel opened on a cavern under the castle, where the storm lords of old had built their landing.

The passage was navigable only during high tide, and was never less than treacherous, but his smuggler's skills had not deserted him. Davos threaded their way deftly between the jagged rocks until the cave mouth loomed up before them. He let the waves carry them inside. They crashed around him, slamming the boat this way and that and soaking them to the skin. A half-seen finger of rock came rushing up out of the gloom, snarling foam, and Davos barely kept them off it with an oar.

Then they were past, engulfed in darkness, and the waters smoothed.

The little boat slowed and swirled. The sound of their breathing echoed until it seemed to surround them. Davos had not expected the blackness. The last time, torches had burned all along the tunnel, and the eyes of starving men had peered down through the murder holes in the ceiling. The portcullis was somewhere ahead, he knew. Davos used the oars to slow them, and they drifted against it almost gently.

"This is as far as we go, unless you have a man inside to lift the gate for us." His whispers scurried across the lapping water like a line of mice on soft pink feet.

"Have we passed within the walls?"

"Yes. Beneath. But we can go no farther. The portcullis goes all the way to the bottom. And the bars are too closely spaced for even a child to squeeze through."

There was no answer but a soft rustling. And then a light bloomed amidst the darkness.

Davos raised a hand to shield his eyes, and his breath caught in his throat. Melisandre had thrown back her cowl and shrugged out of the smothering robe. Beneath, she was naked, and huge with child. Swollen breasts hung heavy against her chest, and her belly bulged as if near to bursting. *"Gods preserve us,"* he whispered, and heard her answering laugh, deep and throaty. Her eyes were hot coals, and the sweat that dappled her skin seemed to glow with a light of its own. Melisandre *shone.*

Panting, she squatted and spread her legs. Blood ran down her thighs, black as ink. Her cry might have been agony or ecstasy or both. And Davos saw the crown of the child's head push its way out of her. Two arms wriggled free, grasping, black fingers coiling around Melisandre's straining thighs, pushing, until the whole of the shadow slid out into the world and rose taller than Davos, tall as the tunnel, towering above the boat. He had only an instant to look at it before it was gone, twisting between the bars of the portcullis and racing across the surface of the water, but that instant was long enough.

He knew that shadow. As he knew the man who'd cast it.

JON

The call came drifting through the black of night. Jon pushed himself onto an elbow, his hand reaching for Longclaw by force of habit as the camp began to stir. *The horn that wakes the sleepers*, he thought.

The long low note lingered at the edge of hearing. The sentries at the ringwall stood still in their footsteps, breath frosting and heads turned toward the west. As the sound of the horn faded, even the wind ceased to blow. Men rolled from their blankets and reached for spears and swordbelts, moving quietly, listening. A horse whickered and was hushed. For a heartbeat it seemed as if the whole forest were holding its breath. The brothers of the Night's Watch waited for a second blast, praying they should not hear it, fearing that they would.

When the silence had stretched unbearably long and the men knew at last that the horn would not wind again, they grinned at one another sheepishly, as if to deny that they had been anxious. Jon Snow fed a few sticks to the fire, buckled on his swordbelt, pulled on his boots, shook the dirt and dew from the cloak, and fastened it around his shoulders. The flames blazed up beside him, welcome heat beating against his face as he dressed. He could hear the Lord Commander moving inside the tent. After a moment Mormont lifted the flap. "One blast?" On his shoulder, his raven sat fluffed and silent, looking miserable.

"One, my lord," Jon agreed. "Brothers returning."

Mormont moved to the fire. "The Halfhand. And past time." He had grown more restive every day they waited, much longer and he would have been fit to whelp cubs. "See that there's hot food for the men and fodder for the horses. I'll see Qhorin at once."

"I'll bring him, my lord." The men from the Shadow Tower had been expected days ago. When they had not appeared, the brothers had begun to wonder. Jon had heard gloomy mutterings around the cookfire, and not just from Dolorous Edd. Ser Ottyn Wythers was for retreating to Castle Black as soon as possible. Ser Mallador Locke would strike for the Shadow Tower, hoping to pick up Qhorin's trail and learn what had befallen him. And Thoren Smallwood wanted to push on into the mountains. "Mance Rayder knows he must battle the Watch," Thoren had declared, "but he will never look for us so far north. If we ride up the Milkwater, we can take him unawares and cut his host to ribbons before he knows we are on him."

"The numbers would be greatly against us," Ser Ottyn had objected. "Craster said he was gathering a great host. Many thousands. Without Qhorin, we are only two hundred."

"Send two hundred wolves against ten thousand sheep, ser, and see what happens," said Smallwood confidently.

"There are goats among these sheep, Thoren," warned Jarman Buckwell. "Aye, and maybe a few lions. Rattleshirt, Harma the Dogshead, Alfyn Crowkiller . . ."

"I know them as well as you do, Buckwell," Thoren Smallwood snapped back. "And I mean to have their heads, every one. These are *wildlings*. No soldiers. A few hundred heroes, drunk most like, amidst a great horde of women, children, and thralls. We will sweep over them and send them howling back to their hovels."

They had argued for many hours, and reached no agreement. The Old Bear was too stubborn to retreat, but neither would he rush headlong up the Milkwater, seeking battle. In the end, nothing had been decided but to wait a few more days for the men from the Shadow Tower, and talk again if they did not appear.

And now they had, which meant that the decision could be delayed no longer. Jon was glad of that much, at least. If they must battle Mance Rayder, let it be soon.

He found Dolorous Edd at the fire, complaining about how difficult it was for him to sleep when people insisted on blowing horns in the woods. Jon gave him something new to complain about. Together they woke Hake, who received the Lord Commander's orders with a stream of curses, but got up all the same and soon had a dozen brothers cutting roots for a soup.

Sam came puffing up as Jon crossed the camp. Under the black hood his face was as pale and round as the moon. "I heard the horn. Has your uncle come back?"

"It's only the men from the Shadow Tower." It was growing harder to cling to the hope of Benjen Stark's safe return. The cloak he had found beneath the Fist could well have belonged to his uncle or one of his men, even the Old Bear admitted as much, though why they would have buried it there, wrapped around the cache of dragonglass, no one could say. "Sam, I have to go."

At the ringwall, he found the guards sliding spikes from the half-frozen earth to make an opening. It was not long until the first of the brothers from the Shadow Tower began wending their way up the slope. All in leather and fur they were, with here and there a bit of steel or bronze; heavy beards covered hard lean faces, and made them look as shaggy as their garrons. Jon was surprised to see some of them were riding two to a horse. When he looked more closely, it was plain that many of them were wounded. *There has been trouble on the way.*

Jon knew Qhorin Halfhand the instant he saw him, though they had never met. The big ranger was half a legend in the Watch; a man of slow words and swift action, tall and straight as a spear, long-limbed and solemn. Unlike his men, he was clean-shaven. His hair fell from beneath his helm in a heavy braid touched with hoarfrost, and the blacks he wore were so faded they might have been greys. Only thumb and forefinger remained on the hand that held the reins; the other fingers had been sheared off catching a wildling's axe that would otherwise have split his skull. It was told that he had thrust his maimed fist into the face of the axeman so the blood spurted into his eyes, and slew him while he was blind. Since that day, the wildlings beyond the Wall had known no foe more implacable.

Jon hailed him. "Lord Commander Mormont would see you at once. I'll show you to his tent."

Qhorin swung down from his saddle. "My men are hungry, and our horses require tending."

"They'll all be seen to."

The ranger gave his horse into the care of one of his men and followed. "You are Jon Snow. You have your father's look."

"Did you know him, my lord?"

"I am no lordling. Only a brother of the Night's Watch. I knew Lord Eddard, yes. And his father before him."

Jon had to hurry his steps to keep up with Qhorin's long strides. "Lord Rickard died before I was born."

"He was a friend to the Watch." Qhorin glanced behind. "It is said that a direwolf runs with you."

"Ghost should be back by dawn. He hunts at night."

They found Dolorous Edd frying a rasher of bacon and boiling a dozen eggs in a kettle over the Old Bear's cookfire. Mormont sat in his wood-and-leather camp chair. "I had begun to fear for you. Did you meet with trouble?"

"We met with Alfyn Crowkiller. Mance had sent him to scout along the Wall, and we chanced on him returning." Qhorin removed his helm. "Alfyn will trouble the realm no longer, but some of his company escaped us. We hunted down as many as we could, but it may be that a few will win back to the mountains."

"And the cost?"

"Four brothers dead. A dozen wounded. A third as many as the foe. And we took captives. One died quickly from his wounds, but the other lived long enough to be questioned."

"Best talk of this inside. Jon will fetch you a horn of ale. Or would you prefer hot spiced wine?"

"Boiled water will suffice. An egg and a bite of bacon."

"As you wish." Mormont lifted the flap of the tent and Qhorin Halfhand stooped and stepped through.

Edd stood over the kettle swishing the eggs about with a spoon. "I envy those eggs," he said. "I could do with a bit of boiling about now. If the kettle were larger, I might jump in. Though I would sooner it were wine than water. There are worse ways to die than warm and drunk. I knew a brother drowned himself in wine once. It was a poor vintage, though, and his corpse did not improve it."

"You *drank* the wine?"

"It's an awful thing to find a brother dead. You'd have need of a drink as well, Lord Snow." Edd stirred the kettle and added a pinch more nutmeg.

Restless, Jon squatted by the fire and poked at it with a stick. He could hear the Old Bear's voice inside the tent, punctuated by the raven's squawks and Qhorin Halfhand's quieter tones, but he could not make out the words. *Alfyn Crowkiller dead, that's good.* He was one of the bloodiest of the wildling raiders, taking his name from the black brothers he'd slain. *So why does Qhorin sound so grave, after such a victory?*

Jon had hoped that the arrival of men from the Shadow Tower would lift the spirits in the camp. Only last night, he was coming back through the dark from a piss when he heard five or six men talking in low voices around the embers of a fire. When he heard Chett muttering that it was past time they turned back, Jon stopped to listen. "It's an old man's folly, this ranging," he heard. "We'll find nothing but our graves in them mountains."

"There's giants in the Frostfangs, and wargs, and worse things," said Lark the Sisterman.

"I'll not be going there, I promise you."

"The Old Bear's not like to give you a choice."

"Might be we won't give him one," said Chett.

Just then one of the dogs had raised his head and growled, and he had to move away quickly, before he was seen. *I was not meant to hear that,* he thought. He considered taking the tale to Mormont, but he could not bring himself to inform on his brothers, even brothers such as Chett and the Sisterman. *It was just empty talk,* he told himself. *They are cold and afraid; we all are.* It was hard waiting here, perched on the stony summit above the forest, wondering what the morrow might bring. *The unseen enemy is always the most fearsome.*

Jon slid his new dagger from its sheath and studied the flames as they played against the shiny black glass. He had fashioned the wooden hilt himself, and wound hempen twine around it to make a grip. Ugly, but it served. Dolorous Edd opined that glass knives were about as useful as nipples on a knight's breastplate, but Jon was not so certain. The dragon-glass blade was sharper than steel, albeit far more brittle.

It must have been buried for a reason.

He had made a dagger for Grenn as well, and another for the Lord Commander. The warhorn he had given to Sam. On closer examination the horn had proved cracked, and even after he had cleaned all the dirt out, Jon had been unable to get any sound from it. The rim was chipped as well, but Sam liked old things, even worthless old things. "Make a drinking horn out of it," Jon told him, "and every time you take a drink you'll remember how you ranged beyond the Wall, all the way to the Fist of the First Men." He gave Sam a spearhead and a dozen arrowheads as well, and passed the rest out among his other friends for luck.

The Old Bear had seemed pleased by the dagger, but he preferred a steel knife at his belt, Jon had noticed. Mormont could offer no answers as to who might have buried the cloak or what it might mean. *Perhaps Qhorin will know.* The Halfhand had ventured deeper into the wild than any other living man.

"You want to serve, or shall I?"

Jon sheathed the dagger. "I'll do it." He wanted to hear what they were saying.

Edd cut three thick slices off a stale round of oat bread, stacked them on a wooden platter, covered them with bacon and bacon drippings, and filled a bowl with hard-cooked eggs. Jon took the bowl in one hand and the platter in the other and backed into the Lord Commander's tent.

Qhorin was seated cross-legged on the floor, his spine as straight as a spear. Candlelight flickered against the hard flat planes of his cheeks as he spoke. ". . . Rattleshirt, the Weeping Man, and every other chief great and small," he was saying. "They have wargs as well, and mammoths, and more strength than we would have dreamed. Or so he claimed. I will not swear as to the truth of it. Ebben believes the man was telling us tales to make his life last a little longer."

"True or false, the Wall must be warned," the Old Bear said as Jon placed the platter between them. "And the king."

"Which king?"

"All of them. The true and the false alike. If they would claim the realm, let them defend it."

The Halfhand helped himself to an egg and cracked it on the edge of the bowl. "These kings will do what they will," he said, peeling away the shell. "Likely it will be little enough. The best hope is Winterfell. The Starks must rally the north."

"Yes. To be sure." The Old Bear unrolled a map, frowned at it, tossed it aside, opened another. He was pondering where the hammer would fall, Jon could see it. The Watch had once manned seventeen castles along the hundred leagues of the Wall, but they had been abandoned one by one as the brotherhood dwindled. Only three were now garrisoned, a fact that Mance Rayder knew as well as they did. "Ser Alliser Thorne will bring back fresh levies from King's Landing, we can hope. If we man Greyguard from the Shadow Tower and the Long Barrow from Eastwatch . . ."

"Greyguard has largely collapsed. Stonedoor would serve better, if the men could be found. Icemark and Deep Lake as well, mayhaps. With daily patrols along the battlements between."

"Patrols, aye. Twice a day, if we can. The Wall itself is a formidable obstacle. Undefended, it cannot stop them, yet it will delay them. The larger the host, the longer they'll require. From the emptiness they've left behind, they must mean to bring their women with them. Their young as well, and beasts . . . have you ever seen a goat climb a ladder? A rope? They will need to build a stair, or a great ramp . . . it will take a moon's turn at the least, perhaps longer. Mance will know his best chance is to pass *beneath* the Wall. Through a gate, or . . ."

"A breach."

Mormont's head came up sharply. "What?"

"They do not plan to climb the Wall nor to burrow beneath it, my lord. They plan to break it."

"The Wall is seven hundred feet high, and so thick at the base that it would take a hundred men a year to cut through it with picks and axes."

"Even so."

Mormont plucked at his beard, frowning. "How?"

"How else? Sorcery." Qhorin bit the egg in half. "Why else would Mance choose to gather his strength in the Frostfangs? Bleak and hard they are, and a long weary march from the Wall."

"I'd hoped he chose the mountains to hide his muster from the eyes of my rangers."

"Perhaps," said Qhorin, finishing the egg, "but there is more, I think. He is seeking something in the high cold places. He is searching for something he needs."

"Something?" Mormont's raven lifted its head and screamed. The sound was sharp as a knife in the closeness of the tent.

"Some power. What it is, our captive could not say. He was questioned perhaps too sharply, and died with much unsaid. I doubt he knew in any case."

Jon could hear the wind outside. It made a high thin sound as it shivered through the stones of the ringwall and tugged at the tent ropes. Mormont rubbed his mouth thoughtfully. "Some power," he repeated. "I must know."

"Then you must send scouts into the mountains."

"I am loath to risk more men."

"We can only die. Why else do we don these black cloaks, but to die in defense of the realm? I would send fifteen men, in three parties of five. One to probe the Milkwater, one the Skirling Pass, one to climb the Giant's Stair. Jarman Buckwell, Thoren Smallwood, and myself to command. To learn what waits in those mountains."

"*Waits,*" the raven cried. "*Waits.*"

Lord Commander Mormont sighed deep in his chest. "I see no other choice," he conceded, "but if you do not return . . ."

"Someone will come down out of the Frostfangs, my lord," the ranger said. "If us, all well and good. If not, it will be Mance Rayder, and you sit square in his path. He cannot march south and leave you behind, to follow and harry his rear. He must attack. This is a strong place."

"Not that strong," said Mormont.

"Belike we shall all die, then. Our dying will buy time for our brothers on the Wall. Time to garrison the empty castles and freeze shut the gates, time to summon lords and kings to their aid, time to hone their axes and repair their catapults. Our lives will be coin well spent."

"*Die,*" the raven muttered, pacing along Mormont's shoulders. "*Die, die, die, die.*" The Old Bear sat slumped and silent, as if the burden of speech had grown too heavy for him to bear. But at last he said, "May the gods forgive me. Choose your men."

Qhorin Halfhand turned his head. His eyes met Jon's, and held them for a long moment. "Very well. I choose Jon Snow."

Mormont blinked. "He is hardly more than a boy. And my steward besides. Not even a ranger."

"Tollett can care for you as well, my lord." Qhorin lifted his maimed, two-fingered hand. "The old gods are still strong beyond the Wall. The gods of the First Men . . . and the Starks."

Mormont looked at Jon. "What is your will in this?"

"To go," he said at once.

The old man smiled sadly. "I thought it might be."

Dawn had broken when Jon stepped from the tent beside Qhorin Half-hand. The wind swirled around them, stirring their black cloaks and sending a scatter of red cinders flying from the fire.

"We ride at noon," the ranger told him. "Best find that wolf of yours."

TYRION

"The queen intends to send Prince Tommen away." They knelt alone in the hushed dimness of the sept, surrounded by shadows and flickering candles, but even so Lancel kept his voice low. "Lord Gyles will take him to Rosby, and conceal him there in the guise of a page. They plan to darken his hair and tell everyone that he is the son of a hedge knight."

"Is it the mob she fears? Or me?"

"Both," said Lancel.

"Ah." Tyrion had known nothing of this ploy. Had Varys's little birds failed him for once? Even spiders must nod, he supposed . . . or was the eunuch playing a deeper and more subtle game than he knew? "You have my thanks, ser."

"Will you grant me the boon I asked of you?"

"Perhaps." Lancel wanted his own command in the next battle. A splendid way to die before he finished growing that mustache, but young knights always think themselves invincible.

Tyrion lingered after his cousin had slipped away. At the Warrior's altar, he used one candle to light another. *Watch over my brother, you bloody bastard, he's one of yours.* He lit a second candle to the Stranger, for himself.

That night, when the Red Keep was dark, Bronn arrived to find him sealing a letter. "Take this to Ser Jacelyn Bywater." The dwarf dribbled hot golden wax down onto the parchment.

"What does it say?" Bronn could not read, so he asked impudent questions.

"That he's to take fifty of his best swords and scout the roseroad." Tyrion pressed his seal into the soft wax.

"Stannis is more like to come up the kingsroad."

"Oh, I know. Tell Bywater to disregard what's in the letter and take his men north. He's to lay a trap along the Rosby road. Lord Gyles will depart for his castle in a day or two, with a dozen men-at-arms, some servants, and my nephew. Prince Tommen may be dressed as a page."

"You want the boy brought back, is that it?"

"No. I want him taken on to the castle." Removing the boy from the city was one of his sister's better notions, Tyrion had decided. At Rosby, Tommen would be safe from the mob, and keeping him apart from his brother also made things more difficult for Stannis; even if he took King's Landing and executed Joffrey, he'd still have a Lannister claimant to contend with. "Lord Gyles is too sickly to run and too craven to fight. He'll command his castellan to open the gates. Once inside the walls, Bywater is to expel the garrison and hold Tommen there safe. Ask him how he likes the sound of *Lord* Bywater."

"Lord Bronn would sound better. I could grab the boy for you just as well. I'll dandle him on my knee and sing him nursery songs if there's a lordship in it."

"I need you here," said Tyrion. *And I don't trust you with my nephew.* Should any ill befall Joffrey, the Lannister claim to the Iron Throne would rest on Tommen's young shoulders. Ser Jacelyn's gold cloaks would defend the boy; Bronn's sellswords were more apt to sell him to his enemies.

"What should the new lord do with the old one?"

"Whatever he pleases, so long as he remembers to feed him. I don't want him dying." Tyrion pushed away from the table. "My sister will send one of the Kingsguard with the prince."

Bronn was not concerned. "The Hound is Joffrey's dog, he won't leave him. Ironhand's gold cloaks should be able to handle the others easy enough."

"If it comes to killing, tell Ser Jacelyn I won't have it done in front of Tommen." Tyrion donned a heavy cloak of dark brown wool. "My nephew is tenderhearted."

"Are you certain he's a Lannister?"

"I'm certain of nothing but winter and battle," he said. "Come. I'm riding with you part of the way."

"Chataya's?"

"You know me too well."

They left through a postern gate in the north wall. Tyrion put his heels into his horse and clattered down Shadowblack Lane. A few furtive shapes darted into alleys at the sound of hoofbeats on the cobbles, but no one dared accost them. The council had extended his curfew; it was death to be taken on the streets after the evenfall bells had sung. The measure had restored a degree of peace to King's Landing and quartered the number of corpses found in the alleys of a morning, yet Varys said the people cursed him for it. *They should be thankful they have the breath to curse.* A pair of gold cloaks confronted them as they were making their way along Coppersmith's Wynd, but when they realized whom they'd challenged they begged the Hand's pardons and waved them on. Bronn turned south for the Mud Gate and they parted company.

Tyrion rode on toward Chataya's, but suddenly his patience deserted him. He twisted in the saddle, scanning the street behind. There were no signs of followers. Every window was dark or tightly shuttered. He heard nothing but the wind swirling down the alleys. *If Cersei has someone stalking me tonight, he must be disguised as a rat.* "Bugger it all," he muttered. He was sick of caution. Wheeling his horse around, he dug in his spurs. *If anyone's after me, we'll see how well they ride.* He flew through the moonlight streets, clattering over cobbles, darting down narrow alleys and up twisty wynds, racing to his love.

As he hammered on the gate he heard music wafting faintly over the spiked stone walls. One of the Ibbenese ushered him inside. Tyrion gave the man his horse and said, "Who is that?" The diamond-shaped panes of the longhall windows shone with yellow light, and he could hear a man singing.

The Ibbenese shrugged. "Fatbelly singer."

The sound swelled as he walked from the stable to the house. Tyrion had never been fond of singers, and he liked this one even less than the run of the breed, sight unseen. When he pushed open the door, the man broke off. "My lord Hand." He knelt, balding and kettle-bellied, murmuring, "An honor, an honor."

"M'lord." Shae smiled at the sight of him. He liked that smile, the quick unthinking way it came to her pretty face. The girl wore her purple silk, belted with a cloth-of-silver sash. The colors favored her dark hair and the smooth cream of her skin.

"Sweetling," he called her. "And who is this?"

The singer raised his eyes. "I am called Symon Silver Tongue, my lord. A player, a singer, a taleteller—"

"And a great fool," Tyrion finished. "What did you call me, when I entered?"

"Call? I only . . ." The silver in Symon's tongue seemed to have turned to lead. "My lord Hand, I said, an honor . . ."

"A wiser man would have pretended not to recognize me. Not that I would have been fooled, but you ought to have tried. What am I to do with you now? You know of my sweet Shae, you know where she dwells, you know that I visit by night alone."

"I swear, I'll tell no one . . ."

"On that much we agree. Good night to you." Tyrion led Shae up the stairs.

"My singer may never sing again now," she teased. "You've scared the voice from him."

"A little fear will help him reach those high notes."

She closed the door to their bedchamber. "You won't hurt him, will you?" She lit a scented candle and knelt to pull off his boots. "His songs cheer me on the nights you don't come."

"Would that I could come every night," he said as she rubbed his bare feet. "How well does he sing?"

"Better than some. Not so good as others."

Tyrion opened her robe and buried his face between her breasts. She always smelled clean to him, even in this reeking sty of a city. "Keep him if you like, but keep him close. I won't have him wandering the city spreading tales in pot-shops."

"He won't—" she started.

Tyrion covered her mouth with his own. He'd had talk enough; he needed the sweet simplicity of the pleasure he found between Shae's thighs. Here, at least, he was welcome, wanted.

Afterward, he eased his arm out from under her head, slipped on his tunic, and went down to the garden. A half-moon silvered the leaves of the fruit trees and shone on the surface of the stone bathing pond. Tyrion seated himself beside the water. Somewhere off to his right a cricket was chirping, a curiously homey sound. *It is peaceful here,* he thought, *but for how long?*

A whiff of something rank made him turn his head. Shae stood in the door behind him, dressed in the silvery robe he'd given her. *I loved a maid as white as winter, with moonglow in her hair.* Behind her stood one of the begging brothers, a portly man in filthy patched robes, his bare feet crusty with dirt, a bowl hung about his neck on a leather thong where a septon would have worn a crystal. The smell of him would have gagged a rat.

"Lord Varys has come to see you," Shae announced.

The begging brother blinked at her, astonished. Tyrion laughed. "To be sure. How is it you knew him when I did not?"

She shrugged. "It's still him. Only dressed different."

"A different look, a different smell, a different way of walking," said Tyrion. "Most men would be deceived."

"And most women, maybe. But not whores. A whore learns to see the man, not his garb, or she turns up dead in an alley."

Varys looked pained, and not because of the false scabs on his feet. Tyrion chuckled. "Shae, would you bring us some wine?" He might need a drink. Whatever brought the eunuch here in the dead of night was not like to be good.

"I almost fear to tell you why I've come, my lord," Varys said when Shae had left them. "I bring dire tidings."

"You ought to dress in black feathers, Varys, you're as bad an omen as any raven." Awkwardly, Tyrion pushed to his feet, half afraid to ask the next question. "Is it Jaime?" *If they have harmed him, nothing will save them.*

"No, my lord. A different matter. Ser Cortnay Penrose is dead. Storm's End has opened its gates to Stannis Baratheon."

Dismay drove all other thoughts from Tyrion's mind. When Shae returned with the wine, he took one sip and flung the cup away to explode against the side of the house. She raised a hand to shield herself from the shards as the wine ran down the stones in long fingers, black in the moonlight. "*Damn* him!" Tyrion said.

Varys smiled, showing a mouth full of rotted teeth. "Who, my lord? Ser Cortnay or Lord Stannis?"

"Both of them." Storm's End was strong, it should have been able to hold out for half a year or more . . . time enough for his father to finish with Robb Stark. "How did this happen?"

Varys glanced at Shae. "My lord, must we trouble your sweet lady's sleep with such grim and bloody talk?"

"A lady might be afraid," said Shae, "but I'm not."

"You should be," Tyrion told her. "With Storm's End fallen, Stannis will soon turn his attention toward King's Landing." He regretted flinging away that wine now. "Lord Varys, give us a moment, and I'll ride back to the castle with you."

"I shall wait in the stables." He bowed and stomped off.

Tyrion drew Shae down beside him. "You are not safe here."

"I have my walls, and the guards you gave me."

"Sellswords," Tyrion said. "They like my gold well enough, but will they die for it? As for these walls, a man could stand on another's shoulders and be over in a heartbeat. A manse much like this one was burned during the riots. They killed the goldsmith who owned it for the crime of having a full larder, just as they tore the High Septon to pieces, raped Lollys half a hundred times, and smashed Ser Aron's skull in. What do you think they would do if they got their hands on the Hand's lady?"

"The Hand's whore, you mean?" She looked at him with those big bold eyes of hers. "Though I would be your lady, m'lord. I'd dress in all the beautiful things you gave me, in satin and samite and cloth-of-gold, and I'd wear your jewels and hold your hand and sit by you at feasts. I could give you sons, I know I could . . . and I vow I'd never shame you."

My love for you shames me enough. "A sweet dream, Shae. Now put it aside, I beg you. It can never be."

"Because of the queen? I'm not afraid of her either."

"I am."

"Then *kill* her and be done with it. It's not as if there was any love between you."

Tyrion sighed. "She's my sister. The man who kills his own blood is cursed forever in the sight of gods and men. Moreover, whatever you and I may think of Cersei, my father and brother hold her dear. I can scheme with any man in the Seven Kingdoms, but the gods have not equipped me to face Jaime with swords in hand."

"The Young Wolf and Lord Stannis have swords and they don't scare you."

How little you know, sweetling. "Against them I have all the power of House Lannister. Against Jaime or my father, I have no more than a twisted back and a pair of stunted legs."

"You have me." Shae kissed him, her arms sliding around his neck as she pressed her body to his.

The kiss aroused him, as her kisses always did, but this time Tyrion gently disentangled himself. "Not now. Sweetling, I have . . . well, call it the seed of a plan. I think I might be able to bring you into the castle kitchens."

Shae's face went still. "The kitchens?"

"Yes. If I act through Varys, no one will be the wiser."

She giggled. "M'lord, I'd poison you. Every man who's tasted my cooking has told me what a good whore I am."

"The Red Keep has sufficient cooks. Butchers and bakers too. You'd need to pose as a scullion."

"A pot girl," she said, "in scratchy brown roughspun. Is that how m'lord wants to see me?"

"M'lord wants to see you alive," Tyrion said. "You can scarcely scour pots in silk and velvet."

"Has m'lord grown tired of me?" She reached a hand under his tunic and found his cock. In two quick strokes she had it hard. "*He* still wants me." She laughed. "Would you like to fuck your kitchen wench, m'lord? You can dust me with flour and suck gravy off my titties if you . . ."

"Stop it." The way she was acting reminded him of Dancy, who had tried so hard to win her wager. He yanked her hand away to keep her from further mischief. "This is not the time for bed sport, Shae. Your life may be at stake."

Her grin was gone. "If I've displeased m'lord, I never meant it, only . . . couldn't you just give me more guards?"

Tyrion breathed a deep sigh. *Remember how young she is*, he told himself. He took her hand. "Your gems can be replaced, and new gowns can be sewn twice as lovely as the old. To me, you're the most precious thing within these walls. The Red Keep is not safe either, but it's a deal safer than here. I want you there."

"In the kitchens." Her voice was flat. "Scouring pots."

"For a short while."

"My father made me his kitchen wench," she said, her mouth twisting. "That was why I ran off."

"You told me you ran off because your father made you his whore," he reminded her.

"That too. I didn't like scouring his pots no more than I liked his cock in me." She tossed her head. "Why can't you keep me in your tower? Half the lords at court keep bedwarmers."

"I was expressly forbidden to take you to court."

"By your stupid father." Shae pouted. "You're old enough to keep all the whores you want. Does he take you for a beardless boy? What could he do, spank you?"

He slapped her. Not hard, but hard enough. "Damn you," he said. "*Damn* you. *Never* mock me. Not *you*."

For a moment Shae did not speak. The only sound was the cricket, chirping, chirping. "Beg pardon, m'lord," she said at last, in a heavy wooden voice. "I never meant to be impudent."

And I never meant to strike you. Gods be good, am I turning into Cersei? "That was ill done," he said. "On both our parts. Shae, you do not understand." Words he had never meant to speak came tumbling out of him like mummers from a hollow horse. "When I was thirteen, I wed a crofter's daughter. Or so I thought her. I was blind with love for her, and thought she felt the same for me, but my father rubbed my face in the truth. My bride was a whore Jaime had hired to give me my first taste of manhood." *And I believed all of it, fool that I was.* "To drive the lesson home, Lord Tywin gave my wife to a barracks of his guardsmen to use as they pleased, and commanded me to watch." *And to take her one last time, after the rest were done. One last time, with no trace of love or tenderness remaining.* "So you will remember her as she truly is," he said, *and I should have defied him, but my cock betrayed me, and I did as I was bid.* "After he was done with her, my father had the marriage undone. It was as if we had never been wed, the septons said." He squeezed her hand. "Please, let's have no more talk of the Tower of the Hand. You will be in the kitchens only a little while. Once we're done with Stannis, you'll have another manse, and silks as soft as your hands."

Shae's eyes had grown large but he could not read what lay behind them. "My hands won't be soft if I clean ovens and scrape plates all day. Will you still want them touching you when they're all red and raw and cracked from hot water and lye soap?"

"More than ever," he said. "When I look at them, they'll remind me how brave you were."

He could not say if she believed him. She lowered her eyes. "I am yours to command, m'lord."

It was as much acceptance as she could give tonight, he saw that plain enough. He kissed her cheek where he'd struck her, to take some sting from the blow. "I will send for you."

Varys was waiting in the stables, as promised. His horse looked spavined and half-dead. Tyrion mounted up; one of the sellswords opened the gates. They rode out in silence. *Why did I tell her about Tysha, gods help me!* he asked himself, suddenly afraid. There were some secrets that should never be spoken, some shames a man should take to his grave. What did he want from her, forgiveness? The way she had looked at him, what did that mean? Did she hate the thought of scouring pots that much, or was it his confession? *How could I tell her that and still think she would love me!* part of him said, and another part mocked, saying, *Fool of a dwarf, it is only the gold and jewels the whore loves.*

His scarred elbow was throbbing, jarred every time the horse set down a hoof. Sometimes he could almost fancy he heard the bones grinding together inside. Perhaps he should see a maester, get some potion for the pain . . . but since Pycelle had revealed himself for what he was, Tyrion Lannister mistrusted the maesters. The gods only knew who they were conspiring with, or what they had mixed in those potions they gave you. "Varys," he said. "I need to bring Shae into the castle without Cersei becoming aware." Briefly, he sketched out his kitchen scheme.

When he was done, the eunuch made a little clucking sound. "I will do as my lord commands, of course . . . but I must warn you, the kitchens are full of eyes and ears. Even if the girl falls under no particular suspicion, she will be subject to a thousand questions. Where was she born? Who were her parents? How did she come to King's Landing? The truth will never do, so she must lie . . . and lie, and lie." He glanced down at Tyrion. "And such a pretty young kitchen wench will incite lust as well as curiosity. She will be touched, pinched, patted, and fondled.

Pot boys will crawl under her blankets of a night. Some lonely cook may seek to wed her. Bakers will knead her breasts with floured hands."

"I'd sooner have her fondled than stabbed," said Tyrion.

Varys rode on a few paces and said, "It might be that there is another way. As it happens, the maidservant who attends Lady Tanda's daughter has been filching her jewels. Were I to inform Lady Tanda, she would be forced to dismiss the girl at once. And the daughter would require a new maidservant."

"I see." This had possibilities, Tyrion saw at once. A lady's bedmaid wore finer garb than a scullion, and often even a jewel or two. Shae should be pleased by that. And Cersei thought Lady Tanda tedious and hysterical, and Lollys a bovine lackwit. She was not like to pay them any friendly calls.

"Lollys is timid and trusting," Varys said. "She will accept any tale she is told. Since the mob took her maidenhood she is afraid to leave her chambers, so Shae will be out of sight . . . but conveniently close, should you have need of comfort."

"The Tower of the Hand is watched, you know as well as I. Cersei would be certain to grow curious if Lollys's bedmaid starting paying me calls."

"I might be able to slip the child into your bedchamber unseen. Chataya's is not the only house to boast a hidden door."

"A secret access? To *my* chambers?" Tyrion was more annoyed than surprised. Why else would Maegor the Cruel have ordered death for all the builders who had worked on his castle, except to preserve such secrets? "Yes, I suppose there would be. Where will I find the door? In my solar? My bedchamber?"

"My friend, you would not force me to reveal *all* my little secrets, would you?"

"Henceforth think of them as *our* little secrets, Varys." Tyrion glanced up at the eunuch in his smelly mummer's garb. "Assuming you *are* on my side . . ."

"Can you doubt it?"

"Why no, I trust you implicitly." A bitter laugh echoed off the shuttered windows. "I trust you like one of my own blood, in truth. Now tell me how Cortnay Penrose died."

"It is said that he threw himself from a tower."

"Threw *himself*? No, I will not believe that!"

"His guards saw no man enter his chambers, nor did they find any within afterward."

"Then the killer entered earlier and hid under the bed," Tyrion suggested, "or he climbed down from the roof on a rope. Perhaps the guards are lying. Who's to say they did not do the thing themselves?"

"Doubtless you are right, my lord."

His smug tone said otherwise. "But you do not think so? How was it done, then?"

For a long moment Varys said nothing. The only sound was the stately *clack* of horseshoes on cobbles. Finally the eunuch cleared his throat. "My lord, do you believe in the old powers?"

"Magic, you mean?" Tyrion said impatiently. "Bloodspells, curses, shapeshifting, those sorts of things?" He snorted. "Do you mean to suggest that Ser Cortnay was magicked to his death?"

"Ser Cortnay had challenged Lord Stannis to single combat on the morning he died. I ask you, is this the act of a man lost to despair? Then there is the matter of Lord Renly's mysterious and most fortuitous murder, even as his battle lines were forming up to sweep his brother from the field." The eunuch paused a moment. "My lord, you once asked me how it was that I was cut."

"I recall," said Tyrion. "You did not want to talk of it."

"Nor do I, but . . ." This pause was longer than the one before, and when Varys spoke again his voice was different somehow. "I was an orphan boy apprenticed to a traveling folly. Our master owned a fat little cog and we sailed up and down the narrow sea performing in all the Free Cities and from time to time in Oldtown and King's Landing.

"One day at Myr, a certain man came to our folly. After the performance, he made an offer for me that my master found too tempting to refuse. I was in terror. I feared the man meant to use me as I had heard men used small boys, but in truth the only part of me he had need of was my manhood. He gave me a potion that made me powerless to move or speak, yet did nothing to dull my senses. With a long hooked blade, he sliced me root and stem, chanting all the while. I watched him burn my manly parts on a brazier. The flames turned blue, and I heard a voice answer his call, though I did not understand the words they spoke.

"The mummers had sailed by the time he was done with me. Once I had served his purpose, the man had no further interest in me, so he put me out. When I asked him what I should do now, he answered that he supposed I should die. To spite him, I resolved to live. I begged, I stole, and I sold what parts of my body still remained to me. Soon I was as good a thief as any in Myr, and when I was older I learned that often the contents of a man's letters are more valuable than the contents of his purse.

"Yet I still dream of that night, my lord. Not of the sorcerer, nor his blade, nor even the way my manhood shriveled as it burned. I dream of the voice. The voice from the flames. Was it a god, a demon, some conjurer's trick? I could not tell you, and I know all the tricks. All I can say for a certainty is that he called it, and it answered, and since that day I have hated magic and all those who practice it. If Lord Stannis is one such, I mean to see him dead."

When he was done, they rode in silence for a time. Finally Tyrion said, "A harrowing tale. I'm sorry."

The eunuch sighed. "You are sorry, but you do not believe me. No, my lord, no need to apologize. I was drugged and in pain and it was a very long time ago and far across the sea. No doubt I dreamed that voice. I've told myself as much a thousand times."

"I believe in steel swords, gold coins, and men's wits," said Tyrion. "And I believe there once were dragons. I've seen their skulls, after all."

"Let us hope that is the worst thing you ever see, my lord."

"On that we agree." Tyrion smiled. "And for Ser Cortnay's death, well, we know Stannis hired sellsails from the Free Cities. Perhaps he bought himself a skilled assassin as well."

"A *very* skilled assassin."

"There are such. I used to dream that one day I'd be rich enough to send a Faceless Man after my sweet sister."

"Regardless of how Ser Cortnay died," said Varys, "he is dead, the castle fallen. Stannis is free to march."

"Any chance we might convince the Dornishmen to descend on the Marches?" asked Tyrion.

"None."

"A pity. Well, the threat may serve to keep the Marcher lords close to their castles, at least. What news of my father?"

"If Lord Tywin has won across the Red Fork, no word has reached me yet. If he does not hasten, he may be trapped between his foes. The Oakheart leaf and the Rowan tree have been seen north of the Mander."

"No word from Littlefinger?"

"Perhaps he never reached Bitterbridge. Or perhaps he's died there. Lord Tarly has seized Renly's stores and put a great many to the sword, Florents, chiefly. Lord Caswell has shut himself up in his castle."

Tyrion threw back his head and laughed.

Varys reined up, nonplussed. "My lord?"

"Don't you see the jest, Lord Varys?" Tyrion waved a hand at the shuttered windows, at all the sleeping city. "Storm's End is fallen and Stannis is coming with fire and steel and the gods alone know what dark powers, and the good folk don't have Jaime to protect them, nor Robert nor Renly nor Rhaegar nor their precious Knight of Flowers. Only me, the one they hate." He laughed again. "The dwarf, the evil counselor, the twisted little monkey demon. I'm all that stands between them and chaos."

CATELYN

Tell Father I have gone to make him proud." Her brother swung up into his saddle, every inch the lord in his bright mail and flowing mud-and-water cloak. A silver trout ornamented the crest of his greathelm, twin to the one painted on his shield.

"He was always proud of you, Edmure. And he loves you fiercely. Believe that."

"I mean to give him better reason than mere birth." He wheeled his warhorse about and raised a hand. Trumpets sounded, a drum began to boom, the drawbridge descended in fits and starts, and Ser Edmure Tully led his men out from Riverrun with lances raised and banners streaming.

I have a greater host than yours, brother, Catelyn thought as she watched them go. *A host of doubts and fears.*

Beside her, Brienne's misery was almost palpable. Catelyn had ordered garments sewn to her measure, handsome gowns to suit her birth and sex, yet still she preferred to dress in oddments of mail and boiled leather, a swordbelt cinched around her waist. She would have been happier riding to war with Edmure, no doubt, but even walls as strong as Riverrun's required swords to hold them. Her brother had taken every able-bodied man for the fords, leaving Ser Desmond Grell to command a garrison made up of the wounded, the old, and the sick, along with a few squires and some untrained peasant boys still shy of manhood. This, to defend a castle crammed full of women and children.

When the last of Edmure's foot had shuffled under the portcullis, Brienne asked, "What shall we do now, my lady?"

"Our duty." Catelyn's face was drawn as she started across the yard. *I have always done my duty,* she thought. Perhaps that was why her lord father had always cherished her best of all his children. Her two older brothers had both died in infancy, so she had been son as well as daughter to Lord Hoster until Edmure was born. Then her mother had died and her father had told her that she must be the lady of Riverrun now, and she had done that too. And when Lord Hoster promised her to Brandon Stark, she had thanked him for making her such a splendid match.

I gave Brandon my favor to wear, and never comforted Petyr once after he was wounded, nor bid him farewell when Father sent him off. And when Brandon was murdered and Father told me I must wed his brother, I did so gladly, though I never saw Ned's face until our wedding day. I gave my maidenhood to this solemn stranger and sent him off to his war and his king and the woman who bore him his bastard, because I always did my duty.

Her steps took her to the sept, a seven-sided sandstone temple set amidst her mother's gardens and filled with rainbow light. It was crowded when they entered; Catelyn was not alone in her need for prayer. She knelt before the painted marble image of the Warrior and lit a scented candle for Edmure and another for Robb off beyond the hills. *Keep them safe and help them to victory,* she prayed, *and bring peace to the souls of the slain and comfort to those they leave behind.*

The septon entered with his censer and crystal while she was at her prayers, so Catelyn lingered for the celebration. She did not know this septon, an earnest young man close to Edmure's age. He performed his office well enough, and his voice was rich and pleasant when he sang the praises to the Seven, but Catelyn found herself yearning for the thin quavering tones of Septon Osmynd, long dead. Osmynd would have listened patiently to the tale of what she had seen and felt in Renly's pavilion, and he might have known what it meant as well, and what she must do to lay to rest the shadows that stalked her dreams. *Osmynd, my father, Uncle Brynden, old Maester Kym, they always seemed to know everything, but now there is only me, and it seems I know nothing, not even my duty. How can I do my duty if I do not know where it lies!*

Catelyn's knees were stiff by the time she rose, though she felt no wiser. Perhaps she would go to the godswood tonight, and pray to Ned's gods as well. They were older than the Seven.

Outside, she found song of a very different sort. Rymund the Rhymer sat by the brewhouse amidst a circle of listeners, his deep voice ringing as he sang of Lord Deremond at the Bloody Meadow.

And there he stood with sword in hand,
the last of Darry's ten . . .

Brienne paused to listen for a moment, broad shoulders hunched and thick arms crossed against her chest. A mob of ragged boys raced by, screeching and flailing at each other with sticks. *Why do boys so love to play at war?* Catelyn wondered if Rymund was the answer. The singer's voice swelled as he neared the end of his song.

And red the grass beneath his feet,
and red his banners bright,
and red the glow of setting sun
that bathed him in its light.
"Come on, come on," the great lord called,
"my sword is hungry still."
And with a cry of savage rage,
They swarmed across the rill . . .

"Fighting is better than this waiting," Brienne said. "You don't feel so helpless when you fight. You have a sword and a horse, sometimes an axe. When you're armored it's hard for anyone to hurt you."

"Knights die in battle," Catelyn reminded her.

Brienne looked at her with those blue and beautiful eyes. "As ladies die in childbed. No one sings songs about *them*."

"Children are a battle of a different sort." Catelyn started across the yard. "A battle without banners or warhorns, but no less fierce. Carrying a child, bringing it into the world . . . your mother will have told you of the pain . . ."

"I never knew my mother," Brienne said. "My father had ladies . . . a different lady every year, but . . ."

"Those were no ladies," Catelyn said. "As hard as birth can be, Brienne, what comes after is even harder. At times I feel as though I am being torn apart. Would that there were five of me, one for each child, so I might keep them all safe."

"And who would keep *you* safe, my lady?"

Her smile was wan and tired. "Why, the men of my House. Or so my lady mother taught me. My lord father, my brother, my uncle, my husband, they will keep me safe . . . but while they are away from me, I suppose you must fill their place, Brienne."

Brienne bowed her head. "I shall try, my lady."

Later that day, Maester Vyman brought a letter. She saw him at once, hoping for some word from Robb, or from Ser Rodrik in Winterfell, but the message proved to be from one Lord Meadows, who named himself castellan of Storm's End. It was addressed to her father, her brother, her son, "or whoever now holds Riverrun." Ser Cortnay Penrose was dead, the man wrote, and Storm's End had opened its gate to Stannis Baratheon, the trueborn and rightful heir. The castle garrison had sworn their swords to his cause, one and all, and no man of them had suffered harm.

"Save Cortnay Penrose," Catelyn murmured. She had never met the man, yet she grieved to hear of his passing. "Robb should know of this at once," she said. "Do we know where he is?"

"At last word he was marching toward the Crag, the seat of House Westerling," said Maester Vyman. "If I dispatched a raven to Ashemark, it may be that they could send a rider after him."

"Do so."

Catelyn read the letter again after the maester was gone. "Lord Meadows says nothing of Robert's bastard," she confided to Brienne. "I suppose he yielded the boy with the rest, though I confess, I do not understand why Stannis wanted him so badly."

"Perhaps he fears the boy's claim."

"A bastard's claim? No, it's something else . . . what does this child look like?"

"He is seven or eight, comely, with black hair and bright blue eyes. Visitors oft thought him Lord Renly's own son."

"And Renly favored Robert." Catelyn had a glimmer of understanding. "Stannis means to parade his brother's bastard before the realm, so men might see Robert in his face and wonder why there is no such likeness in Joffrey."

"Would that mean so much?"

"Those who favor Stannis will call it proof. Those who support Joffrey will say it means nothing." Her own children had more Tully about them than Stark. Arya was the only one to show much of Ned in her features. *And Jon Snow, but he was never mine.* She found herself thinking of Jon's mother, that shadowy secret love her husband would never speak of. *Does she grieve for Ned as I do? Or did she hate him for leaving her bed for mine? Does she pray for her son as I have prayed for mine?*

They were uncomfortable thoughts, and futile. If Jon had been born of Ashara Dayne of Starfall, as some whispered, the lady was long dead; if not, Catelyn had no clue who or where his mother might be. And it made no matter. Ned was gone now, and his loves and his secrets had all died with him.

Still, she was struck again by how strangely men behaved when it came to their bastards. Ned had always been fiercely protective of Jon, and Ser Cortnay Penrose had given up his life for this Edric Storm, yet

Roose Bolton's bastard had meant less to him than one of his dogs, to judge from the tone of the queer cold letter Edmure had gotten from him not three days past. He had crossed the Trident and was marching on Harrenhal as commanded, he wrote. "A strong castle, and well garrisoned, but His Grace shall have it, if I must kill every living soul within to make it so." He hoped His Grace would weigh that against the crimes of his bastard son, whom Ser Rodrik Cassel had put to death. "A fate he no doubt earned," Bolton had written. "Tainted blood is ever treacherous, and Ramsay's nature was sly, greedy, and cruel. I count myself well rid of him. The trueborn sons my young wife has promised me would never have been safe while he lived."

The sound of hurrying footsteps drove the morbid thoughts from her head. Ser Desmond's squire dashed panting into the room and knelt. "My lady . . . Lannisters . . . across the river."

"Take a long breath, lad, and tell it slowly."

He did as she bid him. "A column of armored men," he reported. "Across the Red Fork. They are flying a purple unicorn below the lion of Lannister."

Some son of Lord Brax. Brax had come to Riverrun once when she was a girl, to propose wedding one of his sons to her or Lysa. She wondered whether it was this same son out there now, leading the attack.

The Lannisters had ridden out of the southeast beneath a blaze of banners, Ser Desmond told her when she ascended to the battlements to join him. "A few outriders, no more," he assured her. "The main strength of Lord Tywin's host is well to the south. We are in no danger here."

South of the Red Fork the land stretched away open and flat. From the watchtower Catelyn could see for miles. Even so, only the nearest ford was visible. Edmure had entrusted Lord Jason Mallister with its defense, as well as that of three others farther upriver. The Lannister riders were milling about uncertainly near the water, crimson and silver banners flapping in the wind. "No more than fifty, my lady," Ser Desmond estimated.

Catelyn watched the riders spread out in a long line. Lord Jason's men waited to receive them behind rocks and grass and hillocks. A trumpet blast sent the horsemen forward at a ponderous walk, splashing down into the current. For a moment they made a brave show, all bright armor and streaming banners, the sun flashing off the points of their lances.

"Now," she heard Brienne mutter.

It was hard to make out what was happening, but the screams of the horses seemed loud even at this remove, and beneath them Catelyn heard the fainter clash of steel on steel. A banner vanished suddenly as its bearer was swept under, and soon after the first dead man drifted past their walls, borne along by the current. By then the Lannisters had pulled back in confusion. She watched as they re-formed, conferred briefly, and galloped back the way they had come. The men on the walls shouted taunts after them, though they were already too far off to hear.

Ser Desmond slapped his belly. "Would that Lord Hoster could have seen that. It would have made him dance."

"My father's dancing days are past, I fear," Catelyn said, "and this fight is just begun. The Lannisters will come again. Lord Tywin has twice my brother's numbers."

"He could have ten times and it would not matter," Ser Desmond said. "The west bank of the Red Fork is higher than the east, my lady, and well wooded. Our bowmen have good cover, and a clear field for their shafts . . . and should any breach occur, Edmure will have his best knights in reserve, ready to ride wherever they are most sorely needed. The river will hold them."

"I pray that you are right," Catelyn said gravely.

That night they came again. She had commanded them to wake her at once if the enemy returned, and well after midnight a serving girl touched her gently by the shoulder. Catelyn sat up at once. "What is it?"

"The ford again, my lady."

Wrapped in a bedrobe, Catelyn climbed to the roof of the keep. From there she could see over the walls and the moonlit river to where the battle raged. The defenders had built watchfires along the bank, and perhaps the Lannisters thought to find them night-blind or unwary. If so, it was folly. Darkness was a chancy ally at best. As they waded in to breast their way across, men stepped in hidden pools and went down splashing, while others stumbled over stones or gashed their feet on the hidden caltrops. The Mallister bowmen sent a storm of fire arrows hissing across the river, strangely beautiful from afar. One man, pierced through a dozen times, his clothes afire, danced and whirled in the knee-deep water until at last he fell and was swept downstream. By the time his body came bobbing past Riverrun, the fires and his life had both been extinguished.

A small victory, Catelyn thought when the fighting had ended and the surviving foemen had melted back into the night, *yet a victory nonetheless.* As they descended the winding turret steps, Catelyn asked Brienne for her thoughts. "That was the brush of Lord Tywin's fingertip, my lady," the girl said. "He is probing, feeling for a weak point, an undefended crossing. If he does not find one, he will curl all his fingers into a fist and try and make one." Brienne hunched her shoulders. "That's what I'd do. Were I him." Her hand went to the hilt of her sword and gave it a little pat, as if to make certain it was still there.

And may the gods help us then, Catelyn thought. Yet there was nothing she could do for it. That was Edmure's battle out there on the river; hers was here inside the castle.

The next morning as she broke her fast, she sent for her father's aged steward, Utherydes Wayn. "Have Ser Cleos Frey brought a flagon of wine. I mean to question him soon, and I want his tongue well loosened."

"As you command, my lady."

Not long after, a rider with the Mallister eagle sewn on his breast arrived with a message from Lord Jason, telling of another skirmish and another victory. Ser Flement Brax had tried to force a crossing at a different ford six leagues to the south. This time the Lannisters shortened their lances and advanced across the river behind on foot, but the Mallister bowmen had rained high arcing shots down over their shields, while the scorpions Edmure had mounted on the riverbank sent heavy stones crashing through to break up the formation. "They left a dozen dead in the water, only two reaching the shallows, where we dealt with them briskly," the rider reported. He also told of fighting farther upstream, where Lord Karyl Vance held the fords. "Those thrusts too were turned aside, at grievous cost to our foes."

Perhaps Edmure was wiser than I knew, Catelyn thought. *His lords all saw the sense in his battle plans, why was I so blind? My brother is not the little boy I remember, no more than Robb is.*

She waited until evening before going to pay her call upon Ser Cleos Frey, reasoning that the longer she delayed, the drunker he was likely to be. As she entered the tower cell, Ser Cleos stumbled to his knees. "My lady, I knew naught of any escape. The Imp said a Lannister must needs have a Lannister escort, on my oath as a knight—"

"Arise, ser." Catelyn seated herself. "I know no grandson of Walder Frey would be an oathbreaker." *Unless it served his purpose.* "You brought peace terms, my brother said."

"I did." Ser Cleos lurched to his feet. She was pleased to see how unsteady he was.

"Tell me," she commanded, and he did.

When he was done, Catelyn sat frowning. Edmure had been right, these were no terms at all, except . . . "Lannister will exchange Arya and Sansa for his brother?"

"Yes. He sat on the Iron Throne and swore it."

"Before witnesses?"

"Before all the court, my lady. And the gods as well. I said as much to Ser Edmure, but he told me it was not possible, that His Grace Robb would never consent."

"He told you true." She could not even say that Robb was wrong. Arya and Sansa were children. The Kingslayer, alive and free, was as dangerous as any man in the realm. That road led nowhere. "Did you see my girls? Are they treated well?"

Ser Cleos hesitated. "I . . . yes, they seemed . . ."

He is fumbling for a lie, Catelyn realized, *but the wine has fuddled his wits.* "Ser Cleos," she said coolly, "you forfeited the protection of your peace banner when your men played us false. Lie to me, and you'll hang from the walls beside them. Believe that. I shall ask you once more—*did you see my daughters?*"

His brow was damp with sweat. "I saw Sansa at the court, the day Tyrion told me his terms. She looked most beautiful, my lady. Perhaps a, a bit wan. Drawn, as it were."

Sansa, but not Arya. That might mean anything. Arya had always been harder to tame. Perhaps Cersei was reluctant to parade her in open court for fear of what she might say or do. They might have her locked safely out of sight. *Or they might have killed her.* Catelyn shoved the thought away. "*His* terms, you said . . . yet Cersei is Queen Regent."

"Tyrion spoke for both of them. The queen was not there. She was indisposed that day, I was told."

"Curious." Catelyn thought back to that terrible trek through the Mountains of the Moon, and the way Tyrion Lannister had somehow seduced that sellsword from her service to his own. *The dwarf is too clever by half.* She could not imagine how he had survived the high road after Lysa had sent him from the Vale, yet it did not surprise her. *He had no part in Ned's murder, at the least. And he came to my defense when the clansmen attacked us. If I could trust his word . . .*

She opened her hands to look down at the scars across her fingers. *His dagger's marks,* she reminded herself. *His dagger, in the hand of the killer he paid to open Bran's throat.* Though the dwarf denied it, to be sure. Even after Lysa locked him in one of her sky cells and threatened him with her moon door, he had still denied it. "He lied," she said, rising abruptly. "The Lannisters are liars every one, and the dwarf is the worst of them. The killer was armed with his own knife."

Ser Cleos stared. "I know nothing of any—"

"You know nothing," she agreed, sweeping from the cell. Brienne fell in beside her, silent. *It is simpler for her,* Catelyn thought with a pang of envy. She was like a man in that. For men the answer was always the same, and never farther away than the nearest sword. For a woman, a mother, the way was stonier and harder to know.

She took a late supper in the Great Hall with her garrison, to give them what encouragement she could. Rymund the Rhymer sang through all the courses, sparing her the need to talk. He closed with the song he had written about Robb's victory at Oxcross. "*And the stars in the night were the eyes of his wolves, and the wind itself was their song.*"

Between the verses, Rymund threw back his head and howled, and by the end, half of the hall was howling along with him, even Desmond Grell, who was well in his cups. Their voices rang off the rafters.

Let them have their songs, if it makes them brave, Catelyn thought, toying with her silver goblet.

"There was always a singer at Evenfall Hall when I was a girl," Brienne said quietly. "I learned all the songs by heart."

"Sansa did the same, though few singers ever cared to make the long journey north to Winterfell." *I told her there would be singers at the king's court, though. I told her she would hear music of all sorts, that her father could find some master to help her learn the high harp. Oh, gods forgive me . . .*

Brienne said, "I remember a woman . . . she came from some place across the narrow sea. I could not even say what language she sang in, but her voice was as lovely as she was. She had eyes the color of plums and her waist was so tiny my father could put his hands around it. His hands were almost as big as mine." She closed her long, thick fingers, as if to hide them.

"Did you sing for your father?" Catelyn asked.

Brienne shook her head, staring down at her trencher as if to find some answer in the gravy.

"For Lord Renly?"

The girl reddened. "Never, I . . . his fool, he made cruel japes sometimes, and I . . ."

"Someday you must sing for me."

"I . . . please, I have no gift." Brienne pushed back from the table. "Forgive me, my lady. Do I have your leave to go?"

Catelyn nodded. The tall, ungainly girl left the hall with long strides, almost unnoticed amidst the revelry. *May the gods go with her,* she thought as she returned listlessly to her supper.

It was three days later when the hammer blow that Brienne had foretold fell, and five days before they heard of it. Catelyn was sitting with her father when Edmure's messenger arrived. The man's armor was dinted, his boots dusty, and he had a ragged hole in his surcoat, but the look on his face as he knelt was enough to tell her that the news was good. "Victory, my lady." He handed her Edmure's letter. Her hand trembled as she broke the seal.

Lord Tywin had tried to force a crossing at a dozen different fords, her brother wrote, but every thrust had been thrown back. Lord Lefford had been drowned, the Crakehall knight called Strongboar taken captive, Ser Addam Marbrand thrice forced to retreat . . . but the fiercest battle had been fought at Stone Mill, where Ser Gregor Clegane had led the assault. So many of his men had fallen that their dead horses threatened to dam the flow. In the end the Mountain and a handful of his best had gained the west bank, but Edmure had thrown his reserve at them, and they had shattered and reeled away bloody and beaten. Ser Gregor himself had lost his horse and staggered back across the Red Fork bleeding from a dozen wounds while a rain of arrows and stones fell all around him. "They shall not cross, Cat," Edmure scrawled, "Lord Tywin is marching to the southeast. A feint perhaps, or full retreat, it matters not. *They shall not cross.*"

Ser Desmond Grell had been elated. "Oh, if only I might have been with him," the old knight said when she read him the letter. "Where is that fool Rymund? There's a song in this, by the gods, and one that even Edmure will want to hear. The mill that ground the Mountain down, I could almost make the words myself, had I the singer's gift."

"I'll hear no songs until the fighting's done," Catelyn said, perhaps too sharply. Yet she allowed Ser Desmond to spread the word, and agreed when he suggested breaking open some casks in honor of Stone Mill. The mood within Riverrun had been strained and somber; they would all be better for a little drink and hope.

That night the castle rang to the sounds of celebration. *"Riverrun!"* the smallfolk shouted, and "Tully! Tully!" They'd come frightened and helpless, and her brother had taken them in when most lords would have closed their gates. Their voices floated in through the high windows, and seeped under the heavy redwood doors. Rymund played his harp, accompanied by a pair of drummers and a youth with a set of reed pipes. Catelyn listened to girlish laughter, and the excited chatter of the green boys her brother had left her for a garrison. Good sounds . . . and yet they did not touch her. She could not share their happiness.

In her father's solar she found a heavy leatherbound book of maps and opened it to the riverlands. Her eyes found the path of the Red Fork and traced it by flickering candlelight. *Marching to the southeast*, she thought. By now they had likely reached the headwaters of the Blackwater Rush, she decided.

She closed the book even more uneasy than before. The gods had granted them victory after victory. At Stone Mill, at Oxcross, in the Battle of the Camps, at the Whispering Wood . . .

But if we are winning, why am I so afraid?

BRAN

The sound was the faintest of *clinks*, a scraping of steel over stone. He lifted his head from his paws, listening, sniffing at the night. The evening's rain had woken a hundred sleeping smells and made them ripe and strong again. Grass and thorns, blackberries broken on the ground, mud, worms, rotting leaves, a rat creeping through the bush. He caught the shaggy black scent of his brother's coat and the sharp coppery tang of blood from the squirrel he'd killed. Other squirrels moved through the branches above, smelling of wet fur and fear, their little claws scratching at the bark. The noise had sounded something like that.

And he heard it again, *clink* and scrape. It brought him to his feet. His ears pricked and his tail rose. He howled, a long deep shivery cry, a howl to wake the sleepers, but the piles of man-rock were dark and dead. A still wet night, a night to drive men into their holes. The rain had stopped, but the men still hid from the damp, huddled by the fires in their caves of piled stone.

His brother came sliding through the trees, moving almost as quiet as another brother he remembered dimly from long ago, the white one with the eyes of blood. *This* brother's eyes were pools of shadow, but the fur on the back of his neck was bristling. He had heard the sounds as well, and known they meant danger.

This time the *clink* and scrape were followed by a slithering and the soft swift patter of skinfeet on stone. The wind brought the faintest whiff of a man-smell he did not know. *Stranger. Danger. Death.*

He ran toward the sound, his brother racing beside him. The stone dens rose before them, walls slick and wet. He bared his teeth, but the man-rock took no notice. A gate loomed up, a black iron snake coiled tight about bar and post. When he crashed against it, the gate shuddered and the snake clanked and slithered and held. Through the bars he could look down the long stone burrow that ran between the walls to the stony field beyond, but there was no way through. He could force his muzzle between the bars, but no more. Many a time his brother had tried to crack the black bones of the gate between his teeth, but they would not break. They had tried to dig under, but there were great flat stones beneath, half-covered by earth and blown leaves.

Snarling, he paced back and forth in front of the gate, then threw himself at it once more. It moved a little and slammed him back. *Locked*, something whispered. *Chained.* The voice he did not hear, the scent without a smell. The other ways were closed as well. Where doors opened in the walls of man-rock, the wood was thick and strong. There was no way out.

There is, the whisper came, and it seemed as if he could see the shadow of a great tree covered in needles, slanting up out of the black earth to ten times the height of a man. Yet when he looked about, it was not there. *The other side of the godswood, the sentinel, hurry, hurry . . .*

Through the gloom of night came a muffled shout, cut short.

Swiftly, swiftly, he whirled and bounded back into the trees, wet leaves rustling beneath his paws, branches whipping at him as he rushed past. He could hear his brother following close. They plunged under the heart tree and around the cold pool, through the blackberry bushes, under a tangle of oaks and ash and hawthorn scrub, to the far side of the wood . . . and there it was, the shadow he'd glimpsed without seeing, the slanting tree pointing at the rooftops. *Sentinel*, came the thought.

He remembered how it was to climb it then. The needles everywhere, scratching at his bare face and falling down the back of his neck, the sticky sap on his hands, the sharp piney smell of it. It was an easy tree for a boy to climb, leaning as it did, crooked, the branches so close together they almost made a ladder, slanting right up to the roof.

Growling, he sniffed around the base of the tree, lifted a leg and marked it with a stream of urine. A low branch brushed his face, and he snapped at it, twisting and pulling until the wood cracked and tore. His mouth was full of needles and the bitter taste of the sap. He shook his head and snarled.

His brother sat back on his haunches and lifted his voice in a ululating howl, his song black with mourning. The way was no way. They were not squirrels, nor the cubs of men, they could not wriggle up the trunks of trees, clinging with soft pink paws and clumsy feet. They were runners, hunters, prowlers.

Off across the night, beyond the stone that hemmed them close, the dogs woke and began to bark. One and then another and then all of them, a great clamor. They smelled it too; the scent of foes and fear.

A desperate fury filled him, hot as hunger. He sprang away from the wall, loped off beneath the trees, the shadows of branch and leaf dappling his grey fur . . . and then he turned and raced back in a rush. His feet flew, kicking up wet leaves and pine needles, and for a little time he was a hunter and an antlered stag was fleeing before him and he could see it, smell it, and he ran full out in pursuit. The smell of fear made his heart thunder and slaver ran from his jaws, and he reached the falling tree in stride and threw himself up the trunk, claws scrabbling at the bark for purchase. Upward he bounded, *up*, two bounds, three, hardly slowing, until he was among the lower limbs. Branches tangled his feet and whipped at his eyes, grey-green needles scattered as he shouldered through them, snapping. He had to slow. Something snagged at his foot and he wrenched it free, snarling. The trunk narrowed under him, the slope steeper, almost straight up, and wet. The bark tore like skin when he tried to claw at it. He was a third of the way up, halfway, more, the roof was almost within reach . . . and then he put down a foot and felt it slip off the curve of wet wood, and suddenly he was sliding, stumbling. He yowled in fear and fury, falling, *falling*, and twisted around while the ground rushed up to break him . . .

And then Bran was back abed in his lonely tower room, tangled in his blankets, his breath coming hard. "Summer," he cried aloud. "Summer." His shoulder seemed to ache, as if he had fallen on it, but he knew it was only the ghost of what the wolf was feeling. *Jojen told it true. I am a beastling.* Outside he could hear the faint barking of dogs. *The sea has come. It's flowing over the walls, just as Jojen saw.* Bran grabbed the bar overhead and pulled himself up, shouting for help. No one came, and after a moment he remembered that no one would. They had taken the guard off his door. Ser Rodrik had needed every man of fighting age he could lay his hands on, so Winterfell had been left with only a token garrison.

The rest had left eight days past, six hundred men from Winterfell and the nearest holdfasts. Cley Cerwyn was bringing three hundred more to join them on the march, and Maester Luwin had sent ravens before them, summoning levies from White Harbor and the barrowlands and even the deep places inside the wolfswood. Torrhen's Square was under attack by some monstrous war chief named Dagmer Cleftjaw. Old Nan said he couldn't be killed, that once a foe had cut his head in two with an axe, but Dagmer was so fierce he'd just pushed the two halves back together and held them until they healed up. *Could Dagmer have won?* Torrhen's Square was many days from Winterfell, yet still . . .

Bran pulled himself from the bed, moving bar to bar until he reached the windows. His fingers fumbled a little as he swung back the shutters. The yard was empty, and all the windows he could see were black. Winterfell slept. *"Hodor!"* he shouted down, as loud as he could. Hodor would be asleep above the stables, but maybe if he yelled loud enough he'd hear, or *somebody* would. *"Hodor, come fast! Osha! Meera, Jojen, anyone!"* Bran cupped his hands around his mouth. *"HOOOOODOOOOOR!"*

But when the door crashed open behind him, the man who stepped through was no one Bran knew. He wore a leather jerkin sewn with overlapping iron disks, and carried a dirk in one hand and an axe strapped to his back. "What do you want?" Bran demanded, afraid. "This is my room. You get out of here."

Theon Greyjoy followed him into the bedchamber. "We're not here to harm you, Bran."

"Theon?" Bran felt dizzy with relief. "Did Robb send you? Is he here too?"

"Robb's far away. He can't help you now."

"Help me?" He was confused. "Don't scare me, Theon."

"I'm *Prince* Theon now. We're both princes, Bran. Who would have dreamed it? But I've taken your castle, my prince."

"Winterfell?" Bran shook his head. "No, you *couldn't.*"

"Leave us, Werlag." The man with the dirk withdrew. Theon seated himself on the bed. "I sent four men over the walls with grappling claws and ropes, and they opened a postern gate for the rest of us. My men are dealing with yours even now. I promise you, Winterfell is mine."

Bran did not understand. "But you're Father's *ward.*"

"And now you and your brother are *my* wards. As soon as the fighting's done, my men will be bringing the rest of your people together in the Great Hall. You and I are going to speak to them. You'll tell them how you've yielded Winterfell to me, and command them to serve and obey their new lord as they did the old."

"I *won't,*" said Bran. "We'll fight you and throw you out. I never yielded, you can't make me say I did."

"This is no game, Bran, so don't play the boy with me, I won't stand for it. The castle is mine, but these people are still yours. If the prince would keep them safe, he'd best do as he's told." He rose and went to the door. "Someone will come dress you and carry you to the Great Hall. Think carefully on what you want to say."

The waiting made Bran feel even more helpless than before. He sat in the window seat, staring out at dark towers and walls black as shadow. Once he thought he heard shouting beyond the Guards Hall, and something that might have been the clash of swords, but he did not have Summer's ears to hear, nor his nose to smell. *Awake, I am still broken, but when I sleep, when I'm Summer, I can run and fight and hear and smell.*

He had expected that Hodor would come for him, or maybe one of the serving girls, but when the door next opened it was Maester Luwin, carrying a candle. "Bran," he said, "you . . . know what has happened? You have been told?" The skin was broken above his left eye, and blood ran down that side of his face.

"Theon came. He said Winterfell was his now."

The maester set down the candle and wiped the blood off his cheek. "They swam the moat. Climbed the walls with hook and rope. Came over wet and dripping, steel in hand." He sat on the chair by the door, as fresh blood flowed. "Alebelly was on the gate, they surprised him in the turret and killed him. Hayhead's wounded as well. I had time to send off two ravens before they burst in. The bird to White Harbor got away, but they brought down the other with an arrow." The maester stared at the rushes. "Ser Rodrik took too many of our men, but I am to blame as much as he is. I never saw this danger, I never . . ."

Jojen saw it, Bran thought. "You better help me dress."

"Yes, that's so." In the heavy ironbound chest at the foot of Bran's bed the maester found smallclothes, breeches, and tunic. "You are the Stark in Winterfell, and Robb's heir. You must look princely." Together they garbed him as befit a lord.

"Theon wants me to yield the castle," Bran said as the maester was fastening the cloak with his favorite wolf's-head clasp of silver and jet.

"There is no shame in that. A lord must protect his smallfolk. Cruel places breed cruel peoples, Bran, remember that as you deal with these ironmen. Your lord father did what he could to gentle Theon, but I fear it was too little and too late."

The ironman who came for them was a squat thick-bodied man with a coal-black beard that covered half his chest. He bore the boy easily enough, though he looked none too happy with the task. Rickon's bedchamber was a half turn down the steps. The four-year-old was cranky at being woken. "I want Mother," he said. "I *want* her. And Shaggydog too."

"Your mother is far away, my prince." Maester Luwin pulled a bedrobe over the child's head. "But I'm here, and Bran." He took Rickon by the hand and led him out.

Below, they came on Meera and Jojen being herded from their room by a bald man whose spear was three feet taller than he was. When Jojen looked at Bran, his eyes were green pools full of sorrow. Other ironmen had rousted the Freys. "Your brother's lost his kingdom," Little Walder told Bran. "You're no prince now, just a hostage."

"So are you," Jojen said, "and me, and all of us."

"No one was talking to you, frogeater."

One of the ironmen went before them carrying a torch, but the rain had started again and soon drowned it out. As they hurried across the yard they could hear the direwolves howling in the godswood. *I hope Summer wasn't hurt falling from the tree.*

Theon Greyjoy was seated in the high seat of the Starks. He had taken off his cloak. Over a shirt of fine mail he wore a black surcoat emblazoned with the golden kraken of his House. His hands rested on the wolves' heads carved at the ends of the wide stone arms. "Theon's sitting in Robb's chair," Rickon said.

"Hush, Rickon." Bran could feel the menace around them, but his brother was too young. A few torches had been lit, and a fire kindled in the great hearth, but most of the hall remained in darkness. There was no place to sit with the benches stacked against the walls, so the castle folk stood in small groups, not daring to speak. He saw Old Nan, her toothless mouth opening and closing. Hayhead was carried in between two of the other guards, a bloodstained bandage wrapped about his bare chest. Poxy Tym wept inconsolably, and Beth Cassel cried with fear.

"What have we here?" Theon asked of the Reeds and Freys.

"These are Lady Catelyn's wards, both named Walder Frey," Maester Luwin explained. "And this is Jojen Reed and his sister Meera, son and daughter to Howland Reed of Greywater Watch, who came to renew their oaths of fealty to Winterfell."

"Some might call that ill-timed," said Theon, "though not for me. Here you are and here you'll stay." He vacated the high seat. "Bring the prince here, Lorren." The black-bearded man dumped Bran onto the stone as if he were a sack of oats.

People were still being driven into the Great Hall, prodded along with shouts and the butts of the spears. Gage and Osha arrived from the kitchens, spotted with flour from making the morning bread. Mikken they dragged in cursing. Farlen entered limping, struggling to support Palla. Her dress had been ripped in two; she held it up with a clenched fist and walked as if every step were agony. Septon Chayle rushed to lend a hand, but one of the ironmen knocked him to the floor.

The last man marched through the doors was the prisoner Reek, whose stench preceded him, ripe and pungent. Bran felt his stomach twist at the smell of him. "We found this one locked in a tower cell," announced his escort, a beardless youth with ginger-colored hair and sodden clothing, doubtless one of those who'd swum the moat. "He says they call him Reek."

"Can't think why," Theon said, smiling. "Do you always smell so bad, or did you just finish fucking a pig?"

"Haven't fucked no one since they took me, m'lord. Heke's me true name. I was in service to the Bastard o' the Dreadfort till the Starks give him an arrow in the back for a wedding gift."

Theon found that amusing. "Who did he marry?"

"The widow o' Hornwood, m'lord."

"That crone? Was he blind? She has teats like empty wineskins, dry and withered."

"It wasn't her teats he wed her for, m'lord."

The ironmen slammed shut the tall doors at the foot of the hall. From the high seat, Bran could see about twenty of them. *He probably left some guards on the gates and the armory.* Even so, there couldn't be more than thirty.

Theon raised his hands for quiet. "You all know me—"

"Aye, we know you for a sack of steaming dung!" shouted Mikken, before the bald man drove the butt of his spear into his gut, then smashed him across the face with the shaft. The smith stumbled to his knees and spat out a tooth.

"Mikken, you be silent." Bran tried to sound stern and lordly, the way Robb did when he made a command, but his voice betrayed him and the words came out in a shrill squeak.

"Listen to your little lordling, Mikken," said Theon. "He has more sense than you do."

A good lord protects his people, he reminded himself. "I've yielded Winterfell to Theon."

"Louder, Bran. And call me prince."

He raised his voice. "I have yielded Winterfell to Prince Theon. All of you should do as he commands you."

"Damned if I will!" bellowed Mikken.

Theon ignored the outburst. "My father has donned the ancient crown of salt and rock, and declared himself King of the Iron Islands. He claims the north as well, by right of conquest. You are all his subjects."

"Bugger that." Mikken wiped the blood from his mouth. "I serve the Starks, not some treasonous squid of—*aah.*" The butt of the spear smashed him face first into the stone floor.

"Smiths have strong arms and weak heads," observed Theon. "But if the rest of you serve me as loyally as you served Ned Stark, you'll find me as generous a lord as you could want."

On his hands and knees, Mikken spat blood. *Please don't*, Bran wished at him, but the blacksmith shouted, "If you think you can hold the north with this sorry lot o'—"

The bald man drove the point of his spear into the back of Mikken's neck. Steel slid through flesh and came out his throat in a welter of blood. A woman screamed, and Meera wrapped her arms around Rickon. *It's blood he drowned on,* Bran thought numbly. *His own blood.*

"Who else has something to say?" asked Theon Greyjoy.

"Hodor hodor hodor hodor," shouted Hodor, eyes wide.

"Someone kindly shut that halfwit up."

Two ironmen began to beat Hodor with the butts of their spears. The stableboy dropped to the floor, trying to shield himself with his hands.

"I will be as good a lord to you as Eddard Stark ever was." Theon raised his voice to be heard above the smack of wood on flesh. "Betray me, though, and you'll wish you hadn't. And don't think the men you see here are the whole of my power. Torrhen's Square and Deepwood Motte will soon be ours as well, and my uncle is sailing up the Saltspear to seize Moat Cailin. If Robb Stark can stave off the Lannisters, he may reign as King of the Trident hereafter, but House Greyjoy holds the north now."

"Stark's lords will fight you," the man Reek called out. "That bloated pig at White Harbor for one, and them Umbers and Karstarks too. You'll need men. Free me and I'm yours."

Theon weighed him a moment. "You're cleverer than you smell, but I could not suffer that stench."

"Well," said Reek, "I could wash some. If I was free."

"A man of rare good sense." Theon smiled. "Bend the knee."

One of the ironmen handed Reek a sword, and he laid it at Theon's feet and swore obedience to House Greyjoy and King Balon. Bran could not look. The green dream was coming true.

"M'lord Greyjoy!" Osha stepped past Mikken's body. "I was brought here captive too. You were there the day I was taken."

I thought you were a friend, Bran thought, hurt.

"I need fighters," Theon declared, "not kitchen sluts."

"It was Robb Stark put me in the kitchens. For the best part of a year, I've been left to scour kettles, scrape grease, and warm the straw for this one." She threw a look at Gage. "I've had a bellyful of it. Put a spear in my hand again."

"I got a spear for you right here," said the bald man who'd killed Mikken. He grabbed his crotch, grinning.

Osha drove her bony knee up between his legs. "You keep that soft pink thing." She wrested the spear from him and used the butt to knock him off his feet. "I'll have me the wood and iron." The bald man writhed on the floor while the other reavers sent up gales of laughter.

Theon laughed with the rest. "You'll do," he said. "Keep the spear; Stygg can find another. Now bend the knee and swear."

When no one else rushed forward to pledge service, they were dismissed with a warning to do their work and make no trouble. Hodor was given the task of bearing Bran back to his bed. His face was all ugly from the beating, his nose swollen and one eye closed. "Hodor," he sobbed between cracked lips as he lifted Bran in huge strong arms and bloody hands and carried him back out into the rain.

ARYA

"There's ghosts, I know there is." Hot Pie was kneading bread, his arms floured up to his elbows. "Pia saw something in the buttery last night."

Arya made a rude noise. Pia was always seeing things in the buttery. Usually they were men. "Can I have a tart?" she asked. "You baked a whole tray."

"I need a whole tray. Ser Amory is partial to them."

She hated Ser Amory. "Let's spit on them."

Hot Pie looked around nervously. The kitchens were full of shadows and echoes, but the other cooks and scullions were all asleep in the cavernous lofts above the ovens. "He'll know."

"He will not," Arya said. "You can't taste *spit*."

"If he does, it's me they'll whip." Hot Pie stopped his kneading. "You shouldn't even *be* here. It's the black of night."

It was, but Arya never minded. Even in the black of night, the kitchens were never still; there was always someone rolling dough for the morning bread, stirring a kettle with a long wooden spoon, or butchering a hog for Ser Amory's breakfast bacon. Tonight it was Hot Pie.

"If Pinkeye wakes and finds you gone—" Hot Pie said.

"Pinkeye never wakes." His true name was Mebble, but everyone called him Pinkeye for his runny eyes. "Not once he's passed out." Each morning he broke his fast with ale. Each evening he fell into a drunken sleep after supper, wine-colored spit running down his chin. Arya would wait until she heard him snoring, then creep barefoot up the servant's stair, making no more noise than the mouse she'd been. She carried neither candle nor taper. Syrio had told her once that darkness could be her friend, and he was right. If she had the moon and the stars to see by, that was enough. "I bet we could escape, and Pinkeye wouldn't even notice I was gone," she told Hot Pie.

"I don't want to escape. It's better here than it was in them woods. I don't want to eat no worms. Here, sprinkle some flour on the board."

Arya cocked her head. "What's that?"

"What? I don't—"

"Listen with your *ears*, not your mouth. That was a warhorn. Two blasts, didn't you hear? And there, that's the portcullis chains, someone's going out or coming in. Want to go see?" The gates of Harrenhal had not been opened since the morning Lord Tywin had marched with his host.

"I'm making the morning bread," Hot Pie complained. "Anyhow I don't like it when it's dark, I told you."

"I'm going. I'll tell you after. Can I have a tart?"

"No."

She filched one anyway, and ate it on her way out. It was stuffed with chopped nuts and fruit and cheese, the crust flaky and still warm from the oven. Eating Ser Amory's tart made Arya feel daring. *Barefoot surefoot lightfoot*, she sang under her breath. *I am the ghost in Harrenhal.*

The horn had stirred the castle from sleep; men were coming out into the ward to see what the commotion was about. Arya fell in with the others. A line of ox carts were rumbling under the portcullis. *Plunder*, she knew at once. The riders escorting the carts spoke in a babble of queer tongues. Their armor glinted pale in the moonlight, and she saw a pair of striped black-and-white zorses. *The Bloody Mummers.* Arya withdrew a little deeper into the shadows, and watched as a huge black bear rolled by, caged in the back of a wagon. Other carts were loaded down with silver plate, weapons and shields, bags of flour, pens of squealing hogs and scrawny dogs and chickens. Arya was thinking how long it had been since she'd had a slice off a pork roast when she saw the first of the prisoners.

By his bearing and the proud way he held his head, he must have been a lord. She could see mail glinting beneath his torn red surcoat. At first Arya took him for a Lannister, but when he passed near a torch she saw his device was a silver fist, not a lion. His wrists were bound tightly, and a rope around one ankle tied him to the man behind him, and him to the man behind him, so the whole column had to shuffle along in a lurching lockstep. Many of the captives were wounded. If any halted, one of the riders would trot up and give him a lick of the whip to get him moving again. She tried to judge how many prisoners there were, but lost count before she got to fifty. There were twice that many at least. Their clothing was stained with mud and blood, and in the torchlight it was hard to make out all their badges and sigils, but some of those Arya glimpsed she recognized. Twin towers. Sunburst. Bloody man. Battle-axe. *The battle-axe is for Cerwyn, and the white sun on black is Karstark. They're northmen. My father's men, and Robb's.* She didn't like to think what that might mean.

The Bloody Mummers began to dismount. Stableboys emerged sleepy from their straw to tend their lathered horses. One of the riders was shouting for ale. The noise brought Ser Amory Lorch out onto the covered gallery above the ward, flanked by two torchbearers. Goat-helmed Vargo Hoat reined up below him. "My lord cathellan," the sellsword said. He had a thick, slobbery voice, as if his tongue was too big for his mouth.

"What's all this, Hoat?" Ser Amory demanded, frowning.

"Captiths. Rooth Bolton thought to croth the river, but my Brafe Companions cut his van to pieceth. Killed many, and thent Bolton running. Thith ith their lord commander, Glover, and the one behind ith Ther Aenyth Frey."

Ser Amory Lorch stared down at the roped captives with his little pig eyes. Arya did not think he was pleased. Everyone in the castle knew that he and Vargo Hoat hated each other. "Very well," he said. "Ser Cadwyn, take these men to the dungeons."

The lord with the mailed fist on his surcoat raised his eyes. "We were promised honorable treatment—" he began.

"*Silenth!*" Vargo Hoat screamed at him, spraying spittle.

Ser Amory addressed the captives. "What Hoat promised you is nothing to me. Lord Tywin made *me* the castellan of Harrenhal, and I shall do with you as I please." He gestured to his guards. "The great cell under the Widow's Tower ought to hold them all. Any who do not care to go are free to die here."

As his men herded off the captives at spearpoint, Arya saw Pinkeye emerge from the stairwell, blinking at the torchlight. If he found her missing, he would shout and threaten to whip the bloody hide off her, but she was not afraid. He was no Weese. He was forever threatening to whip the bloody hide off this one or that one, but Arya never actually knew him to *hit*. Still, it would be better if he never saw her. She glanced around. The oxen were being unharnessed, the carts unloaded, while the Brave Companions clamored for drink and the curious gathered around the caged bear. In the commotion, it was not hard to slip off unseen. She went back the way she had come, wanting to be out of sight before someone noticed her and thought to put her to work.

Away from the gates and the stables, the great castle was largely deserted. The noise dwindled behind her. A swirling wind gusted, drawing a high shivery scream from the cracks in the Wailing Tower. Leaves had begun to fall from the trees in the godswood, and she could hear them moving through the deserted courtyards and between the empty buildings, making a faint skittery sound as the wind drove them across the stones. Now that Harrenhal was near empty once again, sound did queer things here. Sometimes the stones seemed to drink up noise, shrouding the yards in a blanket of silence. Other times, the echoes had a life of their own, so every footfall became the tread of a ghostly army, and every distant voice a ghostly feast. The funny sounds were one of the things that bothered Hot Pie, but not Arya.

Quiet as a shadow, she flitted across the middle bailey, around the Tower of Dread, and through the empty mews, where people said the spirits of dead falcons stirred the air with ghostly wings. She could go where she would. The garrison numbered no more than a hundred men, so small a troop that they were lost in Harrenhal. The Hall of a Hundred Hearths was closed off, along with many of the lesser buildings, even the Wailing Tower. Ser Amory Lorch resided in the castellan's chambers in Kingspyre, themselves as spacious as a lord's, and Arya and the other servants had moved to the cellars beneath him so they would be close at hand. While Lord Tywin had been in residence, there was always a man-at-arms wanting to know your business. But now there were only a hundred men left to guard a thousand doors, and no one seemed to know who should be where, or care much.

As she passed the armory, Arya heard the ring of a hammer. A deep orange glow shone through the high windows. She climbed to the roof and peeked down. Gendry was beating out a breastplate. When he worked, nothing existed for him but metal, bellows, fire. The hammer was like part of his arm. She watched the play of muscles in his chest and listened to the steel music he made. *He's strong*, she thought. As he took up the long-handled tongs to dip the breastplate into the quenching trough, Arya slithered through the window and leapt down to the floor beside him.

He did not seem surprised to see her. "You should be abed, girl." The breastplate hissed like a cat as he dipped it in the cold water. "What was all that noise?"

"Vargo Hoat's come back with prisoners. I saw their badges. There's a Glover, from Deepwood Motte, he's my father's man. The rest too, mostly." All of a sudden, Arya knew why her feet had brought her here. "You have to help me get them out."

Gendry laughed. "And how do we do that?"

"Ser Amory sent them down to the dungeon. The one under the Widow's Tower, that's just one big cell. You could smash the door open with your hammer—"

"While the guards watch and make bets on how many swings it will take me, maybe?"

Arya chewed her lips. "We'd need to kill the guards."

"How are we supposed to do that?"

"Maybe there won't be a lot of them."

"If there's *two*, that's too many for you and me. You never learned nothing in that village, did you? You try this and Vargo Hoat will cut off your hands and feet, the way he does." Gendry took up the tongs again.

"You're *afraid*."

"Leave me alone, girl."

"Gendry, there's a *hundred* northmen. Maybe more, I couldn't count them all. That's as many as Ser Amory has. Well, not counting the Bloody Mummers. We just have to get them out and we can take over the castle and escape."

"Well, you can't get them out, no more'n you could save Lommy." Gendry turned the breastplate with the tongs to look at it closely. "And if we did escape, where would we go?"

"Winterfell," she said at once. "I'd tell Mother how you helped me, and you could stay—"

"Would m'lady permit? Could I shoe your horses for you, and make swords for your lordly brothers?"

Sometimes he made her so *angry*. "You stop that!"

"Why should I wager my feet for the chance to sweat in Winterfell in place of Harrenhal? You know old Ben Blackthumb? He came here as a boy. Smithed for Lady Whent and her father before her and his father before him, and even for Lord Lothston who held Harrenhal before the Whents. Now he smiths for Lord Tywin, and you know what he says? A sword's a sword, a helm's a helm, and if you reach in the fire you get burned, no matter who you're serving. Lucan's a fair enough master. I'll stay here."

"The queen will catch you, then. She didn't send gold cloaks after Ben *Blackthumb*!"

"Likely it wasn't even me they wanted."

"It was too, you know it. You're *somebody*."

"I'm a 'prentice smith, and one day might' be I'll make a master armorer . . . *if* I don't run off and lose my feet or get myself killed." He turned away from her, picked up his hammer once more, and began to bang.

Arya's hands curled into helpless fists. "The next helm you make, put *mule's ears* on it in place of bull's horns!" She had to flee, or else she would have started hitting him. *He probably wouldn't even feel it if I did. When they find who he is and cut off his stupid mulehead, he'll be sorry he didn't help.* She was better off without him anyhow. He was the one who got her caught at the village.

But thinking of the village made her remember the march, and the storeroom, and the Tickler. She thought of the little boy who'd been hit in the face with the mace, of stupid old All-for-Joffrey, of Lommy Greenhands. *I was a sheep, and then I was a mouse, I couldn't do anything but hide.* Arya chewed her lip and tried to think when her courage had come back. *Jaqen made me brave again. He made me a ghost instead of a mouse.*

She had been avoiding the Lorathi since Weese's death. Chiswyck had been *easy*, anyone could push a man off the wallwalk, but Weese had raised that ugly spotted dog from a pup, and only some dark magic could have turned the animal against him. *Yoren found Jaqen in a black cell, the same as Rorge and Biter,* she remembered. *Jaqen did something horrible and Yoren knew, that's why he kept him in chains.* If the Lorathi was a wizard, Rorge and Biter could be demons he called up from some hell, not men at all.

Jaqen still owed her one death. In Old Nan's stories about men who were given magic wishes by a grumkin, you had to be especially careful with the third wish, because it was the last. Chiswyck and Weese hadn't been very important. *The last death has to count,* Arya told herself every night when she whispered her names. But now she wondered if that was truly the reason she had hesitated. So long as she could kill with a whisper, Arya need not be afraid of anyone . . . but once she used up the last death, she would only be a mouse again.

With Pinkeye awake, she dared not go back to her bed. Not knowing where else to hide, she made for the godswood. She liked the sharp smell of the pines and sentinels, the feel of grass and dirt between her toes, and the sound the wind made in the leaves. A slow little stream meandered through the wood, and there was one spot where it had eaten the ground away beneath a deadfall.

There, beneath rotting wood and twisted splintered branches, she found her hidden sword.

Gendry was too stubborn to make one for her, so she had made her own by breaking the bristles off a broom. Her blade was much too light and had no proper grip, but she liked the sharp jagged splintery end.

Whenever she had a free hour she stole away to work at the drills Syrio had taught her, moving barefoot over the fallen leaves, slashing at branches and whacking down leaves. Sometimes she even climbed the trees and danced among the upper branches, her toes gripping the limbs as she moved back and forth, teetering a little less every day as her balance returned to her. Night was the best time; no one ever bothered her at night.

Arya climbed. Up in the kingdom of the leaves, she unsheathed and for a time forgot them all, Ser Amory and the Mummers and her father's men alike, losing herself in the feel of rough wood beneath the soles of her feet and the *swish* of sword through air. A broken branch became Joffrey. She struck at it until it fell away. The queen and Ser Ilyn and Ser Meryn and the Hound were only leaves, but she killed them all as well, slashing them to wet green ribbons. When her arm grew weary, she sat with her legs over a high limb to catch her breath in the cool dark air, listening to the squeak of bats as they hunted. Through the leafy canopy she could see the bone-white branches of the heart tree. *It looks just like the one in Winterfell from here.* If only it had been . . . then when she climbed down she would have been home again, and maybe find her father sitting under the weirwood where he always sat.

Shoving her sword through her belt, she slipped down branch to branch until she was back on the ground. The light of the moon painted the limbs of the weirwood silvery white as she made her way toward it, but the five-pointed red leaves turned black by night. Arya stared at the face carved into its trunk. It was a terrible face, its mouth twisted, its eyes flaring and full of hate. Is that what a god looked like? Could gods be hurt, the same as people? *I should pray*, she thought suddenly.

Arya went to her knees. She wasn't sure how she should begin. She clasped her hands together. *Help me, you old gods*, she prayed silently. *Help me get those men out of the dungeon so we can kill Ser Amory, and bring me home to Winterfell. Make me a water dancer and a wolf and not afraid again, ever.*

Was that enough? Maybe she should pray aloud if she wanted the old gods to hear. Maybe she should pray longer. Sometimes her father had prayed a long time, she remembered. But the old gods had never helped him. Remembering that made her angry. "You should have saved him," she scolded the tree. "He prayed to you all the time. I don't care if you help me or not. I don't think you could even if you wanted to."

"Gods are not mocked, girl."

The voice startled her. She leapt to her feet and drew her wooden sword. Jaqen H'ghar stood so still in the darkness that he seemed one of the trees. "A man comes to hear a name. One and two and then comes three. A man would have done."

Arya lowered the splintery point toward the ground. "How did you know I was here?"

"A man sees. A man hears. A man knows."

She regarded him suspiciously. Had the gods sent him? "How'd you make the dog kill Weese? Did you call Rorge and Biter up from hell? Is Jaqen H'ghar your true name?"

"Some men have many names. Weasel. Arry. *Arya*."

She backed away from him, until she was pressed against the heart tree. "Did Gendry tell?"

"A man knows," he said again. "My lady of Stark."

Maybe the gods *had* sent him in answer to her prayers. "I need you to help me get those men out of the dungeons. That Glover and those others, all of them. We have to kill the guards and open the cell somehow—"

"A girl forgets," he said quietly. "Two she has had, three were owed. If a guard must die, she needs only speak his name."

"But *one* guard won't be enough, we need to kill them all to open the cell." Arya bit her lip hard to stop from crying. "I want you to save the northmen like I saved you."

He looked down at her pitilessly. "Three lives were snatched from a god. Three lives must be repaid. The gods are not mocked." His voice was silk and steel.

"I never mocked." She thought for a moment. "The name . . . can I name *anyone*? And you'll kill him?"

Jaqen H'ghar inclined his head. "A man has said."

"*Anyone?*" she repeated. "A man, a woman, a little baby, or Lord Tywin, or the High Septon, or your father?"

"A man's sire is long dead, but did he live, and did you know his name, he would die at your command."

"Swear it," Arya said. "Swear it by the gods."

"By all the gods of sea and air, and even him of fire, I swear it." He placed a hand in the mouth of the weirwood. "By the seven new gods and the old gods beyond count, I swear it."

He has sworn. "Even if I named the king . . ."

"Speak the name, and death will come. On the morrow, at the turn of the moon, a year from this day, it will come. A man does not fly like a bird, but one foot moves and then another and one day a man is there, and a king dies." He knelt beside her, so they were face-to-face. "A girl whispers if she fears to speak aloud. Whisper it now. Is it *Joffrey?*"

Arya put her lips to his ear. "It's *Jaqen H'ghar*."

Even in the burning barn, with walls of flame towering all around and him in chains, he had not seemed so distraught as he did now. "A girl . . . she makes a jest."

"You swore. The gods heard you swear."

"The gods did hear." There was a knife in his hand suddenly, its blade thin as her little finger. Whether it was meant for her or him, Arya could not say. "A girl will weep. A girl will lose her only friend."

"You're not my friend. A friend would *help* me." She stepped away from him, balanced on the balls of her feet in case he threw his knife. "I'd never kill a *friend.*"

Jaqen's smile came and went. "A girl might . . . name another name then, if a friend did help?"

"A girl might," she said. "If a friend did help."

The knife vanished. "Come."

"Now?" She had never thought he would act so quickly.

"A man hears the whisper of sand in a glass. A man will not sleep until a girl unsays a certain name. Now, evil child."

I'm not an evil child, she thought, *I am a direwolf, and the ghost in Harrenhal.* She put her broomstick back in its hiding place and followed him from the godswood.

Despite the hour, Harrenhal stirred with fitful life. Vargo Hoat's arrival had thrown off all the routines. Ox carts, oxen, and horses had all vanished from the yard, but the bear cage was still there. It had been hung from the arched span of the bridge that divided the outer and middle wards, suspended on heavy chains, a few feet off the ground. A ring of torches bathed the area in light. Some of the boys from the stables were tossing stones to make the bear roar and grumble. Across the ward, light spilled through the door of the Barracks Hall, accompanied by the clatter of tankards and men calling for more wine. A dozen voices took up a song in a guttural tongue strange to Arya's ears.

They're drinking and eating before they sleep, she realized. *Pinkeye would have sent to wake me, to help with the serving. He'll know I'm not abed.* But likely he was busy pouring for the Brave Companions and those of Ser Amory's garrison who had joined them. The noise they were making would be a good distraction.

"The hungry gods will feast on blood tonight, if a man would do this thing," Jaqen said. "Sweet girl, kind and gentle. Unsay one name and say another and cast this mad dream aside."

"I won't."

"Just so." He seemed resigned. "The thing will be done, but a girl must obey. A man has no time for talk."

"A girl will obey," Arya said. "What should I do?"

"A hundred men are hungry, they must be fed, the lord commands hot broth. A girl must run to the kitchens and tell her pie boy."

"Broth," she repeated. "Where will you be?"

"A girl will help make broth, and wait in the kitchens until a man comes for her. Go. Run."

Hot Pie was pulling his loaves from the ovens when she burst into the kitchen, but he was no longer alone. They'd woken the cooks to feed Vargo Hoat and his Bloody Mummers. Serving men were carrying off baskets of Hot Pie's bread and tarts, the chief cook was carving cold slices off a ham, spit boys were turning rabbits while the pot girls basted them with honey, women were chopping onions and carrots. "What do you want, Weasel?" the chief cook asked when he saw her.

"Broth," she announced. "My lord wants broth."

He jerked his carving knife at the black iron kettles hung over the flames. "What do you think that is? Though I'd soon as piss in it as serve it to that goat. Can't even let a man have a night's sleep." He spat. "Well, never you mind, run back and tell him a kettle can't be hurried."

"I'm to wait here until it's done."

"Then stay out of the way. Or better yet, make yourself of use. Run to the buttery; his goatship will be wanting butter and cheese. Wake up Pia and tell her she'd best be nimble for once, if she wants to keep both of her feet."

She ran as fast as she could. Pia was awake in the loft, moaning under one of the Mummers, but she slipped back into her clothes quick enough when she heard Arya shout. She filled six baskets with crocks of butter and big wedges of stinky cheese wrapped in cloth. "Here, help me with these," she told Arya.

"I can't. But you better hurry or Vargo Hoat will chop off your foot." She darted off before Pia could grab her. On the way back, she wondered why none of the captives had their hands or feet chopped off. Maybe Vargo Hoat was afraid to make Robb angry. Though he didn't seem the sort to be afraid of *anyone.*

Hot Pie was stirring the kettles with a long wooden spoon when Arya returned to the kitchens. She grabbed up a second spoon and started to help. For a moment she thought maybe she should tell him, but then she remembered the village and decided not to. *He'd only yield again.*

Then she heard the ugly sound of Rorge's voice. *"Cook,"* he shouted. "We'll take your bloody broth." Arya let go of the spoon in dismay. *I never told him to bring them.* Rorge wore his iron helmet, with the nasal that half hid his missing nose. Jaqen and Biter followed him into the kitchen.

"The bloody broth isn't bloody ready yet," the cook said. "It needs to simmer. We only now put in the onions and—"

"Shut your hole, or I'll shove a spit up your ass and we'll baste you for a turn or two. I said broth and I said now."

Hissing, Biter grabbed a handful of half-charred rabbit right off the spit, and tore into it with his pointed teeth while honey dripped between his fingers.

The cook was beaten. "Take your bloody broth, then, but if the goat asks why it tastes so thin, you tell him."

Biter licked the grease and honey off his fingers as Jaqen H'ghar donned a pair of heavy padded mitts. He gave a second pair to Arya. "A weasel will help." The broth was boiling hot, and the kettles were heavy. Arya and Jaqen wrestled one between them, Rorge carried one by himself, and Biter grabbed two more, hissing in pain when the handles burned his hands. Even so, he did not drop them. They lugged the kettles out of the kitchens and across the ward. Two guards had been posted at the door of the Widow's Tower. "What's this?" one said to Rorge.

"A pot of boiling piss, want some?"

Jaqen smiled disarmingly. "A prisoner must eat too."

"No one said nothing about—"

Arya cut him off. "It's for *them*, not you."

The second guard waved them past. "Bring it down, then."

Inside the door a winding stair led down to the dungeons. Rorge led the way, with Jaqen and Arya bringing up the rear. "A girl will stay out of the way," he told her.

The steps opened onto a dank stone vault, long, gloomy, and windowless. A few torches burned in sconces at the near end where a group of Ser Amory's guards sat around a scarred wooden table, talking and playing at tiles. Heavy iron bars separated them from where the captives were crowded together in the dark. The smell of the broth brought many up to the bars.

Arya counted eight guards. They smelled the broth as well. "There's the ugliest serving wench I ever saw," their captain said to Rorge. "What's in the kettle?"

"Your cock and balls. You want to eat or not?"

One of the guards had been pacing, one standing near the bars, a third sitting on the floor with his back to the wall, but the prospect of food drew all of them to the table.

"About bloody time they fed us."

"That onions I smell?"

"So where's the bread?"

"Fuck, we need bowls, cups, spoons—"

"No you don't." Rorge heaved the scalding hot broth across the table, full in their faces. Jaqen H'ghar did the same. Biter threw his kettles too, swinging them underarm so they spun across the dungeon, raining soup. One caught the captain in the temple as he tried to rise. He went down like a sack of sand and lay still. The rest were screaming in agony, praying, or trying to crawl off.

Arya pressed back against the wall as Rorge began to cut throats. Biter preferred to grab the men behind the head and under the chin and crack their necks with a single twist of his huge pale hands. Only one of the guards managed to get a blade out. Jaqen danced away from his slash, drew his own sword, drove the man back into a corner with a flurry of blows, and killed him with a thrust to the heart. The Lorathi brought the blade to Arya still red with heart's blood and wiped it clean on the front of her shift. "A girl should be bloody too. This is her work."

The key to the cell hung from a hook on the wall above the table. Rorge took it down and opened the door. The first man through was the lord with the mailed fist on his surcoat. "Well done," he said. "I am Robett Glover."

"My lord." Jaqen gave him a bow.

Once freed, the captives stripped the dead guards of their weapons and darted up the steps with steel in hand. Their fellows crowded after them, bare-handed. They went swiftly, and with scarcely a word. None of them seemed quite so badly wounded as they had when Vargo Hoat had marched them through the gates of Harrenhal. "This of the soup, that was clever," the man Glover was saying. "I did not expect that. Was it Lord Hoat's idea?"

Rorge began to laugh. He laughed so hard that snot flew out the hole where his nose had been. Biter sat on top of one of the dead men, holding a limp hand as he gnawed at the fingers. Bones cracked between his teeth.

"Who are you men?" A crease appeared between Robett Glover's brows. "You were not with Hoat when he came to Lord Bolton's encampment. Are you of the Brave Companions?"

Rorge wiped the snot off his chin with the back of his hand. "We are now."

"This man has the honor to be Jaqen H'ghar, once of the Free.City of Lorath. This man's discourteous companions are named Rorge and Biter. A lord will know which is Biter." He waved a hand toward Arya. "And here—"

"I'm Weasel," she blurted, before he could tell who she *really* was. She did not want her name said here, where Rorge might hear, and Biter, and all these others she did not know.

She saw Glover dismiss her. "Very well," he said. "Let's make an end to this bloody business."

When they climbed back up the winding stair, they found the door guards lying in pools of their own blood. Northmen were running across the ward. Arya heard shouts. The door of Barracks Hall burst open and a wounded man staggered out screaming. Three others ran after him and silenced him with spear and sword. There was fighting around the gatehouse as well. Rorge and Biter rushed off with Glover, but Jaqen H'ghar knelt beside Arya. "A girl does not understand?"

"Yes I do," she said, though she didn't, not truly.

The Lorathi must have seen it on her face. "A goat has no loyalty. Soon a wolf banner is raised here, I think. But first a man would hear a certain name unsaid."

"I take back the name." Arya chewed her lip. "Do I still have a third death?"

"A girl is greedy." Jaqen touched one of the dead guards and showed her his bloody fingers. "Here is three and there is four and eight more lie dead below. The debt is paid."

"The debt is paid," Arya agreed reluctantly. She felt a little sad. Now she was just a mouse again.

"A god has his due. And now a man must die." A strange smile touched the lips of Jaqen H'ghar.

"Die?" she said, confused. What did he mean? "But I unsaid the name. You don't need to die now."

"I do. My time is done." Jaqen passed a hand down his face from forehead to chin, and where it went he changed. His cheeks grew fuller, his eyes closer; his nose hooked, a scar appeared on his right cheek where no scar had been before. And when he shook his head, his long straight hair, half red and half white, dissolved away to reveal a cap of tight black curls.

Arya's mouth hung open. "Who are you?" she whispered, too astonished to be afraid. "How did you do that? Was it hard?"

He grinned, revealing a shiny gold tooth. "No harder than taking a new name, if you know the way."

"Show me," she blurted. "I want to do it too."

"If you would learn, you must come with me."

Arya grew hesitant. "Where?"

"Far and away, across the narrow sea."

"I can't. I have to go home. To Winterfell."

"Then we must part," he said, "for I have duties too." He lifted her hand and pressed a small coin into her palm. "Here."

"What is it?"

"A coin of great value."

Arya bit it. It was so hard it could only be iron. "Is it worth enough to buy a horse?"

"It is not meant for the buying of horses."

"Then what good is it?"

"As well ask what good is life, what good is death? If the day comes when you would find me again, give that coin to any man from Braavos, and say these words to him—*valar morghulis.*"

"*Valar morghulis,*" Arya repeated. It wasn't hard. Her fingers closed tight over the coin. Across the yard, she could hear men dying. "Please don't go, Jaqen."

"Jaqen is as dead as Arry," he said sadly, "and I have promises to keep. *Valar morghulis,* Arya Stark. Say it again."

"*Valar morghulis,*" she said once more, and the stranger in Jaqen's clothes bowed to her and stalked off through the darkness, cloak swirling. She was alone with the dead men. *They deserved to die,* Arya told herself, remembering all those Ser Amory Lorch had killed at the holdfast by the lake.

The cellars under Kingspyre were empty when she returned to her bed of straw. She whispered her names to her pillow, and when she was done she added, "*Valar morghulis,*" in a small soft voice, wondering what it meant.

Come dawn, Pinkeye and the others were back, all but one boy who'd been killed in the fighting for no reason that anyone could say. Pinkeye went up alone to see how matters stood by light of day, complaining all the while that his old bones could not abide steps. When he returned, he told them that Harrenhal had been taken. "Them Bloody Mummers killed some of Ser Amory's lot in their beds, and the rest at table after they were good and drunk. The new lord will be here before the day's out, with his whole host. He's from the wild north up where that Wall is, and they say he's a hard one. This lord or that lord, there's still work to be done. Any foolery and I'll whip the skin off your back." He looked at Arya when he said that, but never said a word to her about where she had been the night before.

All morning she watched the Bloody Mummers strip the dead of their valuables and drag the corpses to the Flowstone Yard, where a pyre was laid to dispose of them. Shagwell the Fool hacked the heads off two dead knights and pranced about the castle swinging them by the hair and making them talk. "What did you die of?" one head asked. "Hot weasel soup," replied the second.

Arya was set to mopping up dried blood. No one said a word to her beyond the usual, but every so often she would notice people looking at her strangely. Robett Glover and the other men they'd freed must have talked about what had happened down in the dungeon, and then Shagwell and his stupid talking heads started in about the weasel soup. She would have told him to shut up, but she was scared to. The fool was half-mad, and she'd heard that he'd once killed a man for not laughing at one of his japes. *He better shut his mouth or I'll put him on my list with the rest,* she thought as she scrubbed at a reddish-brown stain.

It was almost evenfall when the new master of Harrenhal arrived. He had a plain face, beardless and ordinary, notable only for his queer pale eyes. Neither plump, thin, nor muscular, he wore black ringmail and a spotted pink cloak. The sigil on his banner looked like a man dipped in blood. "On your knees for the Lord of the Dreadfort!" shouted his squire, a boy no older than Arya, and Harrenhal knelt.

Vargo Hoat came forward. "My lord, Harrenhal ith yourth."

The lord gave answer, but too softly for Arya to hear. Robett Glover and Ser Aenys Frey, freshly bathed and clad in clean new doublets and cloaks, came up to join them. After some brief talk, Ser Aenys led them over to Rorge and Biter. Arya was surprised to see them still here; somehow she would have expected them to vanish when Jaqen did. Arya heard the harsh sound of Rorge's voice, but not what he was saying. Then Shagwell pounced on her, dragging her out across the yard. "My lord, my lord," he sang, tugging at her wrist, "here's the weasel who made the soup!"

"Let go," Arya said, wriggling out of his grasp.

The lord regarded her. Only his eyes moved; they were very pale, the color of ice. "How old are you, child?"

She had to think for a moment to remember. "Ten."

"Ten, my lord," he reminded her. "Are you fond of animals?"

"Some kinds. My lord."

A thin smile twitched across his lips. "But not lions, it would seem. Nor manticores."

She did not know what to say to that, so she said nothing.

"They tell me you are called Weasel. That will not serve. What name did your mother give you?"

She bit her lip, groping for another name. Lommy had called her Lumpyhead, Sansa used Horseface, and her father's men once dubbed her Arya Underfoot, but she did not think any of those were the sort of name he wanted.

"Nymeria," she said. "Only she called me Nan for short."

"You will call me my lord when you speak to me, Nan," the lord said mildly. "You are too young to be a Brave Companion, I think, and of the wrong sex. Are you afraid of leeches, child?"

"They're only leeches. My lord."

"My squire could take a lesson from you, it would seem. Frequent leechings are the secret of a long life. A man must purge himself of bad blood. You will do, I think. For so long as I remain at Harrenhal, Nan, you shall be my cupbearer, and serve me at table and in chambers."

This time she knew better than to say that she'd sooner work in the stables. "Yes, your lord. I mean, my lord."

The lord waved a hand. "Make her presentable," he said to no one in particular, "and make certain she knows how to pour wine without spilling it." Turning away, he lifted a hand and said, "Lord Hoat, see to those banners above the gatehouse."

Four Brave Companions climbed to the ramparts and hauled down the lion of Lannister and Ser Amory's own black manticore. In their place they raised the flayed man of the Dreadfort and the direwolf of Stark. And that evening, a page named Nan poured wine for Roose Bolton and Vargo Hoat as they stood on the gallery, watching the Brave Companions parade Ser Amory Lorch naked through the middle ward. Ser Amory pleaded and sobbed and clung to the legs of his captors, until Rorge pulled him loose, and Shagwell kicked him down into the bear pit.

The bear is all in black, Arya thought. *Like Yoren.* She filled Roose Bolton's cup, and did not spill a drop.

DAENERYS

In this city of splendors, Dany had expected the House of the Undying Ones to be the most splendid of all, but she emerged from her palanquin to behold a grey and ancient ruin.

Long and low, without towers or windows, it coiled like a stone serpent through a grove of black-barked trees whose inky blue leaves made the stuff of the sorcerous drink the Qartheen called *shade of the evening*. No other buildings stood near. Black tiles covered the palace roof, many fallen or broken; the mortar between the stones was dry and crumbling. She understood now why Xaro Xhoan Daxos called it the Palace of Dust. Even Drogon seemed disquieted by the sight of it. The black dragon *hissed*, smoke seeping out between his sharp teeth.

"Blood of my blood," Jhogo said in Dothraki, "this is an evil place, a haunt of ghosts and *maegi*. See how it drinks the morning sun? Let us go before it drinks us as well."

Ser Jorah Mormont came up beside them. "What power can they have if they live in *that*?"

"Heed the wisdom of those who love you best," said Xaro Xhoan Daxos, lounging inside the palanquin. "Warlocks are bitter creatures who eat dust and drink of shadows. They will give you naught. They have naught to give."

Aggo put a hand on his *arakh*. "*Khaleesi*, it is said that many go into the Palace of Dust, but few come out."

"It is said," Jhogo agreed.

"We are blood of your blood," said Aggo, "sworn to live and die as you do. Let us walk with you in this dark place, to keep you safe from harm."

"Some places even a *khal* must walk alone," Dany said.

"Take me, then," Ser Jorah urged. "The risk—"

"Queen Daenerys must enter alone, or not at all." The warlock Pyat Pree stepped out from under the trees. *Has he been there all along?* Dany wondered. "Should she turn away now, the doors of wisdom shall be closed to her forevermore."

"My pleasure barge awaits, even now," Xaro Xhoan Daxos called out. "Turn away from this folly, most stubborn of queens. I have flutists who will soothe your troubled soul with sweet music, and a small girl whose tongue will make you sigh and melt."

Ser Jorah Mormont gave the merchant prince a sour look. "Your Grace, remember Mirri Maz Duur."

"I do," Dany said, suddenly decided. "I remember that she had knowledge. And she was only a *maegi*."

Pyat Pree smiled thinly. "The child speaks as sagely as a crone. Take my arm, and let me lead you."

"I am no child." Dany took his arm nonetheless.

It was darker than she would have thought under the black trees, and the way was longer. Though the path seemed to run straight from the street to the door of the palace, Pyat Pree soon turned aside. When she questioned him, the warlock said only, "The front way leads in, but never out again. Heed my words, my queen. The House of the Undying Ones was not made for mortal men. If you value your soul, take care and do just as I tell you."

"I will do as you say," Dany promised.

"When you enter, you will find yourself in a room with four doors: the one you have come through and three others. Take the door to your right. Each time, the door to your right. If you should come upon a stairwell, climb. Never go down, and never take any door but the first door to your right."

"The door to my right," Dany repeated. "I understand. And when I leave, the opposite?"

"By no means," Pyat Pree said. "Leaving and coming, it is the same. Always up. Always the door to your right. Other doors may open to you. Within, you will see many things that disturb you. Visions of loveliness and visions of horror, wonders and terrors. Sights and sounds of days gone by and days to come and days that never were. Dwellers and servitors may speak to you as you go. Answer or ignore them as you choose, but *enter no room* until you reach the audience chamber."

"I understand."

"When you come to the chamber of the Undying, be patient. Our little lives are no more than a flicker of a moth's wing to them. Listen well, and write each word upon your heart."

When they reached the door—a tall oval mouth, set in a wall fashioned in the likeness of a human face—the smallest dwarf Dany had ever seen was waiting on the threshold. He stood no higher than her knee, his faced pinched and pointed, snoutish, but he was dressed in delicate livery of purple and blue, and his tiny pink hands held a silver tray. Upon it rested a slender crystal glass filled with a thick blue liquid: *shade of the evening*, the wine of warlocks. "Take and drink," urged Pyat Pree.

"Will it turn my lips blue?"

"One flute will serve only to unstop your ears and dissolve the caul from off your eyes, so that you may hear and see the truths that will be laid before you."

Dany raised the glass to her lips. The first sip tasted like ink and spoiled meat, foul, but when she swallowed it seemed to come to life within her. She could feel tendrils spreading through her chest, like fingers of fire coiling around her heart, and on her tongue was a taste like honey and anise and cream, like mother's milk and Drogo's seed, like red meat and hot blood and molten gold. It was all the tastes she had ever known, and none of them . . . and then the glass was empty.

"Now you may enter," said the warlock. Dany put the glass back on the servitor's tray, and went inside.

She found herself in a stone anteroom with four doors, one on each wall. With never a hesitation, she went to the door on her right and stepped through. The second room was a twin to the first. Again she turned to the right-hand door. When she pushed it open she faced yet another small antechamber with four doors. *I am in the presence of sorcery.*

The fourth room was oval rather than square and walled in wormeaten wood in place of stone. Six passages led out from it in place of four. Dany chose the rightmost, and entered a long, dim, high-ceilinged hall. Along the right hand was a row of torches burning with a smoky orange light, but the only doors were to her left. Drogon unfolded wide black wings and beat the stale air. He flew twenty feet before thudding to an undignified crash. Dany strode after him.

The mold-eaten carpet under her feet had once been gorgeously colored, and whorls of gold could still be seen in the fabric, glinting broken amidst the faded grey and mottled green. What remained served to muffle her footfalls, but that was not all to the good. Dany could hear sounds within the walls, a faint scurrying and scrabbling that made her think of rats. Drogon heard them too. His head moved as he followed the sounds, and when they stopped he gave an angry scream. Other sounds, even more disturbing, came through some of the closed doors. One shook and thumped, as if someone were trying to break through. From another came a dissonant piping that made the dragon lash his tail wildly from side to side. Dany hurried quickly past.

Not all the doors were closed. *I will not look,* Dany told herself, but the temptation was too strong.

In one room, a beautiful woman sprawled naked on the floor while four little men crawled over her. They had rattish pointed faces and tiny pink hands, like the servitor who had brought her the glass of shade. One was pumping between her thighs. Another savaged her breasts, worrying at the nipples with his wet red mouth, tearing and chewing.

Farther on she came upon a feast of corpses. Savagely slaughtered, the feasters lay strewn across overturned chairs and hacked trestle tables, asprawl in pools of congealing blood. Some had lost limbs, even heads. Severed hands clutched bloody cups, wooden spoons, roast fowl, heels of bread. In a throne above them sat a dead man with the head of a wolf. He wore an iron crown and held a leg of lamb in one hand as a king might hold a scepter, and his eyes followed Dany with mute appeal.

She fled from him, but only as far as the next open door. *I know this room,* she thought. She remembered those great wooden beams and the carved animal faces that adorned them. And there outside the window, a lemon tree! The sight of it made her heart ache with longing. *It is the house with the red door, the house in Braavos.* No sooner had she thought it than old Ser Willem came into the room, leaning heavily on his stick. "Little princess, there you are," he said in his gruff kind voice. "Come," he said, "come to me, my lady, you're home now, you're safe now." His big wrinkled hand reached for her, soft as old leather, and Dany wanted to take it and hold it and kiss it, she wanted that as much as she had ever wanted anything. Her foot edged forward, and then she thought, *He's dead, he's dead, the sweet old bear, he died a long time ago.* She backed away and ran.

The long hall went on and on and on, with endless doors to her left and only torches to her right. She ran past more doors than she could count, closed doors and open ones, doors of wood and doors of iron, carved doors and plain ones, doors with pulls and doors with locks and doors with knockers. Drogon lashed against her back, urging her on, and Dany ran until she could run no more.

Finally a great pair of bronze doors appeared to her left, grander than the rest. They swung open as she neared, and she had to stop and look. Beyond loomed a cavernous stone hall, the largest she had ever seen. The skulls of dead dragons looked down from its walls. Upon a towering barbed throne sat an old man in rich robes, an old man with dark eyes and long silver-grey hair. "Let him be king over charred bones and cooked meat," he said to a man below him. "Let him be the king of ashes." Drogon shrieked, his claws digging through silk and skin, but the king on his throne never heard, and Dany moved on.

Viserys, was her first thought the next time she paused, but a second glance told her otherwise. The man had her brother's hair, but he was taller, and his eyes were a dark indigo rather than lilac. "Aegon," he said to a woman nursing a newborn babe in a great wooden bed. "What better name for a king?"

"Will you make a song for him?" the woman asked.

"He has a song," the man replied. "He is the prince that was promised, and his is the song of ice and fire." He looked up when he said it and his eyes met Dany's, and it seemed as if he saw her standing there beyond the door. "There must be one more," he said, though whether he was speaking to her or the woman in the bed she could not say. "The dragon has three heads." He went to the window seat, picked up a harp, and ran his fingers lightly over its silvery strings. Sweet sadness filled the room as man and wife and babe faded like the morning mist, only the music lingering behind to speed her on her way.

It seemed as though she walked for another hour before the long hall finally ended in a steep stone stair, descending into darkness. Every door, open or closed, had been to her left. Dany looked back behind her. The torches were going out, she realized with a start of fear. Perhaps twenty still burned. Thirty at most. One more guttered out even as she watched, and the darkness came a little farther down the hall, creeping toward her. And as she listened it seemed as if she heard something else coming, shuffling and dragging itself slowly along the faded carpet. Terror filled her. She could not go back and she was afraid to stay here, but how could she go on? There was no door on her right, and the steps went down, not up.

Yet another torch went out as she stood pondering, and the sounds grew faintly louder. Drogon's long neck snaked out and he opened his mouth to scream, steam rising from between his teeth. *He hears it too.* Dany turned to the blank wall once more, but there was nothing. *Could there be a secret door, a door I cannot see?* Another torch went out. Another. *The first door on the right, he said, always the first door on the right. The first door on the right* . . .

It came to her suddenly. . . . *is the last door on the left!*

She flung herself through. Beyond was another small room with four doors. To the right she went, and to the right, and to the right, and to the right, and to the right, and to the right, and to the right, until she was dizzy and out of breath once more.

When she stopped, she found herself in yet another dank stone chamber . . . but this time the door opposite was round, shaped like an open mouth, and Pyat Pree stood outside in the grass beneath the trees. "Can it be that the Undying are done with you so soon?" he asked in disbelief when he saw her.

"So soon?" she said, confused. "I've walked for hours, and still not found them."

"You have taken a wrong turning. Come, I will lead you." Pyat Pree held out his hand.

Dany hesitated. There was a door to her right, still closed . . .

"That's not the way," Pyat Pree said firmly, his blue lips prim with disapproval. "The Undying Ones will not wait forever."

"Our little lives are no more than a flicker of a moth's wing to them," Dany said, remembering.

"Stubborn child. You will be lost, and never found."

She walked away from him, to the door on the right.

"No," Pyat screeched. "No, to me, come to me, to *meeeeeee*." His face crumbled inward, changing to something pale and wormlike.

Dany left him behind, entering a stairwell. She began to climb. Before long her legs were aching. She recalled that the House of the Undying Ones had seemed to have no towers.

Finally the stair opened. To her right, a set of wide wooden doors had been thrown open. They were fashioned of ebony and weirwood, the black and white grains swirling and twisting in strange interwoven patterns. They were very beautiful, yet somehow frightening. *The blood of the dragon must not be afraid*. Dany said a quick prayer, begging the Warrior for courage and the Dothraki horse god for strength. She made herself walk forward.

Beyond the doors was a great hall and a splendor of wizards. Some wore sumptuous robes of ermine, ruby velvet, and cloth of gold. Others fancied elaborate armor studded with gemstones, or tall pointed hats speckled with stars. There were women among them, dressed in gowns of surpassing loveliness. Shafts of sunlight slanted through windows of stained glass, and the air was alive with the most beautiful music she had ever heard.

A kingly man in rich robes rose when he saw her, and smiled. "Daenerys of House Targaryen, be welcome. Come and share the food of forever. We are the Undying of Qarth."

"Long have we awaited you," said a woman beside him, clad in rose and silver. The breast she had left bare in the Qartheen fashion was as perfect as a breast could be.

"We knew you were to come to us," the wizard king said. "A thousand years ago we knew, and have been waiting all this time. We sent the comet to show you the way."

"We have knowledge to share with you," said a warrior in shining emerald armor, "and magic weapons to arm you with. You have passed every trial. Now come and sit with us, and all your questions shall be answered."

She took a step forward. But then Drogon leapt from her shoulder. He flew to the top of the ebony-and-weirwood door, perched there, and began to bite at the carved wood.

"A willful beast," laughed a handsome young man. "Shall we teach you the secret speech of dragonkind? Come, come."

Doubt seized her. The great door was so heavy it took all of Dany's strength to budge it, but finally it began to move. Behind was another door, hidden. It was old grey wood, splintery and plain . . . but it stood to the right of the door through which she'd entered. The wizards were beckoning her with voices sweeter than song. She ran from them, Drogon flying back down to her. Through the narrow door she passed, into a chamber awash in gloom.

A long stone table filled this room. Above it floated a human heart, swollen and blue with corruption, yet still alive. It beat, a deep ponderous throb of sound, and each pulse sent out a wash of indigo light. The figures around the table were no more than blue shadows. As Dany walked to the empty chair at the foot of the table, they did not stir, nor speak, nor turn to face her. There was no sound but the slow, deep beat of the rotting heart.

. . . *mother of dragons* . . . came a voice, part whisper and part moan. . . . *dragons* . . . *dragons* . . . *dragons* . . . other voices echoed in the gloom. Some were male and some female. One spoke with the timbre of a child. The floating heart pulsed from dimness to darkness. It was hard to summon the will to speak, to recall the words she had practiced so assiduously. "I am Daenerys Stormborn of House Targaryen, Queen of the Seven Kingdoms of Westeros." *Do they hear me? Why don't they move?* She sat, folding her hands in her lap. "Grant me your counsel, and speak to me with the wisdom of those who have conquered death."

Through the indigo murk, she could make out the wizened features of the Undying One to her right, an old old man, wrinkled and hairless. His flesh was a ripe violet-blue, his lips and nails bluer still, so dark they were almost black. Even the whites of his eyes were blue. They stared unseeing at the ancient woman on the opposite side of the table, whose gown of pale silk had rotted on her body. One withered breast was left bare in the Qartheen manner, to show a pointed blue nipple hard as leather.

She is not breathing. Dany listened to the silence. *None of them are breathing, and they do not move, and those eyes see nothing. Could it be that the Undying Ones were dead?*

Her answer was a whisper as thin as a mouse's whisker. . . . *we live . . . live . . . live . . .* it sounded. Myriad other voices whispered echoes. . . . *and know . . . know . . . know . . . know . . .*

"I have come for the gift of truth," Dany said. "In the long hall, the things I saw . . . were they true visions, or lies? Past things, or things to come? What did they mean?"

. . . the shape of shadows . . . morrows not yet made . . . drink from the cup of ice . . . drink from the cup of fire . . .

. . . mother of dragons . . . child of three . . .

"Three?" She did not understand.

. . . three heads has the dragon . . . the ghost chorus yammered inside her skull with never a lip moving, never a breath stirring the still blue air. *. . . mother of dragons . . . child of storm . . .* The whispers became a swirling song. *. . . three fires must you light . . . one for life and one for death and one to love . . .* Her own heart was beating in unison to the one that floated before her, blue and corrupt . . . *three mounts must you ride . . . one to bed and one to dread and one to love . . .* The voices were growing louder, she realized, and it seemed her heart was slowing, and even her breath. *. . . three treasons will you know . . . once for blood and once for gold and once for love . . .*

"I don't . . ." Her voice was no more than a whisper, almost as faint as theirs. What was happening to her? "I don't understand," she said, more loudly. Why was it so hard to talk here? "Help me. Show me."

. . . help her . . . the whispers mocked. *. . . show her . . .*

Then phantoms shivered through the murk, images in indigo. Viserys screamed as the molten gold ran down his cheeks and filled his mouth. A tall lord with copper skin and silver-gold hair stood beneath the banner of a fiery stallion, a burning city behind him. Rubies flew like drops of blood from the chest of a dying prince, and he sank to his knees in the water and with his last breath murmured a woman's name. *. . . mother of dragons, daughter of death . . .* Glowing like sunset, a red sword was raised in the hand of a blue-eyed king who cast no shadow. A cloth dragon swayed on poles amidst a cheering crowd. From a smoking tower, a great stone beast took wing, breathing shadow fire. *. . . mother of dragons, slayer of lies . . .* Her silver was trotting through the grass, to a darkling stream beneath a sea of stars. A corpse stood at the prow of a ship, eyes bright in his dead face, grey lips smiling sadly. A blue flower grew from a chink in a wall of ice, and filled the air with sweetness. *. . . mother of dragons, bride of fire . . .*

Faster and faster the visions came, one after the other, until it seemed as if the very air had come alive. Shadows whirled and danced inside a tent, boneless and terrible. A little girl ran barefoot toward a big house with a red door. Mirri Maz Duur shrieked in the flames, a dragon bursting from her brow. Behind a silver horse the bloody corpse of a naked man bounced and dragged. A white lion ran through grass taller than a man. Beneath the Mother of Mountains, a line of naked crones crept from a great lake and knelt shivering before her, their grey heads bowed. Ten thousand slaves lifted bloodstained hands as she raced by on her silver, riding like the wind. *"Mother!"* they cried. *"Mother, mother!"* They were reaching for her, touching her, tugging at her cloak, the hem of her skirt, her foot, her leg, her breast. They wanted her, needed her, the fire, the life, and Dany gasped and opened her arms to give herself to them . . .

But then black wings buffeted her round the head, and a scream of fury cut the indigo air, and suddenly the visions were gone, ripped away, and Dany's gasp turned to horror. The Undying were all around her, blue and cold, whispering as they reached for her, pulling, stroking, tugging at her clothes, touching her with their dry cold hands, twining their fingers through her hair. All the strength had left her limbs. She could not move. Even her heart had ceased to beat. She felt a hand on her bare breast, twisting her nipple. Teeth found the soft skin of her throat. A mouth descended on one eye, licking, sucking, *biting* . . .

Then indigo turned to orange, and whispers turned to screams. Her heart was pounding, racing, the hands and mouths were gone, heat washed over her skin, and Dany blinked at a sudden glare. Perched above her, the dragon spread his wings and tore at the terrible dark heart, ripping the rotten flesh to ribbons, and when his head snapped forward, fire flew from his open jaws, bright and hot. She could hear the shrieks of the Undying as they burned, their high thin papery voices crying out in tongues long dead. Their flesh was crumbling parchment, their bones dry wood soaked in tallow. They danced as the flames consumed them; they staggered and writhed and spun and raised blazing hands on high, their fingers bright as torches.

Dany pushed herself to her feet and bulled through them. They were light as air, no more than husks, and they fell at a touch. The whole room was ablaze by the time she reached the door. *"Drogon,"* she called, and he flew to her through the fire.

Outside a long dim passageway stretched serpentine before her, lit by the flickering orange glare from behind. Dany ran, searching for a door, a door to her right, a door to her left, any door, but there was nothing, only twisty stone walls, and a floor that seemed to move slowly under her feet, writhing as if to trip her. She kept her feet and ran faster, and suddenly the door was there ahead of her, a door like an open mouth.

When she spilled out into the sun, the bright light made her stumble. Pyat Pree was gibbering in some unknown tongue and hopping from one foot to the other. When Dany looked behind her, she saw thin tendrils of smoke forcing their way through cracks in the ancient stone walls of the Palace of Dust, and rising from between the black tiles of the roof.

Howling curses, Pyat Pree drew a knife and danced toward her, but Drogon flew at his face. Then she heard the *crack* of Jhogo's whip, and never was a sound so sweet. The knife went flying, and an instant later Rakharo was slamming Pyat to the ground. Ser Jorah Mormont knelt beside Dany in the cool green grass and put his arm around her shoulder.

TYRION

"If you die stupidly, I'm going to feed your body to the goats," Tyrion threatened as the first load of Stone Crows pushed off from the quay.

Shagga laughed. "The Halfman has no goats."

"I'll get some just for you."

Dawn was breaking, and pale ripples of light shimmered on the surface of the river, shattering under the poles and re-forming when the ferry had passed. Timett had taken his Burned Men into the kingswood two days before. Yesterday the Black Ears and Moon Brothers followed, today the Stone Crows.

"Whatever you do, don't try and fight a battle," Tyrion said. "Strike at their camps and baggage train. Ambush their scouts and hang the bodies from trees ahead of their line of march, loop around and cut down stragglers. I want night attacks, so many and so sudden that they'll be afraid to sleep—"

Shagga laid a hand atop Tyrion's head. "All this I learned from Dolf son of Holger before my beard had grown. This is the way of war in the Mountains of the Moon."

"The kingswood is not the Mountains of the Moon, and you won't be fighting Milk Snakes and Painted Dogs. And *listen* to the guides I'm sending, they know this wood as well as you know your mountains. Heed their counsel and they'll serve you well."

"Shagga will listen to the Halfman's pets," the clansman promised solemnly. And then it was time for him to lead his garron onto the ferry. Tyrion watched them push off and pole out toward the center of the Blackwater. He felt a queer twinge in the pit of his stomach as Shagga faded in the morning mist. He was going to feel naked without his clansmen.

He still had Bronn's hirelings, near eight hundred of them now, but sellswords were notoriously fickle. Tyrion had done what he could to buy their continued loyalty, promising Bronn and a dozen of his best men lands and knighthoods when the battle was won. They'd drunk his wine, laughed at his jests, and called each other *ser* until they were all staggering . . . all but Bronn himself, who'd only smiled that insolent dark smile of his and afterward said, "They'll kill for that knighthood, but don't ever think they'll die for it."

Tyrion had no such delusion.

The gold cloaks were almost as uncertain a weapon. Six thousand men in the City Watch, thanks to Cersei, but only a quarter of them could be relied upon. "There's few out-and-out traitors, though there's some, even your spider hasn't found them all," Bywater had warned him. "But there's hundreds greener than spring grass, men who joined for bread and ale and safety. No man likes to look craven in the sight of his fellows, so they'll fight brave enough at the start, when it's all warhorns and blowing banners. But if the battle looks to be going sour they'll break, and they'll break bad. The first man to throw down his spear and run will have a thousand more trodding on his heels."

To be sure, there were seasoned men in the City Watch, the core of two thousand who'd gotten their gold cloaks from Robert, not Cersei. Yet even those . . . a watchman was not truly a soldier, Lord Tywin Lannister had been fond of saying. Of knights and squires and men-at-arms, Tyrion had no more than three hundred. Soon enough, he must test the truth of another of his father's sayings: One man on a wall was worth ten beneath it.

Bronn and the escort were waiting at the foot of the quay, amidst swarming beggars, strolling whores, and fishwives crying the catch. The fishwives did more business than all the rest combined. Buyers flocked around the barrels and stalls to haggle over winkles, clams, and river pike. With no other food coming into the city, the price of fish was ten times what it had been before the war, and still rising. Those who had coin came to the riverfront each morning and each evening, in hopes of bringing home an eel or a pot of red crabs; those who did not slipped between the stalls hoping to steal, or stood gaunt and forlorn beneath the walls.

The gold cloaks cleared a path through the press, shoving people aside with the shafts of their spears. Tyrion ignored the muttered curses as best he could. A fish came sailing out of the crowd, slimy and rotten. It landed at his feet and flew to pieces. He stepped over it gingerly and climbed into his saddle. Children with swollen bellies were already fighting over pieces of the stinking fish.

Mounted, he gazed along the riverfront. Hammers rang in the morning air as carpenters swarmed over the Mud Gate, extending wooden hoardings from the battlements. Those were coming well. He was a deal less pleased by the clutter of ramshackle structures that had been allowed to grow up behind the quays, attaching themselves to the city walls like barnacles on the hull of a ship; bait shacks and pot-shops, warehouses, merchants' stalls, alehouses, the cribs where the cheaper sort of whores spread their legs. *It has to go, every bit of it.* As it was, Stannis would hardly need scaling ladders to storm the walls.

He called Bronn to his side. "Assemble a hundred men and burn everything you see here between the water's edge and the city walls." He waved his stubby fingers, taking in all the waterfront squalor. "I want nothing left standing, do you understand?"

The black-haired sellsword turned his head, considering the task. "Them as own all this won't like that much."

"I never imagined they would. So be it; they'll have something else to curse the evil monkey demon for."

"Some may fight."

"See that they lose."

"What do we do with those that live here?"

"Let them have a reasonable time to remove their property, and then move them out. Try not to kill any of them, they're not the enemy. And no more rapes! Keep your men in line, damn it."

"They're sellswords, not septons," said Bronn. "Next you'll be telling me you want them sober."

"It couldn't hurt."

Tyrion only wished he could as easily make city walls twice as tall and three times as thick. Though perhaps it did not matter. Massive walls and tall towers had not saved Storm's End, nor Harrenhal, nor even Winterfell.

He remembered Winterfell as he had last seen it. Not as grotesquely huge as Harrenhal, nor as solid and impregnable to look at as Storm's End, yet there had been a great strength in those stones, a sense that within those walls a man might feel safe. The news of the castle's fall had come as a wrenching shock. "The gods give with one hand and take with the other," he muttered under his breath when Varys told him. They had given the Starks Harrenhal and taken Winterfell, a dismal exchange.

No doubt he should be rejoicing. Robb Stark would have to turn north now. If he could not defend his own home and hearth, he was no sort of king at all. It meant reprieve for the west, for House Lannister, and yet . . .

Tyrion had only the vaguest memory of Theon Greyjoy from his time with the Starks. A callow youth, always smiling, skilled with a bow; it was hard to imagine him as Lord of Winterfell. The Lord of Winterfell would always be a Stark.

He remembered their godswood; the tall sentinels armored in their grey-green needles, the great oaks, the hawthorn and ash and soldier pines, and at the center the heart tree standing like some pale giant frozen in time. He could almost smell the place, earthy and brooding, the smell of centuries, and he remembered how dark the wood had been even by day. *That wood was Winterfell. It was the north. I never felt so out of place as I did when I walked there, so much an unwelcome intruder.* He wondered if the Greyjoys would feel it too. The castle might well be theirs, but never that godswood. Not in a year, or ten, or fifty.

Tyrion Lannister walked his horse slowly toward the Mud Gate. *Winterfell is nothing to you,* he reminded himself. *Be glad the place has fallen, and look to your own walls.* The gate was open. Inside, three great trebuchets stood side by side in the market square, peering over the battlements like three huge birds. Their throwing arms were made from the trunks of old oaks, and banded with iron to keep them from splitting. The gold cloaks had named them the Three Whores, because they'd be giving Lord Stannis such a lusty welcome. *Or so we hope.*

Tyrion put his heels into his horse and trotted through the Mud Gate, breasting the human tide. Once beyond the Whores, the press grew thinner and the street opened up around him.

The ride back to the Red Keep was uneventful, but at the Tower of the Hand he found a dozen angry trader captains waiting in his audience chamber to protest the seizure of their ships. He gave them a sincere apology and promised compensation once the war was done. That did little to appease them. "What if you should lose, my lord?" one Braavosi asked.

"Then apply to King Stannis for your compensation."

By the time he rid himself of them, bells were ringing and Tyrion knew he would be late for the installation. He waddled across the yard almost at a run and crowded into the back of the castle sept as Joffrey fastened white silk cloaks about the shoulders of the two newest members of his Kingsguard. The rite seemed to require that everyone stand, so Tyrion saw nothing but a wall of courtly arses. On the other hand, once the new High Septon was finished leading the two knights through their solemn vows and anointing them in the names of the Seven, he would be well positioned to be first out the doors.

He approved of his sister's choice of Ser Balon Swann to take the place of the slain Preston Greenfield. The Swanns were Marcher lords, proud, powerful, and cautious. Pleading illness, Lord Gulian Swann had remained in his castle, taking no part in the war, but his eldest son had ridden with Renly and now Stannis, while Balon, the younger, served at King's Landing. If he'd had a third son, Tyrion suspected he'd be off with Robb Stark. It was not perhaps the most honorable course, but it showed good sense; whoever won the Iron Throne, the Swanns intended to survive. In addition to being well born, young Ser Balon was valiant, courtly, and skilled at arms; good with a lance, better with a morningstar, superb with the bow. He would serve with honor and courage.

Alas, Tyrion could not say the same for Cersei's second choice. Ser Osmund Kettleblack *looked* formidable enough. He stood six feet and six inches, most of it sinew and muscle, and his hook nose, bushy eyebrows, and spade-shaped brown beard gave his face a fierce aspect, so long as he did not smile. Lowborn, no more than a hedge knight, Kettleblack was utterly dependent on Cersei for his advancement, which was doubtless why she'd picked him. "Ser Osmund is as loyal as he is brave," she'd told Joffrey when she put forward his name. It was true, unfortunately. The good Ser Osmund had been selling her secrets to Bronn since the day she'd hired him, but Tyrion could scarcely *tell* her that.

He supposed he ought not complain. The appointment gave him another ear close to the king, unbeknownst to his sister. And even if Ser Osmund proved an utter craven, he would be no worse than Ser Boros Blount, currently residing in a dungeon at Rosby. Ser Boros had been escorting Tommen and Lord Gyles when Ser Jacelyn Bywater and his gold cloaks had surprised them, and had yielded up his charge with an alacrity that would have enraged old Ser Barristan Selmy as much as it did Cersei; a knight of the Kingsguard was supposed to die in defense of the king and royal family. His sister had insisted that Joffrey strip Blount of his white cloak on the grounds of treason and cowardice. *And now she replaces him with another man just as hollow.*

The praying, vowing, and anointing seemed to take most of the morning. Tyrion's legs soon began to ache. He shifted his weight from one foot to the other, restless. Lady Tanda stood several rows up, he saw, but her daughter was not with her. He had been half hoping to catch a glimpse of Shae. Varys said she was doing well, but he would prefer to see for himself.

"Better a lady's maid than a pot girl," Shae had said when Tyrion told her the eunuch's scheme. "Can I take my belt of silver flowers and my gold collar with the black diamonds you said looked like my eyes? I won't wear them if you say I shouldn't."

Loath as he was to disappoint her, Tyrion had to point out that while Lady Tanda was by no means a clever woman, even she might wonder if her daughter's bedmaid seemed to own more jewelry than her daughter. "Choose two or three dresses, no more," he commanded her. "Good wool, no silk, no samite, and no fur. The rest I'll keep in my own chambers for when you visit me." It was not the answer Shae had wanted, but at least she was safe.

When the investiture was finally done Joffrey marched out between Ser Balon and Ser Osmund in their new white cloaks, while Tyrion lingered for a word with the new High Septon (who was *his* choice, and wise enough to know who put the honey on his bread). "I want the gods on our side," Tyrion told him bluntly. "Tell them that Stannis has vowed to burn the Great Sept of Baelor."

"Is it true, my lord?" asked the High Septon, a small, shrewd man with a wispy white beard and wizened face.

Tyrion shrugged. "It may be. Stannis burned the godswood at Storm's End as an offering to the Lord of Light. If he'd offend the old gods, why should he spare the new? Tell them that. Tell them that any man who thinks to give aid to the usurper betrays the gods as well as his rightful king."

"I shall, my lord. And I shall command them to pray for the health of the king and his Hand as well."

Hallyne the Pyromancer was waiting on him when Tyrion returned to his solar, and Maester Frenken had brought messages. He let the alchemist wait a little longer while he read what the ravens had brought him. There was an old letter from Doran Martell, warning him that Storm's End had fallen, and a much more intriguing one from Balon Greyjoy on Pyke, who styled himself *King of the Isles and the North*. He invited King Joffrey to send an envoy to the Iron Islands to fix the borders between their realms and discuss a possible alliance.

Tyrion read the letter three times and set it aside. Lord Balon's longships would have been a great help against the fleet sailing up from Storm's End, but they were thousands of leagues away on the wrong side of Westeros, and Tyrion was far from certain that he wanted to give away half the realm. *Perhaps I should spill this one in Cersei's lap, or take it to the council.*

Only then did he admit Hallyne with the latest tallies from the alchemists. "This cannot be true," said Tyrion as he pored over the ledgers. "Almost thirteen thousand jars? Do you take me for a fool? I'm not about to pay the king's gold for empty jars and pots of sewage sealed with wax, I warn you."

"No, no," Hallyne squeaked, "the sums are accurate, I swear. We have been, hmmm, most fortunate, my lord Hand. Another cache of Lord Rossart's was found, more than three hundred jars. Under the Dragonpit! Some whores have been using the ruins to entertain their patrons, and one of them fell through a patch of rotted floor into a cellar. When he felt the jars, he mistook them for wine. He was so drunk he broke the seal and drank some."

"There was a prince who tried that once," said Tyrion dryly. "I haven't seen any dragons rising over the city, so it would seem it didn't work this time either." The Dragonpit atop the hill of Rhaenys had been abandoned for a century and a half. He supposed it was as good a place as any to store wildfire, and better than most, but it would have been nice if the late Lord Rossart had *told* someone. "Three hundred jars, you say? That still does not account for these totals. You are several *thousand* jars ahead of the best estimate you gave me when last we met."

"Yes, yes, that's so." Hallyne mopped at his pale brow with the sleeve of his black-and-scarlet robe. "We have been working very hard, my lord Hand, hmmm."

"That would doubtless explain why you are making so much more of the substance than before." Smiling, Tyrion fixed the pyromancer with his mismatched stare. "Though it does raise the question of why you did not begin working hard until now."

Hallyne had the complexion of a mushroom, so it was hard to see how he could turn any paler, yet somehow he managed. "We *were*, my lord Hand, my brothers and I have been laboring day and night from the first, I assure you. It is only, hmmm, we have made so much of the substance that we have become, hmmm, more *practiced* as it were, and also"—the alchemist shifted uncomfortably—"certain spells, hmmm, ancient secrets of our order, very delicate, very troublesome, but necessary if the substance is to be, hmmm, all it should be . . ."

Tyrion was growing impatient. Ser Jacelyn Bywater was likely here by now, and Ironhand misliked waiting. "Yes, you have secret spells; how splendid. What of them?"

"They, hmmm, seem to be working better than they were." Hallyne smiled weakly. "You don't suppose there are any dragons about, do you?"

"Not unless you found one under the Dragonpit. Why?"

"Oh, pardon, I was just remembering something old Wisdom Pollitor told me once, when I was an acolyte. I'd asked him why so many of our spells seemed, well, not as *effectual* as the scrolls would have us believe, and he said it was because magic had begun to go out of the world the day the last dragon died."

"Sorry to disappoint you, but I've seen no dragons. I have noticed the

King's Justice lurking about, however. Should any of these fruits you're selling me turn out to be filled with anything but wildfire, you'll be seeing him as well."

Hallyne fled so quickly that he almost bowled over Ser Jacelyn—no, *Lord* Jacelyn, he must remember that. Ironhand was mercifully direct, as ever. He'd returned from Rosby to deliver a fresh levy of spearmen recruited from Lord Gyles's estates and resume his command of the City Watch. "How does my nephew fare?" Tyrion asked when they were done discussing the city's defenses.

"Prince Tommen is hale and happy, my lord. He has adopted a fawn some of my men brought home from a hunt. He had one once before, he says, but Joffrey skinned her for a jerkin. He asks about his mother sometimes, and often begins letters to the Princess Myrcella, though he never seems to finish any. His brother, however, he does not seem to miss at all."

"You have made suitable arrangements for him, should the battle be lost?"

"My men have their instructions."

"Which are?"

"You commanded me to tell no one, my lord."

That made him smile. "I'm pleased you remember." Should King's Landing fall, he might well be taken alive. Better if he did not know where Joffrey's heir might be found.

Varys appeared not long after Lord Jacelyn had left. "Men are such faithless creatures," he said by way of greeting.

Tyrion sighed. "Who's the traitor today?"

The eunuch handed him a scroll. "So much villainy, it sings a sad song for our age. Did honor die with our fathers?"

"My father is not dead yet." Tyrion scanned the list. "I know some of these names. These are rich men. Traders, merchants, craftsmen. Why should they conspire against us?"

"It seems they believe that Lord Stannis must win, and wish to share his victory. They call themselves the Antler Men, after the crowned stag."

"Someone should tell them that Stannis changed his sigil. Then they can be the Hot Hearts." It was no matter for jests, though; it appeared that these Antler Men had armed several hundred followers, to seize the Old Gate once battle was joined, and admit the enemy to the city. Among the names on the list was the master armorer Salloreon. "I suppose this means I won't be getting that terrifying helm with the demon horns," Tyrion complained as he scrawled the order for the man's arrest.

THEON

One moment he was asleep; the next, awake.

Kyra nestled against him, one arm draped lightly over his, her breasts brushing his back. He could hear her breathing, soft and steady. The sheet was tangled about them. It was the black of night. The bedchamber was dark and still.

What is it? Did I hear something? Someone?

Wind sighed faintly against the shutters. Somewhere, far off, he heard the yowl of a cat in heat. Nothing else. *Sleep, Greyjoy,* he told himself. *The castle is quiet, and you have guards posted. At your door, at the gates, on the armory.*

He might have put it down to a bad dream, but he did not remember dreaming. Kyra had worn him out. Until Theon had sent for her, she had lived all of her eighteen years in the winter town without ever setting foot inside the walls of the castle. She came to him wet and eager and lithe as a weasel, and there had been a certain undeniable spice to fucking a common tavern wench in Lord Eddard Stark's own bed.

She murmured sleepily as Theon slid out from under her arm and got to his feet. A few embers still smoldered in the hearth. Wex slept on the floor at the foot of the bed, rolled up inside his cloak and dead to the world. Nothing moved. Theon crossed to the window and threw open the shutters. Night touched him with cold fingers, and gooseprickles rose on his bare skin. He leaned against the stone sill and looked out on dark towers, empty yards, black sky, and more stars than a man could ever count if he lived to be a hundred. A half-moon floated above the Bell Tower and cast its reflection on the roof of the glass gardens. He heard no alarums, no voices, not so much as a footfall.

All's well, Greyjoy. Hear the quiet? You ought to be drunk with joy. You took Winterfell with fewer than thirty men, a feat to sing of. Theon started back to bed. He'd roll Kyra on her back and fuck her again, that ought to banish these phantoms. Her gasps and giggles would make a welcome respite from this silence.

He stopped. He had grown so used to the howling of the direwolves that he scarcely heard it anymore . . . but some part of him, some hunter's instinct, heard its absence.

Urzen stood outside his door, a sinewy man with a round shield slung over his back. "The wolves are quiet," Theon told him. "Go see what they're doing, and come straight back." The thought of the direwolves running loose gave him a queasy feeling. He remembered the day in the wolfswood when the wildlings had attacked Bran. Summer and Grey Wind had torn them to pieces.

When he prodded Wex with the toe of his boot, the boy sat up and rubbed his eyes. "Make certain Bran Stark and his little brother are in their beds, and be quick about it."

"M'lord?" Kyra called sleepily.

"Go back to sleep, this does not concern you." Theon poured himself a cup of wine and drank it down. All the time he was listening, hoping to hear a howl. *Too few men,* he thought sourly. *I have too few men. If Asha does not come . . .*

Wex returned the quickest, shaking his head side to side. Cursing, Theon found his tunic and breeches on the floor where he had dropped them in his haste to get at Kyra. Over the tunic he donned a jerkin of iron-studded leather, and he belted a longsword and dagger at his waist. His hair was wild as the wood, but he had larger concerns.

By then Urzen was back. "The wolves be gone."

Theon told himself he must be as cold and deliberate as Lord Eddard. "Rouse the castle," he said. "Herd them out into the yard, everyone, we'll see who's missing. And have Lorren make a round of the gates. Wex, with me."

He wondered if Stygg had reached Deepwood Motte yet. The man was not as skilled a rider as he claimed—none of the ironmen were much good in the saddle—but there'd been time enough. Asha might well be on her way. *And if she learns that I have lost the Starks . . .* It did not bear thinking about.

Bran's bedchamber was empty, as was Rickon's half a turn below. Theon cursed himself. He should have kept a guard on them, but he'd deemed it more important to have men walking the walls and protecting the gates than to nursemaid a couple of children, one a cripple.

Outside he heard sobbing as the castle folk were pulled from their beds and driven into the yard. *I'll give them reason to sob. I've used them gently, and this is how they repay me.* He'd even had two of his own men whipped bloody for raping that kennel girl, to show them he meant to be just. *They still blame me for the rape, though. And the rest.* He deemed that unfair. Mikken had killed himself with his mouth, just as Benfred had. As for Chayle, he had to give *someone* to the Drowned God, his men expected it. "I bear you no ill will," he'd told the septon before they threw him down the well, "but you and your gods have no place here now." You'd think the others might be grateful he hadn't chosen one of them, but no. He wondered how many of them were part of this plot against him.

Urzen returned with Black Lorren. "The Hunter's Gate," Lorren said. "Best come see."

The Hunter's Gate was conveniently sited close to the kennels and kitchens. It opened directly on fields and forests, allowing riders to come and go without first passing through the winter town, and so was favored by hunting parties. "Who had the guard here?" Theon demanded.

"Drennan and Squint."

Drennan was one of the men who'd raped Palla. "If they've let the boys escape, I'll have more than a little skin off their back this time, I swear it."

"No need for that," Black Lorren said curtly.

Nor was there. They found Squint floating facedown in the moat, his entrails drifting behind him like a nest of pale snakes. Drennan lay half-naked in the gatehouse, in the snug room where the drawbridge was worked. His throat had been opened ear to ear. A ragged tunic concealed the half-healed scars on his back, but his boots were scattered amidst the rushes, and his breeches tangled about his feet. There was cheese on a small table near the door, beside an empty flagon. And two cups.

Theon picked one up and sniffed at the dregs of wine in the bottom. "Squint was up on the wallwalk, no?"

"Aye," said Lorren.

Theon flung the cup into the hearth. "I'd say Drennan was pulling down his breeches to stick it in the woman when she stuck it in him. His own cheese knife, by the look of it. Someone find a pike and fish the other fool out of the moat."

The other fool was in a deal worse shape than Drennan. When Black Lorren drew him out of the water, they saw that one of his arms had been wrenched off at the elbow, half of his neck was missing, and there was a ragged hole where his navel and groin once had been. The pike tore through his bowels as Lorren was pulling him in. The stench was awful.

"The direwolves," Theon said. "Both of them, at a guess." Disgusted, he walked back to the drawbridge. Winterfell was encircled by two massive granite walls, with a wide moat between them. The outer wall stood eighty feet high, the inner more than a hundred. Lacking men, Theon had been forced to abandon the outer defenses and post his guards along the higher inner walls. He dared not risk having them on the wrong side of the moat should the castle rise against him.

There had to be two or more, he decided. *While the woman was entertaining Drennan, the others freed the wolves.*

Theon called for a torch and led them up the steps to the wallwalk. He swept the flame low before him, looking for . . . *there*. On the inside of the rampart and in the wide crenel between two upthrust merlons. "Blood," he announced, "clumsily mopped up. At a guess, the woman killed Drennan and lowered the drawbridge. Squint heard the clank of chains, came to have a look, and got this far. They pushed the corpse through the crenel into the moat so he wouldn't be found by another sentry."

Urzen peered along the walls. "The other watch turrets are not far. I see torches burning—"

"Torches, but no guards," Theon said testily. "Winterfell has more turrets than I have men."

"Four guards at the main gate," said Black Lorren, "and five walking the walls beside Squint."

Urzen said, "If he had sounded his horn—"

I am served by fools. "Try and imagine it was you up here, Urzen. It's dark and cold. You have been walking sentry for hours, looking forward to the end of your watch. Then you hear a noise and move toward the gate, and suddenly you see *eyes* at the top of the stair, glowing green and gold in the torchlight. Two shadows come rushing toward you faster than you can believe. You catch a glimpse of teeth, start to level your spear, and they *slam* into you and open your belly, tearing through leather as if it were cheesecloth." He gave Urzen a hard shove. "And now you're down on your back, your guts are spilling out, and one of them has his teeth around your neck." Theon grabbed the man's scrawny throat, tightened his fingers, and smiled. "Tell me, at what moment during all of this do you stop to *blow your fucking horn?*" He shoved Urzen away roughly, sending him stumbling back against a merlon. The man rubbed his throat. *I should have had those beasts put down the day we took the castle*, he thought angrily. *I'd seen them kill, I knew how dangerous they were.*

"We must go after them," Black Lorren said.

"Not in the dark." Theon did not relish the idea of chasing direwolves through the wood by night; the hunters could easily become the hunted. "We'll wait for daylight. Until then, I had best go speak with my loyal subjects."

Down in the yard, a uneasy crowd of men, women, and children had been pushed up against the wall. Many had not been given time to dress; they covered themselves with woolen blankets, or huddled naked under cloaks or bedrobes. A dozen ironmen hemmed them in, torches in one hand and weapons in the other. The wind was gusting, and the flickering orange light reflected dully off steel helms, thick beards, and unsmiling eyes.

Theon walked up and down before the prisoners, studying the faces. They *all* looked guilty to him. "How many are missing?"

"Six." Reek stepped up behind him, smelling of soap, his long hair moving in the wind. "Both Starks, that bog boy and his sister, the halfwit from the stables, and your wildling woman."

Osha. He had suspected her from the moment he saw that second cup. *I should have known better than to trust that one. She's as unnatural as Asha. Even their names sound alike.*

"Has anyone had a look at the stables?"

"Aggar says no horses are missing."

"Dancer is still in his stall?"

"Dancer?" Reek frowned. "Aggar says the horses are all there. Only the halfwit is missing."

They're afoot, then. That was the best news he'd heard since he woke. Bran would be riding in his basket on Hodor's back, no doubt. Osha would need to carry Rickon; his little legs wouldn't take him far on their own. Theon was confident that he'd soon have them back in his hands. "Bran and Rickon have fled," he told the castle folk, watching their eyes. "Who knows where they've gone?" No one answered. "They could not have escaped without help," Theon went on. "Without food, clothing, weapons." He had locked away every sword and axe in Winterfell, but no doubt some had been hidden from him. "I'll have the names of all those who aided them. All those who turned a blind eye." The only sound was the wind. "Come first light, I mean to bring them back." He hooked his thumbs through his swordbelt. "I need huntsmen. Who wants a nice warm wolfskin to see them through the winter? Gage?" The cook had always greeted him cheerfully when he returned from the hunt, to ask whether he'd brought anything choice for the table, but he had nothing to say now. Theon walked back the way he had come, searching their faces for the least sign of guilty knowledge. "The wild is no place for a cripple. And Rickon, young as he is, how long will he last out there? Nan, think how frightened he must be." The old woman had nattered at him for ten years, telling her endless stories, but now she gaped at him as if he were some stranger. "I might have killed every man of you and given your women to my soldiers for their pleasure, but instead I protected you. Is this the thanks you offer?" Joseth who'd groomed his horses, Farlen who'd taught him all he knew of hounds, Barth the brewer's wife who'd been his first—not one of them would meet his eyes. *They hate me*, he realized.

Reek stepped close. "Strip off their skins," he urged, his thick lips glistening. "Lord Bolton, he used to say a naked man has few secrets, but a flayed man's got none."

The flayed man was the sigil of House Bolton, Theon knew; ages past, certain of their lords had gone so far as to cloak themselves in the skins of dead enemies. A number of Starks had ended thus. Supposedly all that had stopped a thousand years ago, when the Boltons had bent their knees to Winterfell. *Or so they say, but old ways die hard, as well I know.*

"There will be no flaying in the north so long as I rule in Winterfell," Theon said loudly. *I am your only protection against the likes of him*, he wanted to scream. He could not be that blatant, but perhaps some were clever enough to take the lesson.

The sky was greying over the castle walls. Dawn could not be far off. "Joseth, saddle Smiler and a horse for yourself. Murch, Gariss, Poxy Tym, you'll come as well." Murch and Gariss were the best huntsmen in the castle, and Tym was a fine bowman. "Aggar, Rednose, Gelmarr, Reek, Wex." He needed his own to watch his back. "Farlen, I'll want hounds, and you to handle them."

The grizzled kennelmaster crossed his arms. "And why would I care to hunt down my own trueborn lords, and babes at that?"

Theon moved close. "I am your trueborn lord now, and the man who keeps Palla safe."

He saw the defiance die in Farlen's eyes. "Aye, m'lord."

Stepping back, Theon glanced about to see who else he might add. "Maester Luwin," he announced.

"I know nothing of hunting."

No, but I don't trust you in the castle in my absence. "Then it's past time you learned."

"Let me come too. I want that wolfskin cloak." A boy stepped forward, no older than Bran. It took Theon a moment to remember him. "I've hunted lots of times before," Walder Frey said. "Red deer and elk, and even boar."

His cousin laughed at him. "He rode on a boar hunt with his father, but they never let him near the boar."

Theon look at the boy doubtfully. "Come if you like, but if you can't keep up, don't think that I'll nurse you along." He turned back to Black

Lorren. "Winterfell is yours in my absence. If we do not return, do with it as you will." *That bloody well ought to have them praying for my success.*

They assembled by the Hunter's Gate as the first pale rays of the sun brushed the top of the Bell Tower, their breath frosting in the cold morning air. Gelmarr had equipped himself with a longaxe whose reach would allow him to strike before the wolves were on him. The blade was heavy enough to kill with a single blow. Aggar wore steel greaves. Reek arrived carrying a boar spear and an overstuffed washerwoman's sack bulging with god knows what. Theon had his bow; he needed nothing else. Once he had saved Bran's life with an arrow. He hoped he would not need to take it with another, but if it came to that, he would.

Eleven men, two boys, and a dozen dogs crossed the moat. Beyond the outer wall, the tracks were plain to read in the soft ground; the pawprints of the wolves, Hodor's heavy tread, the shallower marks left by the feet of the two Reeds. Once under the trees, the stony ground and fallen leaves made the trail harder to see, but by then Farlen's red bitch had the scent. The rest of the dogs were close behind, the hounds sniffing and barking, a pair of monstrous mastiffs bringing up the rear. Their size and ferocity might make the difference against a cornered direwolf.

He'd have guessed that Osha might run south to Ser Rodrik, but the trail led north by northwest, into the very heart of the wolfswood. Theon did not like that one bit. It would be a bitter irony if the Starks made for Deepwood Motte and delivered themselves right into Asha's hands. *I'd sooner have them dead*, he thought bitterly. *It is better to be seen as cruel than foolish.*

Wisps of pale mist threaded between the trees. Sentinels and soldier pines grew thick about here, and there was nothing as dark and gloomy as an evergreen forest. The ground was uneven, and the fallen needles disguised the softness of the turf and made the footing treacherous for the horses, so they had to go slowly. *Not as slowly as a man carrying a cripple, though, or a bony harridan with a four-year-old on her back.* He told himself to be patient. He'd have them before the day was out.

Maester Luwin trotted up to him as they were following a game trail along the lip of a ravine. "Thus far hunting seems indistinguishable from riding through the woods, my lord."

Theon smiled. "There are similarities. But with hunting, there's blood at the end."

"Must it be so? This flight was great folly, but will you not be merciful? These are your foster brothers we seek."

"No Stark but Robb was ever brotherly toward me, but Bran and Rickon have more value to me living than dead."

"The same is true of the Reeds. Moat Cailin sits on the edge of the bogs. Lord Howland can make your uncle's occupation a visit to hell if he chooses, but so long as you hold his heirs he must stay his hand."

Theon had not considered that. In truth, he had scarcely considered the mudmen at all, beyond eyeing Meera once or twice and wondering if she was still a maiden. "You may be right. We will spare them if we can."

"And Hodor too, I hope. The boy is simple, you know that. He does as he is told. How many times has he groomed your horse, soaped your saddle, scoured your mail?"

Hodor was nothing to him. "If he does not fight us, we will let him live." Theon pointed a finger. "But say one word about sparing the wildling, and you can die with her. She swore me an oath, and pissed on it."

The maester inclined his head. "I make no apologies for oathbreakers. Do what you must. I thank you for your mercy."

Mercy, thought Theon as Luwin dropped back. *There's a bloody trap. Too much and they call you weak, too little and you're monstrous.* Yet the maester had given him good counsel, he knew. His father thought only in terms of conquest, but what good was it to take a kingdom if you could not hold it? Force and fear could carry you only so far. A pity Ned Stark had taken his daughters south; elsewise Theon could have tightened his grip on Winterfell by marrying one of them. Sansa was a pretty little thing too, and by now likely even ripe for bedding. But she was a thousand leagues away, in the clutches of the Lannisters. A shame.

The wood grew ever wilder. The pines and sentinels gave way to huge dark oaks. Tangles of hawthorn concealed treacherous gullies and cuts. Stony hills rose and fell. They passed a crofter's cottage, deserted and overgown, and skirted a flooded quarry where the still water had a sheen as grey as steel. When the dogs began to bay, Theon figured the fugitives were near at hand. He spurred Smiler and followed at a trot, but what he found was only the carcass of a young elk . . . or what remained of it.

He dismounted for a closer look. The kill was still fresh, and plainly the work of wolves. The dogs sniffed round it eagerly, and one of the mastiffs buried his teeth in a haunch until Farlen shouted him off. *No part of this animal has been butchered*, Theon realized. *The wolves ate, but not the men.* Even if Osha did not want to risk a fire, she ought to have cut them a few steaks. It made no sense to leave so much good meat to rot. "Farlen, are you certain we're on the right trail?" he demanded. "Could your dogs be chasing the wrong wolves?"

"My bitch knows the smell of Summer and Shaggy well enough."

"I hope so. For your sake."

Less than an hour later, the trail led down a slope toward a muddy brook swollen by the recent rains. It was there the dogs lost the scent. Farlen and Wex waded across with the hounds and came back shaking their heads while the animals ranged up and down the far bank, sniffing. "They went in here, m'lord, but I can't see where they come out," the kennelmaster said.

Theon dismounted and knelt beside the stream. He dipped a hand in it. The water was cold. "They won't have stayed long in this," he said. "Take half the dogs downstream, I'll go up—"

Wex clapped his hands together loudly.

"What is it?" Theon said.

The mute boy pointed.

The ground near the water was sodden and muddy. The tracks the wolves had left were plain enough. "Pawprints, yes. So?"

Wex drove his heel into the mud, and pivoted his foot this way and that. It left a deep gouge.

Joseth understood. "A man the size of Hodor ought to have left a deep print in this mud," he said. "More so with the weight of a boy on his back. Yet the only boot prints here are our own. See for yourself."

Appalled, Theon saw it was true. The wolves had gone into the turgid brown water alone. "Osha must have turned aside back of us. Before the elk, most likely. She sent the wolves on by themselves, hoping we'd chase after them." He rounded on his huntsmen. "If you two have played me false—"

"There's been only the one trail, my lord, I swear it," said Gariss defensively. "And the direwolves would never have parted from them boys. Not for long."

That's so, Theon thought. Summer and Shaggydog might have gone off to hunt, but soon or late they would return to Bran and Rickon. "Gariss, Murch, take four dogs and double back, find where we lost them. Aggar, you watch them, I'll have no trickery. Farlen and I will follow the direwolves. Give a blast on the horn when you pick up the trail. Two blasts if you catch sight of the beasts themselves. Once we find where they went, they'll lead us back to their masters."

He took Wex, the Frey boy, and Gynir Rednose to search upstream. He and Wex rode on one side of the brook, Rednose and Walder Frey on the other, each with a pair of hounds. The wolves might have come out on either bank. Theon kept an eye out for tracks, spoor, broken branches, any hint as to where the direwolves might have left the water. He spied the prints of deer, elk, and badger easily enough. Wex surprised a vixen drinking at the stream, and Walder flushed three rabbits from the underbrush and managed to put an arrow in one. They saw the claw marks where a bear had shredded the bark of a tall birch. But of the direwolves there was no sign.

A little farther, Theon told himself. *Past that oak, over that rise, past the next bend of the stream, we'll find something there*. He pressed on long after he knew he should turn back, a growing sense of anxiety gnawing at his belly. It was midday when he wrenched Smiler's head round in disgust and gave up.

Somehow Osha and the wretched boys were eluding him. It should not have been possible, not on foot, burdened with a cripple and a young child. Every passing hour increased the likelihood that they would make good their escape. *If they reach a village* . . . The people of the north would never deny Ned Stark's sons, Robb's brothers. They'd have mounts to speed them on their way, food. Men would fight for the honor of protecting them. The whole bloody north would rally around them.

The wolves went downstream, that's all. He clung to that thought. *That red bitch will sniff where they came out of the water and we'll be after them again.*

But when they joined up with Farlen's party, one look at the kennelmaster's face smashed all of Theon's hopes to shards. "The only thing those dogs are fit for is a bear baiting," he said angrily. "Would that I had a bear."

"The dogs are not at fault." Farlen knelt between a mastiff and his precious red bitch, a hand on each. "Running water don't hold no scents, m'lord."

"The wolves had to come out of the stream *somewhere*."

"No doubt they did. Upstream or down. We keep on, we'll find the place, but which way?"

"I never knew a wolf to run up a streambed for miles," said Reek. "A man might. If he knew he was being hunted, he might. But a wolf?"

Yet Theon wondered. These beasts were not as other wolves. *I should have skinned the cursed things.*

It was the same tale all over again when they rejoined Gariss, Murch, and Aggar. The huntsmen had retraced their steps halfway to Winterfell without finding any sign of where the Starks might have parted company with the direwolves. Farlen's hounds seemed as frustrated as their masters, sniffing forlornly at trees and rocks and snapping irritably at each other.

Theon dared not admit defeat. "We'll return to the brook. Search again. This time we'll go as far as we must."

"We won't find them," the Frey boy said suddenly. "Not so long as the frogeaters are with them. Mudmen are sneaks, they won't fight like decent folks, they skulk and use poison arrows. You never see them, but they see you. Those who go into the bogs after them get lost and never come out. Their houses *move*, even the castles like Greywater Watch." He glanced nervously at greenery that encircled them on all sides. "They might be out there right now, listening to everything we say."

Farlen laughed to show what he thought of that notion. "My dogs would smell anything in them bushes. Be all over them before you could break wind, boy."

"Frogeaters don't smell like men," Frey insisted. "They have a boggy stink, like frogs and trees and scummy water. Moss grows under their arms in place of hair, and they can live with nothing to eat but mud and breathe swamp water."

Theon was about to tell him what he ought to do with his wet nurse's fable when Maester Luwin spoke up. "The histories say the crannogmen grew close to the children of the forest in the days when the greenseers tried to bring the hammer of the waters down upon the Neck. It may be that they have secret knowledge."

Suddenly the wood seemed a deal darker than it had a moment before, as if a cloud had passed before the sun. It was one thing to have some fool boy spouting folly, but maesters were supposed to be wise. "The only children that concern me are Bran and Rickon," Theon said. "Back to the stream. Now."

For a moment he did not think they were going to obey, but in the end old habit asserted itself. They followed sullenly, but they followed. The Frey boy was as jumpy as those rabbits he'd flushed earlier. Theon put men on either bank and followed the current. They rode for miles, going slow and careful, dismounting to lead the horses over treacherous ground, letting the good-for-bear-bait hounds sniff at every bush. Where a fallen tree dammed the flow, the hunters were forced to loop around a deep green pool, but if the direwolves had done the same they'd left neither print nor spoor. The beasts had taken to swimming, it seemed. *When I catch them, they'll have all the swimming they can stomach. I'll give them both to the Drowned God.*

When the woods began to darken, Theon Greyjoy knew he was beaten. Either the crannogmen *did* know the magic of the children of the forest, or else Osha had deceived them with some wildling trick. He made them press on through the dusk, but when the last light faded Joseth finally worked up the courage to say, "This is fruitless, my lord. We will lame a horse, break a leg."

"Joseth has the right of it," said Maester Luwin. "Groping through the woods by torchlight will avail us nothing."

Theon could taste bile at the back of his throat, and his stomach was a nest of snakes twining and snapping at each other. If he crept back to Winterfell empty-handed, he might as well dress in motley henceforth and wear a pointed hat; the whole north would know him for a fool. *And when my father hears, and Asha . . .*

"M'lord prince." Reek urged his horse near. "Might be them Starks never came this way. If I was them, I would have gone north and east, maybe. To the Umbers. Good Stark men, they are. But their lands are a long way. The boys will shelter someplace nearer. Might be I know where."

Theon looked at him suspiciously. "Tell me."

"You know that old mill, sitting lonely on the Acorn Water? We stopped there when I was being dragged to Winterfell a captive. The miller's wife sold us hay for our horses while that old knight clucked over her brats. Might be the Starks are hiding there."

Theon knew the mill. He had even tumbled the miller's wife a time or two. There was nothing special about it, or her. "Why there? There are a dozen villages and holdfasts just as close."

Amusement shone in those pale eyes. "Why? Now that's past knowing. But they're there, I have a feeling."

He was growing sick of the man's sly answers. *His lips look like two worms fucking.* "What are you saying? If you've kept some knowledge from me—"

"M'lord prince?" Reek dismounted, and beckoned Theon to do the same. When they were both afoot, he pulled open the cloth sack he'd fetched from Winterfell. "Have a look here."

It was growing hard to see. Theon thrust his hand into the sack impatiently, groping amongst soft fur and rough scratchy wool. A sharp point pricked his skin, and his fingers closed around something cold and hard. He drew out a wolf's-head brooch, silver and jet. Understanding came suddenly. His hand closed into a fist. "Gelmarr," he said, wondering whom he could trust. *None of them.* "Aggar. Rednose. With us. The rest of you may return to Winterfell with the hounds. I'll have no further need of them. I know where Bran and Rickon are hiding now."

"Prince Theon," Maester Luwin entreated, "you will remember your promise? Mercy, you said."

"Mercy was for this morning," said Theon. *It is better to be feared than laughed at.* "Before they made me angry."

JON

They could see the fire in the night, glimmering against the side of the mountain like a fallen star. It burned redder than the other stars, and did not twinkle, though sometimes it flared up bright and sometimes dwindled down to no more than a distant spark, dull and faint.

Half a mile ahead and two thousand feet up, Jon judged, *and perfectly placed to see anything moving in the pass below.*

"Watchers in the Skirling Pass," wondered the oldest among them. In the spring of his youth, he had been squire to a king, so the black brothers still called him Squire Dalbridge. "What is it Mance Rayder fears, I wonder?"

"If he knew they'd lit a fire, he'd flay the poor bastards," said Ebben, a squat bald man muscled like a bag of rocks.

"Fire is life up here," said Qhorin Halfhand, "but it can be death as well." By his command, they'd risked no open flames since entering the mountains. They ate cold salt beef, hard bread, and harder cheese, and slept clothed and huddled beneath a pile of cloaks and furs, grateful for each other's warmth. It made Jon remember cold nights long ago at Winterfell, when he'd shared a bed with his brothers. These men were brothers too, though the bed they shared was stone and earth.

"They'll have a horn," said Stonesnake.

The Halfhand said, "A horn they must not blow."

"That's a long cruel climb by night," Ebben said as he eyed the distant spark through a cleft in the rocks that sheltered them. The sky was cloudless, the jagged mountains rising black on black until the very top, where their cold crowns of snow and ice shone palely in the moonlight.

"And a longer fall," said Qhorin Halfhand. "Two men, I think. There are like to be two up there, sharing the watch."

"Me." The ranger they called Stonesnake had already shown that he was the best climber among them. It would have to be him.

"And me," said Jon Snow.

Qhorin Halfhand looked at him. Jon could hear the wind keening as it shivered through the high pass above them. One of the garrons whickered and pawed at the thin stony soil of the hollow where they had taken shelter. "The wolf will remain with us," Qhorin said. "White fur is seen too easily by moonlight." He turned to Stonesnake. "When it's done, throw down a burning brand. We'll come when we see it fall."

"No better time to start than now," said Stonesnake.

They each took a long coil of rope. Stonesnake carried a bag of iron spikes as well, and a small hammer with its head wrapped in thick felt. Their garrons they left behind, along with their helms, mail, and Ghost. Jon knelt and let the direwolf nuzzle him before they set off. "Stay," he commanded. "I'll be back for you."

Stonesnake took the lead. He was a short wiry man, near fifty and grey of beard but stronger than he seemed, and he had the best night eyes of anyone Jon had ever known. He needed them tonight. By day the mountains were blue-grey, brushed with frost, but once the sun vanished behind the jagged peaks they turned black. Now the rising moon had limned them in white and silver.

The black brothers moved through black shadows amidst black rocks, working their way up a steep, twisting trail as their breath frosted in the black air. Jon felt almost naked without his mail, but he did not miss its weight. This was hard going, and slow. To hurry here was to risk a broken ankle or worse. Stonesnake seemed to know where to put his feet as if by instinct, but Jon needed to be more careful on the broken, uneven ground.

The Skirling Pass was really a series of passes, a long twisting course that went up around a succession of icy wind-carved peaks and down through hidden valleys that seldom saw the sun. Apart from his companions, Jon had glimpsed no living man since they'd left the wood behind and begun to make their way upward. The Frostfangs were as cruel as any place the gods had made, and as inimical to men. The wind cut like a knife up here, and shrilled in the night like a mother mourning her slain children. What few trees they saw were stunted, grotesque things growing sideways out of cracks and fissures. Tumbled shelves of rock often overhung the trail, fringed with hanging icicles that looked like long white teeth from a distance.

Yet even so, Jon Snow was not sorry he had come. There were wonders here as well. He had seen sunlight flashing on icy thin waterfalls as they plunged over the lips of sheer stone cliffs, and a mountain meadow full of autumn wildflowers, blue coldsnaps and bright scarlet frostfires and stands of piper's grass in russet and gold. He had peered down ravines so deep and black they seemed certain to end in some hell, and he had ridden his garron over a wind-eaten bridge of natural stone with nothing but sky to either side. Eagles nested in the heights and came down to hunt the valleys, circling effortlessly on great blue-grey wings that seemed almost part of the sky. Once he had watched a shadowcat stalk a ram, flowing down the mountainside like liquid smoke until it was ready to pounce.

Now it is our turn to pounce. He wished he could move as sure and silent as that shadowcat, and kill as quickly. Longclaw was sheathed across his back, but he might not have room to use it. He carried dirk and dagger for closer work. *They will have weapons as well, and I am not armored.* He wondered who would prove the shadowcat by night's end, and who the ram.

For a long way they stayed to the trail, following its twists and turns as it snaked along the side of the mountain, upward, ever upward. Sometimes the mountain folded back on itself and they lost sight of the fire, but soon or late it would always reappear. The path Stonesnake chose would never have served for the horses. In places Jon had to put his back to the cold stone and shuffle along sideways like a crab, inch by inch. Even where the track widened it was treacherous; there were cracks big enough to swallow a man's leg, rubble to stumble over, hollow places where the water pooled by day and froze hard by night. *One step and then another,* Jon told himself. *One step and then another, and I will not fall.*

He had not shaved since leaving the Fist of the First Men, and the hair on his lip was soon stiff with frost. Two hours into the climb, the wind kicked up so fiercely that it was all he could do to hunch down and cling to the rock, praying he would not be blown off the mountain. *One step and then another,* he resumed when the gale subsided. *One step and then another, and I will not fall.*

Soon they were high enough so that looking down was best not considered. There was nothing below but yawning blackness, nothing above but moon and stars. "The mountain is your mother," Stonesnake had told him during an easier climb a few days past. "Cling to her, press your face up against her teats, and she won't drop you." Jon had made a joke of it, saying how he'd always wondered who his mother was, but never thought to find her in the Frostfangs. It did not seem nearly so amusing now. *One step and then another*, he thought, clinging tight.

The narrow track ended abruptly where a massive shoulder of black granite thrust out from the side of the mountain. After the bright moonlight, its shadow was so black that it felt like stepping into a cave. "Straight up here," the ranger said in a quiet voice. "We want to get above them." He peeled off his gloves, tucked them through his belt, tied one end of his rope around his waist, the other end around Jon. "Follow me when the rope grows taut." The ranger did not wait for an answer but started at once, moving upward with fingers and feet, faster than Jon would have believed. The long rope unwound slowly. Jon watched him closely, making note of how he went, and where he found each handhold, and when the last loop of hemp uncoiled, he took off his own gloves and followed, much more slowly.

Stonesnake had passed the rope around the smooth spike of rock he was waiting on, but as soon as Jon reached him he shook it loose and was off again. This time there was no convenient cleft when he reached the end of their tether, so he took out his felt-headed hammer and drove a spike deep into a crack in the stone with a series of gentle taps. Soft as the sounds were, they echoed off the stone so loudly that Jon winced with every blow, certain that the wildlings must hear them too. When the spike was secure, Stonesnake secured the rope to it, and Jon started after him. *Suck on the mountain's teat*, he reminded himself. *Don't look down. Keep your weight above your feet. Don't look down. Look at the rock in front of you. There's a good handhold, yes. Don't look down. I can catch a breath on that ledge there, all I need to do is reach it. Never look down.*

Once his foot slipped as he put his weight on it and his heart stopped in his chest, but the gods were good and he did not fall. He could feel the cold seeping off the rock into his fingers, but he dared not don his gloves; gloves would slip, no matter how tight they seemed, cloth and fur moving between skin and stone, and up here that could kill him. His burned hand was stiffening up on him, and soon it began to ache. Then he ripped open his thumbnail somehow, and after that he left smears of blood wherever he put his hand. He hoped he still had all his fingers by the end of the climb.

Up they went, and up, and up, black shadows creeping across the moonlit wall of rock. Anyone down on the floor of the pass could have seen them easily, but the mountain hid them from the view of the wildlings by their fire. They were close now, though. Jon could sense it. Even so, he did not think of the foes who were waiting for him, all unknowing, but of his brother at Winterfell. *Bran used to love to climb. I wish I had a tenth part of his courage.*

The wall was broken two-thirds of the way up by a crooked fissure of icy stone. Stonesnake reached down a hand to help him up. He had donned his gloves again, so Jon did the same. The ranger moved his head to the left, and the two of them crawled along the shelf three hundred yards or more, until they could see the dull orange glow beyond the lip of the cliff.

The wildlings had built their watchfire in a shallow depression above the narrowest part of the pass, with a sheer drop below and rock behind to shelter them from the worst of the wind. That same windbreak allowed the black brothers to crawl within a few feet of them, creeping along on their bellies until they were looking down on the men they must kill.

One was asleep, curled up tight and buried beneath a great mound of skins. Jon could see nothing of him but his hair, bright red in the firelight. The second sat close to the flames, feeding them twigs and branches and complaining of the wind in a querulous tone. The third watched the pass, though there was little to see, only a vast bowl of darkness ringed by the snowy shoulders of the mountains. It was the watcher who wore the horn.

Three. For a moment Jon was uncertain. *There was only supposed to be two.* One was asleep, though. And whether there was two or three or twenty, he still must do what he had come to do. Stonesnake touched his arm, pointed at the wildling with the horn. Jon nodded toward the one by the fire. It felt queer, picking a man to kill. Half the days of his life had been spent with sword and shield, training for this moment. *Did Robb feel this way before his first battle?* he wondered, but there was no time to ponder the question. Stonesnake moved as fast as his namesake, leaping down on the wildlings in a rain of pebbles. Jon slid Longclaw from its sheath and followed.

It all seemed to happen in a heartbeat. Afterward Jon could admire the courage of the wildling who reached first for his horn instead of his blade. He got it to his lips, but before he could sound it Stonesnake knocked the horn aside with a swipe of his shortsword. Jon's man leapt to his feet, thrusting at his face with a burning brand. He could feel the heat of the flames as he flinched back. Out of the corner of his eye, he saw the sleeper stirring, and knew he must finish his man quick. When the brand swung again, he bulled into it, swinging the bastard sword with both hands. The Valyrian steel sheared through leather, fur, wool, and flesh, but when the wildling fell he twisted, ripping the sword from Jon's grasp. On the ground the sleeper sat up beneath his furs. Jon slid his dirk free, grabbing the man by the hair and jamming the point of the knife up under his chin as he reached for his—no, *her*—

His hand froze. "A girl."

"A watcher," said Stonesnake. "A wildling. Finish her."

Jon could see fear and fire in her eyes. Blood ran down her white throat from where the point of his dirk had pricked her. *One thrust and it's done*, he told himself. He was so close he could smell onion on her breath. *She is no older than I am.* Something about her made him think of Arya, though they looked nothing at all alike. "Will you yield?" he asked, giving the dirk a half turn. *And if she doesn't?*

"I yield." Her words steamed in the cold air.

"You're our captive, then." He pulled the dirk away from the soft skin of her throat.

"Qhorin said nothing of taking captives," said Stonesnake.

"He never said not to." Jon let go his grip on the girl's hair, and she scuttled backward, away from them.

"She's a spearwife." Stonesnake gestured at the long-hafted axe that lay beside her sleeping furs. "She was reaching for that when you grabbed her. Give her half a chance and she'll bury it between your eyes."

"I won't give her half a chance." Jon kicked the axe well out of the girl's reach. "Do you have a name?"

"Ygritte." Her hand rubbed at her throat and came away bloody. She stared at the wetness.

Sheathing his dirk, he wrenched Longclaw free from the body of the man he'd killed. "You are my captive, Ygritte."

"I gave you my name."

"I'm Jon Snow."

She flinched. "An evil name."

"A bastard name," he said. "My father was Lord Eddard Stark of Winterfell."

The girl watched him warily, but Stonesnake gave a mordant chuckle. "It's the captive supposed to tell things, remember?" The ranger thrust a long branch into the fire. "Not that she will. I've known wildlings to bite off their own tongues before they'd answer a question." When the end of the branch was blazing merrily, he took two steps and flung it out over the pass. It fell through the night spinning until it was lost to sight.

"You ought to burn them you killed," said Ygritte.

"Need a bigger fire for that, and big fires burn bright." Stonesnake turned, his eyes scanning the black distance for any spark of light. "Are there more wildlings close by, is that it?"

"Burn them," the girl repeated stubbornly, "or it might be you'll need them swords again."

Jon remembered dead Othor and his cold black hands. "Maybe we should do as she says."

"There are other ways." Stonesnake knelt beside the man he'd slain, stripped him of cloak and boots and belt and vest, then hoisted the body over one thin shoulder and carried it to the edge. He grunted as he tossed it over. A moment later they heard a wet, heavy smack well below them. By then the ranger had the second body down to the skin and was dragging it by the arms. Jon took the feet and together they flung the dead man out in the blackness of the night.

Ygritte watched and said nothing. She was older than he'd thought at first, Jon realized; maybe as old as twenty, but short for her age, bandy-legged, with a round face, small hands, and a pug nose. Her shaggy mop of red hair stuck out in all directions. She looked plump as she crouched there, but most of that was layers of fur and wool and leather. Underneath all that she could be as skinny as Arya.

"Were you sent to watch for us?" Jon asked her.

"You, and others."

Stonesnake warmed his hands over the fire. "What waits beyond the pass?"

"The free folk."

"How many?"

"Hundreds and thousands. More than you ever saw, crow." She smiled. Her teeth were crooked, but very white.

She doesn't know how many. "Why come here?"

Ygritte fell silent.

"What's in the Frostfangs that your king could want? You can't stay here, there's no food."

She turned her face away from him.

"Do you mean to march on the Wall? When?"

She stared at the flames as if she could not hear him.

"Do you know anything of my uncle, Benjen Stark?"

Ygritte ignored him. Stonesnake laughed. "If she spits out her tongue, don't say I didn't warn you."

A low rumbling growl echoed off the rock. *Shadowcat,* Jon knew at once. As he rose he heard another, closer at hand. He pulled his sword and turned, listening.

"They won't trouble us," Ygritte said. "It's the dead they've come for. Cats can smell blood six miles off. They'll stay near the bodies till they've eaten every last stringy shred o' meat, and cracked the bones for the marrow."

Jon could hear the sounds of their feeding echoing off the rocks. It gave him an uneasy feeling. The warmth of the fire made him realize how bone-tired he was, but he dared not sleep. He had taken a captive, and it was on him to guard her. "Were they your kin?" he asked her quietly. "The two we killed?"

"No more than you are."

"Me?" He frowned. "What do you mean?"

"You said you were the Bastard o' Winterfell."

"I am."

"Who was your mother?"

"Some woman. Most of them are." Someone had said that to him once. He did not remember who.

She smiled again, a flash of white teeth. "And she never sung you the song o' the winter rose?"

"I never knew my mother. Or any such song."

"Bael the Bard made it," said Ygritte. "He was King-beyond-the-Wall a long time back. All the free folk know his songs, but might be you don't sing them in the south."

"Winterfell's not in the south," Jon objected.

"Yes it is. Everything below the Wall's south to us."

He had never thought of it that way. "I suppose it's all in where you're standing."

"Aye," Ygritte agreed. "It always is."

"Tell me," Jon urged her. It would be hours before Qhorin came up, and a story would help keep him awake. "I want to hear this tale of yours."

"Might be you won't like it much."

"I'll hear it all the same."

"Brave black crow," she mocked. "Well, long before he was king over the free folk, Bael was a great raider."

Stonesnake gave a snort. "A murderer, robber, and raper, is what you mean."

"That's all in where you're standing too," Ygritte said. "The Stark in Winterfell wanted Bael's head, but never could take him, and the taste o' failure galled him. One day in his bitterness he called Bael a craven who preyed only on the weak. When word o' that got back, Bael vowed to teach the lord a lesson. So he scaled the Wall, skipped down the kingsroad, and walked into Winterfell one winter's night with harp in hand, naming himself Sygerrik of Skagos. *Sygerrik* means 'deceiver' in the Old Tongue, that the First Men spoke, and the giants still speak.

"North or south, singers always find a ready welcome, so Bael ate at Lord Stark's own table, and played for the lord in his high seat until half the night was gone. The old songs he played, and new ones he'd made himself, and he played and sang so well that when he was done, the lord offered to let him name his own reward. 'All I ask is a flower,'

Bael answered, 'the fairest flower that blooms in the gardens o'
Winterfell.'

"Now as it happened the winter roses had only then come into bloom,
and no flower is so rare nor precious. So the Stark sent to his glass
gardens and commanded that the most beautiful o' the winter roses be
plucked for the singer's payment. And so it was done. But when morning
come, the singer had vanished . . . and so had Lord Brandon's maiden
daughter. Her bed they found empty, but for the pale blue rose that Bael
had left on the pillow where her head had lain."

Jon had never heard this tale before. "Which Brandon was this supposed to be? Brandon the Builder lived in the Age of Heroes, thousands of
years before Bael. There was Brandon the Burner and his father Brandon
the Shipwright, but—"

"This was Brandon the Daughterless," Ygritte said sharply. "Would
you hear the tale, or no?"

He scowled. "Go on."

"Lord Brandon had no other children. At his behest, the black crows
flew forth from their castles in the hundreds, but nowhere could they
find any sign o' Bael or this maid. For most a year they searched, till the
lord lost heart and took to his bed, and it seemed as though the line o'
Starks was at its end. But one night as he lay waiting to die, Lord Brandon heard a child's cry. He followed the sound and found his daughter
back in her bedchamber, asleep with a babe at her breast."

"Bael had brought her back?"

"No. They had been in Winterfell all the time, hiding with the dead
beneath the castle. The maid loved Bael so dearly she bore him a son, the
song says . . . though if truth be told, all the maids love Bael in them
songs he wrote. Be that as it may, what's certain is that Bael left the child
in payment for the rose he'd plucked unasked, and that the boy grew to
be the next Lord Stark. So there it is—you have Bael's blood in you, same
as me."

"It never happened," Jon said.

She shrugged. "Might be it did, might be it didn't. It is a good song,
though. My mother used to sing it to me. She was a woman too, Jon
Snow. Like yours." She rubbed her throat where his dirk had cut her.
"The song ends when they find the babe, but there is a darker end to the
story. Thirty years later, when Bael was King-beyond-the-Wall and led
the free folk south, it was young Lord Stark who met him at the Frozen
Ford . . . and killed him, for Bael would not harm his own son when
they met sword to sword."

"So the son slew the father instead," said Jon.

"Aye," she said, "but the gods hate kinslayers, even when they kill
unknowing. When Lord Stark returned from the battle and his mother

saw Bael's head upon his spear, she threw herself from a tower in her grief. Her son did not long outlive her. One o' his lords peeled the skin off him and wore him for a cloak."

"Your Bael was a liar," he told her, certain now.

"No," Ygritte said, "but a bard's truth is different than yours or mine. Anyway, you asked for the story, so I told it." She turned away from him, closed her eyes, and seemed to sleep.

Dawn and Qhorin Halfhand arrived together. The black stones had turned to grey and the eastern sky had gone indigo when Stonesnake spied the rangers below, wending their way upward. Jon woke his captive and held her by the arm as they descended to meet them. Thankfully, there was another way off the mountain to the north and west, along paths much gentler than the one that had brought them up here. They were waiting in a narrow defile when their brothers appeared, leading their garrons. Ghost raced ahead at first scent of them. Jon squatted to let the direwolf close his jaws around his wrist, tugging his hand back and forth. It was a game they played. But when he glanced up, he saw Ygritte watching with eyes as wide and white as hen's eggs.

Qhorin Halfhand made no comment when he saw the prisoner. "There were three," Stonesnake told him. No more than that.

"We passed two," Ebben said, "or what the cats had left of them." He eyed the girl sourly, suspicion plain on his face.

"She yielded," Jon felt compelled to say.

Qhorin's face was impassive. "Do you know who I am?"

"Qhorin Halfhand." The girl looked half a child beside him, but she faced him boldly.

"Tell me true. If I fell into the hands of your people and yielded myself, what would it win me?"

"A slower death than elsewise."

The big ranger looked to Jon. "We have no food to feed her, nor can we spare a man to watch her."

"The way before us is perilous enough, lad," said Squire Dalbridge. "One shout when we need silence, and every man of us is doomed."

Ebben drew his dagger. "A steel kiss will keep her quiet."

Jon's throat was raw. He looked at them all helplessly. "She yielded herself to me."

"Then you must do what needs be done," Qhorin Halfhand said. "You are the blood of Winterfell and a man of the Night's Watch." He looked at the others. "Come, brothers. Leave him to it. It will go easier for him if we do not watch." And he led them up the steep twisting trail toward the pale pink glow of the sun where it broke through a mountain cleft, and before very long only Jon and Ghost remained with the wildling girl.

He thought Ygritte might try to run, but she only stood there, waiting, looking at him. "You never killed a woman before, did you?" When he shook his head, she said, "We die the same as men. But you don't need to do it. Mance would take you, I know he would. There's secret ways. Them crows would never catch us."

"I'm as much a crow as they are," Jon said.

She nodded, resigned. "Will you burn me, after?"

"I can't. The smoke might be seen."

"That's so." She shrugged. "Well, there's worse places to end up than the belly of a shadowcat."

He pulled Longclaw over a shoulder. "Aren't you afraid?"

"Last night I was," she admitted. "But now the sun's up." She pushed her hair aside to bare her neck, and knelt before him. "Strike hard and true, crow, or I'll come back and haunt you."

Longclaw was not so long or heavy a sword as his father's Ice, but it was Valyrian steel all the same. He touched the edge of the blade to mark where the blow must fall, and Ygritte shivered. "That's cold," she said. "Go on, be quick about it."

He raised Longclaw over his head, both hands tight around the grip. *One cut, with all my weight behind it.* He could give her a quick clean death, at least. He was his father's son. Wasn't he? Wasn't he?

"Do it," she urged him after a moment. "Bastard. *Do it.* I can't stay brave forever." When the blow did not fall she turned her head to look at him.

Jon lowered his sword. "Go," he muttered.

Ygritte stared.

"Now," he said, "before my wits return. *Go."*

She went.

SANSA

The southern sky was black with smoke. It rose swirling off a hundred distant fires, its sooty fingers smudging out the stars. Across the Blackwater Rush, a line of flame burned nightly from horizon to horizon, while on this side the Imp had fired the whole riverfront: docks and warehouses, homes and brothels, everything outside the city walls.

Even in the Red Keep, the air tasted of ashes. When Sansa found Ser Dontos in the quiet of the godswood, he asked if she'd been crying. "It's only from the smoke," she lied. "It looks as though half the kingswood is burning."

"Lord Stannis wants to smoke out the Imp's savages." Dontos swayed as he spoke, one hand on the trunk of a chestnut tree. A wine stain discolored the red-and-yellow motley of his tunic. "They kill his scouts and raid his baggage train. And the wildlings have been lighting fires too. The Imp told the queen that Stannis had better train his horses to eat ash, since he would find no blade of grass. I heard him say so. I hear all sorts of things as a fool that I never heard when I was a knight. They talk as though I am not there, and"—he leaned close, breathing his winey breath right in her face—"the Spider pays in gold for any little trifle. I think Moon Boy has been his for years."

He is drunk again. My poor Florian he names himself, and so he is. But he is all I have. "Is it true Lord Stannis burned the godswood at Storm's End?"

Dontos nodded. "He made a great pyre of the trees as an offering to his new god. The red priestess made him do it. They say she rules him now, body and soul. He's vowed to burn the Great Sept of Baelor too, if he takes the city."

"Let him." When Sansa had first beheld the Great Sept with its marble walls and seven crystal towers, she'd thought it was the most beautiful building in the world, but that had been before Joffrey beheaded her father on its steps. "I want it burned."

"Hush, child, the gods will hear you."

"Why should they? They never hear my prayers."

"Yes they do. They sent me to you, didn't they?"

Sansa picked at the bark of a tree. She felt light-headed, almost feverish. "They sent you, but what good have you done? You promised you would take me home, but I'm still here."

Dontos patted her arm. "I've spoken to a certain man I know, a good friend to me . . . and you, my lady. He will hire a swift ship to take us to safety, when the time is right."

"The time is right now," Sansa insisted, "before the fighting starts. They've forgotten about me. I know we could slip away if we tried."

"Child, child." Dontos shook his head. "Out of the castle, yes, we could do that, but the city gates are more heavily guarded than ever, and the Imp has even closed off the river."

It was true. The Blackwater Rush was as empty as Sansa had ever seen it. All the ferries had been withdrawn to the north bank, and the trading galleys had fled or been seized by the Imp to be made over for battle. The only ships to be seen were the king's war galleys. They rowed endlessly up and down, staying to the deep water in the middle of the river and exchanging flights of arrows with Stannis's archers on the south shore.

Lord Stannis himself was still on the march, but his vanguard had appeared two nights ago during the black of the moon. King's Landing had woken to the sight of their tents and banners. They were five thousand, Sansa had heard, near as many as all the gold cloaks in the city. They flew the red or green apples of House Fossoway, the turtle of Estermont, and the fox-and-flowers of Florent, and their commander was Ser Guyard Morrigen, a famous southron knight who men now called Guyard the Green. His standard showed a crow in flight, its black wings spread wide against a storm-green sky. But it was the pale yellow banners that worried the city. Long ragged tails streamed behind them like flickering flames, and in place of a lord's sigil they bore the device of a god: the burning heart of the Lord of Light.

"When Stannis comes, he'll have ten times as many men as Joffrey does, everyone says so."

Dontos squeezed her shoulder. "The size of his host does not matter, sweetling, so long as they are on the wrong side of the river. Stannis cannot cross without ships."

"He *has* ships. More than Joffrey."

"It's a long sail from Storm's End, the fleet will need to come up Massey's Hook and through the Gullet and across Blackwater Bay. Perhaps the good gods will send a storm to sweep them from the seas." Dontos gave a hopeful smile. "It is not easy for you, I know. You must be patient, child. When my friend returns to the city, we shall have our ship. Have faith in your Florian, and try not to be afraid."

Sansa dug her nails into her hand. She could feel the fear in her tummy, twisting and pinching, worse every day. Nightmares of the day Princess Myrcella had sailed still troubled her sleep; dark suffocating dreams that woke her in the black of night, struggling for breath. She could hear the people screaming at her, screaming without words, like animals. They had hemmed her in and thrown filth at her and tried to pull her off her horse, and would have done worse if the Hound had not cut his way to her side. They had torn the High Septon to pieces and smashed in Ser Aron's head with a rock. *Try not to be afraid!* he said.

The whole city was afraid. Sansa could see it from the castle walls. The smallfolk were hiding themselves behind closed shutters and barred doors as if that would keep them safe. The last time King's Landing had fallen, the Lannisters looted and raped as they pleased and put hundreds to the sword, even though the city had opened its gates. This time the Imp meant to fight, and a city that fought could expect no mercy at all.

Dontos was prattling on. "If I were still a knight, I should have to put on armor and man the walls with the rest. I ought to kiss King Joffrey's feet and thank him sweetly."

"If you thanked him for making you a fool, he'd make you a knight again," Sansa said sharply.

Dontos chuckled. "My Jonquil's a clever girl, isn't she?"

"Joffrey and his mother say I'm stupid."

"Let them. You're safer that way, sweetling. Queen Cersei and the Imp and Lord Varys and their like, they all watch each other keen as hawks, and pay this one and that one to spy out what the others are doing, but no one ever troubles themselves about Lady Tanda's daughter, do they?" Dontos covered his mouth to stifle a burp. "Gods preserve you, my little Jonquil." He was growing weepy. The wine did that to him. "Give your Florian a little kiss now. A kiss for luck." He swayed toward her.

Sansa dodged the wet groping lips, kissed him lightly on an unshaven cheek, and bid him good night. It took all her strength not to weep. She had been weeping too much of late. It was unseemly, she knew, but she could not seem to help herself; the tears would come, sometimes over a trifle, and nothing she did could hold them back.

The drawbridge to Maegor's Holdfast was unguarded. The Imp had moved most of the gold cloaks to the city walls, and the white knights of the Kingsguard had duties more important than dogging her heels. Sansa could go where she would so long as she did not try to leave the castle, but there was nowhere she wanted to go.

She crossed over the dry moat with its cruel iron spikes and made her way up the narrow turnpike stair, but when she reached the door of her bedchamber she could not bear to enter. The very walls of the room made her feel trapped; even with the window opened wide it felt as though there were no air to breathe.

Turning back to the stair, Sansa climbed. The smoke blotted out the stars and the thin crescent of moon, so the roof was dark and thick with shadows. Yet from here she could see everything: the Red Keep's tall towers and great cornerforts, the maze of city streets beyond, to south and west the river running black, the bay to the east, the columns of smoke and cinders, and fires, fires everywhere. Soldiers crawled over the city walls like ants with torches, and crowded the hoardings that had sprouted from the ramparts. Down by the Mud Gate, outlined against the drifting smoke, she could make out the vague shape of the three huge catapults, the biggest anyone had ever seen, overtopping the walls by a good twenty feet. Yet none of it made her feel less fearful. A stab went through her, so sharp that Sansa sobbed and clutched at her belly. She might have fallen, but a shadow moved suddenly, and strong fingers grabbed her arm and steadied her.

She grabbed a merlon for support, her fingers scrabbling at the rough stone. "Let go of me," she cried. "Let go."

"The little bird thinks she has wings, does she? Or do you mean to end up crippled like that brother of yours?"

Sansa twisted in his grasp. "I wasn't going to fall. It was only . . . you startled me, that's all."

"You mean I scared you. And still do."

She took a deep breath to calm herself. "I thought I was alone, I . . ." She glanced away.

"The little bird still can't bear to look at me, can she?" The Hound released her. "You were glad enough to see my face when the mob had you, though. Remember?"

Sansa remembered all too well. She remembered the way they had howled, the feel of the blood running down her cheek from where the stone had struck her, and the garlic stink on the breath of the man who had tried to pull her from her horse. She could still feel the cruel pinch of fingers on her wrist as she lost her balance and began to fall.

She'd thought she was going to die then, but the fingers had twitched, all five at once, and the man had shrieked loud as a horse. When his hand fell away, another hand, stronger, shoved her back into her saddle. The man with the garlicky breath was on the ground, blood pumping out the stump of his arm, but there were others all around, some with clubs in hand. The Hound leapt at them, his sword a blur of steel that trailed a red mist as it swung. When they broke and ran before him he had laughed, his terrible burned face for a moment transformed.

She made herself look at that face now, really look. It was only courteous, and a lady must never forget her courtesies. *The scars are not the worst part, nor even the way his mouth twitches. It's his eyes.* She had never seen eyes so full of anger. "I . . . I should have come to you after," she said haltingly. "To thank you, for . . . for saving me . . . you were so brave."

"Brave?" His laugh was half a snarl. "A dog doesn't need courage to chase off rats. They had me thirty to one, and not a man of them dared face me."

She hated the way he talked, always so harsh and angry. "Does it give you joy to scare people?"

"No, it gives me joy to kill people." His mouth twitched. "Wrinkle up your face all you like, but spare me this false piety. You were a high lord's get. Don't tell me Lord Eddard Stark of Winterfell never killed a man."

"That was his duty. He never liked it."

"Is that what he told you?" Clegane laughed again. "Your father lied. Killing is the sweetest thing there is." He drew his longsword. "*Here's* your truth. Your precious father found that out on Baelor's steps. Lord of Winterfell, Hand of the King, Warden of the North, the mighty Eddard Stark, of a line eight thousand years old . . . but Ilyn Payne's blade went through his neck all the same, didn't it? Do you remember the dance he did when his head came off his shoulders?"

Sansa hugged herself, suddenly cold. "Why are you always so hateful? I was *thanking* you . . ."

"Just as if I was one of those true knights you love so well, yes. What do you think a knight is *for*, girl? You think it's all taking favors from ladies and looking fine in gold plate? Knights are for *killing*." He laid the edge of his longsword against her neck, just under her ear. Sansa could feel the sharpness of the steel. "I killed my first man at twelve. I've lost count of how many I've killed since then. High lords with old names, fat rich men dressed in velvet, knights puffed up like bladders with their honors, yes, and women and children too—they're all meat, and I'm the butcher. Let them have their lands and their gods and their gold. Let them have their *sers*." Sandor Clegane spat at her feet to show what he thought of that. "So long as I have this," he said, lifting the sword from her throat, "there's no man on earth I need fear."

Except your brother, Sansa thought, but she had better sense than to say it aloud. *He is a dog, just as he says. A half-wild, mean-tempered dog that bites any hand that tries to pet him, and yet will savage any man who tries to hurt his masters.* "Not even the men across the river?"

Clegane's eyes turned toward the distant fires. "All this burning." He sheathed his sword. "Only cowards fight with fire."

"Lord Stannis is no coward."

"He's not the man his brother was either. Robert never let a little thing like a river stop him."

"What will you do when he crosses?"

"Fight. Kill. Die, maybe."

"Aren't you afraid? The gods might send you down to some terrible hell for all the evil you've done."

"What evil?" He laughed. "What gods?"

"The gods who made us all."

"All?" he mocked. "Tell me, little bird, what kind of god makes a monster like the Imp, or a halfwit like Lady Tanda's daughter? If there are gods, they made sheep so wolves could eat mutton, and they made the weak for the strong to play with."

"True knights protect the weak."

He snorted. "There are no true knights, no more than there are gods. If you can't protect yourself, die and get out of the way of those who can. Sharp steel and strong arms rule this world, don't ever believe any different."

Sansa backed away from him. "You're awful."

"I'm honest. It's the world that's awful. Now fly away, little bird, I'm sick of you peeping at me."

Wordless, she fled. She was afraid of Sandor Clegane . . . and yet, some part of her wished that Ser Dontos had a little of the Hound's ferocity. *There are gods,* she told herself, *and there are true knights too. All the stories can't be lies.*

That night Sansa dreamed of the riot again. The mob surged around her, shrieking, a maddened beast with a thousand faces. Everywhere she turned she saw faces twisted into monstrous inhuman masks. She wept and told them she had never done them hurt, yet they dragged her from her horse all the same. "No," she cried, "no, please, don't, *don't,*" but no one paid her any heed. She shouted for Ser Dontos, for her brothers, for her dead father and her dead wolf, for gallant Ser Loras who had given her a red rose once, but none of them came. She called for the heroes from the songs, for Florian and Ser Ryam Redwyne and Prince Aemon the Dragonknight, but no one heard. Women swarmed over her like weasels, pinching her legs and kicking her in the belly, and someone hit her in the face and she felt her teeth shatter. Then she saw the bright glimmer of steel. The knife plunged into her belly and tore and tore and tore, until there was nothing left of her down there but shiny wet ribbons.

When she woke, the pale light of morning was slanting through her window, yet she felt as sick and achy as if she had not slept at all. There was something sticky on her thighs. When she threw back the blanket and saw the blood, all she could think was that her dream had somehow come true. She remembered the knives inside her, twisting and ripping. She squirmed away in horror, kicking at the sheets and falling to the floor, breathing raggedly, naked, bloodied, and afraid.

But as she crouched there, on her hands and knees, understanding came. "No, please," Sansa whimpered, "please, no." She didn't want this happening to her, not now, not here, not now, not now, not now, not now.

Madness took hold of her. Pulling herself up by the bedpost, she went to the basin and washed between her legs, scrubbing away all the stickiness. By the time she was done, the water was pink with blood. When her maidservants saw it they would *know*. Then she remembered the bedclothes. She rushed back to the bed and stared in horror at the dark red stain and the tale it told. All she could think was that she had to get rid of it, or else they'd see. She couldn't let them see, or they'd marry her to Joffrey and make her lay with him.

Snatching up her knife, Sana hacked at the sheet, cutting out the stain. *If they ask me about the hole, what will I say?* Tears ran down her face. She pulled the torn sheet from the bed, and the stained blanket as well. *I'll have to burn them.* She balled up the evidence, stuffed it in the fireplace, drenched it in oil from her bedside lamp, and lit it afire. Then she realized that the blood had soaked through the sheet into the feather-bed, so she bundled that up as well, but it was big and cumbersome, hard to move. Sansa could get only half of it into the fire. She was on her knees, struggling to shove the mattress into the flames as thick grey smoke eddied around her and filled the room, when the door burst open and she heard her maid gasp.

In the end it took three of them to pull her away. And it was all for nothing. The bedclothes were burnt, but by the time they carried her off her thighs were bloody again. It was as if her own body had betrayed her to Joffrey, unfurling a banner of Lannister crimson for all the world to see.

When the fire was out, they carried off the singed featherbed, fanned away the worst of the smoke, and brought up a tub. Women came and went, muttering and looking at her strangely. They filled the tub with scalding hot water, bathed her and washed her hair and gave her a cloth to wear between her legs. By then Sansa was calm again, and ashamed for her folly. The smoke had ruined most of her clothing. One of the women went away and came back with a green wool shift that was almost her size. "It's not as pretty as your own things, but it will serve," she announced when she'd pulled it down over Sansa's head. "Your shoes weren't burned, so at least you won't need to go barefoot to the queen."

Cersei Lannister was breaking her fast when Sansa was ushered into her solar. "You may sit," the queen said graciously. "Are you hungry?" She gestured at the table. There was porridge, honey, milk, boiled eggs, and crisp fried fish.

The sight of the food made Sansa feel ill. Her tummy was tied in a knot. "No, thank you, Your Grace."

"I don't blame you. Between Tyrion and Lord Stannis, everything I eat tastes of ash. And now you're setting fires as well. What did you hope to accomplish?"

Sansa lowered her head. "The blood frightened me."

"The blood is the seal of your womanhood. Lady Catelyn might have prepared you. You've had your first flowering, no more."

Sansa had never felt less flowery. "My lady mother told me, but I . . . I thought it would be different."

"Different how?"

"I don't know. Less . . . less messy, and more magical."

Queen Cersei laughed. "Wait until you birth a child, Sansa. A woman's life is nine parts mess to one part magic, you'll learn that soon enough . . . and the parts that look like magic often turn out to be messiest of all." She took a sip of milk. "So now you are a woman. Do you have the least idea of what that means?"

"It means that I am now fit to be wedded and bedded," said Sansa, "and to bear children for the king."

The queen gave a wry smile. "A prospect that no longer entices you as it once did, I can see. I will not fault you for that. Joffrey has always been difficult. Even his birth . . . I labored a day and a half to bring him forth. You cannot imagine the pain, Sansa. I screamed so loudly that I fancied Robert might hear me in the kingswood."

"His Grace was not with you?"

"Robert? Robert was hunting. That was his custom. Whenever my time was near, my royal husband would flee to the trees with his huntsmen and hounds. When he returned he would present me with some pelts or a stag's head, and I would present him with a baby.

"Not that I *wanted* him to stay, mind you. I had Grand Maester Pycelle and an army of midwives, and I had my brother. When they told Jaime he was not allowed in the birthing room, he smiled and asked which of them proposed to keep him out.

"Joffrey will show you no such devotion, I fear. You could thank your sister for that, if she weren't dead. He's never been able to forget that day on the Trident when you saw her shame him, so he shames you in turn. You're stronger than you seem, though. I expect you'll survive a bit of humiliation. I did. You may never love the king, but you'll love his children."

"I love His Grace with all my heart," Sansa said.

The queen sighed. "You had best learn some new lies, and quickly. Lord Stannis will not like that one, I promise you."

"The new High Septon said that the gods will never permit Lord Stannis to win, since Joffrey is the rightful king."

A half smile flickered across the queen's face. "Robert's trueborn son and heir. Though Joff would cry whenever Robert picked him up. His Grace did not like that. His bastards had always gurgled at him happily, and sucked his finger when he put it in their little baseborn mouths. Robert wanted smiles and cheers, always, so he went where he found them, to his friends and his whores. Robert wanted to be loved. My brother Tyrion has the same disease. Do you want to be loved, Sansa?"

"Everyone wants to be loved."

"I see flowering hasn't made you any brighter," said Cersei. "Sansa, permit me to share a bit of womanly wisdom with you on this very special day. Love is poison. A sweet poison, yes, but it will kill you all the same."

JON

It was dark in the Skirling Pass. The great stone flanks of the mountains hid the sun for most of the day, so they rode in shadow, the breath of man and horse steaming in the cold air. Icy fingers of water trickled down from the snowpack above into small frozen pools that cracked and broke beneath the hooves of their garrons. Sometimes they would see a few weeds struggling from some crack in the rock or a splotch of pale lichen, but there was no grass, and they were above the trees now.

The track was as steep as it was narrow, wending its way ever upward. Where the pass was so constricted that rangers had to go single file, Squire Dalbridge would take the lead, scanning the heights as he went, his longbow ever close to hand. It was said he had the keenest eyes in the Night's Watch.

Ghost padded restlessly by Jon's side. From time to time he would stop and turn, his ears pricked, as if he heard something behind them. Jon did not think the shadowcats would attack living men, not unless they were starving, but he loosened Longclaw in its scabbard even so.

A wind-carved arch of grey stone marked the highest point of the pass. Here the way broadened as it began its long descent toward the valley of the Milkwater. Qhorin decreed that they would rest here until the shadows began to grow again. "Shadows are friends to men in black," he said.

Jon saw the sense of that. It would be pleasant to ride in the light for a time, to let the bright mountain sun soak through their cloaks and chase the chill from their bones, but they dared not. Where there were three watchers there might be others, waiting to sound the alarm.

Stonesnake curled up under his ragged fur cloak and was asleep almost at once. Jon shared his salt beef with Ghost while Ebben and Squire Dalbridge fed the horses. Qhorin Halfhand sat with his back to a rock, honing the edge of his longsword with long slow strokes. Jon watched the ranger for a few moments, then summoned his courage and went to him. "My lord," he said, "you never asked me how it went. With the girl."

"I am no lord, Jon Snow." Qhorin slid the stone smoothly along the steel with his two-fingered hand.

"She told me Mance would take me, if I ran with her."

"She told you true."

"She even claimed we were kin. She told me a story . . ."

". . . of Bael the Bard and the rose of Winterfell. So Stonesnake told me. It happens I know the song. Mance would sing it of old, when he came back from a ranging. He had a passion for wildling music. Aye, and for their women as well."

"You knew him?"

"We all knew him." His voice was sad.

They were friends as well as brothers, Jon realized, *and now they are sworn foes.* "Why did he desert?"

"For a wench, some say. For a crown, others would have it." Qhorin tested the edge of his sword with the ball of his thumb. "He liked women, Mance did, and he was not a man whose knees bent easily, that's true. But it was more than that. He loved the wild better than the Wall. It was in his blood. He was wildling born, taken as a child when some raiders were put to the sword. When he left the Shadow Tower he was only going home again."

"Was he a good ranger?"

"He was the best of us," said the Halfhand, "and the worst as well. Only fools like Thoren Smallwood despise the wildlings. They are as brave as we are, Jon. As strong, as quick, as clever. But they have no discipline. They name themselves the free folk, and each one thinks himself as good as a king and wiser than a maester. Mance was the same. He never learned how to obey."

"No more than me," said Jon quietly.

Qhorin's shrewd grey eyes seemed to see right through him. "So you let her go?" He did not sound the least surprised.

"You know?"

"Now. Tell me why you spared her."

It was hard to put into words. "My father never used a headsman. He said he owed it to men he killed to look into their eyes and hear their last words. And when I looked into Ygritte's eyes, I . . ." Jon stared down at his hands helplessly. "I know she was an enemy, but there was no evil in her."

"No more than in the other two."

"It was their lives or ours," Jon said. "If they had seen us, if they had sounded that horn . . ."

"The wildlings would hunt us down and slay us, true enough."

"Stonesnake has the horn now, though, and we took Ygritte's knife and axe. She's behind us, afoot, unarmed . . ."

"And not like to be a threat," Qhorin agreed. "If I had needed her dead, I would have left her with Ebben, or done the thing myself."

"Then why did you command it of me?"

"I did not command it. I told you to do what needed to be done, and left you to decide what that would be." Qhorin stood and slid his long-sword back into its scabbard. "When I want a mountain scaled, I call on Stonesnake. Should I need to put an arrow through the eye of some foe across a windy battlefield, I summon Squire Dalbridge. Ebben can make any man give up his secrets. To lead men you must know them, Jon Snow. I know more of you now than I did this morning."

"And if I had slain her?" asked Jon.

"She would be dead, and I would know you better than I had before. But enough talk. You ought be sleeping. We have leagues to go, and dangers to face. You will need your strength."

Jon did not think sleep would come easily, but he knew the Halfhand was right. He found a place out of the wind, beneath an overhang of rock, and took off his cloak to use it for a blanket. "Ghost," he called. "Here. To me." He always slept better with the great white wolf beside him; there was comfort in the smell of him, and welcome warmth in that shaggy pale fur. This time, though, Ghost did no more than look at him. Then he turned away and padded around the garrons, and quick as that he was gone. *He wants to hunt,* Jon thought. Perhaps there were goats in these mountains. The shadowcats must live on something. "Just don't try and bring down a 'cat," he muttered. Even for a direwolf, that would be dangerous. He tugged his cloak over him and stretched out beneath the rock.

When he closed his eyes, he dreamed of direwolves.

There were five of them when there should have been six, and they were scattered, each apart from the others. He felt a deep ache of empti-ness, a sense of incompleteness. The forest was vast and cold, and they were so small, so lost. His brothers were out there somewhere, and his sister, but he had lost their scent. He sat on his haunches and lifted his head to the darkening sky, and his cry echoed through the forest, a long lonely mournful sound. As it died away, he pricked up his ears, listening for an answer, but the only sound was the sigh of blowing snow.

Jon?

The call came from behind him, softer than a whisper, but strong too. Can a shout be silent? He turned his head, searching for his brother, for a glimpse of a lean grey shape moving beneath the trees, but there was nothing, only . . .

A weirwood.

It seemed to sprout from solid rock, its pale roots twisting up from a myriad of fissures and hairline cracks. The tree was slender compared to other weirwoods he had seen, no more than a sapling, yet it was growing as he watched, its limbs thickening as they reached for the sky. Wary, he circled the smooth white trunk until he came to the face. Red eyes looked at him. Fierce eyes they were, yet glad to see him. The weirwood had his brother's face. Had his brother always had three eyes?

Not always, came the silent shout. *Not before the crow.*

He sniffed at the bark, smelled wolf and tree and boy, but behind that there were other scents, the rich brown smell of warm earth and the hard grey smell of stone and something else, something terrible. Death, he knew. He was smelling death. He cringed back, his hair bristling, and bared his fangs.

Don't be afraid, I like it in the dark. No one can see you, but you can see them. But first you have to open your eyes. See? Like this. And the tree reached down and touched him.

And suddenly he was back in the mountains, his paws sunk deep in a drift of snow as he stood upon the edge of a great precipice. Before him the Skirling Pass opened up into airy emptiness, and a long vee-shaped valley lay spread beneath him like a quilt, awash in all the colors of an autumn afternoon.

A vast blue-white wall plugged one end of the vale, squeezing between the mountains as if it had shouldered them aside, and for a moment he thought he had dreamed himself back to Castle Black. Then he realized he was looking at a river of ice several thousand feet high. Under that glittering cold cliff was a great lake, its deep cobalt waters reflecting the snowcapped peaks that ringed it. There were men down in the valley, he saw now; many men, thousands, a huge host. Some were tearing great holes in the half-frozen ground, while others trained for war. He watched as a swarming mass of riders charged a shield wall, astride horses no larger than ants. The sound of their mock battle was a rustling of steel leaves, drifting faintly on the wind. Their encampment had no plan to it; he saw no ditches, no sharpened stakes, no neat rows of horse lines. Everywhere crude earthen shelters and hide tents sprouted haphazardly, like a pox on the face of the earth. He spied untidy mounds of hay, smelled goats and sheep, horses and pigs, dogs in great profusion. Tendrils of dark smoke rose from a thousand cookfires.

This is no army, no more than it is a town. This is a whole people come together.

Across the long lake, one of the mounds moved. He watched it more closely and saw that it was not dirt at all, but alive, a shaggy lumbering beast with a snake for a nose and tusks larger than those of the greatest boar that had ever lived. And the thing riding it was huge as well, and his shape was wrong, too thick in the leg and hips to be a man.

Then a sudden gust of cold made his fur stand up, and the air thrilled to the sound of wings. As he lifted his eyes to the ice-white mountain heights above, a shadow plummeted out of the sky. A shrill scream split the air. He glimpsed blue-grey pinions spread wide, shutting out the sun . . .

"Ghost!" Jon shouted, sitting up. He could still feel the talons, the *pain.* "Ghost, to me!"

Ebben appeared, grabbed him, shook him. "Quiet! You mean to bring the wildlings down on us? What's wrong with you, boy?"

"A dream," said Jon feebly. "I was Ghost, I was on the edge of the mountain looking down on a frozen river, and something attacked me. A bird . . . an eagle, I think . . ."

Squire Dalbridge smiled. "It's always pretty women in my dreams. Would that I dreamed more often."

Qhorin came up beside him. "A frozen river, you say?"

"The Milkwater flows from a great lake at the foot of a glacier," Stonesnake put in.

"There was a tree with my brother's face. The wildlings . . . there were *thousands,* more than I ever knew existed. And giants riding mammoths." From the way the light had shifted, Jon judged that he had been asleep for four or five hours. His head ached, and the back of his neck where the talons had burned through him. *But that was in the dream.*

"Tell me all that you remember, from first to last," said Qhorin Halfhand.

Jon was confused. "It was only a dream."

"A wolf dream," the Halfhand said. "Craster told the Lord Commander that the wildlings were gathering at the source of the Milkwater. That may be why you dreamed it. Or it may be that you saw what waits for us, a few hours farther on. Tell me."

It made him feel half a fool to talk of such things to Qhorin and the other rangers, but he did as he was commanded. None of the black brothers laughed at him, however. By the time he was done, even Squire Dalbridge was no longer smiling.

"Skinchanger?" said Ebben grimly, looking at the Halfhand. *Does he mean the eagle?* Jon wondered. *Or me?* Skinchangers and wargs belonged in Old Nan's stories, not in the world he had lived in all his life. Yet here, in this strange bleak wilderness of rock and ice, it was not hard to believe.

"The cold winds are rising. Mormont feared as much. Benjen Stark felt it as well. Dead men walk and the trees have eyes again. Why should we balk at wargs and giants?"

"Does this mean my dreams are true as well?" asked Squire Dalbridge. "Lord Snow can keep his mammoths, I want my women."

"Man and boy I've served the Watch, and ranged as far as any," said Ebben. "I've seen the bones of giants, and heard many a queer tale, but no more. I want to see them with my own eyes."

"Be careful they don't see you, Ebben," Stonesnake said.

Ghost did not reappear as they set out again. The shadows covered the floor of the pass by then, and the sun was sinking fast toward the jagged twin peaks of the huge mountain the rangers named Forktop. *If the dream was true . . .* Even the thought scared him. Could the eagle have hurt Ghost, or knocked him off the precipice? And what about the weirwood with his brother's face, that smelled of death and darkness?

The last ray of sun vanished behind the peaks of Forktop. Twilight filled the Skirling Pass. It seemed to grow colder almost at once. They were no longer climbing. In fact, the ground had begun to descend, though as yet not sharply. It was littered with cracks and broken boulders and tumbled heaps of rock. *It will be dark soon, and still no sight of Ghost.* It was tearing Jon apart, yet he dare not shout for the direwolf as he would have liked. Other things might be listening as well.

"Qhorin," Squire Dalbridge called softly. "There. Look."

The eagle was perched on a spine of rock far above them, outlined against the darkening sky. *We've seen other eagles,* Jon thought. *That need not be the one I dreamed of.*

Even so, Ebben would have loosed a shaft at it, but the squire stopped him. "The bird's well out of bowshot."

"I don't like it watching us."

The squire shrugged. "Nor me, but you won't stop it. Only waste a good arrow."

Qhorin sat in his saddle, studying the eagle for a long time. "We press on," he finally said. The rangers resumed their descent.

Ghost, Jon wanted to shout, *where are you?*

He was about to follow Qhorin and the others when he glimpsed a flash of white between two boulders. *A patch of old snow,* he thought, until he saw it stir. He was off his horse at once. As he went to his knees,

Ghost lifted his head. His neck glistened wetly, but he made no sound when Jon peeled off a glove and touched him. The talons had torn a bloody path through fur and flesh, but the bird had not been able to snap his neck.

Qhorin Halfhand was standing over him. "How bad?"

As if in answer, Ghost struggled to his feet.

"The wolf is strong," the ranger said. "Ebben, water. Stonesnake, your skin of wine. Hold him still, Jon."

Together they washed the caked blood from the direwolf's fur. Ghost struggled and bared his teeth when Qhorin poured the wine into the ragged red gashes the eagle had left him, but Jon wrapped his arms around him and murmured soothing words, and soon enough the wolf quieted. By the time they'd ripped a strip from Jon's cloak to wrap the wounds, full dark had settled. Only a dusting of stars set the black of sky apart from the black of stone. "Do we press on?" Stonesnake wanted to know.

Qhorin went to his garron. "Back, not on."

"Back?" Jon was taken by surprise.

"Eagles have sharper eyes than men. We are seen. So now we run." The Halfhand wound a long black scarf around his face and swung up into the saddle.

The other rangers exchanged a look, but no man thought to argue. One by one they mounted and turned their mounts toward home. "Ghost, come," he called, and the direwolf followed, a pale shadow moving through the night.

All night they rode, feeling their way up the twisting pass and through the stretches of broken ground. The wind grew stronger. Sometimes it was so dark that they dismounted and went ahead on foot, each man leading his garron. Once Ebben suggested that some torches might serve them well, but Qhorin said, "No fire," and that was the end of that. They reached the stone bridge at the summit and began to descend again. Off in the darkness a shadowcat screamed in fury, its voice bouncing off the rocks so it seemed as though a dozen other 'cats were giving answer. Once Jon thought he saw a pair of glowing eyes on a ledge overhead, as big as harvest moons.

In the black hour before dawn, they stopped to let the horses drink and fed them each a handful of oats and a twist or two of hay. "We are not far from the place the wildlings died," said Qhorin. "From there, one man could hold a hundred. The right man." He looked at Squire Dalbridge.

The squire bowed his head. "Leave me as many arrows as you can spare, brothers." He stroked his longbow. "And see my garron has an apple when you're home. He's earned it, poor beastie."

He's staying to die, Jon realized.

Qhorin clasped the squire's forearm with a gloved hand. "If the eagle flies down for a look at you . . ."

". . . he'll sprout some new feathers."

The last Jon saw of Squire Dalbridge was his back as he clambered up the narrow path to the heights.

When dawn broke, Jon looked up into a cloudless sky and saw a speck moving through the blue. Ebben saw it too, and cursed, but Qhorin told him to be quiet. "Listen."

Jon held his breath, and heard it. Far away and behind them, the call of a hunting horn echoed against the mountains.

"And now they come," said Qhorin.

TYRION

Pod dressed him for his ordeal in a plush velvet tunic of Lannister crimson and brought him his chain of office. Tyrion left it on the bedside table. His sister misliked being reminded that he was the King's Hand, and he did not wish to inflame the relations between them any further.

Varys caught up with him as he was crossing the yard. "My lord," he said, a little out of breath. "You had best read this at once." He held out a parchment in a soft white hand. "A report from the north."

"Good news or bad?" Tyrion asked.

"That is not for me to judge."

Tyrion unrolled the parchment. He had to squint to read the words in the torchlit yard. "Gods be good," he said softly. "Both of them?"

"I fear so, my lord. It is so sad. So grievous sad. And them so young and innocent."

Tyrion remembered how the wolves had howled when the Stark boy had fallen. *Are they howling now, I wonder?* "Have you told anyone else?" he asked.

"Not as yet, though of course I must."

He rolled up the letter. "I'll tell my sister." He wanted to see how she took the news. He wanted that very much.

The queen looked especially lovely that night. She wore a low-cut gown of deep green velvet that brought out the color of her eyes. Her golden hair tumbled across her bare shoulders, and around her waist was a woven belt studded with emeralds. Tyrion waited until he had been seated and served a cup of wine before thrusting the letter at her. He said not a word. Cersei blinked at him innocently and took the parchment from his hand.

"I trust you're pleased," he said as she read. "You wanted the Stark boy dead, I believe."

Cersei made a sour face. "It was Jaime who threw him from that window, not me. For love, he said, as if that would please me. It was a stupid thing to do, and dangerous besides, but when did our sweet brother ever stop to think?"

"The boy saw you," Tyrion pointed out.

"He was a child. I could have frightened him into silence." She looked at the letter thoughtfully. "Why must I suffer accusations every time some Stark stubs his toe? This was Greyjoy's work, I had nothing to do with it."

"Let us hope Lady Catelyn believes that."

Her eyes widened. "She wouldn't—"

"—kill Jaime? Why not? What would you do if Joffrey and Tommen were murdered?"

"I still hold Sansa!" the queen declared.

"We still hold Sansa," he corrected her, "and we had best take good care of her. Now where is this supper you've promised me, sweet sister?"

Cersei set a tasty table, that could not be denied. They started with a creamy chestnut soup, crusty hot bread, and greens dressed with apples and pine nuts. Then came lamprey pie, honeyed ham, buttered carrots, white beans and bacon, and roast swan stuffed with mushrooms and oysters. Tyrion was exceedingly courteous; he offered his sister the choice portions of every dish, and made certain he ate only what she did. Not that he truly thought she'd poison him, but it never hurt to be careful.

The news about the Starks had soured her, he could see. "We've had no word from Bitterbridge?" she asked anxiously as she speared a bit of apple on the point of her dagger and ate it with small, delicate bites.

"None."

"I've never trusted Littlefinger. For enough coin, he'd go over to Stannis in a heartbeat."

"Stannis Baratheon is too bloody righteous to buy men. Nor would he make a comfortable lord for the likes of Petyr. This war has made for some queer bedfellows, I agree, but those two? No."

As he carved some slices off the ham, she said, "We have Lady Tanda to thank for the pig."

"A token of her love?"

"A bribe. She begs leave to return to her castle. Your leave as well as mine. I suspect she fears you'll arrest her on the road, as you did Lord Gyles."

"Does she plan to make off with the heir to the throne?" Tyrion served his sister a cut of ham and took one for himself. "I'd sooner she remain. If she wants to feel safe, tell her to bring down her garrison from Stokeworth. As many men as she has."

"If we need men so badly, why did you send away your savages?" A certain testiness crept into Cersei's voice.

"It was the best use I could have made of them," he told her truthfully. "They're fierce warriors, but not soldiers. In formal battle, discipline is more important than courage. They've already done us more good in the kingswood than they would ever have done us on the city walls."

As the swan was being served, the queen questioned him about the conspiracy of the Antler Men. She seemed more annoyed than afraid. "Why are we plagued with so many treasons? What injury has House Lannister ever done these wretches?"

"None," said Tyrion, "but they think to be on the winning side . . . which makes them fools as well as traitors."

"Are you certain you've found them all?"

"Varys says so." The swan was too rich for his taste.

A line appeared on Cersei's pale white brow, between those lovely eyes. "You put too much trust in that eunuch."

"He serves me well."

"Or so he'd have you believe. You think you're the only one he whispers secrets to? He gives each of us just enough to convince us that we'd be helpless without him. He played the same game with me, when I first wed Robert. For years, I was convinced I had no truer friend at court, but now . . ." She studied his face for a moment. "He says you mean to take the Hound from Joffrey."

Damn Varys. "I need Clegane for more important duties."

"Nothing is more important than the life of the king."

"The life of the king is not at risk. Joff will have brave Ser Osmund guarding him, and Meryn Trant as well." *They're good for nothing better.* "I need Balon Swann and the Hound to lead sorties, to make certain Stannis gets no toehold on our side of the Blackwater."

"Jaime would lead the sorties himself."

"From Riverrun? That's quite a sortie."

"Joff's only a boy."

"A boy who wants to be part of this battle, and for once he's showing some sense. I don't intend to put him in the thick of the fighting, but he needs to be seen. Men fight more fiercely for a king who shares their peril than one who hides behind his mother's skirts."

"He's *thirteen*, Tyrion."

"Remember Jaime at thirteen? If you want the boy to be his father's son, let him play the part. Joff wears the finest armor gold can buy, and he'll have a dozen gold cloaks around him at all times. If the city looks to be in the least danger of falling, I'll have him escorted back to the Red Keep at once."

He had thought that might reassure her, but he saw no sign of pleasure in those green eyes. "*Will* the city fall?"

"No." *But if it does, pray that we can hold the Red Keep long enough for our lord father to march to our relief.*

"You've lied to me before, Tyrion."

"Always with good reason, sweet sister. I want amity between us as much as you do. I've decided to release Lord Gyles." He had kept Gyles safe for just this gesture. "You can have Ser Boros Blount back as well."

The queen's mouth tightened. "Ser Boros can rot at Rosby," she said, "but Tommen—"

"—stays where he is. He's safer under Lord Jacelyn's protection than he would ever have been with Lord Gyles."

Serving men cleared away the swan, hardly touched. Cersei beckoned for the sweet. "I hope you like blackberry tarts."

"I love all sorts of tarts."

"Oh, I've known that a long while. Do you know why Varys is so dangerous?"

"Are we playing at riddles now? No."

"He doesn't have a cock."

"Neither do you." *And don't you just hate that, Cersei?*

"Perhaps I'm dangerous too. You, on the other hand, are as big a fool as every other man. That worm between your legs does half your thinking."

Tyrion licked the crumbs off his fingers. He did not like his sister's smile. "Yes, and just now my worm is thinking that perhaps it is time I took my leave."

"Are you unwell, brother?" She leaned forward, giving him a good look at the top of her breasts. "Suddenly you appear somewhat flustered."

"Flustered?" Tyrion glanced at the door. He thought he'd heard something outside. He was beginning to regret coming here alone. "You've never shown much interest in my cock before."

"It's not your cock that interests me, so much as what you stick it in. I don't depend on the eunuch for everything, as you do. I have my own ways of finding out things . . . especially things that people don't want me to know."

"What are you trying to say?"

"Only this—*I have your little whore.*"

Tyrion reached for his wine cup, buying a moment to gather his thoughts. "I thought men were more to your taste."

"You're such a droll little fellow. Tell me, have you married this one yet?" When he gave her no answer she laughed and said, "Father will be ever so relieved."

His belly felt as if it were full of eels. How had she found Shae? Had Varys betrayed him? Or had all his precautions been undone by his impatience the night he rode directly to the manse? "Why should you care who I choose to warm my bed?"

"A Lannister always pays his debts," she said. "You've been scheming against me since the day you came to King's Landing. You sold Myrcella, stole Tommen, and now you plot to have Joff killed. You want him dead so you can rule through Tommen."

Well, I can't say the notion isn't tempting. "This is madness, Cersei. Stannis will be here in days. You need me."

"For what? Your great prowess in battle?"

"Bronn's sellswords will never fight without me," he lied.

"Oh, I think they will. It's your gold they love, not your impish wit. Have no fear, though, they won't be without you. I won't say I haven't thought of slitting your throat from time to time, but Jaime would never forgive me if I did."

"And the whore?" He would not call her by name. *If I can convince her Shae means nothing to me, perhaps . . .*

"She'll be treated gently enough, so long as no harm comes to my sons. If Joff should be killed, however, or if Tommen should fall into the hands of our enemies, your little cunt will die more painfully than you can possibly imagine."

She truly believes I mean to kill my own nephew. "The boys are safe," he promised her wearily. "Gods be good, Cersei, they're my own blood! What sort of man do you take me for?"

"A small and twisted one."

Tyrion stared at the dregs on the bottom of his wine cup. *What would Jaime do in my place?* Kill the bitch, most likely, and worry about the consequences afterward. But Tyrion did not have a golden sword, nor the skill to wield one. He loved his brother's reckless wrath, but it was their lord father he must try and emulate. *Stone, I must be stone, I must be Casterly Rock, hard and unmovable. If I fail this test, I had as lief seek out the nearest grotesquerie.* "For all I know, you've killed her already," he said.

"Would you like to see her? I thought you might." Cersei crossed the room and threw open the heavy oaken door. "Bring in my brother's whore."

Ser Osmund's brothers Osney and Osfryd were peas from the same pod, tall men with hooked noses, dark hair, and cruel smiles. She hung between them, eyes wide and white in her dark face. Blood trickled from her broken lip, and he could see bruises through her torn clothing. Her hands were bound with rope, and they'd gagged her so she could not speak.

"You said she wouldn't be hurt."

"She fought." Unlike his brothers, Osney Kettleblack was clean-shaven, so the scratches showed plainly on his bare cheeks. "Got claws like a shadowcat, this one."

"Bruises heal," said Cersei in a bored tone. "The whore will live. So long as Joff does."

Tyrion wanted to laugh at her. It would have been so sweet, so very very sweet, but it would have given the game away. *You've lost, Cersei, and the Kettleblacks are even bigger fools than Bronn claimed.* All he needed to do was say the words.

Instead he looked at the girl's face and said, "You swear you'll release her after the battle?"

"If you release Tommen, yes."

He pushed himself to his feet. "Keep her then, but keep her safe. If these animals think they can use her . . . well, sweet sister, let me point out that a scale tips two ways." His tone was calm, flat, uncaring; he'd reached for his father's voice, and found it. "Whatever happens to her happens to Tommen as well, and that includes the beatings and rapes." *If she thinks me such a monster, I'll play the part for her.*

Cersei had not expected that. "You would not dare."

Tyrion made himself smile, slow and cold. Green and black, his eyes laughed at her. "Dare? I'll do it myself."

His sister's hand flashed at his face, but he caught her wrist and bent it back until she cried out. Osfryd moved to her rescue. "One more step and I'll break her arm," the dwarf warned him. The man stopped. "You remember when I said you'd never hit me again, Cersei?" He shoved her to the floor and turned back to the Kettleblacks. "Untie her and remove that gag."

The rope had been so tight as to cut off the blood to her hands. She cried out in pain as the circulation returned. Tyrion massaged her fingers gently until feeling returned. "Sweetling," he said, "you must be brave. I am sorry they hurt you."

"I know you'll free me, my lord."

"I will," he promised, and Alayaya bent over and kissed him on the brow. Her broken lips left a smear of blood on his forehead. *A bloody kiss is more than I deserve,* Tyrion thought. *She would never have been hurt but for me.*

Her blood still marked him as he looked down at the queen. "I have never liked you, Cersei, but you were my own sister, so I never did you harm. You've ended that. I will hurt you for this. I don't know how yet, but give me time. A day will come when you think yourself safe and happy, and suddenly your joy will turn to ashes in your mouth, and you'll know the debt is paid."

In war, his father had told him once, the battle is over in the instant one army breaks and flees. No matter that they're as numerous as they were a moment before, still armed and armored; once they had run before you they would not turn to fight again. So it was with Cersei. "Get out!" was all the answer she could summon. "Get out of my sight!"

Tyrion bowed. "Good night, then. And pleasant dreams."

He made his way back to the Tower of the Hand with a thousand armored feet marching through his skull. *I ought to have seen this coming the first time I slipped through the back of Chataya's wardrobe.* Perhaps he had not *wanted* to see. His legs were aching badly by the time he had made the climb. He sent Pod for a flagon of wine and pushed his way into his bedchamber.

Shae sat cross-legged in the canopied bed, nude but for the heavy golden chain that looped across the swell of her breasts: a chain of linked golden hands, each clasping the next.

Tyrion had not expected her. "What are you doing here?"

Laughing, she stroked the chain. "I wanted some hands on my titties . . . but these little gold ones are cold."

For a moment he did know what to say. How could he tell her that another woman had taken the beating meant for her, and might well die in her place should some mischance of battle fell Joffrey? He wiped Alayaya's blood from his brow with the heel of his hand. "The Lady Lollys—"

"She's asleep. Sleep's all she ever wants to do, the great cow. She sleeps and she eats. Sometimes she falls asleep while she's eating. The food falls under the blankets and she *rolls* in it, and I have to clean her." She made a disgusted face. "All they did was *fuck* her."

"Her mother says she's sick."

"She has a baby in her belly, that's all."

Tyrion gazed around the room. Everything seemed much as he left it. "How did you enter? Show me the hidden door."

She gave a shrug. "Lord Varys made me wear a hood. I couldn't see, except . . . there was one place, I got a peep at the floor out the bottom of the hood. It was all tiles, you know, the kind that make a picture?"

"A mosaic?"

Shae nodded. "They were colored red and black. I think the picture was a dragon. Otherwise, everything was dark. We went down a ladder and walked a long ways, until I was all twisted around. Once we stopped so he could unlock an iron gate. I brushed against it when we went through. The dragon was past the gate. Then we went up another ladder, with a tunnel at the top. I had to stoop, and I think Lord Varys was crawling."

Tyrion made a round of the bedchamber. One of the sconces looked loose. He stood on his toes and tried to turn it. It revolved slowly, scraping against the stone wall. When it was upside down, the stub of the candle fell out. The rushes scattered across the cold stone floor did not show any particular disturbance. "Doesn't m'lord want to bed me?" asked Shae.

"In a moment." Tyrion threw open his wardrobe, shoved the clothing aside, and pushed against the rear panel. What worked for a whorehouse might work for a castle as well . . . but no, the wood was solid, unyielding. A stone beside the window seat drew his eye, but all his tugging and prodding went for naught. He returned to the bed frustrated and annoyed.

Shae undid his laces and threw her arms around his neck. "Your shoulders feel as hard as rocks," she murmured. "Hurry, I want to feel you inside me." Yet as her legs locked around his waist, his manhood left him. When she felt him go soft, Shae slid down under the sheets and took him in her mouth, but even that could not rouse him.

After a few moments he stopped her. "What's wrong?" she asked. All the sweet innocence of the world was written there in the lines of her young face.

Innocence? Fool, she's a whore, Cersei was right, you think with your cock, fool, fool.

"Just go to sleep, sweetling," he urged, stroking her hair. Yet long after Shae had taken his advice, Tyrion himself still lay awake, his fingers cupped over one small breast as he listened to her breathing.

CATELYN

The Great Hall of Riverrun was a lonely place for two to sit to supper. Deep shadows draped the walls. One of the torches had guttered out, leaving only three. Catelyn sat staring into her wine goblet. The vintage tasted thin and sour on her tongue. Brienne was across from her. Between them, her father's high seat was as empty as the rest of the hall. Even the servants were gone. She had given them leave to join the celebration.

The walls of the keep were thick, yet even so, they could hear the muffled sounds of revelry from the yard outside. Ser Desmond had brought twenty casks up from the cellars, and the smallfolk were celebrating Edmure's imminent return and Robb's conquest of the Crag by hoisting horns of nut-brown ale.

I cannot blame them, Catelyn thought. *They do not know. And if they did, why should they care? They never knew my sons. Never watched Bran climb with their hearts in their throats, pride and terror so mingled they seemed as one, never heard him laugh, never smiled to see Rickon trying so fiercely to be like his older brothers.* She stared at the supper set before her: trout wrapped in bacon, salad of turnip greens and red fennel and sweetgrass, pease and onions and hot bread. Brienne was eating methodically, as if supper were another chore to be accomplished. *I am become a sour woman,* Catelyn thought. *I take no joy in mead nor meat, and song and laughter have become suspicious strangers to me. I am a creature of grief and dust and bitter longings. There is an empty place within me where my heart was once.*

The sound of the other woman's eating had become intolerable to her. "Brienne, I am no fit company. Go join the revels, if you would. Drink a horn of ale and dance to Rymund's harping."

"I am not made for revels, my lady." Her big hands tore apart a heel of black bread. Brienne stared at the chunks as if she had forgotten what they were. "If you command it, I . . ."

Catelyn could sense her discomfort. "I only thought you might enjoy happier company than mine."

"I'm well content." The girl used the bread to sop up some of the bacon grease the trout had been fried in.

"There was another bird this morning." Catelyn did not know why she said it. "The maester woke me at once. That was dutiful, but not kind. Not kind at all." She had not meant to tell Brienne. No one knew but her and Maester Vyman, and she had meant to keep it that way until . . . until . . .

Until what? Foolish woman, will holding it secret in your heart make it any less true? If you never tell, never speak of it, will it become only a dream, less than a dream, a nightmare half-remembered? Oh, if only the gods would be so good.

"Is it news of King's Landing?" asked Brienne.

"Would that it was. The bird came from Castle Cerwyn, from Ser Rodrik, my castellan." *Dark wings, dark words.* "He has gathered what power he could and is marching on Winterfell, to take the castle back." How unimportant all that sounded now. "But he said . . . he wrote . . . he told me, he . . ."

"My lady, what is it? Is it some news of your sons?"

Such a simple question that was; would that the answer could be as simple. When Catelyn tried to speak, the words caught in her throat. "I have no sons but Robb." She managed those terrible words without a sob, and for that much she was glad.

Brienne looked at her with horror. "My lady?"

"Bran and Rickon tried to escape, but were taken at a mill on the Acorn Water. Theon Greyjoy has mounted their heads on the walls of Winterfell. Theon Greyjoy, who ate at my table since he was a boy of ten." *I have said it, gods forgive me. I have said it and made it true.*

Brienne's face was a watery blur. She reached across the table, but her fingers stopped short of Catelyn's, as if the touch might be unwelcome. "I . . . there are no words, my lady. My good lady. Your sons, they . . . they're with the gods now."

"Are they?" Catelyn said sharply. "What god would let this happen? Rickon was only a baby. How could he deserve such a death? And

Bran . . . when I left the north, he had not opened his eyes since his fall. I had to go before he woke. Now I can never return to him, or hear him laugh again." She showed Brienne her palms, her fingers. "These scars . . . they sent a man to cut Bran's throat as he lay sleeping. He would have died then, and me with him, but Bran's wolf tore out the man's throat." That gave her a moment's pause. "I suppose Theon killed the wolves too. He must have, elsewise . . . I was certain the boys would be safe so long as the direwolves were with them. Like Robb with his Grey Wind. But my daughters have no wolves now."

The abrupt shift of topic left Brienne bewildered. "Your daughters . . ."

"Sansa was a lady at three, always so courteous and eager to please. She loved nothing so well as tales of knightly valor. Men would say she had my look, but she will grow into a woman far more beautiful than I ever was, you can see that. I often sent away her maid so I could brush her hair myself. She had auburn hair, lighter than mine, and so thick and soft . . . the red in it would catch the light of the torches and shine like copper.

"And Arya, well . . . Ned's visitors would oft mistake her for a stableboy if they rode into the yard unannounced. Arya was a trial, it must be said. Half a boy and half a wolf pup. Forbid her anything and it became her heart's desire. She had Ned's long face, and brown hair that always looked as though a bird had been nesting in it. I despaired of ever making a lady of her. She collected scabs as other girls collect dolls, and would say anything that came into her head. I think she must be dead too." When she said that, it felt as though a giant hand were squeezing her chest. "I want them all dead, Brienne. Theon Greyjoy first, then Jaime Lannister and Cersei and the Imp, every one, every one. But my girls . . . my girls will . . ."

"The queen . . . she has a little girl of her own," Brienne said awkwardly. "And sons too, of an age with yours. When she hears, perhaps she . . . she may take pity, and . . ."

"Send my daughters back unharmed?" Catelyn smiled sadly. "There is a sweet innocence about you, child. I could wish . . . but no. Robb will avenge his brothers. Ice can kill as dead as fire. *Ice* was Ned's greatsword. Valyrian steel, marked with the ripples of a thousand foldings, so sharp I feared to touch it. Robb's blade is dull as a cudgel compared to Ice. It will not be easy for him to get Theon's head off, I fear. The Starks do not use headsmen. Ned always said that the man who passes the sentence should swing the blade, though he never took any joy in the duty. But *I* would, oh, yes." She stared at her scarred hands, opened and closed them, then slowly raised her eyes. "I've sent him wine."

"Wine?" Brienne was lost. "Robb? Or . . . Theon Greyjoy?"

"The Kingslayer." The ploy had served her well with Cleos Frey. *I hope you're thirsty, Jaime. I hope your throat is dry and tight.* "I would like you to come with me."

"I am yours to command, my lady."

"Good." Catelyn rose abruptly. "Stay, finish your meal in peace. I will send for you later. At midnight."

"So late, my lady?"

"The dungeons are windowless. One hour is much like another down there, and for me, all hours are midnight." Her footsteps rang hollowly when Catelyn left the hall. As she climbed to Lord Hoster's solar, she could hear them outside, shouting, "Tully!" and "A cup! A cup to the brave young lord!" *My father is not dead,* she wanted to shout down at them. *My sons are dead, but my father lives, damn you all, and he is your lord still.*

Lord Hoster was deep in sleep. "He had a cup of dreamwine not so long ago, my lady," Maester Vyman said. "For the pain. He will not know you are here."

"It makes no matter," Catelyn said. *He is more dead than alive, yet more alive than my poor sweet sons.*

"My lady, is there aught I might do for you? A sleeping draught, perhaps?"

"Thank you, Maester, but no. I will not sleep away my grief. Bran and Rickon deserve better from me. Go and join the celebration, I will sit with my father for a time."

"As you will, my lady." Vyman bowed and left her.

Lord Hoster lay on his back, mouth open, his breath a faint whistling sigh. One hand hung over the edge of the mattress, a pale frail fleshless thing, but warm when she touched it. She slid her fingers through his and closed them. *No matter how tightly I hold him, I cannot keep him here,* she thought sadly. *Let him go.* Yet her fingers would not seem to unbend.

"I have no one to talk with, Father," she told him. "I pray, but the gods do not answer." Lightly she kissed his hand. The skin was warm, blue veins branching like rivers beneath his pale translucent skin. Outside the greater rivers flowed, the Red Fork and the Tumblestone, and they would flow forever, but not so the rivers in her father's hand. Too soon that current would grow still. "Last night I dreamed of that time Lysa and I got lost while riding back from Seagard. Do you remember? That strange fog came up and we fell behind the rest of the party. Everything was grey, and I could not see a foot past the nose of my horse. We lost the road. The branches of the trees were like long skinny arms reaching out to grab us as we passed. Lysa started to cry, and when I shouted the fog seemed to swallow the sound. But Petyr knew where we were, and he rode back and found us . . .

"But there's no one to find me now, is there? This time I have to find our own way, and it is hard, so hard.

"I keep remembering the Stark words. Winter has come, Father. For me. For me. Robb must fight the Greyjoys now as well as the Lannisters, and for what? For a gold hat and an iron chair? Surely the land has bled enough. I want my girls back, I want Robb to lay down his sword and pick some homely daughter of Walder Frey to make him happy and give him sons. I want Bran and Rickon back, I want . . ." Catelyn hung her head. "I *want,*" she said once more, and then her words were gone.

After a time the candle guttered and went out. Moonlight slanted between the slats of the shutters, laying pale silvery bars across her father's face. She could hear the soft whisper of his labored breathing, the endless rush of waters, the faint chords of some love song drifting up from the yard, so sad and sweet. *"I loved a maid as red as autumn,"* Rymund sang, *"with sunset in her hair."*

Catelyn never noticed when the singing ended. Hours had passed, yet it seemed only a heartbeat before Brienne was at the door. "My lady," she announced softly. "Midnight has come."

Midnight has come, Father, she thought, *and I must do my duty.* She let go of his hand.

The gaoler was a furtive little man with broken veins in his nose. They found him bent over a tankard of ale and the remains of a pigeon pie, more than a little drunk. He squinted at them suspiciously. "Begging your forgiveness, m'lady, but Lord Edmure says no one is to see the Kingslayer without a writing from him, with his seal upon it."

"*Lord* Edmure? Has my father died, and no one told me?"

The gaoler licked his lips. "No, m'lady, not as I knows."

"You will open the cell, or you will come with me to Lord Hoster's solar and tell him why you saw fit to defy me."

His eyes fell. "As m'lady says." The keys were chained to the studded leather belt that girdled his waist. He muttered under his breath as he sorted through them, until he found the one that fit the door to the Kingslayer's cell.

"Go back to your ale and leave us," she commanded. An oil lamp hung from a hook on the low ceiling. Catelyn took it down and turned up the flame. "Brienne, see that I am not disturbed."

Nodding, Brienne took up a position just outside the cell, her hand resting on the pommel of her sword. "My lady will call if she has need of me."

Catelyn shouldered aside the heavy wood-and-iron door and stepped into foul darkness. This was the bowels of Riverrun, and smelled the part. Old straw crackled underfoot. The walls were discolored with patches of nitre. Through the stone, she could hear the faint rush of the Tumblestone. The lamplight revealed a pail overflowing with feces in one corner and a huddled shape in another. The flagon of wine stood beside the door, untouched. *So much for that ploy. I ought to be thankful that the gaoler did not drink it himself, I suppose.*

Jaime raised his hands to cover his face, the chains around his wrists clanking. "Lady Stark," he said, in a voice hoarse with disuse. "I fear I am in no condition to receive you."

"Look at me, ser."

"The light hurts my eyes. A moment, if you would." Jaime Lannister had been allowed no razor since the night he was taken in the Whispering Wood, and a shaggy beard covered his face, once so like the queen's. Glinting gold in the lamplight, the whiskers made him look like some great yellow beast, magnificent even in chains. His unwashed hair fell to his shoulders in ropes and tangles, the clothes were rotting on his body, his face was pale and wasted . . . and even so, the power and the beauty of the man were still apparent.

"I see you had no taste for the wine I sent you."

"Such sudden generosity seemed somewhat suspect."

"I can have your head off anytime I want. Why would I need to poison you?"

"Death by poison can seem natural. Harder to claim that my head simply fell off." He squinted up from the floor, his cat-green eyes slowly becoming accustomed to the light. "I'd invite you to sit, but your brother has neglected to provide me a chair."

"I can stand well enough."

"Can you? You look terrible, I must say. Though perhaps it's just the light in here." He was fettered at wrist and ankle, each cuff chained to the others, so he could neither stand nor lie comfortably. The ankle chains were bolted to the wall. "Are my bracelets heavy enough for you, or did you come to add a few more? I'll rattle them prettily if you like."

"You brought this on yourself," she reminded him. "We granted you the comfort of a tower cell befitting your birth and station. You repaid us by trying to escape."

"A cell is a cell. Some under Casterly Rock make this one seem a sunlit garden. One day perhaps I'll show them to you."

If he is cowed, he hides it well, Catelyn thought. "A man chained hand and foot should keep a more courteous tongue in his mouth, ser. I did not come here to be threatened."

"No? Then surely it was to have your pleasure of me? It's said that widows grow weary of their empty beds. We of the Kingsguard vow never to wed, but I suppose I could still service you if that's what you need. Pour us some of that wine and slip out of that gown and we'll see if I'm up to it."

Catelyn stared down at him in revulsion. *Was there ever a man as beautiful or as vile as this one?* "If you said that in my son's hearing, he would kill you for it."

"Only so long as I was wearing these." Jaime Lannister rattled his chains at her. "We both know the boy is afraid to face me in single combat."

"My son may be young, but if you take him for a fool, you are sadly mistaken . . . and it seems to me that you were not so quick to make challenges when you had an army at your back."

"Did the old Kings of Winter hide behind their mothers' skirts as well?"

"I grow weary of this, ser. There are things I must know."

"Why should I tell you anything?"

"To save your life."

"You think I fear death?" That seemed to amuse him.

"You should. Your crimes will have earned you a place of torment in the deepest of the seven hells, if the gods are just."

"What gods are those, Lady Catelyn? The trees your husband prayed to? How well did they serve him when my sister took his head off?" Jaime gave a chuckle. "If there are gods, why is the world so full of pain and injustice?"

"Because of men like you."

"There are no men like me. There's only me."

There is nothing here but arrogance and pride, and the empty courage of a madman. I am wasting my breath with this one. If there was ever a spark of honor in him, it is long dead. "If you will not speak with me, so be it. Drink the wine or piss in it, ser, it makes no matter to me."

Her hand was at the door pull when he said, "Lady Stark." She turned, waited. "Things go to rust in this damp," Jaime went on. "Even a man's courtesies. Stay, and you shall have your answers . . . for a price."

He has no shame. "Captives do not set prices."

"Oh, you'll find mine modest enough. Your turnkey tells me nothing but vile lies, and he cannot even keep them straight. One day he says Cersei has been flayed, and the next it's my father. Answer my questions and I'll answer yours."

"Truthfully?"

"Oh, it's *truth* you want? Be careful, my lady. Tyrion says that people often claim to hunger for truth, but seldom like the taste when it's served up."

"I am strong enough to hear anything you care to say."

"As you will, then. But first, if you'd be so kind . . . the wine. My throat is raw."

Catelyn hung the lamp from the door and moved the cup and flagon closer. Jaime sloshed the wine around his mouth before he swallowed. "Sour and vile," he said, "but it will do." He put his back to the wall, drew his knees up to his chest, and stared at her. "Your first question, Lady Catelyn?"

Not knowing how long this game might continue, Catelyn wasted no time. "Are you Joffrey's father?"

"You would never ask unless you knew the answer."

"I want it from your own lips."

He shrugged. "Joffrey is mine. As are the rest of Cersei's brood, I suppose."

"You admit to being your sister's lover?"

"I've always loved my sister, and you owe me two answers. Do all my kin still live?"

"Ser Stafford Lannister was slain at Oxcross, I am told."

Jaime was unmoved. "Uncle Dolt, my sister called him. It's Cersei and Tyrion who concern me. As well as my lord father."

"They live, all three." *But not long, if the gods are good.*

Jaime drank some more wine. "Ask your next."

Catelyn wondered if he would dare answer her next question with anything but a lie. "How did my son Bran come to fall?"

"I flung him from a window."

The easy way he said it took her voice away for an instant. *If I had a knife, I would kill him now,* she thought, until she remembered the girls. Her throat constricted as she said, "You were a knight, sworn to defend the weak and innocent."

"He was weak enough, but perhaps not so innocent. He was spying on us."

"Bran would not spy."

"Then blame those precious gods of yours, who brought the boy to our window and gave him a glimpse of something he was never meant to see."

"Blame the *gods*?" she said, incredulous. "Yours was the hand that threw him. You meant for him to die."

His chains chinked softly. "I seldom fling children from towers to improve their health. Yes, I meant for him to die."

"And when he did not, you knew your danger was worse than ever, so you gave your catspaw a bag of silver to make certain Bran would never wake."

"Did I now?" Jaime lifted his cup and took a long swallow. "I won't deny we talked of it, but you were with the boy day and night, your maester and Lord Eddard attended him frequently, and there were guards, even those damned direwolves . . . it would have required cutting my way through half of Winterfell. And why bother, when the boy seemed like to die of his own accord?"

"If you lie to me, this session is at an end." Catelyn held out her hands, to show him her fingers and palms. "The man who came to slit Bran's throat gave me these scars. You swear you had no part in sending him?"

"On my honor as a Lannister."

"Your honor as a Lannister is worth less than *this*." She kicked over the waste pail. Foul-smelling brown ooze crept across the floor of the cell, soaking into the straw.

Jaime Lannister backed away from the spill as far as his chains would allow. "I may indeed have shit for honor, I won't deny it, but I have never yet hired anyone to do my killing. Believe what you will, Lady Stark, but if I had wanted your Bran dead I would have slain him myself."

Gods be merciful, he's telling the truth. "If you did not send the killer, your sister did."

"If so, I'd know. Cersei keeps no secrets from me."

"Then it was the Imp."

"Tyrion is as innocent as your Bran. *He* wasn't climbing around outside of anyone's window, spying."

"Then why did the assassin have his dagger?"

"What dagger was this?"

"It was so long," she said, holding her hands apart, "plain, but finely made, with a blade of Valyrian steel and a dragonbone hilt. Your brother won it from Lord Baelish at the tourney on Prince Joffrey's name day."

Lannister poured, drank, poured, and stared into his wine cup. "This wine seems to be improving as I drink it. Imagine that. I seem to remember that dagger, now that you describe it. Won it, you say? How?"

"Wagering on you when you tilted against the Knight of Flowers." Yet when she heard her own words Catelyn knew she had gotten it wrong. "No . . . was it the other way?"

"Tyrion always backed me in the lists," Jaime said, "but that day Ser Loras unhorsed me. A mischance, I took the boy too lightly, but no matter. Whatever my brother wagered, he lost . . . but that dagger *did* change hands, I recall it now. Robert showed it to me that night at the feast. His Grace loved to salt my wounds, especially when drunk. And when was he not drunk?"

Tyrion Lannister had said much the same thing as they rode through the Mountains of the Moon, Catelyn remembered. She had refused to believe him. Petyr had sworn otherwise, Petyr who had been almost a brother, Petyr who loved her so much he fought a duel for her hand . . .

and yet if Jaime and Tyrion told the same tale, what did that mean? The brothers had not seen each other since departing Winterfell more than a year ago. "Are you trying to deceive me?" Somewhere there was a trap here.

"I've admitted to shoving your precious urchin out a window, what would it gain me to lie about this knife?" He tossed down another cup of wine. "Believe what you will, I'm past caring what people say of me. And it's my turn. Have Robert's brothers taken the field?"

"They have."

"Now there's a niggardly response. Give me more than that, or your next answer will be as poor."

"Stannis marches against King's Landing," she said grudgingly. "Renly is dead, murdered at Bitterbridge by his brother, through some black art I do not understand."

"A pity," Jaime said. "I rather liked Renly, though Stannis is quite another tale. What side have the Tyrells taken?"

"Renly, at first. Now, I could not say."

"Your boy must be feeling lonely."

"Robb was sixteen a few days past . . . a man grown, and a king. He's won every battle he's fought. The last word we had from him, he had taken the Crag from the Westerlings."

"He hasn't faced my father yet, has he?"

"When he does, he'll defeat him. As he did you."

"He took me unawares. A craven's trick."

"You dare talk of tricks? Your brother Tyrion sent us cutthroats in envoy's garb, under a peace banner."

"If it were one of your sons in this cell, wouldn't his brothers do as much for him?"

My son has no brothers, she thought, but she would not share her pain with a creature such as this.

Jaime drank some more wine. "What's a brother's life when honor is at stake, eh?" Another sip. "Tyrion is clever enough to realize that your son will never consent to ransom me."

Catelyn could not deny it. "Robb's bannermen would sooner see you dead. Rickard Karstark in particular. You slew two of his sons in the Whispering Wood."

"The two with the white sunburst, were they?" Jaime gave a shrug. "If truth be told, it was *your* son that I was trying to slay. The others got in my way. I killed them in fair fight, in the heat of battle. Any other knight would have done the same."

"How can you still count yourself a knight, when you have forsaken every vow you ever swore?"

Jaime reached for the flagon to refill his cup. "So many vows . . .

they make you swear and swear. Defend the king. Obey the king. Keep his secrets. Do his bidding. Your life for his. But obey your father. Love your sister. Protect the innocent. Defend the weak. Respect the gods. Obey the laws. It's too much. No matter what you do, you're forsaking one vow or the other." He took a healthy swallow of wine and closed his eyes for an instant, leaning his head back against the patch of nitre on the wall. "I was the youngest man ever to wear the white cloak."

"And the youngest to betray all it stood for, Kingslayer."

"*Kingslayer*," he pronounced carefully. "And such a king he was!" He lifted his cup. "To Aerys Targaryen, the Second of His Name, Lord of the Seven Kingdoms and *Protector* of the Realm. And to the sword that opened his throat. A *golden* sword, don't you know. Until his blood ran red down the blade. Those are the Lannister colors, red and gold."

As he laughed, she realized the wine had done its work; Jaime had drained most of the flagon, and he was drunk. "Only a man like you would be proud of such an act."

"I told you, there are no men like me. Answer me this, Lady Stark— did your Ned ever tell you the manner of his father's death? Or his brother's?"

"They strangled Brandon while his father watched, and then killed Lord Rickard as well." An ugly tale, and sixteen years old. Why was he asking about it now?

"Killed, yes, but *how*?"

"The cord or the axe, I suppose."

Jaime took a swallow, wiped his mouth. "No doubt Ned wished to spare you. His sweet young bride, if not quite a maiden. Well, you wanted truth. Ask me. We made a bargain, I can deny you nothing. Ask."

"Dead is dead." *I do not want to know this.*

"Brandon was different from his brother, wasn't he? He had blood in his veins instead of cold water. More like me."

"Brandon was nothing like you."

"If you say so. You and he were to wed."

"He was on his way to Riverrun when . . ." Strange, how telling it still made her throat grow tight, after all these years. ". . . when he heard about Lyanna, and went to King's Landing instead. It was a rash thing to do." She remembered how her own father had raged when the news had been brought to Riverrun. *The gallant fool,* was what he called Brandon.

Jaime poured the last half cup of wine. "He rode into the Red Keep with a few companions, shouting for Prince Rhaegar to come out and die. But Rhaegar wasn't there. Aerys sent his guards to arrest them all for plotting his son's murder. The others were lords' sons too, it seems to me."

"Ethan Glover was Brandon's squire," Catelyn said. "He was the only one to survive. The others were Jeffory Mallister, Kyle Royce, and Elbert Arryn, Jon Arryn's nephew and heir." It was queer how she still remembered the names, after so many years. "Aerys accused them of treason and summoned their fathers to court to answer the charge, with the sons as hostages. When they came, he had them murdered without trial. Fathers and sons both."

"There were trials. Of a sort. Lord Rickard demanded trial by combat, and the king granted the request. Stark armored himself as for battle, thinking to duel one of the Kingsguard. Me, perhaps. Instead they took him to the throne room and suspended him from the rafters while two of Aerys's pyromancers kindled a blaze beneath him. The king told him that *fire* was the champion of House Targaryen. So all Lord Rickard needed to do to prove himself innocent of treason was . . . well, not burn.

"When the fire was blazing, Brandon was brought in. His hands were chained behind his back, and around his neck was a wet leathern cord attached to a device the king had brought from Tyrosh. His legs were left free, though, and his longsword was set down just beyond his reach.

"The pyromancers roasted Lord Rickard slowly, banking and fanning that fire carefully to get a nice even heat. His cloak caught first, and then his surcoat, and soon he wore nothing but metal and ashes. Next he would start to cook, Aerys promised . . . unless his son could free him. Brandon tried, but the more he struggled, the tighter the cord constricted around his throat. In the end he strangled himself.

"As for Lord Rickard, the steel of his breastplate turned cherry-red before the end, and his gold melted off his spurs and dripped down into the fire. I stood at the foot of the Iron Throne in my white armor and white cloak, filling my head with thoughts of Cersei. After, Gerold Hightower himself took me aside and said to me, 'You swore a vow to guard the king, not to judge him.' That was the White Bull, loyal to the end and a better man than me, all agree."

"Aerys . . ." Catelyn could taste bile at the back of her throat. The story was so hideous she suspected it had to be true. "Aerys was mad, the whole realm knew it, but if you would have me believe you slew him to avenge Brandon Stark . . ."

"I made no such claim. The Starks were nothing to me. I will say, I think it passing odd that I am loved by one for a kindness I never did, and reviled by so many for my finest act. At Robert's coronation, I was made to kneel at the royal feet beside Grand Maester Pycelle and Varys the eunuch, so that he might *forgive* us our crimes before he took us into his service. As for your Ned, he should have kissed the hand that slew Aerys, but he preferred to scorn the arse he found sitting on Robert's throne. I think Ned Stark loved Robert better than he ever loved his brother or his father . . . or even you, my lady. He was never unfaithful to Robert, was he?" Jaime gave a drunken laugh. "Come, Lady Stark, don't you find this all terribly amusing?"

"I find nothing about you amusing, Kingslayer."

"That name again. I don't think I'll fuck you after all, Littlefinger had you first, didn't he? I never eat off another man's trencher. Besides, you're not half so lovely as my sister." His smile cut. "I've never lain with any woman but Cersei. In my own way, I have been truer than your Ned ever was. Poor old dead Ned. So who has shit for honor now, I ask you? What was the name of that bastard he fathered?"

Catelyn took a step backward. *"Brienne."*

"No, that wasn't it." Jaime Lannister upended the flagon. A trickle ran down onto his face, bright as blood. "Snow, that was the one. Such a *white* name . . . like the pretty cloaks they give us in the Kingsguard when we swear our pretty oaths."

Brienne pushed open the door and stepped inside the cell. "You called, my lady?"

"Give me your sword." Catelyn held out her hand.

THEON

The sky was a gloom of cloud, the woods dead and frozen. Roots grabbed at Theon's feet as he ran, and bare branches lashed his face, leaving thin stripes of blood across his cheeks. He crashed through heedless, breathless, icicles flying to pieces before him. *Mercy,* he sobbed. From behind came a shuddering howl that curdled his blood. *Mercy, mercy.* When he glanced back over his shoulder he saw them coming, great wolves the size of horses with the heads of small children. *Oh, mercy, mercy.* Blood dripped from their mouths black as pitch, burning holes in the snow where it fell. Every stride brought them closer. Theon tried to run faster, but his legs would not obey. The trees all had faces, and they were laughing at him, laughing, and the howl came again. He could smell the hot breath of the beasts behind him, a stink of brimstone and corruption. *They're dead, dead, I saw them killed,* he tried to shout, *I saw their heads dipped in tar,* but when he opened his mouth only a moan emerged, and then something *touched* him and he whirled, shouting . . .

. . . flailing for the dagger he kept by his bedside and managing only to knock it to the floor. Wex danced away from him. Reek stood behind the mute, his face lit from below by the candle he carried. "What?" Theon cried. *Mercy.* "What do you want? Why are you in my bedchamber? *Why?*"

"My lord prince," said Reek, "your sister has come to Winterfell. You asked to be informed at once if she arrived."

"Past time," Theon muttered, pushing his fingers through his hair. He had begun to fear that Asha meant to leave him to his fate. *Mercy.* He glanced outside the window, where the first vague light of dawn was just brushing the towers of Winterfell. "Where is she?"

"Lorren took her and her men to the Great Hall to break their fast. Will you see her now?"

"Yes." Theon pushed off the blankets. The fire had burned down to embers. "Wex, hot water." He could not let Asha see him disheveled and soaked with sweat. *Wolves with children's faces . . .* He shivered. "Close the shutters." The bedchamber felt as cold as the dream forest had been.

All his dreams had been cold of late, and each more hideous than the one before. Last night he had dreamed himself back in the mill again, on his knees dressing the dead. Their limbs were already stiffening, so they seemed to resist sullenly as he fumbled at them with half-frozen fingers, tugging up breeches and knotting laces, yanking fur-trimmed boots over hard unbending feet, buckling a studded leather belt around a waist no bigger than the span of his hands. "This was never what I wanted," he told them as he worked. "They gave me no choice." The corpses made no answer, but only grew colder and heavier.

The night before, it had been the miller's wife. Theon had forgotten her name, but he remembered her body, soft pillowy breasts and stretch marks on her belly, the way she clawed his back when he fucked her. Last night in his dream he had been in bed with her once again, but this time she had teeth above *and* below, and she tore out his throat even as she was gnawing off his manhood. It was madness. He'd seen her die too. Gelmarr had cut her down with one blow of his axe as she cried to Theon for mercy. *Leave me, woman. It was him who killed you, not me. And he's dead as well.* At least Gelmarr did not haunt Theon's sleep.

The dream had receded by the time Wex returned with the water. Theon washed the sweat and sleep from his body and took his own good time dressing. Asha had let him wait long enough; now it was her turn. He chose a satin tunic striped black and gold and a fine leather jerkin with silver studs . . . and only then remembered that his wretched sister put more stock in blades than beauty. Cursing, he tore off the clothes and dressed again, in felted black wool and ringmail. Around his waist he buckled sword and dagger, remembering the night she had humiliated him at his own father's table. *Her sweet suckling babe, yes. Well, I have a knife too, and know how to use it.*

Last of all, he donned his crown, a band of cold iron slim as a finger, set with heavy chunks of black diamond and nuggets of gold. It was misshapen and ugly, but there was no help for that. Mikken lay buried in the lichyard, and the new smith was capable of little more than nails and horseshoes. Theon consoled himself with the reminder that it was only a prince's crown. He would have something much finer when he was crowned king.

Outside his door, Reek waited with Urzen and Kromm. Theon fell in with them. These days, he took guards with him everywhere he went, even to the privy. Winterfell wanted him dead. The very night they had returned from Acorn Water, Gelmarr the Grim had tumbled down some steps and broken his back. The next day, Aggar turned up with his throat slit ear to ear. Gynir Rednose became so wary that he shunned wine, took to sleeping in byrnie, coif, and helm, and adopted the noisiest dog in the kennels to give him warning should anyone try to steal up on his sleeping place. All the same, one morning the castle woke to the sound of the little dog barking wildly. They found the pup racing around the well, and Rednose floating in it, drowned.

He could not let the killings go unpunished. Farlen was as likely a suspect as any, so Theon sat in judgment, called him guilty, and condemned him to death. Even that went sour. As he knelt to the block, the kennelmaster said, "M'lord Eddard always did his own killings." Theon had to take the axe himself or look a weakling. His hands were sweating, so the shaft twisted in his grip as he swung and the first blow landed between Farlen's shoulders. It took three more cuts to hack through all that bone and muscle and sever the head from the body, and afterward he was sick, remembering all the times they'd sat over a cup of mead talking of hounds and hunting. *I had no choice,* he wanted to scream at the corpse. *The ironborn can't keep secrets, they had to die, and someone had to take the blame for it.* He only wished he had killed him cleaner. Ned Stark had never needed more than a single blow to take a man's head.

The killings stopped after Farlen's death, but even so his men continued sullen and anxious. "They fear no foe in open battle," Black Lorren told him, "but it is another thing to dwell among enemies, never knowing if the washerwoman means to kiss you or kill you, or whether the serving boy is filling your cup with ale or bale. We would do well to leave this place."

"I am the Prince of Winterfell!" Theon had shouted. "This is my seat, no man will drive me from it. No, nor woman either!"

Asha. It was her doing. My own sweet sister, may the Others bugger her with a sword. She wanted him dead, so she could steal his place as their father's heir. That was why she had let him languish here, ignoring the urgent commands he had sent her.

He found her in the high seat of the Starks, ripping a capon apart with her fingers. The hall rang with the voices of her men, sharing stories with Theon's own as they drank together. They were so loud that his entrance went all but unnoticed. "Where are the rest?" he demanded of Reek. There were no more than fifty men at the trestle tables, most of them his. Winterfell's Great Hall could have seated ten times the number.

"This is the whole o' the company, m'lord prince."

"The *whole*—how many men did she bring?"

"Twenty, by my count."

Theon Greyjoy strode to where his sister was sprawled. Asha was laughing at something one of her men had said, but broke off at his approach. "Why, 'tis the Prince of Winterfell." She tossed a bone to one of the dogs sniffing about the hall. Under that hawk's beak of a nose, her wide mouth twisted in a mocking grin. "Or is it Prince of Fools?"

"Envy ill becomes a maid."

Asha sucked grease from her fingers. A lock of black hair fell across her eyes. Her men were shouting for bread and bacon. They made a deal of noise, as few as they were. "Envy, Theon?"

"What else would you call it? With thirty men, I captured Winterfell in a night. You needed a thousand and a moon's turn to take Deepwood Motte."

"Well, I'm no great warrior like you, brother." She quaffed half a horn of ale and wiped her mouth with the back of her hand. "I saw the heads above your gates. Tell me true, which one gave you the fiercest fight, the cripple or the babe?"

Theon could feel the blood rushing to his face. He took no joy from those heads, no more than he had in displaying the headless bodies of the children before the castle. Old Nan stood with her soft toothless mouth opening and closing soundlessly, and Farlen threw himself at Theon, snarling like one of his hounds. Urzen and Cadwyl had to beat him senseless with the butts of their spears. *How did I come to this!* he remembered thinking as he stood over the fly-speckled bodies.

Only Maester Luwin had the stomach to come near. Stone-faced, the small grey man had begged leave to sew the boys' heads back onto their shoulders, so they might be laid in the crypts below with the other Stark dead.

"No," Theon had told him. "Not the crypts."

"But why, my lord? Surely they cannot harm you now. It is where they belong. All the bones of the Starks—"

"I said *no*." He needed the heads for the wall, but he had burned the headless bodies that very day, in all their finery. Afterward he had knelt amongst the bones and ashes to retrieve a slag of melted silver and cracked jet, all that remained of the wolf's-head brooch that had once been Bran's. He had it still.

"I treated Bran and Rickon generously," he told his sister. "They brought their fate on themselves."

"As do we all, little brother."

His patience was at an end. "How do you expect me to hold Winterfell if you bring me only twenty men?"

"Ten," Asha corrected. "The others return with me. You wouldn't want your own sweet sister to brave the dangers of the wood without an escort, would you? There are direwolves prowling the dark." She uncoiled from the great stone seat and rose to her feet. "Come, let us go somewhere we can speak more privily."

She was right, he knew, though it galled him that she would make that decision. *I should never have come to the hall*, he realized belatedly. *I should have summoned her to me.*

It was too late for that now, however. Theon had no choice but to lead Asha to Ned Stark's solar. There, before the ashes of a dead fire, he blurted, "Dagmer's lost the fight at Torrhen's Square—"

"The old castellan broke his shield wall, yes," Asha said calmly. "What did you expect? This Ser Rodrik knows the land intimately, as the Cleftjaw does not, and many of the northmen were mounted. The ironborn lack the discipline to stand a charge of armored horse. Dagmer lives, be grateful for that much. He's leading the survivors back toward the Stony Shore."

She knows more than I do, Theon realized. That only made him angrier. "The victory has given Leobald Tallhart the courage to come out from behind his walls and join Ser Rodrik. And I've had reports that Lord Manderly has sent a dozen barges upriver packed with knights, warhorses, and siege engines. The Umbers are gathering beyond the Last River as well. I'll have an *army* at my gates before the moon turns, and you bring me only *ten men*?"

"I need not have brought you any."

"I commanded you—"

"*Father* commanded me to take Deepwood Motte," she snapped. "He said nothing of me having to rescue my little brother."

"Bugger Deepwood," he said. "It's a wooden pisspot on a hill. Winterfell is the heart of the land, but how am I to hold it without a garrison?"

"You might have thought of that before you took it. Oh, it was cleverly done, I'll grant you. If only you'd had the good sense to raze the castle and carry the two little princelings back to Pyke as hostages, you might have won the war in a stroke."

"You'd like that, wouldn't you? To see my prize reduced to ruins and ashes."

"Your prize will be the doom of you. Krakens rise from the *sea*, Theon, or did you forget that during your years among the wolves? Our strength is in our longships. My wooden pisspot sits close enough to the sea for supplies and fresh men to reach me whenever they are needful. But Winterfell is hundreds of leagues inland, ringed by woods, hills, and hostile holdfasts and castles. And every man in a thousand leagues is your enemy now, make no mistake. You made certain of that when you mounted those heads on your gatehouse." Asha shook her head. "How could you be such a bloody fool? *Children . . .*"

"They defied me!" he shouted in her face. "And it was blood for blood besides, two sons of Eddard Stark to pay for Rodrik and Maron." The words tumbled out heedlessly, but Theon knew at once that his father would approve. "I've laid my brothers' ghosts to rest."

"Our brothers," Asha reminded him, with a half smile that suggested she took his talk of vengeance well salted. "Did you bring their ghosts from Pyke, brother? And here I thought they haunted only Father."

"When has a maid ever understood a man's need for revenge?" Even if his father did not appreciate the gift of Winterfell, he *must* approve of Theon avenging his brothers!

Asha snorted back a laugh. "This Ser Rodrik may well feel the same manly need, did you think of that? You are blood of my blood, Theon, whatever else you may be. For the sake of the mother who bore us both, return to Deepwood Motte with me. Put Winterfell to the torch and fall back while you still can."

"No." Theon adjusted his crown. "I took this castle and I mean to hold it."

His sister looked at him a long time. "Then hold it you shall," she said, "for the rest of your life." She sighed. "I say it tastes like folly, but what would a shy maid know of such things?" At the door she gave him one last mocking smile. "You ought to know, that's the ugliest crown I've ever laid eyes on. Did you make it yourself?"

She left him fuming, and lingered no longer than was needful to feed and water her horses. Half the men she'd brought returned with her as threatened, riding out the same Hunter's Gate that Bran and Rickon had used for their escape.

Theon watched them go from atop the wall. As his sister vanished into the mists of the wolfswood he found himself wondering why he had not listened and gone with her.

"Gone, has she?" Reek was at his elbow.

Theon had not heard him approach, nor smelled him either. He could not think of anyone he wanted to see less. It made him uneasy to see the man walking around breathing, with what he knew. *I should have had him killed after he did the others,* he reflected, but the notion made him nervous. Unlikely as it seemed, Reek could read and write, and he was possessed of enough base cunning to have hidden an account of what they'd done.

"M'lord prince, if you'll pardon me saying, it's not right for her to abandon you. And ten men, that won't be near enough."

"I am well aware of that," Theon said. *So was Asha.*

"Well, might be I could help you," said Reek. "Give me a horse and bag o' coin, and I could find you some good fellows."

Theon narrowed his eyes. "How many?"

"A hundred, might be. Two hundred. Maybe more." He smiled, his pale eyes glinting. "I was born up north here. I know many a man, and many a man knows Reek."

Two hundred men were not an army, but you didn't need thousands to hold a castle as strong as Winterfell. So long as they could learn which end of a spear did the killing, they might make all the difference. "Do as you say and you'll not find me ungrateful. You can name your own reward."

"Well, m'lord, I haven't had no woman since I was with Lord Ramsay," Reek said. "I've had my eye on that Palla, and I hear she's already been had, so . . ."

He had gone too far with Reek to turn back now. "Two hundred men and she's yours. But a man less and you can go back to fucking pigs."

Reek was gone before the sun went down, carrying a bag of Stark silver and the last of Theon's hopes. *Like as not, I'll never see the wretch again,* he thought bitterly, but even so the chance had to be taken.

That night he dreamed of the feast Ned Stark had thrown when King Robert came to Winterfell. The hall rang with music and laughter, though the cold winds were rising outside. At first it was all wine and roast meat, and Theon was making japes and eyeing the serving girls and having himself a fine time . . . until he noticed that the room was growing darker. The music did not seem so jolly then; he heard discords and strange silences, and notes that hung in the air bleeding. Suddenly the wine turned bitter in his mouth, and when he looked up from his cup he saw that he was dining with the dead.

King Robert sat with his guts spilling out on the table from the great gash in his belly, and Lord Eddard was headless beside him. Corpses lined the benches below, grey-brown flesh sloughing off their bones as they raised their cups to toast, worms crawling in and out of the holes that were their eyes. He knew them, every one; Jory Cassel and Fat Tom, Porther and Cayn and Hullen the master of horse, and all the others who had ridden south to King's Landing never to return. Mikken and Chayle sat together, one dripping blood and the other water. Benfred Tallhart and his Wild Hares filled most of a table. The miller's wife was there as well, and Farlen, even the wildling Theon had killed in the wolfswood the day he had saved Bran's life.

But there were others with faces he had never known in life, faces he had seen only in stone. The slim, sad girl who wore a crown of pale blue roses and a white gown spattered with gore could only be Lyanna. Her brother Brandon stood beside her, and their father Lord Rickard just behind. Along the walls figures half-seen moved through the shadows, pale shades with long grim faces. The sight of them sent fear shivering through Theon sharp as a knife. And then the tall doors opened with a crash, and a freezing gale blew down the hall, and Robb came walking out of the night. Grey Wind stalked beside, eyes burning, and man and wolf alike bled from half a hundred savage wounds.

Theon woke with a scream, startling Wex so badly that the boy ran naked from the room. When his guards burst in with drawn swords, he ordered them to bring him the maester. By the time Luwin arrived rumpled and sleepy, a cup of wine had steadied Theon's hands, and he was feeling ashamed of his panic. "A dream," he muttered, "that was all it was. It meant nothing."

"Nothing," Luwin agreed solemnly. He left a sleeping draught, but Theon poured it down the privy shaft the moment he was gone. Luwin was a man as well as a maester, and the man had no love for him. *He wants me to sleep, yes . . . to sleep and never wake. He'd like that as much as Asha would.*

He sent for Kyra, kicked shut the door, climbed on top of her, and fucked the wench with a fury he'd never known was in him. By the time he finished, she was sobbing, her neck and breasts covered with bruises and bite marks. Theon shoved her from the bed and threw her a blanket. "Get out."

Yet even then, he could not sleep.

Come dawn, he dressed and went outside, to walk along the outer walls. A brisk autumn wind was swirling through the battlements. It reddened his cheeks and stung his eyes. He watched the forest go from grey to green below him as light filtered through the silent trees. On his left he could see tower tops above the inner wall, their roofs gilded by the rising sun. The red leaves of the weirwood were a blaze of flame among the green. *Ned Stark's tree*, he thought, and *Stark's wood, Stark's castle, Stark's sword, Stark's gods. This is their place, not mine. I am a Greyjoy of Pyke, born to paint a kraken on my shield and sail the great salt sea. I should have gone with Asha.*

On their iron spikes atop the gatehouse, the heads waited.

Theon gazed at them silently while the wind tugged on his cloak with small ghostly hands. The miller's boys had been of an age with Bran and Rickon, alike in size and coloring, and once Reek had flayed the skin from their faces and dipped their heads in tar, it was easy to see familiar features in those misshapen lumps of rotting flesh. People were such fools. *If we'd said they were rams' heads, they would have seen horns.*

SANSA

They had been singing in the sept all morning, since the first report of enemy sails had reached the castle. The sound of their voices mingled with the whicker of horses, the clank of steel, and the groaning hinges of the great bronze gates to make a strange and fearful music. *In the sept they sing for the Mother's mercy but on the walls it's the Warrior they pray to, and all in silence.* She remembered how Septa Mordane used to tell them that the Warrior and the Mother were only two faces of the same great god. *But if there is only one, whose prayers will be heard?*

Ser Meryn Trant held the blood bay for Joffrey to mount. Boy and horse alike wore gilded mail and enameled crimson plate, with matching golden lions on their heads. The pale sunlight flashed off the golds and reds every time Joff moved. *Bright, shining, and empty,* Sansa thought.

The Imp was mounted on a red stallion, armored more plainly than the king in battle gear that made him look like a little boy dressed up in his father's clothes. But there was nothing childish about the battle-axe slung below his shield. Ser Mandon Moore rode at his side, white steel icy bright. When Tyrion saw her he turned his horse her way. "Lady Sansa," he called from the saddle, "surely my sister has asked you to join the other highborn ladies in Maegor's?"

"She has, my lord, but King Joffrey sent for me to see him off. I mean to visit the sept as well, to pray."

"I won't ask for whom." His mouth twisted oddly; if that was a smile, it was the queerest she had ever seen. "This day may change all. For you as well as for House Lannister. I ought to have sent you off with Tommen, now that I think on it. Still, you should be safe enough in Maegor's, so long as—"

"*Sansa!*" The boyish shout rang across the yard; Joffrey had seen her. "Sansa, here!"

He calls me as if he were calling a dog, she thought.

"His Grace has need of you," Tyrion Lannister observed. "We'll talk again after the battle, if the gods permit."

Sansa threaded her way through a file of gold-cloaked spearmen as Joffrey beckoned her closer. "It will be battle soon, everyone says so."

"May the gods have mercy on us all."

"My uncle's the one who will need mercy, but I won't give him any." Joffrey drew his sword. The pommel was a ruby cut in the shape of a heart, set between a lion's jaws. Three fullers were deeply incised in the blade. "My new blade, Hearteater."

He'd owned a sword named Lion's Tooth once, Sansa remembered. Arya had taken it from him and thrown it in a river. *I hope Stannis does the same with this one.* "It is beautifully wrought, Your Grace."

"Bless my steel with a kiss." He extended the blade down to her. "Go on, kiss it."

He had never sounded more like a stupid little boy. Sansa touched her lips to the metal, thinking that she would kiss any number of swords sooner than Joffrey. The gesture seemed to please him, though. He sheathed the blade with a flourish. "You'll kiss it again when I return, and taste my uncle's blood."

Only if one of your Kingsguard kills him for you. Three of the White Swords would go with Joffrey and his uncle: Ser Meryn, Ser Mandon, and Ser Osmund Kettleblack. "Will you lead your knights into battle?" Sansa asked, hoping.

"I would, but my uncle the Imp says my uncle Stannis will never cross the river. I'll command the Three Whores, though. I'm going to see to the traitors myself." The prospect made Joff smile. His plump pink lips always made him look pouty. Sansa had liked that once, but now it made her sick.

"They say my brother Robb always goes where the fighting is thickest," she said recklessly. "Though he's older than Your Grace, to be sure. A man grown."

That made him frown. "I'll deal with your brother after I'm done with my traitor uncle. I'll gut him with Hearteater, you'll see." He wheeled his horse about and spurred toward the gate. Ser Meryn and Ser Osmund fell in to his right and left, the gold cloaks following four abreast. The Imp and Ser Mandon Moore brought up the rear. The guards saw them off with shouts and cheers. When the last was gone, a sudden stillness settled over the yard, like the hush before a storm.

Through the quiet, the singing pulled at her. Sansa turned toward the sept. Two stableboys followed, and one of the guards whose watch was ended. Others fell in behind them.

Sansa had never seen the sept so crowded, nor so brightly lit; great shafts of rainbow-colored sunlight slanted down through the crystals in the high windows, and candles burned on every side, their little flames twinkling like stars. The Mother's altar and the Warrior's swam in light, but Smith and Crone and Maid and Father had their worshipers as well, and there were even a few flames dancing below the Stranger's half-human face . . . for what was Stannis Baratheon, if not the Stranger come to judge them? Sansa visited each of the Seven in turn, lighting a candle at each altar, and then found herself a place on the benches between a wizened old washerwoman and a boy no older than Rickon, dressed in the fine linen tunic of a knight's son. The old woman's hand was bony and hard with callus, the boy's small and soft, but it was good to have someone to hold on to. The air was hot and heavy, smelling of incense and sweat, crystal-kissed and candle-bright; it made her dizzy to breathe it.

She knew the hymn; her mother had taught it to her once, a long time ago in Winterfell. She joined her voice to theirs.

> *Gentle Mother, font of mercy,*
> *save our sons from war, we pray,*
> *stay the swords and stay the arrows,*
> *let them know a better day.*
> *Gentle Mother, strength of women,*
> *help our daughters through this fray,*
> *soothe the wrath and tame the fury,*
> *teach us all a kinder way.*

Across the city, thousands had jammed into the Great Sept of Baelor on Visenya's Hill, and they would be singing too, their voices swelling out over the city, across the river, and up into the sky. *Surely the gods must hear us,* she thought.

Sansa knew most of the hymns, and followed along on those she did not know as best she could. She sang along with grizzled old serving men and anxious young wives, with serving girls and soldiers, cooks and falconers, knights and knaves, squires and spit boys and nursing mothers. She sang with those inside the castle walls and those without, sang with all the city. She sang for mercy, for the living and the dead alike, for Bran and Rickon and Robb, for her sister Arya and her bastard brother Jon

Snow, away off on the Wall. She sang for her mother and her father, for her grandfather Lord Hoster and her uncle Edmure Tully, for her friend Jeyne Poole, for old drunken King Robert, for Septa Mordane and Ser Dontos and Jory Cassel and Maester Luwin, for all the brave knights and soldiers who would die today, and for the children and the wives who would mourn them, and finally, toward the end, she even sang for Tyrion the Imp and for the Hound. *He is no true knight but he saved me all the same*, she told the Mother. *Save him if you can, and gentle the rage inside him.*

But when the septon climbed on high and called upon the gods to protect and defend their true and noble king, Sansa got to her feet. The aisles were jammed with people. She had to shoulder through while the septon called upon the Smith to lend strength to Joffrey's sword and shield, the Warrior to give him courage, the Father to defend him in his need. *Let his sword break and his shield shatter*, Sansa thought coldly as she shoved out through the doors, *let his courage fail him and every man desert him.*

A few guards paced along on the gatehouse battlements, but otherwise the castle seemed empty. Sansa stopped and listened. Away off, she could hear the sounds of battle. The singing almost drowned them out, but the sounds were there if you had the ears to hear: the deep moan of warhorns, the creak and thud of catapults flinging stones, the splashes and splinterings, the crackle of burning pitch and *thrum* of scorpions loosing their yard-long iron-headed shafts . . . and beneath it all, the cries of dying men.

It was another sort of song, a terrible song. Sansa pulled the hood of her cloak up over her ears, and hurried toward Maegor's Holdfast, the castle-within-a-castle where the queen had promised they would all be safe. At the foot of the drawbridge, she came upon Lady Tanda and her two daughters. Falyse had arrived yesterday from Castle Stokeworth with a small troop of soldiers. She was trying to coax her sister onto the bridge, but Lollys clung to her maid, sobbing, "I don't want to, I don't want to, I don't want to."

"The battle is *begun*," Lady Tanda said in a brittle voice.

"I don't want to, I don't want to."

There was no way Sansa could avoid them. She greeted them courteously. "May I be of help?"

Lady Tanda flushed with shame. "No, my lady, but we thank you kindly. You must forgive my daughter, she has not been well."

"I don't want to." Lollys clutched at her maid, a slender, pretty girl with short dark hair who looked as though she wanted nothing so much as to shove her mistress into the dry moat, onto those iron spikes. "Please, please, I don't want to."

Sansa spoke to her gently. "We'll all be thrice protected inside, and there's to be food and drink and song as well."

Lollys gaped at her, mouth open. She had dull brown eyes that always seemed to be wet with tears. "I don't want to."

"You *have* to," her sister Falyse said sharply, "and that is the end of it. Shae, help me." They each took an elbow, and together half dragged and half carried Lollys across the bridge. Sansa followed with their mother. "She's been sick," Lady Tanda said. *If a babe can be termed a sickness,* Sansa thought. It was common gossip that Lollys was with child.

The two guards at the door wore the lion-crested helms and crimson cloaks of House Lannister, but Sansa knew they were only dressed-up sellswords. Another sat at the foot of the stair—a real guard would have been standing, not sitting on a step with his halberd across his knees— but he rose when he saw them and opened the door to usher them inside.

The Queen's Ballroom was not a tenth the size of the castle's Great Hall, only half as big as the Small Hall in the Tower of the Hand, but it could still seat a hundred, and it made up in grace what it lacked in space. Beaten silver mirrors backed every wall sconce, so the torches burned twice as bright; the walls were paneled in richly carved wood, and sweet-smelling rushes covered the floors. From the gallery above drifted down the merry strains of pipes and fiddle. A line of arched windows ran along the south wall, but they had been closed off with heavy draperies. Thick velvet hangings admitted no thread of light, and would muffle the sound of prayer and war alike. *It makes no matter,* Sansa thought. *The war is with us.*

Almost every highborn woman in the city sat at the long trestle tables, along with a handful of old men and young boys. The women were wives, daughters, mothers, and sisters. Their men had gone out to fight Lord Stannis. Many would not return. The air was heavy with the knowledge. As Joffrey's betrothed, Sansa had the seat of honor on the queen's right hand. She was climbing the dais when she saw the man standing in the shadows by the back wall. He wore a long hauberk of oiled black mail, and held his sword before him: her father's greatsword, Ice, near as tall as he was. Its point rested on the floor, and his hard bony fingers curled around the crossguard on either side of the grip. Sansa's breath caught in her throat. Ser Ilyn Payne seemed to sense her stare. He turned his gaunt, pox-ravaged face toward her.

"What is *he* doing here?" she asked Osfryd Kettleblack. He captained the queen's new red cloak guard.

Osfryd grinned. "Her Grace expects she'll have need of him before the night's done."

Ser Ilyn was the King's Justice. There was only one service he might be needed for. *Whose head does she want?*

"All rise for Her Grace, Cersei of House Lannister, Queen Regent and Protector of the Realm," the royal steward cried.

Cersei's gown was snowy linen, white as the cloaks of the Kingsguard. Her long dagged sleeves showed a lining of gold satin. Masses of bright yellow hair tumbled to her bare shoulders in thick curls. Around her slender neck hung a rope of diamonds and emeralds. The white made her look strangely innocent, almost maidenly, but there were points of color on her cheeks.

"Be seated," the queen said when she had taken her place on the dais, "and be welcome." Osfryd Kettleblack held her chair; a page performed the same service for Sansa. "You look pale, Sansa," Cersei observed. "Is your red flower still blooming?"

"Yes."

"How apt. The men will bleed out there, and you in here." The queen signaled for the first course to be served.

"Why is Ser Ilyn here?" Sansa blurted out.

The queen glanced at the mute headsman. "To deal with treason, and to defend us if need be. He was a knight before he was a headsman." She pointed her spoon toward the end of the hall, where the tall wooden doors had been closed and barred. "When the axes smash down those doors, you may be glad of him."

I would be gladder if it were the Hound, Sansa thought. Harsh as he was, she did not believe Sandor Clegane would let any harm come to her. "Won't your guards protect us?"

"And who will protect us from my guards?" The queen gave Osfryd a sideways look. "Loyal sellswords are rare as virgin whores. If the battle is lost, my guards will trip on those crimson cloaks in their haste to rip them off. They'll steal what they can and flee, along with the serving men, washerwomen, and stableboys, all out to save their own worthless hides. Do you have any notion what happens when a city is sacked, Sansa? No, you wouldn't, would you? All you know of life you learned from singers, and there's such a dearth of good sacking songs."

"True knights would never harm women and children." The words rang hollow in her ears even as she said them.

"True knights." The queen seemed to find that wonderfully amusing. "No doubt you're right. So why don't you just eat your broth like a good girl and wait for Symeon Star-Eyes and Prince Aemon the Dragonknight to come rescue you, sweetling. I'm sure it won't be very long now."

DAVOS

Blackwater Bay was rough and choppy, whitecaps everywhere. *Black Betha* rode the flood tide, her sail cracking and snapping at each shift of wind. *Wraith* and *Lady Marya* sailed beside her, no more than twenty yards between their hulls. His sons could keep a line. Davos took pride in that.

Across the sea warhorns boomed, deep throaty moans like the calls of monstrous serpents, repeated ship to ship. "Bring down the sail," Davos commanded. "Lower mast. Oarsmen to your oars." His son Matthos relayed the commands. The deck of *Black Betha* churned as crewmen ran to their tasks, pushing through the soldiers who always seemed to be in the way no matter where they stood. Ser Imry had decreed that they would enter the river on oars alone, so as not to expose their sails to the scorpions and spitfires on the walls of King's Landing.

Davos could make out *Fury* well to the southeast, her sails shimmering golden as they came down, the crowned stag of Baratheon blazoned on the canvas. From her decks Stannis Baratheon had commanded the assault on Dragonstone sixteen years before, but this time he had chosen to ride with his army, trusting *Fury* and the command of his fleet to his wife's brother Ser Imry, who'd come over to his cause at Storm's End with Lord Alester and all the other Florents.

Davos knew *Fury* as well as he knew his own ships. Above her three hundred oars was a deck given over wholly to scorpions, and topside she mounted catapults fore and aft, large enough to fling barrels of burning pitch. A most formidable ship, and very swift as well, although Ser Imry had packed her bow to stern with armored knights and men-at-arms, at some cost to her speed.

The warhorns sounded again, commands drifting back from the *Fury*. Davos felt a tingle in his missing fingertips. "Out oars," he shouted. "Form line." A hundred blades dipped down into the water as the oarmaster's drum began to boom. The sound was like the beating of a great slow heart, and the oars moved at every stroke, a hundred men pulling as one.

Wooden wings had sprouted from the *Wraith* and *Lady Marya* as well. The three galleys kept pace, their blades churning the water. "Slow cruise," Davos called. Lord Velaryon's silver-hulled *Pride of Driftmark* had moved into her position to port of *Wraith*, and *Bold Laughter* was coming up fast, but *Harridan* was only now getting her oars into the water and *Seahorse* was still struggling to bring down her mast. Davos looked astern. Yes, there, far to the south, that could only be *Swordfish*, lagging as ever. She dipped two hundred oars and mounted the largest ram in the fleet, though Davos had grave doubts about her captain.

He could hear soldiers shouting encouragement to each other across the water. They'd been little more than ballast since Storm's End, and were eager to get at the foe, confident of victory. In that, they were of one mind with their admiral, Lord High Captain Ser Imry Florent.

Three days past, he had summoned all his captains to a war council aboard the *Fury* while the fleet lay anchored at the mouth of the Wendwater, in order to acquaint them with his dispositions. Davos and his sons had been assigned a place in the second line of battle, well out on the dangerous starboard wing. "A place of honor," Allard had declared, well satisfied with the chance to prove his valor. "A place of peril," his father had pointed out. His sons had given him pitying looks, even young Maric. *The Onion Knight has become an old woman*, he could hear them thinking, *still a smuggler at heart*.

Well, the last was true enough, he would make no apologies for it. *Seaworth* had a lordly ring to it, but down deep he was still Davos of Flea Bottom, coming home to his city on its three high hills. He knew as much of ships and sails and shores as any man in the Seven Kingdoms, and had fought his share of desperate fights sword to sword on a wet deck. But to this sort of battle he came a maiden, nervous and afraid. Smugglers do not sound warhorns and raise banners. When they smell danger, they raise sail and run before the wind.

Had he been admiral, he might have done it all differently. For a start, he would have sent a few of his swiftest ships to probe upriver and see what awaited them, instead of smashing in headlong. When he had suggested as much to Ser Imry, the Lord High Captain had thanked him courteously, but his eyes were not as polite. *Who is this lowborn craven?* those eyes asked. *Is he the one who bought his knighthood with an onion?*

With four times as many ships as the boy king, Ser Imry saw no need for caution or deceptive tactics. He had organized the fleet into ten lines of battle, each of twenty ships. The first two lines would sweep up the river to engage and destroy Joffrey's little fleet, or "the boy's toys" as Ser Imry dubbed them, to the mirth of his lordly captains. Those that followed would land companies of archers and spearmen beneath the city walls, and only then join the fight on the river. The smaller, slower ships to the rear would ferry over the main part of Stannis's host from the south bank, protected by Salladhor Saan and his Lyseni, who would stand out in the bay in case the Lannisters had other ships hidden up along the coast, poised to sweep down on their rear.

To be fair, there was reason for Ser Imry's haste. The winds had not used them kindly on the voyage up from Storm's End. They had lost two cogs to the rocks of Shipbreaker Bay on the very day they set sail, a poor way to begin. One of the Myrish galleys had foundered in the Straits of Tarth, and a storm had overtaken them as they were entering the Gullet, scattering the fleet across half the narrow sea. All but twelve ships had finally regrouped behind the sheltering spine of Massey's Hook, in the calmer waters of Blackwater Bay, but not before they had lost considerable time.

Stannis would have reached the Rush days ago. The kingsroad ran from Storm's End straight to King's Landing, a much shorter route than by sea, and his host was largely mounted; near twenty thousand knights, light horse, and freeriders, Renly's unwilling legacy to his brother. They would have made good time, but armored destriers and twelve-foot lances would avail them little against the deep waters of the Blackwater Rush and the high stone walls of the city. Stannis would be camped with his lords on the south bank of the river, doubtless seething with impatience and wondering what Ser Imry had done with his fleet.

Off Merling Rock two days before, they had sighted a half-dozen fishing skiffs. The fisherfolk had fled before them, but one by one they had been overtaken and boarded. "A small spoon of victory is just the thing to settle the stomach before battle," Ser Imry had declared happily. "It makes the men hungry for a larger helping." But Davos had been more interested in what the captives had to say about the defenses at King's Landing. The dwarf had been busy building some sort of boom to close off the mouth of the river, though the fishermen differed as to whether the work had been completed or not. He found himself wishing it had. If the river was closed to them, Ser Imry would have no choice but to pause and take stock.

The sea was full of sound: shouts and calls, warhorns and drums and the trill of pipes, the slap of wood on water as thousands of oars rose and fell. *"Keep line,"* Davos shouted. A gust of wind tugged at his old green cloak. A jerkin of boiled leather and a pothelm at his feet were his only armor. At sea, heavy steel was as like to cost a man his life as to save it, he believed. Ser Imry and the other highborn captains did not share his view; they glittered as they paced their decks.

Harridan and *Seahorse* had slipped into their places now, and Lord Celtigar's *Red Claw* beyond them. To starboard of Allard's *Lady Marya* were the three galleys that Stannis had seized from the unfortunate Lord Sunglass, *Piety*, *Prayer*, and *Devotion*, their decks crawling with archers. Even *Swordfish* was closing, lumbering and rolling through a thickening sea under both oars and sail. *A ship of that many oars ought to be much faster*, Davos reflected with disapproval. *It's that ram she carries, it's too big, she has no balance.*

The wind was gusting from the south, but under oars it made no matter. They would be sweeping in on the flood tide, but the Lannisters would have the river current to their favor, and the Blackwater Rush flowed strong and swift where it met the sea. The first shock would inevitably favor the foe. *We are fools to meet them on the Blackwater,* Davos thought. In any encounter on the open sea, their battle lines would envelop the enemy fleet on both flanks, driving them inward to destruction. On the river, though, the numbers and weight of Ser Imry's ships would count for less. They could not dress more than twenty ships abreast, lest they risk tangling their oars and colliding with each other.

Beyond the line of warships, Davos could see the Red Keep up on Aegon's High Hill, dark against a lemon sky, with the mouth of the Rush opening out below. Across the river the south shore was black with men and horses, stirring like angry ants as they caught sight of the approaching ships. Stannis would have kept them busy building rafts and fletching arrows, yet even so the waiting would have been a hard thing to bear. Trumpets sounded from among them, tiny and brazen, soon swallowed by the roar of a thousand shouts. Davos closed his stubby hand around the pouch that held his fingerbones, and mouthed a silent prayer for luck.

Fury herself would center the first line of battle, flanked by the *Lord Steffon* and the *Stag of the Sea*, each of two hundred oars. On the port and starboard wings were the hundreds: *Lady Harra, Brightfish, Laughing Lord, Sea Demon, Horned Honor, Ragged Jenna, Trident Three, Swift Sword, Princess Rhaenys, Dog's Nose, Sceptre, Faithful, Red Raven, Queen Alysanne, Cat, Courageous,* and *Dragonsbane*. From every stern streamed the fiery heart of the Lord of Light, red and yellow and orange. Behind Davos and his sons came another line of hundreds commanded by knights and lordly captains, and then the smaller, slower Myrish contingent, none dipping more than eighty oars. Farther back would come the sailed ships, carracks and lumbering great cogs, and last of all Salladhor Saan in his proud *Valyrian*, a towering three-hundred, paced by the rest of his galleys with their distinctive striped hulls. The flamboyant Lyseni princeling had not been pleased to be assigned the rear guard, but it was clear that Ser Imry trusted him no more than Stannis did. *Too many complaints, and too much talk of the gold he was owed.* Davos was sorry nonetheless. Salladhor Saan was a resourceful old pirate, and his crews were born seamen, fearless in a fight. They were wasted in the rear.

Ahooooooooooooooooooooooooooo. The call rolled across whitecaps and churning oars from the forecastle of the *Fury:* Ser Imry was sounding the attack. *Ahooooooooooooooooooooo, ahooooooooooooooooooooooo.*

Swordfish had joined the line at last, though she still had her sail raised. "Fast cruise," Davos barked. The drum began to beat more quickly, and the stroke picked up, the blades of the oars cutting water, *splash-swoosh, splash-swoosh, splash-swoosh.* On deck, soldiers banged sword against shield, while archers quietly strung their bows and pulled the first arrow from the quivers at their belts. The galleys of the first line of battle obscured his vision, so Davos paced the deck searching for a better view. He saw no sign of any boom; the mouth of the river was open, as if to swallow them all. Except . . .

In his smuggling days, Davos had often jested that he knew the waterfront at King's Landing a deal better than the back of his hand, since he had not spent a good part of his life sneaking in and out of the back of his hand. The squat towers of raw new stone that stood opposite one another at the mouth of the Blackwater might mean nothing to Ser Imry Florent, but to him it was as if two extra fingers had sprouted from his knuckles.

Shading his eyes against the westering sun, he peered at those towers more closely. They were too small to hold much of a garrison. The one on the north bank was built against the bluff with the Red Keep frowning above; its counterpart on the south shore had its footing in the water. *They dug a cut through the bank,* he knew at once. That would make the tower very difficult to assault; attackers would need to wade through the water or bridge the little channel. Stannis had posted bowmen below, to fire up at the defenders whenever one was rash enough to lift his head above the ramparts, but otherwise had not troubled.

Something flashed down low where the dark water swirled around the base of the tower. It was sunlight on steel, and it told Davos Seaworth all he needed to know. *A chain boom . . . and yet they have not closed the river against us. Why?*

He could make a guess at that as well, but there was no time to consider the question. A shout went up from the ships ahead, and the warhorns blew again: the enemy was before them.

Between the flashing oars of *Sceptre* and *Faithful*, Davos saw a thin line of galleys drawn across the river, the sun glinting off the gold paint that marked their hulls. He knew those ships as well as he knew his own. When he had been a smuggler, he'd always felt safer knowing whether the sail on the horizon marked a fast ship or a slow one, and whether her captain was a young man hungry for glory or an old one serving out his days.

Ahooooooooooooooooooooooooooooo, the warhorns called. "Battle speed," Davos shouted. On port and starboard he heard Dale and Allard giving the same command. Drums began to beat furiously, oars rose and fell, and *Black Betha* surged forward. When he glanced toward *Wraith*, Dale gave him a salute. *Swordfish* was lagging once more, wallowing in the wake of the smaller ships to either side; elsewise the line was straight as a shield wall.

The river that had seemed so narrow from a distance now stretched wide as a sea, but the city had grown gigantic as well. Glowering down from Aegon's High Hill, the Red Keep commanded the approaches. Its iron-crowned battlements, massive towers, and thick red walls gave it the aspect of a ferocious beast hunched above river and streets. The bluffs on which it crouched were steep and rocky, spotted with lichen and gnarled thorny trees. The fleet would have to pass below the castle to reach the harbor and city beyond.

The first line was in the river now, but the enemy galleys were backing water. *They mean to draw us in. They want us jammed close, constricted, no way to sweep around their flanks . . . and with that boom behind us.* He paced his deck, craning his neck for a better look at Joffrey's fleet. The boy's toys included the ponderous *Godsgrace*, he saw, the old slow *Prince Aemon*, the *Lady of Silk* and her sister *Lady's Shame*, *Wildwind*, *Kingslander*, *White Hart*, *Lance*, *Seaflower*. But where was the *Lionstar*? Where was the beautiful *Lady Lyanna* that King Robert had named in honor of the maid he'd loved and lost? And where was *King Robert's Hammer*? She was the largest war galley in the royal fleet, four hundred oars, the only warship the boy king owned capable of overmatching *Fury*. By rights she should have formed the heart of any defense.

Davos tasted a trap, yet he saw no sign of any foes sweeping in behind them, only the great fleet of Stannis Baratheon in their ordered ranks, stretching back to the watery horizon. *Will they raise the chain and cut us in two?* He could not see what good that would serve. The ships left out in the bay could still land men north of the city; a slower crossing, but safer.

A flight of flickering orange birds took wing from the castle, twenty or thirty of them; pots of burning pitch, arcing out over the river trailing threads of flame. The waters ate most, but a few found the decks of galleys in the first line of battle, spreading flame when they shattered. Men-at-arms were scrambling on *Queen Alysanne*'s deck, and he could see smoke rising from three different spots on *Dragonsbane*, nearest the bank. By then a second flight was on its way, and arrows were falling as well, hissing down from the archers' nests that studded the towers above. A soldier tumbled over *Cat*'s gunwale, crashed off the oars, and sank. *The first man to die today*, Davos thought, *but he will not be the last.*

Atop the Red Keep's battlements streamed the boy king's banners: the crowned stag of Baratheon on its gold field, the lion of Lannister on crimson. More pots of pitch came flying. Davos heard men shriek as fire spread across *Courageous*. Her oarsmen were safe below, protected from missiles by the half deck that sheltered them, but the men-at-arms crowded topside were not so fortunate. The starboard wing was taking all the damage, as he had feared. *It will be our turn soon*, he reminded himself, uneasy. *Black Betha* was well in range of the firepots, being the sixth ship out from the north bank. To starboard, she had only Allard's *Lady Marya*, the ungainly *Swordfish*—so far behind now that she was nearer the third line than the second—and *Piety*, *Prayer*, and *Devotion*, who would need all the godly intervention they could get, placed as vulnerably as they were.

As the second line swept past the twin towers, Davos took a closer look. He could see three links of a huge chain snaking out from a hole no bigger than a man's head and disappearing under the water. The towers had a single door, set a good twenty feet off the ground. Bowmen on the roof of the northern tower were firing down at *Prayer* and *Devotion*. The archers on *Devotion* fired back, and Davos heard a man scream as the arrows found him.

"Captain ser." His son Matthos was at his elbow. "Your helm." Davos took it with both hands and slid it over his head. The pothelm was visorless; he hated having his vision impeded.

By then the pitch pots were raining down around them. He saw one shatter on the deck of *Lady Marya*, but Allard's crew quickly beat it out. To port, warhorns sounded from the *Pride of Driftmark*. The oars flung up sprays of water with every stroke. The yard-long shaft of a scorpion came down not two feet from Matthos and sank into the wood of the deck, thrumming. Ahead, the first line was within bowshot of the enemy; flights of arrows flew between the ships, hissing like striking snakes.

South of the Blackwater, Davos saw men dragging crude rafts toward the water while ranks and columns formed up beneath a thousand streaming banners. The fiery heart was everywhere, though the tiny black stag imprisoned in the flames was too small to make out. *We should be flying the crowned stag,* he thought. *The stag was King Robert's sigil, the city would rejoice to see it. This stranger's standard serves only to set men against us.*

He could not behold the fiery heart without thinking of the shadow Melisandre had birthed in the gloom beneath Storm's End. *At least we fight this battle in the light, with the weapons of honest men,* he told himself. The red woman and her dark children would have no part of it. Stannis had shipped her back to Dragonstone with his bastard nephew Edric Storm. His captains and bannermen had insisted that a battlefield was no place for a woman. Only the queen's men had dissented, and then not loudly. All the same, the king had been on the point of refusing them until Lord Bryce Caron said, "Your Grace, if the sorceress is with us, afterward men will say it was her victory, not yours. They will say you owe your crown to her spells." That had turned the tide. Davos himself had held his tongue during the arguments, but if truth be told, he had not been sad to see the back of her. He wanted no part of Melisandre or her god.

To starboard, *Devotion* drove toward shore, sliding out a plank. Archers scrambled into the shallows, holding their bows high over their heads to keep the strings dry. They splashed ashore on the narrow strand beneath the bluffs. Rocks came bouncing down from the castle to crash among them, and arrows and spears as well, but the angle was steep and the missiles seemed to do little damage.

Prayer landed two dozen yards upstream and *Piety* was slanting toward the bank when the defenders came pounding down the riverside, the hooves of their warhorses sending up gouts of water from the shallows. The knights fell among the archers like wolves among chickens, driving them back toward the ships and into the river before most could notch an arrow. Men-at-arms rushed to defend them with spear and axe, and in three heartbeats the scene had turned to blood-soaked chaos. Davos recognized the dog's-head helm of the Hound. A white cloak streamed from his shoulders as he rode his horse up the plank onto the deck of *Prayer*, hacking down anyone who blundered within reach.

Beyond the castle, King's Landing rose on its hills behind the encircling walls. The riverfront was a blackened desolation; the Lannisters had burned everything and pulled back within the Mud Gate. The charred spars of sunken hulks sat in the shallows, forbidding access to the long stone quays. *We shall have no landing there.* He could see the tops of three huge trebuchets behind the Mud Gate. High on Visenya's

Hill, sunlight blazed off the seven crystal towers of the Great Sept of Baelor.

Davos never saw the battle joined, but he heard it; a great rending crash as two galleys came together. He could not say which two. Another impact echoed over the water an instant later, and then a third. Beneath the screech of splintering wood, he heard the deep *thrum-thump* of the *Fury*'s fore catapult. *Stag of the Sea* split one of Joffrey's galleys clean in two, but *Dog's Nose* was afire and *Queen Alysanne* was locked between *Lady of Silk* and *Lady's Shame*, her crew fighting the boarders rail-to-rail.

Directly ahead, Davos saw the enemy's *Kingslander* drive between *Faithful* and *Sceptre*. The former slid her starboard oars out of the way before impact, but *Sceptre*'s portside oars snapped like so much kindling as *Kingslander* raked along her side. "Loose," Davos commanded, and his bowmen sent a withering rain of shafts across the water. He saw *Kingslander*'s captain fall, and tried to recall the man's name.

Ashore, the arms of the great trebuchets rose one, two, three, and a hundred stones climbed high into the yellow sky. Each one was as large as a man's head; when they fell they sent up great gouts of water, smashed through oak planking, and turned living men into bone and pulp and gristle. All across the river the first line was engaged. Grappling hooks were flung out, iron rams crashed through wooden hulls, boarders swarmed, flights of arrows whispered through each other in the drifting smoke, and men died . . . but so far, none of his.

Black Betha swept upriver, the sound of her oarmaster's drum thundering in her captain's head as he looked for a likely victim for her ram. The beleaguered *Queen Alysanne* was trapped between two Lannister warships, the three made fast by hooks and lines.

"*Ramming speed!*" Davos shouted.

The drumbeats blurred into a long fevered hammering, and *Black Betha* flew, the water turning white as milk as it parted for her prow. Allard had seen the same chance; *Lady Marya* ran beside them. The first line had been transformed into a confusion of separate struggles. The three tangled ships loomed ahead, turning, their decks a red chaos as men hacked at each other with sword and axe. *A little more*, Davos Seaworth beseeched the Warrior, *bring her around a little more, show me her broadside.*

The Warrior must have been listening. *Black Betha* and *Lady Marya* slammed into the side of *Lady's Shame* within an instant of each other, ramming her fore and aft with such force that men were thrown off the deck of *Lady of Silk* three boats away. Davos almost bit his tongue off when his teeth jarred together. He spat out blood. *Next time close your mouth, you fool.* Forty years at sea, and yet this was the first time he'd rammed another ship. His archers were loosing arrows at will.

"Back water," he commanded. When *Black Betha* reversed her oars, the river rushed into the splintered hole she left, and *Lady's Shame* fell to pieces before his eyes, spilling dozens of men into the river. Some of the living swam; some of the dead floated; the ones in heavy mail and plate sank to the bottom, the quick and the dead alike. The pleas of drowning men echoed in his ears.

A flash of green caught his eye, ahead and off to port, and a nest of writhing emerald serpents rose burning and hissing from the stern of *Queen Alysanne.* An instant later Davos heard the dread cry of *"Wildfire!"*

He grimaced. Burning pitch was one thing, wildfire quite another. Evil stuff, and well-nigh unquenchable. Smother it under a cloak and the cloak took fire; slap at a fleck of it with your palm and your hand was aflame. "Piss on wildfire and your cock burns off," old seamen liked to say. Still, Ser Imry had warned them to expect a taste of the alchemists' vile *substance.* Fortunately, there were few true pyromancers left. *They will soon run out,* Ser Imry had assured them.

Davos reeled off commands; one bank of oars pushed off while the other backed water, and the galley came about. *Lady Marya* had won clear too, and a good thing; the fire was spreading over *Queen Alysanne* and her foes faster than he would have believed possible. Men wreathed in green flame leapt into the water, shrieking like nothing human. On the walls of King's Landing, spitfires were belching death, and the great trebuchets behind the Mud Gate were throwing boulders. One the size of an ox crashed down between *Black Betha* and *Wraith*, rocking both ships and soaking every man on deck. Another, not much smaller, found *Bold Laughter.* The Velaryon galley exploded like a child's toy dropped from a tower, spraying splinters as long as a man's arm.

Through black smoke and swirling green fire, Davos glimpsed a swarm of small boats bearing downriver: a confusion of ferries and wherries, barges, skiffs, rowboats, and hulks that looked too rotten to float. It stank of desperation; such driftwood could not turn the tide of a fight, only get in the way. The lines of battle were hopelessly ensnarled, he saw. Off to port, *Lord Steffon, Ragged Jenna,* and *Swift Sword* had broken through and were sweeping upriver. The starboard wing was heavily engaged, however, and the center had shattered under the stones of those trebuchets, some captains turning downstream, others veering to port, anything to escape that crushing rain. *Fury* had swung her aft catapult to fire back at the city, but she lacked the range; the barrels of pitch were shattering under the walls. *Sceptre* had lost most of her oars, and *Faithful* had been rammed and was starting to list. He took *Black Betha* between them, and struck a glancing blow at Queen Cersei's ornate carved-and-gilded pleasure barge, laden with soldiers instead of sweetmeats now. The collision spilled a dozen of them into the river, where *Betha*'s archers picked them off as they tried to stay afloat.

Matthos's shout alerted him to the danger from port; one of the Lannister galleys was coming about to ram. "Hard to starboard," Davos shouted. His men used their oars to push free of the barge, while others turned the galley so her prow faced the onrushing *White Hart.* For a moment he feared he'd been too slow, that he was about to be sunk, but the current helped swing *Black Betha,* and when the impact came it was only a glancing blow, the two hulls scraping against each other, both ships snapping oars. A jagged piece of wood flew past his head, sharp as any spear. Davos flinched. "Board her!" he shouted. Grappling lines were flung. He drew his sword and led them over the rail himself.

The crew of the *White Hart* met them at the rail, but *Black Betha*'s men-at-arms swept over them in a screaming steel tide. Davos fought through the press, looking for the other captain, but the man was dead before he reached him. As he stood over the body, someone caught him from behind with an axe, but his helm turned the blow, and his skull was left ringing when it might have been split. Dazed, it was all he could do to roll. His attacker charged screaming. Davos grasped his sword in both hands and drove it up point first into the man's belly.

One of his crewmen pulled him back to his feet. "Captain ser, the *Hart* is ours." It was true, Davos saw. Most of the enemy were dead, dying, or yielded. He took off his helm, wiped blood from his face, and made his way back to his own ship, trodding carefully on boards slimy with men's guts. Matthos lent him a hand to help him back over the rail.

For those few instants, *Black Betha* and *White Hart* were the calm eye in the midst of the storm. *Queen Alysanne* and *Lady of Silk*, still locked together, were a ranging green inferno, drifting downriver and dragging pieces of *Lady's Shame.* One of the Myrish galleys had slammed into them and was now afire as well. *Cat* was taking on men from the fast-sinking *Courageous.* The captain of *Dragonsbane* had driven her between two quays, ripping out her bottom; her crew poured ashore with the archers and men-at-arms to join the assault on the walls. *Red Raven*, rammed, was slowly listing. *Stag of the Sea* was fighting fires and boarders both, but the fiery heart had been raised over Joffrey's *Loyal Man. Fury*, her proud bow smashed in by a boulder, was engaged with *Godsgrace.* He saw Lord Velaryon's *Pride of Driftmark* crash between two Lannister river runners, overturning one and lighting the other up with fire arrows. On the south bank, knights were leading their mounts aboard the cogs, and some of the smaller galleys were already making their way across, laden with men-at-arms. They had to thread cautiously between sinking ships and patches of drifting wildfire. The whole of King Stannis's fleet was in the river now, save for Salladhor Saan's Lyseni. Soon enough they would control the Blackwater. *Ser Imry will have his victory*, Davos thought, *and Stannis will bring his host across, but gods be good, the cost of this . . .*

"Captain ser!" Matthos touched his shoulder.

It was *Swordfish*, her two banks of oars lifting and falling. She had never brought down her sails, and some burning pitch had caught in her rigging. The flames spread as Davos watched, creeping out over ropes and sails until she trailed a head of yellow flame. Her ungainly iron ram, fashioned after the likeness of the fish from which she took her name, parted the surface of the river before her. Directly ahead, drifting toward her and swinging around to present a tempting plump target, was one of the Lannister hulks, floating low in the water. Slow green blood was leaking out between her boards.

When he saw that, Davos Seaworth's heart stopped beating.

"No," he said. "No, *NOOOOOO!*" Above the roar and crash of battle, no one heard him but Matthos. Certainly the captain of the *Swordfish* did not, intent as he was on finally spearing something with his ungainly fat sword. The *Swordfish* went to battle speed. Davos lifted his maimed hand to clutch at the leather pouch that held his fingerbones.

With a grinding, splintering, tearing crash, *Swordfish* split the rotted hulk asunder. She burst like an overripe fruit, but no fruit had ever screamed that shattering wooden scream. From inside her Davos saw green gushing from a thousand broken jars, poison from the entrails of a dying beast, glistening, shining, spreading across the surface of the river . . .

"Back water," he roared. "Away. Get us off her, back water, back water!" The grappling lines were cut, and Davos felt the deck move under his feet as *Black Betha* pushed free of *White Hart*. Her oars slid down into the water.

Then he heard a short sharp *woof*, as if someone had blown in his ear. Half a heartbeat later came the roar. The deck vanished beneath him, and black water smashed him across the face, filling his nose and mouth. He was choking, drowning. Unsure which way was up, Davos wrestled the river in blind panic until suddenly he broke the surface. He spat out water, sucked in air, grabbed hold of the nearest chunk of debris, and held on.

Swordfish and the hulk were gone, blackened bodies were floating downstream beside him, and choking men clinging to bits of smoking wood. Fifty feet high, a swirling demon of green flame danced upon the river. It had a dozen hands, in each a whip, and whatever they touched burst into fire. He saw *Black Betha* burning, and *White Hart* and *Loyal*

Man to either side. *Piety, Cat, Courageous, Sceptre, Red Raven, Harridan, Faithful, Fury,* they had all gone up, *Kingslander* and *Godsgrace* as well, the demon was eating his own. Lord Velaryon's shining *Pride of Driftmark* was trying to turn, but the demon ran a lazy green finger across her silvery oars and they flared up like so many tapers. For an instant she seemed to be stroking the river with two banks of long bright torches.

The current had him in its teeth by then, spinning him around and around. He kicked to avoid a floating patch of wildfire. *My sons,* Davos thought, but there was no way to look for them amidst the roaring chaos. Another hulk heavy with wildfire went up behind him. The Blackwater itself seemed to boil in its bed, and burning spars and burning men and pieces of broken ships filled the air.

I'm being swept out into the bay. It wouldn't be as bad there; he ought to be able to make shore, he was a strong swimmer. Salladhor Saan's galleys would be out in the bay as well, Ser Imry had commanded them to stand off . . .

And then the current turned him about again, and Davos saw what awaited him downstream.

The chain. Gods save us, they've raised the chain.

Where the river broadened out into Blackwater Bay, the boom stretched taut, a bare two or three feet above the water. Already a dozen galleys had crashed into it, and the current was pushing others against them. Almost all were aflame, and the rest soon would be. Davos could make out the striped hulls of Salladhor Saan's ships beyond, but he knew he would never reach them. A wall of red-hot steel, blazing wood, and swirling green flame stretched before him. The mouth of the Blackwater Rush had turned into the mouth of hell.

TYRION

Motionless as a gargoyle, Tyrion Lannister hunched on one knee atop a merlon. Beyond the Mud Gate and the desolation that had once been the fishmarket and wharves, the river itself seemed to have taken fire. Half of Stannis's fleet was ablaze, along with most of Joffrey's. The kiss of wildfire turned proud ships into funeral pyres and men into living torches. The air was full of smoke and arrows and screams.

Downstream, commoners and highborn captains alike could see the hot green death swirling toward their rafts and carracks and ferries, borne on the current of the Blackwater. The long white oars of the Myrish galleys flashed like the legs of maddened centipedes as they fought to come about, but it was no good. The centipedes had no place to run.

A dozen great fires raged under the city walls, where casks of burning pitch had exploded, but the wildfire reduced them to no more than candles in a burning house, their orange and scarlet pennons fluttering insignificantly against the jade holocaust. The low clouds caught the color of the burning river and roofed the sky in shades of shifting green, eerily beautiful. *A terrible beauty. Like dragonfire.* Tyrion wondered if Aegon the Conqueror had felt like this as he flew above his Field of Fire.

The furnace wind lifted his crimson cloak and beat at his bare face, yet he could not turn away. He was dimly aware of the gold cloaks cheering from the hoardings. He had no voice to join them. It was a half victory. *It will not be enough.*

He saw another of the hulks he'd stuffed full of King Aerys's fickle fruits engulfed by the hungry flames. A fountain of burning jade rose from the river, the blast so bright he had to shield his eyes. Plumes of fire thirty and forty feet high danced upon the waters, crackling and hissing. For a few moments they washed out the screams. There were hundreds in the water, drowning or burning or doing a little of both.

Do you hear them shrieking, Stannis? Do you see them burning? This is your work as much as mine. Somewhere in that seething mass of men south of the Blackwater, Stannis was watching too, Tyrion knew. He'd never had his brother Robert's thirst for battle. He would command from the rear, from the reserve, much as Lord Tywin Lannister was wont to do. Like as not, he was sitting a warhorse right now, clad in bright armor, his crown upon his head. *A crown of red gold, Varys says, its points fashioned in the shapes of flames.*

"My ships." Joffrey's voice cracked as he shouted up from the wallwalk, where he huddled with his guards behind the ramparts. The golden circlet of kingship adorned his battle helm. "My *Kingslander's* burning, *Queen Cersei, Loyal Man.* Look, that's *Seaflower,* there." He pointed with his new sword, out to where the green flames were licking at *Seaflower's* golden hull and creeping up her oars. Her captain had turned her upriver, but not quickly enough to evade the wildfire.

She was doomed, Tyrion knew. *There was no other way. If we had not come forth to meet them, Stannis would have sensed the trap.* An arrow could be aimed, and a spear, even the stone from a catapult, but wildfire had a will of its own. Once loosed, it was beyond the control of mere men. "It could not be helped," he told his nephew. "Our fleet was doomed in any case."

Even from atop the merlon—he had been too short to see over the ramparts, so he'd had them boost him up—the flames and smoke and chaos of battle made it impossible for Tyrion to see what was happening downriver under the castle, but he had seen it a thousand times in his mind's eye. Bronn would have whipped the oxen into motion the moment Stannis's flagship passed under the Red Keep; the chain was ponderous heavy, and the great winches turned but slowly, creaking and rumbling. The whole of the usurper's fleet would have passed by the time the first glimmer of metal could be seen beneath the water. The links would emerge dripping wet, some glistening with mud, link by link by link, until the whole great chain stretched taut. King Stannis had rowed his fleet up the Blackwater, but he would not row out again.

Even so, some were getting away. A river's current was a tricky thing, and the wildfire was not spreading as evenly as he had hoped. The main channel was all aflame, but a good many of the Myrmen had made for the south bank and looked to escape unscathed, and at least eight ships had landed under the city walls. *Landed or wrecked, but it comes to the same thing, they've put men ashore.* Worse, a good part of the south wing of the enemy's first two battle lines had been well upstream of the inferno when the hulks went up. Stannis would be left with thirty or forty galleys, at a guess; more than enough to bring his whole host across, once they had regained their courage.

That might take a bit of time; even the bravest would be dismayed after watching a thousand or so of his fellows consumed by wildfire. Hallyne said that sometimes the substance burned so hot that flesh melted like tallow. Yet even so . . .

Tyrion had no illusions where his own men were concerned. *If the battle looks to be going sour they'll break, and they'll break bad,* Jacelyn Bywater had warned him, so the only way to win was to make certain the battle stayed sweet, start to finish.

He could see dark shapes moving through the charred ruins of the riverfront wharfs. *Time for another sortie,* he thought. Men were never so vulnerable as when they first staggered ashore. He must not give the foe time to form up on the north bank.

He scrambled down off the merlon. "Tell Lord Jacelyn we've got enemy on the riverfront," he said to one of the runners Bywater had assigned him. To another he said, "Bring my compliments to Ser Arneld and ask him to swing the Whores thirty degrees west." The angle would allow them to throw farther, if not as far out into the water.

"Mother promised I could have the Whores," Joffrey said. Tyrion was annoyed to see that the king had lifted the visor of his helm again. Doubtless the boy was cooking inside all that heavy steel . . . but the last thing he needed was some stray arrow punching through his nephew's eye.

He clanged the visor shut. "Keep that closed, Your Grace; your sweet person is precious to us all." *And you don't want to spoil that pretty face, either.* "The Whores are yours." It was as good a time as any; flinging more firepots down onto burning ships seemed pointless. Joff had the Antler Men trussed up naked in the square below, antlers nailed to their heads. When they'd been brought before the Iron Throne for justice, he had promised to send them to Stannis. A man was not as heavy as a boulder or a cask of burning pitch, and could be thrown a deal farther. Some of the gold cloaks had been wagering on whether the traitors would fly all the way across the Blackwater. "Be quick about it, Your Grace," he told Joffrey. "We'll want the trebuchets throwing stones again soon enough. Even wildfire does not burn forever."

Joffrey hurried off happy, escorted by Ser Meryn, but Tyrion caught Ser Osmund by the wrist before he could follow. "Whatever happens, keep him safe and *keep him there,* is that understood?"

"As you command." Ser Osmund smiled amiably.

Tyrion had warned Trant and Kettleblack what would happen to them should any harm come to the king. And Joffrey had a dozen veteran gold cloaks waiting at the foot of the steps. *I'm protecting your wretched bastard as well as I can, Cersei,* he thought bitterly. *See you do the same for Alayaya.*

No sooner was Joff off than a runner came panting up the steps. "My lord, hurry!" He threw himself to one knee. "They've landed men on the tourney grounds, hundreds! They're bringing a ram up to the King's Gate."

Tyrion cursed and made for the steps with a rolling waddle. Podrick Payne waited below with their horses. They galloped off down River Row, Pod and Ser Mandon Moore coming hard behind him. The shuttered houses were steeped in green shadow, but there was no traffic to get in their way; Tyrion had commanded that the street be kept clear, so the defenders could move quickly from one gate to the next. Even so, by the time they reached the King's Gate, he could hear a booming crash of wood on wood that told him the battering ram had been brought into play. The groaning of the great hinges sounded like the moans of a dying giant. The gatehouse square was littered with the wounded, but he saw lines of horses as well, not all of them hurt, and sellswords and gold cloaks enough to form a strong column. "Form up," he shouted as he leapt to the ground. The gate moved under the impact of another blow. "Who commands here? You're going out."

"No." A shadow detached itself from the shadow of the wall, to become a tall man in dark grey armor. Sandor Clegane wrenched off his helm with both hands and let it fall to the ground. The steel was scorched and dented, the left ear of the snarling hound sheared off. A gash above one eye had sent a wash of blood down across the Hound's old burn scars, masking half his face.

"Yes." Tyrion faced him.

Clegane's breath came ragged. "Bugger that. And you."

A sellsword stepped up beside him. "We been out. Three times. Half our men are killed or hurt. Wildfire bursting all around us, horses screaming like men and men like horses—"

"Did you think we hired you to fight in a tourney? Shall I bring you a nice iced milk and a bowl of raspberries? No? Then get on your fucking horse. You too, dog."

The blood on Clegane's face glistened red, but his eyes showed white. He drew his longsword.

He is afraid, Tyrion realized, shocked. *The Hound is frightened.* He tried to explain their need. "They've taken a ram to the gate, you can hear them, we need to disperse them—"

"Open the gates. When they rush inside, surround them and kill them." The Hound thrust the point of his longsword into the ground and leaned upon the pommel, swaying. "I've lost half my men. Horse as well. I'm not taking more into that fire."

Ser Mandon Moore moved to Tyrion's side, immaculate in his enameled white plate. "The King's Hand commands you."

"Bugger the King's Hand." Where the Hound's face was not sticky with blood, it was pale as milk. "Someone bring me a drink." A gold cloak officer handed him a cup. Clegane took a swallow, spit it out, flung the cup away. "Water? Fuck your water. Bring me wine."

He is dead on his feet. Tyrion could see it now. *The wound, the fire . . . he's done, I need to find someone else, but who? Ser Mandon?* He looked at the men and knew it would not do. Clegane's fear had shaken them. Without a leader, they would refuse as well, and Ser Mandon . . . a dangerous man, Jaime said, yes, but not a man other men would follow.

In the distance Tyrion heard another great crash. Above the walls, the darkening sky was awash with sheets of green and orange light. How long could the gate hold?

This is madness, he thought, *but sooner madness than defeat. Defeat is death and shame.* "Very well, *I'll* lead the sortie."

If he thought that would shame the Hound back to valor, he was wrong. Clegane only laughed. *"You?"*

Tyrion could see the disbelief on their faces. "Me. Ser Mandon, you'll bear the king's banner. Pod, my helm." The boy ran to obey. The Hound leaned on that notched and blood-streaked sword and looked at him with those wide white eyes. Ser Mandon helped Tyrion mount up again. *"Form up!"* he shouted.

His big red stallion wore crinet and chamfron. Crimson silk draped his hindquarters, over a coat of mail. The high saddle was gilded. Podrik Payne handed up helm and shield, heavy oak emblazoned with a golden hand on red, surrounded by small golden lions. He walked his horse in a circle, looking at the little force of men. Only a handful had responded to his command, no more than twenty. They sat their horses with eyes as white as the Hound's. He looked contemptuously at the others, the knights and sellswords who had ridden with Clegane. "They say I'm half a man," he said. "What does that make the lot of you?"

That shamed them well enough. A knight mounted, helmetless, and rode to join the others. A pair of sellswords followed. Then more. The King's Gate shuddered again. In a few moments the size of Tyrion's command had doubled. He had them trapped. *If I fight, they must do the same, or they are less than dwarfs.*

"You won't hear me shout out Joffrey's name," he told them. "You won't hear me yell for Casterly Rock either. This is your city Stannis means to sack, and that's your gate he's bringing down. So come with me and kill the son of a bitch!" Tyrion unsheathed his axe, wheeled the stallion around, and trotted toward the sally port. He *thought* they were following, but never dared to look.

SANSA

The torches shimmered brightly against the hammered metal of the wall sconces, filling the Queen's Ballroom with silvery light. Yet there was still darkness in that hall. Sansa could see it in the pale eyes of Ser Ilyn Payne, who stood by the back door still as stone, taking neither food nor wine. She could hear it in Lord Gyles's racking cough, and the whispered voice of Osney Kettleblack when he slipped in to bring Cersei the tidings.

Sansa was finishing her broth when he came the first time, entering through the back. She glimpsed him talking to his brother Osfryd. Then he climbed the dais and knelt beside the high seat, smelling of horse, four long thin scratches on his cheek crusted with scabs, his hair falling down past his collar and into his eyes. For all his whispering, Sansa could not help but hear. "The fleets are locked in battle. Some archers got ashore, but the Hound's cut them to pieces, Y'Grace. Your brother's raising his chain, I heard the signal. Some drunkards down to Flea Bottom are smashing doors and climbing through windows. Lord Bywater's sent the gold cloaks to deal with them. Baelor's Sept is jammed full, everyone praying."

"And my son?"

"The king went to Baelor's to get the High Septon's blessing. Now he's walking the walls with the Hand, telling the men to be brave, lifting their spirits as it were."

Cersei beckoned to her page for another cup of wine, a golden vintage from the Arbor, fruity and rich. The queen was drinking heavily, but the wine only seemed to make her more beautiful; her cheeks were flushed, and her eyes had a bright, feverish heat to them as she looked down over the hall. *Eyes of wildfire,* Sansa thought.

Musicians played. Jugglers juggled. Moon Boy lurched about the hall on stilts making mock of everyone, while Ser Dontos chased serving girls on his broomstick horse. The guests laughed, but it was a joyless laughter, the sort of laughter that can turn into sobbing in half a heartbeat. *Their bodies are here, but their thoughts are on the city walls, and their hearts as well.*

After the broth came a salad of apples, nuts, and raisins. At any other time, it might have made a tasty dish, but tonight all the food was flavored with fear. Sansa was not the only one in the hall without an appetite. Lord Gyles was coughing more than he was eating, Lollys Stokeworth sat hunched and shivering, and the young bride of one of Ser Lancel's knights began to weep uncontrollably. The queen commanded Maester Frenken to put her to bed with a cup of dreamwine. "Tears," she said scornfully to Sansa as the woman was led from the hall. "The woman's weapon, my lady mother used to call them. The man's weapon is a sword. And that tells us all you need to know, doesn't it?"

"Men must be very brave, though," said Sansa. "To ride out and face swords and axes, everyone trying to kill you . . ."

"Jaime told me once that he only feels truly alive in battle and in bed." She lifted her cup and took a long swallow. Her salad was untouched. "I would sooner face any number of swords than sit helpless like this, pretending to enjoy the company of this flock of frightened hens."

"You asked them here, Your Grace."

"Certain things are expected of a queen. They will be expected of you should you ever wed Joffrey. Best learn." The queen studied the wives, daughters, and mothers who filled the benches. "Of themselves the hens are nothing, but their cocks are important for one reason or another, and some may survive this battle. So it behooves me to give their women my protection. If my wretched dwarf of a brother should somehow manage to prevail, they will return to their husbands and fathers full of tales about how brave I was, how my courage inspired them and lifted their spirits, how I never doubted our victory even for a moment."

"And if the castle should fall?"

"You'd like that, wouldn't you?" Cersei did not wait for a denial. "If I'm not betrayed by my own guards, I may be able to hold here for a time. Then I can go to the walls and offer to yield to Lord Stannis in person. That will spare us the worst. But if Maegor's Holdfast should fall before Stannis can come up, why then, most of my guests are in for a bit of rape,

I'd say. And you should never rule out mutilation, torture, and murder at times like these."

Sansa was horrified. "These are women, unarmed, and gently born."

"Their birth protects them," Cersei admitted, "though not as much as you'd think. Each one's worth a good ransom, but after the madness of battle, soldiers often seem to want flesh more than coin. Even so, a golden shield is better than none. Out in the streets, the women won't be treated near as tenderly. Nor will our servants. Pretty things like that serving wench of Lady Tanda's could be in for a lively night, but don't imagine the old and the infirm and the ugly will be spared. Enough drink will make blind washerwomen and reeking pig girls seem as comely as you, sweetling."

"*Me?*"

"*Try* not to sound so like a mouse, Sansa. You're a woman now, remember? And betrothed to my firstborn." The queen sipped at her wine. "Were it anyone else outside the gates, I might hope to beguile him. But this is Stannis Baratheon. I'd have a better chance of seducing his horse." She noticed the look on Sansa's face, and laughed. "Have I shocked you, my lady?" She leaned close. "You little fool. Tears are not a woman's *only* weapon. You've got another one between your legs, and you'd best learn to use it. You'll find men use their swords freely enough. Both kinds of swords."

Sansa was spared the need to reply when two Kettleblacks reentered the hall. Ser Osmund and his brothers had become great favorites about the castle; they were always ready with a smile and a jest, and got on with grooms and huntsmen as well as they did with knights and squires. With the serving wenches they got on best of all, it was gossiped. Of late Ser Osmund had taken Sandor Clegane's place by Joffrey's side, and Sansa had heard the women at the washing well saying he was as strong as the Hound, only younger and faster. If that was so, she wondered why she had never once heard of these Kettleblacks before Ser Osmund was named to the Kingsguard.

Osney was all smiles as he knelt beside the queen. "The hulks have gone up, Y'Grace. The whole Blackwater's awash with wildfire. A hundred ships burning, maybe more."

"And my son?"

"He's at the Mud Gate with the Hand and the Kingsguard, Y'Grace. He spoke to the archers on the hoardings before, and gave them a few tips on handling a crossbow, he did. All agree, he's a right brave boy."

"He'd best remain a right *live* boy." Cersei turned to his brother Osfryd, who was taller, sterner, and wore a drooping black mustache. "Yes?"

Osfryd had donned a steel halfhelm over his long black hair, and the look on his face was grim. "Y'Grace," he said quietly, "the boys caught a groom and two maidservants trying to sneak out a postern with three of the king's horses."

"The night's first traitors," the queen said, "but not the last, I fear. Have Ser Ilyn see to them, and put their heads on pikes outside the stables as a warning." As they left, she turned to Sansa. "Another lesson you should learn, if you hope to sit beside my son. Be gentle on a night like this and you'll have treasons popping up all about you like mushrooms after a hard rain. The only way to keep your people loyal is to make certain they fear you more than they do the enemy."

"I will remember, Your Grace," said Sansa, though she had always heard that love was a surer route to the people's loyalty than fear. *If I am ever a queen, I'll make them love me.*

Crabclaw pies followed the salad. Then came mutton roasted with leeks and carrots, served in trenchers of hollowed bread. Lollys ate too fast, got sick, and retched all over herself and her sister. Lord Gyles coughed, drank, coughed, drank, and passed out. The queen gazed down in disgust to where he sprawled with his face in his trencher and his hand in a puddle of wine. "The gods must have been mad to waste manhood on the likes of him, and I must have been mad to demand his release."

Osfryd Kettleblack returned, crimson cloak swirling. "There's folks gathering in the square, Y'Grace, asking to take refuge in the castle. Not a mob, rich merchants and the like."

"Command them to return to their homes," the queen said. "If they won't go, have our crossbowmen kill a few. No sorties; I won't have the gates opened for any reason."

"As you command." He bowed and moved off.

The queen's face was hard and angry. "Would that I could take a sword to their necks myself." Her voice was starting to slur. "When we were little, Jaime and I were so much alike that even our lord father could not tell us apart. Sometimes as a lark we would dress in each other's clothes and spend a whole day each as the other. Yet even so, when Jaime was given his first sword, there was none for me. 'What do *I* get?' I remember asking. We were so much alike, I could never understand why they treated us so *differently*. Jaime learned to fight with sword and lance and mace, while I was taught to smile and sing and please. He was heir to Casterly Rock, while I was to be sold to some stranger like a horse, to be ridden whenever my new owner liked, beaten whenever he liked, and cast aside in time for a younger filly. Jaime's lot was to be glory and power, while mine was birth and moonblood."

"But you were queen of all the Seven Kingdoms," Sansa said.

"When it comes to swords, a queen is only a woman after all."

Cersei's wine cup was empty. The page moved to fill it again, but she turned it over and shook her head. "No more. I must keep a clear head."

The last course was goat cheese served with baked apples. The scent of cinnamon filled the hall as Osney Kettleblack slipped in to kneel once more between them. "Y'Grace," he murmured. "Stannis has landed men on the tourney grounds, and there's more coming across. The Mud Gate's under attack, and they've brought a ram to the King's Gate. The Imp's gone out to drive them off."

"That will fill them with fear," the queen said dryly. "He hasn't taken Joff, I hope."

"No, Y'Grace, the king's with my brother at the Whores, flinging Antler Men into the river."

"With the Mud Gate under assault? Folly. Tell Ser Osmund I want him out of there at once, it's too dangerous. Fetch him back to the castle."

"The Imp said—"

"It's what *I* said that ought concern you." Cersei's eyes narrowed. "Your brother will do as he's told, or I'll see to it that he leads the next sortie himself, and you'll go with him."

After the meal had been cleared away, many of the guests asked leave to go to the sept. Cersei graciously granted their request. Lady Tanda and her daughters were among those who fled. For those who remained, a singer was brought forth to fill the hall with the sweet music of the high harp. He sang of Jonquil and Florian, of Prince Aemon the Dragonknight and his love for his brother's queen, of Nymeria's ten thousand ships. They were beautiful songs, but terribly sad. Several of the women began to weep, and Sansa felt her own eyes growing moist.

"Very good, dear." The queen leaned close. "You want to practice those tears. You'll need them for King Stannis."

Sansa shifted nervously. "Your Grace?"

"Oh, spare me your hollow courtesies. Matters must have reached a desperate strait out there if they need a dwarf to lead them, so you might as well take off your mask. I know all about your little treasons in the godswood."

"The godswood?" *Don't look at Ser Dontos, don't, don't,* Sansa told herself. *She doesn't know, no one knows, Dontos promised me, my Florian would never fail me.* "I've done no treasons. I only visit the godswood to pray."

"For Stannis. Or your brother, it's all the same. Why else seek your father's gods? You're praying for our defeat. What would you call that, if not treason?"

"I pray for Joffrey," she insisted nervously.

"Why, because he treats you so sweetly?" The queen took a flagon of sweet plum wine from a passing serving girl and filled Sansa's cup. "Drink," she commanded coldly. "Perhaps it will give you the courage to deal with truth for a change."

Sansa lifted the cup to her lips and took a sip. The wine was cloyingly sweet, but very strong.

"You can do better than that," Cersei said. "Drain the cup, Sansa. Your queen commands you."

It almost gagged her, but Sansa emptied the cup, gulping down the thick sweet wine until her head was swimming.

"More?" Cersei asked.

"No. Please."

The queen looked displeased. "When you asked about Ser Ilyn earlier, I lied to you. Would you like to hear the truth, Sansa? Would you like to know why he's really here?"

She did not dare answer, but it did not matter. The queen raised a hand and beckoned, never waiting for a reply. Sansa had not even seen Ser Ilyn return to the hall, but suddenly there he was, striding from the shadows behind the dais as silent as a cat. He carried Ice unsheathed. Her father had always cleaned the blade in the godswood after he took a man's head, Sansa recalled, but Ser Ilyn was not so fastidious. There was blood drying on the rippling steel, the red already fading to brown. "Tell Lady Sansa why I keep you by us," said Cersei.

Ser Ilyn opened his mouth and emitted a choking rattle. His pox-scarred face had no expression.

"He's here for us, he says," the queen said. "Stannis may take the city and he may take the throne, but I will not suffer him to judge me. I do not mean for him to have us alive."

"*Us?*"

"You heard me. So perhaps you had best pray again, Sansa, and for a different outcome. The Starks will have no joy from the fall of House Lannister, I promise you." She reached out and touched Sansa's hair, brushing it lightly away from her neck.

TYRION

The slot in his helm limited Tyrion's vision to what was before him, but when he turned his head he saw three galleys beached on the tourney grounds, and a fourth, larger than the others, standing well out into the river, firing barrels of burning pitch from a catapult.

"Wedge," Tyrion commanded as his men streamed out of the sally port. They formed up in spearhead, with him at the point. Ser Mandon Moore took the place to his right, flames shimmering against the white enamel of his armor, his dead eyes shining passionlessly through his helm. He rode a coal-black horse barded all in white, with the pure white shield of the Kingsguard strapped to his arm. On the left, Tyrion was surprised to see Podrick Payne, a sword in his hand. "You're too young," he said at once. "Go back."

"I'm your squire, my lord."

Tyrion could spare no time for argument. "With me, then. Stay close." He kicked his horse into motion.

They rode knee to knee, following the line of the looming walls. Joffrey's standard streamed crimson and gold from Ser Mandon's staff, stag and lion dancing hoof to paw. They went from a walk to a trot, wheeling wide around the base of the tower. Arrows darted from the city walls while stones spun and tumbled overhead, crashing down blindly onto earth and water, steel and flesh. Ahead loomed the King's Gate and a surging mob of soldiers wrestling with a huge ram, a shaft of black oak with an iron head. Archers off the ships surrounded them, loosing their shafts at whatever defenders showed themselves on the gatehouse walls. "Lances," Tyrion commanded. He sped to a canter.

The ground was sodden and slippery, equal parts mud and blood. His stallion stumbled over a corpse, his hooves sliding and churning the earth, and for an instant Tyrion feared his charge would end with him tumbling from the saddle before he even reached the foe, but somehow he and his horse both managed to keep their balance. Beneath the gate men were turning, hurriedly trying to brace for the shock. Tyrion lifted his axe and shouted, *"King's Landing!"* Other voices took up the cry, and now the arrowhead flew, a long scream of steel and silk, pounding hooves and sharp blades kissed by fire.

Ser Mandon dropped the point of his lance at the last possible instant, and drove Joffrey's banner through the chest of a man in a studded jerkin, lifting him full off his feet before the shaft snapped. Ahead of Tyrion was a knight whose surcoat showed a fox peering through a ring of flowers. *Florent* was his first thought, but *helmless* ran a close second. He smashed the man in the face with all the weight of axe and arm and charging horse, taking off half his head. The shock of impact numbed his shoulder. *Shagga would laugh at me,* he thought, riding on.

A spear thudded against his shield. Pod galloped beside him, slashing down at every foe they passed. Dimly, he heard cheers from the men on the walls. The battering ram crashed down into the mud, forgotten in an instant as its handlers fled or turned to fight. Tyrion rode down an archer, opened a spearman from shoulder to armpit, glanced a blow off a swordfish-crested helm. At the ram his big red reared but the black stallion leapt the obstacle smoothly and Ser Mandon flashed past him, death in snow-white silk. His sword sheared off limbs, cracked heads, broke shields asunder—though few enough of the enemy had made it across the river with shields intact.

Tyrion urged his mount over the ram. Their foes were fleeing. He moved his head right to left and back again, but saw no sign of Podrick Payne. An arrow clattered against his cheek, missing his eye slit by an inch. His jolt of fear almost unhorsed him. *If I'm to sit here like a stump, I had as well paint a target on my breastplate.*

He spurred his horse back into motion, trotting over and around a scatter of corpses. Downriver, the Blackwater was jammed with the hulks of burning galleys. Patches of wildfire still floated atop the water, sending fiery green plumes swirling twenty feet into the air. They had dispersed the men on the battering ram, but he could see fighting all along the riverfront. Ser Balon Swann's men, most like, or Lancel's, trying to throw the enemy back into the water as they swarmed ashore off the burning ships. "We'll ride for the Mud Gate," he commanded.

Ser Mandon shouted, *"The Mud Gate!"* And they were off again. *"King's Landing!"* his men cried raggedly, and *"Halfman! Halfman!"* He wondered who had taught them that. Through the steel and padding of his helm, he heard anguished screams, the hungry crackle of flame, the shuddering of warhorns, and the brazen blast of trumpets. Fire was everywhere. *Gods be good, no wonder the Hound was frightened. It's the flames he fears . . .*

A splintering crash rang across the Blackwater as a stone the size of a horse landed square amidships on one of the galleys. *Ours or theirs?* Through the roiling smoke, he could not tell. His wedge was gone; every man was his own battle now. *I should have turned back,* he thought, riding on.

The axe was heavy in his fist. A handful still followed him, the rest dead or fled. He had to wrestle his stallion to keep his head to the east. The big destrier liked fire no more than Sandor Clegane had, but the horse was easier to cow.

Men were crawling from the river, men burned and bleeding, coughing up water, staggering, most dying. He led his troop among them, delivering quicker cleaner deaths to those strong enough to stand. The war shrank to the size of his eye slit. Knights twice his size fled from him, or stood and died. They seemed little things, and fearful. *"Lannister!"* he shouted, slaying. His arm was red to the elbow, glistening in the light off the river. When his horse reared again, he shook his axe at the stars and heard them call out *"Halfman! Halfman!"* Tyrion felt drunk.

The battle fever. He had never thought to experience it himself, though Jaime had told him of it often enough. How time seemed to blur and slow and even stop, how the past and the future vanished until there was nothing but the instant, how fear fled, and thought fled, and even your body. "You don't feel your wounds then, or the ache in your back from the weight of the armor, or the sweat running down into your eyes. You stop feeling, you stop thinking, you stop being *you*, there is only the fight, the foe, this man and then the next and the next and the next, and you know they are afraid and tired but you're not, you're alive, and death is all around you but their swords move so slowly, you can dance through them laughing." *Battle fever. I am half a man and drunk with slaughter, let them kill me if they can!*

They tried. Another spearman ran at him. Tyrion lopped off the head of his spear, then his hand, then his arm, trotting around him in a circle. An archer, bowless, thrust at him with an arrow, holding it as if it were a knife. The destrier kicked at the man's thigh to send him sprawling, and Tyrion barked laughter. He rode past a banner planted in the mud, one of Stannis's fiery hearts, and chopped the staff in two with a swing of his axe. A knight rose up from nowhere to hack at his shield with a two-handed greatsword, again and again, until someone thrust a dagger under his arm. One of Tyrion's men, perhaps. He never saw.

"I yield, ser," a different knight called out, farther down the river. "Yield. Ser knight, I yield to you. My pledge, here, here." The man lay in a puddle of black water, offering up a lobstered gauntlet in token of submission. Tyrion had to lean down to take it from him. As he did, a pot of wildfire burst overhead, spraying green flame. In the sudden stab of light he saw that the puddle was not black but red. The gauntlet still had the knight's hand in it. He flung it back. "Yield," the man sobbed hopelessly, helplessly. Tyrion reeled away.

A man-at-arms grabbed the bridle of his horse and thrust at Tyrion's face with a dagger. He knocked the blade aside and buried the axe in the nape of the man's neck. As he was wresting it free, a blaze of white appeared at the edge of his vision. Tyrion turned, thinking to find Ser Mandon Moore beside him again, but this was a different white knight. Ser Balon Swann wore the same armor, but his horse trappings bore the battling black-and-white swans of his House. *He's more a spotted knight than a white one*, Tyrion thought inanely. Every bit of Ser Balon was spattered with gore and smudged by smoke. He raised his mace to point downriver. Bits of brain and bone clung to its head. "My lord, look."

Tyrion swung his horse about to peer down the Blackwater. The current still flowed black and strong beneath, but the surface was a roil of blood and flame. The sky was red and orange and garish green. "What?" he said. Then he saw.

Steel-clad men-at-arms were clambering off a broken galley that had smashed into a pier. *So many, where are they coming from?* Squinting into the smoke and glare, Tyrion followed them back out into the river. Twenty galleys were jammed together out there, maybe more, it was hard to count. Their oars were crossed, their hulls locked together with grappling lines, they were impaled on each other's rams, tangled in webs of fallen rigging. One great hulk floated hull up between two smaller ships. Wrecks, but packed so closely that it was possible to leap from one deck to the other and so cross the Blackwater.

Hundreds of Stannis Baratheon's boldest were doing just that. Tyrion saw one great fool of a knight trying to ride across, urging a terrified horse over gunwales and oars, across tilting decks slick with blood and crackling with green fire. *We made them a bloody bridge*, he thought in dismay. Parts of the bridge were sinking and other parts were afire and the whole thing was creaking and shifting and like to burst asunder at any moment, but that did not seem to stop them. "Those are brave men," he told Ser Balon in admiration. "Let's go kill them."

He led them through the guttering fires and the soot and ash of the riverfront, pounding down a long stone quay with his own men and Ser

Balon's behind him. Ser Mandon fell in with them, his shield a ragged ruin. Smoke and cinders swirled through the air, and the foe broke before their charge, throwing themselves back into the water, knocking over other men as they fought to climb up. The foot of the bridge was a half-sunken enemy galley with *Dragonsbane* painted on her prow, her bottom ripped out by one of the sunken hulks Tyrion had placed between the quays. A spearman wearing the red crab badge of House Celtigar drove the point of his weapon up through the chest of Balon Swann's horse before he could dismount, spilling the knight from the saddle. Tyrion hacked at the man's head as he flashed by, and by then it was too late to rein up. His stallion leapt from the end of the quay and over a splintered gunwale, landing with a splash and a scream in ankle-deep water. Tyrion's axe went spinning, followed by Tyrion himself, and the deck rose up to give him a wet smack.

Madness followed. His horse had broken a leg and was screaming horribly. Somehow he managed to draw his dagger, and slit the poor creature's throat. The blood gushed out in a scarlet fountain, drenching his arms and chest. He found his feet again and lurched to the rail, and then he was fighting, staggering and splashing across crooked decks awash with water. Men came at him. Some he killed, some he wounded, and some went away, but always there were more. He lost his knife and gained a broken spear, he could not have said how. He clutched it and stabbed, shrieking curses. Men ran from him and he ran after them, clambering up over the rail to the next ship and then the next. His two white shadows were always with him; Balon Swann and Mandon Moore, beautiful in their pale plate. Surrounded by a circle of Velaryon spearmen, they fought back to back; they made battle as graceful as a dance.

His own killing was a clumsy thing. He stabbed one man in the kidney when his back was turned, and grabbed another by the leg and upended him into the river. Arrows hissed past his head and clattered off his armor; one lodged between shoulder and breastplate, but he never felt it. A naked man fell from the sky and landed on the deck, body bursting like a melon dropped from a tower. His blood spattered through the slit of Tyrion's helm. Stones began to plummet down, crashing through the decks and turning men to pulp, until the whole bridge gave a shudder and twisted violently underfoot, knocking him sideways.

Suddenly the river was pouring into his helm. He ripped it off and crawled along the listing deck until the water was only neck deep. A groaning filled the air, like the death cries of some enormous beast. *The ship*, he had time to think, *the ship's about to tear loose.* The broken galleys were ripping apart, the bridge breaking apart. No sooner had he come to that realization than he heard a sudden *crack*, loud as thunder, the deck lurched beneath him, and he slid back down into the water.

The list was so steep he had to climb back up, hauling himself along a snapped line inch by bloody inch. Out of the corner of his eye, he saw the hulk they'd been tangled with drifting downstream with the current, spinning slowly as men leapt over her side. Some wore Stannis's flaming heart, some Joffrey's stag-and-lion, some other badges, but it seemed to make no matter. Fires were burning upstream and down. On one side of him was a raging battle, a great confusion of bright banners waving above a sea of struggling men, shield walls forming and breaking, mounted knights cutting through the press, dust and mud and blood and smoke. On the other side, the Red Keep loomed high on its hill, spitting fire. They were on the wrong sides, though. For a moment Tyrion thought he was going mad, that Stannis and the castle had traded places. *How could Stannis cross to the north bank?* Belatedly he realized that the deck was turning, and somehow he had gotten spun about, so castle and battle had changed sides. *Battle, what battle, if Stannis hasn't crossed who is he fighting?* Tyrion was too tired to make sense of it. His shoulder ached horribly, and when he reached up to rub it he saw the arrow, and remembered. *I have to get off this ship.* Downstream was nothing but a wall of fire, and if the wreck broke loose the current would take him right into it.

Someone was calling his name faintly through the din of battle. Tyrion tried to shout back. "Here! Here, I'm here, help me!" His voice sounded so thin he could scarcely hear himself. He pulled himself up the slanting deck, and grabbed for the rail. The hull slammed into the next galley over and rebounded so violently he was almost knocked into the water. Where had all his strength gone? It was all he could do to hang on.

"MY LORD! TAKE MY HAND! MY LORD TYRION!"

There on the deck of the next ship, across a widening gulf of black water, stood Ser Mandon Moore, a hand extended. Yellow and green fire shone against the white of his armor, and his lobstered gauntlet was sticky with blood, but Tyrion reached for it all the same, wishing his arms were longer. It was only at the very last, as their fingers brushed across the gap, that something niggled at him . . . Ser Mandon was holding out his *left* hand, why . . .

Was that why he reeled backward, or did he see the sword after all? He would never know. The point slashed just beneath his eyes, and he felt its cold hard touch and then a blaze of pain. His head spun around as if he'd been slapped. The shock of the cold water was a second slap more jolting than the first. He flailed for something to grab on to, knowing that once he went down he was not like to come back up. Somehow his hand found the splintered end of a broken oar. Clutching it tight as a desperate lover, he shinnied up foot by foot. His eyes were full of water, his mouth was full of blood, and his head throbbed horribly. *Gods give me strength to reach the deck* . . . There was nothing else, only the oar, the water, the deck.

Finally he rolled over the side and lay breathless and exhausted, flat on his back. Balls of green and orange flame crackled overhead, leaving streaks between the stars. He had a moment to think how pretty it was before Ser Mandon blocked out the view. The knight was a white steel shadow, his eyes shining darkly behind his helm. Tyrion had no more strength than a rag doll. Ser Mandon put the point of his sword to the hollow of his throat and curled both hands around the hilt.

And suddenly he lurched to the left, staggering into the rail. Wood split, and Ser Mandon Moore vanished with a shout and a splash. An instant later, the hulls came slamming together again, so hard the deck seemed to jump. Then someone was kneeling over him. "Jaime?" he croaked, almost choking on the blood that filled his mouth. Who else would save him, if not his brother?

"Be still, my lord, you're hurt bad." *A boy's voice, that makes no sense*, thought Tyrion. It sounded almost like Pod.

SANSA

When Ser Lancel Lannister told the queen that the battle was
lost, she turned her empty wine cup in her hands and said,
"Tell my brother, ser." Her voice was distant, as if the
news were of no great interest to her.

"Your brother's likely dead." Ser Lancel's surcoat was soaked with the
blood seeping out under his arm. When he had arrived in the hall, the
sight of him had made some of the guests scream. "He was on the bridge
of boats when it broke apart, we think. Ser Mandon's likely gone as well,
and no one can find the Hound. Gods be damned, Cersei, *why* did you
have them fetch Joffrey back to the castle? The gold cloaks are throwing
down their spears and running, hundreds of them. When they saw the
king leaving, they lost all heart. The whole Blackwater's awash with
wrecks and fire and corpses, but we could have held if—"

Osney Kettleblack pushed past him. "There's fighting on both sides of
the river now, Y'Grace. It may be that some of Stannis's lords are fighting each other, no one's sure, it's all confused over there. The Hound's
gone, no one knows where, and Ser Balon's fallen back inside the city.
The riverside's theirs. They're ramming at the King's Gate again, and Ser
Lancel's right, your men are deserting the walls and killing their own
officers. There's mobs at the Iron Gate and the Gate of the Gods fighting
to get out, and Flea Bottom's one great drunken riot."

Gods be good, Sansa thought, *it is happening, Joffrey's lost his head
and so have I.* She looked for Ser Ilyn, but the King's Justice was not to

be seen. *I can feel him, though. He's close, I'll not escape him, he'll have my head.*

Strangely calm, the queen turned to his brother Osfryd. "Raise the drawbridge and bar the doors. No one enters or leaves Maegor's without my leave."

"What about them women who went to pray?"

"They chose to leave my protection. Let them pray; perhaps the gods will defend them. Where's my son?"

"The castle gatehouse. He wanted to command the crossbowmen. There's a mob howling outside, half of them gold cloaks who came with him when we left the Mud Gate."

"Bring him inside Maegor's *now.*"

"*No!*" Lancel was so angry he forgot to keep his voice down. Heads turned toward them as he shouted, "We'll have the Mud Gate all over again. Let him stay where he is, he's the *king—*"

"He's my son." Cersei Lannister rose to her feet. "You claim to be a Lannister as well, cousin, prove it. Osfryd, why are you standing there? *Now* means today."

Osfryd Kettleblack hurried from the hall, his brother with him. Many of the guests were rushing out as well. Some of the women were weeping, some praying. Others simply remained at the tables and called for more wine. "Cersei," Ser Lancel pleaded, "if we lose the castle, Joffrey will be killed in any case, you know that. Let him stay, I'll keep him by me, I swear—"

"Get out of my way." Cersei slammed her open palm into his wound. Ser Lancel cried out in pain and almost fainted as the queen swept from the room. She spared Sansa not so much as a glance. *She's forgotten me. Ser Ilyn will kill me and she won't even think about it.*

"Oh, gods," an old woman wailed. "We're lost, the battle's lost, she's running." Several children were crying. *They can smell the fear.* Sansa found herself alone on the dais. Should she stay here, or run after the queen and plead for her life?

She never knew why she got to her feet, but she did. "Don't be afraid," she told them loudly. "The queen has raised the drawbridge. This is the safest place in the city. There's thick walls, the moat, the spikes . . ."

"What's happened?" demanded a woman she knew slightly, the wife of a lesser lordling. "What did Osney tell her? Is the king hurt, has the city fallen?"

"*Tell us,*" someone else shouted. One woman asked about her father, another her son.

Sansa raised her hands for quiet. "Joffrey's come back to the castle. He's not hurt. They're still fighting, that's all I know, they're fighting bravely. The queen will be back soon." The last was a lie, but she had to soothe them. She noticed the fools standing under the galley. "Moon Boy, make us laugh."

Moon Boy did a cartwheel, and vaulted on top of a table. He grabbed up four wine cups and began to juggle them. Every so often one of them would come down and smash him in the head. A few nervous laughs echoed through the hall. Sansa went to Ser Lancel and knelt beside him. His wound was bleeding afresh where the queen had struck him. "Madness," he gasped. "Gods, the Imp was right, was right . . ."

"Help him," Sansa commanded two of the serving men. One just looked at her and ran, flagon and all. Other servants were leaving the hall as well, but she could not help that. Together, Sansa and the serving man got the wounded knight back on his feet. "Take him to Maester Frenken." Lancel was one of *them*, yet somehow she still could not bring herself to wish him dead. *I am soft and weak and stupid, just as Joffrey says. I should be killing him, not helping him.*

The torches had begun to burn low, and one or two had flickered out. No one troubled to replace them. Cersei did not return. Ser Dontos climbed the dais while all eyes were on the other fool. "Go back to your bedchamber, sweet Jonquil," he whispered. "Lock yourself in, you'll be safer there. I'll come for you when the battle's done."

Someone will come for me, Sansa thought, *but will it be you, or will it be Ser Ilyn?* For a mad moment she thought of begging Dontos to defend her. He had been a knight too, trained with the sword and sworn to defend the weak. *No. He has not the courage, or the skill. I would only be killing him as well.*

It took all the strength she had in her to walk slowly from the Queen's Ballroom when she wanted so badly to run. When she reached the steps, she *did* run, up and around until she was breathless and dizzy. One of the guards knocked into her on the stair. A jeweled wine cup and a pair of silver candlesticks spilled out of the crimson cloak he'd wrapped them in and went clattering down the steps. He hurried after them, paying Sansa no mind once he decided she was not going to try and take his loot.

Her bedchamber was black as pitch. Sansa barred the door and fumbled through the dark to the window. When she ripped back the drapes, her breath caught in her throat.

The southern sky was aswirl with glowing, shifting colors, the reflections of the great fires that burned below. Baleful green tides moved against the bellies of the clouds, and pools of orange light spread out across the heavens. The reds and yellows of common flame warred against the emeralds and jades of wildfire, each color flaring and then fading, birthing armies of short-lived shadows to die again an instant later. Green dawns gave way to orange dusks in half a heartbeat. The air itself smelled *burnt*, the way a soup kettle sometimes smelled if it was left on the fire too long and all the soup boiled away. Embers drifted through the night air like swarms of fireflies.

Sansa backed away from the window, retreating toward the safety of her bed. *I'll go to sleep*, she told herself, *and when I wake it will be a new day, and the sky will be blue again. The fighting will be done and someone will tell me whether I'm to live or die.* "Lady," she whimpered softly, wondering if she would meet her wolf again when she was dead.

Then something stirred behind her, and a hand reached out of the dark and grabbed her wrist.

Sansa opened her mouth to scream, but another hand clamped down over her face, smothering her. His fingers were rough and callused, and sticky with blood. "Little bird. I knew you'd come." The voice was a drunken rasp.

Outside, a swirling lance of jade light spit at the stars, filling the room with green glare. She saw him for a moment, all black and green, the blood on his face dark as tar, his eyes glowing like a dog's in the sudden glare. Then the light faded and he was only a hulking darkness in a stained white cloak.

"If you scream I'll kill you. Believe that." He took his hand from her mouth. Her breath was coming ragged. The Hound had a flagon of wine on her bedside table. He took a long pull. "Don't you want to ask who's winning the battle, little bird?"

"Who?" she said, too frightened to defy him.

The Hound laughed. "I only know who's lost. Me."

He is drunker than I've ever seen him. He was sleeping in my bed. What does he want here? "What have you lost?"

"All." The burnt half of his face was a mask of dried blood. "Bloody dwarf. Should have killed him. Years ago."

"He's dead, they say."

"Dead? No. Bugger that. I don't want him dead." He cast the empty flagon aside. "I want him *burned*. If the gods are good, they'll burn him, but I won't be here to see. I'm going."

"Going?" She tried to wriggle free, but his grasp was iron.

"The little bird repeats whatever she hears. *Going*, yes."

"Where will you go?"

"Away from here. Away from the fires. Go out the Iron Gate, I suppose. North somewhere, anywhere."

"You won't get out," Sansa said. "The queen's closed up Maegor's, and the city gates are shut as well."

"Not to me. I have the white cloak. And I have *this*." He patted the pommel of his sword. "The man who tries to stop me is a dead man. Unless he's on fire." He laughed bitterly.

"Why did you come here?"

"You promised me a song, little bird. Have you forgotten?"

She didn't know what he meant. She couldn't sing for him now, here, with the sky aswirl with fire and men dying in their hundreds and their thousands. "I can't," she said. "Let me go, you're scaring me."

"Everything scares you. Look at me. *Look* at me."

The blood masked the worst of his scars, but his eyes were white and wide and terrifying. The burnt corner of his mouth twitched and twitched again. Sansa could smell him; a stink of sweat and sour wine and stale vomit, and over it all the reek of blood, blood, blood.

"I could keep you safe," he rasped. "They're all afraid of me. No one would hurt you again, or I'd kill them." He yanked her closer, and for a moment she thought he meant to kiss her. He was too strong to fight. She closed her eyes, wanting it to be over, but nothing happened. "Still can't bear to look, can you?" she heard him say. He gave her arm a hard wrench, pulling her around and shoving her down onto the bed. "I'll have that song. Florian and Jonquil, you said." His dagger was out, poised at her throat. "Sing, little bird. Sing for your little life."

Her throat was dry and tight with fear, and every song she had ever known had fled from her mind. *Please don't kill me*, she wanted to scream, *please don't*. She could feel him twisting the point, pushing it into her throat, and she almost closed her eyes again, but then she remembered. It was not the song of Florian and Jonquil, but it was a song. Her voice sounded small and thin and tremulous in her ears.

> *Gentle Mother, font of mercy,*
> *save our sons from war, we pray,*
> *stay the swords and stay the arrows,*
> *let them know a better day.*
> *Gentle Mother, strength of women,*
> *help our daughters through this fray,*
> *soothe the wrath and tame the fury,*
> *teach us all a kinder way.*

She had forgotten the other verses. When her voice trailed off, she feared he might kill her, but after a moment the Hound took the blade from her throat, never speaking.

Some instinct made her lift her hand and cup his cheek with her fingers. The room was too dark for her to see him, but she could feel the stickiness of the blood, and a wetness that was not blood. "Little bird," he said once more, his voice raw and harsh as steel on stone. Then he rose from the bed. Sansa heard cloth ripping, followed by the softer sound of retreating footsteps.

When she crawled out of bed, long moments later, she was alone. She found his cloak on the floor, twisted up tight, the white wool stained by blood and fire. The sky outside was darker by then, with only a few pale green ghosts dancing against the stars. A chill wind was blowing, banging the shutters. Sansa was cold. She shook out the torn cloak and huddled beneath it on the floor, shivering.

How long she stayed there she could not have said, but after a time she heard a bell ringing, far off across the city. The sound was a deep-throated bronze booming, coming faster with each knell. Sansa was wondering what it might mean when a second bell joined in, and a third, their voices calling across the hills and hollows, the alleys and towers, to every corner of King's Landing. She threw off the cloak and went to her window.

The first faint hint of dawn was visible in the east, and the Red Keep's own bells were ringing now, joining in the swelling river of sound that flowed from the seven crystal towers of the Great Sept of Baelor. They had rung the bells when King Robert died, she remembered, but this was different, no slow dolorous death knell but a joyful thunder. She could hear men shouting in the streets as well, and something that could only be cheers.

It was Ser Dontos who brought her the word. He staggered through her open door, wrapped her in his flabby arms, and whirled her around and around the room, whooping so incoherently that Sansa understood not a word of it. He was as drunk as the Hound had been, but in him it was a dancing happy drunk. She was breathless and dizzy when he let her down. "What is it?" She clutched at a bedpost. "What's happened? Tell me!"

"It's done! Done! Done! The city is saved. Lord Stannis is dead, Lord Stannis is fled, no one knows, no one cares, his host is broken, the danger's done. Slaughtered, scattered, or gone over, they say. Oh, the bright banners! The banners, Jonquil, the banners! Do you have any wine? We ought to drink to this day, yes. It means you're safe, don't you see?"

"Tell me what's happened!" Sansa shook him.

Ser Dontos laughed and hopped from one leg to the other, almost falling. "They came up through the ashes while the river was burning. The river, Stannis was neck deep in the river, and they took him from the rear. Oh, to be a knight again, to have been part of it! His own men hardly fought, they say. Some ran but more bent the knee and went over, shouting for Lord Renly! What must Stannis have thought when he heard that? I had it from Osney Kettleblack who had it from Ser Osmund, but Ser Balon's back now and his men say the same, and the gold cloaks as well. We're delivered, sweetling! They came up the roseroad and along the riverbank, through all the fields Stannis had burned, the ashes puffing up around their boots and turning all their armor grey, but oh! the *banners* must have been bright, the golden rose and golden lion and all the others, the Marbrand tree and the Rowan, Tarly's huntsman and Redwyne's grapes and Lady Oakheart's leaf. All the westermen, all the power of Highgarden and Casterly Rock! Lord Tywin himself had their right wing on the north side of the river, with Randyll Tarly commanding the center and Mace Tyrell the left, but the vanguard won the fight. They plunged through Stannis like a lance through a pumpkin, every man of them howling like some demon in steel. And do you know who led the vanguard? Do you? Do you? *Do you?*"

"Robb?" It was too much to be hoped, but . . .

"It was *Lord Renly!* Lord Renly in his green armor, with the fires shimmering off his golden antlers! Lord Renly with his tall spear in his hand! They say he killed Ser Guyard Morrigen himself in single combat, and a dozen other great knights as well. It was Renly, it was Renly, it was Renly! Oh! the banners, darling Sansa! Oh! to be a knight!"

DAENERYS

She was breaking her fast on a bowl of cold shrimp-and-persimmon soup when Irri brought her a Qartheen gown, an airy confection of ivory samite patterned with seed pearls. "Take it away," Dany said. "The docks are no place for lady's finery."

If the Milk Men thought her such a savage, she would dress the part for them. When she went to the stables, she wore faded sandsilk pants and woven grass sandals. Her small breasts moved freely beneath a painted Dothraki vest, and a curved dagger hung from her medallion belt. Jhiqui had braided her hair Dothraki fashion, and fastened a silver bell to the end of the braid. "I have won no victories," she tried telling her handmaid when the bell tinkled softly.

Jhiqui disagreed. "You burned the *maegi* in their house of dust and sent their souls to hell."

That was Drogon's victory, not mine, Dany wanted to say, but she held her tongue. The Dothraki would esteem her all the more for a few bells in her hair. She chimed as she mounted her silver mare, and again with every stride, but neither Ser Jorah nor her bloodriders made mention of it. To guard her people and her dragons in her absence, she chose Rakharo. Jhogo and Aggo would ride with her to the waterfront.

They left the marble palaces and fragrant gardens behind and made their way through a poorer part of the city where modest brick houses turned blind walls to the street. There were fewer horses and camels to be seen, and a dearth of palanquins, but the streets teemed with children, beggars, and skinny dogs the color of sand. Pale men in dusty linen skirts stood beneath arched doorways to watch them pass. *They know who I am, and they do not love me.* Dany could tell from the way they looked at her.

Ser Jorah would sooner have tucked her inside her palanquin, safely hidden behind silken curtains, but she refused him. She had reclined too long on satin cushions, letting oxen bear her hither and yon. At least when she rode she felt as though she was getting somewhere.

It was not by choice that she sought the waterfront. She was fleeing again. Her whole life had been one long flight, it seemed. She had begun running in her mother's womb, and never once stopped. How often had she and Viserys stolen away in the black of night, a bare step ahead of the Usurper's hired knives? But it was run or die. Xaro had learned that Pyat Pree was gathering the surviving warlocks together to work ill on her.

Dany had laughed when he told her. "Was it not you who told me warlocks were no more than old soldiers, vainly boasting of forgotten deeds and lost prowess?"

Xaro looked troubled. "And so it was, then. But now? I am less certain. It is said that the glass candles are burning in the house of Urrathon Night-Walker, that have not burned in a hundred years. Ghost grass grows in the Garden of Gehane, phantom tortoises have been seen carrying messages between the windowless houses on Warlock's Way, and all the rats in the city are chewing off their tails. The wife of Mathos Mallarawan, who once mocked a warlock's drab moth-eaten robe, has gone mad and will wear no clothes at all. Even fresh-washed silks make her feel as though a thousand insects were crawling on her skin. And Blind Sybassion the Eater of Eyes can see again, or so his slaves do swear. A man must wonder." He sighed. "These are strange times in Qarth. And strange times are bad for trade. It grieves me to say so, yet it might be best if you left Qarth entirely, and sooner rather than later." Xaro stroked her fingers reassuringly. "You need not go alone, though. You have seen dark visions in the Palace of Dust, but Xaro has dreamed brighter dreams. I see you happily abed, with our child at your breast. Sail with me around the Jade Sea, and we can yet make it so! It is not too late. Give me a son, my sweet song of joy!"

Give you a dragon, you mean. "I will not wed you, Xaro."

His face had grown cold at that. "Then go."

"But where?"

"Somewhere far from here."

Well, perhaps it was time. The people of her *khalasar* had welcomed the chance to recover from the ravages of the red waste, but now that they were plump and rested once again, they began to grow unruly. Dothraki were not accustomed to staying long in one place. They were a warrior people, not made for cities. Perhaps she had lingered in Qarth too long, seduced by its comforts and its beauties. It was a city that always promised more than it would give you, it seemed to her, and her welcome here had turned sour since the House of the Undying had collapsed in a great gout of smoke and flame. Overnight the Qartheen had come to remember that dragons were *dangerous*. No longer did they vie with each other to give her gifts. Instead the Tourmaline Brotherhood had called openly for her expulsion, and the Ancient Guild of Spicers for her death. It was all Xaro could do to keep the Thirteen from joining them.

But where am I to go? Ser Jorah proposed that they journey farther east, away from her enemies in the Seven Kingdoms. Her bloodriders would sooner have returned to their great grass sea, even if it meant braving the red waste again. Dany herself had toyed with the idea of settling in Vaes Tolorro until her dragons grew great and strong. But her heart was full of doubts. Each of these felt wrong, somehow . . . and even when she decided where to go, the question of how she would get there remained troublesome.

Xaro Xhoan Daxos would be no help to her, she knew that now. For all his professions of devotion, he was playing his own game, not unlike Pyat Pree. The night he asked her to leave, Dany had begged one last favor of him. "An army, is it?" Xaro asked. "A kettle of gold? A galley, perhaps?"

Dany blushed. She hated begging. "A ship, yes."

Xaro's eyes had glittered as brightly as the jewels in his nose. "I am a trader, *Khaleesi*. So perhaps we should speak no more of giving, but rather of trade. For one of your dragons, you shall have ten of the finest ships in my fleet. You need only say that one sweet word."

"No," she said.

"Alas," Xaro sobbed, "that was not the word I meant."

"Would you ask a mother to sell one of her children?"

"Whyever not? They can always make more. Mothers sell their children every day."

"Not the Mother of Dragons."

"Not even for twenty ships?"

"Not for a hundred."

His mouth curled downward. "I do not have a hundred. But you have three dragons. Grant me one, for all my kindnesses. You will still have two, and thirty ships as well."

Thirty ships would be enough to land a small army on the shore of Westeros. *But I do not have a small army.* "How many ships do you own, Xaro?"

"Eighty-three, if one does not count my pleasure barge."

"And your colleagues in the Thirteen?"

"Among us all, perhaps a thousand."

"And the Spicers and the Tourmaline Brotherhood?"

"Their trifling fleets are of no account."

"Even so," she said, "tell me."

"Twelve or thirteen hundred for the Spicers. No more than eight hundred for the Brotherhood."

"And the Asshai'i, the Braavosi, the Summer Islanders, the Ibbenese, and all the other peoples who sail the great salt sea, how many ships do they have? All together?"

"Many and more," he said irritably. "What does this matter?"

"I am trying to set a price on one of the three living dragons in the world." Dany smiled at him sweetly. "It seems to me that one-third of all the ships in the world would be fair."

Xaro's tears ran down his cheeks on either side of his jewel-encrusted nose. "Did I not warn you not to enter the Palace of Dust? This is the very thing I feared. The whispers of the warlocks have made you as mad as Mallarawan's wife. A third of all the ships in the world? Pah. Pah, I say. Pah."

Dany had not seen him since. His seneschal brought her messages, each cooler than the last. She must quit his house. He was done feeding her and her people. He demanded the return of his gifts, which she had accepted in bad faith. Her only consolation was that at least she'd had the great good sense not to marry him.

The warlocks whispered of three treasons . . . once for blood and once for gold and once for love. The first traitor was surely Mirri Maz Duur, who had murdered Khal Drogo and their unborn son to avenge her people. Could Pyat Pree and Xaro Xhoan Daxos be the second and the third? She did not think so. What Pyat did was not for gold, and Xaro had never truly loved her.

The streets grew emptier as they passed through a district given over to gloomy stone warehouses. Aggo went before her and Jhogo behind, leaving Ser Jorah Mormont at her side. Her bell rang softly, and Dany found her thoughts returning to the Palace of Dust once more, as the tongue returns to a space left by a missing tooth. *Child of three,* they had called her, *daughter of death, slayer of lies, bride of fire.* So many threes. Three fires, three mounts to ride, three treasons. "The dragon has three heads," she sighed. "Do you know what that means, Jorah?"

"Your Grace? The sigil of House Targaryen is a three-headed dragon, red on black."

"I know that. But there are no three-headed dragons."

"The three heads were Aegon and his sisters."

"Visenya and Rhaenys," she recalled. "I am descended from Aegon and Rhaenys through their son Aenys and their grandson Jaehaerys."

"Blue lips speak only lies, isn't that what Xaro told you? Why do you care what the warlocks whispered? All they wanted was to suck the life from you, you know that now."

"Perhaps," she said reluctantly. "Yet the things I saw . . ."

"A dead man in the prow of a ship, a blue rose, a banquet of blood . . . what does any of it mean, *Khaleesi*? A mummer's dragon, you said. What *is* a mummer's dragon, pray?"

"A cloth dragon on poles," Dany explained. "Mummers use them in their follies, to give the heroes something to fight."

Ser Jorah frowned.

Dany could not let it go. *"His is the song of ice and fire,* my brother said. I'm certain it was my brother. Not Viserys, Rhaegar. He had a harp with silver strings."

Ser Jorah's frown deepened until his eyebrows came together. "Prince Rhaegar played such a harp," he conceded. "You saw him?"

She nodded. "There was a woman in a bed with a babe at her breast. My brother said the babe was the prince that was promised and told her to name him Aegon."

"Prince Aegon was Rhaegar's heir by Elia of Dorne," Ser Jorah said. "But if he was this prince that was promised, the promise was broken along with his skull when the Lannisters dashed his head against a wall."

"I remember," Dany said sadly. "They murdered Rhaegar's daughter as well, the little princess. Rhaenys, she was named, like Aegon's sister. There was no Visenya, but he said the dragon has three heads. What is the song of ice and fire?"

"It's no song I've ever heard."

"I went to the warlocks hoping for answers, but instead they've left me with a hundred new questions."

By then there were people in the streets once more. "Make way," Aggo shouted, while Jhogo sniffed at the air suspiciously. "I smell it, *Khaleesi,*" he called. "The poison water." The Dothraki distrusted the sea and all that moved upon it. Water that a horse could not drink was water they wanted no part of. *They will learn,* Dany resolved. *I braved their sea with Khal Drogo. Now they can brave mine.*

Qarth was one of the world's great ports, its great sheltered harbor a riot of color and clangor and strange smells. Winesinks, warehouses, and gaming dens lined the streets, cheek by jowl with cheap brothels and the temples of peculiar gods. Cutpurses, cutthroats, spellsellers, and moneychangers mingled with every crowd. The waterfront was one great marketplace where the buying and selling went on all day and all night, and goods might be had for a fraction of what they cost at the bazaar, if a man did not ask where they came from. Wizened old women bent like hunchbacks sold flavored waters and goat's milk from glazed ceramic jugs strapped to their shoulders. Seamen from half a hundred nations wandered amongst the stalls, drinking spiced liquors and trading jokes in queer-sounding tongues. The air smelled of salt and frying fish, of hot tar and honey, of incense and oil and sperm.

Aggo gave an urchin a copper for a skewer of honey-roasted mice and nibbled them as he rode. Jhogo bought a handful of fat white cherries. Elsewhere they saw beautiful bronze daggers for sale, dried squids and carved onyx, a potent magical elixir made of virgin's milk and shade of the evening, even dragon's eggs which looked suspiciously like painted rocks.

As they passed the long stone quays reserved for the ships of the Thirteen, she saw chests of saffron, frankincense, and pepper being off-loaded from Xaro's ornate *Vermillion Kiss*. Beside her, casks of wine, bales of sourleaf, and pallets of striped hides were being trundled up the gangplank onto the *Bride in Azure*, to sail on the evening tide. Farther along, a crowd had gathered around the Spicer galley *Sunblaze* to bid on slaves. It was well known that the cheapest place to buy a slave was right off the ship, and the banners floating from her masts proclaimed that the *Sunblaze* had just arrived from Astapor on Slaver's Bay.

Dany would get no help from the Thirteen, the Tourmaline Brotherhood, or the Ancient Guild of Spicers. She rode her silver past several miles of their quays, docks, and storehouses, all the way out to the far end of the horseshoe-shaped harbor where the ships from the Summer Islands, Westeros, and the Nine Free Cities were permitted to dock.

She dismounted beside a gaming pit where a basilisk was tearing a big red dog to pieces amidst a shouting ring of sailors. "Aggo, Jhogo, you will guard the horses while Ser Jorah and I speak to the captains."

"As you say, *Khaleesi*. We will watch you as you go."

It was good to hear men speaking Valyrian once more, and even the Common Tongue, Dany thought as they approached the first ship. Sailors, dockworkers, and merchants alike gave way before her, not knowing what to make of this slim young girl with silver-gold hair who dressed in the Dothraki fashion and walked with a knight at her side. Despite the heat of the day, Ser Jorah wore his green wool surcoat over chainmail, the black bear of Mormont sewn on his chest.

But neither her beauty nor his size and strength would serve with the men whose ships they needed.

"You require passage for a hundred Dothraki, all their horses, yourself and this knight, and three *dragons*?" said the captain of the great cog *Ardent Friend* before he walked away laughing. When she told a Lyseni on the *Trumpeteer* that she was Daenerys Stormborn, Queen of the Seven Kingdoms, he gave her a deadface look and said, "Aye, and I'm

Lord Tywin Lannister and shit gold every night." The cargomaster of the Myrish galley *Silken Spirit* opined that dragons were too dangerous at sea, where any stray breath of flame might set the rigging afire. The owner of *Lord Faro's Belly* would risk dragons, but not Dothraki. "I'll have no such godless savages in my *Belly*, I'll not." The two brothers who captained the sister ships *Quicksilver* and *Greyhound* seemed sympathetic and invited them into the cabin for a glass of Arbor red. They were so courteous that Dany was hopeful for a time, but in the end the price they asked was far beyond her means, and might have been beyond Xaro's. *Pinchbottom Petto* and *Sloe-Eyed Maid* were too small for her needs, *Bravo* was bound for the Jade Sea, and *Magister Manolo* scarce looked seaworthy.

As they made their way toward the next quay, Ser Jorah laid a hand against the small of her back. "Your Grace. You are being followed. No, do not turn." He guided her gently toward a brass-seller's booth. "This is a noble work, my queen," he proclaimed loudly, lifting a large platter for her inspection. "See how it shines in the sun?"

The brass was polished to a high sheen. Dany could see her face in it . . . and when Ser Jorah angled it to the right, she could see behind her. "I see a fat brown man and an older man with a staff. Which is it?"

"Both of them," Ser Jorah said. "They have been following us since we left *Quicksilver*."

The ripples in the brass stretched the strangers queerly, making one man seem long and gaunt, the other immensely squat and broad. "A most excellent brass, great lady," the merchant exclaimed. "Bright as the sun! And for the Mother of Dragons, only thirty honors."

The platter was worth no more than three. "Where are my guards?" Dany declared. "This man is trying to rob me!" For Jorah, she lowered her voice and spoke in the Common Tongue. "They may not mean me ill. Men have looked at women since time began, perhaps it is no more than that."

The brass-seller ignored their whispers. "Thirty? Did I say thirty? Such a fool I am. The price is twenty honors."

"All the brass in this booth is not worth twenty honors," Dany told him as she studied the reflections. The old man had the look of Westeros about him, and the brown-skinned one must weigh twenty stone. *The Usurper offered a lordship to the man who kills me, and these two are far from home. Or could they be creatures of the warlocks, meant to take me unawares?*

"Ten, *Khaleesi*, because you are so lovely. Use it for a looking glass. Only brass this fine could capture such beauty."

"It might serve to carry nightsoil. If you threw it away, I might pick it up, so long as I did not need to stoop. But *pay* for it?" Dany shoved the platter back into his hands. "Worms have crawled up your nose and eaten your wits."

"Eight honors," he cried. "My wives will beat me and call me fool, but I am a helpless child in your hands. Come, eight, that is less than it is worth."

"What do I need with dull brass when Xaro Xhoan Daxos feeds me off plates of gold?" As she turned to walk off, Dany let her glance sweep over the strangers. The brown man was near as wide as he'd looked in the platter, with a gleaming bald head and the smooth cheeks of a eunuch. A long curving *arakh* was thrust through the sweat-stained yellow silk of his bellyband. Above the silk, he was naked but for an absurdly tiny iron-studded vest. Old scars crisscrossed his tree-trunk arms, huge chest, and massive belly, pale against his nut-brown skin.

The other man wore a traveler's cloak of undyed wool, the hood thrown back. Long white hair fell to his shoulders, and a silky white beard covered the lower half of his face. He leaned his weight on a hardwood staff as tall as he was. *Only fools would stare so openly if they meant me harm.* All the same, it might be prudent to head back toward Jhogo and Aggo. "The old man does not wear a sword," she said to Jorah in the Common Tongue as she drew him away.

The brass merchant came hopping after them. "Five honors, for five it is yours, it was meant for you."

Ser Jorah said, "A hardwood staff can crack a skull as well as any mace."

"Four! I know you want it!" He danced in front of them, scampering backward as he thrust the platter at their faces.

"Do they follow?"

"Lift that up a little higher," the knight told the merchant. "Yes. The old man pretends to linger at a potter's stall, but the brown one has eyes only for you."

"Two honors! Two! Two!" The merchant was panting heavily from the effort of running backward.

"Pay him before he kills himself," Dany told Ser Jorah, wondering what she was going to do with a huge brass platter. She turned back as he reached for his coins, intending to put an end to this mummer's farce. The blood of the dragon would not be herded through the bazaar by an old man and a fat eunuch.

A Qartheen stepped into her path. "Mother of Dragons, for you." He knelt and thrust a jewel box into her face.

Dany took it almost by reflex. The box was carved wood, its mother-of-pearl lid inlaid with jasper and chalcedony. "You are too generous." She opened it. Within was a glittering green scarab carved from onyx and emerald. *Beautiful*, she thought. *This will help pay for our passage.* As she reached inside the box, the man said, "I am so sorry," but she hardly heard.

The scarab unfolded with a hiss.

Dany caught a glimpse of a malign black face, almost human, and an arched tail dripping venom . . . and then the box flew from her hand in pieces, turning end over end. Sudden pain twisted her fingers. As she cried out and clutched her hand, the brass merchant let out a shriek, a woman screamed, and suddenly the Qartheen were shouting and pushing each other aside. Ser Jorah slammed past her, and Dany stumbled to one knee. She heard the *hiss* again. The old man drove the butt of his staff into the ground, Aggo came riding through an eggseller's stall and vaulted from his saddle, Jhogo's whip cracked overhead, Ser Jorah slammed the eunuch over the head with the brass platter, sailors and whores and merchants were fleeing or shouting or both . . .

"Your Grace, a thousand pardons." The old man knelt. "It's dead. Did I break your hand?"

She closed her fingers, wincing. "I don't think so."

"I had to knock it away," he started, but her bloodriders were on him before he could finish. Aggo kicked his staff away and Jhogo seized him round the shoulders, forced him to his knees, and pressed a dagger to his throat. "*Khaleesi*, we saw him strike you. Would you see the color of his blood?"

"Release him." Dany climbed to her feet. "Look at the bottom of his staff, blood of my blood." Ser Jorah had been shoved off his feet by the eunuch. She ran between them as *arakh* and longsword both came flashing from their sheaths. "Put down your steel! Stop it!"

"Your Grace?" Mormont lowered his sword only an inch. "These men attacked you."

"They were defending me." Dany snapped her hand to shake the sting from her fingers. "It was the other one, the Qartheen." When she looked around he was gone. "He was a Sorrowful Man. There was a manticore in that jewel box he gave me. This man knocked it out of my hand." The brass merchant was still rolling on the ground. She went to him and helped him to his feet. "Were you stung?"

"No, good lady," he said, shaking, "or else I would be dead. But it touched me, *aieeee*, when it fell from the box it landed on my arm." He had soiled himself, she saw, and no wonder.

She gave him a silver for his trouble and sent him on his way before she turned back to the old man with the white beard. "Who is it that I owe my life to?"

"You owe me nothing, Your Grace. I am called Arstan, though Belwas named me Whitebeard on the voyage here." Though Jhogo had released him, the old man remained on one knee. Aggo picked up his staff, turned it over, cursed softly in Dothraki, scraped the remains of the manticore off on a stone, and handed it back.

"And who is Belwas?" she asked.

The huge brown eunuch swaggered forward, sheathing his *arakh*. "I am Belwas. Strong Belwas they name me in the fighting pits of Meereen. Never did I lose." He slapped his belly, covered with scars. "I let each man cut me once, before I kill him. Count the cuts and you will know how many Strong Belwas has slain."

Dany had no need to count his scars; there were many, she could see at a glance. "And why are you here, Strong Belwas?"

"From Meereen I am sold to Qohor, and then to Pentos and the fat man with sweet stink in his hair. He it was who send Strong Belwas back across the sea, and old Whitebeard to serve him."

The fat man with sweet stink in his hair . . . "Illyrio?" she said. "You were sent by Magister Illyrio?"

"We were, Your Grace," old Whitebeard replied. "The Magister begs your kind indulgence for sending us in his stead, but he cannot sit a horse as he did in his youth, and sea travel upsets his digestion." Earlier he had spoken in the Valyrian of the Free Cities, but now he changed to the Common Tongue. "I regret if we caused you alarm. If truth be told, we were not certain, we expected someone more . . . more . . ."

"Regal?" Dany laughed. She had no dragon with her, and her raiment was hardly queenly. "You speak the Common Tongue well, Arstan. Are you of Westeros?"

"I am. I was born on the Dornish Marches, Your Grace. As a boy I squired for a knight of Lord Swann's household." He held the tall staff upright beside him like a lance in need of a banner. "Now I squire for Belwas."

"A bit old for such, aren't you?" Ser Jorah had shouldered his way to her side, holding the brass platter awkwardly under his arm. Belwas's hard head had left it badly bent.

"Not too old to serve my liege, Lord Mormont."

"You know me as well?"

"I saw you fight a time or two. At Lannisport where you near un-horsed the Kingslayer. And on Pyke, there as well. You do not recall, Lord Mormont?"

Ser Jorah frowned. "Your face seems familiar, but there were hundreds at Lannisport and thousands on Pyke. And I am no lord. Bear Island was taken from me. I am but a knight."

"A knight of my Queensguard." Dany took his arm. "And my true friend and good counselor." She studied Arstan's face. He had a great dignity to him, a quiet strength she liked. "Rise, Arstan Whitebeard. Be welcome, Strong Belwas. Ser Jorah you know. Ko Aggo and Ko Jhogo are blood of my blood. They crossed the red waste with me, and saw my dragons born.''

"Horse boys." Belwas grinned toothily. "Belwas has killed many horse boys in the fighting pits. They jingle when they die."

Aggo's *arakh* leapt to his hand. "Never have I killed a fat brown man. Belwas will be the first."

"Sheath your steel, blood of my blood," said Dany, "this man comes to serve me. Belwas, you will accord all respect to my people, or you will leave my service sooner than you'd wish, and with more scars than when you came."

The gap-toothed smile faded from the giant's broad brown face, replaced by a confused scowl. Men did not often threaten Belwas, it would seem, and less so girls a third his size.

Dany gave him a smile, to take a bit of the sting from the rebuke. "Now tell me, what would Magister Illyrio have of me, that he would send you all the way from Pentos?"

"He would have dragons," said Belwas gruffly, "and the girl who makes them. He would have you."

"Belwas has the truth of us, Your Grace," said Arstan. "We were told to find you and bring you back to Pentos. The Seven Kingdoms have need of you. Robert the Usurper is dead, and the realm bleeds. When we set sail from Pentos there were four kings in the land, and no justice to be had."

Joy bloomed in her heart, but Dany kept it from her face. "I have three dragons," she said, "and more than a hundred in my *khalasar*, with all their goods and horses."

"It is no matter," boomed Belwas. "We take all. The fat man hires three ships for his little silverhair queen."

"It is so, Your Grace," Arstan Whitebeard said. "The great cog *Saduleon* is berthed at the end of the quay, and the galleys *Summer Sun* and *Joso's Prank* are anchored beyond the breakwater."

Three heads has the dragon, Dany thought, wondering. "I shall tell my people to make ready to depart at once. But the ships that bring me home must bear different names."

"As you wish," said Arstan. "What names would you prefer?"

"*Vhagar*," Daenerys told him. "*Meraxes*. And *Balerion*. Paint the names on their hulls in golden letters three feet high, Arstan. I want every man who sees them to know the dragons are returned."

ARYA

The heads had been dipped in tar to slow the rot. Every morning when Arya went to the well to draw fresh water for Roose Bolton's basin, she had to pass beneath them. They faced outward, so she never saw their faces, but she liked to pretend that one of them was Joffrey's. She tried to picture how his pretty face would look dipped in tar. *If I was a crow I could fly down and peck off his stupid fat pouty lips.*

The heads never lacked for attendants. The carrion crows wheeled about the gatehouse in raucous unkindness and quarreled upon the ramparts over every eye, screaming and cawing at each other and taking to the air whenever a sentry passed along the battlements. Sometimes the maester's ravens joined the feast as well, flapping down from the rookery on wide black wings. When the ravens came the crows would scatter, only to return the moment the larger birds were gone.

Do the ravens remember Maester Tothmure? Arya wondered. *Are they sad for him? When they quork at him, do they wonder why he doesn't answer?* Perhaps the dead could speak to them in some secret tongue the living could not hear.

Tothmure had been sent to the axe for dispatching birds to Casterly Rock and King's Landing the night Harrenhal had fallen, Lucan the armorer for making weapons for the Lannisters, Goodwife Harra for telling Lady Whent's household to serve them, the steward for giving Lord Tywin the keys to the treasure vault. The cook was spared (some said because he'd made the weasel soup), but stocks were hammered together for pretty Pia and the other women who'd shared their favors with Lannister soldiers. Stripped and shaved, they were left in the middle ward beside the bear pit, free for the use of any man who wanted them.

Three Frey men-at-arms were using them that morning as Arya went to the well. She tried not to look, but she could hear the men laughing. The pail was very heavy once full. She was turning to bring it back to Kingspyre when Goodwife Amabel seized her arm. The water went sloshing over the side onto Amabel's legs. "You did that on purpose," the woman screeched.

"What do you want?" Arya squirmed in her grasp. Amabel had been half-crazed since they'd cut Harra's head off.

"See there?" Amabel pointed across the yard at Pia. "When this northman falls you'll be where she is."

"Let me go." She tried to wrench free, but Amabel only tightened her fingers.

"He will fall too, Harrenhal pulls them all down in the end. Lord Tywin's won now, he'll be marching back with all his power, and then it will be his turn to punish the disloyal. And don't think he won't know what you did!" The old woman laughed. "I may have a turn at you myself. Harra had an old broom, I'll save it for you. The handle's cracked and splintery—"

Arya swung the bucket. The weight of the water made it turn in her hands, so she didn't smash Amabel's head in as she wanted, but the woman let go of her anyway when the water came out and drenched her. "Don't ever touch me," Arya shouted, "or I'll kill you. You get away."

Sopping, Goodwife Amabel jabbed a thin finger at the flayed man on the front of Arya's tunic. "You think you're safe with that little bloody man on your teat, but you're not! The Lannisters are coming! See what happens when they get here."

Three-quarters of the water had splashed out on the ground, so Arya had to return to the well. If I told Lord Bolton what she said, her head would be up next to Harra's before it got dark, she thought as she drew up the bucket again. She wouldn't, though.

Once, when there had been only half as many heads, Gendry had caught Arya looking at them. "Admiring your work?" he asked.

He was angry because he'd liked Lucan, she knew, but it still wasn't fair. "It's Steelshanks Walton's work," she said defensively. "And the Mummers, and Lord Bolton."

"And who gave us all them? You and your weasel soup."

Arya punched his arm. "It was just hot broth. You hated Ser Amory too."

"I hate this lot worse. Ser Amory was fighting for his lord, but the Mummers are sellswords and turncloaks. Half of them can't even speak the Common Tongue. Septon Utt likes little boys, Qyburn does black magic, and your friend Biter *eats* people."

The worst thing was, she couldn't even say he was wrong. The Brave Companions did most of the foraging for Harrenhal, and Roose Bolton had given them the task of rooting out Lannisters. Vargo Hoat had divided them into four bands, to visit as many villages as possible. He led the largest group himself, and gave the others to his most trusted captains. She had heard Rorge laughing over Lord Vargo's way of finding traitors. All he did was return to places he had visited before under Lord Tywin's banner and seize those who had helped him. Many had been bought with Lannister silver, so the Mummers often returned with bags of coin as well as baskets of heads. "A riddle!" Shagwell would shout gleefully. "If Lord Bolton's goat eats the men who fed Lord Lannister's goat, how many goats are there?"

"One," Arya said when he asked her.

"Now there's a weasel clever as a goat!" the fool tittered.

Rorge and Biter were as bad as the others. Whenever Lord Bolton took a meal with the garrison, Arya would see them there among the rest. Biter gave off a stench like bad cheese, so the Brave Companions made him sit down near the foot of the table where he could grunt and hiss to himself and tear his meat apart with fingers and teeth. He would *sniff* at Arya when she passed, but it was Rorge who scared her most. He sat up near Faithful Ursywck, but she could feel his eyes crawling over her as she went about her duties.

Sometimes she wished she had gone off across the narrow sea with Jaqen H'ghar. She still had the stupid coin he'd given her, a piece of iron no larger than a penny and rusted along the rim. One side had writing on it, queer words she could not read. The other showed a man's head, but so worn that all his features had rubbed off. *He said it was of great value, but that was probably a lie too, like his name and even his face.* That made her so angry that she threw the coin away, but after an hour she got to feeling bad and went and found it again, even though it wasn't worth anything.

She was thinking about the côin as she crossed the Flowstone Yard, struggling with the weight of the water in her pail. "Nan," a voice called out. "Put down that pail and come help me."

Elmar Frey was no older than she was, and short for his age besides. He had been rolling a barrel of sand across the uneven stone, and was red-faced from exertion. Arya went to help him. Together they pushed the barrel all the way to the wall and back again, then stood it upright.

She could hear the sand shifting around inside as Elmar pried open the lid and pulled out a chainmail hauberk. "Do you think it's clean enough?" As Roose Bolton's squire, it was his task to keep his mail shiny bright.

"You need to shake out the sand. There's still spots of rust. See?" She pointed. "You'd best do it again."

"You do it." Elmar could be friendly when he needed help, but afterward he would always remember that he was a squire and she was only a serving girl. He liked to boast how he was the son of the Lord of the Crossing, not a nephew or a bastard or a grandson but a trueborn *son*, and on account of that he was going to marry a princess.

Arya didn't care about his precious princess, and didn't like him giving her commands. "I have to bring m'lord water for his basin. He's in his bedchamber being leeched. Not the regular black leeches but the big pale ones."

Elmar's eyes got as big as boiled eggs. Leeches terrified him, especially the big pale ones that looked like jelly until they filled up with blood. "I forgot, you're too skinny to push such a heavy barrel."

"I forgot, you're stupid." Arya picked up the pail. "Maybe you should get leeched too. There's leeches in the Neck as big as pigs." She left him there with his barrel.

The lord's bedchamber was crowded when she entered. Qyburn was in attendance, and dour Walton in his mail shirt and greaves, plus a dozen Freys, all brothers, half brothers, and cousins. Roose Bolton lay abed, naked. Leeches clung to the inside of his arms and legs and dotted his pallid chest, long translucent things that turned a glistening pink as they fed. Bolton paid them no more mind than he did Arya.

"We must not allow Lord Tywin to trap us here at Harrenhal," Ser Aenys Frey was saying as Arya filled the washbasin. A grey stooped giant of a man with watery red eyes and huge gnarled hands, Ser Aenys had brought fifteen hundred Frey swords south to Harrenhal, yet it often seemed as if he were helpless to command even his own brothers. "The castle is so large it requires an army to hold it, and once surrounded we cannot *feed* an army. Nor can we hope to lay in sufficient supplies. The country is ash, the villages given over to wolves, the harvest burnt or stolen. Autumn is on us, yet there is no food in store and none being planted. We live on forage, and if the Lannisters deny that to us, we will be down to rats and shoe leather in a moon's turn."

"I do not mean to be besieged here." Roose Bolton's voice was so soft that men had to strain to hear it, so his chambers were always strangely hushed.

"What, then?" demanded Ser Jared Frey, who was lean, balding, and pockmarked. "Is Edmure Tully so drunk on his victory that he thinks to give Lord Tywin battle in the open field?"

If he does he'll beat them, Arya thought. *He'll beat them as he did on the Red Fork, you'll see.* Unnoticed, she went to stand by Qyburn.

"Lord Tywin is many leagues from here," Bolton said calmly. "He has many matters yet to settle at King's Landing. He will not march on Harrenhal for some time."

Ser Aenys shook his head stubbornly. "You do not know the Lannisters as we do, my lord. King Stannis thought that Lord Tywin was a thousand leagues away as well, and it undid him."

The pale man in the bed smiled faintly as the leeches nursed of his blood. "I am not a man to be undone, ser."

"Even if Riverrun marshals all its strength and the Young Wolf wins back from the west, how can we hope to match the numbers Lord Tywin can send against us? When he comes, he will come with far more power than he commanded on the Green Fork. Highgarden has joined itself to Joffrey's cause, I remind you!"

"I had not forgotten."

"I have been Lord Tywin's captive once," said Ser Hosteen, a husky man with a square face who was said to be the strongest of the Freys. "I have no wish to enjoy Lannister hospitality again."

Ser Harys Haigh, who was a Frey on his mother's side, nodded vigorously. "If Lord Tywin could defeat a seasoned man like Stannis Baratheon, what chance will our boy king have against him?" He looked round to his brothers and cousins for support, and several of them muttered agreement.

"Someone must have the courage to say it," Ser Hosteen said. "The war is lost. King Robb must be made to see that."

Roose Bolton studied him with pale eyes. "His Grace has defeated the Lannisters every time he has faced them in battle."

"He has lost the north," insisted Hosteen Frey. "He has lost *Winterfell*! His brothers are dead . . ."

For a moment Arya forgot to breathe. *Dead? Bran and Rickon, dead? What does he mean? What does he mean about Winterfell, Joffrey could never take Winterfell, never, Robb would never let him.* Then she remembered that Robb was not at Winterfell. He was away in the west, and Bran was crippled, and Rickon only four. It took all her strength to remain still and silent, the way Syrio Forel had taught her, to stand there like a stick of furniture. She felt tears gathering in her eyes, and willed them away. *It's not true, it can't be true, it's just some Lannister lie.*

"Had Stannis won, all might have been different," Ronel Rivers said wistfully. He was one of Lord Walder's bastards.

"Stannis lost," Ser Hosteen said bluntly. "Wishing it were otherwise will not make it so. King Robb must make his peace with the Lannisters. He must put off his crown and bend the knee, little as he may like it."

"And who will tell him so?" Roose Bolton smiled. "It is a fine thing to have so many valiant brothers in such troubled times. I shall think on all you've said."

His smile was dismissal. The Freys made their courtesies and shuffled out, leaving only Qyburn, Steelshanks Walton, and Arya. Lord Bolton beckoned her closer. "I am bled sufficiently. Nan, you may remove the leeches."

"At once, my lord." It was best never to make Roose Bolton ask twice. Arya wanted to ask him what Ser Hosteen had meant about Winterfell, but she dared not. *I'll ask Elmar,* she thought. *Elmar will tell me.* The leeches wriggled slowly between her fingers as she plucked them carefully from the lord's body, their pale bodies moist to the touch and distended with blood. *They're only leeches,* she reminded herself. *If I closed my hand, they'd squish between my fingers.*

"There is a letter from your lady wife." Qyburn pulled a roll of parchment from his sleeve. Though he wore maester's robes, there was no chain about his neck; it was whispered that he had lost it for dabbling in necromancy.

"You may read it," Bolton said.

The Lady Walda wrote from the Twins almost every day, but all the letters were the same. "I pray for you morn, noon, and night, my sweet lord," she wrote, "and count the days until you share my bed again. Return to me soon, and I will give you many trueborn sons to take the place of your dear Domeric and rule the Dreadfort after you." Arya pictured a plump pink baby in a cradle, covered with plump pink leeches.

She brought Lord Bolton a damp washcloth to wipe down his soft hairless body. "I will send a letter of my own," he told the onetime maester.

"To the Lady Walda?"

"To Ser Helman Tallhart."

A rider from Ser Helman had come two days past. Tallhart men had taken the castle of the Darrys, accepting the surrender of its Lannister garrison after a brief siege.

"Tell him to put the captives to the sword and the castle to the torch, by command of the king. Then he is to join forces with Robett Glover and strike east toward Duskendale. Those are rich lands, and hardly touched by the fighting. It is time they had a taste. Glover has lost a castle, and Tallhart a son. Let them take their vengeance on Duskendale."

"I shall prepare the message for your seal, my lord."

Arya was glad to hear that the castle of the Darrys would be burned. That was where they'd brought her when she'd been caught after her fight with Joffrey, and where the queen had made her father kill Sansa's wolf. *It deserves to burn.* She wished that Robett Glover and Ser Helman Tallhart would come back to Harrenhal, though; they had marched too quickly, before she'd been able to decide whether to trust them with her secret.

"I will hunt today," Roose Bolton announced as Qyburn helped him into a quilted jerkin.

"Is it safe, my lord?" Qyburn asked. "Only three days past, Septon Utt's men were attacked by wolves. They came right into his camp, not five yards from the fire, and killed two horses."

"It is wolves I mean to hunt. I can scarcely sleep at night for the howling." Bolton buckled on his belt, adjusting the hang of sword and dagger. "It's said that direwolves once roamed the north in great packs of a hundred or more, and feared neither man nor mammoth, but that was long ago and in another land. It is queer to see the common wolves of the south so bold."

"Terrible times breed terrible things, my lord."

Bolton showed his teeth in something that might have been a smile. "Are these times so terrible, Maester?"

"Summer is gone and there are four kings in the realm."

"One king may be terrible, but four?" He shrugged. "Nan, my fur cloak." She brought it to him. "My chambers will be clean and orderly upon my return," he told her as she fastened it. "And tend to Lady Walda's letter."

"As you say, my lord."

The lord and maester swept from the room, giving her not so much as a backward glance. When they were gone, Arya took the letter and carried it to the hearth, stirring the logs with a poker to wake the flames anew. She watched the parchment twist, blacken, and flare up. *If the Lannisters hurt Bran and Rickon, Robb will kill them every one. He'll never bend the knee, never, never, never. He's not afraid of any of them.* Curls of ash floated up the chimney. Arya squatted beside the fire, watching them rise through a veil of hot tears. *If Winterfell is truly gone, is this my home now? Am I still Arya, or only Nan the serving girl, for forever and forever and forever?*

She spent the next few hours tending to the lord's chambers. She swept out the old rushes and scattered fresh sweet-smelling ones, laid a fresh fire in the hearth, changed the linens and fluffed the featherbed, emptied the chamber pots down the privy shaft and scrubbed them out, carried an armload of soiled clothing to the washerwomen, and brought up a bowl of crisp autumn pears from the kitchen. When she was done with the bedchamber, she went down half a flight of stairs to do the same in the great solar, a spare drafty room as large as the halls of many a smaller castle. The candles were down to stubs, so Arya changed them out. Under the windows was a huge oaken table where the lord wrote his letters. She stacked the books, changed the candles, put the quills and inks and sealing wax in order.

A large ragged sheepskin was tossed across the papers. Arya had started to roll it up when the colors caught her eye: the blue of lakes and rivers, the red dots where castles and cities could be found, the green of woods. She spread it out instead. THE LANDS OF THE TRIDENT, said the ornate script beneath the map. The drawing showed everything from the Neck to the Blackwater Rush. *There's Harrenhal at the top of the big lake*, she realized, *but where's Riverrun?* Then she saw. *It's not so far . . .*

The afternoon was still young by the time she was done, so Arya took herself off to the godswood. Her duties were lighter as Lord Bolton's cupbearer than they had been under Weese or even Pinkeye, though they required dressing like a page and washing more than she liked. The hunt would not return for hours, so she had a little time for her needlework.

She slashed at birch leaves till the splintery point of the broken broomstick was green and sticky. "Ser Gregor," she breathed. "Dunsen, Polliver, Raff the Sweetling." She spun and leapt and balanced on the balls of her feet, darting this way and that, knocking pinecones flying. "The Tickler," she called out one time, "the Hound," the next. "Ser Ilyn, Ser Meryn, Queen Cersei." The bole of an oak loomed before her, and she lunged to drive her point through it, grunting "Joffrey, Joffrey, Joffrey." Her arms and legs were dappled by sunlight and the shadows of leaves. A sheen of sweat covered her skin by the time she paused. The heel of her right foot was bloody where she'd skinned it, so she stood one-legged before the heart tree and raised her sword in salute. *"Valar morghulis,"* she told the old gods of the north. She liked how the words sounded when she said them.

As Arya crossed the yard to the bathhouse, she spied a raven circling down toward the rookery, and wondered where it had come from and what message it carried. *Might be it's from Robb, come to say it wasn't true about Bran and Rickon.* She chewed on her lip, hoping. *If I had wings I could fly back to Winterfell and see for myself. And if it was true, I'd just fly away, fly up past the moon and the shining stars, and see all the things in Old Nan's stories, dragons and sea monsters and the Titan of Braavos, and maybe I wouldn't ever fly back unless I wanted to.*

The hunting party returned near evenfall with nine dead wolves. Seven were adults, big grey-brown beasts, savage and powerful, their mouths drawn back over long yellow teeth by their dying snarls. But the other two had only been pups. Lord Bolton gave orders for the skins to be sewn into a blanket for his bed. "Cubs still have that soft fur, my lord," one of his men pointed out. "Make you a nice warm pair of gloves."

Bolton glanced up at the banners waving above the gatehouse towers. "As the Starks are wont to remind us, winter is coming. Have it done." When he saw Arya looking on, he said, "Nan, I'll want a flagon of hot spice wine, I took a chill in the woods. See that it doesn't get cold. I'm of a mind to sup alone. Barley bread, butter, and boar."

"At once, my lord." That was always the best thing to say.

Hot Pie was making oatcakes when she entered the kitchen. Three other cooks were boning fish, while a spit boy turned a boar over the flames. "My lord wants his supper, and hot spice wine to wash it down," Arya announced, "and he doesn't want it cold." One of the cooks washed his hands, took out a kettle, and filled it with a heavy, sweet red. Hot Pie was told to crumble in the spices as the wine heated. Arya went to help.

"I can do it," he said sullenly. "I don't need you to show me how to spice wine."

He hates me too, or else he's scared of me. She backed away, more sad than angry. When the food was ready, the cooks covered it with a silver cover and wrapped the flagon in a thick towel to keep it warm. Dusk was settling outside. On the walls the crows muttered round the heads like courtiers round a king. One of the guards held the door to Kingspyre. "Hope that's not weasel soup," he jested.

Roose Bolton was seated by the hearth reading from a thick leatherbound book when she entered. "Light some candles," he commanded her as he turned a page. "It grows gloomy in here."

She placed the food at his elbow and did as he bid her, filling the room with flickering light and the scent of cloves. Bolton turned a few more pages with his finger, then closed the book and placed it carefully in the fire. He watched the flames consume it, pale eyes shining with reflected light. The old dry leather went up with a *whoosh,* and the yellow pages stirred as they burned, as if some ghost were reading them. "I will have no further need of you tonight," he said, never looking at her.

She should have gone, silent as a mouse, but something had hold of her. "My lord," she asked, "will you take me with you when you leave Harrenhal?"

He turned to stare at her, and from the look in his eyes it was as if his supper had just spoken to him. "Did I give you leave to question me, Nan?"

"No, my lord." She lowered her eyes.

"You should not have spoken, then. Should you?"

"No. My lord."

For a moment he looked amused. "I will answer you, just this once. I mean to give Harrenhal to Lord Vargo when I return to the north. You will remain here, with him."

"But I don't—" she started.

He cut her off. "I am not in the habit of being questioned by servants, Nan. Must I have your tongue out?"

He would do it as easily as another man might cuff a dog, she knew. "No, my lord."

"Then I'll hear no more from you?"

"No, my lord."

"Go, then. I shall forget this insolence."

Arya went, but not to her bed. When she stepped out into the darkness of the yard, the guard on the door nodded at her and said, "Storm coming. Smell the air?" The wind was gusting, flames swirling off the torches mounted atop the walls beside the rows of heads. On her way to the godswood, she passed the Wailing Tower where once she had lived in fear of Weese. The Freys had taken it for their own since Harrenhal's fall. She could hear angry voices coming from a window, many men talking and arguing all at once. Elmar was sitting on the steps outside, alone.

"What's wrong?" Arya asked him when she saw the tears shining on his cheeks.

"My princess," he sobbed. "We've been dishonored, Aenys says. There was a bird from the Twins. My lord father says I'll need to marry someone else, or be a septon."

A stupid princess, she thought, *that's nothing to cry over.* "My brothers might be dead," she confided.

Elmar gave her a scornful look. "No one cares about a serving girl's brothers."

It was hard not to hit him when he said that. "I hope your princess dies," she said, and ran off before he could grab her.

In the godswood she found her broomstick sword where she had left it, and carried it to the heart tree. There she knelt. Red leaves rustled. Red eyes peered inside her. *The eyes of the gods.* "Tell me what to do, you gods," she prayed.

For a long moment there was no sound but the wind and the water and the creak of leaf and limb. And then, far far off, beyond the godswood and the haunted towers and the immense stone walls of Harrenhal, from somewhere out in the world, came the long lonely howl of a wolf. Gooseprickles rose on Arya's skin, and for an instant she felt dizzy. Then, so faintly, it seemed as if she heard her father's voice. "When the snows fall and the white winds blow, the lone wolf dies, but the pack survives," he said.

"But there is no pack," she whispered to the weirwood. Bran and

Rickon were dead, the Lannisters had Sansa, Jon had gone to the Wall. "I'm not even me now, I'm Nan."

"You are Arya of Winterfell, daughter of the north. You told me you could be strong. You have the wolf blood in you."

"The wolf blood." Arya remembered now. "I'll be as strong as Robb. I said I would." She took a deep breath, then lifted the broomstick in both hands and brought it down across her knee. It broke with a loud *crack*, and she threw the pieces aside. *I am a direwolf, and done with wooden teeth.*

That night she lay in her narrow bed upon the scratchy straw, listening to the voices of the living and the dead whisper and argue as she waited for the moon to rise. They were the only voices she trusted anymore. She could hear the sound of her own breath, and the wolves as well, a great pack of them now. *They are closer than the one I heard in the godswood*, she thought. *They are calling to me.*

Finally she slipped from under the blanket, wriggled into a tunic, and padded barefoot down the stairs. Roose Bolton was a cautious man, and the entrance to Kingspyre was guarded day and night, so she had to slip out of a narrow cellar window. The yard was still, the great castle lost in haunted dreams. Above, the wind keened through the Wailing Tower.

At the forge she found the fires extinguished and the doors closed and barred. She crept in a window, as she had once before. Gendry shared a mattress with two other apprentice smiths. She crouched in the loft for a long time before her eyes adjusted enough for her to be sure that he was the one on the end. Then she put a hand over his mouth and pinched him. His eyes opened. He could not have been very deeply asleep. *"Please,"* she whispered. She took her hand off his mouth and pointed.

For a moment she did not think he understood, but then he slid out from under the blankets. Naked, he padded across the room, shrugged into a loose roughspun tunic, and climbed down from the loft after her. The other sleepers did not stir. "What do you want now?" Gendry said in a low angry voice.

"A sword."

"Blackthumb keeps all the blades locked up, I told you that a hundred times. Is this for Lord Leech?"

"For me. Break the lock with your hammer."

"They'll break my hand," he grumbled. "Or worse."

"Not if you run off with me."

"Run, and they'll catch you and kill you."

"They'll do you worse. Lord Bolton is giving Harrenhal to the Bloody Mummers, he told me so."

Gendry pushed black hair out of his eyes. "So?"

She looked right at him, fearless. "So when Vargo Hoat's the lord, he's going to cut off the feet of all the servants to keep them from running away. The smiths too."

"That's only a story," he said scornfully.

"No, it's true, I heard Lord Vargo say so," she lied. "He's going to cut one foot off everyone. The left one. Go to the kitchens and wake Hot Pie, he'll do what you say. We'll need bread or oakcakes or something. You get the swords and I'll do the horses. We'll meet near the postern in the east wall, behind the Tower of Ghosts. No one ever comes there."

"I know that gate. It's guarded, same as the rest."

"So? You won't forget the swords?"

"I never said I'd come."

"No. But if you do, you won't forget the swords?"

He frowned. "No," he said at last. "I guess I won't."

Arya reentered Kingspyre the same way she had left it, and stole up the winding steps listening for footfalls. In her cell, she stripped to the skin and dressed herself carefully, in two layers of smallclothes, warm stockings, and her cleanest tunic. It was Lord Bolton's livery. On the breast was sewn his sigil, the flayed man of the Dreadfort. She tied her shoes, threw a wool cloak over her skinny shoulders, and knotted it under her throat. Quiet as a shadow, she moved back down the stairs. Outside the lord's solar she paused to listen at the door, easing it open slowly when she heard only silence.

The sheepskin map was on the table, beside the remains of Lord Bolton's supper. She rolled it up tight and thrust it through her belt. He'd left his dagger on the table as well, so she took that too, just in case Gendry lost his courage.

A horse neighed softly as she slipped into the darkened stables. The grooms were all asleep. She prodded one with her toe until he sat up groggily and said, "Eh? Whas?"

"Lord Bolton requires three horses saddled and bridled."

The boy got to his feet, pushing straw from his hair. "Wha, at this hour? Horses, you say?" He blinked at the sigil on her tunic. "Whas he want horses for, in the dark?"

"Lord Bolton is not in the habit of being questioned by servants." She crossed her arms.

The stableboy was still looking at the flayed man. He knew what it meant. "Three, you say?"

"One two three. Hunting horses. Fast and surefoot." Arya helped him with the bridles and saddles, so he would not need to wake any of the others. She hoped they would not hurt him afterward, but she knew they probably would.

Leading the horses across the castle was the worst part. She stayed in the shadow of the curtain wall whenever she could, so the sentries walking their rounds on the ramparts above would have needed to look almost straight down to see her. *And if they do, what of it? I'm my lord's own cupbearer.* It was a chill dank autumn night. Clouds were blowing in from the west, hiding the stars, and the Wailing Tower screamed mournfully at every gust of wind. *It smells like rain.* Arya did not know whether that would be good or bad for their escape.

No one saw her, and she saw no one, only a grey and white cat creeping along atop the godswood wall. It stopped and spit at her, waking memories of the Red Keep and her father and Syrio Forel. "I could catch you if I wanted," she called to it softly, "but I have to go, cat." The cat hissed again and ran off.

The Tower of Ghosts was the most ruinous of Harrenhal's five immense towers. It stood dark and desolate behind the remains of a collapsed sept where only rats had come to pray for near three hundred years. It was there she waited to see if Gendry and Hot Pie would come. It seemed as though she waited a long time. The horses nibbled at the weeds that grew up between the broken stones while the clouds swallowed the last of the stars. Arya took out the dagger and sharpened it to keep her hands busy. Long smooth strokes, the way Syrio had taught her. The sound calmed her.

She heard them coming long before she saw them. Hot Pie was breathing heavily, and once he stumbled in the dark, barked his shin, and cursed loud enough to wake half of Harrenhal. Gendry was quieter, but the swords he was carrying rang together as he moved. "Here I am." She stood. "Be quiet or they'll hear you."

The boys picked their way toward her over tumbled stones. Gendry was wearing oiled chainmail under his cloak, she saw, and he had his blacksmith's hammer slung across his back. Hot Pie's red round face peered out from under a hood. He had a sack of bread dangling from his right hand and a big wheel of cheese under his left arm. "There's a guard on that postern," said Gendry quietly. "I told you there would be."

"You stay here with the horses," said Arya. "I'll get rid of him. Come quick when I call."

Gendry nodded. Hot Pie said, "Hoot like an owl when you want us to come."

"I'm not an owl," said Arya. "I'm a wolf. I'll howl."

Alone, she slid through the shadow of the Tower of Ghosts. She walked fast, to keep ahead of her fear, and it felt as though Syrio Forel walked beside her, and Yoren, and Jaqen H'ghar, and Jon Snow. She had not taken the sword Gendry had brought her, not yet. For this the dagger would be better. It was good and sharp. This postern was the least of Harrenhal's gates, a narrow door of stout oak studded with iron nails, set in an angle of the wall beneath a defensive tower. Only one man was set to guard it, but she knew there would be sentries up in that tower as well, and others nearby walking the walls. Whatever happened, she must be quiet as a shadow. *He must not call out.* A few scattered raindrops had begun to fall. She felt one land on her brow and run slowly down her nose.

She made no effort to hide, but approached the guard openly, as if Lord Bolton himself had sent her. He watched her come, curious as to what might bring a page here at this black hour. When she got closer, she saw that he was a northman, very tall and thin, huddled in a ragged fur cloak. That was bad. She might have been able to trick a Frey or one of the Brave Companions, but the Dreadfort men had served Roose Bolton their whole life, and they knew him better than she did. *If I tell him I am Arya Stark and command him to stand aside* . . . No, she dare not. He was a northman, but not a Winterfell man. He belonged to Roose Bolton.

When she reached him she pushed back her cloak so he would see the flayed man on her breast. "Lord Bolton sent me."

"At this hour? Why for?"

She could see the gleam of steel under the fur, and she did not know if she was strong enough to drive the point of the dagger through chainmail. *His throat, it must be his throat, but he's too tall, I'll never reach it.* For a moment she did not know what to say. For a moment she was a little girl again, and scared, and the rain on her face felt like tears.

"He told me to give all his guards a silver piece, for their good service." The words seemed to come out of nowhere.

"Silver, you say?" He did not believe her, but he *wanted* to; silver was silver, after all. "Give it over, then."

Her fingers dug down beneath her tunic and came out clutching the coin Jaqen had given her. In the dark the iron could pass for tarnished silver. She held it out . . . and let it slip through her fingers.

Cursing her softly, the man went to a knee to grope for the coin in the dirt, and there was his neck right in front of her. Arya slid her dagger out and drew it across his throat, as smooth as summer silk. His blood covered her hands in a hot gush and he tried to shout but there was blood in his mouth as well.

"Valar morghulis," she whispered as he died.

When he stopped moving, she picked up the coin. Outside the walls of Harrenhal, a wolf howled long and loud. She lifted the bar, set it aside, and pulled open the heavy oak door. By the time Hot Pie and Gendry came up with the horses, the rain was falling hard. "You killed him!" Hot Pie gasped.

"What did you think I would do?" Her fingers were sticky with blood, and the smell was making her mare skittish. *It's no matter,* she thought, swinging up into the saddle. *The rain will wash them clean again.*

SANSA

The throne room was a sea of jewels, furs, and bright fabrics. Lords and ladies filled the back of the hall and stood beneath the high windows, jostling like fishwives on a dock.

The denizens of Joffrey's court had striven to outdo each other today. Jalabhar Xho was all in feathers, a plumage so fantastic and extravagant that he seemed like to take flight. The High Septon's crystal crown fired rainbows through the air every time he moved his head. At the council table, Queen Cersei shimmered in a cloth-of-gold gown slashed in burgundy velvet, while beside her Varys fussed and simpered in a lilac brocade. Moon Boy and Ser Dontos wore new suits of motley, clean as a spring morning. Even Lady Tanda and her daughters looked pretty in matching gowns of turquoise silk and vair, and Lord Gyles was coughing into a square of scarlet silk trimmed with golden lace. King Joffrey sat above them all, amongst the blades and barbs of the Iron Throne. He was in crimson samite, his black mantle studded with rubies, on his head his heavy golden crown.

Squirming through a press of knights, squires, and rich townfolk, Sansa reached the front of the gallery just as a blast of trumpets announced the entry of Lord Tywin Lannister.

He rode his warhorse down the length of the hall and dismounted before the Iron Throne. Sansa had never seen such armor; all burnished red steel, inlaid with golden scrollwork and ornamentation. His rondels were sunbursts, the roaring lion that crowned his helm had ruby eyes, and a lioness on each shoulder fastened a cloth-of-gold cloak so long and heavy that it draped the hindquarters of his charger. Even the horse's armor was gilded, and his bardings were shimmering crimson silk emblazoned with the lion of Lannister.

The Lord of Casterly Rock made such an impressive figure that it was a shock when his destrier dropped a load of dung right at the base of the throne. Joffrey had to step gingerly around it as he descended to embrace his grandfather and proclaim him Savior of the City. Sansa covered her mouth to hide a nervous smile.

Joff made a show of asking his grandfather to assume governance of the realm, and Lord Tywin solemnly accepted the responsibility, "until Your Grace does come of age." Then squires removed his armor and Joff fastened the Hand's chain of office around his neck. Lord Tywin took a seat at the council table beside the queen. After the destrier was led off and his homage removed, Cersei nodded for the ceremonies to continue.

A fanfare of brazen trumpets greeted each of the heroes as he stepped between the great oaken doors. Heralds cried his name and deeds for all to hear, and the noble knights and highborn ladies cheered as lustily as cutthroats at a cockfight. Pride of place was given to Mace Tyrell, the Lord of Highgarden, a once-powerful man gone to fat, yet still handsome. His sons followed him in; Ser Loras and his older brother Ser Garlan the Gallant. The three dressed alike, in green velvet trimmed with sable.

The king descended the throne once more to greet them, a great honor. He fastened about the throat of each a chain of roses wrought in soft yellow gold, from which hung a golden disc with the lion of Lannister picked out in rubies. "The roses support the lion, as the might of Highgarden supports the realm," proclaimed Joffrey. "If there is any boon you would ask of me, ask and it shall be yours."

And now it comes, thought Sansa.

"Your Grace," said Ser Loras, "I beg the honor of serving in your Kingsguard, to defend you against your enemies."

Joffrey drew the Knight of Flowers to his feet and kissed him on his cheek. "Done, brother."

Lord Tyrell bowed his head. "There is no greater pleasure than to serve the King's Grace. If I was deemed worthy to join your royal council, you would find none more loyal or true."

Joff put a hand on Lord Tyrell's shoulder and kissed him when he stood. "Your wish is granted."

Ser Garlan Tyrell, five years senior to Ser Loras, was a taller bearded version of his more famous younger brother. He was thicker about the chest and broader at the shoulders, and though his face was comely enough, he lacked Ser Loras's startling beauty. "Your Grace," Garlan said when the king approached him, "I have a maiden sister, Margaery, the delight of our House. She was wed to Renly Baratheon, as you know, but Lord Renly went to war before the marriage could be consummated, so she remains innocent. Margaery has heard tales of your wisdom, courage, and chivalry, and has come to love you from afar. I beseech you to send for her, to take her hand in marriage, and to wed your House to mine for all time."

King Joffrey made a show of looking surprised. "Ser Garlan, your sister's beauty is famed throughout the Seven Kingdoms, but I am promised to another. A king must keep his word."

Queen Cersei got to her feet in a rustle of skirts. "Your Grace, in the judgment of your small council, it would be neither proper nor wise for you to wed the daughter of a man beheaded for treason, a girl whose brother is in open rebellion against the throne even now. Sire, your councillors beg you, for the good of your realm, set Sansa Stark aside. The Lady Margaery will make you a far more suitable queen."

Like a pack of trained dogs, the lords and ladies in the hall began to shout their pleasure. *"Margaery,"* they called. "Give us Margaery!" and "No traitor queens! Tyrell! Tyrell!"

Joffrey raised a hand. "I would like to heed the wishes of my people, Mother, but I took a holy vow."

The High Septon stepped forward. "Your Grace, the gods hold bethrothal solemn, but your father, King Robert of blessed memory, made this pact before the Starks of Winterfell had revealed their falseness. Their crimes against the realm have freed you from any promise you might have made. So far as the Faith is concerned, there is no valid marriage contract 'twixt you and Sansa Stark."

A tumult of cheering filled the throne room, and cries of *"Margaery, Margaery"* erupted all around her. Sansa leaned forward, her hands tight around the gallery's wooden rail. She knew what came next, but she was still frightened of what Joffrey might say, afraid that he would refuse to release her even now, when his whole kingdom depended upon it. She felt as if she were back again on the marble steps outside the Great Sept of Baelor, waiting for her prince to grant her father mercy, and instead hearing him command Ilyn Payne to strike off his head. *Please,* she prayed fervently, *make him say it, make him say it.*

Lord Tywin was looking at his grandson. Joff gave him a sullen glance, shifted his feet, and helped Ser Garlan Tyrell to rise. "The gods are good. I am free to heed my heart. I will wed your sweet sister, and gladly, ser." He kissed Ser Garlan on a bearded cheek as the cheers rose all around them.

Sansa felt curiously light-headed. *I am free.* She could feel eyes upon her. *I must not smile,* she reminded herself. The queen had warned her; no matter what she felt inside, the face she showed the world must look distraught. "I will not have my son humiliated," Cersei said. "Do you hear me?"

"Yes. But if I'm not to be queen, what will become of me?"

"That will need to be determined. For the moment, you shall remain here at court, as our ward."

"I want to go home."

The queen was irritated by that. "You should have learned by now, none of us get the things we want."

I have, though, Sansa thought. *I am free of Joffrey. I will not have to kiss him, nor give him my maidenhood, nor bear him children. Let Margaery Tyrell have all that, poor girl.*

By the time the outburst died down, the Lord of Highgarden had been seated at the council table, and his sons had joined the other knights and lordlings beneath the windows. Sansa tried to look forlorn and abandoned as other heroes of the Battle of the Blackwater were summoned forth to receive their rewards.

Paxter Redwyne, Lord of the Arbor, marched down the length of the hall flanked by his twin sons Horror and Slobber, the former limping from a wound taken in the battle. After them followed Lord Mathis Rowan in a snowy doublet with a great tree worked upon the breast in gold thread; Lord Randyll Tarly, lean and balding, a greatsword across his back in a jeweled scabbard; Ser Kevan Lannister, a thickset balding man with a close-trimmed beard; Ser Addam Marbrand, coppery hair streaming to his shoulders; the great western lords Lydden, Crakehall, and Brax.

Next came four of lesser birth who had distinguished themselves in the fighting: the one-eyed knight Ser Philip Foote, who had slain Lord Bryce Caron in single combat; the freerider Lothor Brune, who'd cut his way through half a hundred Fossoway men-at-arms to capture Ser Jon of the green apple and kill Ser Bryan and Ser Edwyd of the red, thereby winning himself the name Lothor Apple-Eater; Willit, a grizzled man-at-arms in the service of Ser Harys Swyft, who'd pulled his master from beneath his dying horse and defended him against a dozen attackers; and a downy-cheeked squire named Josmyn Peckledon, who had killed two knights, wounded a third, and captured two more, though he could not have been more than fourteen. Willit was borne in on a litter, so grievous were his wounds.

Ser Kevan had taken a seat beside his brother Lord Tywin. When the heralds had finished telling of each hero's deeds, he rose. "It is His Grace's wish that these good men be rewarded for their valor. By his decree, Ser Philip shall henceforth be Lord Philip of House Foote, and to him shall go all the lands, rights, and incomes of House Caron. Lothor Brune to be raised to the estate of knighthood, and granted land and keep in the riverlands at war's end. To Josmyn Peckledon, a sword and suit of plate, his choice of any warhorse in the royal stables, and knighthood as soon as he shall come of age. And lastly, for Goodman Willit, a spear with a silver-banded haft, a hauberk of new-forged ringmail, and a full helm with visor. Further, the goodman's sons shall be taken into the service of House Lannister at Casterly Rock, the elder as a squire and the younger as a page, with the chance to advance to knighthood if they serve loyally and well. To all this, the King's Hand and the small council consent."

The captains of the king's warships *Wildwind*, *Prince Aemon*, and *River Arrow* were honored next, along with some under officers from *Godsgrace*, *Lance*, *Lady of Silk*, and *Ramshead*. As near as Sansa could tell, their chief accomplishment had been surviving the battle on the river, a feat that few enough could boast. Hallyne the Pyromancer and the masters of the Alchemists' Guild received the king's thanks as well, and Hallyne was raised to the style of lord, though Sansa noted that neither lands nor castle accompanied the title, which made the alchemist no more a *true* lord than Varys was. A more significant lordship by far was granted to Ser Lancel Lannister. Joffrey awarded him the lands, castle, and rights of House Darry, whose last child lord had perished during the fighting in the riverlands, "leaving no trueborn heirs of lawful Darry blood, but only a bastard cousin."

Ser Lancel did not appear to accept the title; the talk was, his wound might cost him his arm or even his life. The Imp was said to be dying as well, from a terrible cut to the head.

When the herald called, *"Lord Petyr Baelish,"* he came forth dressed all in shades of rose and plum, his cloak patterned with mockingbirds. She could see him smiling as he knelt before the Iron Throne. *He looks so pleased.* Sansa had not heard of Littlefinger doing anything especially heroic during the battle, but it seemed he was to be rewarded all the same.

Ser Kevan got back to his feet. "It is the wish of the King's Grace that his loyal councillor Petyr Baelish be rewarded for faithful service to crown and realm. Be it known that Lord Baelish is granted the castle of Harrenhal with all its attendant lands and incomes, there to make his seat and rule henceforth as Lord Paramount of the Trident. Petyr Baelish and his sons and grandsons shall hold and enjoy these honors until the end of time, and all the lords of the Trident shall do him homage as their rightful liege. The King's Hand and the small council consent."

On his knees, Littlefinger raised his eyes to King Joffrey. "I thank you humbly, Your Grace. I suppose this means I'll need to see about getting some sons and grandsons."

Joffrey laughed, and the court with him. *Lord Paramount of the Trident*, Sansa thought, *and Lord of Harrenhal as well.* She did not understand why that should make him so happy; the honors were as empty as the title granted to Hallyne the Pyromancer. Harrenhal was cursed, everyone knew that, and the Lannisters did not even hold it at present. Besides, the lords of the Trident were sworn to Riverrun and House Tully, and to the King in the North; they would never accept Littlefinger as their liege. *Unless they are made to. Unless my brother and my uncle and my grandfather are all cast down and killed.* The thought made Sansa anxious, but she told herself she was being silly. *Robb has beaten them every time. He'll beat Lord Baelish too, if he must.*

More than six hundred new knights were made that day. They had held their vigil in the Great Sept of Baelor all through the night and crossed the city barefoot that morning to prove their humble hearts. Now they came forward dressed in shifts of undyed wool to receive their knighthoods from the Kingsguard. It took a long time, since only three of the Brothers of the White Sword were on hand to dub them. Mandon Moore had perished in the battle, the Hound had vanished, Aerys Oakheart was in Dorne with Princess Myrcella, and Jaime Lannister was Robb's captive, so the Kingsguard had been reduced to Balon Swann, Meryn Trant, and Osmund Kettleblack. Once knighted, each man rose, buckled on his swordbelt, and stood beneath the windows. Some had bloody feet from their walk through the city, but they stood tall and proud all the same, it seemed to Sansa.

By the time all the new knights had been given their *sers* the hall was growing restive, and none more so than Joffrey. Some of those in the gallery had begun to slip quietly away, but the notables on the floor were trapped, unable to depart without the king's leave. Judging by the way he was fidgeting atop the Iron Throne, Joff would willingly have granted it, but the day's work was far from done. For now the coin was turned over, and the captives were ushered in.

There were great lords and noble knights in that company too: sour old Lord Celtigar, the Red Crab; Ser Bonifer the Good; Lord Estermont, more ancient even than Celtigar; Lord Varner, who hobbled the length of the hall on a shattered knee, but would accept no help; Ser Mark Mullendore, grey-faced, his left arm gone to the elbow; fierce Red Ronnet of Griffin Roost; Ser Dermot of the Rainwood; Lord Willum and his sons Josua and Elyas; Ser Jon Fossoway; Ser Timon the Scrapesword; Aurane, the bastard of Driftmark; Lord Staedmon, called Pennylover; hundreds of others.

Those who had changed their allegiance during the battle needed only to swear fealty to Joffrey, but the ones who had fought for Stannis until the bitter end were compelled to speak. Their words decided their fate. If they begged forgiveness for their treasons and promised to serve loyally henceforth, Joffrey welcomed them back into the king's peace and restored them to all their lands and rights. A handful remained defiant, however. "Do not imagine this is done, boy," warned one, the bastard son of some Florent or other. "The Lord of Light protects King Stannis, now and always. All your swords and all your scheming shall not save you when his hour comes."

"*Your* hour is come right now." Joffrey beckoned to Ser Ilyn Payne to take the man out and strike his head off. But no sooner had that one been dragged away than a knight of solemn mien with a fiery heart on his surcoat shouted out, "Stannis is the true king! A monster sits the Iron Throne, an abomination born of incest!"

"Be silent," Ser Kevan Lannister bellowed.

The knight raised his voice instead. "Joffrey is the black worm eating the heart of the realm! Darkness was his father, and death his mother! Destroy him before he corrupts you all! Destroy them all, queen whore and king worm, vile dwarf and whispering spider, the false flowers. Save yourselves!" One of the gold cloaks knocked the man off his feet, but he continued to shout. "The scouring fire will come! King Stannis will return!"

Joffrey lurched to his feet. "*I'm* king! Kill him! Kill him now! I command it." He chopped down with his hand, a furious, angry gesture . . . and screeched in pain when his arm brushed against one of the sharp metal fangs that surrounded him. The bright crimson samite of his sleeve turned a darker shade of red as his blood soaked through it. "*Mother!*" he wailed.

With every eye on the king, somehow the man on the floor wrested a spear away from one of the gold cloaks, and used it to push himself back to his feet. "The throne denies him!" he cried. "*He is no king!*"

Cersei was running toward the throne, but Lord Tywin remained still as stone. He had only to raise a finger, and Ser Meryn Trant moved forward with drawn sword. The end was quick and brutal. The gold cloaks seized the knight by the arms. "*No king!*" he cried again as Ser Meryn drove the point of his longsword through his chest.

Joff fell into his mother's arms. Three maesters came hurrying forward, to bundle him out through the king's door. Then everyone began talking at once. When the gold cloaks dragged off the dead man, he left a trail of bright blood across the stone floor. Lord Baelish stroked his beard while Varys whispered in his ear. *Will they dismiss us now?* Sansa wondered. A score of captives still waited, though whether to pledge fealty or shout curses, who could say?

Lord Tywin rose to his feet. "We continue," he said in a clear strong voice that silenced the murmurs. "Those who wish to ask pardon for their treasons may do so. We will have no more follies." He moved to the Iron Throne and there seated himself on a step, a mere three feet off the floor.

The light outside the windows was fading by the time the session drew to a close. Sansa felt limp with exhaustion as she made her way down from the gallery. She wondered how badly Joffrey had cut himself. *They say the Iron Throne can be perilous cruel to those who were not meant to sit it.*

Back in the safety of her own chambers, she hugged a pillow to her face to muffle a squeal of joy. *Oh, gods be good, he did it, he put me aside in front of everyone.* When a serving girl brought her supper, she almost kissed her. There was hot bread and fresh-churned butter, a thick beef soup, capon and carrots, and peaches in honey. *Even the food tastes sweeter,* she thought.

Come dark, she slipped into a cloak and left for the godswood. Ser Osmund Kettleblack was guarding the drawbridge in his white armor. Sansa tried her best to sound miserable as she bid him a good evening. From the way he leered at her, she was not sure she had been wholly convincing.

Dontos waited in the leafy moonlight. "Why so sadface?" Sansa asked him gaily. "You were there, you heard. Joff put me aside, he's done with me, he's . . ."

He took her hand. "Oh, Jonquil, my poor Jonquil, you do not understand. Done with you? They've scarcely begun."

Her heart sank. "What do you mean?"

"The queen will never let you go, never. You are too valuable a hostage. And Joffrey . . . sweetling, he is still king. If he wants you in his bed, he will have you, only now it will be bastards he plants in your womb instead of trueborn sons."

"No," Sansa said, shocked. "He let me go, he . . ."

Ser Dontos planted a slobbery kiss on her ear. "Be brave. I swore to see you home, and now I can. The day has been chosen."

"When?" Sansa asked. "When will we go?"

"The night of Joffrey's wedding. After the feast. All the necessary arrangements have been made. The Red Keep will be full of strangers. Half the court will be drunk and the other half will be helping Joffrey bed his bride. For a little while, you will be forgotten, and the confusion will be our friend."

"The wedding won't be for a moon's turn yet. Margaery Tyrell is at Highgarden, they've only now sent for her."

"You've waited so long, be patient awhile longer. Here, I have something for you." Ser Dontos fumbled in his pouch and drew out a silvery spiderweb, dangling it between his thick fingers.

It was a hair net of fine-spun silver, the strands so thin and delicate the net seemed to weigh no more than a breath of air when Sansa took it in her fingers. Small gems were set wherever two strands crossed, so dark they drank the moonlight. "What stones are these?"

"Black amethysts from Asshai. The rarest kind, a deep true purple by daylight."

"It's very lovely," Sansa said, thinking, *It is a ship I need, not a net for my hair.*

"Lovelier than you know, sweet child. It's magic, you see. It's justice you hold. It's vengeance for your father." Dontos leaned close and kissed her again. "It's *home.*"

THEON

Maester Luwin came to him when the first scouts were seen outside the walls. "My lord prince," he said, "you must yield."

Theon stared at the platter of oakcakes, honey, and blood sausage they'd brought him to break his fast. Another sleepless night had left his nerves raw, and the very sight of food sickened him. "There has been no reply from my uncle?"

"None," the maester said. "Nor from your father on Pyke."

"Send more birds."

"It will not serve. By the time the birds reach—"

"*Send them!*" Knocking the platter of food aside with a swipe of his arm, he pushed off the blankets and rose from Ned Stark's bed naked and angry. "Or do you want me dead? Is that it, Luwin? The truth now."

The small grey man was unafraid. "My order serves."

"Yes, but whom?"

"The realm," Maester Luwin said, "and Winterfell. Theon, once I taught you sums and letters, history and warcraft. And might have taught you more, had you wished to learn. I will not claim to bear you any great love, no, but I cannot hate you either. Even if I did, so long as you hold Winterfell I am bound by oath to give you counsel. So now I counsel you to *yield*."

Theon stooped to scoop a puddled cloak off the floor, shook off the rushes, and draped it over his shoulders. *A fire, I'll have a fire, and clean garb. Where's Wex? I'll not go to my grave in dirty clothes.*

"You have no hope of holding here," the maester went on. "If your lord father meant to send you aid, he would have done so by now. It is the Neck that concerns him. The battle for the north will be fought amidst the ruins of Moat Cailin."

"That may be so," said Theon. "And so long as I hold Winterfell, Ser Rodrik and Stark's lords bannermen cannot march south to take my uncle in the rear." *I am not so innocent of warcraft as you think, old man.* "I have food enough to stand a year's siege, if need be."

"There will be no siege. Perhaps they will spend a day or two fashioning ladders and tying grapnels to the ends of ropes. But soon enough they will come over your walls in a hundred places at once. You may be able to hold the keep for a time, but the castle will fall within the hour. You would do better to open your gates and ask for—"

"—*mercy?* I know what kind of mercy they have for me."

"There is a way."

"I am ironborn," Theon reminded him. "I have my own way. What choice have they left me? No, don't answer, I've heard enough of your *counsel.* Go and send those birds as I commanded, and tell Lorren I want to see him. And Wex as well. I'll have my mail scoured clean, and my garrison assembled in the yard."

For a moment he thought the maester was going to defy him. But finally Luwin bowed stiffly. "As you command."

They made a pitifully small assembly; the ironmen were few, the yard large. "The northmen will be on us before nightfall," he told them. "Ser Rodrik Cassel and all the lords who have come to his call. I will not run from them. I took this castle and I mean to hold it, to live or die as Prince of Winterfell. But I will not command any man to die with me. If you leave now, before Ser Rodrik's main force is upon us, there's still a chance you may win free." He unsheathed his longsword and drew a line in the dirt. "Those who would stay and fight, step forward."

No one spoke. The men stood in their mail and fur and boiled leather, as still as if they were made of stone. A few exchanged looks. Urzen shuffled his feet. Dykk Harlaw hawked and spat. A finger of wind ruffled Endehar's long fair hair.

Theon felt as though he were drowning. *Why am I surprised?* he thought bleakly. His father had forsaken him, his uncles, his sister, even that wretched creature Reek. Why should his men prove any more loyal? There was nothing to say, nothing to do. He could only stand there beneath the great grey walls and the hard white sky, sword in hand, waiting, waiting . . .

Wex was the first to cross the line. Three quick steps and he stood at Theon's side, slouching. Shamed by the boy, Black Lorren followed, all scowls. "Who else?" he demanded. Red Rolfe came forward. Kromm. Werlag. Tymor and his brothers. Ulf the Ill. Harrag Sheepstealer. Four Harlaws and two Botleys. Kenned the Whale was the last. Seventeen in all.

Urzen was among those who did not move, and Stygg, and every man of the ten that Asha had brought from Deepwood Motte. "Go, then," Theon told them. "Run to my sister. She'll give you all a warm welcome, I have no doubt."

Stygg had the grace at least to look ashamed. The rest moved off without a word. Theon turned to the seventeen who remained. "Back to the walls. If the gods should spare us, I shall remember every man of you."

Black Lorren stayed when the others had gone. "The castle folk will turn on us soon as the fight begins."

"I know that. What would you have me do?"

"Put them out," said Lorren. "Every one."

Theon shook his head. "Is the noose ready?"

"It is. You mean to use it?"

"Do you know a better way?"

"Aye. I'll take my axe and stand on that drawbridge, and let them come try me. One at a time, two, three, it makes no matter. None will pass the moat while I still draw breath."

He means to die, thought Theon. *It's not victory he wants, it's an end worthy of a song.* "We'll use the noose."

"As you say," Lorren replied, contempt in his eyes.

Wex helped garb him for battle. Beneath his black surcoat and golden mantle was a shirt of well-oiled ringmail, and under that a layer of stiff boiled leather. Once armed and armored, Theon climbed the watchtower at the angle where the eastern and southern walls came together to have a look at his doom. The northmen were spreading out to encircle the castle. It was hard to judge their numbers. A thousand at least; perhaps twice that many. *Against seventeen.* They'd brought catapults and scorpions. He saw no siege towers rumbling up the kingsroad, but there was timber enough in the wolfswood to build as many as were required.

Theon studied their banners through Maester Luwin's Myrish lens tube. The Cerwyn battle-axe flapped bravely wherever he looked, and there were Tallhart trees as well, and mermen from White Harbor. Less common were the sigils of Flint and Karstark. Here and there he even saw the bull moose of the Hornwoods. *But no Glovers, Asha saw to them, no Boltons from the Dreadfort, no Umbers come down from the shadow of the Wall.* Not that they were needed. Soon enough the boy Cley Cerwyn appeared before the gates carrying a peace banner on a tall staff, to announce that Ser Rodrik Cassel wished to parley with Theon Turncloak.

Turncloak. The name was bitter as bile. He had gone to Pyke to lead his father's longships against Lannisport, he remembered. "I shall be out shortly," he shouted down. "Alone."

Black Lorren disapproved. "Only blood can wash out blood," he declared. "Knights may keep their truces with other knights, but they are not so careful of their honor when dealing with those they deem outlaw."

Theon bristled. "I am the Prince of Winterfell and heir to the Iron Islands. Now go find the girl and do as I told you."

Black Lorren gave him a murderous look. "Aye, Prince."

He's turned against me too, Theon realized. Of late it seemed to him as if the very stones of Winterfell had turned against him. *If I die, I die friendless and abandoned.* What choice did that leave him, but to live?

He rode to the gatehouse with his crown on his head. A woman was drawing water from the well, and Gage the cook stood in the door of the kitchens. They hid their hatred behind sullen looks and faces blank as slate, yet he could feel it all the same.

When the drawbridge was lowered, a chill wind sighed across the moat. The touch of it made him shiver. *It is the cold, nothing more,* Theon told himself, *a shiver, not a tremble. Even brave men shiver.* Into the teeth of that wind he rode, under the portcullis, over the drawbridge. The outer gates swung open to let him pass. As he emerged beneath the walls, he could sense the boys watching from the empty sockets where their eyes had been.

Ser Rodrik waited in the market astride his dappled gelding. Beside him, the direwolf of Stark flapped from a staff borne by young Cley Cerwyn. They were alone in the square, though Theon could see archers on the roofs of surrounding houses, spearmen to his right, and to his left a line of mounted knights beneath the merman-and-trident of House Manderly. *Every one of them wants me dead.* Some were boys he'd drunk with, diced with, even wenched with, but that would not save him if he fell into their hands.

"Ser Rodrik." Theon reined to a halt. "It grieves me that we must meet as foes."

"My own grief is that I must wait a while to hang you." The old knight spat onto the muddy ground. "Theon Turncloak."

"I am a Greyjoy of Pyke," Theon reminded him. "The cloak my father swaddled me in bore a kraken, not a direwolf."

"For ten years you have been a ward of Stark."

"Hostage and prisoner, I call it."

"Then perhaps Lord Eddard should have kept you chained to a

dungeon wall. Instead he raised you among his own sons, the sweet boys you have butchered, and to my undying shame I trained you in the arts of war. Would that I had thrust a sword through your belly instead of placing one in your hand."

"I came out to parley, not to suffer your insults. Say what you have to say, old man. What would you have of me?"

"Two things," the old man said. "Winterfell, and your life. Command your men to open the gates and lay down their arms. Those who murdered no children shall be free to walk away, but you shall be held for King Robb's justice. May the gods take pity on you when he returns."

"Robb will never look on Winterfell again," Theon promised. "He will break himself on Moat Cailin, as every southron army has done for ten thousand years. We hold the north now, ser."

"You hold three castles," replied Ser Rodrik, "and this one I mean to take back, Turncloak."

Theon ignored that. "Here are *my* terms. You have until evenfall to disperse. Those who swear fealty to Balon Greyjoy as their king and to myself as Prince of Winterfell will be confirmed in their rights and properties and suffer no harm. Those who defy us will be destroyed."

Young Cerwyn was incredulous. "Are you mad, Greyjoy?"

Ser Rodrik shook his head. "Only vain, lad. Theon has always had too lofty an opinion of himself, I fear." The old man jabbed a finger at him. "Do not imagine that I need wait for Robb to fight his way up the Neck to deal with the likes of you. I have near two thousand men with me . . . and if the tales be true, you have no more than fifty."

Seventeen, in truth. Theon made himself smile. "I have something better than men." And he raised a fist over his head, the signal Black Lorren had been told to watch for.

The walls of Winterfell were behind him, but Ser Rodrik faced them squarely and could not fail to see. Theon watched his face. When his chin quivered under those stiff white whiskers, he knew just what the old man was seeing. *He is not surprised,* he thought with sadness, *but the fear is there.*

"This is craven," Ser Rodrik said. "To use a child so . . . this is despicable."

"Oh, I know," said Theon. "It's a dish I tasted myself, or have you forgotten? I was ten when I was taken from my father's house, to make certain he would raise no more rebellions."

"It is not the same!"

Theon's face was impassive. "The noose I wore was not made of hempen rope, that's true enough, but I felt it all the same. And it chafed, Ser Rodrik. It chafed me raw." He had never quite realized that until now, but as the words came spilling out he saw the truth of them.

"No harm was ever done you."

"And no harm will be done your Beth, so long as you—"

Ser Rodrik never gave him the chance to finish. *"Viper,"* the knight declared, his face red with rage beneath those white whiskers. "I gave you the chance to save your men and die with some small shred of honor, Turncloak. I should have known that was too much to ask of a childkiller." His hand went to the hilt of his sword. "I ought cut you down here and now and put an end to your lies and deceits. By the gods, I should."

Theon did not fear a doddering old man, but those watching archers and that line of knights were a different matter. If the swords came out his chances of getting back to the castle alive were small to none. "Forswear your oath and murder me, and you will watch your little Beth strangle at the end of a rope."

Ser Rodrik's knuckles had gone white, but after a moment he took his hand off the swordhilt. "Truly, I have lived too long."

"I will not disagree, ser. Will you accept my terms?"

"I have a duty to Lady Catelyn and House Stark."

"And your own House? Beth is the last of your blood."

The old knight drew himself up straight. "I offer myself in my daughter's place. Release her, and take me as your hostage. Surely the castellan of Winterfell is worth more than a child."

"Not to me." *A valiant gesture, old man, but I am not that great a fool.* "Not to Lord Manderly or Leobald Tallhart either, I'd wager." *Your sorry old skin is worth no more to them than any other man's.* "No, I'll keep the girl . . . and keep her safe, so long as you do as I've commanded you. Her life is in your hands."

"Gods be good, Theon, how can you do this? You know I must attack, have *sworn* . . ."

"If this host is still in arms before my gate when the sun sets, Beth will hang," said Theon. "Another hostage will follow her to the grave at first light, and another at sunset. Every dawn and every dusk will mean a death, until you are gone. I have no lack of hostages." He did not wait for a reply, but wheeled Smiler around and rode back toward the castle. He went slowly at first, but the thought of those archers at his back soon drove him to a canter. The small heads watched him come from their spikes, their tarred and flayed faces looming larger with every yard, between them stood little Beth Cassel, noosed and crying. Theon put his heel into Smiler and broke into a hard gallop. Smiler's hooves clattered on the drawbridge, like drumbeats.

In the yard he dismounted and handed his reins to Wex. "It may stay them," he told Black Lorren. "We'll know by sunset. Take the girl in till then, and keep her somewhere safe." Under the layers of leather, steel, and wool, he was slick with sweat. "I need a cup of wine. A vat of wine would do even better."

A fire had been laid in Ned Stark's bedchamber. Theon sat beside it and filled a cup with a heavy-bodied red from the castle vaults, a wine as sour as his mood. *They will attack,* he thought gloomily, staring at the flames. *Ser Rodrik loves his daughter, but he is still castellan, and most of all a knight.* Had it been Theon with a noose around his neck and Lord Balon commanding the army without, the warhorns would already have sounded the attack, he had no doubt. He should thank the gods that Ser Rodrik was not ironborn. The men of the green lands were made of softer stuff, though he was not certain they would prove soft enough.

If not, if the old man gave the command to storm the castle regardless, Winterfell would fall; Theon entertained no delusions on that count. His seventeen might kill three, four, five times their own number, but in the end they would be overwhelmed.

Theon stared at the flames over the rim of his wine goblet, brooding on the injustice of it all. "I rode beside Robb Stark in the Whispering Wood," he muttered. He had been frightened that night, but not like this. It was one thing to go into battle surrounded by friends, and another to perish alone and despised. *Mercy,* he thought miserably.

When the wine brought no solace, Theon sent Wex to fetch his bow and took himself to the old inner ward. There he stood, loosing shaft after shaft at the archery butts until his shoulders ached and his fingers were bloody, pausing only long enough to pull the arrows from the targets for another round. *I saved Bran's life with this bow,* he reminded himself. *Would that I could save my own.* Women came to the well, but did not linger; whatever they saw on Theon's face sent them away quickly.

Behind him the broken tower stood, its summit as jagged as a crown where fire had collapsed the upper stories long ago. As the sun moved, the shadow of the tower moved as well, gradually lengthening, a black arm reaching out for Theon Greyjoy. By the time the sun touched the wall, he was in its grasp. *If I hang the girl, the northmen will attack at once,* he thought as he loosed a shaft. *If I do not hang her, they will know my threats are empty.* He knocked another arrow to his bow. *There is no way out, none.*

"If you had a hundred archers as good as yourself, you might have a chance to hold the castle," a voice said softly.

When he turned, Maester Luwin was behind him. "Go away," Theon told him. "I have had enough of your counsel."

"And life? Have you had enough of that, my lord prince?"

He raised the bow. "One more word and I'll put this shaft through your heart."

"You won't."

Theon bent the bow, drawing the grey goose
cheek. "Care to make a wager?"

"I am your last hope, Theon."

I have no hope, he thought. Yet he lowered the bow
said, "I will not run."

"I do not speak of running. Take the black."

"The Night's Watch?" Theon let the bow unbend slowly and pointed
the arrow at the ground.

"Ser Rodrik has served House Stark all his life, and House Stark has
always been a friend to the Watch. He will not deny you. Open your
gates, lay down your arms, accept his terms, and he *must* let you take
the black."

A brother of the Night's Watch. It meant no crown, no sons, no
wife . . . but it meant life, and life with honor. Ned Stark's own brother
had chosen the Watch, and Jon Snow as well.

*I have black garb aplenty, once I tear the krakens off. Even my horse
is black. I could rise high in the Watch—chief of rangers, likely even
Lord Commander. Let Asha keep the bloody islands, they're as dreary
as she is. If I served at Eastwatch, I could command my own ship, and
there's fine hunting beyond the Wall. As for women, what wildling
woman wouldn't want a prince in her bed?* A slow smile crept across his
face. *A black cloak can't be turned. I'd be as good as any man . . .*

"PRINCE THEON!" The sudden shout shattered his daydream.
Kromm was loping across the ward. "The northmen—"

He felt a sudden sick sense of dread. "Is it the attack?"

Maester Luwin clutched his arm. "There's still time. Raise a peace
banner—"

"They're fighting," Kromm said urgently. "More men came up, hundreds of them, and at first they made to join the others. But now they've
fallen on them!"

"Is it Asha?" Had she come to save him after all?

But Kromm gave a shake of his head. "No. These are *northmen*, I tell
you. With a bloody man on their banner."

The flayed man of the Dreadfort. Reek had belonged to the Bastard of
Bolton before his capture, Theon recalled. It was hard to believe that a
vile creature like him could sway the Boltons to change their allegiance,
but nothing else made sense. "I'll see this for myself," Theon said.

Maester Luwin trailed after him. By the time they reached the battlements, dead men and dying horses were strewn about the market square
outside the gates. He saw no battle lines, only a swirling chaos of banners and blades. Shouts and screams rang through the cold autumn air.
Ser Rodrik seemed to have the numbers, but the Dreadfort men were

r led, and had taken the others unawares. Theon watched them
arge and wheel and charge again, chopping the larger force to bloody
pieces every time they tried to form up between the houses. He could
hear the crash of iron axeheads on oaken shields over the terrified
trumpeting of a maimed horse. The inn was burning, he saw.

Black Lorren appeared beside him and stood silently for a time. The
sun was low in the west, painting the fields and houses all a glowing red.
A thin wavering cry of pain drifted over the walls, and a warhorn
sounded off beyond the burning houses. Theon watched a wounded man
drag himself painfully across the ground, smearing his life's blood in the
dirt as he struggled to reach the well that stood at the center of the
market square. He died before he got there. He wore a leather jerkin and
conical halfhelm, but no badge to tell which side he'd fought on.

The crows came in the blue dust, with the evening stars. "The
Dothraki believe the stars are spirits of the valiant dead," Theon said.
Maester Luwin had told him that, a long time ago.

"Dothraki?"

"The horselords across the narrow sea."

"Oh. Them." Black Lorren frowned through his beard. "Savages believe all manner of foolish things."

As the night grew darker and the smoke spread it was harder to make
out what was happening below, but the din of steel gradually diminished
to nothing, and the shouts and warhorns gave way to moans and piteous
wailing. Finally a column of mounted men rode out of the drifting
smoke. At their head was a knight in dark armor. His rounded helm
gleamed a sullen red, and a pale pink cloak streamed from his shoulders.
Outside the main gate he reined up, and one of his men shouted for the
castle to open.

"Are you friend or foe?" Black Lorren bellowed down.

"Would a foe bring such fine gifts?" Red Helm waved a hand, and
three corpses were dumped in front of the gates. A torch was waved
above the bodies, so the defenders upon the walls might see the faces of
the dead.

"The old castellan," said Black Lorren.

"With Leobald Tallhart and Cley Cerwyn." The boy lord had taken an
arrow in the eye, and Ser Rodrik had lost his left arm at the elbow.
Maester Luwin gave a wordless cry of dismay, turned away from the
battlements, and fell to his knees sick.

"The great pig Manderly was too craven to leave White Harbor, or we
would have brought him as well," shouted Red Helm.

I am saved, Theon thought. So why did he feel so empty? This was
victory, sweet victory, the deliverance he had prayed for. He glanced at

Maester Luwin. *To think how close I came to yielding, and taking the black . . .*

"Open the gates for our friends." Perhaps tonight Theon would sleep without fear of what his dreams might bring.

The Dreadfort men made their way across the moat and through the inner gates. Theon descended with Black Lorren and Maester Luwin to meet them in the yard. Pale red pennons trailed from the ends of a few lances, but many more carried battle-axes and greatswords and shields hacked half to splinters. "How many men did you lose?" Theon asked Red Helm as he dismounted.

"Twenty or thirty." The torchlight glittered off the chipped enamel of his visor. His helm and gorget were wrought in the shape of a man's face and shoulders, skinless and bloody, mouth open in a silent howl of anguish.

"Ser Rodrik had you five-to-one."

"Aye, but he thought us friends. A common mistake. When the old fool gave me his hand, I took half his arm instead. Then I let him see my face." The man put both hands to his helm and lifted it off his head, holding it in the crook of his arm.

"Reek," Theon said, disquieted. *How did a serving man get such fine armor?*

The man laughed. "The wretch is dead." He stepped closer. "The girl's fault. If she had not run so far, his horse would not have lamed, and we might have been able to flee. I gave him mine when I saw the riders from the ridge. I was done with her by then, and he liked to take his turn while they were still warm. I had to pull him off her and shove my clothes into his hands—calfskin boots and velvet doublet, silver-chased swordbelt, even my sable cloak. Ride for the Dreadfort, I told him, bring all the help you can. Take my horse, he's swifter, and here, wear the ring my father gave me, so they'll know you came from me. He'd learned better than to question me. By the time they put that arrow through his back, I'd smeared myself with the girl's filth and dressed in his rags. They might have hanged me anyway, but it was the only chance I saw." He rubbed the back of his hand across his mouth. "And now, my sweet prince, there was a woman promised me, if I brought two hundred men. Well, I brought three times as many, and no green boys nor fieldhands neither, but my father's own garrison."

Theon had given his word. This was not the time to flinch. *Pay him his pound of flesh and deal with him later.* "Harrag," he said, "go to the kennels and bring Palla out for . . . ?"

"Ramsay." There was a smile on his plump lips, but none in those pale pale eyes. "Snow, my wife called me before she ate her fingers, but I say Bolton." His smile curdled. "So you'd offer me a kennel girl for my good service, is that the way of it?"

There was a tone in his voice Theon did not like, no more than he liked the insolent way the Dreadfort men were looking at him. "She was what was promised."

"She smells of dogshit. I've had enough of bad smells, as it happens. I think I'll have your bedwarmer instead. What do you call her? Kyra?"

"Are you mad?" Theon said angrily. "I'll have you—"

The Bastard's backhand caught him square, and his cheekbone shattered with a sickening crunch beneath the lobstered steel. The world vanished in a red roar of pain.

Sometime later, Theon found himself on the ground. He rolled onto his stomach and swallowed a mouthful of blood. *Close the gates!* he tried to shout, but it was too late. The Dreadfort men had cut down Red Rolfe and Kenned, and more were pouring through, a river of mail and sharp swords. There was a ringing in his ears, and horror all around him. Black Lorren had his sword out, but there were already four of them pressing in on him. He saw Ulf go down with a crossbow bolt through the belly as he ran for the Great Hall. Maester Luwin was trying to reach him when a knight on a warhorse planted a spear between his shoulders, then swung back to ride over him. Another man whipped a torch round and round his head and then lofted it toward the thatched roof of the stables. *"Save me the Freys,"* the Bastard was shouting as the flames roared upward, *"and burn the rest. Burn it, burn it all."*

The last thing Theon Greyjoy saw was Smiler, kicking free of the burning stables with his mane ablaze, screaming, rearing . . .

TYRION

He dreamed of a cracked stone ceiling and the smells of blood and shit and burnt flesh. The air was full of acrid smoke. Men were groaning and whimpering all around him, and from time to time a scream would pierce the air, thick with pain. When he tried to move, he found that he had fouled his own bedding. The smoke in the air made his eyes water. *Am I crying?* He must not let his father see. He was a Lannister of Casterly Rock. *A lion, I must be a lion, live a lion, die a lion.* He hurt so much, though. Too weak to groan, he lay in his own filth and shut his eyes. Nearby someone was cursing the gods in a heavy, monotonous voice. He listened to the blasphemies and wondered if he was dying. After a time the room faded.

He found himself outside the city, walking through a world without color. Ravens soared through a grey sky on wide black wings, while carrion crows rose from their feasts in furious clouds wherever he set his steps. White maggots burrowed through black corruption. The wolves were grey, and so were the silent sisters; together they stripped the flesh from the fallen. There were corpses strewn all over the tourney fields. The sun was a hot white penny, shining down upon the grey river as it rushed around the charred bones of sunken ships. From the pyres of the dead rose black columns of smoke and white-hot ashes. *My work,* thought Tyrion Lannister. *They died at my command.*

At first there was no sound in the world, but after a time he began to hear the voices of the dead, soft and terrible. They wept and moaned, they begged for an end to pain, they cried for help and wanted their mothers. Tyrion had never known his mother. He wanted Shae, but she was not there. He walked alone amidst grey shadows, trying to remember . . .

The silent sisters were stripping the dead men of their armor and clothes. All the bright dyes had leached out from the surcoats of the slain; they were garbed in shades of white and grey, and their blood was black and crusty. He watched their naked bodies lifted by arm and leg, to be carried swinging to the pyres to join their fellows. Metal and cloth were thrown in the back of a white wooden wagon, pulled by two tall black horses.

So many dead, so very many. Their corpses hung limply, their faces slack or stiff or swollen with gas, unrecognizable, hardly human. The garments the sisters took from them were decorated with black hearts, grey lions, dead flowers, and pale ghostly stags. Their armor was all dented and gashed, the chainmail riven, broken, slashed. *Why did I kill them all?* He had known once, but somehow he had forgotten.

He would have asked one of the silent sisters, but when he tried to speak he found he had no mouth. Smooth seamless skin covered his teeth. The discovery terrified him. How could he live without a mouth? He began to run. The city was not far. He would be safe inside the city, away from all these dead. He did not belong with the dead. He had no mouth, but he was still a living man. *No, a lion, a lion, and alive.* But when he reached the city walls, the gates were shut against him.

It was dark when he woke again. At first he could see nothing, but after a time the vague outlines of a bed appeared around him. The drapes were drawn, but he could see the shape of carved bedposts, and the droop of the velvet canopy over his head. Under him was the yielding softness of a featherbed, and the pillow beneath his head was goose down. *My own bed, I am in my own bed, in my own bedchamber.*

It was warm inside the drapes, under the great heap of furs and blankets that covered him. He was sweating. *Fever,* he thought groggily. He felt so weak, and the pain stabbed through him when he struggled to lift his hand. He gave up the effort. His head felt enormous, as big as the bed, too heavy to raise from the pillow. His body he could scarcely feel at all. *How did I come here?* He tried to remember. The battle came back in fits and flashes. The fight along the river, the knight who'd offered up his gauntlet, the bridge of ships . . .

Ser Mandon. He saw the dead empty eyes, the reaching hand, the green fire shining against the white enamel plate. Fear swept over him in a cold rush; beneath the sheets he could feel his bladder letting go. He would have cried out, if he'd had a mouth. *No, that was the dream,* he thought, his head pounding. *Help me, someone help me. Jaime, Shae, Mother, someone . . . Tysha . . .*

No one heard. No one came. Alone in the dark, he fell back into piss-scented sleep. He dreamed his sister was standing over his bed, with their lord father beside her, frowning. It had to be a dream, since Lord Tywin was a thousand leagues away, fighting Robb Stark in the west. Others came and went as well. Varys looked down on him and sighed, but Littlefinger made a quip. *Bloody treacherous bastard,* Tyrion thought venomously, *we sent you to Bitterbridge and you never came back.* Sometimes he could hear them talking to one another, but he did not understand the words. Their voices buzzed in his ears like wasps muffled in thick felt.

He wanted to ask if they'd won the battle. *We must have, else I'd be a head on a spike somewhere. If I live, we won.* He did not know what pleased him more: the victory, or the fact he had been able to reason it out. His wits were coming back to him, however slowly. That was good. His wits were all he had.

The next time he woke, the draperies had been pulled back, and Podrick Payne stood over him with a candle. When he saw Tyrion open his eyes he ran off. *No, don't go, help me, help,* he tried to call, but the best he could do was a muffled moan. *I have no mouth.* He raised a hand to his face, his every movement pained and fumbling. His fingers found stiff cloth where they should have found flesh, lips, teeth. *Linen.* The lower half of his face was bandaged tightly, a mask of hardened plaster with holes for breathing and feeding.

A short while later Pod reappeared. This time a stranger was with him, a maester chained and robed. "My lord, you must be still," the man murmured. "You are grievous hurt. You will do yourself great injury. Are you thirsty?"

He managed an awkward nod. The maester inserted a curved copper funnel through the feeding hole over his mouth and poured a slow trickle down his throat. Tyrion swallowed, scarcely tasting. Too late he realized the liquid was milk of the poppy. By the time the maester removed the funnel from his mouth, he was already spiraling back to sleep.

This time he dreamed he was at a feast, a victory feast in some great hall. He had a high seat on the dais, and men were lifting their goblets and hailing him as hero. Marillion was there, the singer who'd journeyed with them through the Mountains of the Moon. He played his woodharp and sang of the Imp's daring deeds. Even his father was smiling with approval. When the song was over, Jaime rose from his place, commanded Tyrion to kneel, and touched him first on one shoulder and then on the other with his golden sword, and he rose up a knight. Shae was waiting to embrace him. She took him by the hand, laughing and teasing, calling him her giant of Lannister.

He woke in darkness to a cold empty room. The draperies had been drawn again. Something felt wrong, turned around, though he could not have said what. He was alone once more. Pushing back the blankets, he tried to sit, but the pain was too much and he soon subsided, breathing raggedly. His face was the least part of it. His right side was one huge ache, and a stab of pain went through his chest whenever he lifted his arm. *What's happened to me?* Even the battle seemed half a dream when he tried to think back on it. *I was hurt more badly than I knew. Ser Mandon . . .*

The memory frightened him, but Tyrion made himself hold it, turn it in his head, stare at it hard. *He tried to kill me, no mistake. That part was not a dream. He would have cut me in half if Pod had not . . . Pod, where's Pod?*

Gritting his teeth, he grabbed hold of the bed hangings and yanked. The drapes ripped free of the canopy overhead and tumbled down, half on the rushes and half on him. Even that small effort had dizzied him. The room whirled around him, all bare walls and dark shadows, with a single narrow window. He saw a chest he'd owned, an untidy pile of his clothing, his battered armor. *This is not my bedchamber,* he realized. *Not even the Tower of the Hand.* Someone had moved him. His shout of anger came out as a muffled moan. *They have moved me here to die,* he thought as he gave up the struggle and closed his eyes once more. The room was dank and cold, and he was burning.

He dreamed of a better place, a snug little cottage by the sunset sea. The walls were lopsided and cracked and the floor had been made of packed earth, but he had always been warm there, even when they let the fire go out. *She used to tease me about that,* he remembered. *I never thought to feed the fire, that had always been a servant's task.* "We have no servants," she would remind me, and I would say, "You have me, I'm your servant," and she would say, "A lazy servant. What do they do with lazy servants in Casterly Rock, my lord?" and he would tell her, "They kiss them." That would always make her giggle. "They do not neither. They beat them, I bet," she would say, but he would insist, "No, they kiss them, just like this." He would show her how. "They kiss their fingers first, every one, and they kiss their wrists, yes, and inside their elbows. Then they kiss their funny ears, all our servants have funny ears. Stop laughing! And they kiss their cheeks and they kiss their noses with the little bump in them, there, so, like that, and they kiss their sweet brows and their hair and their lips, their . . . mmmm . . . mouths . . . so . . ."

They would kiss for hours, and spend whole days doing no more than lolling in bed, listening to the waves, and touching each other. Her body was a wonder to him, and she seemed to find delight in his. Sometimes she would sing to him. *I loved a maid as fair as summer, with sunlight in her hair.* "I love you, Tyrion," she would whisper before they went to sleep at night. "I love your lips. I love your voice, and the words you say to me, and how you treat me gentle. I love your face."

"*My* face?"

"Yes. Yes. I love your hands, and how you touch me. Your cock, I love your cock, I love how it feels when it's in me."

"It loves you too, my lady."

"I love to say your name. Tyrion Lannister. It goes with mine. Not the Lannister, t'other part. Tyrion and Tysha. Tysha and Tyrion. Tyrion. My lord Tyrion . . ."

Lies, he thought, *all feigned, all for gold, she was a whore, Jaime's whore, Jaime's gift, my lady of the lie.* Her face seemed to fade away, dissolving behind a veil of tears, but even after she was gone he could still hear the faint, far-off sound of her voice, calling his name. ". . . my lord, can you hear me? My lord? Tyrion? My lord? My lord?"

Through a haze of poppied sleep, he saw a soft pink face leaning over him. He was back in the dank room with the torn bed hangings, and the face was wrong, not hers, too round, with a brown fringe of beard. "Do you thirst, my lord? I have your milk, your good milk. You must not fight, no, don't try to move, you need your rest." He had the copper funnel in one damp pink hand and a flask in the other.

As the man leaned close, Tyrion's fingers slid underneath his chain of many metals, grabbed, pulled. The maester dropped the flask, spilling milk of the poppy all over the blanket. Tyrion twisted until he could feel the links digging into the flesh of the man's fat neck. "*No. More*," he croaked, so hoarse he was not certain he had even spoken. But he must have, for the maester choked out a reply. "Unhand, please, my lord . . . need your milk, the pain . . . the chain, don't, unhand, no . . ."

The pink face was beginning to purple when Tyrion let go. The maester reeled back, sucking in air. His reddened throat showed deep white gouges where the links had pressed. His eyes were white too. Tyrion raised a hand to his face and made a ripping motion over the hardened mask. And again. And again.

"You . . . you want the bandages off, is that it?" the maester said at last. "But I'm not to . . . that would be . . . be most unwise, my lord. You are not yet healed, the queen would . . ."

The mention of his sister made Tyrion growl. *Are you one of hers, then?* He pointed a finger at the maester, then coiled his hand into a fist. Crushing, choking, a promise, unless the fool did as he was bid.

Thankfully, he understood. "I . . . I will do as my lord commands, to be sure, but . . . this is unwise, your wounds . . ."

"*Do. It.*" Louder that time.

Bowing, the man left the room, only to return a few moments later, bearing a long knife with a slender sawtooth blade, a basin of water, a pile of soft cloths, and several flasks. By then Tyrion had managed to squirm backward a few inches, so he was half sitting against his pillow. The maester bade him be very still as he slid the tip of the knife in under his chin, beneath the mask. *A slip of the hand here, and Cersei will be free of me,* he thought. He could feel the blade sawing through the stiffened linen, only inches above his throat.

Fortunately this soft pink man was not one of his sister's braver creatures. After a moment he felt cool air on his cheeks. There was pain as well, but he did his best to ignore that. The maester discarded the bandages, still crusty with potion. "Be still now, I must wash out the wound." His touch was gentle, the water warm and soothing. *The wound,* Tyrion thought, remembering a sudden flash of bright silver that seemed to pass just below his eyes. "This is like to sting some," the maester warned as he wet a cloth with wine that smelled of crushed herbs. It did more than sting. It traced a line of fire all the way across Tyrion's face, and twisted a burning poker up his nose. His fingers clawed the bedclothes and he sucked in his breath, but somehow he managed not to scream. The maester was clucking like an old hen. "It would have been wiser to leave the mask in place until the flesh had knit, my lord. Still, it looks clean, good, good. When we found you down in that cellar among the dead and dying, your wounds were filthy. One of your ribs was broken, doubtless you can feel it, the blow of some mace perhaps, or a fall, it's hard to say. And you took an arrow in the arm, there where it joins the shoulder. It showed signs of mortification, and for a time I feared you might lose the limb, but we treated it with boiling wine and maggots, and now it seems to be healing clean . . ."

"Name," Tyrion breathed up at him. "*Name.*"

The maester blinked. "Why, you are Tyrion Lannister, my lord. Brother to the queen. Do you remember the battle? Sometimes with head wounds—"

"*Your* name." His throat was raw, and his tongue had forgotten how to shape the words.

"I am Maester Ballabar."

"Ballabar," Tyrion repeated. "Bring me. Looking glass."

"My lord," the maester said, "I would not counsel . . . that might be, ah, unwise, as it were . . . your wound . . ."

"*Bring* it," he had to say. His mouth was stiff and sore, as if a punch had split his lip. "And drink. *Wine.* No poppy."

The maester rose flush-faced and hurried off. He came back with a flagon of pale amber wine and a small silvered looking glass in an ornate golden frame. Sitting on the edge of the bed, he poured half a cup of wine and held it to Tyrion's swollen lips. The trickle went down cool, though he could hardly taste it. *"More,"* he said when the cup was empty. Maester Ballabar poured again. By the end of the second cup, Tyrion Lannister felt strong enough to face his face.

He turned over the glass, and did not know whether he ought to laugh or cry. The gash was long and crooked, starting a hair under his left eye and ending on the right side of his jaw. Three-quarters of his nose was gone, and a chunk of his lip. Someone had sewn the torn flesh together with catgut, and their clumsy stitches were still in place across the seam of raw, red, half-healed flesh. *"Pretty,"* he croaked, flinging the glass aside.

He remembered now. The bridge of boats, Ser Mandon Moore, a hand, a sword coming at his face. *If I had not pulled back, that cut would have taken off the top of my head.* Jaime had always said that Ser Mandon was the most dangerous of the Kingsguard, because his dead empty eyes gave no hint to his intentions. *I should never have trusted any of them.* He'd known that Ser Meryn and Ser Boros were his sister's, and Ser Osmund later, but he had let himself believe that the others were not wholly lost to honor. *Cersei must have paid him to see that I never came back from the battle. Why else? I never did Ser Mandon any harm that I know of.* Tyrion touched his face, plucking at the proud flesh with blunt thick fingers. *Another gift from my sweet sister.*

The maester stood beside the bed like a goose about to take flight. "My lord, there, there will most like be a scar . . ."

"Most like?" His snort of laughter turned into a wince of pain. There would be a scar, to be sure. Nor was it likely that his nose would be growing back anytime soon. It was not as if his face had ever been fit to look at. "Teach me, not to, play with, axes." His grin felt tight. "Where, are we? What, what place?" It hurt to talk, but Tyrion had been too long in silence.

"Ah, you are in Maegor's Holdfast, my lord. A chamber over the Queen's Ballroom. Her Grace wanted you kept close, so she might watch over you herself."

I'll wager she did. "Return me," Tyrion commanded. "Own bed. Own chambers." *Where I will have my own men about me, and my own maester too, if I find one I can trust.*

"Your own . . . my lord, that would not be possible. The King's Hand has taken up residence in your former chambers."

"I. Am. King's Hand." He was growing exhausted by the effort of speaking, and confused by what he was hearing.

Maester Ballabar looked distressed. "No, my lord, I . . . you were wounded, near death. Your lord father has taken up those duties now. Lord Tywin, he . . ."

"Here?"

"Since the night of the battle. Lord Tywin saved us all. The smallfolk say it was King Renly's ghost, but wiser men know better. It was your father and Lord Tyrell, with the Knight of Flowers and Lord Littlefinger. They rode through the ashes and took the usurper Stannis in the rear. It was a great victory, and now Lord Tywin has settled into the Tower of the Hand to help His Grace set the realm to rights, gods be praised."

"Gods be praised," Tyrion repeated hollowly. His bloody father *and* bloody Littlefinger and *Renly's ghost*? "I want . . ." *Who do I want?* He could not tell pink Ballabar to fetch him Shae. Who could he send for, who could he trust? Varys? Bronn? Ser Jacelyn? ". . . my squire," he finished. "Pod. Payne." *It was Pod on the bridge of boats, the lad saved my life.*

"The boy? The odd boy?"

"Odd boy. Podrick. Payne. You go. Send *him*."

"As you will, my lord." Maester Ballabar bobbed his head and hurried out. Tyrion could feel the strength seeping out of him as he waited. He wondered how long he had been here, asleep. *Cersei would have me sleep forever, but I won't be so obliging.*

Podrick Payne entered the bedchamber timid as a mouse. "My lord?" He crept close to the bed. *How can a boy so bold in battle be so frightened in a sickroom?* Tyrion wondered. "I meant to stay by you, but the maester sent me away."

"Send *him* away. Hear me. Talk's hard. Need dreamwine. *Dreamwine*, not milk of the poppy. Go to Frenken. *Frenken*, not Ballabar. Watch him make it. Bring it here." Pod stole a glance at Tyrion's face, and just as quickly averted his eyes. *Well, I cannot blame him for that.* "I want," Tyrion went on, "mine own. Guard. Bronn. Where's Bronn?"

"They made him a knight."

Even frowning hurt. "Find him. Bring him."

"As you say. My lord. Bronn."

Tyrion seized the lad's wrist. "Ser Mandon?"

The boy flinched. "I n-never meant to k-k-k-k-"

"*Dead?* You're, certain? *Dead?*"

He shuffled his feet, sheepish. "Drowned."

"Good. Say nothing. Of him. Of me. Any of it. *Nothing*."

By the time his squire left, the last of Tyrion's strength was gone as well. He lay back and closed his eyes. Perhaps he would dream of Tysha again. *I wonder how she'd like my face now*, he thought bitterly.

JON

When Qhorin Halfhand told him to find some brush for a fire, Jon knew their end was near.

It will be good to feel warm again, if only for a little while, he told himself while he hacked bare branches from the trunk of a dead tree. Ghost sat on his haunches watching, silent as ever. *Will he howl for me when I'm dead, as Bran's wolf howled when he fell?* Jon wondered. *Will Shaggydog howl, far off in Winterfell, and Grey Wind and Nymeria, wherever they might be?*

The moon was rising behind one mountain and the sun sinking behind another as Jon struck sparks from flint and dagger, until finally a wisp of smoke appeared. Qhorin came and stood over him as the first flame rose up flickering from the shavings of bark and dead dry pine needles. "As shy as a maid on her wedding night," the big ranger said in a soft voice, "and near as fair. Sometimes a man forgets how pretty a fire can be."

He was not a man you'd expect to speak of maids and wedding nights. So far as Jon knew, Qhorin had spent his whole life in the Watch. *Did he ever love a maid or have a wedding?* He could not ask. Instead he fanned the fire. When the blaze was all acrackle, he peeled off his stiff gloves to warm his hands, and sighed, wondering if ever a kiss had felt as good. The warmth spread through his fingers like melting butter.

The Halfhand eased himself to the ground and sat cross-legged by the fire, the flickering light playing across the hard planes of his face. Only the two of them remained of the five rangers who had fled the Skirling Pass, back into the blue-grey wilderness of the Frostfangs.

At first Jon had nursed the hope that Squire Dalbridge would keep the wildlings bottled up in the pass. But when they'd heard the call of a far-off horn every man of them knew the squire had fallen. Later they spied the eagle soaring through the dusk on great blue-grey wings and Stone-snake unslung his bow, but the bird flew out of range before he could so much as string it. Ebben spat and muttered darkly of wargs and skinchangers.

They glimpsed the eagle twice more the day after, and heard the hunting horn behind them echoing against the mountains. Each time it seemed a little louder, a little closer. When night fell, the Halfhand told Ebben to take the squire's garron as well as his own, and ride east for Mormont with all haste, back the way they had come. The rest of them would draw off the pursuit. "Send Jon," Ebben had urged. "He can ride as fast as me."

"Jon has a different part to play."

"He is half a boy still."

"No," said Qhorin, "he is a man of the Night's Watch."

When the moon rose, Ebben parted from them. Stonesnake went east with him a short way, then doubled back to obscure their tracks, and the three who remained set off toward the southwest.

After that the days and nights blurred one into the other. They slept in their saddles and stopped only long enough to feed and water the garrons, then mounted up again. Over bare rock they rode, through gloomy pine forests and drifts of old snow, over icy ridges and across shallow rivers that had no names. Sometimes Qhorin or Stonesnake would loop back to sweep away their tracks, but it was a futile gesture. They were watched. At every dawn and every dusk they saw the eagle soaring between the peaks, no more than a speck in the vastness of the sky.

They were scaling a low ridge between two snowcapped peaks when a shadowcat came snarling from its lair, not ten yards away. The beast was gaunt and half-starved, but the sight of it sent Stonesnake's mare into a panic; she reared and ran, and before the ranger could get her back under control she had stumbled on the steep slope and broken a leg.

Ghost ate well that day, and Qhorin insisted that the rangers mix some of the garron's blood with their oats, to give them strength. The taste of that foul porridge almost choked Jon, but he forced it down. They each cut a dozen strips of raw stringy meat from the carcass to chew on as they rode, and left the rest for the shadowcats.

There was no question of riding double. Stonesnake offered to lay in wait for the pursuit and surprise them when they came. Perhaps he could take a few of them with him down to hell. Qhorin refused. "If any man in the Night's Watch can make it through the Frostfangs alone and afoot, it is you, brother. You can go over mountains that a horse must go around. Make for the Fist. Tell Mormont what Jon saw, and how. Tell him that the old powers are waking, that he faces giants and wargs and worse. Tell him that the trees have eyes again."

He has no chance, Jon thought when he watched Stonesnake vanish over a snow-covered ridge, a tiny black bug crawling across a rippling expanse of white.

After that, every night seemed colder than the night before, and more lonely. Ghost was not always with them, but he was never far either. Even when they were apart, Jon sensed his nearness. He was glad for that. The Halfhand was not the most companionable of men. Qhorin's long grey braid swung slowly with the motion of his horse. Often they would ride for hours without a word spoken, the only sounds the soft scrape of horseshoes on stone and the keening of the wind, which blew endlessly through the heights. When he slept, he did not dream; not of wolves, nor his brothers, nor anything. *Even dreams cannot live up here,* he told himself.

"Is your sword sharp, Jon Snow?" asked Qhorin Halfhand across the flickering fire.

"My sword is Valyrian steel. The Old Bear gave it to me."

"Do you remember the words of your vow?"

"Yes." They were not words a man was like to forget. Once said, they could never be unsaid. They changed your life forever.

"Say them again with me, Jon Snow."

"If you like." Their voices blended as one beneath the rising moon, while Ghost listened and the mountains themselves bore witness. "Night gathers, and now my watch begins. It shall not end until my death. I shall take no wife, hold no lands, father no children. I shall wear no crowns and win no glory. I shall live and die at my post. I am the sword in the darkness. I am the watcher on the walls. I am the fire that burns against the cold, the light that brings the dawn, the horn that wakes the sleepers, the shield that guards the realms of men. I pledge my life and honor to the Night's Watch, for this night and all the nights to come."

When they were done, there was no sound but the faint crackle of the flames and a distant sigh of wind. Jon opened and closed his burnt fingers, holding tight to the words in his mind, praying that his father's gods would give him the strength to die bravely when his hour came. It would not be long now. The garrons were near the end of their strength. Qhorin's mount would not last another day, Jon suspected.

The flames were burning low by then, the warmth fading. "The fire will soon go out," Qhorin said, "but if the Wall should ever fall, all the fires will go out."

There was nothing Jon could say to that. He nodded.

"We may escape them yet," the ranger said. "Or not."

"I'm not afraid to die." It was only half a lie.

"It may not be so easy as that, Jon."

He did not understand. "What do you mean?"

"If we are taken, you must yield."

"Yield?" He blinked in disbelief. The wildlings did not make captives of the men they called the crows. They killed them, except for . . . "They only spare oathbreakers. Those who join them, like Mance Rayder."

"And you."

"No." He shook his head. "Never. I won't."

"You will. I command it of you."

"*Command* it? But . . ."

"Our honor means no more than our lives, so long as the realm is safe. Are you a man of the Night's Watch?"

"Yes, but—"

"There is no *but*, Jon Snow. You are, or you are not."

Jon sat up straight. "I am."

"Then hear me. If we are taken, you will go over to them, as the wildling girl you captured once urged you. They may demand that you cut your cloak to ribbons, that you swear them an oath on your father's grave, that you curse your brothers and your Lord Commander. You must not balk, whatever is asked of you. Do as they bid you . . . but in your heart, remember who and what you are. Ride with them, eat with them, fight with them, for as long as it takes. And *watch*."

"For what?" Jon asked.

"Would that I knew," said Qhorin. "Your wolf saw their diggings in the valley of the Milkwater. What did they seek, in such a bleak and distant place? Did they find it? That is what you must learn, before you return to Lord Mormont and your brothers. That is the duty I lay on you, Jon Snow."

"I'll do as you say," Jon said reluctantly, "but . . . you will tell them, won't you? The Old Bear, at least? You'll tell him that I never broke my oath."

Qhorin Halfhand gazed at him across the fire, his eyes lost in pools of shadow. "When I see him next. I swear it." He gestured at the fire. "More wood. I want it bright and hot."

Jon went to cut more branches, snapping each one in two before tossing it into the flames. The tree had been dead a long time, but it seemed to live again in the fire, as fiery dancers woke within each stick of wood to whirl and spin in their glowing gowns of yellow, red, and orange.

"Enough," Qhorin said abruptly. "Now we ride."

"Ride?" It was dark beyond the fire, and the night was cold. "Ride where?"

"Back." Qhorin mounted his weary garron one more time. "The fire will draw them past, I hope. Come, brother."

Jon pulled on his gloves again and raised his hood. Even the horses seemed reluctant to leave the fire. The sun was long gone, and only the cold silver shine of the half-moon remained to light their way over the treacherous ground that lay behind them. He did not know what Qhorin had in mind, but perhaps it was a chance. He hoped so. *I do not want to play the oathbreaker, even for good reason.*

They went cautiously, moving as silent as man and horse could move, retracing their steps until they reached the mouth of a narrow defile where an icy little stream emerged from between two mountains. Jon remembered the place. They had watered the horses here before the sun went down.

"The water's icing up," Qhorin observed as he turned aside, "else we'd ride in the streambed. But if we break the ice, they are like to see. Keep close to the cliffs. There's a crook a half mile on that will hide us." He rode into the defile. Jon gave one last wistful look to their distant fire, and followed.

The farther in they went, the closer the cliffs pressed to either side. They followed the moonlit ribbon of stream back toward its source. Icicles bearded its stony banks, but Jon could still hear the sound of rushing water beneath the thin hard crust.

A great jumble of fallen rock blocked their way partway up, where a section of the cliff face had fallen, but the surefooted little garrons were able to pick their way through. Beyond, the walls pinched in sharply, and the stream led them to the foot of a tall twisting waterfall. The air was full of mist, like the breath of some vast cold beast. The tumbling waters shone silver in the moonlight. Jon looked about in dismay. *There is no way out.* He and Qhorin might be able to climb the cliffs, but not with the horses. He did not think they would last long afoot.

"Quickly now," the Halfhand commanded. The big man on the small horse rode over the ice-slick stones, right into the curtain of water, and vanished. When he did not reappear, Jon put his heels into his horse and went after. His garron did his best to shy away. The falling water slapped at them with frozen fists, and the shock of the cold seemed to stop Jon's breath.

Then he was through; drenched and shivering, but through.

The cleft in the rock was barely large enough for man and horse to pass, but beyond, the walls opened up and the floor turned to soft sand. Jon could feel the spray freezing in his beard. Ghost burst through the waterfall in an angry rush, shook droplets from his fur, sniffed at the darkness suspiciously, then lifted a leg against one rocky wall. Qhorin had already dismounted. Jon did the same. "You knew this place was here."

"When I was no older than you, I heard a brother tell how he followed a shadowcat through these falls." He unsaddled his horse, removed her bit and bridle, and ran his fingers through her shaggy mane. "There is a way through the heart of the mountain. Come dawn, if they have not found us, we will press on. The first watch is mine, brother." Qhorin seated himself on the sand, his back to a wall, no more than a vague black shadow in the gloom of the cave. Over the rush of falling waters, Jon heard a soft sound of steel on leather that could only mean that the Halfhand had drawn his sword.

He took off his wet cloak, but it was too cold and damp here to strip down any further. Ghost stretched out beside him and licked his glove before curling up to sleep. Jon was grateful for his warmth. He wondered if the fire was still burning outside, or if it had gone out by now. *If the Wall should ever fall, all the fires will go out.* The moon shone through the curtain of falling water to lay a shimmering pale stripe across the sand, but after a time that too faded and went dark.

Sleep came at last, and with it nightmares. He dreamed of burning castles and dead men rising unquiet from their graves. It was still dark when Qhorin woke him. While the Halfhand slept, Jon sat with his back to the cave wall, listening to the water and waiting for the dawn.

At break of day, they each chewed a half-frozen strip of horsemeat, then saddled their garrons once again, and fastened their black cloaks around their shoulders. During his watch the Halfhand had made a half-dozen torches, soaking bundles of dry moss with the oil he carried in his saddlebag. He lit the first one now and led the way down into the dark, holding the pale flame up before him. Jon followed with the horses. The stony path twisted and turned, first down, then up, then down more steeply. In spots it grew so narrow it was hard to convince the garrons they could squeeze through. *By the time we come out we will have lost them,* he told himself as they went. *Not even an eagle can see through solid stone. We will have lost them, and we will ride hard for the Fist, and tell the Old Bear all we know.*

But when they emerged back into the light long hours later, the eagle was waiting for them, perched on a dead tree a hundred feet up the slope. Ghost went bounding up the rocks after it, but the bird flapped its wings and took to the air.

Qhorin's mouth tightened as he followed its flight with his eyes.

"Here is as good a place as any to make a stand," he declared. "The mouth of the cave shelters us from above, and they cannot get behind us without passing through the mountain. Is your sword sharp, Jon Snow?"

"Yes," he said.

"We'll feed the horses. They've served us bravely, poor beasts."

Jon gave his garron the last of the oats and stroked his shaggy mane while Ghost prowled restlessly amongst the rocks. He pulled his gloves on tighter and flexed his burnt fingers. *I am the shield that guards the realms of men.*

A hunting horn echoed through the mountains, and a moment later Jon heard the baying of hounds. "They will be with us soon," announced Qhorin. "Keep your wolf in hand."

"Ghost, to me," Jon called. The direwolf returned reluctantly to his side, tail held stiffly behind him.

The wildlings came boiling over a ridge not half a mile away. Their hounds ran before them, snarling grey-brown beasts with more than a little wolf in their blood. Ghost bared his teeth, his fur bristling. "Easy," Jon murmured. "Stay." Overhead he heard a rustle of wings. The eagle landed on an outcrop of rock and screamed in triumph.

The hunters approached warily, perhaps fearing arrows. Jon counted fourteen, with eight dogs. Their large round shields were made of skins stretched over woven wicker and painted with skulls. About half of them hid their faces behind crude helms of wood and boiled leather. On either wing, archers notched shafts to the strings of small wood-and-horn bows, but did not loose. The rest seemed to be armed with spears and mauls. One had a chipped stone axe. They wore only what bits of armor they had looted from dead rangers or stolen during raids. Wildlings did not mine or smelt, and there were few smiths and fewer forges north of the Wall.

Qhorin drew his longsword. The tale of how he had taught himself to fight with his left hand after losing half of his right was part of his legend; it was said that he handled a blade better now than he ever had before. Jon stood shoulder to shoulder with the big ranger and pulled Longclaw from its sheath. Despite the chill in the air, sweat stung his eyes.

Ten yards below the cave mouth the hunters halted. Their leader came on alone, riding a beast that seemed more goat than horse, from the surefooted way it climbed the uneven slope. As man and mount grew nearer Jon could hear them clattering; both were armored in bones. Cow bones, sheep bones, the bones of goats and aurochs and elk, the great bones of the hairy mammoths . . . and human bones as well.

"Rattleshirt," Qhorin called down, icy-polite.

"To crows I be the Lord o' Bones." The rider's helm was made from the broken skull of a giant, and all up and down his arms bearclaws had been sewn to his boiled leather.

Qhorin snorted. "I see no lord. Only a dog dressed in chickenbones, who rattles when he rides."

The wildling hissed in anger, and his mount reared. He *did* rattle, Jon could hear it; the bones were strung together loosely, so they clacked and clattered when he moved. "It's *your* bones I'll be rattling soon, Halfhand. I'll boil the flesh off you and make a byrnie from your ribs. I'll carve your teeth to cast me runes, and eat me oaten porridge from your skull."

"If you want my bones, come get them."

That, Rattleshirt seemed reluctant to do. His numbers meant little in the close confines of the rocks where the black brothers had taken their stand; to winkle them out of the cave the wildlings would need to come up two at a time. But another of his company edged a horse up beside him, one of the fighting women called *spearwives*. "We are four-and-ten to two, crows, and eight dogs to your wolf," she called. "Fight or run, you are ours."

"Show them," commanded Rattleshirt.

The woman reached into a bloodstained sack and drew out a trophy. Ebben had been bald as an egg, so she dangled the head by an ear. "He died brave," she said.

"But he died," said Rattleshirt, "same like you." He freed his battle-axe, brandishing it above his head. Good steel it was, with a wicked gleam to both blades; Ebben was never a man to neglect his weapons. The other wildlings crowded forward beside him, yelling taunts. A few chose Jon for their mockery. "Is that your wolf, boy?" a skinny youth called, unlimbering a stone flail. "He'll be my cloak before the sun is down." On the other side of the line, another spearwife opened her ragged furs to show Jon a heavy white breast. "Does the baby want his momma? Come, have a suck o' this, boy." The dogs were barking too.

"They would shame us into folly." Qhorin gave Jon a long look. "Remember your orders."

"Belike we need to flush the crows," Rattleshirt bellowed over the clamor. "Feather them!"

"*No!*" The word burst from Jon's lips before the bowmen could loose. He took two quick steps forward. "We yield!"

"They warned me bastard blood was craven," he heard Qhorin Halfhand say coldly behind him. "I see it is so. Run to your new masters, coward."

Face reddening, Jon descended the slope to where Rattleshirt sat his horse. The wildling stared at him through the eyeholes of his helm, and said, "The free folk have no need of cravens."

"He is no craven." One of the archers pulled off her sewn sheepskin helm and shook out a head of shaggy red hair. "This is the Bastard o' Winterfell, who spared me. Let him live."

Jon met Ygritte's eyes, and had no words.

"Let him die," insisted the Lord of Bones. "The black crow is a tricksy bird. I trust him not."

On a rock above them, the eagle flapped its wings and split the air with a scream of fury.

"The bird hates you, Jon Snow," said Ygritte. "And well he might. He was a man, before you killed him."

"I did not know," said Jon truthfully, trying to remember the face of the man he had slain in the pass. "You told me Mance would take me."

"And he will," Ygritte said.

"Mance is not here," said Rattleshirt. "Ragwyle, gut him."

The big spearwife narrowed her eyes and said, "If the crow would join the free folk, let him show us his prowess and prove the truth of him."

"I'll do whatever you ask." The words came hard, but Jon said them.

Rattleshirt's bone armor clattered loudly as he laughed. "Then kill the Halfhand, bastard."

"As if he could," said Qhorin. *"Turn*, Snow, and die."

And then Qhorin's sword was coming at him and somehow Longclaw leapt upward to block. The force of impact almost knocked the bastard blade from Jon's hand, and sent him staggering backward. *You must not balk, whatever is asked of you.* He shifted to a two-hand grip, quick enough to deliver a stroke of his own, but the big ranger brushed it aside with contemptuous ease. Back and forth they went, black cloaks swirling, the youth's quickness against the savage strength of Qhorin's left-hand cuts. The Halfhand's longsword seemed to be everywhere at once, raining down from one side and then the other, driving him where he would, keeping him off balance. Already he could feel his arms growing numb.

Even when Ghost's teeth closed savagely around the ranger's calf, somehow Qhorin kept his feet. But in that instant, as he twisted, the opening was there. Jon planted and pivoted. The ranger was leaning away, and for an instant it seemed that Jon's slash had not touched him. Then a string of red tears appeared across the big man's throat, bright as a ruby necklace, and the blood gushed out of him, and Qhorin Halfhand fell.

Ghost's muzzle was dripping red, but only the point of the bastard blade was stained, the last half inch. Jon pulled the direwolf away and knelt with one arm around him. The light was already fading in Qhorin's eyes. ". . . sharp," he said, lifting his maimed fingers. Then his hand fell, and he was gone.

He knew, he thought numbly. *He knew what they would ask of me.*

He thought of Samwell Tarly then, of Grenn and Dolorous Edd, of Pyp and Toad back at Castle Black. Had he lost them all, as he had lost Bran and Rickon and Robb? Who was he now? What was he?

"Get him up." Rough hands dragged him to his feet. Jon did not resist. "Do you have a name?"

Ygritte answered for him. "His name is Jon Snow. He is Eddard Stark's blood, of Winterfell."

Ragwyle laughed. "Who would have thought it? Qhorin Halfhand slain by some lordling's byblow."

"Gut him." That was Rattleshirt, still ahorse. The eagle flew to him and perched atop his bony helm, screeching.

"He yielded," Ygritte reminded them.

"Aye, and slew his brother," said a short homely man in a rust-eaten iron halfhelm.

Rattleshirt rode closer, bones clattering. "The wolf did his work for him. It were foully done. The Halfhand's death was mine."

"We all saw how eager you were to take it," mocked Ragwyle.

"He is a warg," said the Lord of Bones, "and a crow. I like him not."

"A warg he may be," Ygritte said, "but that has never frightened us." Others shouted agreement. Behind the eyeholes of his yellowed skull Rattleshirt's stare was malignant, but he yielded grudgingly. *These are a free folk indeed*, thought Jon.

They burned Qhorin Halfhand where he'd fallen, on a pyre made of pine needles, brush, and broken branches. Some of the wood was still green, and it burned slow and smoky, sending a black plume up into the bright hard blue of the sky. Afterward Rattleshirt claimed some charred bones, while the others threw dice for the ranger's gear. Ygritte won his cloak.

"Will we return by the Skirling Pass?" Jon asked her. He did not know if he could face those heights again, or if his garron could survive a second crossing.

"No," she said. "There's nothing behind us." The look she gave him was sad. "By now Mance is well down the Milkwater, marching on your Wall."

BRAN

The ashes fell like a soft grey snow.

He padded over dry needles and brown leaves, to the edge of the wood where the pines grew thin. Beyond the open fields he could see the great piles of man-rock stark against the swirling flames. The wind blew hot and rich with the smell of blood and burnt meat, so strong he began to slaver.

Yet as one smell drew them onward, others warned them back. He sniffed at the drifting smoke. *Men, many men, many horses, and fire, fire, fire.* No smell was more dangerous, not even the hard cold smell of iron, the stuff of man-claws and hardskin. The smoke and ash clouded his eyes, and in the sky he saw a great winged snake whose roar was a river of flame. He bared his teeth, but then the snake was gone. Behind the cliffs tall fires were eating up the stars.

All through the night the fires crackled, and once there was a great roar and a crash that made the earth jump under his feet. Dogs barked and whined and horses screamed in terror. Howls shuddered through the night; the howls of the man-pack, wails of fear and wild shouts, laughter and screams. No beast was as noisy as man. He pricked up his ears and listened, and his brother growled at every sound. They prowled under the trees as a piney wind blew ashes and embers through the sky. In time the flames began to dwindle, and then they were gone. The sun rose grey and smoky that morning.

Only then did he leave the trees, stalking slow across the fields. His brother ran with him, drawn to the smell of blood and death. They padded silent through the dens the men had built of wood and grass and mud. Many and more were burned and many and more were collapsed; others stood as they had before. Yet nowhere did they see or scent a living man. Crows blanketed the bodies and leapt into the air screeching when his brother and he came near. The wild dogs slunk away before them.

Beneath the great grey cliffs a horse was dying noisily, struggling to rise on a broken leg and screaming when he fell. His brother circled round him, then tore out his throat while the horse kicked feebly and rolled his eyes. When he approached the carcass his brother snapped at him and laid back his ears, and he cuffed him with a forepaw and bit his leg. They fought amidst the grass and dirt and falling ashes beside the dead horse, until his brother rolled on his back in submission, tail tucked low. One more bite at his upturned throat; then he fed, and let his brother feed, and licked the blood off his black fur.

The dark place was pulling at him by then, the house of whispers where all men were blind. He could feel its cold fingers on him. The stony smell of it was a whisper up the nose. He struggled against the pull. He did not like the darkness. He was wolf. He was hunter and stalker and slayer, and he belonged with his brothers and sisters in the deep woods, running free beneath a starry sky. He sat on his haunches, raised his head, and howled. *I will not go*, he cried. *I am wolf, I will not go.* Yet even so the darkness thickened, until it covered his eyes and filled his nose and stopped his ears, so he could not see or smell or hear or run, and the grey cliffs were gone and the dead horse was gone and his brother was gone and all was black and still and black and cold and black and dead and black . . .

"Bran," a voice was whispering softly. *"Bran, come back. Come back now, Bran. Bran . . ."*

He closed his third eye and opened the other two, the old two, the blind two. In the dark place all men were blind. But someone was holding him. He could feel arms around him, the warmth of a body snuggled close. He could hear Hodor singing "Hodor, hodor, hodor," quietly to himself.

"Bran?" It was Meera's voice. "You were thrashing, making terrible noises. What did you see?"

"Winterfell." His tongue felt strange and thick in his mouth. *One day when I come back I won't know how to talk anymore.* "It was Winterfell. It was all on fire. There were horse smells, and steel, and blood. They killed everyone, Meera."

He felt her hand on his face, stroking back his hair. "You're all sweaty," she said. "Do you need a drink?"

"A drink," he agreed. She held a skin to his lips, and Bran swallowed so fast the water ran out of the corner of his mouth. He was always weak and thirsty when he came back. And hungry too. He remembered the dying horse, the taste of blood in his mouth, the smell of burnt flesh in the morning air. "How long?"

"Three days," said Jojen. The boy had come up softfoot, or perhaps he had been there all along; in this blind black world, Bran could not have said. "We were afraid for you."

"I was with Summer," Bran said.

"Too long. You'll starve yourself. Meera dribbled a little water down your throat, and we smeared honey on your mouth, but it is not enough."

"I ate," said Bran. "We ran down an elk and had to drive off a treecat that tried to steal him." The cat had been tan-and-brown, only half the size of the direwolves, but fierce. He remembered the musky smell of him, and the way he had snarled down at them from the limb of the oak.

"The wolf ate," Jojen said. "Not you. Take care, Bran. Remember who you are."

He remembered who he was all too well; Bran the boy, Bran the broken. *Better Bran the beastling.* Was it any wonder he would sooner dream his Summer dreams, his wolf dreams? Here in the chill damp darkness of the tomb his third eye had finally opened. He could reach Summer whenever he wanted, and once he had even touched Ghost and talked to Jon. Though maybe he had only dreamed that. He could not understand why Jojen was always trying to pull him back now. Bran used the strength of his arms to squirm to a sitting position. "I have to tell Osha what I saw. Is she here? Where did she go?"

The wildling woman herself gave answer. "Nowhere, m'lord. I've had my fill o' blundering in the black." He heard the scrape of a heel on stone, turned his head toward the sound, but saw nothing. He thought he could smell her, but he wasn't sure. All of them stank alike, and he did not have Summer's nose to tell one from the other. "Last night I pissed on a king's foot," Osha went on. "Might be it was morning, who can say? I was sleeping, but now I'm not." They all slept a lot, not only Bran. There was nothing else to do. Sleep and eat and sleep again, and sometimes talk a little . . . but not too much, and only in whispers, just to be safe. Osha might have liked it better if they had never talked at all, but there was no way to quiet Rickon, or to stop Hodor from muttering, "Hodor, hodor, hodor," endlessly to himself.

"Osha," Bran said, "I saw Winterfell burning." Off to his left, he could hear the soft sound of Rickon's breathing.

"A dream," said Osha.

"A wolf dream," said Bran. "I *smelled* it too. Nothing smells like fire, or blood."

"Whose blood?"

"Men, horses, dogs, everyone. We have to go *see*."

"This scrawny skin of mine's the only one I got," said Osha. "That squid prince catches hold o' me, they'll strip it off my back with a whip."

Meera's hand found Bran's in the darkness and gave his fingers a squeeze. "I'll go if you're afraid."

Bran heard fingers fumbling at leather, followed by the sound of steel on flint. Then again. A spark flew, caught. Osha blew softly. A long pale flame awoke, stretching upward like a girl on her toes. Osha's face floated above it. She touched the flame with the head of a torch. Bran had to squint as the pitch began to burn, filling the world with orange glare. The light woke Rickon, who sat up yawning.

When the shadows moved, it looked for an instant as if the dead were rising as well. Lyanna and Brandon, Lord Rickard Stark their father, Lord Edwyle his father, Lord Willam and his brother Artos the Implacable, Lord Donnor and Lord Beron and Lord Rodwell, one-eyed Lord Jonnel, Lord Barth and Lord Brandon and Lord Cregan who had fought the Dragonknight. On their stone chairs they sat with stone wolves at their feet. This was where they came when the warmth had seeped out of their bodies; this was the dark hall of the dead, where the living feared to tread.

And in the mouth of the empty tomb that waited for Lord Eddard Stark, beneath his stately granite likeness, the six fugitives huddled round their little cache of bread and water and dried meat. "Little enough left," Osha muttered as she blinked down on their stores. "I'd need to go up soon to steal food in any case, or we'd be down to eating Hodor."

"Hodor," Hodor said, grinning at her.

"Is it day or night up there?" Osha wondered. "I've lost all count o' such."

"Day," Bran told her, "but it's dark from all the smoke."

"M'lord is certain?"

Never moving his broken body, he reached out all the same, and for an instant he was seeing double. There stood Osha holding the torch, and Meera and Jojen and Hodor, and the double row of tall granite pillars and long dead lords behind them stretching away into darkness . . . but there was Winterfell as well, grey with drifting smoke, the massive oak-and-iron gates charred and askew, the drawbridge down in a tangle of broken chains and missing planks. Bodies floated in the moat, islands for the crows.

"Certain," he declared.

Osha chewed on that a moment. "I'll risk a look then. I want the lot o' you close behind. Meera, get Bran's basket."

"Are we going home?" Rickon asked excitedly. "I want my horse. And I want applecakes and butter and honey, and Shaggy. Are we going where Shaggydog is?"

"Yes," Bran promised, "but you have to be quiet."

Meera strapped the wicker basket to Hodor's back and helped lift Bran into it, easing his useless legs through the holes. He had a queer flutter in his belly. He knew what awaited them above, but that did not make it any less fearful. As they set off, he turned to give his father one last look, and it seemed to Bran that there was a sadness in Lord Eddard's eyes, as if he did not want them to go. *We have to,* he thought. *It's time.*

Osha carried her long oaken spear in one hand and the torch in the other. A naked sword hung down her back, one of the last to bear Mikken's mark. He had forged it for Lord Eddard's tomb, to keep his ghost at rest. But with Mikken slain and the ironmen guarding the armory, good steel had been hard to resist, even if it meant grave-robbing. Meera had claimed Lord Rickard's blade, though she complained that it was too heavy. Brandon took his namesake's, the sword made for the uncle he had never known. He knew he would not be much use in a fight, but even so the blade felt good in his hand.

But it was only a game, and Bran knew it.

Their footsteps echoed through the cavernous crypts. The shadows behind them swallowed his father as the shadows ahead retreated to unveil other statues; no mere lords, these, but the old Kings in the North. On their brows they wore stone crowns. Torrhen Stark, the King Who Knelt. Edwyn the Spring King. Theon Stark, the Hungry Wolf. Brandon the Burner and Brandon the Shipwright. Jorah and Jonos, Brandon the Bad, Walton the Moon King, Edderion the Bridegroom, Eyron, Benjen the Sweet and Benjen the Bitter, King Edrick Snowbeard. Their faces were stern and strong, and some of them had done terrible things, but they were Starks every one, and Bran knew all their tales. He had never feared the crypts; they were part of his home and who he was, and he had always known that one day he would lie here too.

But now he was not so certain. *If I go up, will I ever come back down? Where will I go when I die?*

"Wait," Osha said when they reached the twisting stone stairs that led up to the surface, and down to the deeper levels where kings more ancient still sat their dark thrones. She handed Meera the torch. "I'll grope my way up." For a time they could hear the sound of her footfalls, but they grew softer and softer until they faded away entirely. "Hodor," said Hodor nervously.

Bran had told himself a hundred times how much he hated hiding down here in the dark, how much he wanted to see the sun again, to ride his horse through wind and rain. But now that the moment was upon him, he was afraid. He'd felt safe in the darkness; when you could not even find your own hand in front of your face, it was easy to believe that no enemies could ever find you either. And the stone lords had given him courage. Even when he could not see them, he had known they were there.

It seemed a long while before they heard anything again. Bran had begun to fear that something had happened to Osha. His brother was squirming restlessly. "I want to *go home!*" he said loudly. Hodor bobbed his head and said, "Hodor." Then they heard the footsteps again, growing louder, and after a few minutes Osha emerged into the light, looking grim. "Something is blocking the door. I can't move it."

"Hodor can move anything," said Bran.

Osha gave the huge stableboy an appraising look. "Might be he can. Come on, then."

The steps were narrow, so they had to climb in single file. Osha led. Behind came Hodor, with Bran crouched low on his back so his head wouldn't hit the ceiling. Meera followed with the torch, and Jojen brought up the rear, leading Rickon by the hand. Around and around they went, and up and up. Bran thought he could smell smoke now, but perhaps that was only the torch.

The door to the crypts was made of ironwood. It was old and heavy, and lay at a slant to the ground. Only one person could approach it at a time. Osha tried once more when she reached it, but Bran could see that it was not budging. "Let Hodor try."

They had to pull Bran from his basket first, so he would not get squished. Meera squatted beside him on the steps, one arm thrown protectively across his shoulders, as Osha and Hodor traded places. "Open the door, Hodor," Bran said.

The huge stableboy put both hands flat on the door, pushed, and grunted. "Hodor?" He slammed a fist against the wood, and it did not so much as jump. "Hodor."

"Use your back," urged Bran. "And your legs."

Turning, Hodor put his back to the wood and shoved. Again. Again. "Hodor!" He put one foot on a higher step so he was bent under the slant of the door and tried to rise. This time the wood groaned and creaked. "*Hodor!*" The other foot came up a step, and Hodor spread his legs apart, braced, and straightened. His face turned red, and Bran could see cords in his neck bulging as he strained against the weight above him. "*Hodor hodor hodor hodor hodor HODOR!*" From above came a dull rumble. Then suddenly the door jerked upward and a shaft of daylight fell across Bran's face, blinding him for a moment. Another shove brought the sound of shifting stone, and then the way was open. Osha poked her spear through and slid out after it, and Rickon squirmed through Meera's legs to follow. Hodor shoved the door open all the way and stepped to the surface. The Reeds had to carry Bran up the last few steps.

The sky was a pale grey, and smoke eddied all around them. They stood in the shadow of the First Keep, or what remained of it. One whole side of the building had torn loose and fallen away. Stone and shattered gargoyles lay strewn across the yard. *They fell just where I did*, Bran thought when he saw them. Some of the gargoyles had broken into so many pieces it made him wonder how he was alive at all. Nearby some crows were pecking at a body crushed beneath the tumbled stone, but he lay facedown and Bran could not say who he was.

The First Keep had not been used for many hundreds of years, but now it was more of a shell than ever. The floors had burned inside it, and all the beams. Where the wall had fallen away, they could see right into the rooms, even into the privy. Yet behind, the broken tower still stood, no more burned than before. Jojen Reed was coughing from the smoke. "Take me home!" Rickon demanded. "I want to be *home!*" Hodor stomped in a circle. "Hodor," he whimpered in a small voice. They stood huddled together with ruin and death all around them.

"We made noise enough to wake a dragon," Osha said, "but there's no one come. The castle's dead and burned, just as Bran dreamed, but we had best—" She broke off suddenly at a noise behind them, and whirled with her spear at the ready.

Two lean dark shapes emerged from behind the broken tower, padding slowly through the rubble. Rickon gave a happy shout of *"Shaggy!"* and the black direwolf came bounding toward him. Summer advanced more slowly, rubbed his head up against Bran's arm, and licked his face.

"We should go," said Jojen. "So much death will bring other wolves besides Summer and Shaggydog, and not all on four feet."

"Aye, soon enough," Osha agreed, "but we need food, and there may be some survived this. Stay together. Meera, keep your shield up and guard our backs."

It took the rest of the morning to make a slow circuit of the castle. The great granite walls remained, blackened here and there by fire but otherwise untouched. But within, all was death and destruction. The doors of the Great Hall were charred and smoldering, and inside the rafters had given way and the whole roof had crashed down onto the floor. The green and yellow panes of the glass gardens were all in shards, the trees and fruits and flowers torn up or left exposed to die. Of the stables, made of wood and thatch, nothing remained but ashes, embers, and dead horses. Bran thought of his Dancer, and wanted to weep. There was a shallow steaming lake beneath the Library Tower, and hot water gushing from a crack in its side. The bridge between the Bell Tower and the rookery had collapsed into the yard below, and Maester Luwin's turret was gone. They saw a dull red glow shining up through the narrow cellar windows beneath the Great Keep, and a second fire still burning in one of the storehouses.

Osha called softly through the blowing smoke as they went, but no one answered. They saw one dog worrying at a corpse, but he ran when he caught the scents of the direwolves; the rest had been slain in the kennels. The maester's ravens were paying court to some of the corpses, while the crows from the broken tower attended others. Bran recognized Poxy Tym, even though someone had taken an axe to his face. One charred corpse, outside the ashen shell of Mother's sept, sat with his arms drawn up and his hands balled into hard black fists, as if to punch anyone who dared approach him. "If the gods are good," Osha said in a low angry voice, "the Others will take them that did this work."

"It was Theon," Bran said blackly.

"No. Look." She pointed across the yard with her spear. "That's one of his ironmen. And there. And that's Greyjoy's warhorse, see? The black one with the arrows in him." She moved among the dead, frowning. "And here's Black Lorren." He had been hacked and cut so badly that his beard looked a reddish-brown now. "Took a few with him, he did." Osha turned over one of the other corpses with her foot. "There's a badge. A little man, all red."

"The flayed man of the Dreadfort," said Bran.

Summer howled, and darted away.

"The godswood." Meera Reed ran after the direwolf, her shield and frog spear to hand. The rest of them trailed after, threading their way through smoke and fallen stones. The air was sweeter under the trees. A few pines along the edge of the wood had been scorched, but deeper in the damp soil and green wood had defeated the flames. "There is a power in living wood," said Jojen Reed, almost as if he knew what Bran was thinking, "a power strong as fire."

On the edge of the black pool, beneath the shelter of the heart tree, Maester Luwin lay on his belly in the dirt. A trail of blood twisted back through damp leaves where he had crawled. Summer stood over him, and Bran thought he was dead at first, but when Meera touched his throat, the maester moaned. "Hodor?" Hodor said mournfully. "Hodor?"

Gently, they eased Luwin onto his back. He had grey eyes and grey hair, and once his robes had been grey as well, but they were darker now where the blood had soaked through. "Bran," he said softly when he saw him sitting tall on Hodor's back. "And Rickon too." He smiled. "The gods are good. I knew . . ."

"Knew?" said Bran uncertainly.

"The legs, I could tell . . . the clothes fit, but the muscles in his legs . . . poor lad . . ." He coughed, and blood came up from inside him. "You vanished . . . in the woods . . . how, though?"

"We never went," said Bran. "Well, only to the edge, and then doubled back. I sent the wolves on to make a trail, but we hid in Father's tomb."

"The crypts." Luwin chuckled, a froth of blood on his lips. When the maester tried to move, he gave a sharp gasp of pain.

Tears filled Bran's eyes. When a man was hurt you took him to the maester, but what could you do when your maester was hurt?

"We'll need to make a litter to carry him," said Osha.

"No use," said Luwin. "I'm dying, woman."

"You *can't*," said Rickon angrily. "No you can't." Beside him, Shaggydog bared his teeth and growled.

The maester smiled. "Hush now, child, I'm much older than you. I can . . . die as I please."

"Hodor, down," said Bran. Hodor went to his knees beside the maester.

"Listen," Luwin said to Osha, "the princes . . . Robb's heirs. Not . . . not together . . . do you hear?"

The wildling woman leaned on her spear. "Aye. Safer apart. But where to take them? I'd thought, might be these Cerwyns . . ."

Maester Luwin shook his head, though it was plain to see what the effort cost him. "Cerwyn boy's dead. Ser Rodrik, Leobald Tallhart, Lady Hornwood . . . all slain. Deepwood fallen, Moat Cailin, soon Torrhen's Square. Ironmen on the Stony Shore. And east, the Bastard of Bolton."

"Then where?" asked Osha.

"White Harbor . . . the Umbers . . . I do not know . . . war everywhere . . . each man against his neighbor, and winter coming . . . such folly, such black mad folly . . ." Maester Luwin reached up and grasped Bran's forearm, his fingers closing with a desperate strength. "You must be strong now. *Strong*."

"I will be," Bran said, though it was hard. *Ser Rodrik killed and Maester Luwin, everyone, everyone . . .*

"Good," the maester said. "A good boy. Your . . . your father's son, Bran. Now *go*."

Osha gazed up at the weirwood, at the red face carved in the pale trunk. "And leave you for the gods?"

"I beg . . ." The maester swallowed. ". . . a . . . a drink of water, and . . . another boon. If you would . . ."

"Aye." She turned to Meera. "Take the boys."

Jojen and Meera led Rickon out between them. Hodor followed. Low branches whipped at Bran's face as they pushed between the trees, and the leaves brushed away his tears. Osha joined them in the yard a few moments later. She said no word of Maester Luwin. "Hodor must stay with Bran, to be his legs," the wildling woman said briskly. "I will take Rickon with me."

"We'll go with Bran," said Jojen Reed.

"Aye, I thought you might," said Osha. "Believe I'll try the East Gate, and follow the kingsroad a ways."

"We'll take the Hunter's Gate," said Meera.

"Hodor," said Hodor.

They stopped at the kitchens first. Osha found some loaves of burned bread that were still edible, and even a cold roast fowl that she ripped in half. Meera unearthed a crock of honey and a big sack of apples. Outside, they made their farewells. Rickon sobbed and clung to Hodor's leg until Osha gave him a smack with the butt end of her spear. Then he followed her quick enough. Shaggydog stalked after them. The last Bran saw of them was the direwolf's tail as it vanished behind the broken tower.

The iron portcullis that closed the Hunter's Gate had been warped so badly by heat it could not be raised more than a foot. They had to squeeze beneath its spikes, one by one.

"Will we go to your lord father?" Bran asked as they crossed the draw-bridge between the walls. "To Greywater Watch?"

Meera looked to her brother for the answer. "Our road is north," Jojen announced.

At the edge of the wolfswood, Bran turned in his basket for one last glimpse of the castle that had been his life. Wisps of smoke still rose into the grey sky, but no more than might have risen from Winterfell's chimneys on a cold autumn afternoon. Soot stains marked some of the arrow loops, and here and there a crack or a missing merlon could be seen in the curtain wall, but it seemed little enough from this distance. Beyond, the tops of the keeps and towers still stood as they had for hundreds of years, and it was hard to tell that the castle had been sacked and burned at all. *The stone is strong*, Bran told himself, *the roots of the trees go deep, and under the ground the Kings of Winter sit their thrones.* So long as those remained, Winterfell remained. It was not dead, just broken. *Like me*, he thought. *I'm not dead either.*

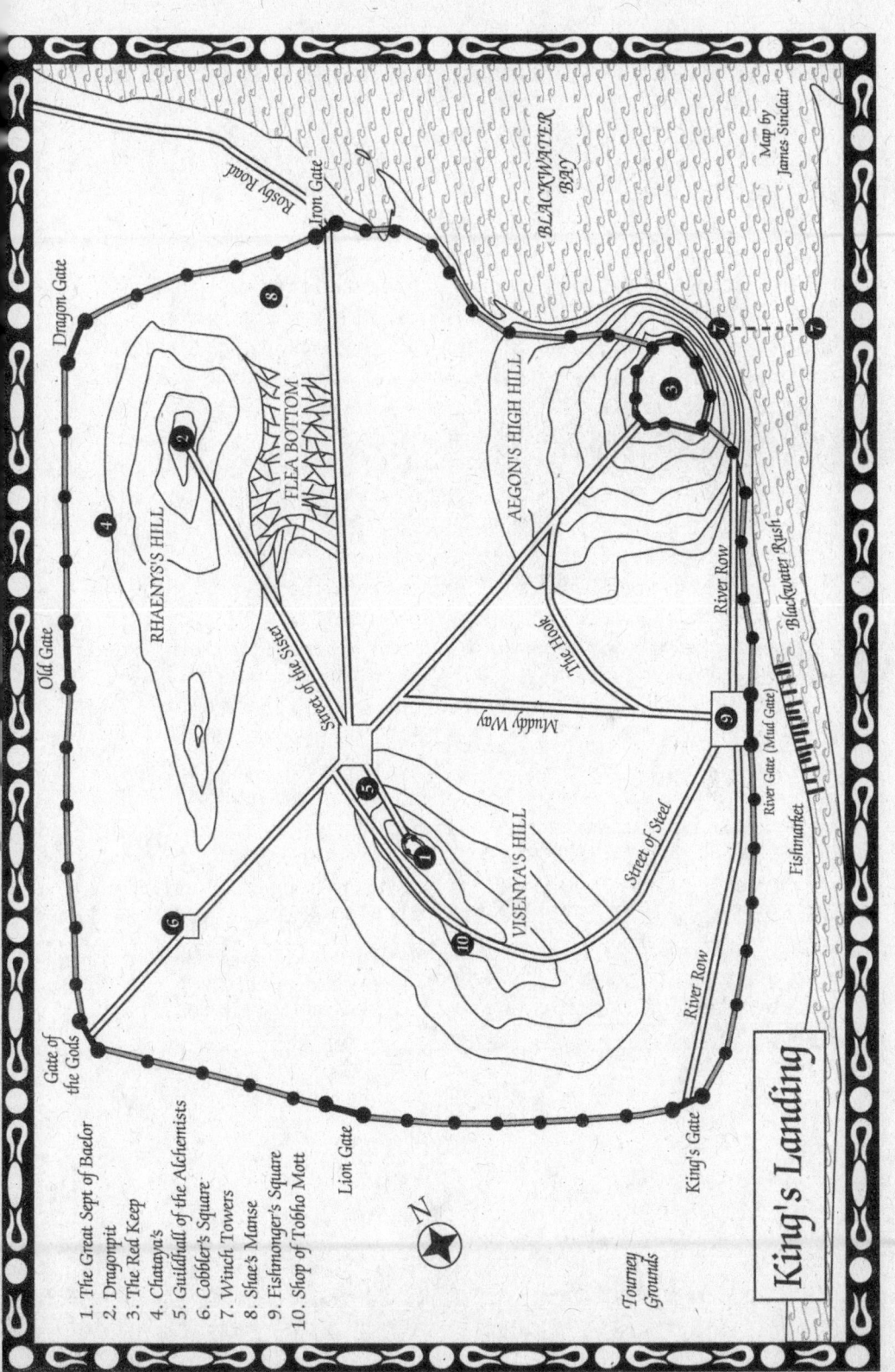

King's Landing

Map by
James Sinclair

1. The Great Sept of Baelor
2. Dragonpit
3. The Red Keep
4. Chataya's
5. Guildhall of the Alchemists
6. Cobbler's Square
7. Winch Towers
8. Shae's Manse
9. Fishmonger's Square
10. Shop of Tobho Mott

BLACKWATER BAY

Rosby Road

Iron Gate

Dragon Gate

Old Gate

Gate of the Gods

Lion Gate

King's Gate

River Gate (Mud Gate)

Blackwater Rush

Fishmarket

River Row

Street of Steel

Muddy Way

The Hook

Street of the Sister

RHAENYS'S HILL

FLEA BOTTOM

AEGON'S HIGH HILL

VISENYA'S HILL

Tourney Grounds

N

Appendix
THE KINGS AND THEIR COURTS

THE KING ON THE IRON THRONE

JOFFREY BARATHEON, the First of His Name, a boy of thirteen years, the eldest son of King Robert I Baratheon and Queen Cersei of House Lannister,

—his mother, QUEEN CERSEI, Queen Regent and Protector of the Realm,

—his sister, PRINCESS MYRCELLA, a girl of nine,

—his brother, PRINCE TOMMEN, a boy of eight, heir to the Iron Throne,

—his uncles, on his father's side:

    —STANNIS BARATHEON, Lord of Dragonstone, styling himself King Stannis the First,

    —RENLY BARATHEON, Lord of Storm's End, styling himself King Renly the First,

—his uncles, on his mother's side:

    —SER JAIME LANNISTER, the Kingslayer, Lord Commander of the Kingsguard, a captive at Riverrun,

    —TYRION LANNISTER, acting Hand of the King,

      —Tyrion's squire, PODRICK PAYNE,

      —Tyrion's guards and sworn swords:

        —BRONN, a sellsword, black of hair and heart,

        —SHAGGA SON OF DOLF, of the Stone Crows,

        —TIMETT SON OF TIMETT, of the Burned Men,

        —CHELLA DAUGHTER OF CHEYK, of the Black Ears,

        —CRAWN SON OF CALOR, of the Moon Brothers,

      —Tyrion's concubine, SHAE, a camp follower, eighteen,

—his small council:

    —GRAND MAESTER PYCELLE,

    —LORD PETYR BAELISH, called LITTLEFINGER, master of coin,

    —LORD JANOS SLYNT, Commander of the City Watch of King's Landing (the "gold cloaks"),

    —VARYS, a eunuch, called the SPIDER, master of whisperers,

—his Kingsguard:

    —SER JAIME LANNISTER, called the KINGSLAYER, Lord Commander, a captive at Riverrun,

    —SANDOR CLEGANE, called the HOUND,

—SER BOROS BLOUNT,
—SER MERYN TRANT,
—SER ARYS OAKHEART,
—SER PRESTON GREENFIELD,
—SER MANDON MOORE,
—his court and retainers:
—SER ILYN PAYNE, the King's Justice, a headsman,
—VYLARR, captain of the Lannister household guards at King's Landing (the "red cloaks"),
—SER LANCEL LANNISTER, formerly squire to King Robert, recently knighted,
—TYREK LANNISTER, formerly squire to King Robert,
—SER ARON SANTAGAR, master-at-arms,
—SER BALON SWANN, second son to Lord Gulian Swann of Stonehelm,
—LADY ERMESANDE HAYFORD, a babe at the breast,
—SER DONTOS HOLLARD, called the RED, a drunk,
—JALABHAR XHO, an exiled prince from the Summer Isles,
—MOON BOY, a jester and fool,
—LADY TANDA STOKEWORTH,
   —FALYSE, her elder daughter,
   —LOLLYS, her younger daughter, a maiden of thirty-three years,
—LORD GYLES ROSBY,
—SER HORAS REDWYNE and his twin SER HOBBER REDWYNE, sons of the Lord of the Arbor,
—the people of King's Landing:
—the City Watch (the "gold cloaks"):
   —JANOS SLYNT, Lord of Harrenhal, Lord Commander,
      —MORROS, his eldest son and heir,
   —ALLAR DEEM, Slynt's chief sergeant,
   —SER JACELYN BYWATER, called IRONHAND, captain of the River Gate,
—HALLYNE THE PYROMANCER, a Wisdom of the Guild of Alchemists,
—CHATAYA, owner of an expensive brothel,
   —ALAYAYA, DANCY, MAREI, some of her girls,
—TOBHO MOTT, a master armorer,
—SALLOREON, a master armorer,
—IRONBELLY, a blacksmith,
—LOTHAR BRUNE, a freerider,
—SER OSMUND KETTLEBLACK, a hedge knight of unsavory reputation,
   —OSFRYD and OSNEY KETTLEBLACK, his brothers,
—SYMON SILVER TONGUE, a singer.

King Joffrey's banner shows the crowned stag of Baratheon, black on gold, and the lion of Lannister, gold on crimson, combatant.

THE KING IN THE NARROW SEA

STANNIS BARATHEON, the First of His Name, the older of King Robert's brothers, formerly Lord of Dragonstone, secondborn son of Lord Steffon Baratheon and Lady Cassana of House Estermont,
—his wife, LADY SELYSE of House Florent,
   —SHIREEN, their only child, a girl of ten,
—his uncle and cousins:
   —SER LOMAS ESTERMONT, an uncle,
      —his son, SER ANDREW ESTERMONT, a cousin,
—his court and retainers:
   —MAESTER CRESSEN, healer and tutor, an old man,
   —MAESTER PYLOS, his young successor,
   —SEPTON BARRE,
   —SER AXELL FLORENT, castellan of Dragonstone, and uncle to Queen Selyse,
   —PATCHFACE, a lackwit fool,
   —LADY MELISANDRE OF ASSHAI, called the RED WOMAN, a priestess of R'hllor, the Heart of Fire,
   —SER DAVOS SEAWORTH, called the ONION KNIGHT and sometimes SHORTHAND, once a smuggler, captain of *Black Betha*,
      —his wife MARYA, a carpenter's daughter,
         —their seven sons:
            —DALE, captain of the *Wraith*,
            —ALLARD, captain of the *Lady Marya*,
            —MATTHOS, second of *Black Betha*,
            —MARIC, oarmaster of *Fury*,
            —DEVAN, squire to King Stannis,
            —STANNIS, a boy of nine years,
            —STEFFON, a boy of six years,
   —BRYEN FARRING, squire to King Stannis,
—his lords bannermen and sworn swords,
   —ARDRIAN CELTIGAR, Lord of Claw Isle, an old man,
   —MONFORD VELARYON, Lord of the Tides and Master of Driftmark,
   —DURAM BAR EMMON, Lord of Sharp Point, a boy of fourteen years,

—GUNCER SUNGLASS, Lord of Sweetport Sound,
—SER HUBARD RAMBTON,
—SALLADHOR SAAN, of the Free City of Lys, styled Prince of the Narrow Sea,
—MOROSH THE MYRMAN, a sellsail admiral.

King Stannis has taken for his banner the fiery heart of the Lord of Light; a red heart surrounded by orange flames upon a bright yellow field. Within the heart is pictured the crowned stag of House Baratheon, in black.

THE KING IN HIGHGARDEN

RENLY BARATHEON, the First of His Name, the younger of King Robert's brothers, formerly Lord of Storm's End, thirdborn son of Lord Steffon Baratheon and Lady Cassana of House Estermont,
—his new bride, LADY MARGAERY of House Tyrell, a maid of fifteen years,
—his uncle and cousins:
　—SER ELDON ESTERMONT, an uncle,
　　—Ser Eldon's son, SER AEMON ESTERMONT, a cousin,
　　　—Ser Aemon's son, SER ALYN ESTERMONT,
—his lords bannermen:
　—MACE TYRELL, Lord of Highgarden and Hand of the King,
　—RANDYLL TARLY, Lord of Horn Hill,
　—MATHIS ROWAN, Lord of Goldengrove,
　—BRYCE CARON, Lord of the Marches,
　—SHYRA ERROL, Lady of Haystack Hall,
　—ARWYN OAKHEART, Lady of Old Oak,
　—ALESTER FLORENT, Lord of Brightwater Keep,
　—LORD SELWYN OF TARTH, called the EVENSTAR,
　—LEYTON HIGHTOWER, Voice of Oldtown, Lord of the Port,
　—LORD STEFFON VARNER,
—his Rainbow Guard:
　—SER LORAS TYRELL, the Knight of Flowers, Lord Commander,
　—LORD BRYCE CARON, the Orange,
　—SER GUYARD MORRIGEN, the Green,
　—SER PARMEN CRANE, the Purple,
　—SER ROBAR ROYCE, the Red,
　—SER EMMON CUY, the Yellow,
　—BRIENNE OF TARTH, the Blue, also called BRIENNE THE BEAUTY, daughter to Lord Selwyn the Evenstar,
—his knights and sworn swords:
　—SER CORTNAY PENROSE, castellan of Storm's End,
　　—Ser Cortnay's ward, EDRIC STORM, a bastard son of King Robert by Lady Delena of House Florent,

—SER DONNEL SWANN, heir to Stonehelm,
—SER JON FOSSOWAY, of the green-apple Fossoways,
—SER BRYAN FOSSOWAY, SER TANTON FOSSOWAY, and SER EDWYD FOSSOWAY, of the red-apple Fossoways,
—SER COLEN OF GREENPOOLS,
—SER MARK MULLENDORE,
—RED RONNET, the Knight of Griffin's Roost,
—his household,
—MAESTER JURNE, counselor, healer, and tutor.

King Renly's banner is the crowned stag of House Baratheon of Storm's End, black upon a gold field, the same banner flown by his brother King Robert.

THE KING IN THE NORTH

ROBB STARK, Lord of Winterfell and King in the North, eldest son of Eddard Stark, Lord of Winterfell, and Lady Catelyn of House Tully, a boy of fifteen years,
—his direwolf, GREY WIND,
—his mother, LADY CATELYN, of House Tully,
—his siblings:
 —PRINCESS SANSA, a maid of twelve,
  —Sansa's direwolf, {LADY}, killed at Castle Darry,
 —PRINCESS ARYA, a girl of ten,
  —Arya's direwolf, NYMERIA, driven off a year past,
 —PRINCE BRANDON, called Bran, heir to Winterfell and the North, a boy of eight,
  —Bran's direwolf, SUMMER,
 —PRINCE RICKON, a boy of four,
  —Rickon's direwolf, SHAGGYDOG,
—his half brother, JON SNOW, a bastard of fifteen years, a man of the Night's Watch,
  —Jon's direwolf, GHOST,
—his uncles and aunts:
 —{BRANDON STARK}, Lord Eddard's elder brother, slain at the command of King Aerys II Targaryen,
 —BENJEN STARK, Lord Eddard's younger brother, a man of the Night's Watch, lost beyond the Wall,
 —LYSA ARRYN, Lady Catelyn's younger sister, widow of {Lord Jon Arryn}, Lady of the Eyrie,
 —SER EDMURE TULLY, Lady Catelyn's younger brother, heir to Riverrun,
 —SER BRYNDEN TULLY, called the BLACKFISH, Lady Catelyn's uncle,
—his sworn swords and battle companions:
 —THEON GREYJOY, Lord Eddard's ward, heir to Pyke and the Iron Islands,
 —HALLIS MOLLEN, captain of guards for Winterfell,

—JACKS, QUENT, SHADD, guardsmen under Mollen's command,
—SER WENDEL MANDERLY, second son to the Lord of White Harbor,
—PATREK MALLISTER, heir to Seagard,
—DACEY MORMONT, eldest daughter of Lady Maege and heir to Bear Island,
—JON UMBER, called the SMALLJON,
—ROBIN FLINT, SER PERWYN FREY, LUCAS BLACKWOOD,
—his squire, OLYVAR FREY, eighteen,
  —the household at Riverrun:
—MAESTER VYMAN, counselor, healer, and tutor,
—SER DESMOND GRELL, master-at-arms,
—SER ROBIN RYGER, captain of the guard,
—UTHERYDES WAYN, steward of Riverrun,
—RYMUND THE RHYMER, a singer,
  —the household at Winterfell:
—MAESTER LUWIN, counselor, healer, and tutor,
—SER RODRIK CASSEL, master-at-arms,
  —BETH, his young daughter,
—WALDER FREY, called BIG WALDER, a ward of Lady Catelyn, eight years of age,
—WALDER FREY, called LITTLE WALDER, a ward of Lady Catelyn, also eight,
—SEPTON CHAYLE, keeper of the castle sept and library,
—JOSETH, master of horse,
  —BANDY and SHYRA, his twin daughters,
—FARLEN, kennelmaster,
  —PALLA, a kennel girl,
—OLD NAN, storyteller, once a wet nurse, now very aged,
  —HODOR, her great-grandson, a simpleminded stableboy,
—GAGE, the cook,
  —TURNIP, a pot girl and scullion,
  —OSHA, a wildling woman taken captive in the wolfswood, serving as kitchen drudge,
—MIKKEN, smith and armorer,
—HAYHEAD, SKITTRICK, POXY TYM, ALEBELLY, guardsmen,
—CALON, TOM, children of guardsmen,
—his lords bannermen and commanders:
—(with Robb at Riverrun)
  —JON UMBER, called the GREATJON,
  —RICKARD KARSTARK, Lord of Karhold,
  —GALBART GLOVER, of Deepwood Motte,
  —MAEGE MORMONT, Lady of Bear Island,
  —SER STEVRON FREY, eldest son of Lord Walder Frey and heir to the Twins,
    —Ser Stevron's eldest son, SER RYMAN FREY,
      —Ser Ryman's son, BLACK WALDER FREY,
  —MARTYN RIVERS, a bastard son of Lord Walder Frey,
—(with Roose Bolton's host at the Twins),

—ROOSE BOLTON, Lord of the Dreadfort, commanding the larger part of the northern host,
—ROBETT GLOVER, of Deepwood Motte,
—WALDER FREY, Lord of the Crossing,
—SER HELMAN TALLHART, of Torrhen's Square,
—SER AENYS FREY,
—(prisoners of Lord Tywin Lannister),
  —LORD MEDGER CERWYN,
  —HARRION KARSTARK, sole surviving son of Lord Rickard,
  —SER WYLIS MANDERLY, heir to White Harbor,
  —SER JARED FREY, SER HOSTEEN FREY, SER DANWELL FREY, and their bastard half brother, RONEL RIVERS,
—(in the field or at their own castles),
  —LYMAN DARRY, a boy of eight,
  —SHELLA WHENT, Lady of Harrenhal, dispossessed of her castle by Lord Tywin Lannister,
  —JASON MALLISTER, Lord of Seagard,
  —JONOS BRACKEN, Lord of the Stone Hedge,
  —TYTOS BLACKWOOD, Lord of Raventree,
  —LORD KARYL VANCE,
  —SER MARQ PIPER,
  —SER HALMON PAEGE,
—his lord bannermen and castellans in the north:
  —WYMAN MANDERLY, Lord of White Harbor,
  —HOWLAND REED of Greywater Watch, a crannogman,
    —Howland's daughter, MEERA, a maid of fifteen,
    —Howland's son, JOJEN, a boy of thirteen,
  —LADY DONELLA HORNWOOD, a widow and grieving mother,
  —CLEY CERWYN, Lord Medger's heir, a boy of fourteen,
  —LEOBALD TALLHART, younger brother to Ser Helman, castellan at Torrhen's Square,
    —Leobald's wife, BERENA of House Hornwood,
    —Leobald's son, BRANDON, a boy of fourteen,
    —Leobald's son, BEREN, a boy of ten,
    —Ser Helman's son, BENFRED, heir to Torrhen's Square,
    —Ser Helman's daughter, EDDARA, a maid of nine,
  —LADY SYBELLE, wife to Robett Glover, holding Deepwood Motte in his absence,
    —Robett's son, GAWEN, three, heir to Deepwood,
    —Robett's daughter, ERENA, a babe of one,
    —LARENCE SNOW, a bastard son of Lord Hornwood, aged twelve, ward of Galbart Glover,
  —MORS CROWFOOD and HOTHER WHORESBANE of House Umber, uncles to the Greatjon,
  —LADY LYESSA FLINT, mother to Robin,
  —ONDREW LOCKE, Lord of Oldcastle, an old man.

The banner of the King in the North remains as it has for thousands of years: the grey direwolf of the Starks of Winterfell, running across an ice-white field.

THE QUEEN ACROSS THE WATER

DAENERYS TARGARYEN, called Daenerys Stormborn, the Unburnt, Mother of Dragons, *Khaleesi* of the Dothraki, and First of Her Name, sole surviving child of King Aerys II Targaryen by his sister/wife, Queen Rhaella, a widow at fourteen years,
—her new-hatched dragons, DROGON, VISERION, RHAEGAL,
—her brothers:
  —{RHAEGAR}, Prince of Dragonstone and heir to the Iron Throne, slain by King Robert on the Trident,
    —{RHAENYS}, Rhaegar's daughter by Elia of Dorne, murdered during the Sack of King's Landing,
    —{AEGON}, Rhaegar's son by Elia of Dorne, murdered during the Sack of King's Landing,
  —{VISERYS}, styling himself King Viserys, the Third of His Name, called the Beggar King, slain in Vaes Dothrak by the hand of Khal Drogo,
—her husband {DROGO}, a *khal* of the Dothraki, died of wounds gone bad,
  —{RHAEGO}, stillborn son of Daenerys and Khal Drogo, slain in the womb by Mirri Maz Duur,
—her Queensguard:
  —SER JORAH MORMONT, an exile knight, once Lord of Bear Island,
  —JHOGO, *ko* and bloodrider, the whip,
  —AGGO, *ko* and bloodrider, the bow,
  —RAKHARO, *ko* and bloodrider, the *arakh*,
—her handmaids:
  —IRRI, a Dothraki girl,
  —JHIQUI, a Dothraki girl,
  —DOREAH, a Lyseni slave, formerly a whore,
—the three seekers:
  —XARO XHOAN DAXOS, a merchant prince of Qarth,
  —PYAT PREE, a warlock of Qarth,
  —QUAITHE, a masked shadowbinder of Asshai,
—ILLYRIO MOPATIS, a magister of the Free City of Pentos, who arranged

to wed Daenerys to Khal Drogo and conspired to restore Viserys to the Iron Throne.

The banner of the Targaryens is the banner of Aegon the Conqueror, who conquered six of Seven Kingdoms, founded the dynasty, and made the Iron Throne from the swords of his conquered enemies: a three-headed dragon, red on black.

OTHER HOUSES GREAT
AND SMALL

HOUSE ARRYN

House Arryn declared for none of the rival claimants at the outbreak of the war, and kept its strength back to protect the Eyrie and the Vale of Arryn. The Arryn sigil is the moon-and-falcon, white, upon a sky-blue field. Their Arryn words are *As High As Honor.*

ROBERT ARRYN, Lord of the Eyrie, Defender of the Vale, Warden of the East, a sickly boy of eight years,
  —his mother, LADY LYSA, of House Tully, third wife and widow of {Lord Jon Arryn}, late Hand of the King, and sister to Catelyn Stark,
  —his household:
    —MAESTER COLEMON, counselor, healer, and tutor,
    —SER MARWYN BELMORE, captain of guards,
    —LORD NESTOR ROYCE, High Steward of the Vale,
      —Lord Nestor's son, SER ALBAR,
      —MYA STONE, a bastard girl in his service, natural daughter of King Robert,
    —MORD, a brutal gaoler,
    —MARILLION, a young singer,
  —his lords bannermen, suitors, and retainers:
    —LORD YOHN ROYCE, called BRONZE YOHN,
      —Lord Yohn's eldest son, SER ANDAR,
      —Lord Yohn's second son, SER ROBAR, in service to King Renly, Robar the Red of the Rainbow Guard,
      —Lord Yohn's youngest son, {SER WAYMAR}, a man of the Night's Watch, lost beyond the Wall,
    —LORD NESTOR ROYCE, brother of Lord Yohn, High Steward of the Vale,
      —Lord Nestor's son and heir, SER ALBAR,
      —Lord Nestor's daughter, MYRANDA,
    —SER LYN CORBRAY, a suitor to Lady Lysa,
      —MYCHEL REDFORT, his squire,
    —LADY ANYA WAYNWOOD,

—Lady Anya's eldest son and heir, SER MORTON, a suitor to Lady Lysa,
—Lady Anya's second son, SER DONNEL, the Knight of the Gate,
—EON HUNTER, Lord of Longbow Hall, an old man, and a suitor to Lady Lysa.

HOUSE FLORENT

The Florents of Brightwater Keep are sworn bannermen to Highgarden, and followed the Tyrells in declaring for King Renly. They also kept a foot in the other camp, however, since Stannis's queen is a Florent, and her uncle the castellan of Dragonstone. The sigil of House Florent shows a fox head in a circle of flowers.

ALESTER FLORENT, Lord of Brightwater,
—his wife, LADY MELARA, of House Crane,
—their children:
—ALEKYNE, heir to Brightwater,
—MELESSA, wed to Lord Randyll Tarly,
—RHEA, wed to Lord Leyton Hightower,
—his siblings:
—SER AXELL, castellan of Dragonstone,
—{SER RYAM}, died in a fall from a horse,
—Ser Ryam's daughter, QUEEN SELYSE, wed to King Stannis,
—Ser Ryam's eldest son and heir, SER IMRY,
—Ser Ryam's second son, SER ERREN,
—SER COLIN,
—Colin's daughter, DELENA, wed to SER HOSMAN NORCROSS,
—Delena's son, EDRIC STORM, a bastard fathered by King Robert,
—Delena's son, ALESTER NORCROSS,
—Delena's son, RENLY NORCROSS,
—Colin's son, MAESTER OMER, in service at Old Oak,
—Colin's son, MERRELL, a squire on the Arbor,
—his sister, RYLENE, wed to Ser Rycherd Crane.

HOUSE FREY

Powerful, wealthy, and numerous, the Freys are bannermen to House Tully, their swords sworn to the service of Riverrun, but they have not always been diligent in performing their duty. When Robert Baratheon met Rhaegar Targaryen on the Trident, the Freys did not arrive until the battle was done, and thereafter Lord Hoster Tully always called Lord Walder "the Late Lord Frey." Lord Frey agreed to support the cause of the King in the North only after Robb Stark agreed to a betrothal, promising to marry one of his daughters or granddaughters after the war was done. Lord Walder has known ninety-one name days, but only recently took his eighth wife, a girl seventy years his junior. It is said of him that he is the only lord in the Seven Kingdoms who could field an army out of his breeches.

WALDER FREY, Lord of the Crossing,
  —by his first wife, {LADY PERRA, of House Royce}:
  —SER STEVRON, heir to the Twins,
    —m. {Corenna Swann, died of a wasting illness},
    —Stevron's eldest son, SER RYMAN,
      —Ryman's son, EDWYN, wed to Janyce Hunter,
        —Edwyn's daughter, WALDA, a girl of eight,
      —Ryman's son, WALDER, called BLACK WALDER,
      —Ryman's son, PETYR, called PETYR PIMPLE,
        —m. Mylenda Caron,
        —Petyr's daughter, PERRA, a girl of five,
    —m. {Jeyne Lydden, died in a fall from a horse},
    —Stevron's son, AEGON, a halfwit called JINGLEBELL,
    —Stevron's daughter, {MAEGELLE, died in childbed},
      —m. Ser Dafyn Vance,
      —Maegelle's daughter, MARIANNE, a maiden,
      —Maegelle's son, WALDER VANCE, a squire,
      —Maegelle's son, PATREK VANCE,
    —m. {Marsella Waynwood, died in childbed},
    —Stevron's son, WALTON, w. Deana Hardyng,
      —Walton's son, STEFFON, called THE SWEET,

—Walton's daughter, WALDA, called FAIR WALDA,
—Walton's son, BRYAN, a squire,
—SER EMMON, m. Genna of House Lannister,
  —Emmon's son, SER CLEOS, m. Jeyne Darry,
    —Cleos's son, TYWIN, a squire of eleven,
    —Cleos's son, WILLEM, a page at Ashemark,
  —Emmon's son, SER LYONEL, m. Melesa Crakehall,
  —Emmon's son, TION, a squire captive at Riverrun,
  —Emmon's son, WALDER, called RED WALDER, a page at Casterly Rock,
—SER AENYS, m. {Tyana Wylde, died in childbed},
  —Aenys's son, AEGON BLOODBORN, an outlaw,
  —Aenys's son, RHAEGAR, m. Jeyne Beesbury,
    —Rhaegar's son, ROBERT, a boy of thirteen,
    —Rhaegar's daughter, WALDA, a girl of ten, called WHITE WALDA,
    —Rhaegar's son, JONOS, a boy of eight,
—PERRIANE, m. Ser Leslyn Haigh,
  —Perriane's son, SER HARYS HAIGH,
    —Harys's son, WALDER HAIGH, a boy of four,
  —Perriane's son, SER DONNEL HAIGH,
  —Perriane's son, ALYN HAIGH, a squire,
—by his second wife, {LADY CYRENNA, of House Swann}:
—SER JARED, their eldest son, m. {Alys Frey},
  —Jared's son, SER TYTOS, m. Zhoe Blanetree,
    —Tytos's daughter, ZIA, a maid of fourteen,
    —Tytos's son, ZACHERY, a boy of twelve, training at the Sept of Oldtown,
  —Jared's daughter, KYRA, m. Ser Garse Goodbrook,
    —Kyra's son, WALDER GOODBROOK, a boy of nine,
    —Kyra's daughter, JEYNE GOODBROOK, six,
—SEPTON LUCEON, in service at the Great Sept of Baelor in King's Landing,
—by his third wife, {LADY AMAREI of House Crakehall}:
—SER HOSTEEN, their eldest son, m. Bellena Hawick,
  —Hosteen's son, SER ARWOOD, m. Ryella Royce,
    —Arwood's daughter, RYELLA, a girl of five,
    —Arwood's twin sons, ANDROW and ALYN, three,
—LADY LYTHENE, m. Lord Lucias Vypren,
  —Lythene's daughter, ELYANA, m. Ser Jon Wylde,
    —Elyana's son, RICKARD WYLDE, four,
  —Lythene's son, SER DAMON VYPREN,
—SYMOND, m. Betharios of Braavos,
  —Symond's son, ALESANDER, a singer,
  —Symond's daughter, ALYX, a maid of seventeen,
  —Symond's son, BRADAMAR, a boy of ten, fostered on Braavos as a ward of Oro Tendyris, a merchant of that city,
—SER DANWELL, m. Wynafrei Whent,
  —{many stillbirths and miscarriages},

—MERRETT, m. Mariya Darry,
  —Merrett's daughter, AMEREI, called AMI, a widow of sixteen, m. {Ser Pate of the Blue Fork},
  —Merrett's daughter, WALDA, called FAT WALDA, a maid of fifteen years,
  —Merrett's daughter, MARISSA, a maid of thirteen,
  —Merrett's son, WALDER, called LITTLE WALDER, a boy of eight, fostered at Winterfell as a ward of Lady Catelyn Stark,
—{SER GEREMY, drowned}, m. Carolei Waynwood,
  —Geremy's son, SANDOR, a boy of twelve, a squire to Ser Donnel Waynwood,
  —Geremy's daughter, CYNTHEA, a girl of nine, a ward of Lady Anya Waynwood,
—SER RAYMUND, m. Beony Beesbury,
  —Raymund's son, ROBERT, sixteen, in training at the Citadel in Oldtown,
  —Raymund's son, MALWYN, fifteen, apprenticed to an alchemist in Lys,
  —Raymund's twin daughters, SERRA and SARRA, maiden girls of fourteen,
  —Raymund's daughter, CERSEI, six, called LITTLE BEE,
—by his fourth wife, {LADY ALYSSA, of House Blackwood}:
  —LOTHAR, their eldest son, called LAME LOTHAR, m. Leonella Lefford,
    —Lothar's daughter, TYSANE, a girl of seven,
    —Lothar's daughter, WALDA, a girl of four,
    —Lothar's daughter, EMBERLEI, a girl of two,
  —SER JAMMOS, m. Sallei Paege,
    —Jammos's son, WALDER, called BIG WALDER, a boy of eight, fostered at Winterfell as a ward of Lady Catelyn Stark,
    —Jammos's twin sons, DICKON and MATHIS, five,
  —SER WHALEN, m. Sylwa Paege,
    —Whalen's son, HOSTER, a boy of twelve, a squire to Ser Damon Paege,
    —Whalen's daughter, MERIANNE, called MERRY, a girl of eleven,
  —LADY MORYA, m. Ser Flement Brax,
    —Morya's son, ROBERT BRAX, nine, fostered at Casterly Rock as a page,
    —Morya's son, WALDER BRAX, a boy of six,
    —Morya's son, JON BRAX, a babe of three,
  —TYTA, called TYTA THE MAID, a maid of twenty-nine,
—by his fifth wife, {LADY SARYA of House Whent}:
—no progeny,
—by his sixth wife, {LADY BETHANY of House Rosby}:
—SER PERWYN, their eldest son,
—SER BENFREY, m. Jyanna Frey, a cousin,
  —Benfrey's daughter, DELLA, called DEAF DELLA, a girl of three,
  —Benfrey's son, OSMUND, a boy of two,
—MAESTER WILLAMEN, in service at Longbow Hall,

—OLYVAR, a squire in the service of Robb Stark,
—ROSLIN, a maid of sixteen,
—by his seventh wife, {LADY ANNARA of House Farring}:
—ARWYN, a maid of fourteen,
—WENDEL, their eldest son, a boy of thirteen, fostered at Seagard as a page,
—COLMAR, promised to the Faith, eleven,
—WALTYR, called TYR, a boy of ten,
—ELMAR, betrothed to Arya Stark, a boy of nine,
—SHIREI, a girl of six,
—his eighth wife, LADY JOYEUSE of House Erenford,
—no progeny as yet,
—Lord Walder's natural children, by sundry mothers,
—WALDER RIVERS, called BASTARD WALDER,
—Bastard Walder's son, SER AEMON RIVERS,
—Bastard Walder's daughter, WALDA RIVERS,
—MAESTER MELWYS, in service at Rosby,
—JEYNE RIVERS, MARTYN RIVERS, RYGER RIVERS, RONEL RIVERS, MELLARA RIVERS, others.

HOUSE GREYJOY

Balon Greyjoy, Lord of the Iron Islands, previously led a rebellion against the Iron Throne, put down by King Robert and Lord Eddard Stark. Though his son Theon, raised at Winterfell, was one of Robb Stark's supporters and closest companions, Lord Balon did not join the northmen when they marched south into the riverlands.

The Greyjoy sigil is a golden kraken upon a black field. Their words are *We Do Not Sow.*

BALON GREYJOY, Lord of the Iron Islands, King of Salt and Rock, Son of the Sea Wind, Lord Reaper of Pyke, captain of the *Great Kraken*,
—his wife, LADY ALANNYS, of House Harlaw,
  —their children:
  —{RODRIK}, slain at Seagard during Greyjoy's Rebellion,
  —{MARON}, slain at Pyke during Greyjoy's Rebellion,
  —ASHA, captain of the *Black Wind*,
  —THEON, a ward of Lord Eddard Stark at Winterfell,
—his brothers:
  —EURON, called CROW'S EYE, captain of the *Silence*, an outlaw, pirate, and raider,
  —VICTARION, Lord Captain of the Iron Fleet, master of the *Iron Victory*,
  —AERON, called DAMPHAIR, a priest of the Drowned God,
—his household on Pyke:
  —DAGMER called CLEFTJAW, master-at-arms, captain of the *Foamdrinker*,
  —MAESTER WENDAMYR, healer and counselor,
  —HELYA, keeper of the castle,
—people of Lordsport:
  —SIGRIN, a shipwright,
—his lords bannermen,
  —LORD BOTLEY, of Lordsport,
  —LORD WYNCH, of Iron Holt,

—LORD HARLAW, of Harlaw,
—STONEHOUSE, of Old Wyk,
—DRUMM, of Old Wyk,
—GOODBROTHER, of Old Wyk,
—GOODBROTHER, of Great Wyk,
—LORD MERLYN, of Great Wyk,
—SPARR, of Great Wyk,
—LORD BLACKTYDE, of Blacktyde,
—LORD SALTCLIFFE, of Saltcliffe,
—LORD SUNDERLY, of Saltcliffe.

HOUSE LANNISTER

The Lannisters of Casterly Rock remain the principal support of King Joffrey's claim to the Iron Throne. Their sigil is a golden lion upon a crimson field. The Lannister words are *Hear Me Roar!*

TYWIN LANNISTER, Lord of Casterly Rock, Warden of the West, Shield of Lannisport, and Hand of the King, commanding the Lannister host at Harrenhal,
—his wife, {LADY JOANNA}, a cousin, died in childbed,
—their children:
—SER JAIME, called the Kingslayer, Warden of the East and Lord Commander of the Kingsguard, a twin to Queen Cersei,
—QUEEN CERSEI, widow of King Robert, twin to Jaime, Queen Regent and Protector of the Realm,
—TYRION, called the IMP, a dwarf,
—his siblings:
—SER KEVAN, his eldest brother,
—Ser Kevan's wife, DORNA, of House Swyft,
—Lady Dorna's father, SER HARYS SWYFT,
—their children:
—SER LANCEL, formerly a squire to King Robert, knighted after his death,
—WILLEM, twin to Martyn, a squire, taken captive at the Whispering Wood,
—MARTYN, twin to Willem, a squire,
—JANEI, a girl of two,
—GENNA, his sister, wed to Ser Emmon Frey,
—Genna's son, SER CLEOS FREY, taken captive at the Whispering Wood,
—Genna's son, TION FREY, a squire, taken captive at the Whispering Wood,
—{SER TYGETT}, his second brother, died of a pox,
—Tygett's widow, DARLESSA, of House Marbrand,
—Tygett's son, TYREK, squire to the king,

—{GERION}, his youngest brother, lost at sea,
—Gerion's bastard daughter, JOY, eleven,
—his cousin, SER STAFFORD LANNISTER, brother to the late Lady
Joanna,
—Ser Stafford's daughters, CERENNA and MYRIELLE,
—Ser Stafford's son, SER DAVEN,
—his lord bannermen, captains, and commanders:
—SER ADDAM MARBRAND, heir to Ashemark, commander of Lord
Tywin's outriders and scouts,
—SER GREGOR CLEGANE, the Mountain That Rides,
—POLLIVER, CHISWYCK, RAFF THE SWEETLING, DUNSEN, and
THE TICKLER, soldiers in his service,
—LORD LEO LEFFORD,
—SER AMORY LORCH, a captain of foragers,
—LEWYS LYDDEN, Lord of the Deep Den,
—GAWEN WESTERLING, Lord of the Crag, taken captive in the
Whispering Wood and held at Seagard,
—SER ROBERT BRAX, and his brother, SER FLEMENT BRAX,
—SER FORLEY PRESTER, of the Golden Tooth,
—VARGO HOAT, of the Free City of Qohor, captain of the sellsword
company called the Brave Companions,
—MAESTER CREYLEN, his counselor.

HOUSE MARTELL

Dorne was the last of the Seven Kingdoms to swear fealty to the Iron Throne. Blood, custom, and history all set the Dornishmen apart from the other kingdoms. When the war of succession broke out, the Prince of Dorne kept his silence and took no part.

The Martell banner is a red sun pierced by a golden spear. Their words are *Unbowed, Unbent, Unbroken.*

DORAN NYMEROS MARTELL, Lord of Sunspear, Prince of Dorne,
—his wife, MELLARIO, of the Free City of Norvos,
—their children:
—PRINCESS ARIANNE, their eldest daughter, heir to Sunspear,
—PRINCE QUENTYN, their eldest son,
—PRINCE TRYSTANE, their younger son,
—his siblings:
—his sister, {PRINCESS ELIA}, wed to Prince Rhaegar Targaryen, slain during the Sack of King's Landing,
—Elia's daughter, {PRINCESS RHAENYS}, a young girl murdered during the Sack of King's Landing,
—Elia's son, {PRINCE AEGON}, a babe, murdered during the Sack of King's Landing,
—his brother, PRINCE OBERYN, the Red Viper,
—his household:
—AREO HOTAH, a Norvoshi sellsword, captain of guards,
—MAESTER CALEOTTE, counselor, healer, and tutor,
—his lords bannermen:
—EDRIC DAYNE, Lord of Starfall.

The principal houses sworn to Sunspear include Jordayne, Santagar, Allyrion, Toland, Yronwood, Wyl, Fowler, and Dayne.

HOUSE TYRELL

Lord Tyrell of Highgarden declared his support for King Renly after Renly's marriage to his daughter Margaery, and brought most of his principal bannermen to Renly's cause. The Tyrell sigil is a golden rose on a grass-green field. Their words are *Growing Strong*.

MACE TYRELL, Lord of Highgarden, Warden of the South, Defender of the Marches, High Marshal of the Reach, and Hand of the King,
—his wife, LADY ALERIE, of House Hightower of Oldtown,
—their children:
—WILLAS, their eldest son, heir to Highgarden,
—SER GARLAN, called the GALLANT, their second son,
—SER LORAS, the Knight of Flowers, their youngest son, Lord Commander of the Rainbow Guard,
—MARGAERY, their daughter, a maid of fifteen years, recently wed to Renly Baratheon,
—his widowed mother, LADY OLENNA of House Redwyne, called the QUEEN OF THORNS,
—his sisters:
—MINA, wed to Paxter Redwyne, Lord of the Arbor,
—their children:
—SER HORAS REDWYNE, twin to Hobber, mocked as HORROR,
—SER HOBBER REDWYNE, twin to Horas, mocked as SLOBBER,
—DESMERA REDWYNE, a maid of sixteen,
—JANNA, wed to Ser Jon Fossoway,
—his uncles:
—GARTH, called the GROSS, Lord Seneschal of Highgarden,
—Garth's bastard sons, GARSE and GARRETT FLOWERS,
—SER MORYN, Lord Commander of the City Watch of Oldtown,
—MAESTER GORMON, a scholar of the Citadel,

—his household:
  —MAESTER LOMYS, counselor, healer, and tutor,
  —IGON VYRWEL, captain of the guard,
  —SER VORTIMER CRANE, master-at-arms,
  —BUTTERBUMPS, fool and jester, hugely fat.

THE MEN OF THE NIGHT'S WATCH

The Night's Watch protects the realm, and is sworn to take no part in civil wars and contests for the throne. Traditionally, in times of rebellion, they do honor to all kings and obey none.

At Castle Black

JEOR MORMONT, Lord Commander of the Night's Watch, called the OLD BEAR,
- —his steward and squire, JON SNOW, the bastard of Winterfell, called LORD SNOW,
  - —Jon's white direwolf, GHOST,
- —MAESTER AEMON (TARGARYEN), counselor and healer,
  - —SAMWELL TARLY and CLYDAS, his stewards,
- —BENJEN STARK, First Ranger, lost beyond the Wall,
  - —THOREN SMALLWOOD, a senior ranger,
  - —JARMEN BUCKWELL, a senior ranger,
  - —SER OTTYN WYTHERS, SER ALADALE WYNCH, GRENN, PYPAR, MATTHAR, ELRON, LARK called the SISTERMAN, rangers,
- —OTHELL YARWYCK, First Builder,
  - —HALDER, ALBETT, builders,
- —BOWEN MARSH, Lord Steward
  - —CHETT, steward and dog handler,
  - —EDDISON TOLLETT, called DOLOROUS EDD, a dour squire,
- —SEPTON CELLADAR, a drunken devout,
- —SER ENDREW TARTH, master-at-arms,
- —brothers of Castle Black:
  - —DONAL NOYE, armorer and smith, one-armed,
  - —THREE-FINGER HOBB, cook,
  - —JEREN, RAST, CUGEN, recruits still in training,
  - —CONWY, GUEREN, "wandering crows," recruiters who collect orphan boys and criminals for the Wall,
  - —YOREN, the senior of the "wandering crows,"

—PRAED, CUTJACK, WOTH, REYSEN, QYLE, recruits bound for the Wall,
—KOSS, GERREN, DOBBER, KURZ, BITER, RORGE, JAQEN H'GHAR, criminals bound for the Wall,
—LOMMY GREENHANDS, GENDRY, TARBER, HOT PIE, ARRY, orphan boys bound for the Wall.

At Eastwatch-by-the-Sea

COTTER PYKE, Commander, Eastwatch,
—SER ALLISER THORNE, master-at-arms,
—brothers of Eastwatch:
  —DAREON, steward and singer.

At the Shadow Tower

SER DENYS MALLISTER, Commander, Shadow Tower,
—QHORIN called HALFHAND, a senior ranger,
—DALBRIDGE, an elderly squire and senior ranger,
—EBBEN, STONESNAKE, rangers.

ACKNOWLEDGMENTS

More details, more devils.

This time around, the angels who helped me put them to rest included Walter Jon Williams, Sage Walker, Melinda Snodgrass, and Carl Keim.

Thanks as well to my patient editors and publishers: Anne Groell, Nita Taublib, Joy Chamberlain, Jane Johnson, and Malcolm Edwards.

And finally, a tip o' the tilting helm to Parris for her Magic Coffee, the fuel that built the Seven Kingdoms.

Also by
GEORGE R. R. MARTIN

Novels

Fevre Dream

Windhaven

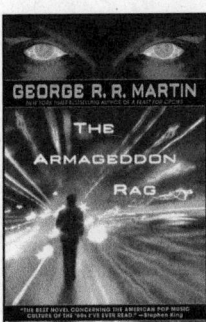

The
Armageddon Rag

Dying of the Light

Short Stories

Dreamsongs:
Volume I

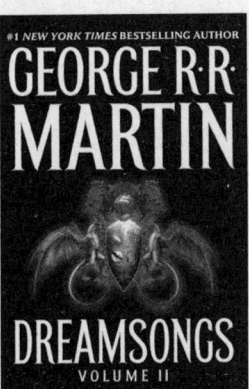

Dreamsongs:
Volume II

Also available in Audio and eBook

THE RANDOM HOUSE PUBLISHING GROUP

www.GeorgeRRMartin.com

ABOUT THE AUTHOR

GEORGE R. R. MARTIN sold his first story in 1971 and hasn't stopped. As a writer-producer, he worked on *The Twilight Zone,* *Beauty and the Beast,* and various feature films and pilots that were never made. In the mid '90s he returned to prose and began work on A Song of Ice and Fire. He has been in the Seven Kingdoms ever since. He lives with the lovely Parris in Santa Fe, New Mexico.

Now, here's a special preview of
the next book in

George R. R. Martin's

landmark series

A STORM OF SWORDS

the riveting sequel to

A GAME OF THRONES

and

A CLASH OF KINGS

On sale now

SANSA

The invitation seemed innocent enough, but every time Sansa read it her tummy tightened into a knot. *She's to be queen now, she's beautiful and rich and everyone loves her, why would she want to sup with a traitor's daughter?* It could be curiosity, she supposed; perhaps Margaery Tyrell wanted to get the measure of the rival she'd displaced. *Does she resent me, I wonder? Does she think I bear her ill will . . .*

Sansa had watched from the castle walls as Margaery Tyrell and her escort made their way up Aegon's High Hill. Joffrey had met his new bride-to-be at the King's Gate to welcome her to the city, and they rode side by side through cheering crowds, Joff glittering in gilded armor and the Tyrell girl splendid in green with a cloak of autumn flowers blowing from her shoulders. She was sixteen, brown-haired and brown-eyed, slender and beautiful. The people called out her name as she passed, held up their children for her blessing, and scattered flowers under the hooves of her horse. Her mother and grandmother followed close behind, riding in a tall wheelhouse whose sides were carved into the shape of a hundred twining roses, every one gilded and shining. The smallfolk cheered them as well.

The same smallfolk who pulled me from my horse and would have killed me, if not for the Hound. Sansa had done nothing to make the commons hate her, no more than Margaery Tyrell had done to win their love. *Does she want me to love her too?* She studied the invitation, which looked to be written in Margaery's own hand. *Does she want my blessing?* Sansa wondered if Joffrey knew of this supper. For all she knew, it might be his doing. That thought made her fearful. If Joff was behind the invitation, he would have some cruel jape planned to shame her in the older girl's eyes. Would he command his Kingsguard to strip her naked once again? The last time he had done that his uncle Tyrion had stopped him, but the Imp could not save her now.

No one can save me but my Florian. Ser Dontos had promised he would help her escape, but not until the night of Joffrey's wedding. The plans had been well laid, her dear devoted knight-turned-fool assured her; there was nothing to do until then but endure, and count the days.

And sup with my replacement . . .

Perhaps she was doing Margaery Tyrell an injustice. Perhaps the invitation was no more than a simple kindness, an act of courtesy. *It might be just a supper.* But this was the Red Keep, this was King's Landing, this was the court of King Joffrey Baratheon, the First of His Name, and if there was one thing that Sansa Stark had learned here, it was mistrust.

Even so, she must accept. She was nothing now, the discarded daughter of a traitor and disgraced sister of a rebel lord. She could scarcely refuse Joffrey's queen-to-be.

I wish the Hound were here. The night of the battle, Sandor Clegane had come to her chambers to take her from the city, but Sansa had refused. Sometimes she lay awake at night, wondering if she'd been wise. She had his stained white cloak hidden in a cedar chest beneath her summer silks. She could not say why she'd kept it. The Hound had turned craven, she heard it said; at the height of the battle, he got so drunk the Imp had to take his men. But Sansa understood. She knew the secret of his burned face. *It was only the fire he feared.* That night, the wildfire had set the river itself ablaze, and filled the very air with green flame. Even in the castle, Sansa had been afraid. Outside . . . she could scarcely imagine it.

Sighing, she got out quill and ink, and wrote Margaery Tyrell a gracious note of acceptance.

When the appointed night arrived, another of the Kingsguard came for her, a man as different from Sandor Clegane as . . . *well, as a flower from a dog.* The sight of Ser Loras Tyrell standing on her threshold made Sansa's heart beat a little faster. This was the first time she had been so close to him since he had returned to King's Landing, leading the vanguard of his father's host. For a moment she did not know what to say. "Ser Loras," she finally managed, "you . . . you look so lovely."

He gave her a puzzled smile. "My lady is too kind. And beautiful besides. My sister awaits you eagerly."

"I have so looked forward to our supper."

"As has Margaery, and my lady grandmother as well." He took her arm and led her toward the steps.

"Your grandmother?" Sansa was finding it hard to walk and talk and think all at the same time, with Ser Loras touching her arm. She could feel the warmth of his hand through the silk.

"Lady Olenna. She is to sup with you as well."

"Oh," said Sansa. *I am talking to him, and he's touching me, he's holding my arm and touching me.* "The Queen of Thorns, she's called. Isn't that right?"

"It is." Ser Loras laughed. *He has the warmest laugh,* she thought as he went on, "You'd best not use that name in her presence, though, or you're like to get pricked."

Sansa reddened. Any fool would have realized that no woman would be happy about being called "the Queen of Thorns." *Maybe I truly am as stupid as Cersei Lannister says.* Desperately she tried to think of something clever and charming to say to him, but her wits had deserted her. She almost told him how beautiful he was, until she remembered that she'd already done that.

He *was* beautiful, though. He seemed taller than he'd been when she'd first met him, but still so lithe and graceful, and Sansa had never seen another boy with such wonderful eyes. *He's no boy, though, he's a man grown, a knight of the Kingsguard.* She thought he looked even finer in white than in the greens and golds of House Tyrell. The only spot of color on him now was the brooch that clasped his cloak; the rose of Highgarden wrought in soft yellow gold, nestled in a bed of delicate green jade leaves.

Ser Balon Swann held the door of Maegor's for them to pass. He was all in white as well, though he did not wear it half so well as Ser Loras. Beyond the spiked moat, two dozen men were taking their practice with sword and shield. With the castle so crowded, the outer ward had been given over to guests to raise their tents and pavilions, leaving only the smaller inner yards for training. One of the Redwyne twins was being driven backward by Ser Tallad, with the eyes on his shield. Chunky Ser Kennos of Kayce, who chuffed and puffed every time he raised his longsword, seemed to be holding his own against Osney Kettleblack, but Osney's brother Ser Osfryd was savagely punishing the frog-faced squire Morros Slynt. Blunted swords or no, Slynt would have a rich crop of bruises by the morrow. It made Sansa wince just to watch. *They have scarcely finished burying the dead from the last battle, and already they are practicing for the next one.*

On the edge of the yard, a lone knight with a pair of golden roses on his shield was holding off three foes. Even as they watched, he caught one of them alongside the head, knocking him senseless. "Is that your brother?" Sansa asked.

"It is, my lady," said Ser Loras. "Garlan often trains against three men, or even four. In battle it is seldom one against one, he says, so he likes to be prepared."

"He must be very brave."

"He is a great knight," Ser Loras replied. "A better sword than me, in truth, though I'm the better lance."

"I remember," said Sansa. "You ride wonderfully, ser."

"My lady is gracious to say so. When has she seen me ride?"

"At the Hand's tourney, don't you remember? You rode a white courser, and your armor was a hundred different kinds of flowers. You gave me a rose. A *red* rose. You threw white roses to the other girls that day." It made her flush to speak of it. "You said no victory was half as beautiful as me."

Ser Loras gave her a modest smile. "I spoke only a simple truth, that any man with eyes could see."

He doesn't remember, Sansa realized, startled. *He is only being kind to me, he doesn't remember me or the rose or any of it.* She had been so certain that it meant something, that it meant *everything.* A *red* rose, not a white. "It was after you unhorsed Ser Robar Royce," she said, desperately.

He took his hand from her arm. "I slew Robar at Storm's End, my lady." It was not a boast; he sounded sad.

Him, and another of King Renly's Rainbow Guard as well, yes. Sansa had heard the women talking of it round the well, but for a moment she'd forgotten. "That was when Lord Renly was killed, wasn't it? How terrible for your poor sister."

"For Margaery?" His voice was tight. "To be sure. She was at Bitterbridge, though. She did not see."

"Even so, when she heard . . ."

Ser Loras brushed the hilt of his sword lightly with his hand. Its grip was white leather, its pommel a rose in alabaster. "Renly is dead. Robar as well. What use to speak of them?"

The sharpness in his tone took her aback. "I . . . my lord, I . . . I did not mean to give offense, ser."

"Nor could you, Lady Sansa," Ser Loras replied, but all the warmth had gone from his voice. Nor did he take her arm again.

They ascended the serpentine steps in a deepening silence.

Oh, why did I have to mention Ser Robar? Sansa thought. *I've ruined everything. He is angry with me now.* She tried to think of something she might say to make amends, but all the words that came to her were lame and weak. *Be quiet, or you will only make it worse,* she told herself.

Lord Mace Tyrell and his entourage had been housed behind the royal sept, in the long slate-roofed keep that had been called the Maidenvault since King Baelor the Blessed had confined his sisters therein, so the sight of them might not tempt him into carnal thoughts. Outside its tall carved doors stood two guards in gilded halfhelms and green cloaks edged in gold satin, the golden rose of Highgarden sewn on their breasts. Both were seven-footers, wide of shoulder and narrow of waist, magnificently muscled. When Sansa got close enough to see their faces, she could not tell one from the other. They had the same strong jaws, the same deep blue eyes, the same thick red mustaches. "Who are they?" she asked Ser Loras, her discomfit forgotten for a moment.

"My grandmother's personal guard," he told her. "Their mother named them Erryk and Arryk, but Grandmother can't tell them apart, so she calls them Left and Right."

Left and Right opened the doors, and Margaery Tyrell herself emerged and swept down the short flight of steps to greet them. "Lady Sansa," she called, "I'm so pleased you came. Be welcome."

Sansa knelt at the feet of her future queen. "You do me great honor, Your Grace."

"Won't you call me Margaery? Please, rise. Loras, help the Lady Sansa to her feet. Might I call you Sansa?"

"If it please you." Ser Loras helped her up.

Margaery dismissed him with a sisterly kiss, and took Sansa by the hand. "Come, my grandmother awaits, and she is not the most patient of ladies."

A fire was crackling in the hearth, and sweet-swelling rushes had been scattered on the floor. Around the long trestle table a dozen women were seated.

Sansa recognized only Lord Tyrell's tall, dignified wife, Lady Alerie, whose long silvery braid was bound with jeweled rings. Margaery performed the other introductions. There were three Tyrell cousins, Megga and Alla and Elinor, all close to Sansa's age. Buxom Lady Janna was Lord Tyrell's sister, and wed to one of the green-apple Fossoways; dainty, bright-eyed Lady Leonette was a Fossoway as well, and wed to Ser Garlan. Septa Nysterica had a homely pox-scarred face but seemed jolly. Pale, elegant Lady Graceford was with child, and Lady Bulwer *was* a child, no more than eight. And "Merry" was what she was to call boisterous plump Meredyth Crane, but most definitely *not* Lady Merryweather, a sultry black-eyed Myrish beauty.

Last of all, Margaery brought her before the wizened white-haired doll of a woman at the head of the table. "I am honored to present my grandmother the Lady Olenna, widow to the late Luthor Tyrell, Lord of Highgarden, whose memory is a comfort to us all."

The old woman smelled of rosewater. *Why, she's just the littlest bit of a thing.* There was nothing the least bit thorny about her. "Kiss me, child," Lady Olenna said, tugging at Sansa's wrist with a soft spotted hand. "It is so kind of you to sup with me and my foolish flock of hens."

Dutifully, Sansa kissed the old woman on the cheek. "It is kind of you to have me, my lady."

"I knew your grandfather, Lord Rickard, though not well."

"He died before I was born."

"I am aware of that, child. It's said that your Tully grandfather is dying too. Lord Hoster, surely they told you? An old man, though not so old as me. Still, night falls for all of us in the end, and too soon for some. You would know that more than most, poor child. You've had your share of grief, I know. We are sorry for your losses."

Sansa glanced at Margaery. "I was saddened when I heard of Lord Renly's death, Your Grace. He was very gallant."

"You are kind to say so," answered Margaery.

Her grandmother snorted. "Gallant, yes, and charming, and very clean. He knew how to dress and he knew how to smile and he knew how to bathe, and somehow he got the notion that this made him fit to be king. The Baratheons have always had some queer notions, to be sure. It comes from their Targaryen blood, I should think." She sniffed. "They tried to marry me to a Targaryen once, but I soon put an end to that."

"Renly was brave and gentle, Grandmother," said Margaery. "Father liked him as well, and so did Loras."

"Loras is young," Lady Olenna said crisply, "and very good at knocking men off horses with a stick. That does not make him wise. As to your father, would that I'd been born a peasant woman with a big wooden spoon, I might have been able to beat some sense into his fat head."

"*Mother*," Lady Alerie scolded.

"Hush, Alerie, don't take that tone with me. And don't call me Mother. If I'd given birth to you, I'm sure I'd remember. I'm only to blame for your husband, the lord oaf of Highgarden."

"Grandmother," Margaery said, "mind your words, or what will Sansa think of us?"

"She might think we have some wits about us. One of us, at any rate." The old woman turned back to Sansa. "It's treason, I warned them, Robert has two sons, and Renly has an older brother, how can he *possibly* have any claim to that ugly iron chair? Tut-tut, says my son, don't you want your sweetling to be queen? You Starks were kings once, the Arryns and the Lannisters as well, and even the Baratheons through the female line, but the Tyrells were no more than stewards until Aegon the Dragon came along and cooked the rightful King of the Reach on the Field of Fire. If truth be told, even our claim to Highgarden is a bit dodgy, just as those dreadful Florents are always whining. 'What does it matter?' you ask, and of course it doesn't, except to oafs like my son. The thought that one day he may see his grandson with his arse on the Iron Throne makes Mace puff up like . . . now, what do you call it? Margaery, you're clever, be a dear and tell your poor old half-daft grandmother the name of that queer fish from the Summer Isles that puffs up to ten times its own size when you poke it."

"They call them puff fish, Grandmother."

"Of course they do. Summer Islanders have no imagination. My son ought to take the puff fish for his sigil, if truth be told. He could put a crown on it, the way the Baratheons do their stag, mayhap that would make him happy. We should have stayed well out of all this bloody foolishness if you ask me, but once the cow's been milked there's no squirting the cream back up her udder. After Lord Puff Fish put that crown on Renly's head, we were into the pudding up to our knees, so here we are to see things through. And what do you say to that, Sansa?"

Sansa's mouth opened and closed. She felt very like a puff fish herself. "The Tyrells can trace their descent back to Garth Greenhand," was the best she could manage at short notice.

The Queen of Thorns snorted. "So can the Florents, the Rowans, the Oakhearts, and half the other noble houses of the south. Garth liked to plant his seed in fertile ground, they say. I shouldn't wonder that more than his hands were green."

"*Sansa*," Lady Alerie broke in, "you must be very hungry. Shall we have a bite of boar together, and some lemon cakes?"

"Lemon cakes are my favorite," Sansa admitted.

"So we have been told," declared Lady Olenna, who obviously had no intention of being hushed. "That Varys creature seemed to think we should be grateful for the information. I've never been quite sure what the *point* of a eunuch is, if truth be told. It seems to me they're only men with the useful bits cut off. Alerie, will you have them bring the food, or do you mean to starve me to death? Here, Sansa, sit here next to me, I'm much less boring than these others. I hope that you're fond of fools."

Sansa smoothed down her skirts and sat. "I think . . . fools, my lady? You mean . . . the sort in motley?"

"Feathers, in this case. What did you imagine I was speaking of? My son? Or these lovely ladies? No, don't blush, with your hair it makes you look like a pomegranate. All men are fools, if truth be told, but the ones in motley are more amusing than ones with crowns. Margaery, child, summon Butterbumps, let us see if we can't make Lady Sansa smile. The rest of you be seated, do I have to tell you everything? Sansa must think that my granddaughter is attended by a flock of sheep."

Butterbumps arrived before the food, dressed in a jester's suit of green and yellow feathers with a floppy coxcomb. An immense round fat man, as big as three Moon Boys, he came cartwheeling into the hall, vaulted onto the table, and laid a gigantic egg right in front of Sansa. "Break it, my lady," he commanded. When she did, a dozen yellow chicks escaped and began running in all directions. *Catch them!* Butterbumps exclaimed. Little Lady Bulwer snagged one and handed it to him, whereby he tilted back his head, popped it into his huge rubbery mouth, and seemed to swallow it whole. When he belched, tiny yellow feathers flew out his nose. Lady Bulwer began to wail in distress, but her tears turned into a sudden squeal of delight when the chick came squirming out of the sleeve of her gown and ran down her arm.

As the servants brought out a broth of leeks and mushrooms, Butterbumps began to juggle and Lady Olenna pushed herself forward to rest her elbows on the table. "Do you know my son, Sansa? Lord Puff Fish of Highgarden?"

"A great lord," Sansa answered politely.

"A great oaf," said the Queen of Thorns. "His father was an oaf as well. My husband, the late Lord Luthor. Oh, I loved him well enough, don't mistake me. A kind man, and not unskilled in the bedchamber, but an appalling oaf all the same. He managed to ride off a cliff whilst hawking. They say he was looking up at the sky and paying no mind to where his horse was taking him.

"And now my oaf son is doing the same, only he's riding a lion instead of a palfrey. It is easy to mount a lion and not so easy to get off, I warned him, but he only chuckles. Should you ever have a son, Sansa, beat him frequently so he learns to mind you. I only had the one boy and I hardly beat him at all, so now he pays more heed to Butterbumps than he does to me. A lion is not a lap cat, I told him, and he gives me a 'tut-tut-Mother.' There is entirely too much tut-tutting in this realm, if you ask me. All these kings would do a deal better if they would put down their swords and listen to their mothers."

Sansa realized that her mouth was open again. She filled it with a spoon of broth while Lady Alerie and the other women were giggling at the spectacle of Butterbumps bouncing oranges off his head, his elbows, and his ample rump.

"I want you to tell me the truth about this royal boy," said Lady Olenna abruptly. "This Joffrey."

Sansa's fingers tightened round her spoon. *The truth? I can't. Don't ask it, please, I can't.* "I . . . I . . . I . . ."

"You, yes. Who would know better? The lad seems kingly enough, I'll grant you. A bit full of himself, but that would be his Lannister blood. We have heard some troubling tales, however. Is there any truth to them? Has this boy mistreated you?"

Sansa glanced about nervously. Butterbumps popped a whole orange into his mouth, chewed and swallowed, slapped his cheek, and blew seeds out of his nose. The women giggled and laughed. Servants were coming and going, and the Maidenvault echoed to the clatter of spoons and plates. One of the chicks hopped back onto the table and ran through Lady Graceford's broth. No one seemed to be paying them any mind, but even so, she was frightened.

Lady Olenna was growing impatient. "Why are you gaping at Butterbumps? I asked a question, I expect an answer. Have the Lannisters stolen your tongue, child?"

Ser Dontos had warned her to speak freely only in the godswood. "Joff . . . King Joffrey, he's . . . His Grace is very fair and handsome, and . . . and as brave as a lion."

"Yes, all the Lannisters are lions, and when a Tyrell breaks wind it smells just like a rose," the old woman snapped. "But how *kind* is he? How clever? Has he a good heart, a gentle hand? Is he chivalrous as befits a king? Will he cherish Margaery and treat her tenderly, protect her honor as he would his own?"

"He will," Sansa lied. "He is very . . . very comely."

"You said that. You know, child, some say that you are as big a fool as Butterbumps here, and I am starting to believe them. *Comely?* I have taught my Margaery what comely is worth, I hope. Somewhat less than a mummer's fart. Aerion Brightfire was comely enough, but a monster all the same. The question is, what is Joffrey?" She reached to snag a passing servant. "I am not fond of leeks. Take this broth away, and bring me some cheese."

"The cheese will be served after the cakes, my lady."

"The cheese will be served when I want it served, and I want it served now." The old woman turned back to Sansa. "Are you frightened, child? No need for that, we're only women here. Tell me the truth, no harm will come to you."

"My father always told the truth." Sansa spoke quietly, but even so, it was hard to get the words out.

"Lord Eddard, yes, he had that reputation, but they named him traitor and took his head off even so." The old woman's eyes bore into her, sharp and bright as the points of swords.

"Joffrey," Sansa said. "Joffrey did that. He promised me he would be merciful, and cut my father's head off. He said *that* was mercy, and he took me up on the walls and made me look at it. The head. He wanted me to weep, but . . ." She stopped abruptly, and covered her mouth. *I've said too much, oh gods be good, they'll know, they'll hear, someone will tell on me.*

"Go on." It was Margaery who urged. Joffrey's own queen-to-be. Sansa did not know how much she had heard.

"I can't." *What if she tells him, what if she tells? He'll kill me for certain then, or give me to Ser Ilyn.* "I never meant . . . my father was a traitor, my brother as well, I have the traitor's blood, please, don't make me say more."

"Calm yourself, child," the Queen of Thorns commanded.

"She's terrified, Grandmother, just look at her."

The old woman called to Butterbumps. "*Fool!* Give us a song. A long one, I should think. 'The Bear and the Maiden Fair' will do nicely."

"It will!" the huge jester replied. "It will do nicely indeed! Shall I sing it standing on my head, my lady?"

"Will that make it sound better?"

"No."

"Stand on your feet, then. We wouldn't want your hat to fall off. As I recall, you never wash your hair."

"As my lady commands." Butterbumps bowed low, let loose of an enormous belch, then straightened, threw out his belly, and bellowed. "*A bear there was, a bear, a BEAR! All black and brown, and covered with hair . . .*"

Lady Olenna squirmed forward. "Even when I was a girl younger than you, it was well known that in the Red Keep the very walls have ears. Well, they will be the better for a song, and meanwhile we girls shall speak freely."

"But," Sansa said, "Varys . . . he *knows*, he always . . ."

"*Sing louder!*" the Queen of Thorns shouted at Butterbumps. "These old ears are almost deaf, you know. Are you whispering at me, you fat fool? I don't pay you for whispers. *Sing!*"

"*. . . THE BEAR!*" thundered Butterbumps, his great deep voice echoing off the rafters. "*OH, COME, THEY SAID, OH COME TO THE FAIR! THE FAIR? SAID HE, BUT I'M A BEAR! ALL BLACK AND BROWN, AND COVERED WITH HAIR!*"

The wrinkled old lady smiled. "At Highgarden we have many spiders amongst the flowers. So long as they keep to themselves we let them spin their little webs, but if they get underfoot we step on them." She patted Sansa on the back of the hand. "Now, child, the truth. What sort of man is this Joffrey, who calls himself Baratheon but looks so very Lannister?"

"*AND DOWN THE ROAD FROM HERE TO THERE. FROM HERE! TO THERE! THREE BOYS, A GOAT, AND A DANCING BEAR!*"

Sansa felt as though her heart had lodged in her throat. The Queen of Thorns was so close she could smell the old woman's sour breath. Her gaunt thin fingers were pinching her wrist. To her other side, Margaery was listening as well. A shiver went through her. "A monster," she whispered, so tremulously she could scarcely hear her own voice. "Joffrey is a monster. He lied about the butcher's boy and made Father kill my wolf. When I displease him, he has the Kingsguard beat me. He's evil and cruel, my lady, it's so. And the queen as well."

Lady Olenna Tyrell and her granddaughter exchanged a look. "Ah," said the old woman, "that's a pity."

Oh, gods, thought Sansa, horrified. *If Margaery won't marry him, Joff will know that I'm to blame.* "Please," she blurted, "don't stop the wedding . . ."

"Have no fear, Lord Puff Fish is determined that Margaery shall be queen. And the word of a Tyrell is worth more than all the gold in Casterly Rock. At least it was in my day. Even so, we thank you for the truth, child."

"*. . . DANCED AND SPUN, ALL THE WAY TO THE FAIR! THE FAIR! THE FAIR!*" Butterbumps hopped and roared and stomped his feet.

"Sansa, would you like to visit Highgarden?" When Margaery Tyrell smiled, she looked very like her brother Loras. "All the autumn flowers are in bloom just now, and there are groves and fountains, shady courtyards, marble colonnades. My lord father always keeps singers at court, sweeter ones than Butters here, and pipers and fiddlers and harpers as well. We have the best horses, and pleasure boats to sail along the Mander. Do you hawk, Sansa?"

"A little," she admitted.

"*OH, SWEET SHE WAS, AND PURE, AND FAIR! THE MAID WITH HONEY IN HER HAIR!*"

"You will love Highgarden as I do, I know it." Margaery brushed back a loose strand of Sansa's hair. "Once you see it, you'll never want to leave. And perhaps you won't have to."

"*HER HAIR! HER HAIR! THE MAID WITH HONEY IN HER HAIR!*"

"Shush, child," the Queen of Thorns said sharply. "Sansa hasn't even told us that she would like to come for a visit."

"Oh, but I would," Sansa said. Highgarden sounded like the place she had always dreamed of, like the beautiful magical court she had once hoped to find at King's Landing.

"*. . . SMELLED THE SCENT ON THE SUMMER AIR. THE BEAR! THE BEAR! ALL BLACK AND BROWN AND COVERED WITH HAIR.*"

"But the queen," Sansa went on, "she won't let me go . . ."

"She will. Without Highgarden, the Lannisters have no hope of keeping Joffrey on his throne. If my son the lord oaf asks, she will have no choice but to grant his request."

"Will he?" asked Sansa. "Will he ask?"

Lady Olenna frowned. "I see no need to give him a choice. Of course, he has no hint of our true purpose."

"*HE SMELLED THE SCENT ON THE SUMMER AIR!*"

Sansa wrinkled her brow. "Our true purpose, my lady?"

"*HE SNIFFED AND ROARED AND SMELLED IT THERE! HONEY ON THE SUMMER AIR!*"

"To see you safely wed, child," the old woman said, as Butterbumps bellowed out the old, old song, "to my grandson."

Wed to Ser Loras, oh . . . Sansa's breath caught in her throat. She remembered Ser Loras in his sparkling sapphire armor, tossing her a rose. Ser Loras in white silk, so pure, innocent, beautiful. The dimples at the corner of his mouth when he smiled. The sweetness of his laugh, the warmth of his hand. She could only imagine what it would be like to pull up his tunic and caress the smooth skin underneath, to stand on her toes and kiss him, to run her fingers through those thick brown curls and drown in his deep brown eyes. A flush crept up her neck.

"*OH, I'M A MAID, AND I'M PURE AND FAIR! I'LL NEVER DANCE WITH A HAIRY BEAR! A BEAR! A BEAR! I'LL NEVER DANCE WITH A HAIRY BEAR!*"

"Would you like that, Sansa?" asked Margaery. "I've never had a sister, only brothers. Oh, please say yes, please say that you will consent to marry my brother."

The words came tumbling out of her. "Yes. I will. I would like that more than anything. To wed Ser Loras, to love him . . ."

"*Loras?*" Lady Olenna sounded annoyed. "Don't be foolish, child. Kingsguard never wed. Didn't they teach you anything in Winterfell? We were speaking of my grandson Willas. He is a bit old for you, to be sure, but a dear boy for all that. Not the least bit oafish, and heir to Highgarden besides."

Sansa felt dizzy; one instant her head was full of dreams of Loras, and the next they had all been snatched away. *Willas? Willas?* "I," she said stupidly. *Courtesy is a lady's armor. You must not offend them, be careful what you say.* "I do not know Ser Willas. I have never had the pleasure, my lady. Is he . . . is he as great a knight as his brothers?"

"*. . . LIFTED HER HIGH INTO THE AIR! THE BEAR! THE BEAR!*"

"No," Margaery said. "He has never taken vows."

Her grandmother frowned. "Tell the girl the truth. The poor lad is crippled, and that's the way of it."

"He was hurt as a squire, riding in his first tourney," Margaery confided. "His horse fell and crushed his leg."

"That snake of a Dornishman was to blame, that Oberyn Martell. And his maester as well."

"*I CALLED FOR A KNIGHT, BUT YOU'RE A BEAR! A BEAR! A BEAR! ALL BLACK AND BROWN AND COVERED WITH HAIR!*"

"Willas has a bad leg but a good heart," said Margaery. "He used to read to me when I was a little girl, and draw me pictures of the stars. You will love him as much as we do, Sansa."

"*SHE KICKED AND WAILED, THE MAID SO FAIR, BUT HE LICKED THE HONEY FROM HER HAIR. HER HAIR! HER HAIR! HE LICKED THE HONEY FROM HER HAIR!*"

"When might I meet him?" asked Sansa, hesitantly.

"Soon," promised Margaery. "When you come to Highgarden, after Joffrey and I are wed. My grandmother will take you."

"I will," said the old woman, patting Sansa's hand and smiling a soft wrinkly smile. "I will indeed."

"*THEN SHE SIGHED AND SQUEALED AND KICKED THE AIR! MY BEAR! SHE SANG. MY BEAR SO FAIR! AND OFF THEY WENT, FROM HERE TO THERE, THE BEAR, THE BEAR, AND THE MAIDEN FAIR.*" Butterbumps roared the last line, leapt into the air, and came down on both feet with a crash that shook the wine cups on the table. The women laughed and clapped.

"I thought that dreadful song would never end," said the Queen of Thorns. "But look, here comes my cheese."